A TEXT BOOK OF

VOICE NETWORK

For

Semester - I

FINAL YEAR DEGREE COURSE IN ELECTRONICS / ELECTRONICS AND TELECOMMUNICATION ENGINEERING / INDUSTRIAL ELECTRONICS/ ELECTRONICS AND COMMUNICATION

Strictly As Per the New Revised Syllabus of

Dr. Babasaheb Ambedkar Marathwada University, Aurangabad

(2013-2014)

R. C. JAISWAL
M.E. (E & TC)
Assistant Professor, E & TC Department,
Pune Institute of Computer Technology,
Dhankawadi, **PUNE.**

Mrs. R. A. APTE
B.E. (E & TC),
Formerly Lecturer, E & TC Department,
Maharashtra Institute of Technology
PUNE.

NIRALI PRAKASHAN

Advancement of knowledge

N2670

VOICE NETWORK (BE - ELECTRONICS GROUP) (BAMU)　　　　ISBN 978-93-83525-74-4

First Edition　:　September 2013

©　　　　:　**Authors**

The text of this publication, or any part thereof, should not be reproduced or transmitted in any form or stored in any computer storage system or device for distribution including photocopy, recording, taping or information retrieval system or reproduced on any disc, tape, perforated media or other information storage device etc., without the written permission of Authors with whom the rights are reserved. Breach of this condition is liable for legal action.

Every effort has been made to avoid errors or omissions in this publication. In spite of this, errors may have crept in. Any mistake, error or discrepancy so noted and shall be brought to our notice shall be taken care of in the next edition. It is notified that neither the publisher nor the authors or seller shall be responsible for any damage or loss of action to any one, of any kind, in any manner, therefrom.

Published By :
NIRALI PRAKASHAN
Abhyudaya Pragati, 1312, Shivaji Nagar,
Off J.M. Road, PUNE – 411005
Tel - (020) 25512336/37/39, Fax - (020) 25511379
Email : niralipune@pragationline.com

DISTRIBUTION CENTRES
PUNE

Nirali Prakashan
119, Budhwar Peth, Jogeshwari Mandir Lane
Pune 411002, Maharashtra
Tel : (020) 2445 2044, 66022708, Fax : (020) 2445 1538
Email : niralilocal@pragationline.com

Nirali Prakashan
S. No. 28/25, Dhyari,
Near Pari Company, Pune 411041
Tel : (020) 24690204Fax : (020) 24690316
Email : bookorder@pragationline.com

MUMBAI
Nirali Prakashan
385, S.V.P. Road, Rasdhara Co-op. Hsg. Society Ltd.,
Girgaum, Mumbai 400004, Maharashtra
Tel : (022) 2385 6339 / 2386 9976, Fax : (022) 2386 9976
Email : niralimumbai@pragationline.com

DISTRIBUTION BRANCHES

NAGPUR
Pratibha Book Distributors
Above Maratha Mandir, Shop No. 3, First Floor,
Rani Jhanshi Square, Sitabuldi, Nagpur 440012,
Maharashtra, Tel : (0712) 254 7129

BENGALURU
Pragati Book House
House No. 1, Sanjeevappa Lane, Avenue Road Cross,
Opp. Rice Church, Bengaluru – 560002.
Tel : (080) 64513344, 64513355,
Mob : 9880582331, 9845021552
Email:bharatsavla@yahoo.com

JALGAON
Nirali Prakashan
34, V. V. Golani Market, Navi Peth, Jalgaon 425001,
Maharashtra, Tel : (0257) 222 0395
Mob : 94234 91860

KOLHAPUR
Nirali Prakashan
New Mahadvar Road,
Kedar Plaza, 1st Floor Opp. IDBI Bank
Kolhapur 416 012, Maharashtra. Mob : 9855046155

CHENNAI
Pragati Books
9/1, Montieth Road, Behind Taas Mahal, Egmore,
Chennai 600008 Tamil Nadu, Tel : (044) 6518 3535,
Mob : 94440 01782 / 98450 21552 / 98805 82331, Email : bharatsavla@yahoo.com

RETAIL OUTLETS
PUNE

Pragati Book Centre
157, Budhwar Peth, Opp. Ratan Talkies,
Pune 411002, Maharashtra
Tel : (020) 2445 8887 / 6602 2707, Fax : (020) 2445 8887

Pragati Book Centre
Amber Chamber, 28/A, Budhwar Peth,
Appa Balwant Chowk, Pune : 411002, Maharashtra,
Tel : (020) 20240335 / 66281669
Email : pbcpune@pragationline.com

Pragati Book Centre
676/B, Budhwar Peth, Opp. Jogeshwari Mandir,
Pune 411002, Maharashtra
Tel : (020) 6601 7784 / 6602 0855

PBC Book Sellers & Stationers
152, Budhwar Peth, Pune 411002, Maharashtra
Tel : (020) 2445 2254 / 6609 2463

MUMBAI
Pragati Book Corner
Indira Niwas, 111 - A, Bhavani Shankar Road, Dadar (W), Mumbai 400028, Maharashtra
Tel : (022) 2422 3526 / 6662 5254, Email : pbcmumbai@pragationline.com

www.pragationline.com　　　　info@pragationline.com

Preface ...

It gives us great pleasure to bring out the book on **"Voice Network"**. This text is designed to explain the various types of Voice Networks in use today.

The book is written mainly for the Final Year Students of E & TC/Electronics Group for the subject **"Voice Network"**. It is written strictly as per the revised syllabus of the Dr. Babasaheb Ambedkar Marathwada University, Aurangabad.

Welcome to the world of Voice Networks. The world is getting networked today. It is making an impact on day-to-day of common man. Businesses and consumers are demanding more interactions with the network.

In view of this, it is necessary to have the fundamental knowledge of the Voice Networks.

This book gives the theoretical and practical knowledge of the different voice networks and voice networking technologies.

This book is organized as follows :

Unit I covers Evolution of Telecommunication, Simple telephone communication, Basics of switching systems, Electronic switching, Digital switching system, Circuit switching, Message switching, Packet switching, Switch signalling - subscriber loop, Interoffice (Common Channel Signalling, Signalling System No. 7).

Unit II covers Introduction, Service level, Traffic usage, Traffic mesurement units, Traffic distribution, Grade of service, Blocking probability, Erlang distribution, Poisson's distribution, Numericals on above topics.

Unit III covers Demand for integration, Problems of integration, ISDN, Basic structure and narrowband ISDN, ISDN interfaces - ISDN terminals, Non-ISDN terminals, ISDN services, Packed switched data, Voice over frame relay, Broadband ISDN, ATM and its interfaces, Public ATM networks.

Unit IV covers Standards for wireless communication systems, Access technologies, Cellular communication fundamentals, GSM architecture and interfaces, Radio link features in GSM system, GSM logical channels and frame structure, Speech coding in GSM, Data services in GSM, Value added services, Privacy and Security in GSM.

Unit V covers CDMA standards, IS-95 system architecture, Air interface, Physical and logical channels of IS-95, CDMA call processing, CDMA 2000 system.

Unit VI covers Introduction to VoIP, Low level protocols - RTP/RTCP/UDP, Speech coding technologies PCM, ADPCM, LPC, Speech Codes ITU series and wireless codes including fixed and variable rare trans-coder technologies including; DTMF generation and detection, Echo cancellation, Voice activity detection and discontinuous transmission (VAD/DTX), Packet loss concealment (PLC)/IP Telephony Protocols - H.323, H.245 Control Signalling, Session Initiation Protocol (SIP), MEGACO and H.248, QoS.

September, 2013   **Authors**

Pune.

Syllabus ...

Unit I : Introduction to Telephone Signalling and Switching

Evolution of Telecommunication, Simple Telephone Communication, Basics of Switching Systems, Electronic Switching, Digital Switching System, Circuit Switching, Message Switching, Packet Switching, Switch Signalling - Subscriber Loop, Interoffice (Common Channel Signalling, Signalling System No. 7).

Unit II : Telecommunication Traffic Engineering

Introduction, Service Level, Traffic Usage, Traffic measurement Units, Traffic Distribution, Grade of Service, Blocking Probability, Erlang Distribution, Poisson's Distribution, Numericals on Above Topics.

Unit III : Data and Voice Integration

Demand for Integration, Problems of Integration, ISDN, Basic Structure and Narrowband ISDN, ISDN Interfaces - ISDN Terminals, Non-ISDN Terminals, ISDN Services, Packed Switched Data, Voice Over Frame Relay, Broadband ISDN, ATM and its Interfaces, Public ATM Networks.

Unit IV : Global System for Mobile Communication

Standards for Wireless Communication Systems, Access Technologies, Cellular Communication Fundamentals, GSM Architecture and Interfaces, Radio Link Features in GSM system, GSM Logical Channels and Frame Structure, Speech Coding in GSM, Data Services in GSM, Value Added services, Privacy and Security in GSM.

Unit V : Code Division Multiple Access

CDMA Standards, IS-95 System Architecture, Air Interface, Physical and Logical Channels of IS-95, CDMA Call Processing, Soft Hand-off, Security and Identification, Wireless Data, CDMA 2000 System.

Unit VI : IP Telephony

Introduction to VoIP, Low level Protocols - RTP/RTCP/UDP, Speech Coding Technologies PCM, ADPCM, LPC, Speech Codes ITU series and Wireless Codes Including Fixed and Variable Rare Trans-coder Technologies including; DTMF Generation and Detection, Echo Cancellation, Voice Activity Detection and Discontinuous Transmission (VAD/DTX), Packet Loss Conceal Meant (PLC)/IP Telephony Protocols - H.323, H.245 Control Signalling, Session Initiation Protocol (SIP), MEGACO and H.248, QoS.

***

Contents ...

***

Unit I

INTRODUCTION TO TELEPHONE SIGNALLING AND SWITCHING

1.1 Introduction

Telecommunication networks carry information signals among entities which are physically (geographically) far away. Such an entity may be a human being attending a telephone, computer, fax machine, etc. For communication between any two entities like a call or data transfer, many more entities might be invoked.

If it is telephonic conversation, the one who initiates the call is the **calling subscriber** and the one for whom the call is made is called the **called subscriber.** For other information transfers, the two communicating entities are called the **source** and **destination.**

Communication is realised only when any entity in one part of the world can communicate with any other entity in rest of the world. Such connectivity in telecommunication networks is achieved by the use of switching systems. In this unit, we will be studying telephone basics, switching, signalling, that is basics of establishing a connectivity between a source and destination.

1.2 Evolution of Telecommunications

Telegraphy was introduced in 1837 in Great Britain and 1845 in France. In March 1876, Alexander Graham Bell demonstrated long distance communication, the possibility of telephony. And this invention was put to use almost immediately.
Graham Bell demonstrated point-to-point telephone connection.

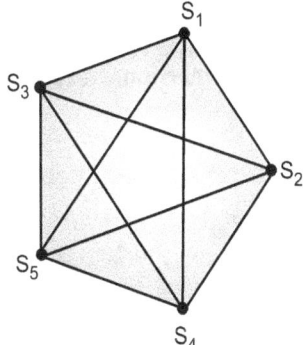

Fig. 1.1: Point-to-Point links in a network

If it is a network of five subscribers, individual links are amongst all. To establish a connection, calling subscriber chooses appropriate link with the called subscriber. To draw attention of called subscriber before information exchange can begin, some form of signalling is required with each link. If called subscriber is engaged, suitable indication should be given to calling subscriber by signalling.

As in Fig. 1.1, there are five subscribers (entities) and ten point-to-point links.

In order to connect 1st entity to all others, $(n - 1)$ links are required (e.g. 1-2, 1-3, 1-4, 1-5).

Because of this 2nd entity is already connected to first.

Therefore, to connect 2nd entity to all others, $(n - 2)$ links are required. (e.g., 2-3, 2-4, 2-5). Similarly, for 3rd, $(n - 3)$ links are required and so on.

$$\therefore \quad \text{Total number of links} \ = \ (n - 1) + (n - 2) + \dots + 1 + 0$$

$$= \ \frac{n\,(n - 1)}{2}$$

Such networks with point-to-point links among all the entities are known as **fully connected networks.** Because of individual links, total number of links becomes too large even for a small number of subscribers.

e.g. for 50 subscribers, we need 1225 links.

As a result of this, implementation of telephony on a large scale demanded telephone sets, pairs of wires and also the switching system/switching office/exchange.

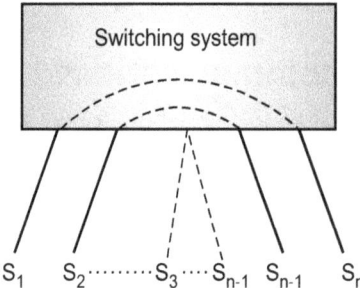

Fig. 1.2: Interconnection with an exchange

In such systems, there is no direct connection among the subscribers, but instead, all subscribers are connected to the exchange (switching system). When a subscriber initiates a call, a connection is established between the two at the exchange. e.g. as in Fig. 1.2, connection between S_1 and S_n and S_2 and S_{n-1}. In such a system, only one link per subscriber is required between the subscriber and the exchange. This limits the total number of links equal to total number of subscribers to that exchange.

Now, signalling is required to draw attention of the switching system/exchange to establish or release a connection. The exchange should also be able to detect if called subscriber is busy and if so, that should be indicated to the calling subscriber. These functions performed by an exchange in establishing and releasing connections are known as **control functions.**

Early and very basic exchanges or switching systems were manual, or needed operator. These had many limitations, so **automatic exchanges** came into existence. They are classified as below.

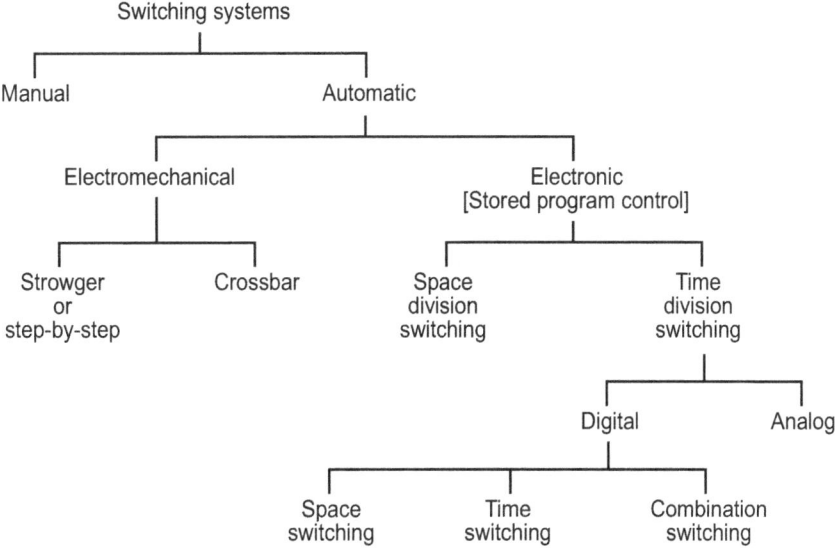

- In Strowger systems, the control functions are performed by circuits associated with the switching element in the system. (For details of Strowger and Crossbar refer to appendix).

- Crossbar systems have hard-wired control subsystems which use relays and latches. But these have limited capability and it is impossible to modify them to provide additional functionalities.

- In electronic systems, control functions are performed by **computer** or **processor.** So these are called as **SPC (Stored Program Control)** systems. New functions, fascilities can be easily added by changing or modifying control program.

- In space division switching, a dedicated path is established between the calling and the called subscribers for the entire duration of the call.

  This technique can be used in Strowger and Crossbar systems.

  An electronic exchange may use crossbar switching matrix for space division switching.

- In time division switching, sampled values of speech signals are transmitted at fixed intervals. This may be analog or digital. (Analog switching: sampled voltage levels and in digital switching: voltage levels are binary coded).

- If the coded values are transferred during the same time interval from input to output, the technique is **space switching**.

- If the values are stored and transferred to the output at a later time interval, technique is called **time switching.**

- A combination switch may also be designed by using a combination of space and time switching techniques.

Subscribers all over the world cannot be connected to a single exchange unless we have a gigantic exchange in the sky and every subscriber has a direct access to it. Communication satellite systems covering the entire globe are available, but capacity of such systems is limited. Major part of telecommunication networks is still **ground based** where subscribers are connected to the exchange via. copper wires. To transfer signal on a pair of wires, it is a must that the subscribers be located within a few kilometers from the exchange, due to technical and engineering constraints.

There can be small exchanges in appropriate geographical location, allowing subscribers in that particular area to communicate. For subscribers in different localities to communicate, it is necessary that switching systems are interconnected to form a network.

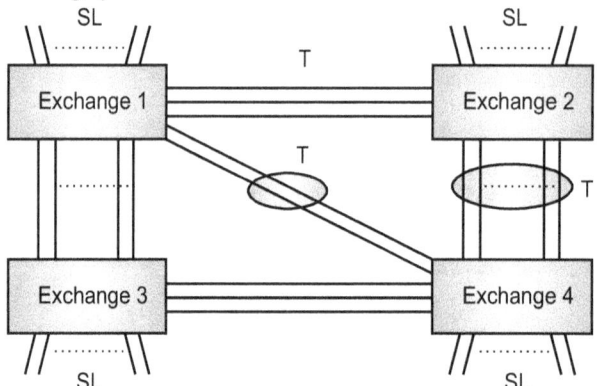

SL: Subscriber lines for a particular exchange

T:Trucks,links running lines between exchanges

Fig. 1.3

The number of trunks (between exchanges) vary and are determined on the basis of traffic between them. As the number of exchanges increases, interconnecting them becomes complex. This problem is handled by introducing a hierarchical structure among the exchanges, and using a number of them in series to establish connection between subscribers.

1.3 Simple Telephone Communication

In the simplest form of a telephone circuit, it is a one way communication between two entities, one receiving (listening) and other transmitting (talking).

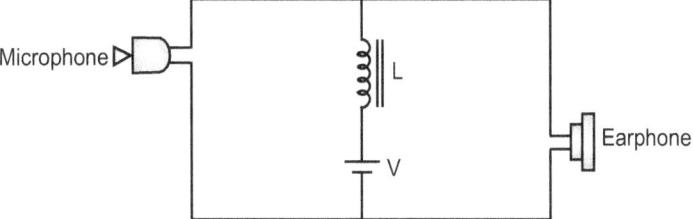

Fig. 1.4: Simple telephone circuit

This **one way communication** is known as **simplex communication**. Microphone and earphone are transducers of telephone system. Microphone converts speech to electrical signals and earphone converts electrical signals to speech (audio). Most commonly used microphone is carbon microphone, which gives strong electrical signals. This quality level is acceptable for telephone conversation.

For working of microphone and earphone please refer appendix.

In normal telephone communication system, information (speech) is transferred both ways. In simplex, one entity was always transmitting and other was always receiving. But in normal telephones, an entity is capable of both receiving and transmitting (sending voice), although they do not take place simultaneously, that is, when one entity is transmitting, the other is receiving and vice-versa. Means an entity is either receiving or sending at an instant of time. Such form of communication, where information transfer takes place both ways - but not simultaneously, is known as **half duplex communication.** If the information takes place in both directions simultaneously, it is called **full duplex communication.**

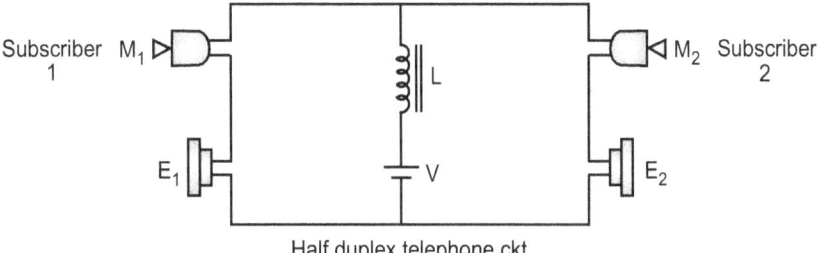

Half duplex telephone ckt.

Fig. 1.5: Half duplex telephone circuit

As seen in Fig. 1.5, there is one transmitter and one receiver (microphone and earphone) at one end, [each subscriber]. In this circuit, speech of 1 is heard by E_2 as well as in E_1, earphone of subscriber 1. Such audio signal heard at the **generating end** is called **sidetone.** A certain amount of sidetone is essential. Human speech and hearing system is a feedback system in which volume of speech is automatically adjusted based on side tone heard by ear. If no sidetone is heard, person tends to shout and if too much sidetone is present, person reduces the speech level. In the above circuit, entire speech intensity is heard as sidetone, which is not desirable.

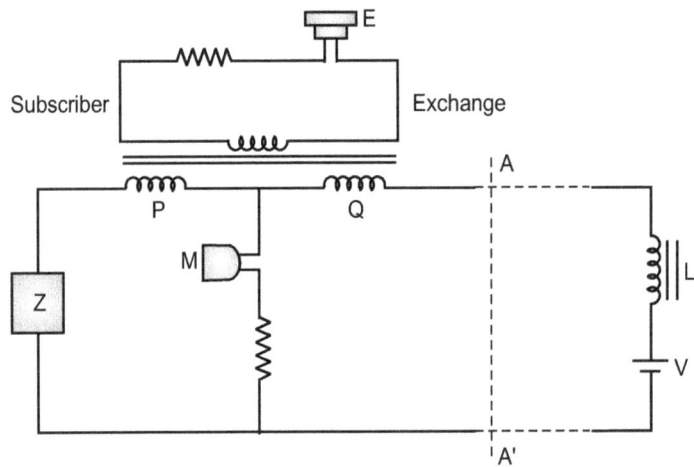

Fig. 1.6: Sidetone coupling

Circuit of Fig. 1.6 gives a small level of sidetone and full speech signal from other entity to the receiver.

Impedance Z is chosen almost equal to impedance equal to impedance to the right of section AA'. Therefore, with proper sidetone coupling, the speech signal from microphone M divides more or less equally in windings P and Q. As these signals are in opposite direction, only a small induced voltage appears in the receiver circuit providing sidetone. When signal is received from other entity, it is in the same direction in both windings P and Q inducing a large signal is receiver circuit.

1.4 Basics of Switching Systems

The purpose of switching is to provide interconnection among all the entities/subscribers on a network without single connections between every pair of entities.

A major component of an exchange is the set of input and output circuits called **inlets** and **outlets.** Primary function of an exchange is to establish an **electrical path** between an **inlet-outlet** pair. The hardware, used for establishing such a connection, is called a **switching matrix** or **switching network.** This switching network is a component of the exchange. [Physically, it will be a big cupboard like structure containing many racks for cards, etc.]

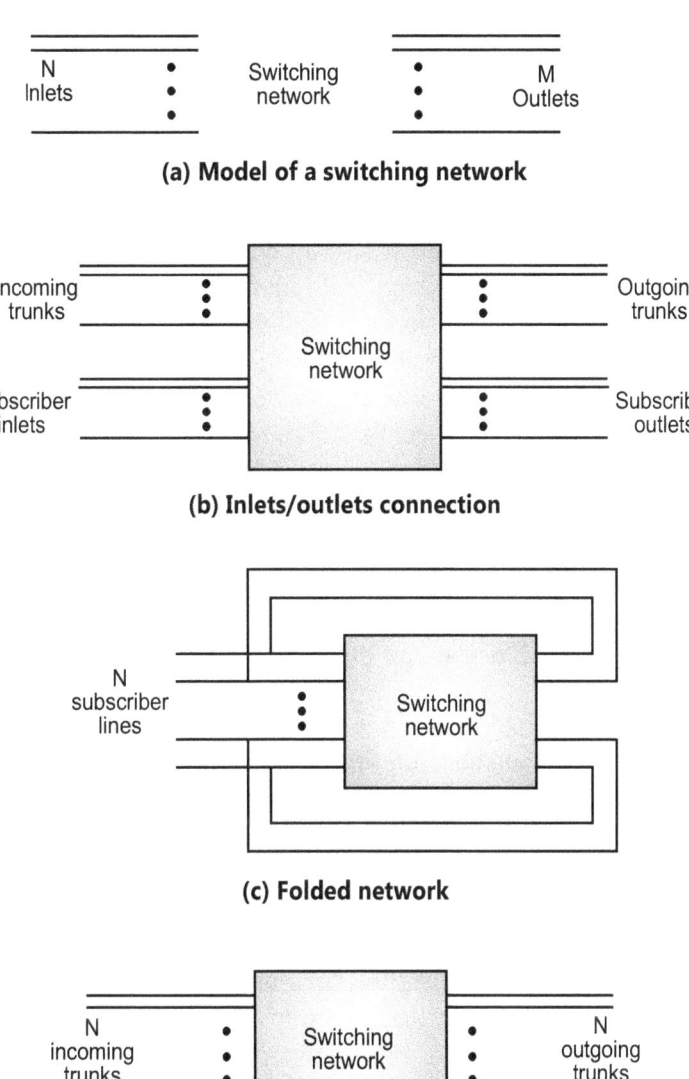

(a) Model of a switching network

(b) Inlets/outlets connection

(c) Folded network

(d) Non-folded network

Fig. 1.7: Switching network configurations

- Fig. 1.7 (a) shows a network with N inlets and M outlets.

  If N = M, the switching network is called a **symmetric network.**

- The inlets/outlets may be connected to local subscriber lines or to trunks from/to other exchange. (Fig. 1.7 (b)).

- When inlets/outlets are connected only to the subscriber lines, output lines are folded back to input and the network is called as **folded network.** (Fig. 1.7 (c)).

If we refer Fig. 1.7 (b), 4 types of connections may be established:

(1)   **Local** call connection between **two subscribers** in the system.
(2)   **Outgoing** call connection between **subscribers** and **outgoing trunk.**
(3)   **Incoming** call connection between **incoming trunk** and local **subscriber.**
(4)   **Transit** call connection between **incoming trunk** and **outgoing trunk.**

In a folded network with N subscribers, there can be maximum N/2 simultaneous calls or information interchanges. The switching network can be designed to provide N/2 simultaneous switching paths. Such network is said to be **non-blocking.** In such non-blocking network, as long as a called subscriber is free, calling subscriber can always get a connection established, because the switching network has that capacity many resources. But, it rarely happens that all the N/2 conversations take place simultaneously. Considering this fact, it may be economical to design a switching network that has simultaneous switching paths equal to average number of calls expected. That means such a network will allow less than N/2 simultaneous conversations. So, it may happen that some expected average number of calls are taking place and a subscriber trying to make a call, requests for a connections, and because there are no free switching paths, he is denied the connection. The subscriber is said to be **blocked** and the switching network is said to be a **blocking network.**

In a blocking network, the number of simultaneous switching paths is less than the maximum number of simultaneous conversations that can take place. The probability that user may get blocked is called **blocking probability.** All the exchanges are designed to meet an estimated maximum average simultaneous traffic (calls), usually known as **busy hour traffic.** Usually, this analysis is done at various different day times (24 hours), that gives the busy hour. The system keeps a record of the calls initiated, completed, terminated, blocked etc. All this information is used to calculate busy hour traffic. Exchanges are designed such that all (switching) resources are common and any required resource is allocated to a conversation as long as it lasts. Good design ensures low blocking probability.

Traffic in telecommunication network is measured by an internationally accepted unit of traffic intensity known as **erlang (E).** A switching resource is said to carry one erlang of traffic, if it is continuously occupied throughout a given period of observation. Traffic engineering will be discussed in Chapter 2.

In a switching network, all the inlet/outlet connections may be used for interexchange transmission. In such case, the exchange does not support local subscribers and is called a **transit exchange.** It is a **non-folded network.** (Fig. 1.7 (d)).
In a non-folded network with N inlets and N outlets, N simultaneous conversations/ information transfers are possible. Therefore, it is non-blocking if N simultaneous switching paths are provided.

- **Switching network provides** the switching **paths. Control subsystem** of the switching system actually **establishes** the path.
- The switching network does not distinguish between inlets/outlets that are connected to subscribers - local links or to trunks.
- Control subsystem distinguishes between these lines and correctly interprets the signalling information received on these lines.
- It senses the end of information transfer and releases the connections.
- Control subsystem gets the signalling information on inlet lines to establish a connection. It sends out signalling information to subscriber or to other exchanges connected to outgoing trunks.
- Signalling is also involved between different subsystems within an exchange.
  The signalling formats and requirements for the subscriber, trunks and subsystems differ significantly. So switching system provides three different forms of signalling:
  (1) Subscriber loop signalling.
  (2) Interexchange signalling.
  (3) Intraexchange or register signalling.

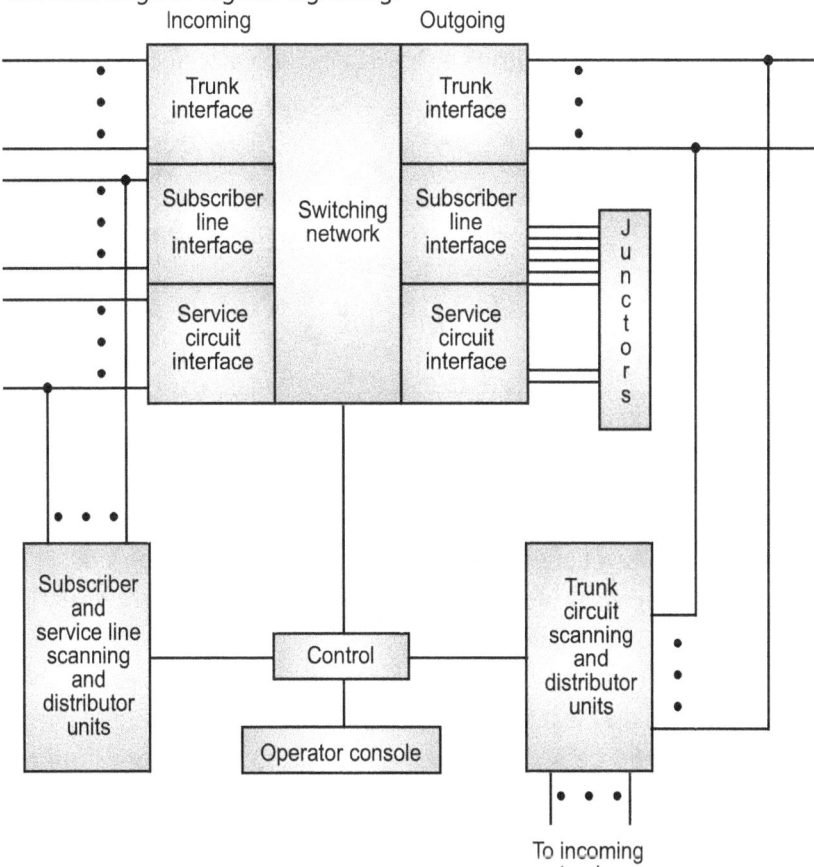

Fig. 1.8: Elements of a switching system

An exchange/switching system has different elements that perform switching, control and signalling functions.

- Some service lines are used for maintenance and testing purposes.

- Subscriber and trunk lines are terminated at respective interfaces.

- **Junctor** circuits imply a folded connection for local subscribers and service circuits.

Some exchanges may provide an internal mechanism for local connections without the use of junctor circuits.

- **Line scanning units sense and obtain signalling information** from respective lines.

- **Distributor units send out signalling information** on respective lines.

- Operator console is used for maintenance and administrative purposes.

- If the control subsystem is an integral part of the switching network, it is known as **direct control switching system.**

- If the control subsystem is outside the switching network, it is known as **common control switching system.** (Indirect control or Register control).

Strowger exchanges are usually direct control systems. Crossbar and electronic exchanges are common control systems. All SPC (Stored Program Control) systems are common control systems.

1.5 Electronic Switch

Before getting into the details of electronic switch, let us study a few basics.

Automatic exchanges have a number of advantages over the manual exchanges:

1. In manual exchange, the subscriber needs to communicate with the operator and common language becomes an important factor. In multilingual areas, this may pose problems, whereas operations in automatic exchanges are language independent.

2. A greater degree of privacy is obtained in automatic exchanges as normally no operator is involved in setting up and monitoring a call.

3. Establishment and release of calls are faster in automatic exchanges. But the operators in manual exchange may take some time to notice the end of conversation and release the circuits. This could be annoying to business subscribers who wish to make many calls in quick succession.

4. In automatic exchanges, time required to establish and release calls remains (almost) the same irrespective of the load on system and time of the day. In manual system, this may not be true.

In manual exchanges, the called subscribers may be most commonly identified by his name, designation, etc. so that operator gets proper information to establish a connection. In automatic exchanges, this is not possible. A formal numbering plan or addressing scheme is required to identify the subscribers. Numbering plan is the one in which a subscriber is identified by a number. This is widely used than using alphanumeric strings identification. A mechanism to transmit the identity of the called subscriber to the exchange is now required at the telephone set. Two methods for this are –

- Pulse dialing.
- Multifrequency dialing.

1.5.1 Pulse Dialing

1. A train of pulses is used to represent a digit in the subscriber number.
2. The number of pulses in the train is equal to the digit value it represents.
3. Zero is represented by 10 pulses.
4. Successive digits in a number are represented by a series of pulse trains.
5. Two successive trains are distinguished from one another by a pause between them, known as **interdigit gap** (200 ms).
6. Pulses are generated by alternately making and breaking the loop circuit between subscriber and exchange.
7. Pulse rate is usually 10 pulses per second with 10% tolerance.
8. Duty cycle of the pulse is normally 33%.

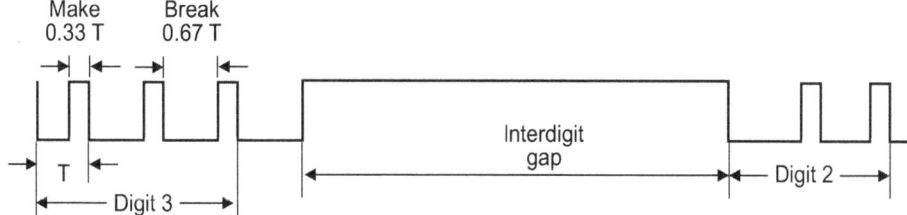

Fig. 1.9: Pulse dialing

Early, rotary dial telephones were used for implementing pulse dialing.

But it involves taking care of many things:

- As pulses are produced by make and break of the subscriber loop, there are chances of sparking inside the instrument.
- Transmitter, receiver and bell circuits may be damaged if pulses pass through them.
- Timing aspects should be independent of user action, because the dialing actions vary from person to person.

As discussed previously, many signaling functions are involved in establishing, maintaining and releasing a call. These are performed by operator in manual exchange. But in automatic exchanges, series of distinctive tones is used.

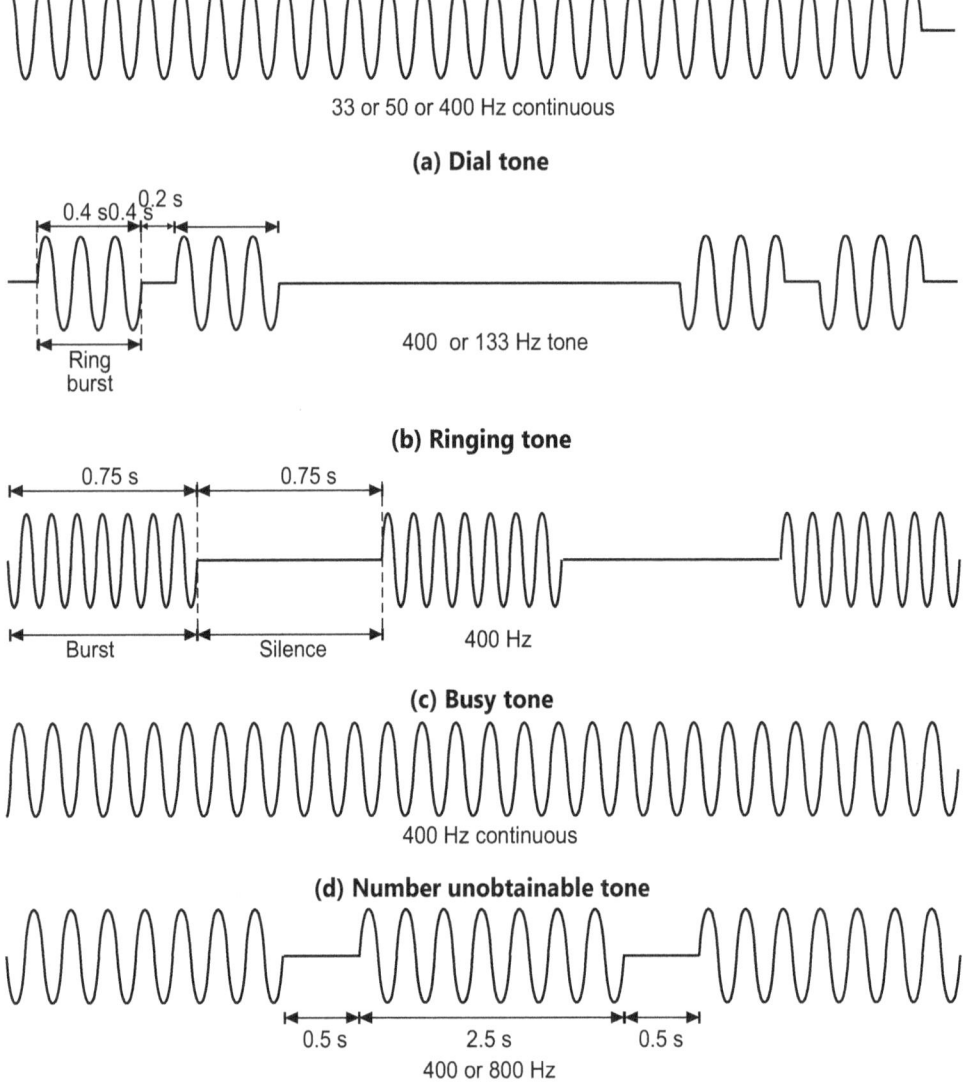

Fig. 1.10: Signaling tones in automatic exchanges and their specifications

(a) **Dial tone** signalling function indicates that the exchange is ready to accept dialed digits from subscriber. Subscriber should start dialing only after hearing this dial tone, or initial pulses may be missed by the exchange. Most often dial tone is sent out by exchange even before the handset is brought near the ear. Dial tone is 33 Hz or 50 Hz or 400 Hz continuous wave. 400 Hz is usually modulated with 25 Hz or 50 Hz.

(b) Ringing tone is sent to the calling subscriber when the called party line is obtained and the exchange sends out ringing current to the telephone set of called party. Ringing tone pattern is similar to that of ringing current, but these are two independent quantities.

(c) Busy tone is sent to the calling subscriber whenever the switching equipment or junction line is not available to put through the call or the called subscriber line is engaged. No distinction is made in these conditions.

(d) Number unobtainable tone is sent to the calling subscriber due to many reasons such as called party line is out of order or disconnected, and an error in dialing leading to the selection of spare line.

(e) Routing tone or call in progress tone is heard by the calling subscriber when his call is routed through a number of different types of exchanges.

With the use of rotary dial telephone around 12 seconds are needed to dial a 7 digit number. From subscriber point of view, a faster dial rate is desirable. Pulse dialing is limited to signalling between the exchange and the subscriber and no signalling is possible end to end, that is between two subscribers. End-to-end signalling is possible only if signalling is in voice frequency band so that signaling information can be transmitted to any point in the network to which voice can be transmitted. End-to-end signalling is desirable feature. Rotary dial signalling is limited to 10 distinct signals, but a higher number of signals would enhance the signalling capability significantly.

A more convenient method of signalling than rotary dialing is preferable from the point of view of human factors. This consideration led to the development of touch tone dial.

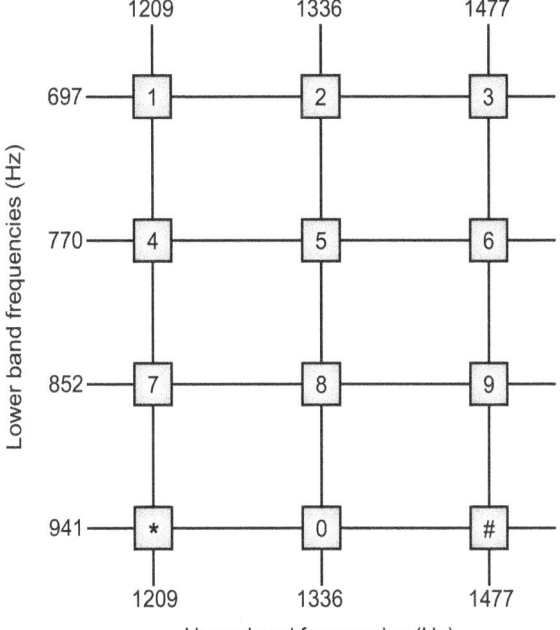

Fig. 1.11: Touch dial arrangement

1.5.2 DTMF Signalling

Rotary dial is replaced by a push button keyboard. **Touching** a **button** generates a **tone.** This tone is a combination of two frequencies: one from upper band and the other from lower band. e.g. touching 5 transmits 770 Hz and 1336 Hz. (Similar to operation of 4×3 matrix.) In an extended design, 1633 Hz can be provided in upper band giving 16 different signals (4×4). But this design is used only in military and special applications.

- As the touch tone signalling is in voice band, it faces the problem of **talk off**. Talk off means the speech signals may be mistaken for touch tone signals. This may lead to wrong control actions like abrupt call termination.

- Another aspect of talk off is that the speech signal may interfere with touch tone signalling if both happen at the same time.

So protection against talk off and design of touch tone signalling include the following factors:

1. **Choice of code:**

Imitation of code signals by speech and music should be difficult. Single frequency tones should be avoided. Some form of **multifrequency code** can be used.

2. **Band separation:**

Chosen frequencies are placed in two separate bands and a restriction is applied that one frequency from each band is chosen to form a code word. (One from higher band and other from lower). Band separation of touch tone frequencies reduces the probability of speech being able to produce touch tone combinations. As in above
Fig. 1.11, for 7 frequencies, [4 in lower band and 3 in upper band], 12 distinct signals are represented. Since two frequencies are mixed from a set of 7 frequencies, this touch tone scheme is called **DTMF - Dual Tone Multifrequency Signalling**.

At the receivers band separation filters can be used.

3. **Choice of frequencies:**

This is dictated by the attenuation and delay distortion characteristics of telephone network circuits for voice band frequencies.

A flat amplitude response with low attenuation and uniform delay response with a low relative delay value are desirable.

Actual range chosen for touch tone dialing is 700-1700 Hz, for defining both - upper and lower frequency bands.

Frequency spacing depends on the accuracies with which signal frequencies can be produced. Accuracy of ± 1.5% is obtainable easily at telephone sets.

Specific values of frequencies can be chosen to avoid simple harmonic relations like 1 : 2 and 2 : 3 between two adjacent frequencies in the same band and between pairs of frequencies in two different bands.

4. Choice of power levels:

Since signalling information does not bear the redundancy of spoken words and sentences, it is desirable that signal power be as large as possible. A nominal value of 1 dB above 1 mW is provided at the telephone set for combined signal power of two frequencies.

It is observed that increase in attenuation in subscriber loop between 697 Hz and 1633 Hz can be as much as 4 dB. To compensate for this, upper band frequencies are transmitted at level of 3 dB higher than that of lower band frequencies. The nominal output levels are chosen as –3.5 dBm and –0.5 dBm for lower and upper band frequencies.

5. Signalling duration:

A minimum of 40 ms has been chosen for both signal and intersignal intervals. This allows dialing rate of over 10 signals per second.

Now see how this touch tone dialing enables end-to-end signalling. Subscriber calling airline office, if he is placed on IVRS (Interactive Voice Response System) or DIVA (Data Voice Answer), he gets voice announcements like - press/dial 1 for reservation, press/dial 2 for checking status of flights, press/dial 0 for operator assistance.

1.5.3 Stored Program Control (SPC)

Everybody is aware of modern digital computers and clearly understands the concept of 'running a program' or 'executing a software' on a computer.

Similar to these concepts, we say that if the exchange control functions are carried by executing a program, it becomes SPC (Stored Program Control) exchange.

It immediately introduces full scale automation of exchange functions, automatic fault diagnosis, centralized maintenance, common channel signalling, interactive man-machine interface.

Introducing computer control to exchanges was a bit tough, because the software must run 24 hours all 365 days in a year and many more years like this. So the computers have to be highly fault tolerant. Development of introducing electronics and computer into exchanges led to the development of full-fledged electronic switching system, including electronic switching network. There are basically two approaches to organize stored program control i.e. centralized and distributed.

1.5.4 Centralized SPC

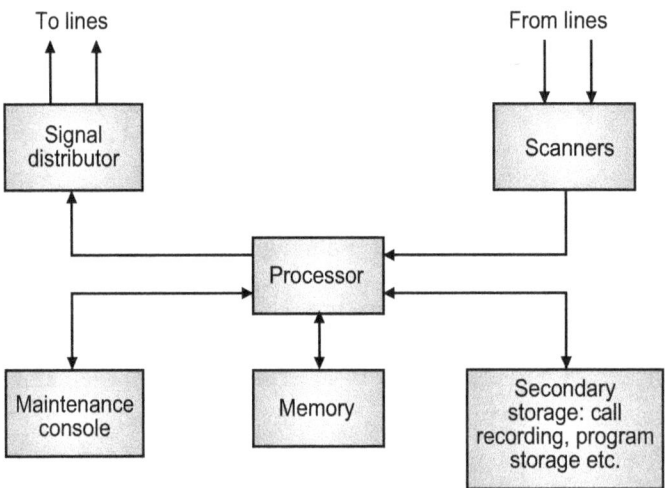

Fig. 1.12: Typical centralized SPC organisation

- In centralized control, all the control equipments are replaced by a single processor which has to be powerful. It must be capable of processing 10-100 calls per second, depending on load on the system and simultaneously it should perform other tasks.

- Centralized SPC may use more than 1 processor for redundancy purposes. Each processor has access to all the exchange resources like scanners, distribution points and each processor is capable of executing all control functions.

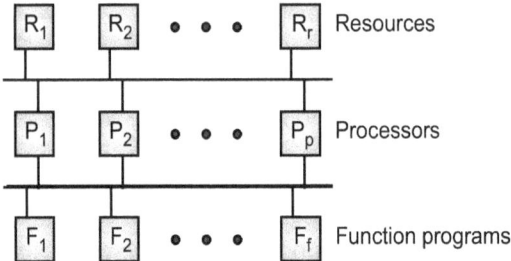

Fig. 1.13: A redundant centralized control structure

- Also, the redundancy may be provided at the level of exchange resources and function programs.

- In almost all present day electronic exchanges, using centralized control, only a two processor configuration is used. Dual processor architecture can operate in:

  (1) Standby mode,

  (2) Synchronous duplex mode,

  (3) Load sharing mode.

(1) Standby Mode:

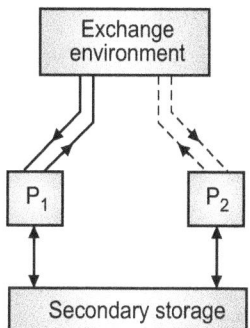

P$_{\overline{1}}$Active processor   P$_{\overline{2}}$ Standby processor

Fig. 1.14: Standby dual processor configuration

- Here, one processor is active and other is on standby, both hardware and software-wise. Standby processor comes online only when active processor fails. Very important requirement here is that standby processor should be able to reconstitute the state of exchange, when it gains the control. [e.g. links and trunks being occupied/free, network paths connected etc. i.e. all call related status].

- Active processor copies status of system periodically into secondary storage. After switch over, the secondary processor loads the most recent update and continues.

(2) Synchronous Duplex Mode:

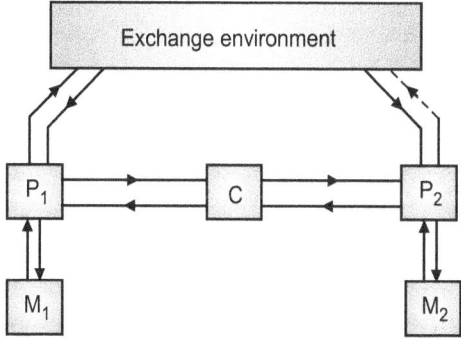

C = ComparatorM = MemoryP = Processor

Fig. 1.15: Synchronous duplex operation

- Here, hardware coupling is provided between two processors which execute same set of instructions and compare the results continuously. If a mismatch occurs, faulty processor is identified and taken out of service within a few milliseconds.

- In normal operation, both processors have the same data in memory all the times and both receive information/status from exchange simultaneously. One of the processor is actually controlling the exchange. Other one is synchronized with it, but it does not control.

- If a fault is detected, processors are developed. A check out program in run to detect the faulty processor. But this does not disturb current calls. Now, other processor operates and controls independently. After repairs when the fault processor is brought back, memory contents of currently active processor are copied to its memory and normal synchronous operation starts.

(3) Load Sharing:

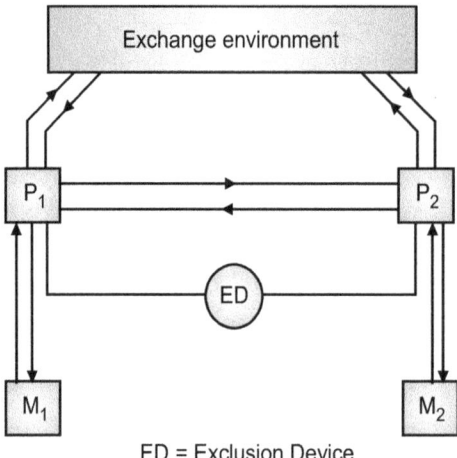

ED = Exclusion Device

Fig. 1.16: Load sharing configuration

- Both processors are active simultaneously and share the load and the resources dynamically. Both processors have access to entire exchange environment.

- Incoming call is assigned randomly or in predetermined order to one of the processors. It then handles that call upto completion.

- Both processors have different memories for storing call data.

- There is an interprocessor link through which the processor exchange information. This is done for mutual co-ordination and to verify 'state of health' of other processor. If the exchange information fails, the processor which detects this, takes the entire load. This load also includes the calls that are already set up by the failing processor.

- Because the resources are shared, one exclusion device is needed, so that both the processors do not seek the same resource at the same time. This device, which set by one processor, prohibits access to that particular device/resource by other processor, until is reset by the first processor.

- Under normal operation, each processor handles half the calls. Load sharing configuration improves the performance as capacities of both are available to handle the overload.

- Main purpose of redundant configuration is to increase the overall availability of the system.

1.5.5 Distributed SPC

- In distributed control, the control functions are shared by many processors within the exchange itself. This structure offers better availability and reliability than centralized SPC.

- Exchange control functions may be decomposed horizontally or vertically.

- In horizontal decomposition, each processor performs only one or some of the exchange control functions.

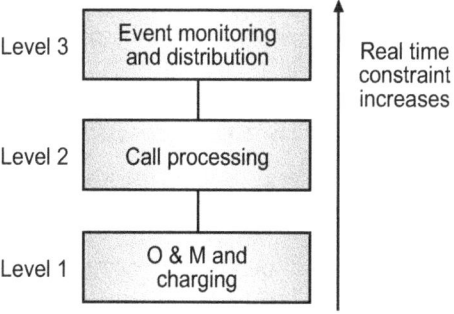

Fig. 1.17: Levels of control functions

- A chain of different processors is used to perform event monitoring, call processing and O and M functions. Entire chain may be duplicated for redundancy.

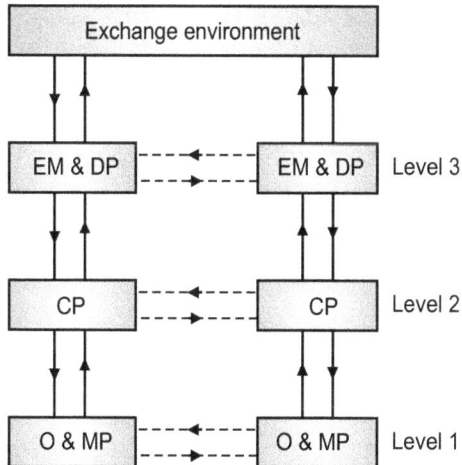

Fig. 1.18: Dual chain distributed control

- In vertical decomposition, the exchange environment is divided into several blocks and each block is assigned to a processor. That processor performs all control functions related to that block. Total control system now consists of several control units coupled together.

- Processor in each block can be duplicated for redundancy. Because of this modular arrangement, exchange expansion is possible easily.

- Since the processors perform specific functions in distributed control, they can be specially designed to carry out these functions efficiently.

- As seen in Fig. 1.18, level 3 processor handles scanning, distribution and marking functions.

- Level 2 processor, also called as switching processor, is designed to ensure 99.9% availability, fault tolerance and security, and to handle a traffic load 40% higher than normal load. Level 1 processor handles O and M functions like - traffic monitoring, adding new line/trunk for operation, detect and locate faults, run diagnostic programs, etc.

- It was mentioned earlier that in space division networks, a crosspoint switching element is used to establish a specific connection between two subscribers.
  (For details see Principles of Crossbar Switching in Appendix).

- A crosspoint is usable for establishing more than 1 connection. This sharing leads to reduction in number of switching elements required in the network.
  A switching element, once allotted, remains dedicated to that connection for the entire call duration. That means a crosspoint is dedicated to one active speech circuit (one conversation/call). A dedicated crosspoint is required because continuous analog speech waveform is passed through the switch in space division switching.

1.6 Digital Switching

- Speech produces narrow band of frequencies 100 Hz to 10 kHz. If all frequencies in speech are transmitted, speech appears to be very natural. But speech remains understandable even if some upper and lower frequencies of speech spectrum are omitted. A **reduction** in **bandwidth** is desirable as it **reduces** the **cost** of **communication.** An acceptable level of intelligibility of speech is obtained by transmitting frequencies in the range of 300 Hz to 3.4 kHz. Such band limited speech signal is often called 'toll' quality speech. Most commercial speech communication systems are designed to have a bandwidth of 3.1 kHz.

- A channel in communication system has a finite transmission loss and is subject to addition of noise. When the length of path increases, signal to noise ratio at the receiving end decreases. In worst cases, signal may be completely masked by the additive noise, particularly when signal level is low. In analog voice transmission, the effect of noise and interference is most noticeable during speech pauses when the signal amplitude is almost zero. Even low noise can be quite annoying during speech pauses.

- Digital speech transmission overcomes many of problems in analog systems. In digital system speech and speech pauses are encoded with data pattern (some coding format) and are transmitted at a constant power level. During signal regeneration, when signal is brought to original level, almost all noise is eliminated. Thus the idle channel noise is determined by the encoding process and not by transmission link.

- The ability to reject crosstalk is superior in digital system than in analog systems. Low level crosstalks are eliminated because of constant amplitude signals. High amplitude crosstalks result in detection errors and are therefore, unintelligible.

- Other advantages of digital systems are their ability to support non-voice services (like picture, video, text, etc.) and easy data encryption and performance monitoring.

- The signal structure in a digital system is independent of the nature of traffic and hence the quality of received signal is guaranteed without knowing the traffic type.

- Digital systems require greater bandwidth than analog systems. Sometimes, this is a big disadvantage. But the advantages are much more, so digital systems are opted for.

- In digital transmission, sampled values of speech are sent as PAM (Pulse Amplitude Modulated) or PCM (Pulse Code Modulated) binary words. You are well aware of these techniques. With 8 kHz sampling rate, (satisfying Nyquist criteria for bandwidth of speech) a sample occurs every 125 μs. In **digital** domain, the **sample values** can be **passed** from an **inlet** to an **outlet** in a few **microseconds** (μs) or less, through a switching element. As a result, during
  125 μs sampling interval, a dedicated switching element remains unused for most of the time, say for over 120 μs. If by some mechanism, that switching element is assigned to different inlet-outlet pairs, for few microseconds each, the same single switching element can be used for transmitting speech samples from a number of inlets to corresponding outlets. That means, a **switching element** can be **shared** by a number of **simultaneously active speech circuits.** This is the principle of **time division switching.**

1.6.1 Basic Time Division Space Switching

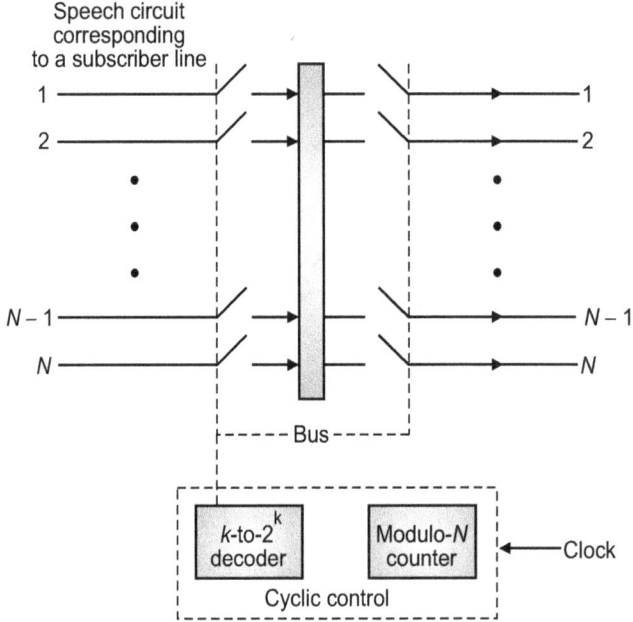

(a) Switching structure

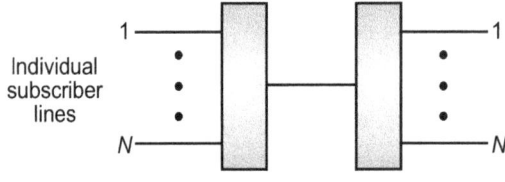

(b) Two-stage equivalent

Fig. 1.19: Simple PAM time division switching

- Shown above in Fig. 1.19 (a), is a simple N × N time division space switch.

- The same is represented as N × 1 and 1 × N : 2 stage representation, having one interconnecting link.

- Speech is carried as PAM analog or PCM digital samples at 125 μs intervals.

- When PAM samples are switched in time division manner, switching is known as **analog time division switching.**

- If PCM, binary samples are switched, switching is known as **digital time division switching.**

- As in Fig. 1.19 (a), bus connects the chosen inlet to outlet by suitable control mechanism and speech samples are transferred.

- Depending on PAM or PCM, analog or digital bus is used.

- The number of **simultaneous conversations,** SC, that can be supported on this network, is **inversely proportional** to time required to **select** and **connect** an **inlet-outlet pair** and **transfer** the **sample** from inlet and outlet.

$$SC = \frac{125}{t_s}$$

t_s is in microseconds, the time to set up a connection and transfer the sample.

- The selection of inlet/outlet is controlled dynamically.

- Simplest form of control is selection in cyclic manner.

- In this case, there is a fixed one-to-one correspondence between inlets and outlets. This implies, if cycle starts like 1, 2, ... N, 1 2, ... N, then, inlet i is always connected to outlet i.

- Effectively, it just happens that a single switching element is used/shared by all N pairs.

- Since all inlets/outlets are scanned within 125 μs, switching capacity of network is same as the number of inlets/outlets and the switch is
non-blocking. But it lacks full availability as it is not possible to connect any inlet to any outlet.

- If we make one of the controls memory based full availability can be obtained.

Input Controlled Time Division Space Switch:

- Input side is cyclically switched.
- There is control memory on output side. This contains the addresses of the outlets in the order in which they are to be connected to inlets. These are stored in contiguous locations. e.g. if address sequence 4-7-1-5 is stored in locations 1, 2, 3, 4 of the control memory, it implies that inlet 1 is connected to outlet 4, inlet 2 to outlet 7, 3 to 1, 4 to 5.
- This switch is said to be **input controlled** or input driven, as the outlet is selected depending upon the inlet that is being scanned at any instant.
- The modulo N counter of cyclic control also acts as MAR (Memory Address Register) of the control memory.
- Control memory has N words (for N inlets) and width is $\log_2 N$ bits to address the N outlets.

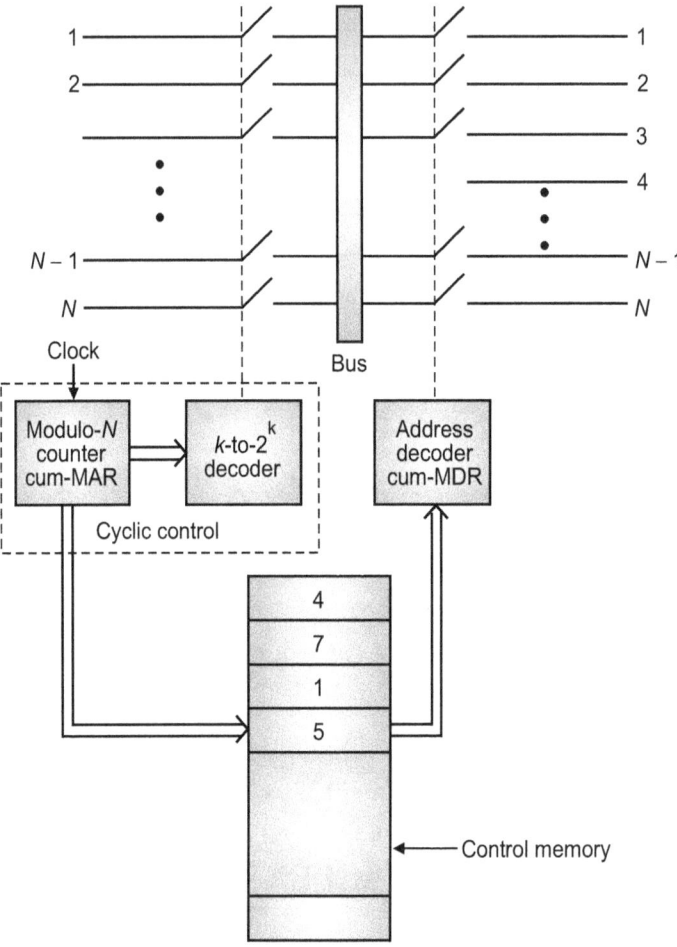

Fig. 1.20: Input-controlled time division space switch

- Cyclic control implies that all subscriber lines are scanned irrespective of whether they are active or not.
- For an active inlet i, the corresponding outlet address is contained in i^{th} location of control memory.
- It is read and passed to address decoder, also acting as MDR - Memory Data Register of control memory.
- Decoder output enables power outlet to be connected to the bus and then sample is transferred from inlet to outlet.
- Thus, any inlet can be connected to any outlet ensuring full availability.
- In case the inlet is not active, corresponding location in control memory contains a null value and thus, does not allow decoder to enable any output line.

- A single switching element is being time shared by N connections, and a physical connection is established between inlet and outlet for the duration of sample transfer (t_S), this switching technique is **time division space switching.**

Output Controlled Time Division Space Switch:

On similar lines, a fully available time division space switch can be designed with cyclic control for outlets and control memory based selection for inlets. Here, the switch is called **output controlled,** because each location of control memory is rigidly associated with a given outlet.

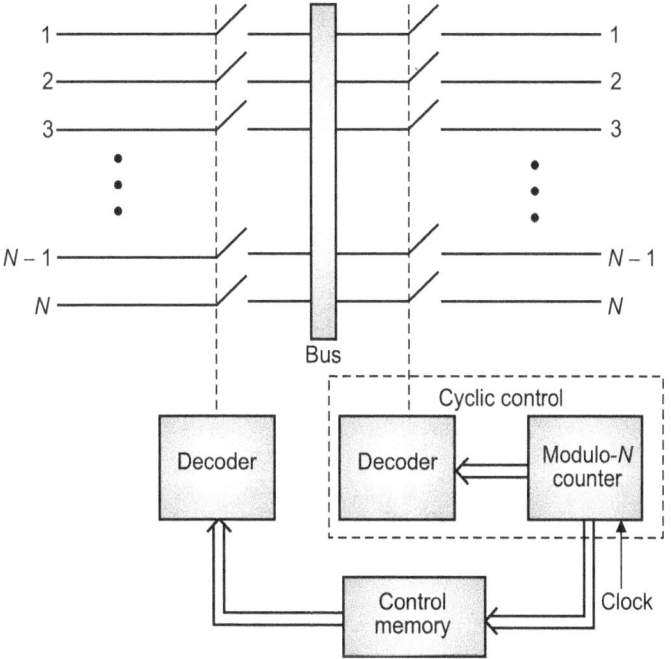

Fig. 1.21: Output-controlled time division space switch

- These switches are capable of supporting broadcast connections.

  [Broadcast: Data from same inlet is transferred to all outlets].
- So far we have assumed that samples are transferred from inlet to outlet. In practical conversation, speech is exchanged both ways.
- For this two independent buses may be used, so that data transfers can take place simultaneously in opposite directions.
- Or a single bus may be used to organize the two-way data transfer, first in one direction and then in opposite direction.
- Digital bus usually supports parallel data transfer.
- Input or output controlled configuration can be used to support folded network connections. They also support two-way transfer for folded networks.

- The use of cyclic control in input or output controlled switches restricts the number of subscribers on the system rather than switching capacity. This is because with cyclic control, all the lines are scanned irrespective of whether they are active or not.
- In practice, the number of active subscribers is only about 20% of the total.

Memory Controlled Time Division Space Switch:

A switch configuration based on the use of control memory for controlling both inlets and outlets can be designed. It can permit a much larger number of subscribers than the switching capacity of the network and this is called as memory controlled time division space switch.

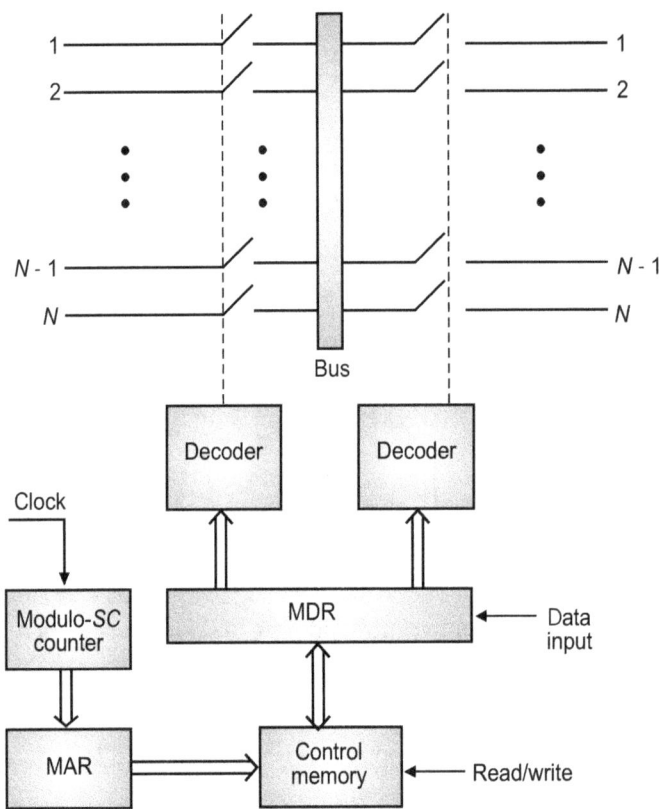

MDR = Memory DataAddress, MAR = MemoryAddress Register

Fig. 1.22: Generalised time division space switch

- Here, each word of control memory has two addresses – inlet address and outlet address.
- The memory width is 2 [$\log_2 N$].
- Modulo-SC counter [switching capacity] is updated at the clock rate.
- Control memory words are read out one after other.

- The inlet address is used to connect that inlet to the bus and outlet address is used to connect that particular outlet to the bus.
- Then sample is transferred from inlet to outlet.
- Clock updates counter and cycle is repeated.
- The number of words in control memory and the size of modulo counter are now equal to the switching capacity of the network and have no relation to the number of subscribers.

$$SC = \frac{125}{t_s}$$

$$\text{Clock Rate } = 8.Sc \text{ kHz}$$

$$t_s \quad - \quad t_i + t_m + t_d + t_t$$
$$t_i \quad - \quad \text{Time to increment modulo N counter}$$
$$t_m \quad - \quad \text{Time to read control memory}$$
$$t_d \quad - \quad \text{Time to decode and select inlet and /or outlet}$$
$$t_t \quad - \quad \text{Time to transfer sample from inlet to outlet}$$

[Same equations are applicable for input controlled and output controlled).

1.6.2 Basic Time Division Time Switching

- Another way of organizing time division switching is to use a memory block in place of the bus used earlier, provided we have PCM samples.

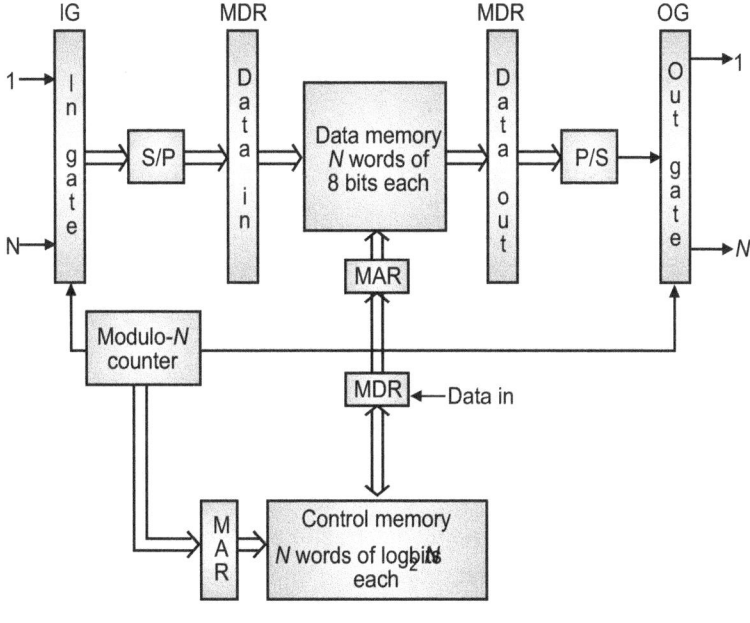

(a) Switching structure

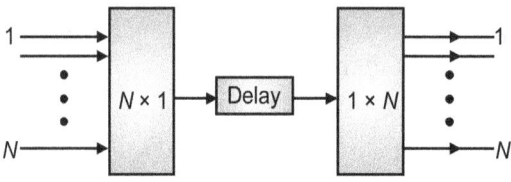

(b) Equivalent circuit

Fig. 1.23: Basic time division time switching

- In this organization, data coming in through inlets are written into data memory and are read out later to the appropriate outlets.

- Usually incoming and outgoing data are in serial form and memory read/write is in parallel form. So serial-to-parallel and then parallel-to-serial conversion is needed.

- There is **no physical connection**, even momentarily between inlets and outlets.

- Information is **not** transferred in **real time,** it is first stored in memory, and later transferred to outlet.

  There is **time delay** between sample acquisition from inlet and its delivery to related outlet.

  So this data memory base scheme is called **time division time switching.**

- This can be controlled in following three ways:

  (1)   Sequential write/random read.

  (2)   Random write/sequential read.

  (3)   Random input/random output.

- In (1) and (2), read and write operations refer to read/write associated with data memory. In both cases, inlets and outlets are scanned sequentially.

- In (3), inlets and outlets are scanned randomly and data memory is accessed sequentially.

  With each of these three forms, time division time switch may be operated in two modes:

  (1)   Phased operation.

  (2)   Slotted operation.

- With **sequential write/random read** control, and with **phased operation**, the inlets are scanned one after other in **first phase** and the data are stored in data memory sequentially.

- The data memory location i corresponds to inlet i (one-to-one correspondence).

- The control memory locations 1, 2, ... N contain the addresses of inlets corresponding to outlets 1, 2, 3, ... N.

- In the **second phase**, inlet addresses are read out from control memory.

  The corresponding locations in the data memory are accessed and the data is transferred to outlets in sequence.

- As any inlet can be connected to any outlet, inlet addresses are randomly distributed in control memory. So read access to data memory in random.

- Write access to data memory in 1st phase is sequential and read access in 2nd phase is random, hence the name describes the control method.

  But inlets, outlets and control memory are accessed sequentially.

- Phase 1: Memory write = 1 per inlet.

  Phase 2: Memory reads = 2 $\varnothing$ $\left.\begin{array}{c} \text{1 control memory} \\ + \\ \text{1 data memory} \end{array}\right\}$ per outlet

$$t_s = N\, t_d + N\, (t_d + t_c)$$

t_d – Read/write time for data memory

t_c – Read/write for control memory

N – N individual subscriber lines

If $t_d = t_c = t_m, (t_m$ in µs$)$

then $\boxed{t_s = 3 \cdot N \cdot t_m}$

But entire operation has to be completed within 125 µs.

∴ $\boxed{N = \dfrac{125}{3\, t_m}}$

- The number of subscribers can be increased by overlapping read cycles of data memory and control memory in second phase.

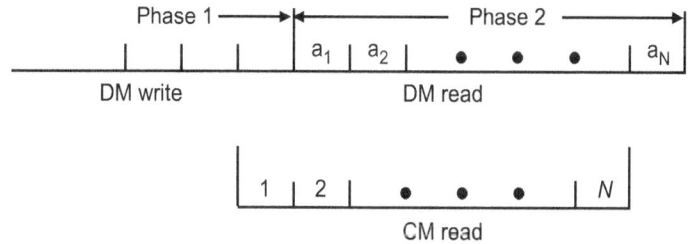

(a) Overlapping of data and control memory reads

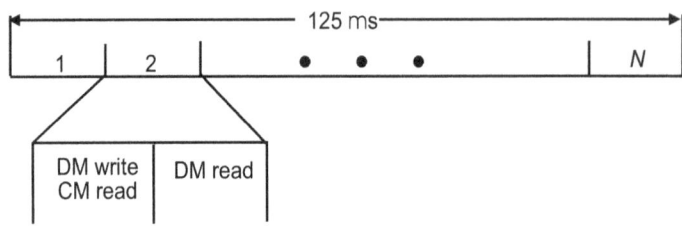

(b) Simultaneous DM write CM read
Fig. 1.24: Two modes of operation of time switches

- As in Fig. 1.24 (a), during **last write** cycle of **phase 1**, the **first location** of **control memory** which contains an inlet address, say a_1, is **read.**
- During **first cycle** of **second phase**, location a_1 of **data memory** and **second** location of **control memory** are read out **simultaneously.**
  So above equation gets modified as,

$$N = \frac{125}{2\, t_m}$$ ... (1.1)

In Slotted Operation:

- The 125 µs period is divided into N subperiods of duration 125/N.
  In each subperiod i, following operations are performed:
  (1)   Read inlet i and store the data in data memory location i.
  (2)   Read the location i of the control memory which contains the value, say j.
  (3)   Read the data memory location j and transfer data to outlet i.
- Operations (1) and (2) can be carried out simultaneously, so that equation (1.1) holds true [Fig. 1.24 (b)].
  Choice of modes is related to design.
- In phased mode, modulo N counter goes through 2 cycles for operation, but in slotted mode, has one cycle.
- In phased mode, Direct Memory Access can be used for data transfer from inlets to outlets. This is not possible in slotted mode.
- In phased mode, the samples are transferred to outlets in the same 125 µs period in which they were acquired. But in slotted mode, sample values may belong to previous 125 µs period, and thus introduces delay of one sample between inlet and outlet.

In Random write/sequential read control in phased operation,

- The control memory contains the addresses of outlets corresponding to the inlets.
- In first phase, control memory is read and inlet data is written into the data memory location specified by the contents of control memory.
- Inlets are scanned sequentially, but written into data memory randomly.
- In second phase, data memory is read out sequentially and data is sent to outlets sequentially.

There is no correspondence between inlets and outlets but there is one-to-one correspondence between outlets and data memory locations.

• The equations studied for sequential write/random read are applicable here also.

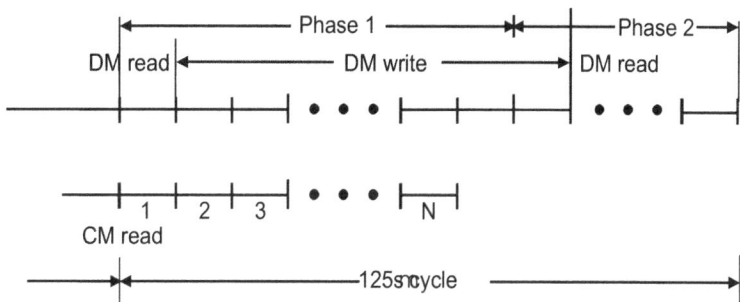

Fig. 1.25: Overlapping of data memory write and control memory read operations

• Here, first read cycle of CM is overlapped with last read cycle of DM in previous 125 μs cycle.

In both the above methods, all inlets and outlets are scanned irrespective of whether they are active or not. So total number of subscribers is limited by the number of read/write operations that can be performed in 125 μs interval.

Or simply, number of subscribers is equal to switching capacity of the system and switches are non-blocking.

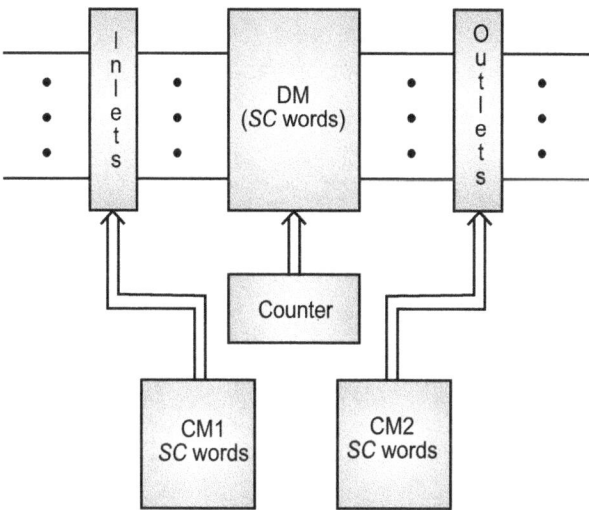

Fig. 1.26: Random input/random output time switch

If we scan only the active subscribers, number of subscribers connected to system can be increased significantly.

The last control method, **random input/random output** permits larger number of subscribers than the switching capacity of the system. The switch in this case is blocking.

- Two control memory modules CM1 and CM2 hold the addresses of active inlets and outlets respectively.

- There is one-to-one **correspondence** between the **locations** of the **two control memories,** that is if **active inlet** is at **x** in **CM1**, address of **outlet** to which inlet is to be connected is at **x** in **CM2**.

- If we consider phased operation, in first phase, addresses of active inlets are read out from CM1, one by one and data is transferred from inlets to the data memory starting from its first location.

- In second phase, addresses of the outlets are read out from CM2, and data from data memory is transferred to outlets specified by these addresses.

- Two read/write operations in each phase give switching capacity,

$$SC = \frac{125}{4t_m}$$

- By overlapping control memory and data memory operations, switching capacity is doubled.

$$SC = \frac{125}{2t_m}$$

- With the VLSI techniques, **dual port** memory chips are available. Using such memory chips, **input** and **output** operations can be done **simultaneously**, again doubling the switching capacity.

$$SC = \frac{125}{t_m}$$

- Entries in the control memory modules specify the active inlet/outlet pairs.

  Whenever a call is set up, corresponding inlet and outlet addresses are entered in CM1 and CM2 respectively at the same location addresses.

- When a call is terminated, corresponding entries are set to null.

- The entries in control memory are managed by any of the three ways:

  (1) By maintaining a free list:

  [A linked list having information about the free locations in control memory.]

  (2) By compacting the entries everytime a call terminates:

  [Gathering all entries of active pairs at the beginning of control memory.]

  (3) By maintaining free and occupied lists.

1.6.3 Time Multiplex Switches

The switches we have seen so far (time division space/time) are used in local exchanges. Now, we have to study the switches that are used in transit exchanges. Those exchanges have time multiplexed switches. Here inlets and outlets are trunks, which carry time division multiplexed data streams.

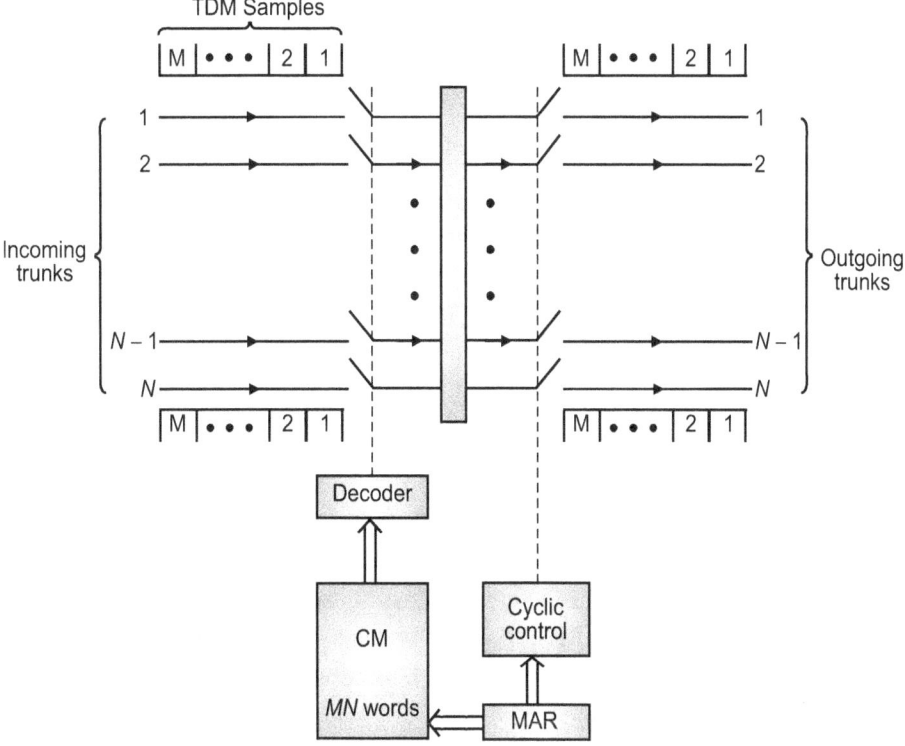

Fig. 1.27: Time multiplexed space switch

Fig. 1.27 shows a time multiplexed time division space switch.

- There are N incoming and N outgoing trunks.
- Each trunk carries a time division multiplexed stream of M samples per frame. Each frame is of 125 μs time duration.
- In one frame time, a total of **MN** speech samples have to be switched.

    One sample duration (125/M μs) is called as a **time slot.**
- In one time slot, N samples are switched.
- Fig. 1.27 shows an output-controlled switch.

- The output is cyclically scanned.
- There are **M locations** in the **control memory for each outlet.** (1: M relation between outlet: CM).
- In total, control memory has **MN words.**

  We can view it as memory of M blocks of N words each. We can also represent a location address in a 2-D form like (i, j).

  i → block address (1 ≤ i ≤ m).

  j → word within that block (1 ≤ j ≤ N).

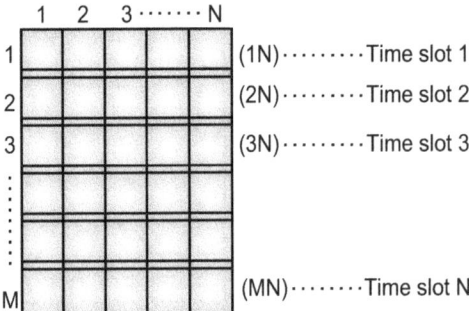

Fig. 1.28

Block address i corresponds to time slot i and j to outlet j.

- First N locations correspond to first time slot (1, 1) to (1, N), next N locations (2, 1) to (2, N) or (N + 1 to 2N with linear addressing) correspond to second time slot.
- If location (i, j) contains inlet address k, it means that inlet k is connected to outlet j during the time slot i. (Recall functioning of output controlled switch).

  [As in Fig. 1.28, address (2, 3) contains value 5. So 5 to 3 connection at time slot 2].

- The number of trunks supported is –

$$N = \frac{125}{Mt_s}$$

t_s – Switching time including memory access time per inlet-outlet pair

- Cost of switch is,

  C = Number of switches + Number of memory words.

$$C = 2N + MN$$

- The number of trunks supported can be increased by splitting control memory into N independent modules of M words each.

  Each module services one input or output line.

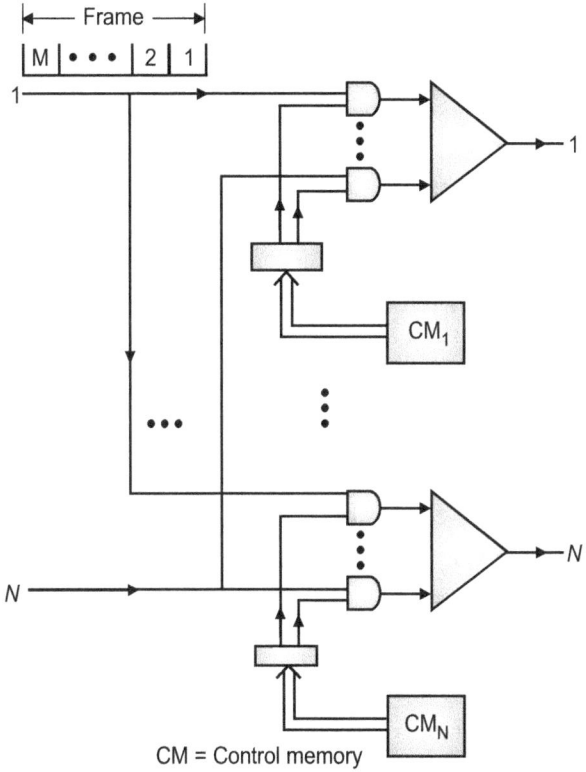

CM = Control memory

Fig. 1.29: Time multiplexed space switch with N control memory modules

- If control memory modules are arranged such that each one services one input and switches input data to proper output during every time slot, the switch is input controlled.
  If all modules serve the output lines by switching the appropriate inputs, the switch is output controlled.
- Fig. 1.29 shows output - controlled configuration. There is one control memory module for each output line.
- These contain the addresses of inlets that should be switched to respective outputs in each of M time slots. Location 1 of every module corresponds to time slot 1, location 2 to time slot 2.
  This implies that all locations corresponding to a particular time slot are read out in parallel.
- There is no constraint on number of trunks supported due to time.

Only constraint is, $\boxed{M = \dfrac{125}{t_m}}$

t_m – Control memory access time.

-              Cost of switch = Number of switches + Memory words.
          Number of switches = N switches of size (N × 1) at each input
    ∴   C = N (N × 1) + MN

$$\boxed{C = N^2 + MN}$$

- Because of broadcast facility, output controlled configurations are preferred over input controlled.
- Time multiplexed space switches do not provide full availability. Sources, trunks and destination have one-to-one time relationship.
- A sample from input slot i can be transferred only to destination i of one or more outlets. For every input, there are N (M − 1) outputs that cannot be reached. In other words, interchange of samples among different time slots is not possible. So it is not fully available.

Time Multiplexed Time Switching:

These switches permit **time slot interchange** (TSI) of sample values. In TSI, speech sample input during one time slot may be sent to output during different time slot. This implies a delay between reception and transmission of a sample.

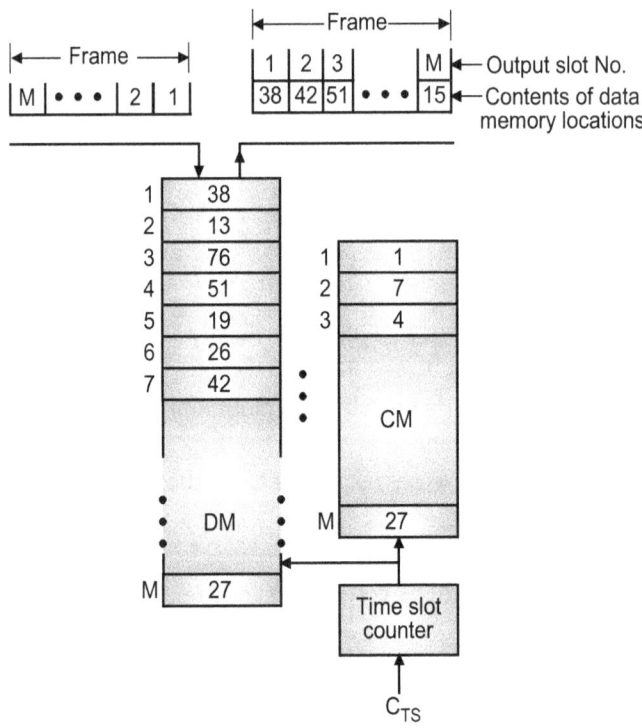

CM = Control Memory, DTS = Time slot clock, DM = Data Memory

(a) Principle of Time Slot Interchange

Fig. 1.30: Time Slot Interchange switch

- Fig. 1.30 (a) illustrates principle of TSI by considering one incoming and one outgoing trunk.
- M channels are multiplexed in each trunk.
- The switch is organized in sequential write/random read manner.
- Time slot duration, $t_{TS} = \dfrac{125}{M}$.

  Time slot clock runs at time slot rate.

  (1 pulse every 125/M µs).

  Time slot counter is incremented by one at the end of each time slot.
- The contents of the counter provide location addresses for data memory and control memory.
- Data memory and control memory are accessed simultaneously at the beginning of time slot.
- Then the contents of control memory are used as the address of data memory. Then data is read out to the output trunk.

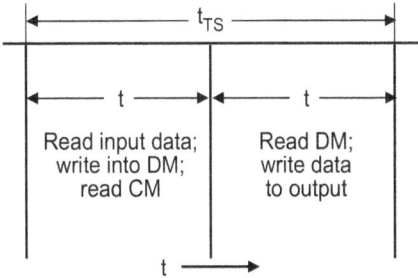

(b) Operations in a time slot

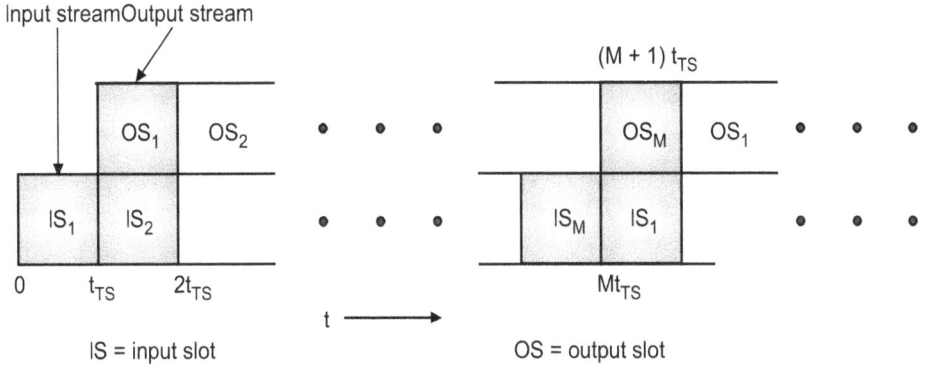

(c) Time relationship between inlet and outlet streams
Fig. 1.30: Time slot interchange switch (cont.)

- Fig. 1.30 (b) shows operations in one time slot.

- **Sample is available** for reading at the **beginning of time slot** and the sample is **ready** for **output** (on output trunk) **at the end of time slot.**

- Even if there is no time slot interchange, a sample is **delayed by a minimum of one time slot,** because of the storage action.

  Time slot switch can be considered to have an inherent delay of one time slot.

- As Fig. 1.30 (c) shows, output stream is delayed by t_{TS} µs as compared to incoming stream.

- Depending on the output time slot to which an input slot contents are switched, sample experiences a delay in the range of t_{TS} to Mt_{TS} µs.

  Refer Fig. 1.30 (a), and observe the entries.

      –   CM[1] = 1 implies input time slot 1 switch to output time slot 1

  $\therefore$ Delay experienced by sample = t_{TS}.

      –   CM[2] = 7 implies input time slot 1 switch to output time slot 2.

  $\therefore$ Delay experienced = $((M - 7) + 2 + 1) \, t_{TS}$

                         = $(M - 4) \, t_{TS}$

      –   CM[3] = 4 implies input time slot 4 switch to output time slot 3

  $\therefore$ Delay experienced = $((M - 4) + 3 + 1) \, t_{TS}$ µs

                         = $M \cdot t_{TS}$

- There are two sequential memory accesses per time slot (CM and DM). So the time constraint is,

$$t_{TS} \; = \; 2 \, t_m$$

$$\boxed{125 = 2 \cdot M \, t_m}$$

t_m – Access time of memory modules in µs.

- As there are no switching elements,

          Cost of switch   = Number of memory locations

$$\boxed{C = 2M}$$

- When there is two-way traffic and network is non-folded, another set of data and control memory is used.

  In second CM, locations 1, 7, 4 contain 1, 2, 3 respectively corresponding to sample entries shown.

  When 125 µs cycle is complete, values in input time slots 1, 7, 4 are interchanged with output time slots 1, 2, 3.

- When network is folded, there is only one set of CM and DM even for two-way traffic.

  CM locations 7, 4 contain 2 and 3. When 125 µs cycle is complete, values in time slots 7 and 2, and in time slots 4 and 3 are interchanged.

  For a folded network, transferring data from same time slots (input time slot 1 to output time slot 1) is irrelevant.

- A TSI switch may be designed to be expanding or concentrating. In such switch, the number of time slots/(samples) per frame in the input (M_1) and output (M_2) are different.
- The switch is **expanding** if $M_2 > M_1$. Here, M_2, output bit rate is higher than input. For a **concentrating** switch, $M_1 > M_2$, the input bit rate is higher.
- This can be realised by delinking read and write operations of DM. They are carried out independently and asynchronously.

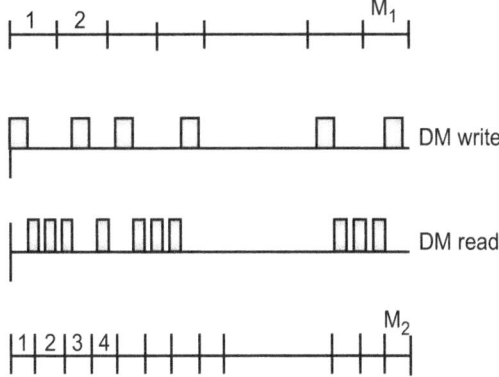

Fig. 1.31: Asynchronous read/write operations

- Time constraint becomes,

$$125 = (M_1 + M_2) t_m$$

- Buffering may be required at input and output to ensure uniform data rates.
- Major application of expanding and concentrating time switches is in combination switching.

Principle configurations of time multiplexed time switches are:

1. Serial-in/Serial-out.
2. Parallel-in/Serial-out.
3. Serial =in/Parallel-out.
4. Parallel-in/Parallel-out.

In these configurations, there are N time multiplexed time streams, each multiplexing M subscribers, at both input and output. So NM subscribers are to be handled in 125 µs.

1. Serial-in/Serial-out:

- This configuration is similar to one we studied in last section. Fig. 1.30 (a), except that there are N input and N output streams.
- Because of multiple input and output streams, gating circuits are required to route data from inlets to data memory and from data memory to outlets. They are equivalent to N × 1 and 1 × N switching matrices.

- Capacities of both, CM and DM, are NM words each. Width of DM word is 8 bits and that of CM word is $\log_2$ MN.

  The time slot counter width is $\log_2$ MN.

- Counter functions as modulo MN counter.

- Samples of first time slot in locations: 1 to N of data memory.

  Samples of second time slot in locations: N + 1 to 2N ...

- Input sample addresses corresponding to first output time slot 1 are stored in locations 1 to N of control memory, for time slot 2 in N +1 to 2N ...

- In each time slot, N data words are to be input and N data words are to be output.

- During first time slot, first slot samples from all input streams are read and stored in data memory. Within the same time duration, data words corresponding to first time slot of all N output streams are read out from data memory and sent to respective output streams.

- Data memory write and control memory read are carried out simultaneously, followed by data memory read.

- Time constraint is,

$$\textbf{125} = \textbf{2 NM t}_m \qquad (\because t_{TS} = 2N\ t_m)$$

2. Parallel-in/Serial-out:

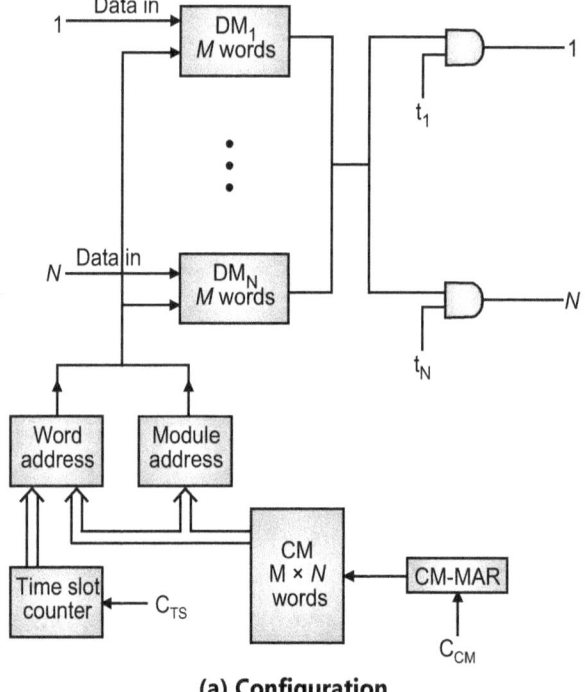

(a) Configuration

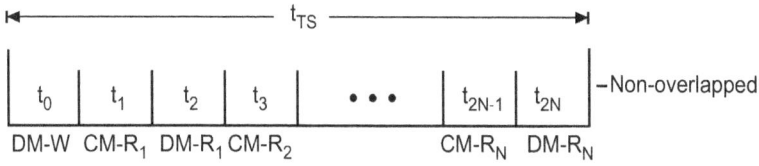

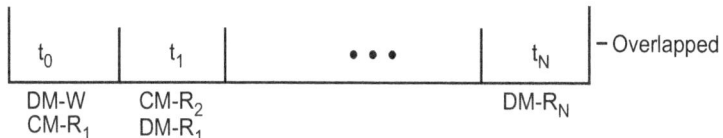

(b) Timing details

Fig. 1.32: Parallel-in/Serial-out configuration

- Data memory is organized as N modules of M words.

- Each module is associated with one input line.

- Time slot duration t_{TS} is divided into N + 1 subslots: $t_0, t_1, ..., t_N$.

  During subslot t_0, data from all input lines are read into respective data memory modules simultaneously.

- A 2-D addressing structure (word address, module address): (time slot n_0, inlet n_0) is used to access data memory words.

  e.g. word 1 corresponds to time slot 1, word 2 corresponds to time slot 2.

- A special control signal is used to enable all the data memory modules for write access during subslot t_0.

- During subslots t_1 to t_N, control memory locations are accessed one after another.

  Then contents of the locations are used to address the data memory for read access and the data words read out are transferred to the corresponding output lines.

- During subslot t_1 of time slot i, data word read from data memory is transferred to the outgoing trunk 1, for insertion in time slot i of this stream. Similar transfers take place during subslots t_2 to t_N to outgoing trunks 2 to N.

- Control memory word width: $\log_2 N + \log_2 M$.

- Control memory clock C_{cm} runs at the rate of one pulse per $t_{TS}/(N + 1)$ µs, except that one pulse is inhibited during subslot t_0.

- Control memory read may be overlapped with data memory. Fig. 1.32 (b) shows this.

- Time constraints now are –

  For non-overlapped operation,

  $$t_{TS} = (2N + 1) t_m, \quad 125 = M (2N + 1) t_m$$

  For overlapped operation,

  $$t_{TS} = (N + 1) t_m, \quad 125 = M(N + 1) t_m$$

- Maximum delay between acquisition and transmission of sample varies between t_0 and $125 - t_N$ μs.

3. Serial-in/Parallel-out:

- Here, data memory modules are associated with the output lines instead of input lines.
- Data input is serial and is carried out during the subslots t_1 to t_N.
- The subslot t_0 is used for parallel read out from all the data memory modules to corresponding output lines.
- It appears that output precedes input. But as the entire operation is cyclic, this is immaterial.

4. Parallel-in/Parallel-out:

Though most complex, this configuration can support largest number of subscribers.

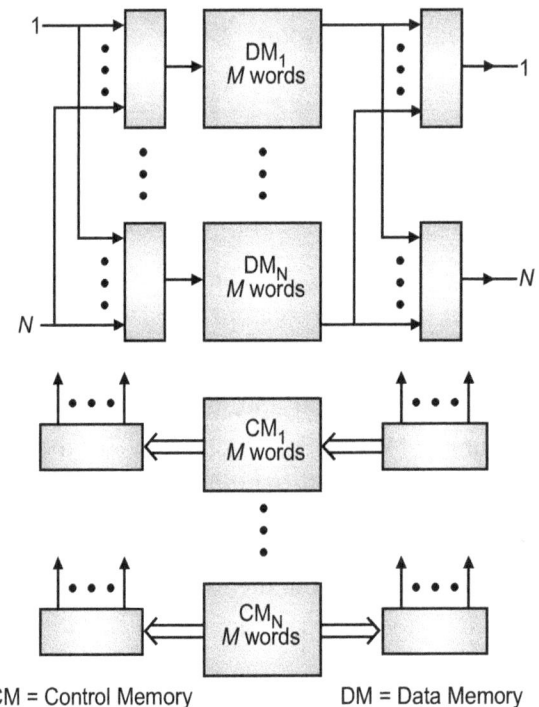

CM = Control Memory   DM = Data Memory

(a) Configuration

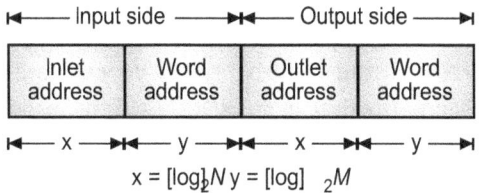

$$x = [\log_2 N \quad y = [\log]_2 M$$

(b) Contents of control memory locations

Fig. 1.33: Parallel-in/Parallel-out time switch

- Both, data memory and control memory are organized as N independent modules of M words each.

  There is one-to-one correspondence between CM and DM modules.

- Address outputs from control memory module i are always used to access words in data memory module i. The correspondence is limited to the module level and does not extend to word level.

- Each location of control memory module contains information about both input side and output side as shown in Fig. 1.33 (b).

- Inlet/outlet address selects one of the N inlet/outlet streams.

  Word address is used to access one of the M words in data memory module corresponding to control memory module from which the word address is read.

- There is one-to-one correspondence between the control memory words and the time slots. The word i in each module contains information pertaining to time slot i.

  There is no such correspondence with data memory words.

- The operation of the switch takes place in three phases in each time slot.

  (1)   Control memory read

  (2)   Data memory write

  (3)   Data memory read.

- Let us consider operation of switch corresponding to time slot 1.

- In first phase, the first location of all control memory modules are read.

  The inlet addresses are decoded and the respective inlets are gated to MDR of Data Memory Modules (DMM).

  The word addresses of input side are transferred to respective MARs of data memory modules.

- In the second phase, a **write** operation is performed in all DMM simultaneously, and the data contained in MDRs are transferred to the respective locations.

- In the third phase, output side word addresses are transferred to respective MARs and a **read** operation is performed in all the DMMs.

The MDRs now contain the data to be transferred to the required outlets.

The outlet addresses from control memory word are decoded to select the respective outlets and the data from MDRs are transferred.

- The time constraint is,

$$t_{TS} = 3t_m$$

It is **independent of N** and thus allows any number of trunks to be supported theoretically. However, practically, engineering constraints limit this number.

1.6.4 Combination Switching

Time multiplexed time division space switches do not provide full availability as they are not capable of performing time slot interchange. Time slot interchange switches are not capable of switching samples across the trunks without the help of some space switching matrices.

So a **combination** of time and space switches leads to configurations that achieve both **time slot interchange** and **sample switching across trunks.** These structures also permit a large number of simultaneous connections to be supported for a given technology.

A combination switch can be built by using a number of stages of time and space switches. Two switch combinations can be **time-space** (TS) or **space-time** (ST) depending on which stage is first.

Two-Stage TS (Time-Space) Switch:

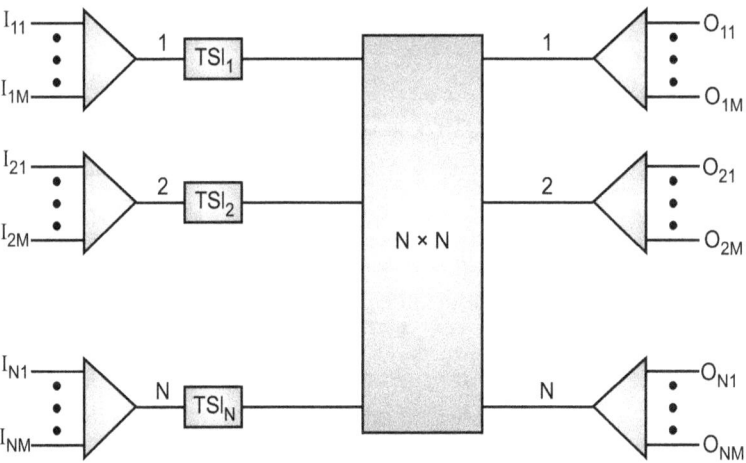

Fig. 1.34: Two-stage TS switch

- As in Fig. 1.34,

  First stage: One time slot interchange per inlet.

  Second stage: $N \times N$ space switch.

  [Memories CM/DM not shown here].

- Each time multiplexed inlet/outlet stream carries M channels.

  A subscriber on the input side is assigned to one of the inlets and a time slot in that inlet.

  I_{47}: Input subscriber assigned to line 4 at time slot 7. (IS_{47}: Its time slot).

  O_{56}: Subscriber connected to outlet 5, time slot 6. (OS_{56}: Its corresponding time slot).

- If communication is between above two subscribers, input sample from IS_{47} is first moved to IS_{46} at the output of TSI switch.

  During time slot 6, connection is established between inlet 4 and outlet 5 at the space switch.

- While this switch configuration ensures full availability, it is not non-blocking.

  Consider two connections: $I_{47} - O_{29}$ and I_{43} and O_{69}. Both samples are from same inlet and are destined to same time slot in different outlets. Both input samples require to be switched to time slot 9, which is not possible. Only one of them can be connected.

- Theoretically TS switch can be made non-blocking by using an expanding time switch and a concentrating space switch.

Two-Stage ST (Space-Time) Switch:

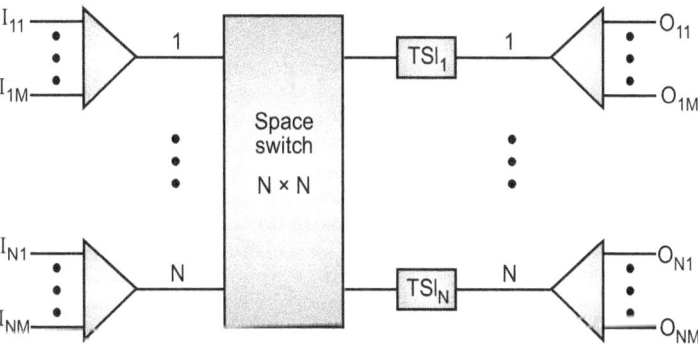

Fig. 1.35: A Space-Time Switch

- Consider a connection between I_{47} and O_{69}.

- During time slot 7, the input sample is switched from inlet 4 to outlet 6 by the space switch.

- It is then switched to time slot 9 by the time switch.

- This switch is also blocking.

  Consider two connections: $I_{75} - O_{96}$ and $I_{85} - O_{92}$.

  Here, only one of the inputs (I_{75}/I_{85}) can be space switched during time slot 5 to the output line 9 and other is blocked.

- Performance of ST and TS switches is identical.

Three-stage Combination Switching:

Three-stage time and space combination switches are more flexible. Most common configurations are:

   (1)   TST (Time-Space-Time) Configuration

   (2)   STS (Space-Time-Space) Configuration

1. TST Configuration:

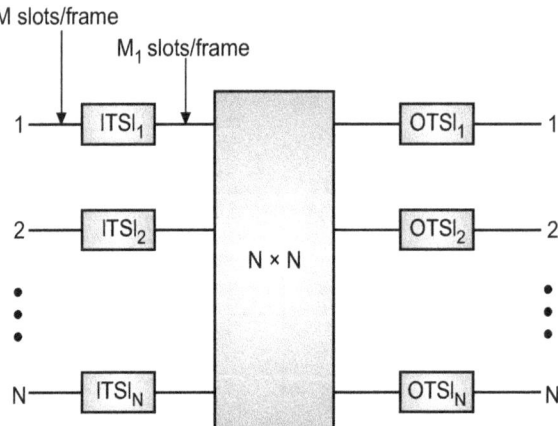

Fig. 1.36: A time-space-time switch

- The two time stages exchange information between external trunks/links and internal space array channels.

- The flexibility that is offered by this configuration is that there is no need to have a fixed space stage time slot for a given input or output time slot.

- An incoming channel time slot may be connected to an outgoing channel time slot using any possible space array time slot. That means, there are many alternative paths between an input and output pair.

- This switch is still blocking.

  Consider a situation when $(M - 1)$ slots in inlet I_j are all busy. Let traffic arrive in M^{th} slot destined to time slot outlet O_k. It is possible that during time slot M, O_k is busy receiving some other output. As a result, blocking occurs.

2. STS Configuration:

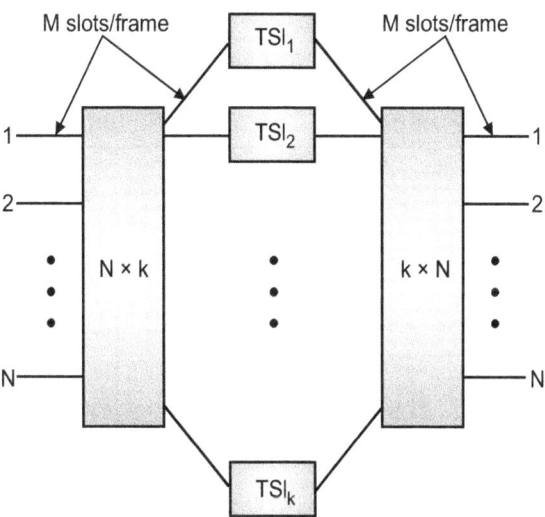

Fig. 1.37: A space-time-space switch

- This consists of $N \times k$ space matrix at the input, an array of k TSI switches in the middle, and $k \times N$ space matrix at the outputs.

- The choice of input and output time slots is fixed for a given connection. But it offers flexibility by the ability to utilize any free TSI switch by space switching on the input and output side.

- There are many alternative paths for a given connection as there are TSI switches. (I_{79} may be connected to O_{84} through TSI_3 as:

  $I_{79} - IS_{79} - IS'_{39} - OS'_{34} - OS_{84} - O_{84}$]

  IS' and OS': Input and output time slots of TST switch.

- Expansion and concentration take place at the space switch level and not at time slot level.

  Time slots are symmetrical throughout the switch.

- Switches are designed to be concentrating when utilization of input links is low.

  When input traffic increases, space expansion in STS switch and time expansion in TST switch are required to maintain low blocking probabilities.

N-stage Combination Switching:

Very large time division switches, supporting 40,000 lines or more can be economically designed by using more than three stages of time and space combination switching. Needless to say they give better flexibility and less blocking.

Typical combinations are shown in Table 1.1.

Table 1.1 (A): Examples of Time-Space Combination Switches

System	Configuration	Traffic Capacity (erlangs)	Maximum Number of Trunks
E10 B (France)	TST	1,600	3,600
No. 4 ESS (USA)	TSSSST	47,000	1,07,520
C-DOT MAX-XL (India)	TST	16,000	40,000
DMS 100 (Folded) (Canada)	TSTS	39,000	61,000
System 12 (USA)	TSTSTSTSTSTS	25,000	60,000
NEAX 61 (Japan)	TSST	22,000	60,000

Table 1.1 (B): Single Stage Vs. Multistage Networks

Single Stage	Multistage
1. Inlet to outlet connection is through a single crosspoint.	1. Inlet to outlet connection is through multiple crosspoints.
2. Use of a single crosspoint per connection results in better quality link.	2. Use of multiple crosspoints may degrade the quality of a connection.
3. Each individual crosspoint can be used for only one inlet/outlet pair connection.	3. Same crosspoint can be used to establish connection between a number of inlet/outlet paired.

Single Stage	Multistage
4. A specific crosspoint is needed for each specific connection.	4. A specific connection may established by using different sets of crosspoint.
5. If a crosspoint fails, associated connection cannot be established. There is no redundancy.	5. Alternative crosspoints and paths are available.
6. Crosspoints are inefficiently used. Only one crosspoint in each row or column of a square or triangular switch matrix is ever in use, even if all the times are active.	7. Number of crosspoints is reduced significantly.
8. A large number of crosspoints in each inlet/outlet leads to capacitive loading.	8. There is no capacitive loading problem.
9. The network is non-blocking in character.	9. The network is blocking in character.
10. Time for establishing a call is less.	10. Time for establishing a call is more.

1.7 Switching Techniques

In last few years, computer and communication technologies are coming together to support many applications and development. Students are well aware of this. One of such developments is data networks which have their beginning in remote computing. Computer users find it convenient if computer access is central or they are centralized systems. Instead of transferring information/data through hard copies or secondary storage devices, it is much more convenient and fast to transmit data on data network. It is a suitable communication network to realize this which would carry data/ information from computer to remote unit or another computer. Earlier PSTN (Public Switched Telephone Network) was used for data transmission. Then progress in this field has led to evolution of modern PDN (Public Data Networks).

So far in previous sections, we were discussing the switches and exchanges related to a call (voice/conversation). When we talk about data, it can be a fax, e-mail messages, text or picture files, etc. Transmission of data is different than voice transmission.

Data transmission in PSTN, limits data rates upto 64 kbps. Use of **modem** is necessary. Students are very much familiar with modems and know its use very well. It converts digital signals to analog at transmitting end and the reverse at the receiving end.

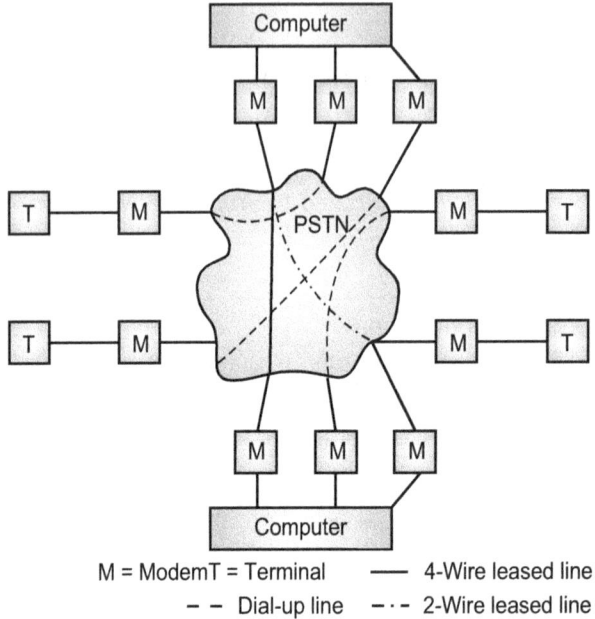

M = Modem T = Terminal   —— 4-Wire leased line
             – – Dial-up line   – · – 2-Wire leased line

Fig. 1.38: Data communication using PSTN

In PSTN, connection can be established using dial up facility or a dedicated non-switched leased line. But basically telephone networks are designed to carry voice traffic. Now, we will see the difference between voice traffic and data traffic.

Differences between Voice and Data Traffic

Voice Traffic	Data Traffic
1. Continuous	Bursty
2. Low bandwidth for long duration	High bandwidth for short duration
3. Typical line utilisation 85-95%	Typical line utilization 5-15%
4. Half duplex	Half or full duplex
5. Real time	Non-real time or near real time
6. Loss acceptable	Loss unacceptable
7. Error tolerable	Error unacceptable

Data traffic is bursty, because, user while sitting at a terminal, may hault for copying files, think in between, or typing something etc. This introduces some long pauses in transmission.

No loss is acceptable, because with a loss, some very important information may be lost or data cannot be reconstructed properly.

You can see there are many differences in voice and data traffic characteristics. This has led to the development of a switching technique. This is better suited for data traffic transmission.

There are two switching techniques for data transmission:

(1) Circuit Switching.

(2) Store and Forward (S and F) Switching.

1.7.1 Circuit Switching

This is analogous to telephone switching.

- In circuit switching, an **electrical path** is established between the **source** and **destination before** any data transfer takes place.

- The electrical path may be realised by physical wires/coaxial cables/radio or satellite links.

- It remains **dedicated** to the communicating **pair** for the **entire duration** of the transmission irrespective of whether data is actually transferred or not.

  No other user can use this path even if it is idle.

- The connection is released only when specifically signalled by either of communicating entities.

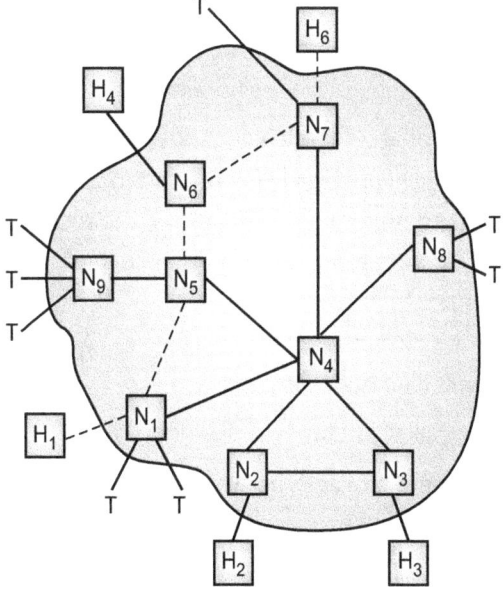

H = Host   N = NodeT=Terminal

Fig. 1.39: Circuit switched network

- When host H_1 wants to transfer data to host computer H_6, a connection request is made to the switching node N_1.

- It then selects a suitable neighbouring node through which the desired connection can be established.

- Next, node N_5 selects onward path through another node (say N_6). N_6 in turn selects N_7.

  So now an electrical path is established between H_1 and H_6 (through nodes $N_1 - N_5 - N_6 - N_7$).

- The path selection is generally based upon a routing algorithm, which takes into account traffic, path length etc. may be a shortest path also. (Same $H_1 - H_6$ connection can be made through $N_1 - N_4 - N_7$).

- Once the path is established, data transfer begins.

- Three phases involved in circuit switched data transfer are:

  (1) Connection establishment (T_c: Time for establishing)

  (2) Data transmission: (T_e: Time for data transmission)

  (3) Connection release: (T_r: Time for path release)

  So total time taken for data transfer through circuit switched connection,

  $$\boxed{T_{CS} = T_e + T_t + T_r}$$

- We ignore the propagation delays as they are very small.

- T_e depends on number of switching nodes in the path between source and destination hosts. Each node (except the last one to which destination host is connected), selects route (or next node) as per the routing algorithm. This involves a certain amount of processing or switching time in each node.

  $$\boxed{T_e = (N - 1)\, T_m}$$

  N – Number of switching nodes in path

  T_m – Average route selection time in each node.

- T_t is dependent on data rate and the size of message.

  $$\boxed{T_t = \frac{M}{R}}$$

  M – Message length in bits.

  R – Data rate in bps.

- T_r is also dependent upon number of switching nodes in a path. Connection release is generally initiated by a 'release signal' which propagates from one end to other. On receiving 'connection release' signal, each node in the circuit performs certain house keeping actions such as making entries in a routing table.

$$\boxed{T_r = N\ T_h}$$

T_h – Time taken to make housekeeping entries

$$\therefore \qquad \boxed{T_{cs} = (N-1)\ T_m + \frac{M}{R} + N\ T_h}$$

- Propagation time is dependent upon the electrical distance between the source and destination, and on the medium of transmission.
  Free space propagation speed ≈ Velocity of electromagnetic waves in vacuum.
  In coaxial cables speed is = 200 m/μs.

- Propagation time, one way (source to destination) can be determined by knowing distance and medium properties. But for each data transfer, the actual protocol used determines how many times the propagation time needs to be counted.
  Consider a simple protocol in which a successful connection establishment is indicated by a signal from destination to source. In this case, twice the propagation time would be counted.
  Here, if we assume no acknowledgement in data transfer and connection release, we can count only one T_p for each of them. (T_p: Transfer + T_p release).

$$\boxed{T_{cs} = (N-1)\ T_m + \frac{M}{R} + N\ T_h + 4\ T_p}$$

- e.g. consider following data and compute data transfer time.
  Switching nodes – 5.
  Establishment time – 2 sec.
  Release time – 0.2 sec.
  Data transfer rate – 2400 bps.
  Message length – 300 bytes.
  Neglecting the propagation time,

$$T_{cs} = (N-1)\ T_m + \frac{M}{R} + N\ T_h$$

$$T_{cs} = (4 \times 2) + \left(300 \times \frac{8}{2400}\right) + (5 \times 0.2)$$

$$= 10\ \text{sec}.$$

[As M is message length in bits, we convert as 300×8].

- In above example, 9 seconds out of total 10 seconds are spent on connection establishment and release and actual transfer lasts only for 1 second.

So circuit switching is inefficient for small messages. Because for those, total data transfer time is dominated by path set up time. But circuit switching is preferred where large volume data transfer is involved.

- Connection establishment time is often a function of load on the network. As load increases, each of the node involved in establishment may have to look for a number of alternative routes before any node is chosen. So path set up time (T_e) increases with load.

Connection release and data transfer times are not significantly affected by the load. Naturally, because once the path is established, it does not affect much.

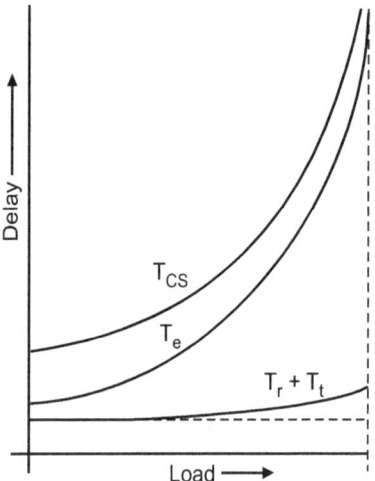

T_{cs}= Total circuit switching delay, T= Connection establishment time

T_r= Connection release time, T= Data transmission time

1.40

Fig. 1.40: Variations of delay components in circuit switching

Fig. 1.40 shows this variation.

Blocking occurs when network is fully loaded.

- Path set up time (20-30 s) turns out to be an excessive overhead for bursty computer traffic which is for few seconds or less.

The entire line quality is affected if there is one bad link in the circuit.

Intercity traffic in PSTNs is carried by high quality coaxial or microwave or satellite links, whereas subscriber links may be of poor quality. And this gives poor quality results although major portion (795%) uses high quality links. This is often termed as 'last mile' problem.

- Speed of operation of the circuit is limited by the slowest link in the circuit. This leads to poor utilization of high capacity links.

Required bandwidth is statically allocated and unused bandwidth is wasted.

- The network does not provide any error control facilities, so they need to be handled by end systems.

1.7.2 Store and Forward (S and F) Switching

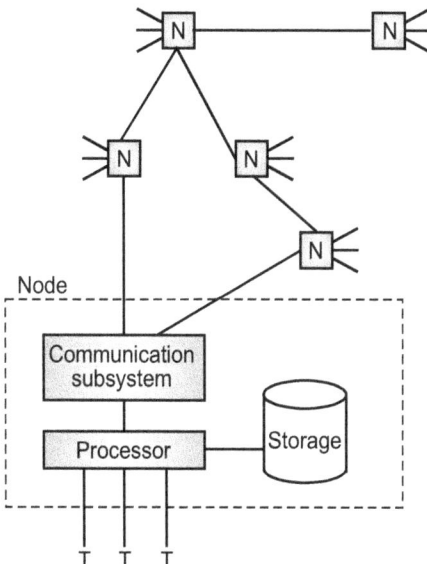

Fig. 1.41: Store and forward network

S and F switching sounds analogous to postal or telegraph system.

- In S and F switching, the switching nodes have the **ability** to **store** user messages and **forward** them towards the **destination** as and when the **links** become **available.**

- For this purpose, each node is equipped with a processor and some buffer storage.

- No end-to-end link is set up prior to data transmission.

- The user deposits the message to the nearest switching node and then, the network takes the responsibility for delivering the message to the destination/host.

- The network moves the user information from node to node. One such movement is called a **'hop'**.

  As communication links are used one at a time, between any two nodes, line speeds are utilized efficiently.

- S and F switching may be classified as:

  (1) Message switching

  (2) Packet switching

(1) Message Switching:

- In message switching, once the transmission is initiated, a **message** is **transmitted completely** without a break from one node to another. That means the message is not split into smaller parts for transmission. Whatever is the data/information sent by user, that is transmitted whole as one message.

- The node processor performs the following functions:

  (1) Receive the full user message and store the same.

  (2) Check the message for data transmission errors and perform error recovery, if required.

  (3) Determine the destination address from the user message.

  (4) Choose an appropriate link towards destination based on certain routing algorithm/criteria.

  (5) Forward the message to next node on the chosen link.

- Message switching has certain drawbacks:

  For long messages, it becomes important to ensure that there is adequate storage space on the receiving node before the transmission is initiated.

  Otherwise, the buffer storage may become full, and a part of the message might not be stored. This requires retransmission of the complete message.

  Similarly, if some error occurs during transmission, the entire message has to be retransmitted.

  Such retransmission of complete message results in large communication overheads in the network.

  If a high priority short message arrives while a long message is in transmission, it has to wait until that transmission of long message is complete.

- The node processor places the message in buffer storage. This storage can be viewed as a queue. The message is not serviced until the resources that is, the proper link for forward transmission is available. It is called as a delay system, or this queuing theory is called waiting line theory.

  Drawbacks of Message Switching are overcome in packet switching.

(2) Packet Switching:

- In packet switching, original user **messages** are **split** into a number of **packets.** These packets are often fixed in size, and these packets are transmitted in S and F manner.

- Messages are **split** at the **source** host and **reassembled** at the **destination** host.

- Each packet transmission is independent of others.

- The packets of a single message may travel via different routes and arrive at the destination with different delays. But with this type of transmission / switching, it may happen that the packets do not arrive serially (as they were split) at the destination, (or they might arrive out of sequence). So to ease out the reassembly, every packet should carry some information.

Complete address information: Destination identifier (id), source identifier, message identifier and packet identifier, along with the actual user data/ message.

A typical packet format is given in Fig. 1.42 (a).

Header					User data
Destination	Source	Message	Packet	Control	
id	id	id	id		

(a) A typical packet format

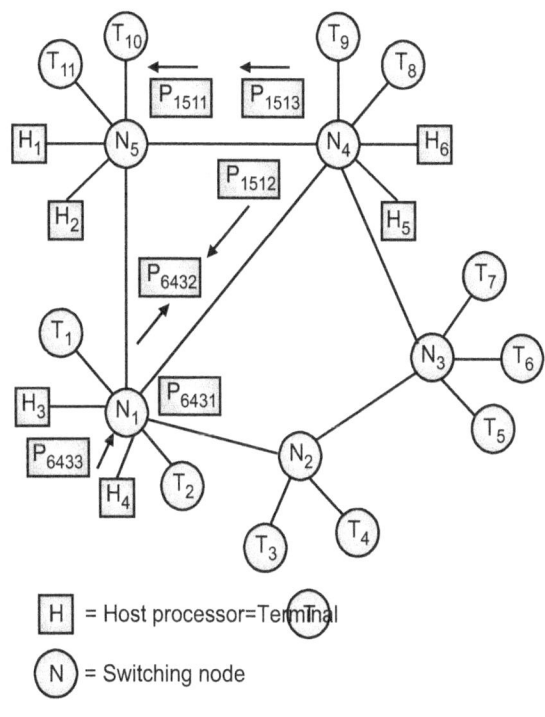

H = Host processor=Terminal

N = Switching node

(b) Packet Switching Network (PSN)

Fig. 1.42: Packet switching

- Packet switching is shown in Fig. 1.42 (b).

As in Fig, 1.42, P_{6432} carries some meaning.

First subscript   : 6 :   Destination host id,

Second subscript   : 4 :   Source host id,

Third subscript   : 3 :   Message id,

Fourth subscript   : 2 :   Packet idd.

So for P_{6432}, we can say second packet of third message originating from source 4, destined to host 6.

- The source host delivers the packets of message in sequence to the network node. Naturally, we expect the packets to arrive at the destination in proper sequence. But as individual packet is routed differently, they arrive out of sequence. So it becomes responsibility of the network to rearrange or reassemble the packets in proper sequence before delivery to the destination host.

- This leads to considerable overhead in terms of buffer storage and processing power at the network nodes and so turns out to be expensive.

- In order to be cost effective, packet networks offer two different forms of services:

(1) Datagram service

(2) Virtual circuit service

In these services, no resequencing is required to be done by the network.

- **Datagram** service is normally used for transmitting **short messages** of one or two packet length.

In case of virtual circuit service, the **route** from source to destination is **fixed** for **all packets** of a message.

- As the packets are delivered to the network in sequence and they follow the same route on a FCFS – First-Come-First-Serve basis, they arrive in sequence at destination.

- But, the transmission of packets may not start until a route is chosen and finalised between source and destination.

- The chosen circuit is not dedicated to a particular connection, as same route can be used for some other transmission. So term **'Virtual Circuit'** describes the connection.

- In virtual circuit, packets need not carry full address information, as all the packets follow the same route.

As soon as a virtual circuit is established between a pair, it is given an identifier (id). This id is sufficient as address in a packet.

- User may want to use the same virtual circuit for a number of messages over a period of time. The circuit established for this is called permanent virtual circuit.

- Delays in S and F networks are:

   (1)   Storage delay, T_s

   (2)   Forwarding delay, T_f

   $\therefore$ S and F delay, $T_{sf} = T_s + T_f$

- As said earlier, a node may be having a number of packets to be sent on outgoing link. These packets are queued and transmitted according to some scheduling and queuing algorithm. (FCFS, priority, etc.) Forwarding delay is largely due to this queuing delay.

- $T_f \qquad\qquad = (N - 1)(T_q + T_m) + T_t$

   T_q – Average queuing delay in each node

   T_m – Processing delay in each node

   T_t – Packet transmission delay

   N – Total nodes involved in the transfer

$(N - 1)$ implies that the destination node does not contribute to any delay as host is attached to it and no other network traffic is on this link.

- If transfer rate is uniform on all links.

$$T_t = (N + 1)\frac{M}{R} + T_p$$

   $(N + 1)$ –   Number of hops from source to destination

   M –   Message length for message switching

       –   Packet length for packet switching

   T_p –   Total propagation delay from source to destination

If data transfer rates are non-uniform,

$$T_t = M\left(\frac{1}{R_1} + \frac{1}{R_2} + ... + \frac{1}{R_{N+1}}\right)$$

- Queuing delay and forwarding delay is a function of load on the network. As load increases, T_f also increases.

Data transmission delay remains almost constant irrespective of load.

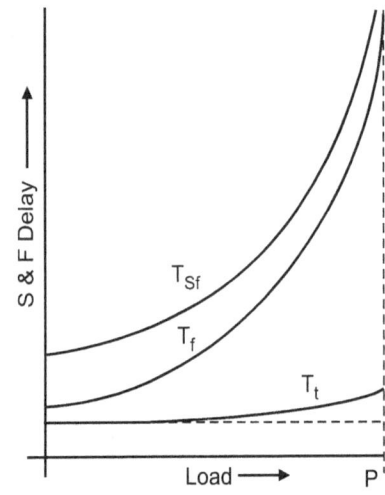

T_f Forwarding delay T_{sf} Store & forward delay
T_t Transmission delay

Fig. 1.43: Variation of delay components in S and F switching

Fig. 1.43 shows these variations.

1.8 Switch Signalling

Signalling systems link variety of switching systems, transmission systems and subscriber equipments in a telecommunication network, and they enable the network to function as a whole.

Three forms of signalling are involved in a telecommunication network.

(1) Subscriber loop signalling.

(2) Intraexchange or register signalling.

(3) Interexchange or inter-register signalling.

- In a telephone network, subscriber loop signalling depends on the type of telephone instrument used. We have seen details of subscriber loop signalling for a rotary dial telephone and also signalling details for a dual tone multifrequency telephone. Multifrequency signalling has brought about new series like Data-In-Voice-Answer, which gives user-to-user signalling facilities.

- The intraexchange signalling is internal to the switching system and depends upon type and design for a switching system, varies from model to model.

- Interexchange signalling takes place between exchanges with common control subsystems, then it is called as inter-register signalling.

   Main purpose of inter-register signalling is the exchange of address digits which pass from exchange to exchange on a link-by-link basis.

Network wide signalling also involves end-to-end signalling between originating and terminating exchange.

Such form of signalling is called line signalling.

- Signalling techniques fall under two major classes: **inchannel signalling and common channel signalling.**

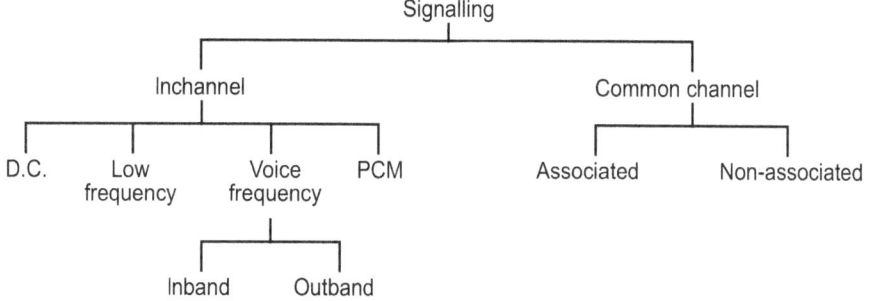

Fig. 1.44: Signalling techniques

- Inchannel signalling, also known as per trunk signalling, uses the same channel which carries user voice or data, to pass control signals related to that channel.

   Inchannel signalling is influenced by various factors associated with information path.

- When unamplified audio line plant which permits an individual metallic signalling path per speech circuit is used, **dc signalling** can be applied. It is simple, reliable and cheap.

- Where amplified audio circuits are in use, **low frequency ac** signalling may be adopted.

- When FDM transmission systems are used, **voice frequency** signalling is used.

- **Inband VF** signalling uses same frequency band as voice - 300 to 3400 Hz. Control signals can be sent everywhere, wherever speech signal can reach. It is independent of transmission system as signal is carried along the same route as voice. But it must be protected against false operation by speech. This is most widely applied signalling system for long distance telephone networks due to its flexibility.

- **Outband VF** signalling uses frequencies above voice band below 4000 Hz. Signalling during speech is possible, allowing continuous supervision and control of the call. Only a narrow bandwidth is available for signalling. Extra electronics is required to handle this, so not used widely.

- Both inband and outband schemes have limited configuration transfer capacity. Modern networks should provide enhanced signalling facilities for the subscriber, switching system and the telephone administration. Such need is met by **Common Channel Signalling [CCS]**.

Difference between Inchannel and Common Channel Signalling

Inchannel Signalling	Common Channel Signalling
1. Trunks are held up during signalling.	1. Trunks are not required for signalling.
2. Signal repertoire is limited.	2. Extensive signal repertoire is possible.
3. Interference between voice and control signals may occur.	3. No interference as the two channels are physically separate.
4. Separate signalling equipment is required for each trunk and hence is expensive.	4. Only one set of signalling equipments is required for a whole group of trunk circuits and therefore CCS is economical.
5. The voice channel being the control channel, there is a possibility of potential misuse by the customers.	5. Control channel is in general inaccessible to users.
6. Signalling is relatively slow.	6. Signalling is significantly fast.
7. Speech circuit reliability is assured.	7. There is no automatic test of the speech circuit.
8. It is difficult to change or add signals.	8. There is flexibility to change or add signals.
9. It is difficult to handle signalling during speech period.	9. There is freedom to handle signals during speech.
10. Reliability of the signalling path is not critical.	10. Reliability of the signalling path is critical.

- CCS can be implemented in two ways:
  Channel associated mode and channel non-associated mode.

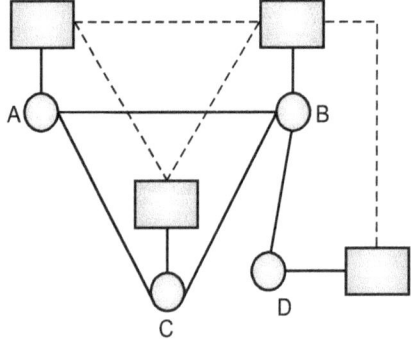

(a) Channel Associated Signalling

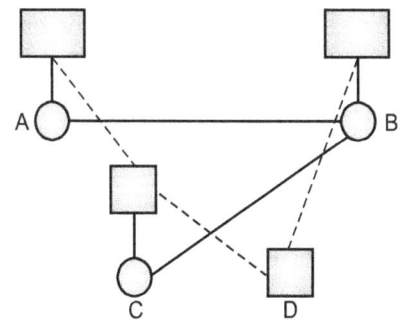

— Speech or information path, ---- Signalling path
○ Switching system, □ Signalling transfer point (STP)

(b) Non-Associated Signalling

Fig. 1.45: Modes of Operation of CCS

- In channel associated mode of CCS, the common signalling closely tracks the trunk groups along the entire length of a connection.

- As in Fig. 1.45 (a), speech paths and their corresponding signalling paths A-B, A-C-B, B-D are shown.

- The signalling in associated mode is still done on a separate signalling channel. The signalling path passes through the same set of switches as does the speech path.

- Network topologies for speech and signalling network are the same.

- Advantages of associated mode are: economic implementation and simple assignment of trunk groups to signalling channels.

- CCS network has two types of nodes:

Signalling Transfer Points (STPs) and Signalling Points (SPs).

STPs have connection with switching centres. It is capable of routing messages and also performs functions of SP.

Control subsystems of switching centres are called as SPs, as signalling originates from them. SP is capable of handling control messages directly addressed to it, but it cannot route messages.

In channel non-associated mode, the signalling information may follow a route that is different from that of speech. As Fig. 1.45 (b) shows,

Speech path	Signalling paths
A-B	A-C-D-B
B-C	B-D-C

- Network topologies for speech and signalling are different.

- At point D in Fig. 1.45 (b), only STP is present, not a switching center i.e. signal messages may be transferred between two end switching systems via any available path in the CCS network.

- A CCS network may use associated signalling in some constituent parts and non-associated signalling in other parts. Such operation is called 'quasi associated signalling'. The signalling paths are not associated, but are fixed for given speech connections.

  We have seen the differences between inchannel and common channel signalling. Some differences need explanation.

- When a called subscriber is busy,

  For inchannel signalling, busy tone originates from the terminating exchange and the switched path is held up as long as the calling subscriber does not go onhook (doesn't hang up). i.e. trunks are held up during signalling.

  In case of CCS, busy tone can be returned by the originating exchange, releving all the intermediate trunks immediately i.e. trunks not required for signalling.

- For signal repertoire, CCS can be configured with the bandwidth required to carry control signals for a rich variety of functions.

- As signalling information is not sent over speech paths in CCS, integrity of speech path is not assured. It is possible that faulty speech link is marked available and a path is established using the same. To avoid this, in CCS, certain checks as routine testing of idle paths and the continuity test of idle path.

  Many speech circuits are served by 1 CCS link and an error or failure of link may affect many speech circuits. So error control and redundant paths are necessary in CCS.

  Most of present day telephone networks are equipped with inchannel signalling systems. But networks with CCS will evolve gradually. At the international level, signalling standards are specified by CCITT. So far, seven international level signalling standards are specified known as **signalling system number** 1-7 (SS1-SS7). There is also a variation of SS5 known as SS5bis. In addition, two regional standards R1 (North America) and R2 (Europe) have also been adopted by CCITT. SS1-SS5 deals with inchannel signalling. SS6 and SS7 are CCS systems.

  [For more information on inchannel signalling refer next section].

1.8.1 Common Channel Signalling

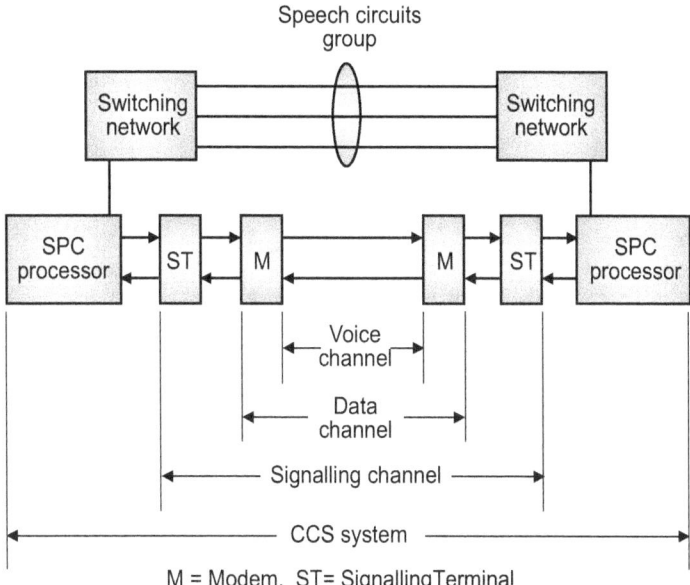

Fig. 1.46: Basic Scheme for CCS

- As seen earlier, signalling is completely separate from switching and speech transmission in CCS.

  Fig. 1.46 shows basic scheme of CCS.

- Here, a separate analog voice channel is used for signalling.

  Modems are used for carrying digital data over analog lines, as signalling in CCS is digital.

- As shown in Fig. 1.46, two signalling channels, one for each direction, (since full duplex communication), are used in dedicated manner to carry signalling information.

  As the channels are dedicated, they are capable of carrying signalling information for a group of circuits.

  Group size is determined by capacity of signalling channel.

  A phase equalized voice channel is capable of supporting a bit rate of 2.4 kbps with acceptable error rates for signalling. At this bit rate, one CCS link can carry signals for 1500-2000 speech circuits.

- The CCS network is basically a store and forward (S and F) network where signalling information travels link-by-link along a route. We have studied S and F networks previously.

- The signalling information in CCS is transferred as messages of varying length, usually defined as one or more fixed length Signalling Units (SUs).

  A message of one signal unit length is called Single Unit Message (SUM) and the other with Multi Unit Message (MUM).

- A single unit is divided into a number of constituent bit fields, each having its own function.

  Typical structures are shown below.

Header	Signalling information	Circuit label	Error check

(a) Single Unit Message

Header		Signalling information	Circuit label	Error check
Sub header	Length	Other signalling information		Error check
Sub header	Length	Address digits		Error check

(b) Three-Unit Message

Fig. 1.47: Typical CCS Signalling Message Formats

- Format of first SU of MUM is identical to SUM.
- In SS6, each SU size: 28 bits.
  Out of 28, last 8 bits: Check bits.
- In SUM,   Header   :   5 bits
      Signalling information :   4 bits
                Circuit label :   11 bits
- In MUM, except for first SU, next SUs have –
                Subheader   :   2 bits
  Length   :   2 bits

  Additional signalling information: 16 bits. Additional signalling information means routing details, address digits, etc.

  Each address digit is 4 bits long.

- A signalling message unit can be an address unit, centralized service message unit, acknowledgement unit, synchronization or idle unit or management message unit.
- In SS6, SUs are grouped in blocks of 12, the last SU being an acknowledgement unit.

SS7:

- The concept of common channel signalling has been further accepted in SS7, which was first defined in 1980, with revisions in 1984 and 1988.

- SS7 has been designed to be an open ended CCS standard that can be used over a variety of digital circuit switched network. While the network being controlled is circuit switched, control signalling uses packet switching. The functions in SS7 are defined assuming packet switching operation, but actual operation can be in circuit switched. This is the case when channel associated signalling mode is chosen for implementation.

- Requirements of ISDN are considered while designing SS7. The internet control and network intelligence essential to ISDN are provided by SS7.

- Although SS7 is suitable for operation over analog channels at speeds less than 64 kbps, it is optimised to work with digital SPC exchanges using 64 kbps digital channels.

- SS7 is suitable for operation over terrestrial and satellite links.

- Protocols architecture is as shown below.

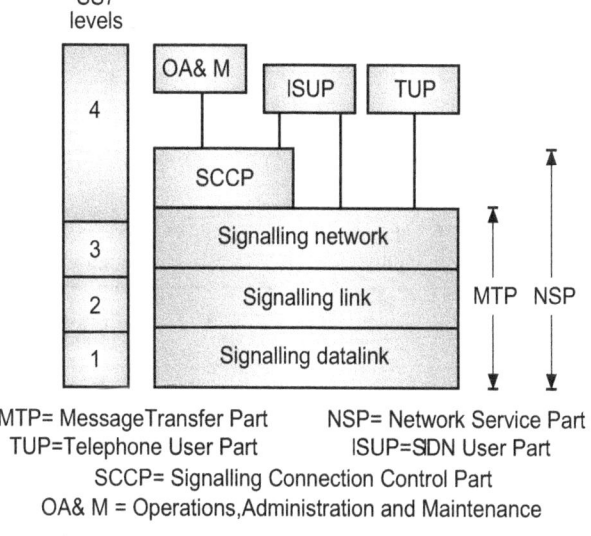

MTP= MessageTransfer Part   NSP= Network Service Part
TUP=Telephone User Part   ISUP=SIDN User Part
SCCP= Signalling Connection Control Part
OA& M = Operations,Administration and Maintenance

Fig. 1.48: Architecture of SS7

- MTP (lower 3 levels) – Message transfer part provides a reliable service for routing messages through SS7 network.

- The lowest layer, signalling data link, is concerned with physical and electrical characteristics of the signalling links between STPs (Signalling Transfer Points) and SPs and between STPs.

- All signalling data links in SS7 are full duplex links dedicated to SS7 traffic.

- The main purpose of second layer, the signalling link is to turn a potentially unreliable physical link into a reliable data link.

  The signalling layer must ensure that –

  (1) There are no losses or duplication of control message.

  (2) Messages are delivered in the same order in which they originate.

  (3) There is a match between receiver capacity and the transmission rates.

  (This implies that the receiver is capable of exercising flow control over the sender).

- There are three types of signalling units defined in SS7:

  (1) Message Signal Unit (MSU).

  (2) Link Status Signal Unit (LSSU).

  (3) Fill In Signal Unit (FISU).

  Formats of these are shown in Fig. 1.49

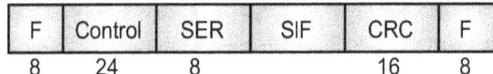

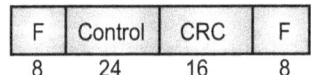

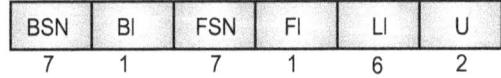

Fig. 1.49: Formats of Signalling Units

- All SUs begin and end with a flag field which has a unique bit pattern (01111110). These flags act as delimiters for the SUs.

  If the SUs are transmitted continuously, then a common flag can be used, acting as closing flag for one SU and opening flag for the next.

- It is possible that unique bit pattern appears inside the SU, destroying synchronization. To avoid this problem, a technique called bit stuffing is used. In this technique, the transmitter inserts an extra 0 whenever it comes across five consecutive 1s in the data part of SU. The receiver on detecting five 1s, deletes the zero following it.

  Thus, only flag pattern contains six 1s.

- All the SUs in SS7 contain 16 bit error checking field (CRC).

- The control field consists of five subfields as in Fig. 1.48 (d). Backward Sequence Number and Backward Indicator bit together permit piggy backed acknowledgement of SU received from other side.

  A negative acknowledgement is indicated by inverting BI bit which remains unchanged for all subsequent positive acknowledgements.

- Forward Sequence Number (FSN) identifies the SU uniquely using modulo 128 count.

- Retransmission is indicated by inverting Forward Indicator (FI) bit which remains unchanged until another retransmission occurs.

- The length of field specifies the length of following information fields, in octets.

  This provides a crosscheck on closing flag.

  It also serves as SU type indicator.

$$0 \ = \ \text{FISU}$$
$$1 \ = \ \text{LSSU}$$
$$3 \text{ to } 63 \ = \ \text{MSU}$$

- The service information octet specifies the type of message and whether the message relates to a national or international network. This (SIF) Signalling Information Field contains level 3 and 4 information. It consists of address label, user data from telephone user part (TUP), ISDN user part (ISUD) or operations, administration and maintenance (OA and M) part.

  Address label field is 32 bits long with a 14 bit signalling link selection subfield.

  A link selection subfield is used to select a path from among alternative routes.

- Level 3, signalling network layer performs functions like message handling and network management.

  Message handling   Discrimination, routing and distribution of messages.

- **Discrimination:** It analyzes the destination code in the address label to decide whether a message is to be routed to another node or message is to be distributed to one of the user parts in the local node. This is done by analyzing type of message information in SER field.

  Discrimination function is needed only in STPs.

- **Routing** function may be invoked by discrimination or by local level 4 entity. Routing decision is based on value in the signalling link selection subfield.

  With 4 bit selection subfield, 16 different routes can be defined through the network.

  In general, all the control signals associated with a single call will follow the same route. This guarantees that the control messages arrive in sequence at the destination.

- Network management function monitors signalling links and overcomes link failures or degradation. This is attempted through redundancy of links and dynamic rerouting.

  Network management is important because failure in the signalling network may affect all the subscribers.

- The Signalling Connection Control Part (SCCP) residing in level 4 was added to SS7 specifications in 1984.

  SCCP and MTP together are referred to as Network Service Part (NSP).

  Main purpose of SCCP is to enhance limited routing, distribution and addressing capabilities of third layer, to meet the needs of those user part requiring enriched information transfer facilities.

  Other modules in level 4 are invoked as per requirements of a service:

  TUP: In response to subscriber actions at telephone.

  Control signalling for TUP deals with establishment, maintenance and termination of telephone calls.

  ISUP: ISDN subscriber calls and related functions.

  OA and M: Messages relating to network management, operations and maintenance.

  SS7 architecture came into existence much after ISO-OSI model and is largely based on work done for ISO-OSI model.

1.8.2 Inchannel Signalling

Table 1.2: CCITT Inchannel Signalling Systems

Signalling system	Signalling technique and application
SS1	500/20 Hz signalling for manual international service.
SS2	600/750 Hz two voice frequency system for semi-automatic service.
SS3	2280 Hz single voice frequency system with limited application in semiautomatic and automatic services.
SS4	2040 and 2400 Hz two VF compound end-to-end analog signalling.
SS5	2400 and 2600 Hz two VF compound analog line signalling and 2/6 multifrequency inband analog inter-register signalling with TASI equipment.
SS5 *bis*	Same as SS5 but for circuits with or without TASI equipment.

Table 1.2 shows different inchannel signalling systems. Early systems SS1, SS2 and SS3 are of historical interest only. At present SS4, SS5, SS5 bis are used.

Other signalling system of interest is PCM signalling and regional R1 and R2.

The international signalling systems SS4, SS5 and SS5 bis adapt inband signalling using a combination of two voice band frequencies or a single voice frequency. In addition, systems SS5 and SS5 bis use multifrequency signalling for

inter-register signalling. In SS4, there is no separate inter-register signalling. We have seen that a compound signal of two voice frequencies is less likely to be imitated by speech than a single frequency of equal duration and it provides a better talk off performance.

Timings for SS4 signalling compound frequencies and single frequency are shown in Table 1.3.

Table 1.3: Timings for SS4 Signalling Elements

Element	Transmitted duration (ms)	Recognition times (ms)
Compound	150 ± 30	80 ± 20
Single-short	100 ± 20	40 ± 10
Single-long	350 ± 70	200 ± 40

Some sample control signals and associated codes are given in Table 1.4.

Table 1.4: Some Control Signals in SS4

Control Signal	Code
Terminal seizure	PX_s
Transit seizure	PY_s
Clear forward	PX_1
Forward transfer	PY_1

$$P = \text{Prefix element}$$
$$X_1 = 2040 \text{ Hz long}$$
$$Y_1 = 2400 \text{ Hz long}$$
$$X_s = 2040 \text{ Hz short}$$
$$Y_s = 2400 \text{ Hz short}$$

Digits of dialled number are transmitted as binary codes.
One of the 2 frequencies:

$$2040 \text{ Hz} + \text{Binary 1}$$
Other, $$2400 \text{ Hz} + \text{Binary 0}$$

Pulse duration: 35 ± 7 ms

SS5:

Initially, SS5 was jointly developed by U.K Post Office and Bell Laboratories for dialing over Time Assigned Speech Interpolation (TASI) equipped transAtlantic cables. The system was subsequently specified by CCITT as a standard in 1964 and has found many applications in world. Most of Atlantic, Pacific and Indian Ocean Circuits use SS5 at present.

- Normal speech activity of a subscriber on call is about 35%. As a result, a full duplex four-wire speech transmission circuits are less than half utilized.
- The **TASI** technique attempts to improve trunk utilization by **assigning a circuit to speech channel** only **when** there is **speech activity.**

  In this way, given number of circuits can support more than double the number of speech channels.
- In TASI, each channel is equipped with a speech detector, which after detecting speech, arranges for a circuit to be assigned to that channel.
- This speech detection and establishment of trunk channel association takes time, so speech burst is clipped for that duration. (Typically 15 ms if channel is available, but increases if traffic is more).
- In order to reduce the extent of interpolation, a circuit is not disassociated from channel for short gaps of speech.

  For this purpose, speech detectors are provided with a short hangover time and a circuit is disconnected only when the speech gap is longer than the detector hangover time.

  Digital counterpart of TASI is known as Digital Speech Interpolation (DSI).

- As with speech bursts, inchannel signalling information also experiences clipping in TASI environment.
- Unless the signals are of sufficient duration, the trunk-channel association and recognition at receiving end cannot be permitted. So there are chances of signals getting lost.
- With pulse signalling, it has been determined that a 500 ms duration is required to account for the extreme trunk-channel association condition.
- So allowing for reliable recognition, a pulse of 850 ± 200 ms duration is considered suitable. But pulse signals of such length would slow down signalling process. Pulse gaps would cause the channel disassociation leading to unnecessary TASI activity.

  And moreover, fixed length pulses cannot take advantage of lightly loaded (low traffic) conditions when channel assignment time is low.
- For these reasons, line signalling in SS5 and SS5 bis is chosen to be **continuously compelled** to ensure that the trunk-channel association is maintained throughout the period of signalling.

  But continuos compelled signalling does not bring out the efficient use of trunks under heavy load conditions as TASI is effectively disabled for the trunk that carries the signalling information.
- Pulse signalling is preferred here and two different techniques are used to maintain trunk-channel association during signalling period.
  (1) The address information is transmitted **en bloc** after gathering all the address digits. The gaps between pulses are ensured to be less than the speech detector hangover time.

  SS5 adapts this en bloc transmission scheme. The en bloc method facilitates checking the validity of the address by digit count and avoids expensive intercontinental circuits to be taken ineffectively during incomplete dialling. But this increases post dialling delay because the digits are accumulated before signalling begins.

  (2) Address digits are transmitted as and when they arrive and a **lock tone** is transmitted during the gaps. SS5 bis uses this method.

  It permits overlapped operation of digits being received and transmitted and reduces post dialling delay. But the trunk is not used efficiently as in en bloc.

  A standard method of transferring signalling information between switching equipment and signalling equipment is required for all signalling systems.

  One such method is provided by ear and mouth (E and M) control. E and M leads constitute a standard interface for delivering and accepting uniform signal conditions.
- There are three types of E and M interfaces - I, II, III.

Type I:

    (1)   Two leads: One for each direction of transmission.

    (2)   It was developed for electromechanical exchanges.

    (3)   M lead: It carries dc signals from switching equipment to signalling equipment (Outgoing part of signalling terminal).

    (4)   E lead: It carries dc signals from incoming part of signalling terminal to switching equipment.

    (5)

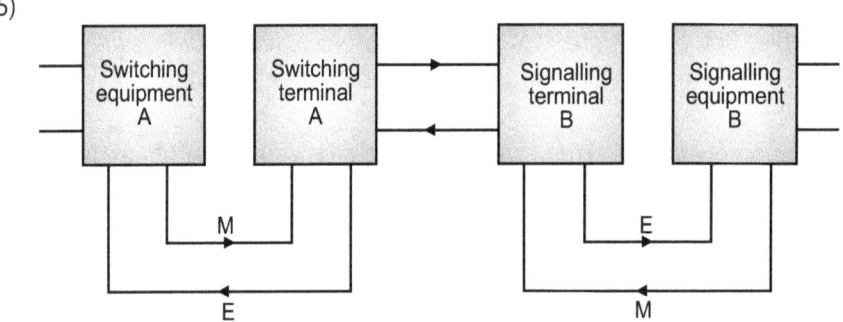

Fig. 1.50: E and M Signalling Control

Type II:

    It is 4-wire, fully looped interface and preferred to electronic switching systems.

Type III:

    Compromise between Type I and II. It uses 3-wire partially looped system.

SOLVED EXAMPLES

Example 1.1: Calculate the number of trunks that can be supported on a time multiplexed space switch. Given that:

    (a)   32 channels are multiplexed in each stream.

    (b)   Control memory access time 100 ns.

    (c)   Bus switching and transfer time is 100 ns/transfer.

Solution:

$$M = 32$$

$$t_s = t_{switch} + t_{transfer}$$

$$= 100 + 100$$

$$= 200 \text{ ns}$$

$$N = \frac{125}{Mt_s}$$

$$= \frac{125}{32 \times 200 \times 10^{-3}}$$

$$\approx 20$$

$$\boxed{\text{Number of trunks supported} = 20}$$

Example 1.2: Calculate maximum access time that can be permitted for data and control memories in TSI switch with single input and single output trunk multiplexing channels. Estimate cost of switch.

Solution: $M = 2500$

There are two sequential memory accesses/time slot.

$$\therefore \qquad t_m = \frac{125}{2M} \ (\mu s)$$

$$= \frac{125}{2 \times 2500}$$

$$= 0.025 \ \mu s$$

$$\boxed{\text{Access time} = 25 \ ns}$$

Cost of switch $= 2M = 5000$ units

$$\boxed{C = 5000 \text{ units}}$$

The equivalent single stage space matrix uses

$$M \times M = 2500 \times 2500$$

$$\therefore \begin{bmatrix} \text{Cost advantage of given} \\ \text{time switch} \end{bmatrix} = \frac{2500 \times 2500}{5000}$$

$$= 1250$$

Example 1.3: Calculate access time of memory modules in parallel-in/serial-out time switch using 64 input and 64 output streams with each stream multiplexing 32 channels.

Solution: Assume overlapped operation.

$M = 32, N = 64.$

$$125 = M (N + 1) t_m$$

$$\therefore \qquad t_m = \frac{125}{M (N + 1)}$$

$$= \frac{125}{32 \times 65}$$

$$= 0.06 \ \mu s$$

$$\boxed{\text{Access time} = 0.06 \ \mu s}$$

Example 1.4: How many subscribers can be supported in bidirectional PAM switching bus, if pulse width of PAM samples is 125 ns?

Solution: $$N = \frac{125}{M \cdot t_s}$$

$M = 2, \quad \cdot \cdot \quad$ Bidirectional bus,

$t_s = 125 + 125 = 250$ ns/channel

$$\therefore \qquad N = \frac{125}{2 \times 250 \text{ ns}}$$

$$\boxed{N = 250}$$

Example 1.5: 1000 inlet and 1000 outlet digital switch is to be built using TSI. Determine the size of control and data memories and speed with which memories have to be accessed.

Solution:

$$CM = 1000 \text{ words} \times 10 \text{ bits}$$

$$DM = 1000 \text{ words} \times 8 \text{ bits}$$

$$\therefore \quad \text{Access time} = \frac{125 \ \mu s}{1000 \times 2}$$

$$= 0.0625 \ \mu s$$

$$= 62.5 \text{ ns}$$

EXERCISE

1. With the help of neat diagram explain principle and working of time slot interchange (TSI) for a time multiplexed time switching system.

2. Explain signalling tones in subscriber loop.

3. Explain inchannel and common channel signalling.

4. With neat diagram, explain the basics of subscriber's telephone circuit. Indicate basic components in telephone and describe its functional operation.

5. What is DTMF dialing? Discuss design considerations for touch tone signalling scheme.

6. With block schematic explain working of output controlled time division space switch. What is expression for switching capacity?

7. Explain with diagram the principle of time division time switching.

8. Write a note on basic scheme for CCS.

9. Is TS network non-blocking? Explain.

10. How are switching systems classified? In what way SPC is superior to hardwired control?

11. What are differences between voice and data traffic?

12. Explain the following switching techniques in detail.

    (a) Time division space switching

    (b) Time division time switching

13. Briefly explain various subscriber loop signaling system used in telephone switching.

14. What are various signaling tones received by subscriber and exchange while setting up the telephone call? State the typical specifications of these tones.

Unit II

TELECOMMUNICATION TRAFFIC ENGINEERING

2.1 Introduction To Traffic Engineering

Traffic engineering provides the basis for the analysis and design of telecommunication networks. It was mentioned earlier about a switch/network being blocking or non-blocking, due to unavailability of switching paths. The calculations and analysis of blocking probability is based on a quantity that specifies the fraction of time for which a subscriber line may be busy. Practically, situation is more complex. Other than switching elements, many other common shared subsystems in telecommunication network contribute to the blocking of a subscriber call. In telephone network, these other resources means digit receivers, interstage switching links, call processors and trunks between the exchanges.

The load or traffic on a network varies during the day at different times. There may be very heavy traffic at certain time and very low traffic at some other time. A cost effective network is to be designed which will provide the required quality of service under such varying traffic conditions. Such a design should be based on formal science, telegraphic theory or traffic engineering. Traffic engineering enables us **to determine the ability** of a telecommunication network **to carry** a **given traffic** at a particular **loss probability**.

It provides a means to determine the quantum of common equipments required to provide a particular level of service for a given traffic pattern and volume.

For Telecommunication network service performance target is to have the resources available for 99.97% of time (excluding planned outages and circumstances beyond telecommunication theory).

The use of mathematical modeling to predict line, equipment and staff capacities for telephone systems is now an accepted technique for fine tuning existing systems, as well as for designing new ones. Traffic engineering techniques are used most often to determine:
- Line and trunk quantities required for an exchange.
- Number of DTMF (Dual tone multifrequency) registers conference trunks, recorded announcement route trunks required.
- Quantities service levels and usage of such special service trunks as foreign exchange, discounted toll trunks and tie trunks (leased lines between exchanges or between various exchange/telephone/cell operators)

- Operator staffing levels and performance predictions as well as the impact of system change on staff quantities.

- Automatic call distributor staffing and service levels.

- In a telephone network, the traffic load on a typical working day during 24 hours is shown in Fig. 2.1.

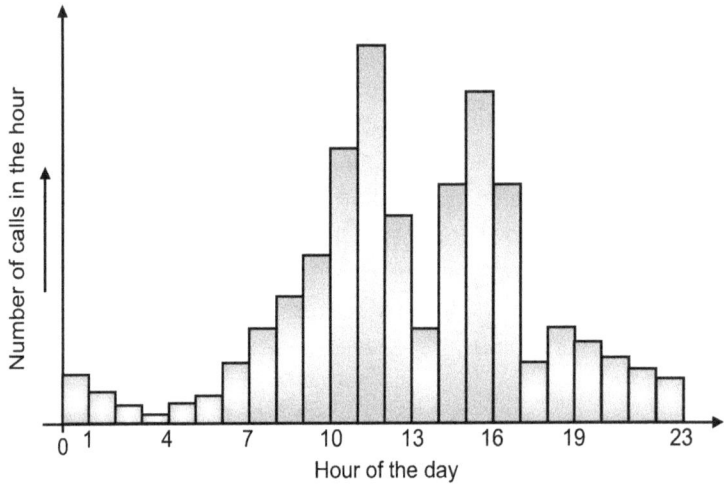

Fig. 2.1: Typical telephone traffic pattern on a working day

- The originating call amplitudes are relative and the actual values depend on the area where the statistics is collected. It may vary from exchange to exchange. However, the traffic pattern is the same irrespective of the area concerned.

- Obviously, there is very less use of network during 0 to 6 hours when most of the population is asleep.

- There is a large peak around mid-forenoon and mid-afternoon, indicating busy office activities.

- The afternoon peak is slightly smaller. The load is low during the lunch hour period (12.00 – 14.00).

- The period 17.00 – 18.00 is again showing a low traffic and signifies that people are on move from offices to residences.

- Again there can be a peak of domestic calls after 18.00 hours when people reach home and the reduced tariff applies. In recent years, the plans for reduced tariff are found to change/vary at different timings, say after 20.00 hours or so. In such condition, the domestic call pattern will be changing accordingly.

- During weekends, holidays, festival days, the traffic pattern is different from the one shown above.

- In a day, the **60 minute interval**, in which **traffic** is the **highest**, is called the **Busy Hour (BH).**

- In Fig. 2.1, 60 min (or 1 hour) period between 11.00 - 12.00 hours is the busy hour.

- This busy hour period may vary from exchange to exchange, depending upon location and community interest of the subscriber.

- Busy hour may show seasonal, weekly and in some places, even daily variations.

- In addition to these variations, there are also unpredictable peaks caused by the stock market activity, weather, natural disaster, international events, sports, etc.

  For example, to enquire about in an earthquake affected area or as had happened recently about Tsunami affected areas in addition to regular, some extra lines were kept open.

- To take into account such fluctuations while designing switching networks, three types of busy hours are defined by CCITT.

    (1) Busy Hour: Continuous 1 hour period lying wholly in time interval concerned, for which the traffic volume or the number of call attempts is greatest.

    (2) Peak Busy Hour: The busy hour each day, it usually varies from day-to-day or over a number of days.

    (3) Time Consistent Busy Hour: The 1 hour period starting at the same time each day for which the average traffic volume or the number of call attempts is greatest over the days under consideration.

    For the ease of records, the busy hour is taken to commence (start) on the hour or half hour only.

- Whenever a call is made, i.e. calling party dials the number, the **call** is said to be **successful** or completed **only if** the called **party answers.** It is said as the call attempt is successful.

- All the call attempts are not successful or they do not make actual conversations for many reasons like – called party busy, no answer from called party, blocking in the trunk groups/exchanges, faulty line, faulty instrument of called party, dead line etc. So number of call attempts is almost never equal to the number of successful calls.

- **Call Completion Rate (CCR)** is defined as the ratio of number of successful calls to number of call attempts.

$$CCR = \frac{\text{Number of successful calls}}{\text{Number of call attempts}}$$

- **Busy Hour Call Attempt (BHCA)** is defined as the number of call attempts in busy hour.

- This parameter BHCA is a very important parameter in deciding the processing capacity of a common control or a stored program control system of an exchange i.e. what is the way in which excessive calls (calls not completed because of any reason) are handled or how they are processed.

- The parameter CCR is used in dimensioning the network capacity i.e. it is the capacity of the network which decides how many calls can be successfully completed. It was mentioned that there are many reasons for all call attempts not being successful conversations. But down the line very basic parameter is the network capacity which plays the major role in figuring CCR.

- Networks are usually designed to provide overall CCR of over 0.70. A **CCR** value of **0.75** is considered **excellent** and attempts to improve it further are not cost effective.

  [75 successful calls out of 100 call attempts.]

- One more related parameter used in traffic engineering is **Busy Hour Calling Rate (BHCR).** It is defined as average number of calls originated by a subscriber during the busy hour.

Example 2.1: An exchange serves 2000 subscribers. If average BHCA is 10,000 and CCR is 60%, calculate busy hour calling rate.

Solution:

$$\text{Average busy hour calls} = \text{Average BHCA} \infty \text{CCR}$$

$$= 10,000 \times \frac{60}{100}$$

$$= 6000 \text{ calls}$$

$$\therefore \quad \text{Busy hour calling rate} = \frac{\text{Average busy hour calls}}{\text{Total number of subscribes}}$$

$$= \frac{6000}{2000} = 3$$

$$\therefore \quad \boxed{\text{BHCR} = 3}$$

- Parameter **BHCR** is useful **in sizing the exchange** to **handle** the peak traffic.

  In **rural** exchange, this BHCR may be as low as **0.2**; but in a **business city**, it may be as high as **three** or **more**.

- It is also very important to know how much of the day's total traffic is carried during the busy hour. This is measured in terms of **day-to-busy hour traffic ratio.** It is the ratio of busy hour calling rate to the average calling rate for the day.

  Typically this ratio is over 20 for city business area and around 6–7 for a rural area.

2.2 Traffic Measurement Units

- The traffic load on a given network may be on local switching unit, inter-office trunk lines or other common subsystems. For further discussion, all common subsystems of telecommunication network are collectively termed as **servers.** (Term link or trunk can be used.)

- The traffic on the network may then be measured in terms of occupancy of servers in the network. Such a measure is called the **traffic intensity** and is defined as,

$$\text{Traffic intensity, } A_0 = \frac{\text{Period for which server is occupied}}{\text{Total period of observation}}$$

Generally, period of observation is taken as one hour. A_0 is dimensionless. It is called **erlang** to honour the Danish telephone engineer A. K. Erlang, who did pioneering work in traffic engineering.

- An erlang is a unit of telecommunications traffic measurement. An erlang represents the continuous use of one voice path. In practice, it is used to describe the total traffic volume of one hour.

- A server is said to have 1 erlang of traffic if it is occupied for the entire period of observation. For example, if a group of users (or a single server) has made 30 calls in one hour, with each call having average call duration of 5 minutes, then the traffic intensity in erlangs is worked out as:

$$\text{Minutes of traffic in one hour} = \text{Number of calls} \times \text{Duration}$$
$$= 30 \times 5$$
$$= 150$$
$$\text{Hours of traffic in one hour} = \frac{150}{60}$$
$$= 2.5$$

$$\therefore \textbf{ Traffic Intensity } = \textbf{2.5 erlangs}$$

- Erlang traffic measurements are made in order to help telecommunication network designers to understand traffic patterns within the network. This is necessary to successfully design the network topology and establish the necessary trunk (server) group sizes.

  These measurements or estimates can be used to work out how many lines are required between a telephone system and exchange or between exchanges etc.

- Several Erlang traffic models exist:

(1) **Erlang B:** This is most commonly used traffic model and is used to find how many links are required if traffic intensity (in erlangs) during the busiest hour is known. The model assumes that all blocked calls are immediately cleared.

(2) **Extended Erlang B:** This model is similar to Erlang B, but takes into account that, a percentage of calls are immediately represented to the system if they encounter blocking (busy signal). The retry percentage can be specified.

(3) **Erlang C:** This model assumes that all blocked calls stay in the system until they can be handled. Such model can be applied to call center or a customer care office, where, if calls are not immediately answered, they enter a queue.

Traffic intensity can be specified over a number of servers.

Example 2.2: In a group of 10 servers, each is occupied for 30 minutes in an observation interval of 2 hours.

Calculate the traffic carried by the group.

Solution:

$$\text{Traffic carried per server} = \frac{\text{Occupied duration}}{\text{Total duration}}$$

$$= \left(\frac{0.5}{1 \times 2}\right) \text{Hours}$$

$$= \left(\frac{30}{120}\right) \text{min}$$

$$= 0.25 \text{ erlangs}$$

$$\text{Total traffic carried by group} = 0.25 \times 10$$

$$= 2.5 \text{ erlangs}$$

Erlang measure indicates the average number of servers occupied and is useful in deriving the average number of calls put through, during the period of observation.

Example 2.3: A group of 20 servers carry a traffic of 10 erlangs. If average duration of calls is 3 minutes, calculate the number of calls put through by a single server and the group as a whole in a one hour period.

Solution: $\quad \text{Traffic per server} = \dfrac{\text{Traffic}}{\text{Number of servers}}$

$$= \frac{10}{20}$$

$$= 0.5 \text{ erlang}$$

This indicates server is busy for 30 minutes in 1 hour.

$$\text{Number of calls put through by 1 server} = \frac{30}{3} = 10 \text{ calls.}$$

$$\text{Total number of calls put through by group} = 10 \times 20$$

$$= 200 \text{ calls}$$

- Traffic intensity is also measured in another way. This measure is known as **Centum Call Second (CCS)** which represents a call time product.

  One CCS means: 1 call for 100 sec. duration or 100 calls for 1 second duration each.

  CCS as a measure of traffic intensity is valid only in telephone circuits. For networks supporting voice, data, etc., erlang is a better measure.

  Calls Seconds (CS) and Call Minutes (CM) are also used as a measure of traffic intensity.

$$1\ E = 36\ CCS\ =\ 3600\ CS = 60\ CM$$

Example 2.4: A subscriber makes 3 phone calls for 3 minutes, 4 min, and 2 min duration in one hour period. Calculate the subscriber traffic in erlangs, CCS and CM.

Solution: Subscriber traffic in erlangs $= \dfrac{\text{Busy period}}{\text{Total period}}$ (both in min.)

$$= \frac{3 + 4 + 2}{60}$$

$$= 0.15\ E$$

$$\text{Traffic in CCS}\ = \frac{(3 + 4 + 2) \times 60}{100}$$

$$= 5.4\ CCS$$

$$\text{Traffic in CM}\ = 3 + 4 + 2$$

$$= 9\ CM$$

When we say, subscriber traffic or trunk traffic, we mean the traffic intensity contributed by a subscriber, or traffic intensity on a trunk.

Traffic intensity is call time product. Therefore, two important parameters required to estimate traffic intensity are:

(1) Average call arrival rate, C (Number of calls/min)

(2) Average holding time per call, t_h (min per call)

Load offered to network is $A = C \cdot t_h$

Example 2.5: Over a 20 min observation interval, 40 subscribers initiate calls. Total duration of calls is 4800 seconds. Calculate load offered to network by the subscribers and the average subscriber traffic.

Solution: Mean arrival rate, $C = \dfrac{40}{20}$ = 2 calls per minute

$$\text{Mean holding time, } t_h\ = \frac{\text{Total duration (min)}}{\text{Calls}}$$

$$= \frac{4800}{40 \times 60}$$

$$= 2 \text{ min per call}$$

$\therefore$ Offered load $= 2 \times 2 = $ **4 erlangs**

Average subscriber traffic $= \dfrac{4}{40} = $ **0.1 erlang**

- Now we say that we have calculated traffic in two ways:
    - (i)   Based on traffic generated by subscribers and
    - (ii)   Based on observation of busy servers in network.
- It may happen that load generated by subscribers exceeds the network capacity. This excess of traffic may be handled in two ways:
    - (1)   The overload traffic may be rejected without being serviced. (calls are lost) – loss system.
    - (2)   It may be held in a queue until network facilities (resources) become available. (calls are delayed) – delay systems.

Conventional automatic telephone exchanges behave like loss systems. Under overload conditions, a user call is blocked. User may get a busy tone or related announcement. So his attempt is not successful. User has to retry and by that time if a resource is free, his call is serviced. (Many attempts may be required @ busy hour.) Operator-oriented manual exchanges can be considered as delay systems. If network is blocked at the time of call, the call is not rejected, but placed in a queue and when the resource is available, that is serviced, the call is made successful without making the user to make another call attempt. There is only one attempt made by user, but is delayed.

Basic performance parameters for loss system are: Grade of Service and blocking probability. For delay systems, the parameter is service delay.

In loss systems, the traffic carried by the network is generally lower than the actual traffic offered to the network by the subscribers. The overload traffic is rejected and hence not carried by the network. Grade of service is a measure of voice service.

2.3 Grade of Service (GOS)

GOS is one aspect of the quality a customer can expect to experience when making a call. The amount of traffic rejected by the network is an index of quality of service offered by the network. In a loss system, grade of service is described as the ratio of calls that are lost due to congestion in the busy hour. It is defined as the ratio of lost traffic to offered traffic.

Grade of Service, GOS $= \dfrac{\text{Number of lost calls}}{\text{Number of offered calls}}$

$$GOS = \frac{A - A_0}{A}$$

A is Offered traffic
A_0 is Carried traffic $\Big\}$ $A - A_0$ is Lost traffic

- Offered traffic is the product of average number of calls generated by the users and the average holding time per call [C. t_h]

- Carried traffic is the average occupancy of the servers in the network.

- Smaller the value of GOS, better is the service. The recommended value of GOS in India is 0.002, which means that 2 calls in every 1000 calls may be lost (or 1 call in 500).

- Usually every common subsystem in network has an associated GOS value. The GOS of the full network is determined by the highest GOS value of the subsystem.

- As the volume of traffic grows with time, the GOS value of a network deteriorates with time.

In order to maintain the value within reasonable limits, initially the network is sized to have much smaller GOS value than the recommended, so that the GOS value continues to be within limits as the network traffic grows.

The Grade Of Service can be measured using different sections of network. When a call is routed, it will pass through several exchanges. If GOS is calculated based on the number of calls rejected by the final circuit group, then the Grade Of Service is determined by the final circuit group blocking criteria.

If GOS is calculated based on number of calls rejected between exchanges, then GOS is determined by the exchange to exchange blocking criteria.

Maintaining Grade Of Service:

The telecommunication service provider is usually aware of the required GOS for a particular product. To achieve and maintain a given Grade Of Service, the operator must ensure that sufficient circuits/routes (or network resources) are available to meet a specific level of demand.

These days, getting daily Grade of Service reports is very common. Every morning a report is generated by the system which tells about all the call history. The report includes hourly information about the calls initiated, i.e. the call attempts, number of calls that were successful, number of calls rejected due to conjestion, how many subscriber lines or trunks were faulty, for how much duration service was not offered because of faults, how many calls were initiated that time, etc. These reports can be analyzed to see which trunks/lines were maximum busy/congested and how many calls were lost because of congestion from these lines only. If congestion is observed continuously and if many calls are being lost, then the system operator/analyst can suggest addition of few more links/trunks serving that particular area. And practically those many new links or trunks can be added which would maintain the specified or required Grade Of Service.

But while allotting new links or trunks, it should be kept in mind that too many circuits will create a situation where an excess capacity might be given which will not be used other than the peak/busy hour (may in off-peak hours they remain idle). This will be causing underutilization of the network.

So complete analysis is to be done before adding new circuits. One approach of maintaining specified GOS is mentioned earlier, providing initially with more GOS. But otherwise, to continue to offer a given Grade Of Service, the number of circuits provided in that circuit group must increase (non-linearly) as the traffic intensity increases.

Blocking Probability:

- The blocking probability P_B is defined as the **probability** that **all the servers** in a system are **busy**.

- When all servers are busy, no further traffic can be carried by the system and the arriving subscriber traffic is blocked.

- It may appear that blocking probability is same as GOS. But this is not the case.

- The fundamental difference is that **GOS** is a measure from **subscriber** point of view, whereas **blocking probability** is a measure from **network** (or switching system/exchange) point of view.

- **GOS** is arrived at by **observing** the number of **rejected** subscriber **calls,** whereas **blocking probability** is arrived at by observing **busy servers** in the switching system.

For example, in a system with equal number of servers and subscribers, GOS = 0, because there is always a server available to the subscriber. On the other hand, there is definite probability that all servers are busy at a given instant and hence the blocking probability is non-zero.

- In order to distinguish between these 2 terms clearly, **GOS** is called **call congestion** or **loss probability** and **blocking probability** is called **time congestion.**

- In case of delay systems, traffic carried by the network is same as load offered to network by subscribers. As the overload traffic is queued, calls are put through network as and when the network facilities are available. GOS definition does not carry any meaning here in case of delay system. (GOS = 0, always for delay systems.)

- For delay systems, **delay probability** is a useful measure which gives the probability that a call experiences delay.

- If the offered load exceeds too much beyond the network capacity, calls undesirably long delays. Under such circumstances, delay systems are said to be unstable as they would never be able to clear the offered load.

  An easy way of bringing the system back to stable operations, is to make it behave like a loss system till the queued up traffic is cleared to an acceptable limit. This technique of maintaining a stable operation is called **flow control.**

- To sum up, we say there are two performance measures:

(1) Subscriber viewpoint:
GOS = Call congestion = Loss probability
(2) Network viewpoint:
Blocking probability = Time congestion

2.4 Quality Of Service (QOS)

QOS refers to the capability of a network to provide better service to selected (given) network traffic and it includes other factors like quality of speech, error-free transmission capability, etc.

QOS is more general than GOS and also refers to lack of noise and tones on the circuit, appropriate loudness levels etc. and includes Grade Of Service.

Quality of Service and Service Level:

When the Internet was first being created, there was no perceived need for a QoS application. So in fact the entire internet ran on a "best effort" system. There were four "type of service" bits and three "precedence" bits provided in each message, but they were largely unused. There are many things that can happen to packets as they travel from origin to destination and they result in the following problems, as seen from the point of view of the sender and receiver.

Dropped packets: The routers might fail to deliver (drop) some packets if they arrive when their buffers are already full. Some, none, or all of the packets might be dropped, depending on the state of the network, and it is impossible to determine what happened in advance. The receiving application must ask for this information to be retransmitted, possibly causing severe delays in the overall transmission.

- **Delay:** It might take a long time for a packet to reach its destination, because it gets held up in long queues, or takes a less direct route to avoid congestion. Alternatively, it might follow a fast, direct route. Thus delay is very unpredictable.

- **Jitter:** Packets from source will reach the destination with different delays. This variation in delay is known as jitter and can seriously affect the quality of streaming audio and/or video.

- **Out-of-order delivery:** When collections of related packets are routed through the Internet, different packets may take different routes, each resulting in a different delay. The result is that the packets arrive in a different order to the one with which they were sent. This problem necessitates special additional protocols responsible for rearranging out-of-order packets once they reach their destination.

- **Error:** Sometimes packets are misdirected, or combined together, or corrupted, while en route. The receiver has to detect this and, just as if the packet was dropped, ask the sender to repeat itself.

Applications requiring QoS:

A defined Quality of Service may be required for certain types of network traffic. For example, streaming multimedia may require guaranteed throughput.

- IP telephony or Voice over IP (VoIP) may require strict limits on jitter and delay.
- Video Teleconferencing (VTC) requires low jitter.
- Dedicated link emulation requires both guaranteed throughput and imposes limits on maximum delay and jitter.
- A safety-critical application, such as remote surgery, may require a guaranteed level of availability (this is also called hard QoS).
- Grid computing applications using Hpc4u middleware that guarantee QoS by offering Fault tolerance mechanisms.

- These types of service are called inelastic, meaning that they require a certain level of bandwidth to function - any more than required is unused, and any less will render the service non-functioning. By contrast, elastic applications can take advantage of however much or little bandwidth is available.

Obtaining QoS:
- Per call
- In call
- In advance: When the expense of mechanisms to provide QoS is justified, network customers and providers typically enter into a contractual agreement termed an SLA (Service Level Agreement) which specifies guarantees for the ability of a network protocol to give guaranteed performance/throughput/ latency bounds based on mutually agreed measures, usually by prioritising traffic.

2.5 Traffic Engineering Theory and Traffic Distributions
- In voice or data communications, subscribers/sources generate calls to servers. When a call arrives at a server, and if a server is available, call is handled. When all servers are busy, the caller can:
  - Receive a busy signal requiring the caller to hang up or try later (retry calling).
  - Automatically get routed to other server.
  - Queue (wait) in some holding facility till server is available.
  - Queue for some tolerable time interval, then disconnect if not served.
- The disposition of call when all servers are busy, has the greatest influence on which formula (model) for analysis to use. So the formulae explained in next sections cover many situations in which sources are blocked or queued when all servers are busy.
- Because the sum of probabilities is one, the probability of a source (caller) being served is one (1) minus the probability of all servers being busy.

  For example, if probability of all servers being busy simultaneously is 10%, then probability of being served is 1 − 0.10 = 0.90 or 90%. That means 10% of callers would encounter a busy signal and 90% would be served.
- The factors dictating the formula that best applies to a given situation include (1) source population (finite or infinite), (2) holding time distribution (constant or exponential) and (3) call disposition when all servers are busy (blocked or queued).
- Most widely used formula types are:
  (1) blocking formulae which assume infinite sources.
  (2) blocking formulae that assume finite sources.
  (3) delay formulae.
- We will be studying these in detail when we analyze LCC, LCH systems.
- Decision tree for formula use is given in Fig. 2.2.

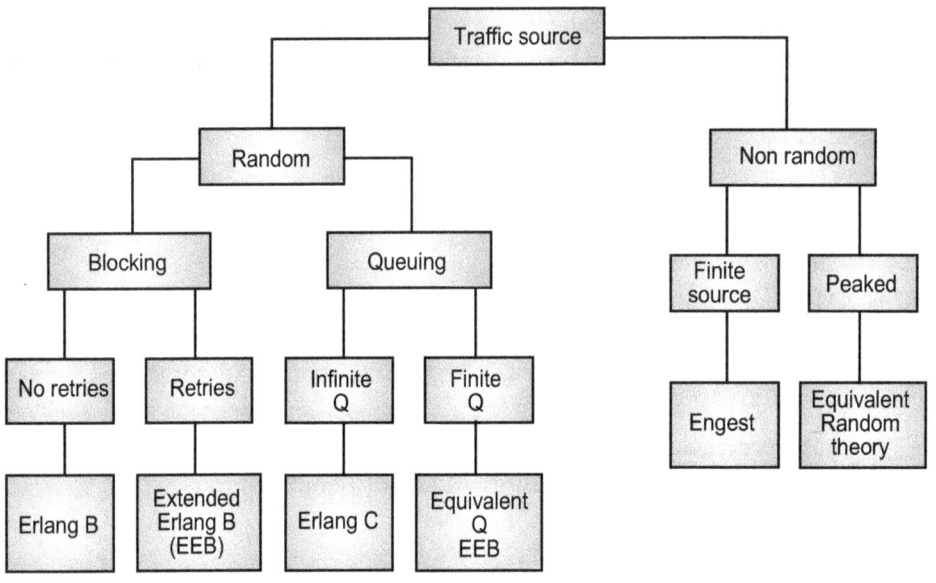

Fig. 2.2: Decision tree for formula use

2.5.1 Concept of Holding Time

It is the call length, call overhead time (queuing time if any). Overheads include the activities necessary on the transmit/receive sides of the call. Outgoing calls incur different activities than do incoming calls.

Major processes are given in Table 2.1.

Table 2.1

Process	Outgoing call	Incoming call
Dialing time (DTMF)	1-7 seconds	1 second
Dialing time (Rotary)	5-12 seconds	5 seconds @ 10 pulse per sec.
Network call setup (SS7)	1-3 seconds	1-3 seconds
Ringing time	12 sec. (2 rings)	12 seconds (2 rings)
Operator answer	5-8 seconds	5-8 seconds
Ringing at station	12 seconds (2 rings)	12 seconds (2 rings)
Conversation time	Variable	Variable

Network call setup may take more time for international calls.

2.5.2 Holding Time Distribution

Generally holding time is considered the talk time, but for trunk sizing, processes in above table should be included.

Voice calls usually have a distribution pattern known as exponential distribution.

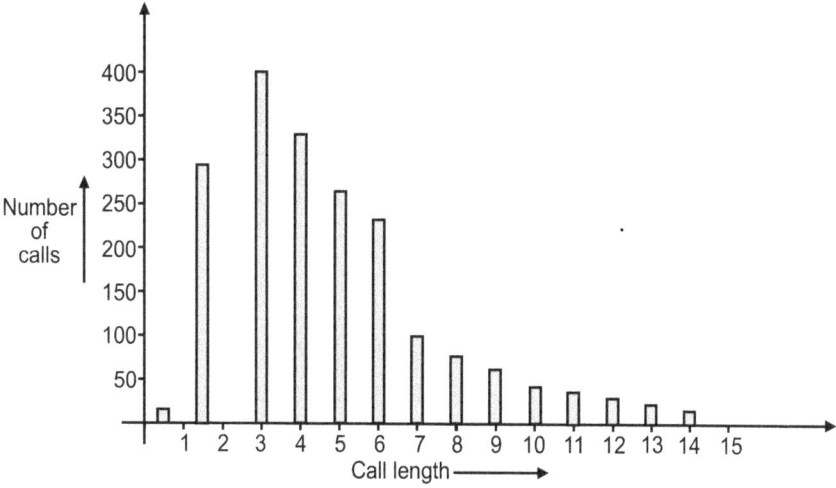

Fig. 2.3: Call holding time distribution (exponential)

(General observation shows this behaviour)

To analyze a model (for telephone/telecommunication) that represents a real life system, it is necessary to use a form that is simple and sufficiently realistic. For queuing theory, it is most convenient to work with probability distributions which exhibit the memoryless property, as it vastly simplifies the mathematics involved. So queuing models (for telephony) are frequently modeled as poisson processes through the use of exponential distribution.

The exponential distribution is the most important time distribution. Its main property is the lack of memory (memoryless). An exponential time interval has no age. The remaining life time is always the same and independent of the actual age. (The Markovian property). This property makes it simple to use exponential time intervals in mathematical models. (Birth and Death processes).

- Combining exponential distributed time intervals in series, we get class of distributions called Erlang distributions.
- For further analysis we need to know about how to describe behaviour of switching system as a random process. We need to study some related basics.

  A **random process** or a **stochastic process** is the one in which one or more **quantities vary with time** in such a way that the **instantaneous values** of the quantities **cannot** be **determined** precisely, but are **predictable** with **certain probability**. The quantities are called random variables.

- Thus a stochastic process is a time indexed function of one or more variables.
  It is generally possible to characterize the behaviour of random process by some statistical properties and thus predict the future performance with a certain probability.

- The telephone traffic qualifies as a stochastic process where number of simultaneously active subscribers and the number of simultaneously busy servers are random variables. It is not possible to precisely estimate the number of simultaneously active subscribers at a given instant of time, but a prediction can be made with a certain probability.

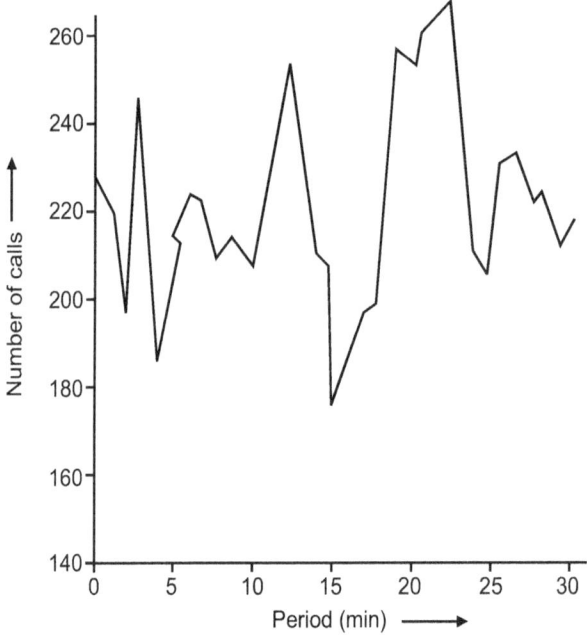

Fig. 2.4: Typical fluctuations in the number of telephone calls

As shown in Fig. 2.4, the pattern signifies a typical random process.

- The values taken by random variables of a random process may be discrete or continuous. In case of telephone traffic, random variable which represents the number of simultaneous calls can take only discrete values. (As against the random variable representing temperature variations in some experiment can take continuous values.

- Time index of random variables can be discrete or continuous. So accordingly we have four different types of stochastic processes.
  (1) Continuous time continuous state.
  (2) Continuous time discrete state.
  (3) Discrete time continuous state.
  (4) Discrete time discrete state.
- A discrete state stochastic process is called **chain**. Statistical properties of a random process may be obtained in two ways:
  (1) By observing its behaviour over a very long period of time **(time statistical parameters).**
  (2) By observing a very large number of statistically identical random sources at any given instant of time **(ensemble statistical parameters).**

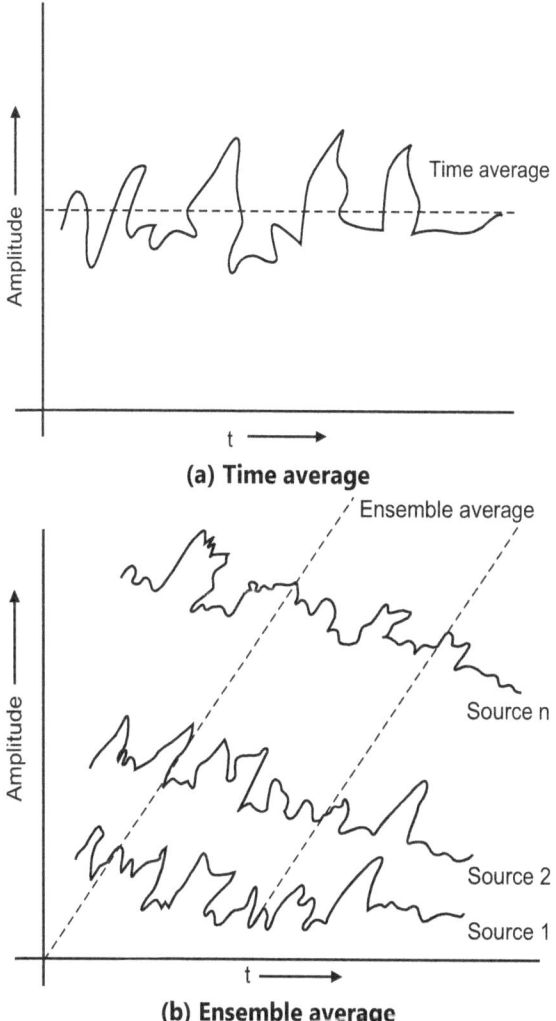

(a) Time average

(b) Ensemble average

Fig. 2.5: Time and Ensemble Averages of Stochastic Averages

- Random processes whose statistical parameters do not change with time are known as **stationary processes.**

  Random processes which have identical time and ensemble averages are known as **ergodic processes**. Ergodic process is stationary, but stationary process need not necessarily be ergodic.

- Telephone traffic is non-stationary. But if we consider the segments 6-9 hours, 10-11 hours, 12-13 hours etc., the traffic may be considered to be stationary. Non-stationary processes are difficult to model and analyze. So we model and analyze telephone traffic in segments when they are considered to be stationary.

- The behaviour of a switching system can be modeled as stochastic process.
  The number of severs busy simultaneously is a discrete random variable.
  The time at which the server becomes busy or free, is also a random process.

- **Markov Process:** Markov processes form an important class of random processes that have some special properties. These were defined and investigated by A.A.Markov.

  A discrete time Markov chain, i.e. discrete time discrete state Markov process is defined as the one which has following property:

$$P[\{X(t_{n+1}) = X_{n+1}\}/X(t_n) = X_n, X(t_{n-1})$$

$$= X_{n-1}, \dots , X(t_1) = X_1\}]$$

$$= P[\{X(t_{n+1}) = X_{n+1}\}/\{X(t_n) = X_n\}]$$

where, $t_1 < t_2 < \dots t_n < t_{n+1}$ and x_i is the ith discrete state space value.

This equation states that:

"The random variable X takes on the **value X_{n+1}** at **time** step **n + 1** is **entirely** determined by **its state value** in **previous time step n.** It is **independent** of its state values in **earlier** time steps, n – 1, n – 2, n – 3 ...etc.

The entire past history of the process is summarized in its current state and hence next state is determined only by current state. If this is the case, the time period, for which the process has stayed in the current state, should not play any role in determining next state. But we require some specification about time that elapses between state transitions. Since the process is random, the time specification should also be in terms of a random variable. This means we are now seeking a probability distribution function for time, which in no way would influence the next state transition of a process i.e. the duration for which a process has stayed in a particular state does not influence the next state transition.

There are only two distribution functions that satisfy this criterion:

  (1) Exponential distribution (continuous).
  (2) Geometric distribution (discrete).

Thus, interstate transition time in discrete time Markov Process is geometrically distributed and in continuous time Markov process, it is exponentially distributed. As these distributions observe the above described property, they are said to be memoryless.

2.5.3 Birth-Death Process

- If we apply the restriction that the state transitions of a Markov chain can occur only to the adjacent states, we obtain **Birth-Death (B-D) Processes.** We talk of population in B-D process.

- The number in the population is a random variable and represents the state value of the process.

- The B-D process moves from its state k to state k – 1 if a death occurs. It moves to state k + 1 if a birth occurs.

- It stays in the same state if there is no birth or death during the time period under consideration.

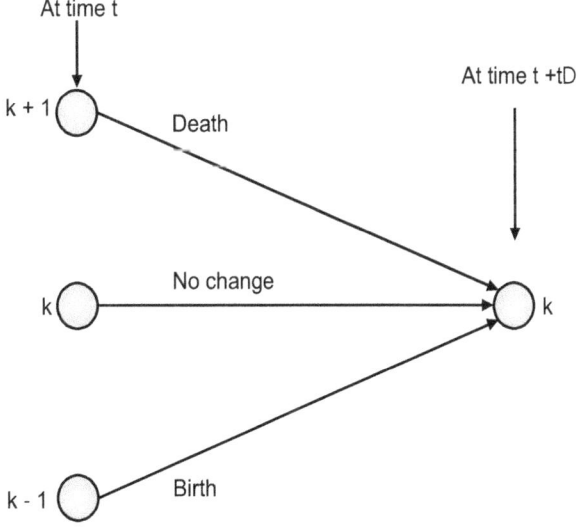

Fig. 2.6: State transitions at a Birth-Death process

- Birth-Death processes are useful for analysis of telecommunication networks. A telecommunication network can be modeled as a B-D process where the number of busy servers represents population, call request means birth and call termination implies a death.

- To analyze a B-D process, we choose a time interval Δt small enough such that,

    (1) There can be only one state transition in Δt.

    (2) There is only one arrival or one termination, but not both.

    (3) There may not be any arrival or termination leaving the state unchanged in time interval Δt.

    We further assume that,

    (1) The probability of an arrival or termination in a particular interval is independent of what had happened in the earlier time intervals.

    (2) Probability of an arrival is directly proportional to the time interval Δt.

- With these assumptions we start the analysis:

    Let, $P_k(t)$ – The probability that the system is in state k at time t i.e., k servers are busy at time t.

                       (λ_k) – Call arrival rate in state k

                       μ_k – Call termination rate in state k

- Then, we have the probabilities in Δt as,

    P [Exactly one arrival]   : $\lambda\,\Delta t$

    P [Exactly one termination]   : $\mu\,\Delta t$

    P [No arrival]   : $1 - \lambda\,\Delta t$

    P [No termination)   : $1 - \mu\,\Delta t$

- Probability of finding the system in state k at time t + Δt is given by,

$$P_k(t + \Delta t) = \underbrace{P_{k-1}(t)\,\lambda_{k-1}\,\Delta t}_{(1)} + \underbrace{P_{k+1}\,t\,\mu_{k+1}\,\Delta t}_{(2)} + \underbrace{(1 - \lambda_k\,\Delta t)(1 - \mu_k\,\Delta t)\,P_k(t)}_{(3)}$$

    (1) The first term represents the possibility of finding the system in state k − 1 at time t and a birth (or call request) occurring during time interval (t, t + Δt).

    (2) The second term gives the possibility of finding the system in state k + 1 at time t and a death (or call termination) occurring during the interval (t, t + Δt).

    (3) The last term represents no arrival and no termination case.

- Expanding above expression and ignoring second order Δt,

$$P_k(t + \Delta t) = P_{k-1}(t)\, \lambda_{k-1}\, \Delta t + P_{k+1}(t)\, \mu_{k+1}\, \Delta t - (\lambda_k + \mu_k)\, P_k(t)\, \Delta t + P_k(t)$$

- We want to determine the dynamics of the system which is given by rate of change of probability P_k with time. Therefore, rearranging the terms, we get,

$$\frac{P_k(t + \Delta t) - P_k(t)}{\Delta t} = P_{k-1}(t)\, \mu_{k-1} + P_{k+1}(t)\, \mu_{k+1} - (\lambda_k + \mu_k)\, P_k(t)$$

In the limit, $\Delta t \to 0$, we get,

$$\boxed{\frac{d\,P_k(t)}{dt} = P_{k-1}(t)\, \lambda_{k-1} + P_{k+1}(t)\, \mu_{k+1} - (\lambda_k + \mu_k)\, P_k(t)}$$

This differential equation governs the dynamics of a B-D process and applies for all values of $k \geq 1$.

For $k = 0$,   number calls in progress, so there cannot be any termination of call, or $\mu_0 = 0$.

There is no state with -1 as the state value.

$\therefore$ For $k = 0$, equation is –

$$\frac{d\,P_0(t)}{dt} = P_1(t)\, \mu_1 - \lambda_0\, P_0(t)$$

Under steady state conditions, the state probabilities reach an equilibrium value and do not change with time. i.e. $P_k(t_1) = P_k(t_2) = P_k(t_i) = P_k$. When commercial offices start functioning around 10.00 hrs, networks pick up traffic and quickly reach a steady state condition when the state probabilities stabilize. Under these conditions, we have,

$$\frac{d\,P_k(t)}{dt} = 0$$

and the B-D process becomes stationary.

$\therefore$ Steady state equations of B-D process are:

$$\boxed{\begin{aligned} P_{k-1}\,\lambda_{k-1} + P_{k+1}\,\mu_{k+1} - (\lambda_k + \mu_k)\, P_k &= 0 \text{ ... for } k \geq 1 \\ P_1\mu_1 - \lambda_0 P_0 &= 0 \text{ ... for } k = 0 \end{aligned}}$$

2.5.4 Poisson Distribution

- Poisson distribution is a **discrete** probability distribution.
- It expresses the probability of a number of events occurring in a fixed time, if these events occur with a known average rate and are independent of the time since last event, or simply, the average number of events that you can expect in a given period.

- So if we can estimate the average number of calls, we expect within an hour, we can predict the probability that the actual number in future hour will exceed the number of trunks available. So we can specify how many trunks will be required to give a particular service level. This analysis gives us Poisson traffic tables.

- Poisson distribution can be applied to incoming traffic (or arrivals) and also to call terminations. Accordingly we have both, Poisson arrival process equation and we first start with incoming traffic

- We said that subscribers generate call is random manner and therefore telecommunication traffic is characterized as a random process.

- Whenever a subscriber originates a call, he adds to the number of calls arriving in the network and has no way by which he can reduce the already arrived calls. So we need to describe an originating process.

- This process can be treated as a special case of B-D process in which death rate is equal to zero, or no death occurring in the process. Such a process is known as **renewal process.**

- It is a **pure birth process** meaning that it can only add to the population and cannot deplete the population by itself.

  [Many subscribers are making calls and all are being serviced, but no call is terminated].

- In the equations, as there is no termination, $\mu_k = 0$.

  $\therefore$ We have,

  $$\frac{d\,P_k\,(t)}{dt} = P_{k-1}\,(t)\,\lambda_{k-1} - \lambda_k P_k\,(t) \text{ ... for } k \geq 1$$

  $$\frac{d\,P_0\,(t)}{dt} = -\lambda_0 P_0\,(t)$$

- Steady state equations are not relevant as we are counting only births (call originations).

- If we start the observation at time $t = 0$, as soon as a birth occurs, say at time $t = t_1$, it is impossible to find the system in state 0. Similarly after i births, it is not possible for the system to be in the state $i - 1$, $i - 2$ etc. In the equations studied so far, birth rate is dependent upon the state of system (λ_k). If we assume a constant birth rate λ, which is independent of the state of the system, we get a **Poisson process.**

- The governing equations are:

  $$\frac{d\,P_k\,(t)}{dt} = \lambda\,P_{k-1}\,(t) - \lambda\,P_k\,(t) \text{ ... for } k \geq 1 \qquad \text{... (2.1)}$$

  $$\frac{d\,P_0\,(t)}{dt} = -\lambda\,P_0\,(t) \text{ ... for } k = 0 \qquad \text{... (2.2)}$$

- To solve the equations, we have to assume certain boundary conditions.

  At time t = 0, system is in state 0, therefore, no births,

  $$\therefore \qquad P_k (0) = \begin{cases} 1 \dots \text{for } k = 0 \\ 0 \dots \text{for } k \neq 0 \end{cases}$$

  With these, solution for equation (2.2) is,

  $$P_0 (t) = e^{-\lambda t} \qquad \qquad \dots (2.3)$$

- For k = 1, from equation (2.1) and equation (2.3),

  $$\frac{d P_1 (t)}{dt} = -\lambda P_1(t) + \lambda e^{-\lambda t}$$

  Solving this, we get,

  $$P_1(t) = \lambda t e^{-\lambda t}$$

- For k = 2, the solution is,

  $$P_2(t) = \frac{(\lambda t)^2 e^{-\lambda t}}{2!}$$

- By induction, general solution is,

  $$\boxed{P_k(t) = \frac{(\lambda t)^{k} - e^{-\lambda t}}{k!}} \text{ – Poisson arrival process equation}$$

  This equation expresses the probability of finding the system with k members in the population at time t. Or in short, it represents the probability of k arrivals in time interval t.

- Equation (2.3) represents the probability of zero arrival in given time interval, i.e. the probability distribution of interarrival times (the time that elapses between two arrivals).

  Thus, in a Poisson process, interarrival time is exponentially distributed.

Example 2.6: A rural telephone exchange normally experiences four call originations per minute. What is probability that exactly eight calls occur in an arbitrarily chosen interval of 30 seconds?

Solution: $\qquad \qquad \lambda = \frac{4}{60} = \frac{1}{15}$ calls per second

t = 30 seconds, $\lambda t = 2$.

$\therefore$ Probability of exactly 8 arrivals.

$$P_8 (30) = \frac{2^8 e^{-2}}{8!}$$

$$P_8 (30) = 0.00086$$

- The above problem shows that the probability of the mentioned event is very low. Now you can understand how useful are these calculations in sizing the switching system.
- It is important to recognize that the assumption of an arrival rate independent of the state of the system in a Poisson process implies that we are dealing with infinite number of sources or essentially constant number of sources.

    If a number of arrivals occur immediately before any subinterval in question, (sudden spurt) some of the sources become busy and cannot generate further requests. The effect of busy sources is to reduce the average arrival rate unless the source population is infinite or large enough such that it is not affected significantly by the busy sources.

Example 2.7: A switching system serves 10,000 subscribers with a traffic intensity of 0.1 E per subscriber. If there is a sudden spurt in the traffic, increasing the average traffic by 50%, what is the effect on arrival rate?

Solution: Total subscribers = 10,000

   (1) Normal traffic = 1000 and

   (2) Increased traffic = 1500 (as 0.1 = T/10,000)

∴ Available subscribers for generating new traffic for (1) Normal traffic = 9000 and (2) Increased traffic = 8500.

$$\therefore \quad \text{Change in arrival rate} \ = \ \frac{\text{Amount of increase}}{\text{Available subscribers}}$$

$$\therefore \quad \text{Change in arrival rate} \ = \ \frac{500}{9000} \times 100$$

$$= \ 5.6\%$$

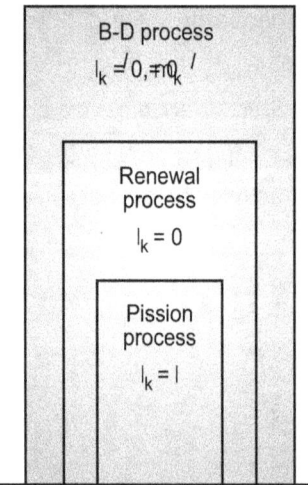

Fig. 2.7: Relationship among different Markov processes

- Fig. 2.7 shows relationship among different Markov processes in the form of Venn diagram. From that we can describe Poisson process as:

  (1) A pure birth process with constant birth rate.

  (2) A birth-death process with zero death rate and a constant birth rate.

  (3) A Markov process with state transitions limited to the next higher state or to the same state and having a constant transition rate.

- In real life Poisson processes we observe are:

  (1) Number of telephone calls arriving at an exchange.

  (2) Number of rainy days in a year.

  (3) Number of typing errors in a manuscript.

  (4) Number of bit errors occurring in data communication system.

- Telephone calls arriving at an exchange follow a Poisson process. But call generation by subscribers is not a Poisson process, but it is a renewal process.

  Superimposition of a large number of renewal processes results in Poisson Process.

- Now we analyze the termination process. In a system modeled as B-D process, the termination phenomenon can be characterized as a **Pure Death Process.**

  We obtain a pure death process from B-D process by setting birth rate equal to zero.

- So equations governing the dynamics of a pure death process are:

$$\frac{d\ P_k(t)}{dt} = \mu_{k+1}\ P_{k+1}\ (t) - \mu_k\ P_k(t) \dots \text{ for } k \geq 1$$

$$\frac{d\ P_0\ (t)}{dt} = \mu_1 P_1(t)$$

- If we assume a constant death rate μ, (similar to constant birth rate), we get the following equations:

$$\frac{d\ P_k(t)}{dt} = \mu\ P_{k+1}\ (t) - \mu\ P_k(t) \dots \text{ for } k \geq 1$$

$$\frac{d\ P_0(t)}{dt} = \mu\ P_1(t) \dots \text{ for } k = 0$$

- Above equations can be solved by assuming suitable boundary conditions.

  We assume, at time t = 0, there are N members in population.

$$\therefore \quad \frac{d\ P_k(t)}{dt} = \mu\ P_{k+1}\ (t) - \mu\ P_k(t) \dots \text{ for } 0 < k < N$$

$$\frac{d\ P_N(t)}{dt} = -\mu\ P_N(t) \dots \text{ for } k = N$$

$$\frac{d\ P_0(t)}{dt} = \mu\ P_1(t) \dots \text{ for } k = 0$$

- Solving these equations, we get,

$$P_N(t) = e^{-\mu t} \text{ ... for } k = N \qquad\qquad ... (2.4)$$

$$P_k(t) = \frac{(\mu t)^{N-k}}{(N-k)!} \cdot e^{-\mu t} \text{ ... for } 0 < k < N \qquad ... (2.5)$$

$$P_0(t) = \frac{(\mu t)^{N-1}}{(N-1)!} \cdot e^{-\mu t} \text{ ... for } k = 0 \qquad ... (2.6)$$

- Equation (2.5) above expresses the probability of no termination or death in a given interval as the population remains at the initial level. This is the probability distribution of how long the system remains in a state without a death (or termination) occurring.

  In other words, this is probability distribution of the service times or holding times in case of calls in a switching system.

  Thus a pure death process has a service time distribution which is exponentially distributed, as required by a Markov Process.

- The holding times of conventional voice conversations are well approximated by an exponential distribution. But for call processing and interoffice signalling, a constant holding time is a better model. In this case, the Poisson equation can be used to determine the probability distribution of active channels. If t_m is the constant holding time, then the probability of finding
  k busy channels at any instant of time is merely the probability that there are
  k arrivals during time interval t_m immediately preceding the instant of observation, given by –

$$P_k(t_m) = \frac{(\lambda t_m)\, e^{(-\lambda t_m)}}{k!}$$

2.5.5 Erlang Distribution

- It is a continuous probability distribution developed by A. K. Erlang to examine the number of calls which might be made at the same time to the exchange. Precisely it was derived to model the total waiting time associated with a queue of requests in an exchange.

- Erlang distribution is a special case of gamma distribution where shape parameter is an integer. It represents the sum of series of exponential distributions.

- There are 2 commonly used versions of Erlang distribution:
  Erlang B – does not allow queuing of blocked calls.

Erlang C – allows unlimited queuing of blocked calls until they are served.

Erlang B and C distributions are still in use for traffic modeling such as design of call centre.

2.6 Blocking Models

We have seen that telecommunication systems can be classified as loss systems or delay systems.

The behaviour of **loss systems** is studied by using **blocking models** and **delay systems** by using **queuing models.**

We are concerned with three aspects while analyzing telecommunication systems.

(1) Modeling the system (B-D process).

(2) Traffic arrival model (Poisson Process).

(3) Service time or holding time distribution. (Exponential or constant time distribution).

In loss systems, the overflow traffic is rejected or we say the overflow traffic experiences blocking from network.

There are 3 ways in which overflow traffic can be handled:

(1) The traffic rejected by one set of resources is cleared by another set of resources in network.

(2) The traffic may return to the same resource after some time.

(3) The traffic may be held by the resource as if it is being serviced, but actually serviced only after the resource is available.

Please understand that case 3 is not queuing of call. The call is accepted, but resource is not immediately allocated. Subscriber proceeds with information exchange (speaking, enquiring). Some part of this initial information may be lost. But resource is allocated quite fast soon enough such that this information loss is unnoticeable by the subscriber within acceptable limits.

So corresponding to above three cases we consider 3 models for loss systems.

(1) Lost calls cleared – LCC

(2) Lost calls returned – LCR

(3) Lost calls held – LCH

2.6.1 Lost Calls Cleared with Infinite Resources

- We will first assume infinite number of subscribers for LCC. So we can use Poisson arrival model for the traffic. The arrival rate is independent of the number of subscribers already busy and remains constant irrespective of the state of the system.

- Usually there are many trunk groups between and among adjacent exchanges.

- Whenever a direct group between 2 exchanges is busy, it is possible to divert the traffic via other exchanges using different trunk groups (analogous as redundant path routing). In this way blocked calls in on trunk group are cleared via other trunk groups.

- LCC model assumes that the subscriber on receiving a busy/engaged tone, hangs up and waits for some time before making another attempt (not immediately or within a short time). Such calls are considered to be cleared by the system and reattempt is treated as new call.

- LCC model is used as a standard for the design and analysis of telecommunication networks in Europe, India and other countries that adapt European practices.

- Main purpose of analysis is to estimate the blocking probability and the Grade of Service. We can express offered traffic A for Poisson arrival process as:

$$A = \lambda t_h \qquad \qquad \text{... (2.7)}$$

where λ = Average Poisson call arrival rate

t_h = Call holding time

- When all servers in the system are busy, any traffic generated by Poisson process is rejected by the system. As overflow traffic is lost, there is a different arrival rate for the network. We call it as effective arrival rate.

∴ Mean effective arrival rate = C_0 and Effective arrival rate in state i: C_i.

- System is said to be in state j when j servers are busy.

- As long as all servers in the system are not busy, entire incoming traffic is carried by network and when all servers are busy, no traffic is accepted by the network. Such a traffic on network is known as **Erlang Traffic** (pure chance traffic of type 1).

- We have,

$$C_i = \lambda \text{ ... for } 0 \leq i < R, \; C_R = 0$$

R – Number of servers in the system.

- The mean effective traffic rate C_0 is calculated as:

$$C_0 = \sum_{i=0}^{R-1} \lambda P_i$$

P_i – The probability that system is in state i.

- System can be in any one of 0, 1, 2, ... R states.

  $\therefore$ We have,

  $$P_0 + P_1 + P_2 + \dots P_R = 1$$

  (Sum of all probabilities = 1)

- Therefore, now we write,

  $$C_o = \lambda \, (P_0 + P_1 + \dots + P_{R-1})$$
  $$= \lambda \, (1 - P_R)$$

- Mean traffic carried by network is given by –

  $$A_o = C_o \, t_h$$
  $$= \lambda \, (1 - P_R) \cdot t_h$$

  $\therefore$ $\qquad\qquad\qquad A_o = A \, (1 - P_R) \qquad\qquad$ ... Using equation (2.7)

  or $\qquad\qquad \boxed{P_R = \dfrac{A - A_o}{A}}$

- The blocking probability P_B is same as the probability that all servers are busy i.e. P_R.

  $\therefore$ For LCC model, where arrival is characterised by Poisson process,

  $$\textbf{GOS} \ = \ \textbf{P}_\textbf{B}$$

- Now we perform the steady state analysis of the B-D process characterizing LCC model. We have seen the arrival process, now we will see the call termination process.

- But here constant death rate is not proper. Call termination rate will be dependent on the number of busy servers in the system i.e. on the state of the system. If a large number of servers are busy, more calls are likely to terminate in a given time and call termination rate will be higher.

- Therefore, termination rate may be considered to be directly proportional to the number of busy servers given by –

  $$\mu_k = k \, \mu \text{ ... for } 0 \le k \le R$$

  μ = Mean call termination rate = $1/t_h$

  μ_k = Call termination rate in state k.

- Substituting values of birth and death rate in steady state equations of B-D process we get,

  $$P_{k-1} \, \lambda + P_{k+1} \, \mu(k + 1) - (\lambda + k\mu) \, P_k = 0$$

- Using equation (2.7), we get,

  $$P_{k+1} = \frac{AP_k + kP_k - AP_{k-1}}{k + 1} \qquad\qquad \text{... for } k > 0$$

$$P_1 = AP_0 \qquad \text{... for } k = 0$$

$$P_2 = \frac{AP_1 + P_1 - AP_0}{2} \qquad \text{... for } k = 1$$

- Substituting P_1, we get,

$$P_2 = \frac{A^2 P_0}{2}$$

Similarly, for $k = 2$, we have,

$$P_3 = \frac{AP_2 + 2P_2 - AP_1}{3}$$

$$= \frac{A^3 P_0}{3 \times 2}$$

$$= \frac{A^3 P_0}{3!}$$

- Generalising, we get,

$$P_j = \frac{A^j P_0}{j!}$$

- For probability,

$$P_0 + AP_0 + ... + \frac{A^R P_0}{R!} = 1$$

$$\therefore \qquad P_0 = \frac{1}{1 + A + \dfrac{A^2}{2!} + ... + \dfrac{A^R}{R!}}$$

- For $k = R$,

$$\therefore \qquad \boxed{P_R = \frac{A^R / R!}{1 + A + \dfrac{A^2}{2!} + ... + \dfrac{A^R}{R!}}}$$

which is Erlang B formula or Loss formula.

2.6.2 Lost Calls Cleared System with Finite Subscribers

In our previous discussion for Erlang B formula, we assumed that call arrivals are independent of the number of active callers. This assumption is justified only when the number of sources is much larger that the number of servers. This may not always be the case in practice.

Consider the case of three stage space division network, where the number of subscribers connected to each input matrix is comparable to the number of servers (alternative paths) available in the network. In such cases, the arrival rate to the system is dependent on the number of subscribers who are not occupied, as the busy subscribers do not generate new calls. The traffic in this case is known as **Engest traffic** or **pure chance traffic of type 2**.

The blocking probabilities in finite source systems are always less than those for infinite source systems, since the arrival rate decreases as the number of busy sources increases.

Let, λ_S – Arrival rate per subscriber

           k – Number of busy subscribers

           N – Total number of subscribers

           R – Number of servers

The arrival rate/offered traffic for system in state k,

$$C_k = (N - k) \lambda_S \text{ ... for } k \leq 0 \leq R$$

- Mean offered traffic rate is,

$$C = \sum_{k=0}^{R} (N - k) \lambda_S P_k = N \lambda_S \sum_{k=0}^{R} P_k - \lambda_S \sum_{k=0}^{R} k \cdot P_k$$

$$= \lambda_S \left(N - \sum_{k=0}^{R} k \cdot P_k \right)$$

$\sum k P_k$ represents the average number of busy servers.

- The carried traffic is average number of calls accepted during the mean service time period. This is same as the average number of busy servers at any given time.

  $\therefore$ $C = \lambda_S (N - A_o)$

- The offered traffic is,

$$A = C \cdot t_h = \lambda_S t_h (N - A_o)$$

- When traffic is in state R, offered traffic rate is $(N - R) \lambda_S$, but now all arrivals are rejected.

  $\therefore$ Lost traffic $= A - A_o = (N - R) \lambda_S \cdot P_R \cdot t_h$

- $$GOS = \frac{N - R}{N - A_o} \cdot P_R$$

- We now calculate the blocking probability. For that we analyze the steady state of B-D process. Arrival process is discussed above. And the termination process is same as for LCC with infinite sources. Termination rate is given by the same equation.

- Substituting for birth and death rates in equations for steady state B-D process, we get,

$$P_{k-1} \lambda_S (N - k + 1) + P_{k+1} \mu (k + 1) - [\lambda_S (N - k) + k\mu] P_k = 0$$

- Rearranging the terms,

$$P_{k+1} = \frac{[(\rho (N - k) + k)] P_k - \rho (N - k + 1) P_{k-1}}{k + 1}$$

$\rho = \dfrac{\lambda_S}{\mu}$, for k = 0: $P_1 = \rho N P_0$

- For k = 1,

$$P_2 = \frac{[(\rho (N - 1) + 1) - \rho (N - 1 + 1) P_0]}{2}$$

$$P_2 = \frac{\rho^2 N (N - 1) P_0}{2}$$

- For k = 2,

$$P_3 = \frac{\rho^3 N (N - 1) (N - 2) P_0}{3 \times 2}$$

- Generalising,

$$P_j = \rho^j \binom{N}{j} P_0$$

$\binom{N}{j} \rightarrow$ Binomial coefficient i.e. $\binom{N}{j} = \dfrac{N!}{j! (N - j)!}$

- For probability,

$$P_0 + \rho \binom{N}{1} P_0 + \rho^2 \binom{N}{2} P_0 + \ldots + \rho^R \binom{N}{R} P_0 = 1$$

$\therefore$

$$P_0 = \frac{1}{1 + \rho \binom{N}{1} + \rho^2 \binom{N}{2} + \ldots + \rho^R \binom{N}{R}}$$

$$P_0 = \frac{1}{\displaystyle\sum_{k=0}^{R} \rho^k \binom{N}{k}}$$

- Blocking Probability,

$$P_B = P_R = \frac{\rho^R \binom{N}{R}}{\displaystyle\sum_{k=0}^{R} \rho^k \binom{N}{k}}$$

- Using above equation and GOS equation, we get,

$$GOS = \frac{N}{N - A_0} \cdot \rho^R \binom{N - 1}{R} \cdot \frac{1}{\displaystyle\sum_{k=0}^{R} \rho^k \binom{N}{k}}$$

$$N - A_O = \frac{N \sum\limits_{k=0}^{R} \rho^k \binom{N}{k} - \sum\limits_{j=0}^{R} j \rho^j \binom{N}{j}}{\sum\limits_{k=0}^{R} \rho^k \binom{N}{k}}$$

- As the limits for summation are same in numerator, we combine the terms, we get,

$$N - A_O = \frac{\sum\limits_{k=0}^{R} \rho^k \binom{N}{k} (N - k)}{\sum\limits_{k=0}^{R} \rho^k \binom{N}{k}}$$

- Simplifying further, we get,

$$N - A_O = \frac{N \sum\limits_{k=0}^{R} \rho^k \binom{N-1}{k}}{\sum\limits_{k=0}^{R} \rho^k \binom{N}{k}}$$

- Substituting for $N - A_O$, we get,

$$GOS = \frac{\rho^R \binom{N-1}{R}}{\sum\limits_{k=0}^{R} \rho^k \binom{N-1}{k}}$$

- For LCC with finite sources, when $R \geq N$ (i.e. servers $\geq$ subscribers), there is no blocking. State probability for that is,

$$P_j = \binom{N}{j} \frac{\rho^j}{\sum\limits_{k=0}^{N} \rho^k \binom{N}{k}} = \binom{N}{j} \frac{\rho^j}{(1 + \rho)^N}$$

Traffic in this case is **Bernouli traffic.**

- Now, we define,　　$a = \dfrac{\rho}{1 + \rho}$

$\rho = a (1 + \rho)$ and $1 - a = \dfrac{1}{1 + \rho}$

Substituting this,

$$P_j = \binom{N}{j} \frac{a^j (1 + \rho)^j}{(1 + \rho)^N}$$

$\therefore$ $$\boxed{P_j = \binom{N}{j} a^j \frac{1}{(1 + \rho)^{N-j}} = \binom{N}{j} a^j (1 - a)^{N-j}}$$

This is **Binomial formula** which implies servers are independent of one another.

- We defined $\rho = \lambda_s\, t_h$, but it does not specify the average activity of a source by itself, and hence cannot be measured directly.

  We can observe the average transmission rate per subscriber based on total traffic (a').

$$a' = \frac{A}{N}$$

$$a' = \rho\left(1 - \frac{A_o}{N}\right) \quad \ldots \text{Refer previous equations}$$

Substituting for A_o,

$$a' = \rho\left[1 - \frac{A}{N}(1 - GOS)\right]$$

Simplifying,

$$a' = \frac{1}{1 + \rho\,(1 - GOS)}$$

For Bernouli traffic, GOS is zero.

$$\therefore \qquad\qquad a' = \frac{\rho}{1 + \rho} = a \text{ (as defined earlier)}$$

Example 2.8: In a telephone system, there are 20 servers and 100 subscribers. On an average there are 10 busy servers at any time. The probability of all servers being busy is 0.2. Calculate GOS assuming (1) Erlang traffic and (2) Engest traffic.

Solution:

(1)   For Erlang traffic, GOS $= P_R$

$\therefore$ GOS $= 0.2$

(2) For Engest traffic,   GOS $= \dfrac{N - R}{N - A_o} \cdot P_R$

N = 100, R = 20, A_o = 10

$\therefore$ GOS $= \dfrac{100 - 20}{100 - 10} \times (0.2)$

$= 0.1875$

You can observe that GOS is lower for LCC with finite sources.

2.6.3 Lost Calls Returned (LCR) System

- In previous discussion for LCC model, we assumed that unsuccessful call attempts were lost and they never returned or the arrival rate into system is no way affected by the calls that are rejected.

  But this is not the case practically. The rejected calls do return to the system in the form of retries resulting in making the offered traffic as:

  Offered traffic = New traffic + Retry traffic.

- Now we have to take into account this returned traffic.

  Model used for analysis is LCR model.

- We make following assumptions:

  (1) No new call is generated when a blocked call is being retried.

  (2) A number of retry attempts may be involved before a call eventually gets serviced.

  (3) Retries are attempted after a random time and each retry time statistically independent of others.

  (4) Typical waiting time before a retry is longer than the average holding time.

- Assumption (3) says that retries are not correlated. If they were related, there would be traffic peaks at some intervals which would be more complicated.

- Assumption (4) allows the system to maintain its statistical equilibrium even in the presence of retry. Bu this, the retry arrivals are made to have the same arrival characteristics as the new traffic. So effectively these assumptions make the retry traffic statistically indistinguishable from the new arrivals. (Retry call is as if it is new call) so blocked calls merely add to the first attempt calls.

- Let, $\lambda \to$ Arrival rate for new calls.

  $$\text{GOS} = P_c \to \text{Call congestion}$$

  i.e. P_c calls are rejected which return to the system as retries. The retries may further experience blocking by a factor of P_c.

  $P_c \times P_c$ calls will be rejected.

  Thus, effective arrival rate,

  $$\lambda' = \lambda + P_c \lambda + P_c^2 \lambda + P_c^3 \lambda + \dots = \frac{\lambda}{1 - P_c} = \frac{\lambda}{1 - \text{GOS}}$$

  This equation relates effective arrival rate to the call congestion. Here it is not possible to directly determine either λ' or P_c, as one is expressed in terms of the other.

They are estimated iteratively using Erlang B formula, starting with λ as initial value of arrival rate.

- The effect of retry traffic is noticeable at high GOS values, but insignificant for low GOS value.

  For a given value of GOS, LCC model permits a larger offered load to the system than LCR model.

2.6.4 Lost Calls Held (LCH) System

- In LCH model, total time spent in the system is independent of the waiting time and it is determined only by the average service time required.

- As soon as a call arrives in the system, it requires service continuously for a period of time. It terminates after that irrespective of whether it is serviced or not. If a call is blocked, a portion of it is lost until server becomes free to service the call.

Fig. 2.8: Lost traffic in LCH model

- An example of LCH model is TASI (Time Assigned speech interpolation) system. In TASI, the number of conversations supported is larger than the number of transmission channels or servers in the system. System exploits silence periods. (no speech) when there is no need for transmitting the signal. The channel is deassigned during the silence period and is used for supporting another conversation which is active.

- If a speech circuit is active when all channels are busy, it is blocked and clipping occurs. Speech segment becomes active irrespective of whether a channel is available or not. Or simply, the duration for which the source is active, is independent of whether it is being serviced or not.

As soon as a call arrives, it is accepted by the system even if server is not available.

So the number of active sources in the system is nothing but the number of call arrivals in time duration, t_h. For infinite population, it is characterized by Poisson arrival process.

Example 2.9: A TASI system has 10 channels and 20 sources connected to it. What is the probability of clipping if activity factor for each source is 0.4?

Solution: Average number of busy servers = 0.4 × 20 = 8.

Clipping will occur if 10 or more sources are in active simultaneously (as number of channels = 10). Probability that 10 or more sources are active, gives the clipping probability.

$$\text{Probability (clipping)} = \sum_{j=10}^{\infty} P_j \, (t = 8)$$

$$= 1 - \sum_{j=0}^{9} P_j \, (t = 8)$$

$$= 1 - e^{-8}\left(1 + 8 + \frac{8^2}{2!} + ... + \frac{8^9}{9!}\right)$$

$$= 0.284$$

2.6.5 Lost Call Delayed/Delay (LCD) Systems

- Delay systems place call or message arrivals in a queue in absence of resources and services them as and when resources become available.

- Delay systems are analyzed using queuing theory (or waiting line theory).

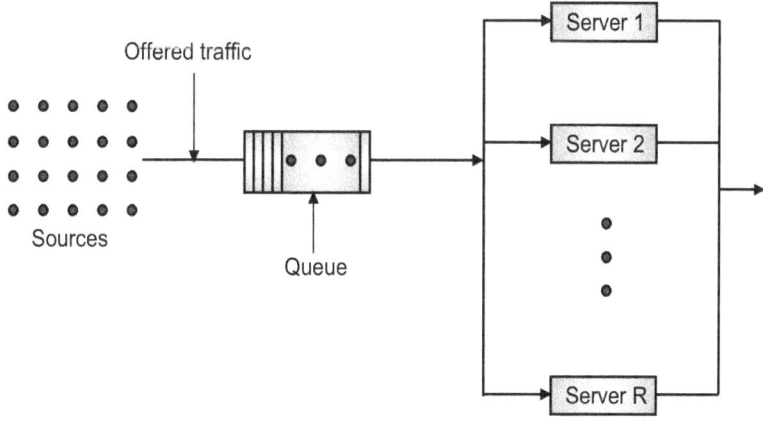

Fig. 2.9: Elements of a Queuing system

Fig. 2.9 shows how the traffic is placed in a queue and allocated a server.

- While analyzing queuing systems, we have to deal with a number of random variables like – waiting request, interarrival time between requests and time spent by a request in the system. Some important ones are listed in Table 2.2.

Table 2.2: Some important Random Variables in a Queuing System

Random variable	Notation
State of the system: number of calls present in the system	k
Queue length: Number of calls or requests waiting to be serviced	k_q
Number of calls in service	k_s
Mean wait time	t_q
Mean service time	t_k
Mean arrival rate	λ
Mean service rate	μ
Mean interarrival time	τ
Probability that there are k calls in the queuing system	P_k
Traffic intensity: λ/μ	ρ
Server utilization: ρ/R	u

- The number of requests present in the system (or state of the system) is given by the sum of requests in the queue and those being serviced. No request is pending in queue unless all servers are busy.

  ∴ We have, $k = k_q + R$

- The mean time a call spends in the system is the sum of mean wait time t_q and mean service or holding time t_h.

- Queuing enables better utilization of servers than a loss system. Queuing has the smoothening effect on traffic flow as far as servers are concerned. Peaks in the arrival process build up the queue. As there is no limit on the number of arrivals occurring in a short period of time, there should be infinite queuing capacity, if loss of traffic is not desired. But practically, only finite queue capacities are possible and therefore, there is a probability, however small it may be, of blocking the delay systems.

  (Servers busy   Queue full   Blocking)

- Assuming that a delay system has infinite queue capacity in an operational sense, the condition for stable operation is,

$$\frac{\text{Mean arrival rate}}{\text{Mean service rate}} < 1$$

or $$\frac{\text{Offered traffic}}{\text{Number of servers}} < 1$$

If this condition is not satisfied, queue would grow infinitely and the system will never be able to clear the traffic offered to it.

- Queuing system is characterized by 6 parameters.

    Notation reads as: A/B/c/K/m/Z.

    A – Arrival process specification

    B – Service time distribution

    c – Number of servers

    K – Queue capacity

    m – Number of sources

    Z – Service discipline

- K and m can be finite or infinite (Default: infinity).

- Z – Discipline can be FCFS (First Come First Serve), random selection, priority based selection, etc.

    (Default: FCFS).

- If K, m, Z are omitted from specifications, we get default values.

- C – Non-zero positive finite number.

- A and B – Any value as shown in Table 2.3.

Table 2.3: Values for Queue Parameters A and B

Values for A and B	Meaning	Remarks
GI	Arrival process with general independent distribution for interarrival time	For A only
G	General (no assumptions) service time distribution	For B only
E_R	Erlang-k interarrival or service time distribution	M stands for Markov
M	Poisson arrival and exponential service time distribution	M stands for Markov
D	Deterministic interarrival or service time distribution	e.g. constant time distributions
H_k	Hyperexponential (with k stages) interarrival or service time distribution	–

- If M/D/4 is the queue specification, it means a queue system with Poisson arrival, deterministic service time distribution, four serves, infinite queue and servers and FCFS discipline.

  If k = 0, it represents a loss system.

- For analysis, we assume infinite sources and infinite queuing capacities exist and discipline is FCFS. We assume Poisson arrival process and service times that are exponentially distributed or constant. So our system is: M/M/R and M/D/R queing system.

- For arrival and service rates, we have,

$$\lambda_k \ = \ \lambda \qquad \dots \qquad \text{for } k = 0, 1, 2, \dots$$

$$\mu_k \ = \ k\mu \qquad \dots \qquad \text{for } k = 0, 1, 2, 3, \dots, R$$

$$\mu_k \ = \ R\mu \qquad \dots \qquad \text{for } k > R$$

- The stability condition demands that,

$$\frac{\lambda}{R\mu} \ < 1 \text{ or } \frac{A}{R} \ < 1$$

- Many results obtained for LCC apply here also. Fundamental difference between LCC and M/M/R delay system is that **state** of **M/M/R** system varies from **0 to infinity;** for **loss system**, from **0 to R**. Any number of calls may enter a delay system and be serviced, or be in the wait state, whereas no calls can enter a loss system once the servers are busy.

$$\therefore P_0 + P_1 + \dots + P_R + P_{R+1} + \dots \ = \ 1$$

$$\therefore \qquad\qquad\qquad P_0 \ = \ 1 - \sum_{k=1}^{\infty} P_k$$

- The loss system and delay system behave identically as long as system is within state R and they behave differently for states equal to or greater than R.

  Substituting birth and death rates for k = R in steady state equation for B-D process,

$$R\mu \, P_{R+1} \ = \ (\lambda + R\mu) \, P_R - \lambda \, P_{R-1}$$

- Using previous results of loss systems,

$$R\mu \cdot P_{R+1} \ = \ (\lambda + R\mu) \frac{A^R}{R!} \cdot P_0 - \lambda \frac{A^{R-1}}{(R-1)!} \, P_0$$

- Simplifying we get,

$$R\mu \, P_{R+1} \ = \ \frac{\lambda A^R}{R!} \cdot P_0$$

or

$$P_{R+1} \ = \ \frac{\lambda}{\mu R} \cdot \frac{A^R}{R!} \cdot P_0 = \frac{A}{R} \cdot \frac{A^R}{R!} \cdot P_0 = \frac{A}{R} \cdot P_R$$

- For k = R + 1, we get,

$$P_{R+2} \ = \ \left(\frac{A}{R}\right)^2 \cdot P_R$$

- Generalizing for k > R,

$$P_k = \left(\frac{A}{R}\right)^{k-R} \cdot P_R$$

- Considering stability condition, we get,

$$\frac{A}{R} + \left(\frac{A}{R}\right)^2 + \left(\frac{A}{R}\right)^3 + \dots = \frac{A/R}{1 - (A/R)} = \frac{A}{R - A}$$

$$\therefore \quad \sum_{k=0}^{R} \frac{A^k}{k!} \cdot P_0 + \frac{A}{R-A} \cdot \frac{A^R}{R!} \cdot P_0 = 1$$

$$\therefore \quad P_0 = \frac{1}{\sum\limits_{k=0}^{R} \dfrac{A^k}{k!} + \dfrac{A^R}{k!} \cdot \dfrac{A}{R-A}}$$

$$P_R = \frac{A^R}{R!} \cdot \frac{1}{\sum\limits_{k=0}^{R} \dfrac{A^k}{k!} + \dfrac{A^R}{R!} \cdot \dfrac{A}{R-A}}$$

- Probability of finding system in state R or above (or probability of message delayed) is,

$$P\,(\text{delay} > 0) = \sum_{k=R}^{\infty} P_k$$

∴ We have,

$$\boxed{P\,(\text{delay} > 0) = \left(1 + \frac{A}{R - A}\right) P_R = \frac{R}{R - A} \cdot P_R}$$

This is known as **Erlang second formula or Erlang delay formula** or **Erlang C formula.**

- For M/M/R queue, waiting time distribution is exponential, given by,

$$P\,(\text{delay} > t) = P\,(\text{delay} < 0)\, c^{[-(R-A)\, t/t_h]}$$

By integrating over time, average waiting time is,

$$t_q = \frac{P\,(\text{delay} > 0) \cdot t_h}{R - A}$$

This equation applies to all arrivals to the system, some of which enter the queue and others which do not.

- Given that message is already put in the queue, average waiting time is,

$$t'_q = \frac{t_h}{R - A}$$

Example 2.10: A PCO is installed in a busy part of a town. 150 people use the booth everyday. Average holding time for call is 1.5 min. There is suggestion from public that another PCO is required in the same locality as the wait times are unduly long. Analyze the situation using M/M/1 queue and determine if the suggestion deserves serious consideration.

Solution: λ = 0.104 per min, t_h = 1.5 min

$A = \lambda \cdot t_h = 0.156$

For a single server case, P_R = A (1 – A) and P (delay > 0) = A = 0.156

∴ t_q = 0.278 min

$t_q^{\,'}$ = 1.78 min.

So no reason for public to complain. But the statement implies that traffic is spread over throughout the day which may not be true. Busy hour traffic is important.

SOLVED EXAMPLES

Example 2.1: During one hour of busy period, 800 calls arrive in an exchange. If average holding time per call is 3 minutes, estimate traffic in erlangs and in CCS units.

Solution: Total duration = 1 hour = 60 min

Average busy period = 3 min/call

Number of calls = 800

∴   Total busy period = 800 ∞ 3

= 2400 min

+ 40 hours

∴   Traffic $= \dfrac{\text{Busy period}}{\text{Total duration}}$

$= \dfrac{40}{1}$ hrs. or $\left(\dfrac{2400}{60}\right)$ min

Traffic = 40 erlangs

1 E = 36 CCS

40 E = 1440 CCS

Example 2.2: 10,000 subscribers are connected to an exchange. If the exchange is designed to achieve a call completion rate of 0.8 when the busy hour calling rate is 4.8, what is BHCA that can be supported by the exchange? What should be call processing time for this exchange?

Solution: Total subscribers = 10,000

CCR = 0.8

BHCR = 4.8

Average busy hour calls = BHCR × Total subscribers

= 4.8 × 10,000

= 48,000

$$\text{BHCA} = \frac{\text{Average busy hour calls}}{\text{CCR}}$$

$$\text{BHCA} = \frac{48000}{0.8}$$

$$= 60{,}000$$

$$\text{Call processing time} = \frac{60 \times 60}{\text{BHCA}}$$

$$= 60 \text{ ms}$$

Example 2.3: A call processor in an exchange requires 120 ms to service a complete call. What is BHCA rating for the processor? If the exchange is capable of carrying 700 erlangs of traffic, what is CCR? Assume average call holding time of 2 min.

Solution: Call holding time, t_h = 2 min

Call service time = 120 ms

Traffic = 700 erlangs

$$\text{BHCA} = \frac{\text{Busy hour period}}{\text{Call completion/Service time}}$$

$$= \frac{60 \times 60}{120 \times 10^{-3}} = 30{,}000$$

$$\text{Traffic} = \frac{\text{Busy period}}{\text{Total duration}}$$

$$700 = \frac{\text{Busy period}}{60}$$

∴   Busy period $= 700 \times 60$

$$= 42000$$

But, t_h = 2 min

∴   Busy period $= \frac{42000}{2}$

$$= 21000$$

$$\text{CCR} = \frac{\text{Busy Period}}{\text{BHCA}}$$

$$= \frac{21000}{30000}$$

$$\text{CCR} = 0.7$$

Example 2.4: During 2 hours busy period, 2400 calls arrive at an exchange. Average holding time per call is 2 min. Calculate traffic load in (1) erlangs, (2) CCS, (3) CS, and (4) CM units.

Solution: Total duration = 2 hours

$$= 120 \text{ min.}$$

$$\text{Total calls} = 2400$$

$$\text{Call holding time } t_h = 2 \text{ min}$$

$$\text{Traffic} = \frac{\text{Busy Period}}{\text{Total duration}}$$

$$= \frac{2400 \times 2}{120}$$

$$= 40 \text{ erlangs} \qquad \text{... Ans.}$$

$$1\,E = 36 \text{ CCS}$$

$$\therefore \qquad 40\,E = 1440 \text{ CCS}$$

$$\text{Traffic in CS} = 144000$$

$$\text{Traffic in CM} = 2400 \text{ CM}$$

$$1\,E = 60 \text{ CM}$$

$$\therefore \qquad 40\,E = 2400 \text{ CM}$$

Example 2.5: The traffic statistics of a company using EPABX indicates 200 outgoing calls are initiated per hour during working hours and 160 calls come in per hour. Each call lasts for 200 seconds on an average. Presuming required GOS = 0.05 for exchange, determine number of lines required between EPABX and main exchange.

Solution:

$$\text{Total calls} = \text{Outgoing} + \text{Incoming}$$

$$= 200 + 160$$

$$= 360 \text{ calls}$$

$$\text{Actual calls} = 360 \text{ calls} - (\text{Calls} \times \text{GOS})$$

$$= 360 - (360 \times 0.5)$$

$$= 342$$

$$\text{Average arrival rate per min} = \frac{342}{60}$$

$$= 5.7 \text{ calls/min}$$

$$\approx 6 \text{ calls/min}$$

$$\text{Each call duration} = 200 \text{ sec.}$$

$$= 3.33 \text{ min per call}$$

$$\therefore \quad \begin{bmatrix} \text{Number of required} \\ \text{lines} \end{bmatrix} = \begin{bmatrix} \text{Average arrival} \\ \text{rate} \end{bmatrix} \times \begin{bmatrix} \text{Call} \\ \text{duration} \end{bmatrix}$$

$$= 5.7 \times 3.33$$

$$\approx 19 \text{ lines}$$

Example 2.6: What is the blocking probability of a PBX to central office trunk group with 10 circuits servicing a first attempt offered traffic load of 7 erlangs? What is the blocking probability if the number of circuits is increased to 13? Assume random retries for all blocked calls.

Solution: 7 erlangs of traffic arises from large number of PBX stations. So we can use infinite source analysis.

$$A = 7 \text{ erlangs}$$
$$N = 10$$
$$\therefore \qquad P_B = \frac{A^N}{N!} \cdot e^{-7}$$
$$= \frac{7^{10}}{10!} \cdot e^{-7}$$
$$P_B = 7.098\%$$

Example 2.7: In an exchange, calls arrive at the rate of 1100 calls per hour, with each call holding for a duration of 3 min. If the demand is serviced by a trunk group of 50 lines, determine GOS.

Solution:
$$\text{Call arrival} = 1100 \text{ calls per hour}$$
$$\text{Call duration} = 3 \text{ min}$$
$$A = \frac{1100}{60} \times 3$$
$$= 55 \text{ lines}$$
$$\text{GOS} = \frac{A - A_o}{A}$$
$$A_o = 50 \text{ lines}$$
$$= \frac{55 - 50}{55}$$
$$\text{GOS} = 0.091$$

Example 2.8: Assume that a trunk group has enough channels to immediately carry all of the traffic offered to it by a Poisson process with an arrival rate of 1 call per min. Assume that average holding time is 2 min. What % of total traffic is carried by first 5 circuits and how much traffic is carried by all remaining circuits.

(Assume traffic is always packed into lowest numbered circuits).

Solution:
$$\text{Call arrival rate, } \lambda = 1 \text{ call/min}$$
$$\text{Average call holding time} = 2 \text{ min}$$
$$\therefore \qquad \lambda t = 2$$
$$P_k = \frac{(\lambda t)^k \cdot e^{-\lambda t}}{k!}$$
$$P_5 = \frac{2^5 \cdot e^{-2}}{5!}$$
$$= 0.036089$$
$$P_6 = \frac{2^6 \cdot e^{-2}}{6!}$$
$$= 0.012029$$

Example 2.9: A message switching network is to be designed for 95% utilization of its transmission links. Assuming exponentially distributed message lengths and arrival rate of 10 messages per min, what is the average waiting time and what is the probability that waiting time exceeds 5 min?

Solution:

$$\lambda = 10 \text{ messages per min}$$

$$t_h = 0.95$$

$$\text{Assume single server, } R = 1$$

$$\therefore \quad P_R = A(1-A)$$

$$P(\text{delay} > 0) = A = 0.95$$

$$\text{Average waiting time} = \frac{t_h}{R-A}$$

$$= \frac{0.95}{1-0.95}$$

$$= 19 \text{ min}$$

Example 2.10: Calculate QOS of an exchange which can cater the traffic of 1170 subscribers at a time out of actually carried traffic of 1200. Calculate number of calls lost per 100 calls.

Solution:

$$QOS = \frac{A - A_0}{A} = \frac{1200 - 1170}{1200}$$

$$= 0.025$$

$$\text{Lost calls} = \frac{1200 - 1170}{100}$$

$$= 0.3$$

EXERCISE

1. What is peak hour, busy hour?
2. Define CCR, BHCA, BHCR, GOS.
3. Describe Erlang and its models.
4. State units of traffic measurement.
5. Comment on how the GOS can be maintained.
6. How blocking probability is related to GOS?
7. State the significance of implementing Poisson and Erlang distribution to telephone traffic.
8. How excess of telephone traffic is taken care of by various blocking models? What happens to the traffic that exceeds the switch capacity?
9. What all factors will be considered while designing a switch?
10. Which all data will you collect, if you are to expand a particular switch?

Unit III

DATA AND VOICE INTEGRATION

INTEGRATED VOICE AND DATA NETWORK

3.1 Introduction

1. Voice/data integration is important to network designers of both, service providers and enterprise.

2. **Service providers are attracted by the lower-cost model – the cost of packet voice is currently estimated to be only 20 to 50 percent of the cost of a traditional circuit-based voice network.**

3. Likewise, enterprise network designers are interested in direct cost savings associated with toll-bypass and tandem switching.

4. Both are also interested in so-called "soft savings" associated with reduced maintenance costs and more efficient network control and management.

5. **Finally, packet-based voice systems offer access to newly enhanced services such as Unified Messaging and application control.**

6. These, in turn, promise to increase the productivity of users and differentiate services.

7. Integration of voice and data technologies has accelerated rapidly in recent years because of both, supply- and demand-side interactions.

8. On the demand side, customers are leveraging investment in network infrastructure to take advantage of integrated applications such as voice applications.

9. On the supply side, vendors have been able to take advantage of break-throughs in many areas, including standards, technology, and network performance.

3.2 Demands and Problems of Integration

3.2.1 Technology

1. Recent advances in technology have also enabled voice integration with data.

2. **For example, new Digital Signal Processor (DSP) technology has allowed analog signals to be processed in the digital domain, which was difficult or impossible only a few years earlier.**

3. These powerful new chips offer tremendous processing speeds, allowing voice to be sampled, digitized, and compressed in real time.

4. Further breakthroughs in the technology allow as many as four voice conversations to be managed at the same time on a single chip, with even greater performance in development.

5. These technologies greatly reduce the cost and complexity of developing products and deploying voice over data solutions.

6. In other areas, the industry has also enjoyed breakthroughs in voice codec (coder/decoder) technology.

7. Previously, it was assumed that voice quality would suffer as bandwidth was decreased in a relatively linear fashion.

8. However, new, sophisticated algorithms employed in new codecs have changed that view.

9. It is now possible to obtain reasonably good sounding voice at a fraction of the bandwidth once required.

10. More importantly, these new algorithms have been incorporated into the standards to allow interoperability of highly compressed voice.

3.2.2 Network Performance

1. Finally, data-networking technology has improved to the point that voice can be carried reliably.

2. Over the last few years, growth in voice traffic has been relatively small, while data traffic has grown exponentially.

3. The result is that data traffic is now greater than voice traffic in many networks.

4. In addition, the relative importance of data traffic has grown, as businesses and organizations have come to base more business practices and policies on the ubiquity of data networks.

5. This increase in importance of data networks has forced a fundamental change in the way data networks are engineered, built, and managed.

6. Typical "best-effort" data modeling has given a way to advanced policy-based networking with managed quality of service to support an even greater range of applications.

7. Voice traffic, as an application on a data network, has benefited greatly from these technologies.

8. For example, support of delay-sensitive SNA traffic over IP networks resulted in breakthroughs in latency management and queuing prioritization, which was then applied to voice traffic.

9. As stated previously, deployment of new technologies and applications must also be driven by greater demand from users.

10. Breakthroughs in technology don't necessarily result in increased deployment, unless they fill a real user need at a reasonable cost.

11. For example, Digital Audio Tape (DAT) technologies never enjoyed widespread use outside the audiophile community because of the high cost and only marginally better perceived performance than analog tapes.

12. Voice/data integration, however, provides users with very real benefits, both now and in the future.

13. Most users of voice/data integration technologies gain in two ways. Packet voice technologies are less expensive, and, in the future, they will offer much greater capabilities compared to today's circuit-based voice systems.

3.2.3 Economic Advantages

1. **It has been estimated that packet voice networking costs only 20 to 30 percent of an equivalent circuit-based voice network.**

2. This is true for both carriers (service providers) and enterprise (private) users.

3. Logically, this implies that enterprise users can operate long-distance voice services between facilities at less cost than purchasing long-distance voice services from a carrier, and it's often true.

4. For example, many enterprise users have deployed integrated voice/data technologies to transport voice over Data Wide-Area Networks (WANs) between traditional PBXs across different geographical locations.

5. The resulting savings in long-distance toll charges often provide payback in as little as six months (especially if international calls are avoided).

6. Using data systems to carry voice as "virtual tie lines" between switches is also useful to service providers.

7. In fact, many new carriers have started to embrace packet-based voice technologies as their primary network infrastructure strategy going forward.

8. However, savings associated with packet voice technologies don't stop with simple transport.

9. It is also possible to switch voice calls in the data domain more economically than traditional circuit-based voice switches.

10. For large, multisite enterprises, the savings result from using the data network to act as a "tandem switch" to route voice calls between PBXs on a call-by-call basis.

11. The resulting voice network structure is simpler to administer and uses a robust, non-blocking switching fabric made up of data systems at its core.

3.2.4 Advances in Applications

1. Real cost savings are sufficient for deployment of voice/data integration technologies.

2. However, there are added benefits, which will become more evident in the future.

3. As applications evolve, organizations will gain increased user productivity from the integration of voice and computer applications.

4. However, as voice/data integration continues, the line between voice and data applications will continue to blur.

5. For example, Unified Messaging systems are now available, that combine voice mail, e-mail, and fax messaging into a single, convenient system.

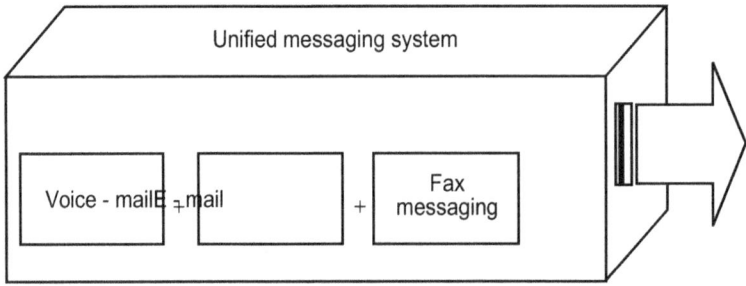

Fig. 3.1: Typical unified messaging system

6. With these advanced systems, users can have e-mail read to them over the phone or can add document attachments to voice mail.

7. At the enterprise level, new applications, such as virtual call centers, allow call center agents to be distributed anywhere within the reach of the data network, while still receiving the full suite of call center functions and features.

8. They can even receive calls over their computers rather than using a traditional telephone instrument, and they can provide "blended contact center" support to answer Web user questions with electronic chat capability and e-mail between voice calls.

9. These capabilities go far beyond simple cost savings and will ultimately make organizations much more effective and profitable.

10. The strong pressures, driving the integration of voice and data networks, have resulted in various solutions to the problem, each with its own strengths and weaknesses.

11. **Three general approaches exist:**

    • **Voice over ATM**   • **Voice over Frame Relay**   • **Voice over IP**

12. There are also mixed solutions, including voice over IP, over Frame Relay, and so on.

13. These are illustrated in Fig. 3.2. The figure shows that voice over ATM and voice over Frame Relay are primarily transport mechanisms between PBXs, while voice over IP can connect all the way to the desktop.

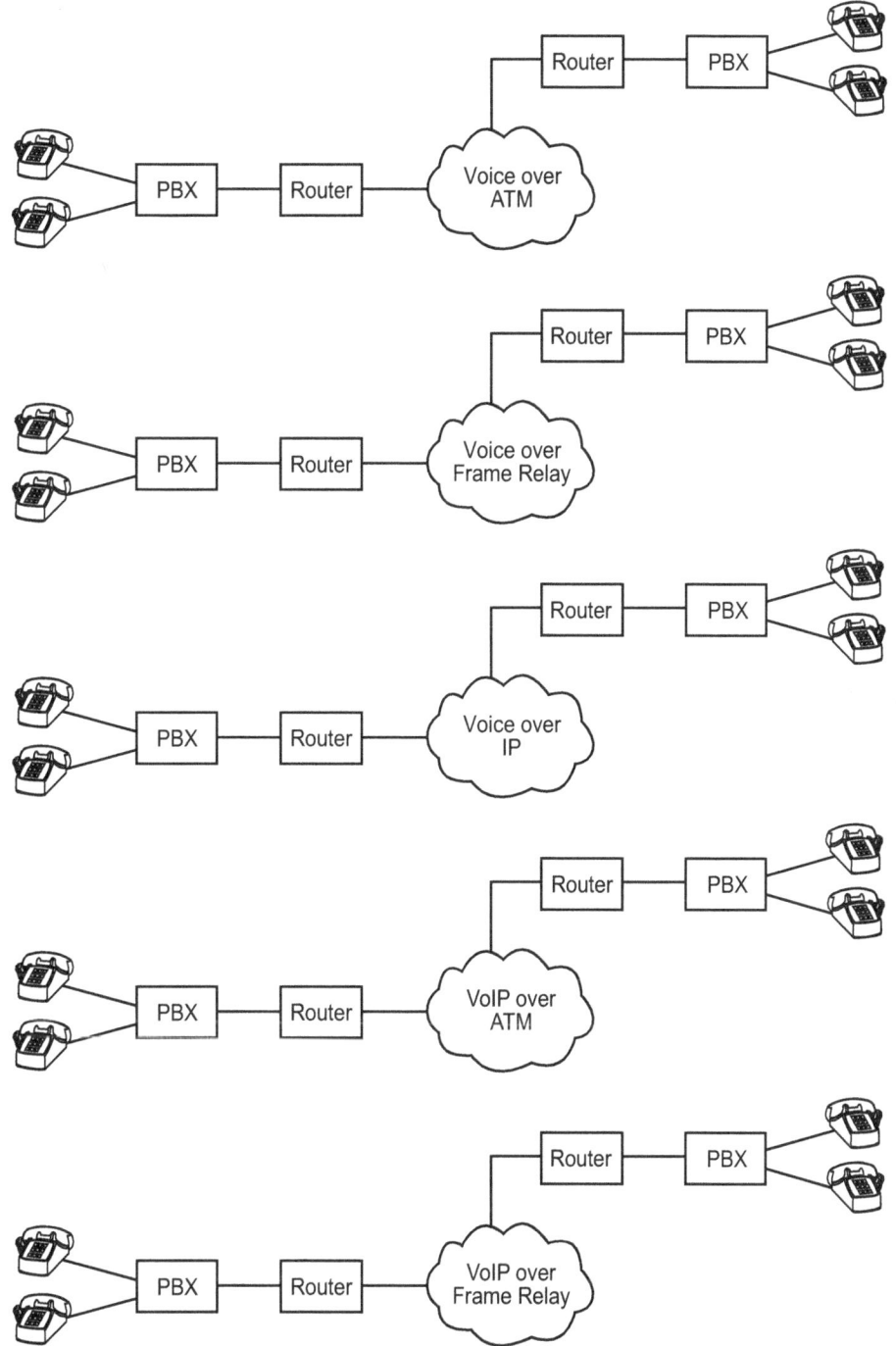

Fig. 3.2: Mixed solutions of voice/data communication

14. The major packet voice technologies are voice over Asynchronous Transfer Mode (ATM), Voice Over Frame Relay, and Voice over Internet Protocol (VoIP).

15. Of these, Frame Relay is transitional; ATM will stay in the backbone as a long-haul transit mode; and Internet Protocol (IP) will ultimately be the end-to-end voice transport method.

16. The current switched voice network will stay in place for at least a decade, slowly replaced by packetized voice.

17. Early consolidation will take place on the Wide-Area Networks that access the Public Switched Telephone Network (PSTN).

18. Small and medium-sized businesses will play a key role in the adoption of converged voice and data, as will new applications that go beyond the notion that "voice rides for free" over a packetized network.

19. Consolidated networks will be critical for reducing the service provider's operational costs, maximizing efficient use of network resources and providing a flexible platform for adapting to a constantly evolving, unpredictable, and increasingly competitive communications landscape.

20. Current interest is focused on integration across packetized networks that are optimized for data but can none-the-less support voice traffic with sufficient quality to meet user requirements.

21. **To ensure the success of packetized multiservice networks, the areas of QoS, features and functionality, and reliability must be at the same level or higher than that of the circuit-switched networks.**

22. QoS is going to be the most important concept in the communications world for the next ten years.

3.2.5 QoS-A Challenge

1. Quality of Service (QoS) is important for the converging networks to be successful.

2. Besides simple assurance, QoS should be clearly defined, quantified, easily expressed and packaged simply enough for people to work with, and pay for.

3. QoS is about providing an environment that preserves the isochronicity of a signal i.e. the signal goes in and comes out, undistorted, perceptually in "real-time."

4. In terms of IP voice and real-time media, this means developing strategies to reduce and regulate end-to-end delays such as codec and packetization delay, transmission and buffering delay, and routing delay. Also of concern are packet loss and jitter.

5. QoS encompasses all seven layers of the Open Systems Interconnection (OSI) Model, as well as every network element from end-to-end, operating systems (real-time scheduling, threads), communications protocols, data networks, scheduling and traffic management issues.

6. **The concept of M3 multi-service, multi-technology and multi-vendor is driving and enabling Next Generation Networks.**

7. But providing QoS assurances in this mixed environment is exceedingly difficult.

8. Each service type has a different concept of what constitutes high quality.

9. Voice services can accept signal loss to some extent, but very little time delay or jitter in order to ensure high call quality.

10. On the other hand, data services can accept time delays to some extent, but not packet loss.

11. Though QoS and bandwidth are related, increasing bandwidth to achieve QoS is not going to solve the problem since it is likely that new applications will fill the available bandwidth in no time.

12. So even with fiber-to-curb and purely optical networks, certain issues may never be resolved.

13. The fundamental trade-off in quality of service is between bandwidth and traffic engineering and prioritization.

14. **As bandwidth becomes more constrained, traffic engineering and prioritization become more important.**

15. QoS is a major concern for the converging network.

16. It's simple economics really. If you give people better quality in any dimension like better sound quality, and better application availability, they will spend more time using your applications and services.

17. Although QoS usually refers to the fidelity of the transmitted voice and facsimile documents, it can also be applied to network availability, use of value added features like conferencing and calling number display, and scalability.

18. **There are three factors that can profoundly impact the QoS. They are delay, jitter, and packet loss.**

19. High end-to-end delay in a voice network gives rise to echo and talker overlap.

20. Echo becomes a problem when the round-trip delay is more than 50 milliseconds.

21. Since echo is perceived as a significant quality problem, converged systems must address the need for echo control and implement some means of echo cancellation.

22. Talker overlap (the problem of one caller stepping on the other talker's speech) becomes significant if the one-way delay becomes greater than 250 milliseconds.

23. The end-to-end delay budget is therefore the major constraint and drives the requirement for reducing delay through a packet network.

24. A technique, called silence suppression, detects whenever there is a gap in the speech and suppresses the transfer of things like pauses, breaths, and other periods of silence.

25. This can amount to 50-60 percent of the time of a call, resulting in considerable bandwidth conservation.

26. **Jitter is the variation in inter-packet arrival time due to variable transmission delay over the network.**

27. Removing jitter requires collecting packets and holding them long enough to allow the slowest packets to arrive in time to be played in the correct sequence.

28. This causes additional delay. The jitter buffers add delay, which is used to remove the packet delay variation that each packet is subjected to as it transits the packet network.

29. IP networks cannot provide a guarantee that there will be no packet loss and the packets will certainly be delivered in order.

30. Packets may be dropped under peak loads and during periods of congestion caused by link failures or inadequate capacity.

31. Due to the time sensitivity of voice transmissions, the normal (Transmission Control Protocol) TCP-based re-transmission schemes are not suitable. Packet losses greater than 10 percent are generally not acceptable.

32. This trade-off, in turn, leads to two global QoS strategies – one linked to bandwidth (RSVP), and the others to prioritization (DifferServ technique).

33. Resource reservation (e.g. RSVP) is where network resources are allocated according to an application's QoS request, subject to bandwidth management policy.

34. Prioritization (e.g. DiffServ technique) is where network traffic is classified and network resources are allocated according to bandwidth management policy.

35. In the latter case, each application traffic flow has an associated Class of Service (CoS), based on which the network elements give preferential treatment to the classes having more stringent requirements.

36. The type of QoS, that is more suitable for an individual flow, depends on the kind of application and the network topology.

37. The most popular QoS protocols are ReSerVation Protocol (RSVP), Differentiated Services (DiffServ technique) and Multi Protocol Label Switching (MPLS).

3.2.6 QoS Solutions

There are three techniques that can be used (separately or in combination) to improve network QoS:

- **Controlling networking environment:** You have to provide a controlled networking environment in which the capacity can be pre-planned and adequate performance can be assumed. This would generally be the case with a private IP network or an Intranet that is owned and operated by a single organization.

- **Using management tools:** You can use management tools to configure the network nodes, monitor performance, and manage capacity and flow on a dynamic basis. Traffic can be prioritized by location, by protocol, or by application type. This allows real-time traffic to be given precedence over   non-critical traffic. Queuing mechanisms can also be manipulated to minimize delays for real-time data flows.

- **Adding control protocols and mechanisms:** You can add control protocols and mechanisms that help to avoid or alleviate the problems inherent in IP networks. Protocols like RTP (Real Time Protocol) and RSVP can also be used to provide greater assurances of controlled QoS within the network. Other mechanisms like admission controls and traffic shaping may also be used to avoid overloading a network.

3.2.7 Markets

1. The coming voice-data integration trend will transcend traditional market segments, encompassing business and residential, local and long-distance, Local-Area Network (LAN) and Wide-Area Network (WAN), wired and wireless, and domestic and international divisions.

2. The benefits of voice-data integration on a single packetized network accrue in a number of areas to service providers and end users alike.

3. For service providers, a single network simplifies network monitoring, troubleshooting and problem resolution, and customer service by consolidating multiple network management systems into a single platform.

4. It also streamlines personnel training requirements, provides economies of scale by consolidating multiple types of traffic instead of having separate overlay networks for each, and enables entirely new value-added, revenue-generating, and customer relationship–building services.

5. For end users, the benefits of a unified network are similar.

6. Network management can be combined under a single umbrella management system; the heretofore separate telecommunications and data communications departments can ultimately be combined; monthly recurring costs for access lines and WAN services can be decreased through the integration of access lines and resulting economies of scale; and, ultimately, a single, internal wiring infrastructure can be used for both, voice and data.

3.2.8 Market Trends

1. Although the days of the PSTN are undeniably numbered, it will coexist with emerging data-centric networks for at least the next decade as networks transit to purely packetized multiservice networks.

2. In addition, traditional service providers are already responding to the threats posed by packetized alternatives by lowering the cost of circuit-switched voice, thereby minimizing the economic incentive for customers to migrate to packetized networks.

3. Competitive pressures due to market dynamics and entries of new players in both the local and long-distance markets are changing the perspective of incumbent carriers, and they are becoming more receptive to offering voice-over-x services.

4. It has also been noted that the deployment models for IP and ATM access both involve the use of gateways between packet networks and the PSTN.

5. This suggests that the PSTN will, in fact, be carrying traffic from packetized networks and will therefore generate revenue.

6. In short, widespread deployment of the pure end-to-end model of packetized voice for businesses that would quickly eliminate carrier circuit-switched revenues will not emerge for several years.

3.2.9 Future Possibilities

1. VoIP is being positioned in all conceivable network configurations and market segments.

2. New IP–based applications will emerge in the next two years that will incorporate video, voice, and data simultaneously for practical business and entertainment purposes.

3. Many of the existing applications are free, which always help to stimulate a market.

4. A related and underestimated application is document sharing which, when used in conjunction with VoIP, has the potential to improve productivity dramatically.

5. There are two important trends to note in the voice-data integration market.

6. Smaller and medium-sized businesses will play an important role in the development of the WAN access integration market and the voice-data integration market in general.

7. Second, the layering of value-added applications on top of multiservice access lines will be important to the success of this market, taking voice-data integration well beyond the simple model of "voice rides for free" over an existing data network.

8. This represents a new phase in the evolution of the voice-data integration market that will be the first step towards the unified networks of the future.

9. This is a step towards fulfilling the promise of the "WAN as a utility" model. Users will view their networks as a utility into which they plug for services, and they may therefore focus on their primary responsibility: running their businesses.

10. This is a new concept for end users, and it will take time for the market to embrace this new concept. Once a threshold is reached, however, it will begin to grow exponentially.

3.2.10 Integrated Voice and Data Network Advantages

1. As businesses grow, the complexity of technology infrastructure can become overwhelming, with the need for more cables, outlets and connections. But that doesn't have to be the case.

2. Integrated Voice and Data network service combines a multi-extension voice-over-Internet phone system, e-mail service and computer network on a single broadband Internet connection. This allows businesses to:

    * **Save money** – You need only one broadband Internet connection and many fewer electrical outlets to support numerous employees. You'll also be able to easily add new e-mail addresses by yourself, using a simple web-based administration form.

    * **Simplify** – You'll dramatically reduce office cabling, and you need only call one service provider for help with phone, computer, Internet, and network issues.

    * **Enhance your brand** – By providing a single phone number for your entire business, including to reach branch offices and tele-workers. Other big-business features of the Internet phone system include an automated phone attendant, extensions and voicemail for each employee, automatic call routing and more.

    * **Evolve** – Integrating voice on data onto a single network provides you with great flexibility, because it is fast and easy to add new features as they become available, or as you need them.

3. What's more, you'll be able to take advantage of new possibilities for improving business and employee productivity.

4. These are just some of the things you can do with an integrated voice and data network:

    * Allow callers to reach you at your regular phone extension even while you work from home or on the road.

    * Receive all your voice, e-mail and fax messages in a single inbox.

    * Record special phone greetings to play, based on time of day or on holidays.

    * Support branch offices, tele-workers and road warriors as easily as if they were at main office.

    * Automatically route callers based on their selections to the best or most available employee.

3.2.11 Integrated Voice and Data Network Applications

Typical applications of a converged voice and data solution include:

- IP Telephony, which converts a voice call into a packet format that can be sent over a data network.

- Unified messaging, allowing all users to manage their voice, fax and e-mail messages from their PCs or laptops.

- Contact centers - large or small, formal or informal, which can be linked to your Web marketing and sales initiatives.

- Computer telephony integration providing the ability to use computer desktops to make and answer calls, store call information, screen pop customer information and address books or track exact call durations for billing purposes.

- Voice networking links to shared applications, such as voice mail systems among different locations.

- Workplace wireless LANs enabling the extension of all the features and benefits on the LAN to a wireless environment, meaning that work can take place anywhere.

- Unified Messaging consolidates voicemail, e-mail and fax messages to the desktop or laptop.

- WLAN extends the capabilities of the existing LAN by delivering voice and data to mobile workers.

- Rich media services to enhance productivity and customer contact with collaborative multimedia capabilities such as instant messaging and chat sessions, video conferencing, personalized call and presence management.

- Computer Telephony Integration (CTI) to combine the intelligence of your phone system with the power of your PC to enable applications such as point-and-click dialing or automatic file retrieval based on your customers' incoming calling line identification.

- Office-to-Office networking to enable four-digit dialing between locations, the ability to transfer voicemail messages to anyone on the network or the option to have voice traffic carried over an existing data network. This is particularly useful for Doctors/Dentists who have more than one office and rotate between locations.

3.2.12 Integrated Voice and Data Network Beneficial for a Business
Save money on long distance:

Voice and fax transmissions can be sent over an existing data network between offices, reducing your business' reliance on long distance services. Administration can also be simplified by managing voice, data, and multimedia locally or remotely.

Improve internal communications:

Help your staff to get critical information when they need it. With a converged solution, your team can share files over the network, talk to co-workers in other offices without toll charges, and retrieve e-mail and voicemail from any location.

Online ordering systems:

Provide new services to help your customers through the purchase process. Say, for example, your product is available through the Web, but a customer would like to talk to a representative before ordering. With a converged network, the client can click on a "Want to Talk" button. Your system selects an appropriate agent and triggers a telephone to call back. You decide how the system selects agents - by product knowledge, or perhaps by time zone. Now you have the best of both worlds: instant and worldwide access to your product with personal service from one of your representatives. This is just one of the many ways, a converged network can help your small business to operate like a larger enterprise.

Increase efficiency:

A converged solution can streamline several separate communication devices as well as a variety of services and applications for maximum efficiency. And you will need only one service contract for your integrated network. Unified Messaging increases efficiency by consolidating voicemail, e-mail, and fax to a computer.

Improve mobility:

A converged voice and data solution helps to solve the business challenge of anywhere, anytime accessibility by providing users with a consistent, reliable, secure mobile experience, regardless of how they are communicating, what device they are using or where they are.

3.2.13 What is Voice Messaging?

Voice messaging systems are designed to take messages but can do so much more:

- Auto attendant directs incoming calls by providing callers with a list of options, which can include reaching an individual, a mailbox or a receptionist. Auto attendant can answer calls when the receptionist is busy or provide information such as office hours when the business is closed. These applications will save your money and increase your productivity giving you a competitive advantage.
- Visual message waiting indication can be provided locally on your phone set or you can be notified of a message at another location or on your cell phone.
- Voice messages can be seamlessly exchanged with other users at different locations when networked together or broadcast messages can be sent to specific departments or the entire company to keep your employees informed of business issues or highlights.
- Unified messaging lets you to manage voice, e-mail and faxes from your computer when you're in the office or remote.

3.2.14 What are Contact Centers?

1. When there are several people answering similar kinds of telephone calls (at an order desk, reservation office, in a customer service department or technical support center), a contact center is the way to go.

2. Contact centers systematically hold calls in a queue and efficiently route them to your staff.

3. A contact center can organize and manage call distribution for as few as two agents to as many as 100+.

4. Systems may have flexible routing and can be customized.

5. You can send VIP callers to special agents automatically, bypassing any hold time or unnecessary prompting to access their account information.

6. Before a call is transferred to an agent, you can broadcast a recorded announcement about a special promotion or new product. (Research has shown that upto 34 percent of callers will ask about a product or service advertised while they are on hold.).

7. In addition, you also have the option to include a multimedia contact center, which allows you to offer enhanced services from your website such as click to talk and web chat to find the information you're looking for.

A contact center will help you:

*   To answer more calls with the same number of staff.

*   To cut long ringing and hold times.

*   To increase revenues.

*   To reduce costs.

*   To improve customer service.

*   Call center reporting software helps you manage the peaks and troughs in call traffic.

3.2.15 Comparing Circuit Switched / Message Switched / DG Packet Switched / VC Packet Switched Networks

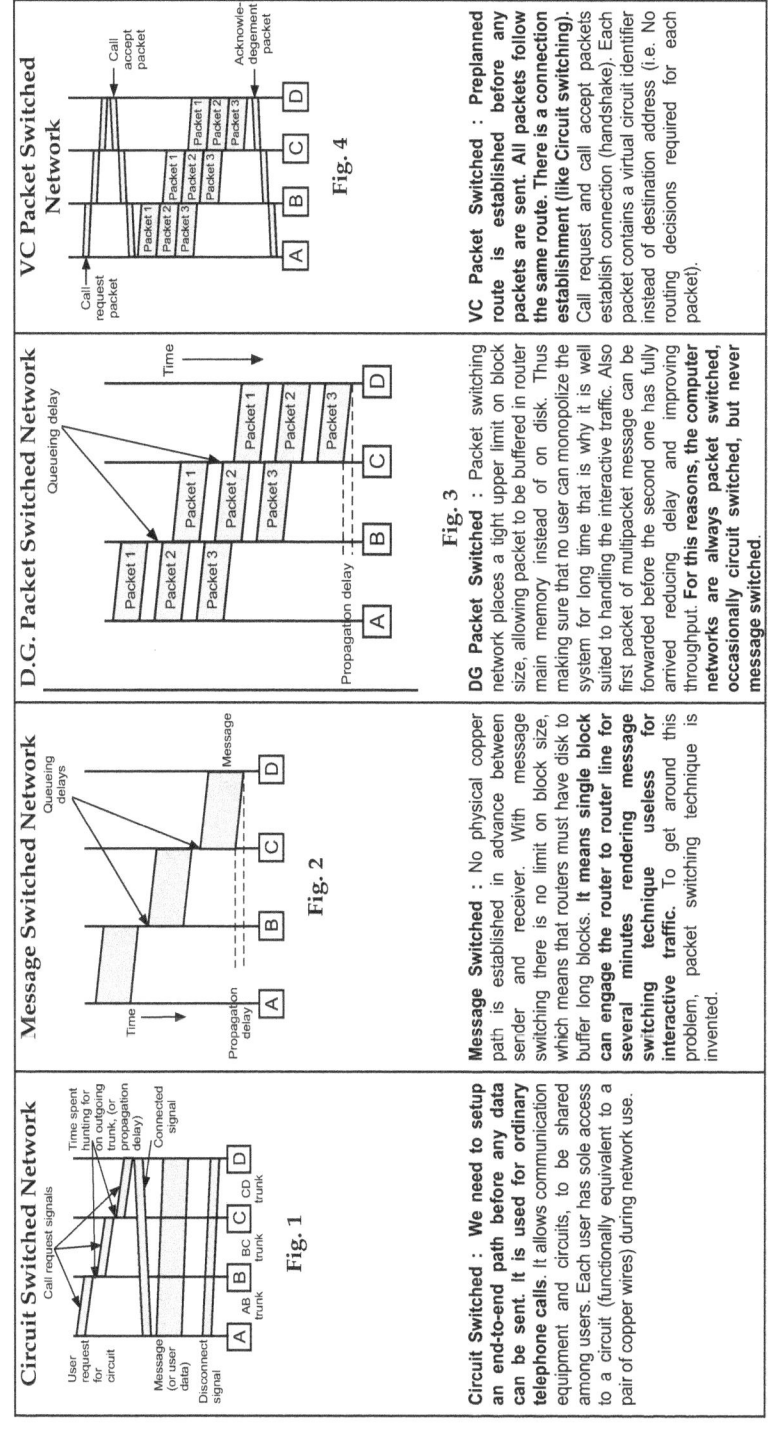

Circuit Switched Network — Fig. 1

Message Switched Network — Fig. 2

D.G. Packet Switched Network — Fig. 3

VC Packet Switched Network — Fig. 4

Circuit Switched : **We need to setup an end-to-end path before any data can be sent. It is used for ordinary telephone calls.** It allows communication equipment and circuits, to be shared among users. Each user has sole access to a circuit (functionally equivalent to a pair of copper wires) during network use.

Message Switched : No physical copper path is established in advance between sender and receiver. With message switching there is no limit on block size, which means that routers must have disk to buffer long blocks. **It means single block can engage the router to router line for several minutes rendering message switching technique useless for interactive traffic.** To get around this problem, packet switching technique is invented.

D.G. Packet Switched : Packet switching network places a tight upper limit on block size, allowing packet to be buffered in router main memory instead of on disk. Thus making sure that no user can monopolize the system for long time that is why it is well suited to handling the interactive traffic. Also first packet of multipacket message can be forwarded before the second one has fully arrived reducing delay and improving throughput. **For this reasons, the computer networks are always packet switched, occasionally circuit switched, but never message switched.**

VC Packet Switched : **Preplanned route is established before any packets are sent. All packets follow the same route. There is a connection establishment (like Circuit switching).** Call request and call accept packets establish connection (handshake). Each packet contains a virtual circuit identifier instead of destination address (i.e. No routing decisions required for each packet).

3.3 ISDN

3.3.1 Introduction

What is ISDN ?

1. Integrated Services Digital Network (ISDN) is a state-of-the-art Public Switched Digital Network for provisioning of different services – voice, data and image transmission over the telephone line through the telephone network.
2. ISDN handles all types of information – voice, data, studio-quality sound, static and moving images.
3. They are all digitized, and transmitted at high speed.
4. ISDN can handle many devices and many telephone numbers on the same line.
5. Upto eight separate telephones, fax machines or computers can be linked to a single Basic Rate ISDN connection and have different phone numbers assigned to them.
6. A Basic Rate ISDN line can support upto two calls at the same time.
7. Any combination of voice, fax or PC connections can take place at the same time, through the same ISDN line.
8. From a digital ISDN telephone, you can place a call to an analogue telephone on the PSTN (Public Switched Telephone Network) and vice-versa.
9. Both networks are interconnected by the network carrier in a way similar to the connection between the mobile phone network and the analogue phone network.
10. For the user, it is completely transparent whether he is calling a GSM (Global System for Mobile) telephone, a conventional telephone or an ISDN digital telephone.
11. The single biggest disadvantage is likely to be your physical location. If you're not in an area that's reasonably close to a telephone company's central office (one with the required equipment already installed), ISDN may not be an option for you. If you live in a metro or near a city, ISDN is an ideal choice. But at other remote locations, ISDN is not available.

Availability:

ISDN service is available by and large in all major cities of India. Also ISDN has overseas connectivity with the following countries: Australia, Austria, Belgium, Canada, Denmark, France, Germany, Ireland, Israel, Italy, Japan, Malaysia, Netherlands, Norway, Philippines, Singapore, Switzerland, Thailand, U.A.E., UK, USA.

Services Provided by ISDN:

Due to the large amounts of information that ISDN lines can carry, ISDN applications are revolutionizing the way businesses communicate. ISDN is not restricted to public telephone networks alone; it may be transmitted via packet switched networks, telex, CATV (Community Antenna TV) networks, etc.

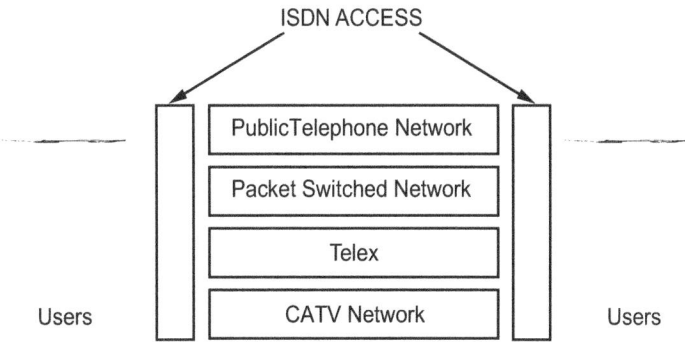

Fig. 3.3: Typical ISDN applications

There are two kinds of services provided by ISDN.

Network Services:

- Network services carry the interactions between the user and the network.
- For example: setting up calls and disconnecting them.

Bearer Services:

- Bearer services carry data between two users.
- For example: voice or fax information encoded as a bit stream.

The following services are offered on a dial-up basis between two ISDN subscribers:

(i) Desktop Video Conferencing on using three ISDN lines at 64/128 kbps.

(ii) High quality video conferencing by using three ISDN lines at 384 kbps.

(iii) Video telephony.

(iv) Teleconferencing, which facilitates the transmission of pictures, documents and drawings etc. apart from voice and images of the participants.

(v) High speed data transmission at 64/128 kbps.

(vi) High speed facsimile at 64/128 kbps with G4 Fax terminal.

(vii) Access to Internet with a higher bandwidth of 64/128 kbps giving significantly improved response time and quality of service.

Supplementary Services:

ISDN, being a Value Added Service, offers many supplementary features/services:

(i) Calling Line Identification Presentation

(ii) Advice of Charge

(iii) Line Hunting

(iv) Closed User Group

(v) User to User Signaling

(vi) Call Waiting

(vii) Call forwarding On No Reply, On Busy, Unconditional

(viii) Multiple Subscriber Number

Bearer Services:

- Circuit switched speech and audio.
- X.25 circuit and packed switched network.
- Frame Relay.
- Circuit switched data.

Teleservices:

- Facsimile – Telephony
- Telex
- Videotext

ISDN Standards:

ISDN is subject to standardization by the ITU-T (International Telecommunication Union-Telecommunication Standard Section) and ETSI (European Telecommunications Standards Institute), which issue recommendations and specifications covering ISDN equipment and interfaces. Standards also exist for types of service, protocols and ISDN numbering.

Operating System Software for ISDN:

- It is of course important to have an operating system, which will support ISDN hardware, allowing your software applications to communicate with and take full advantage of your ISDN terminal adapter.
- First of all, Point-to-Point Protocol (PPP) is the standard Internet access protocol, and it is required for a proper ISDN connection.
- Serial Line Internet Protocol (SLIP) is an older and less efficient protocol, but it is still fairly common.
- SLIP won't work with ISDN, so make sure you have a PPP account. Of course, if your ISP (Internet Service Provider) can provide you with ISDN connectivity, they should know this and it probably won't be an issue.

Different Kinds of ISDN Terminals:

The ISDN telephone line is terminated on a common box called the Network Termination (NT) at the subscriber's premises. The Network Termination unit along with accessories will be provided by the service provider like MTNL or can be procured by the subscriber. The terminal equipment has to be procured by the subscriber himself from the open market.

Types of ISDN Terminal:

(a) ISDN feature phone: This is a simplest type of ISDN phone which has an LCD display and some additional keys.
(b) Terminal adapter (TA).
(c) PC add-on ISDN card.
(d) Video phone.
(e) G4 fax.

Types of Non-ISDN Terminal:

- ISDN terminals such as DTE (Data Terminal Equipment) that predate the ISDN standards are referred to as Terminal Equipment type 2 (TE2).
- Ex. Terminal with physical interface as RS-232 and host computers with X.25 interface.
- This is the old analog telephone.
- Or old-style fax machine.
- Or modem.
- Or whatever we use to hook up to the analog phone line. It can also be other communications equipment that is handled by a TA (Terminal Adapter).

Benefits of ISDN for Network Operators:

1. Avoidance of separate networks for different services.
2. Economical use of the equipment of the digitalized telephone network, especially the copper pair of the subscriber line.
3. Reduction in costs due to simplified operation and maintenance procedures.

How is ISDN line superior to the phone line ?

- The signal on the ISDN line – voice or data, is sent in digital mode.
- The signal level at subscriber's terminal equipment is independent of line length.
- An ISDN subscriber can establish two simultaneous independent calls, which could be voice, data, image or combination of any two, whereas only one call is possible on ordinary telephone lines.
- The call set-up time between two ISDN subscribers is extremely short.

3.3.2 ISDN for Voice, Data and Video

- It is the next-generation, digital telephone network that integrates circuit-switched voice and data services over a common access facility.
- There are two types of ISDN lines. Basic Rate ISDN (BRI) is designed for residential customers and small businesses.
- Primary Rate ISDN (PRI) is designed for larger businesses.

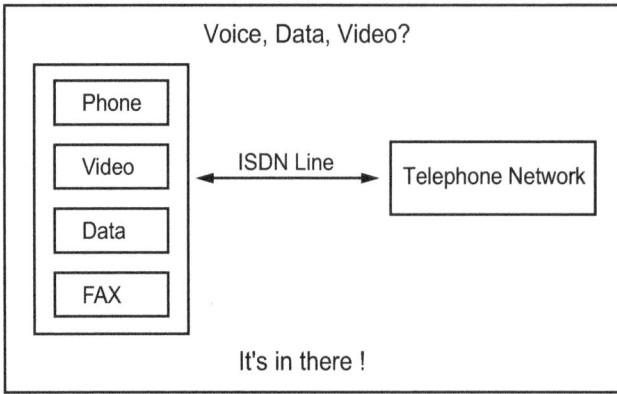

Fig. 3.4: Typical ISDN usage

- ISDN reduces the cost of network administration.

- ISDN simplifies wiring.

- ISDN combines separate voice and data networking requirements.

- ISDN is compatible with BRI/PRI, plus existing analog voice and switched 56 services.

- For residential customers, Basic Rate ISDN (BRI) costs about the equivalent of two phone lines.

- BRI customers can gain high speed Internet access (64 KBPS to 128 KBPS).

- BRI improves the quality of speech in telephone calls. BRI provides an ideal way to keep in touch through personal video conferencing.

- BRI offers improved modem connectivity to non-ISDN systems.

- For business customers, ISDN offers cost savings through the integration of voice and data services.

- PRI provides a great backup solution for leased data lines.

- PRI offers high-quality video conferencing capabilities. PRI costs about the same as standard "channelized T1" services.

3.3.3 Why Digital Communications?

- There are a number of reasons why it is advantageous to carry information, particularly computer data, in a digital format.

- For one, digital lines provide a far cleaner, error-free connection that can ensure reliable transmission worldwide.

- Secondly, digital lines allow equipment that processes data digitally, such as computers or networking routers, to be directly connected, and without the 4 kHz bandwidth limitations imposed by PSTN (voice) telephone lines.

- An ISDN line can carry data at nearly five times the fastest rate achievable using analog modems over PSTN lines.

- Further, while a PSTN line can carry only limited signaling information between the network and the end device (telephone or modem, for example), ISDN lines can carry detailed messages back and forth.

- This information can be used to define multiple incoming callers, to specify the type of incoming data, or to convey useful diagnostic information.

- With digital communications, it is finally possible to carry multiple service types (e.g., voice, computer data, Group 4 fax, motion video) simultaneously on the same network.

- ISDN offers the means to realize a universal in-box integrating voice, voice mail, e-mail, fax and video images from a single application.

3.3.4 ISDN Devices

ISDN Devices:

1. ISDN devices include terminals, terminal adapters (TAs), network-termination devices, line-termination equipment, and exchange-termination equipment.
2. ISDN terminals come in two types. Specialized ISDN terminals are referred to as terminal equipment type 1 (TE1).
3. Non-ISDN terminals, such as DTE, that predates the ISDN standards are referred to as terminal equipment type 2 (TE2).
4. TE1s connect to the ISDN network through a four-wire, twisted-pair digital link. TE2s connect to the ISDN network through a TA.
5. The ISDN TA can be either a standalone device or a board inside the TE2.
6. If the TE2 is implemented as a standalone device, it connects to the TA via a standard physical-layer interface. Examples include RS-232C, V.24, and V.35.
7. Beyond the TE1 and TE2 devices, the next connection point in the ISDN network is the network termination type 1 (NT1) or network termination type 2 (NT2) device.
8. These are network-termination devices that connect the four-wire subscriber wiring to the conventional two-wire local loop.
9. In most other parts of the world, the NT1 is a part of the network provided by the carrier.
10. The NT2 is a more complicated device that typically is found in digital private branch exchanges (PBXs) and that performs layer 2 and 3 protocol functions and concentration services.
11. An NT1/2 device also exists as a single device that combines the functions of an NT1 and an NT2.

ISDN specifies a number of reference points that define logical interfaces between functional groups; such as TAs and NT1s. ISDN reference points include the following:

- **R:** The reference point between non-ISDN equipment and a TA.

- **S:** The reference point between user terminals and the NT2.

- **T:** The reference point between NT1 and NT2 devices.

- **U:** The reference point between NT1 devices and line-termination equipment in the carrier network.

  - Figure 3.5 illustrates a sample ISDN configuration and shows three devices attached to an ISDN switch at the central office.

  - Two of these devices are ISDN-compatible, so they can be attached through an S reference point to NT2 devices.

  - The third device (a standard, non-ISDN telephone) attaches through the reference point to a TA.

  - Any of these devices also could attach to an NT1/2 device, which would replace both the NT1 and the NT2. In addition, although they are not shown, similar user stations are attached to the far-right ISDN switch.

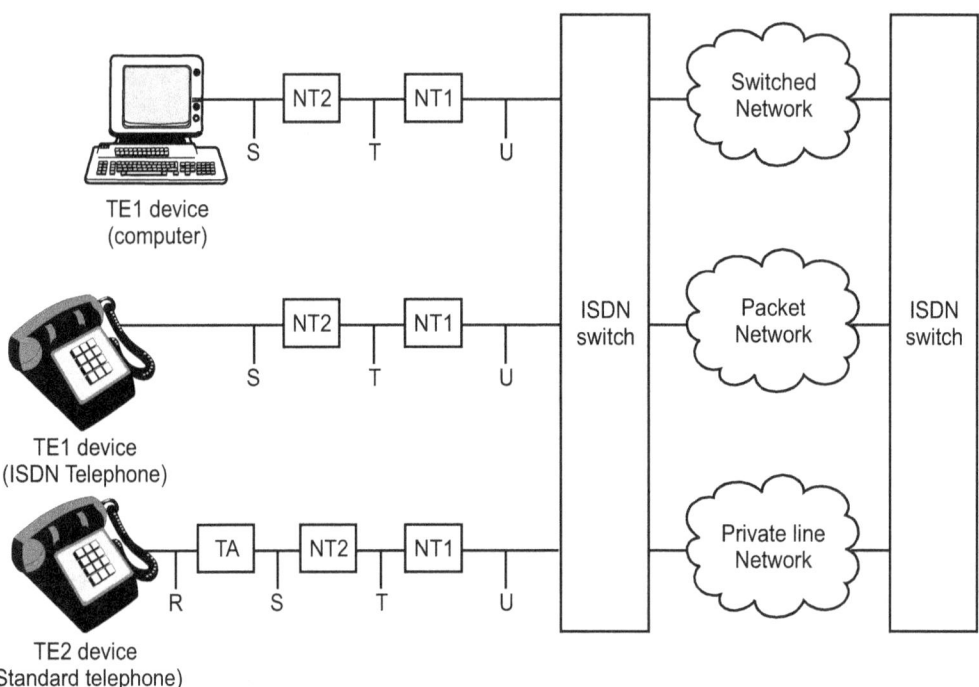

Fig. 3.5: Sample ISDN configuration illustrates relationships between devices and reference points

ISDN Services:

There are two types of services associated with ISDN:

- BRI (Basic Rate Interface) = 2B + 1D
- PRI (Primary Rate Interface) = 23B + 1D
- Hybrid Rate Interface = 1A + 1C

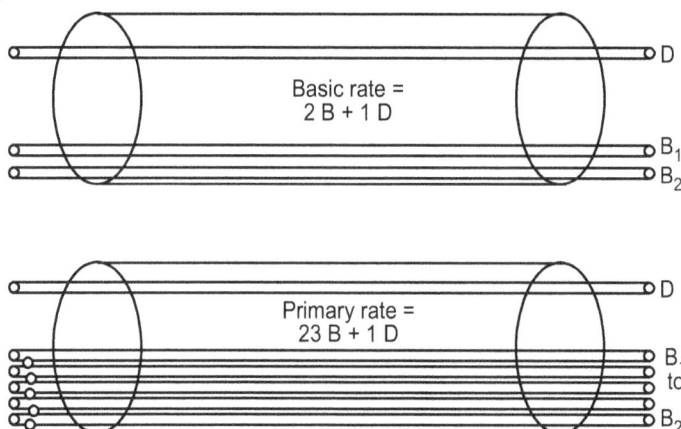

A	=	4 kHz voice channel
B	=	64 kbps voice/data channel
C	=	16 kbps data channel
D	=	16 kbps data channel
E	=	64 kbps data channel
H	=	1920 kbps data channel

Fig. 3.6

3.3.5 ISDN BRI Service

1. The ISDN Basic Rate Interface (BRI) service offers two B channels and one D channel (2B + D).

2. BRI B-channel service operates at 64 kbps and is meant to carry user data.

3. BRI D-channel service operates at 16 kbps and is meant to carry control and signaling information, although it can support user data transmission under certain circumstances.

4. The D channel signaling protocol comprises layers 1 through 3 of the OSI reference model.

5. BRI also provides for framing control and other overhead, bringing its total bit rate to 192 kbps.

6. The BRI physical layer specification is International Telecommunication Union-Telecommunication Standards Section (ITU-T) (formerly the Consultative Committee for International Telegraph and Telephone [CCITT]).

3.3.6 ISDN PRI Service

1. ISDN Primary Rate Interface (PRI) service offers 23 B channels and 1 D channel in North America and Japan, yielding a total bit rate of 1.544 Mbps (the PRI D channel runs at 64 kbps).

2. ISDN PRI in Europe, Australia, and other parts of the world provides 30 B channels plus one 64 kbps D channel and a total interface rate of 2.048 Mbps.

3. ISDN Primary Rate Service offers you the power to create a seamless communication system that speeds and smoothes the flow of information without the expense of dedicated lines, modems, and special cabling.

4. Primary Rate Service links your PBX to advanced central office systems to provide you with global, digital connectivity and the full functionality of ISDN service.

5. Primary Rate Service is the end-to-end digital network architecture that allows users around the world to transmit voice, data, video, and image – separately or simultaneously – over standard telephone lines or fiber optic circuits via standard interface.

6. A single ISDN channel is a fast and flexible information management tool, but Primary Rate Service is two dozen times more powerful - bundling 24 ISDN channels for delivery to your premises.

7. The Primary Rate Service configuration is known as 23B + D: 23B channels for transport of voice, data, video, and image at 64 kbps, plus a single D channel for call setup and control. The 23 B channels can be used as it is, or rearranged in a wide variety of ways to accommodate highly specific user needs.

Key Applications:

*   LAN interconnection
*   Video conferencing
*   Virtual office
*   Backbone LAN access
*   Voice and data integration
*   Image transfer
*   Business continuation and disaster recovery
*   PBX

User Benefits:

- Greater access
- Economy with bandwidth available on demand
- Borderless communications
- Exceptional flexibility
- Digital speed and accuracy
- Fast, reliable backup for lines and host computers

What does a B channel do?

- The B channel carries ISDN Bearer Services across the network and so carries the content of call (the voice, fax or data) between users.
- The B channel is a neutral conduit for bits and carries data at 64000 bits per second (56000 bits per second in some North American networks).
- The ISDN does not need to know what the bits represent. The job of the network is to accept a stream of bits supplied by one user at one end of the B channel and to deliver them to the other user at the opposite end of the channel.
- Within an interface, the B channels are numbered. In a Basic Rate Interface they are numbered 1 and 2; in a Primary Rate Interface, they are numbered 1 to 30 (or 23 in North America).
- When two users are connected, there is no relationship between the channel numbers used at each end.
- You might have one user's B channel number 17 connected with the other user's B channel number 2. The ISDN is responsible for managing this relationship.
- Notice that channel number 17 would only be possible on a PRI, while channel number 2 is possible on both a BRI and a PRI.

ISDN does not restrict the interconnection of B channels between the two kinds of interface.

What does the D channel do ?

The D channel carries the ISDN Network Services between the user and the network. It maintains the user's relationship with the network.

This includes:

- The requests and responses used when you make or receive a call.
- Call progress messages.
- Messages informing you that the called party has closed the call.
- Error messages telling you why a call has not been established for you.

The D channel operates at 16000 bits per second in a BRI and at 64000 bits per second in a PRI.

B & D Channel Characteristics:

- An ISDN channel has two and only two ends. B channels terminate at a user. A B channel can therefore connect two and only two users.
- **B-channel** cannot be Y-shaped. B channels are therefore described as **end-to-end**.
- In the case of the D channel, one end is with the user. The other end is in the network.
- **D-channel is not end-to-end.**
- You cannot normally notice, how the D channels (the red lines) do not pass through the network.
- Notice also how each user has only one D channel and it is not connected in any way with the D channel of the other user.
- The B channel (the blue line) passes directly across the network.

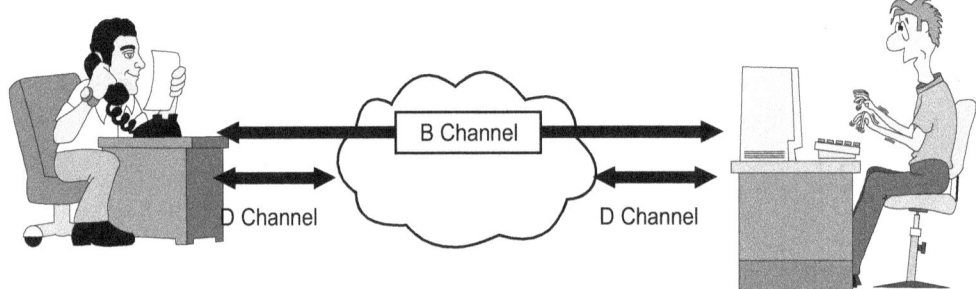

Fig. 3.7: D channel is not end-to-end

How B and D channels share the line: Basic Rate:

- The two B channels and the one D channel that make up a Basic Rate ISDN line are assembled together within the interface using a technique called **Time Division Multiplexing**.

B and D Channel Protocols:

- You must use a protocol to establish meaningful communication across a channel. It is important that both parties to the communication use the same protocol.
- This is particularly important for the D channel. Your signalling requests and responses must be understandable by the network. Even if your ISDN device and ISDN line are both functioning correctly, you might not be able to make successful calls if you're using a D channel protocol that is not the same as the network's.
- ISDN requires that you use a protocol defined by the ITU-T called **Q.931** for signalling in the D channel. However, there are several signalling protocols based on Q.931 in use round the world.
- You have a much greater choice of protocols for the B channel since the B channel is a neutral conduit for data of any type. You can use it to transmit any protocol you wish (e.g. SNA or PPP). However, if the network does not understand the protocol, it cannot give you any assistance if your call has to be delivered to a different type of network (e.g. PSTN), where data conversion is required.

B Channel Characteristics:

- It is important to remember that ISDN channels cannot be divided up into smaller units. Each is provided on an "all or nothing" basis.
- Two users communicating over a B channel have 64000 bits per second available to them. There is nothing they can do to reduce this bandwidth.
- What about the situation where the two users find that 64000 bits per second is not sufficient ? The only solution is to add another B channel. This gives them 128000 bits per second. They are **not** using a single B channel of 128000 bits per second. (Don't forget that the speed of a B channel is defined as 64 000 bits per second. Anything which operates at a different speed is not a B channel).
- This means that they will have two parallel calls between them and the phone bill will show two simultaneous calls.

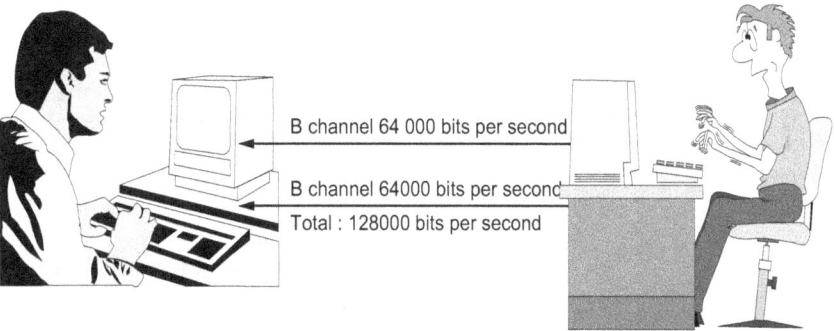

Fig. 3.8: Typical B channel characteristics

Using 2 B Channels:

- Imagine that you are a user communicating with someone else, using two parallel B channels.
- Does the ISDN network care whether these two B channels are connecting the same two users or if they are connecting one user with two others?
- The answer is no. The network treats these as two completely independent calls.

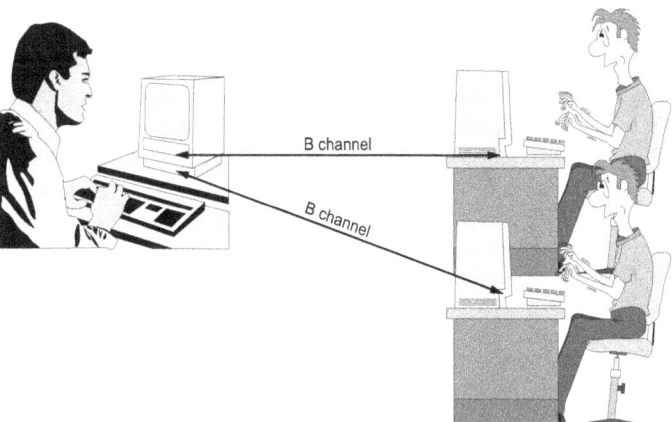

Fig. 3.9: Typical use of 2 B channels

- In the Fig. 3.10, the two users are connected using two B channels in parallel. The ISDN is able to route these B channels independently, because it takes no account of the fact that both the channels connect the same pair of users.
- The speed of the two B channels is identical.
- The time it takes for data to travel from one end of the channel to the other is, however, different.
- One user transmits two items of data simultaneously. One is sent in the B channel, which is routed via satellite; the other is sent in the B channel, which takes the direct route. Will both items of data arrive at the same time?

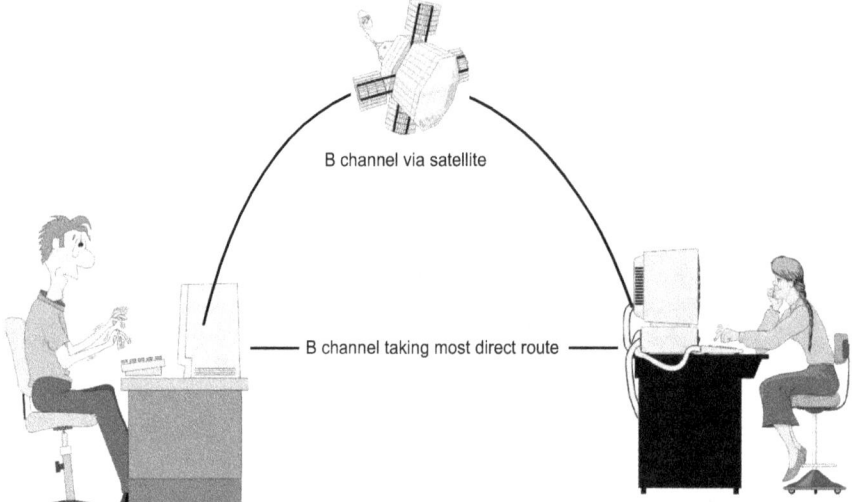

B channel via satellite

B channel taking most direct route

Fig. 3.10: The speed of the two B channels is not identical

- The item of data, which travels down the most direct path, will arrive first. That, which goes via satellite, will arrive later because it has further to travel.
- The ISDN makes no attempt to synchronise the data on the two B channels, possibly because it doesn't understand what the protocol in use. The two B channels are operating independently - the ISDN does not care that they are both connecting the same two users.

Thus regarding B and D channel we can summarize the following points:
- The D channel carries Network Services in the form of signalling. This is the way the user maintains his relationship with the network. Each user has one and only one D channel.
- The B channel carries Bearer Services, which are the communication between two users. A single B channel cannot connect more than two users together.
- B channels and D channels share time on the interface.
- B channels cannot be sub-divided to provide less bandwidth.
- More than one B channel can be used together to provide more bandwidth.

3.3.7 ISDN Operation

1. Each B channel can carry a separate telephone call and usually has its own telephone number, called a **Directory Number** (DN).

2. The two B channels can be combined (bonded) to form a single 128 kbps data channel.

3. The Fig. 3.11 illustrates a minimal ISDN setup connecting two computers.

4. The incoming twisted pair enters a box provided by the telephone company called the network terminator (NT1), which breaks the 144 kbps channel into the two B and single D sub-channels.

5. The B channels carry customer voice or data signals.

6. The D channel carries signals between your ISDN equipment and the phone company's central office.

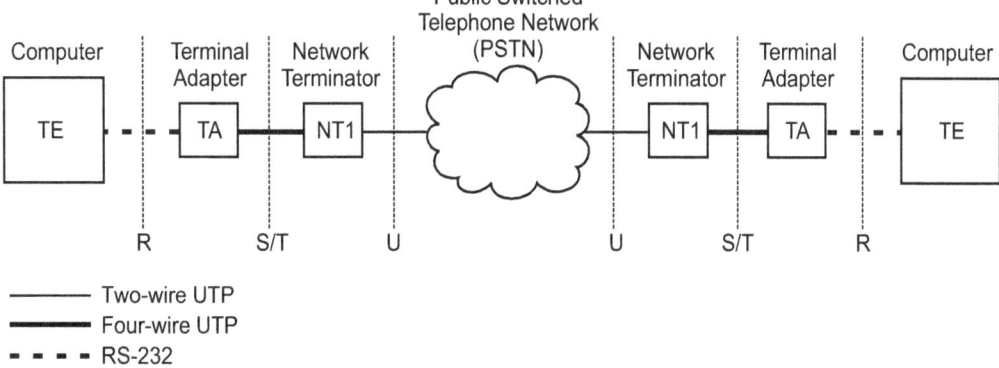

Fig. 3.11: Simple ISDN communication setup between two computers

7. A single four-wire cable carries the 2 B channels and the D channel to a **Terminal Adapter** (TA).

8. The function of this device is to connect any and all **Terminal Equipment** (TE) - computers, fax machines, Local Area Networks, or telephones - to one or both of the **B** channels.

9. In this example, the **TA** is shown as a separate unit, but it could be housed within the computer as an add-in card or integrated feature, or integrated with the **NT1** into a single box as a modem replacement or stand-alone TCP/IP router (network layer device).

10. Also shown are the external ISDN reference points - **R, S/T** and **U.** Each type of reference point represents a different type of interface.

11. The **U** reference point is the incoming unshielded twisted pair (UTP). The **S/T** reference point is a four-wire UTP cable.

12. A typical **TA** for data-only applications might simply emulate a pair of modems, translating standard modem setup and dialing commands into ISDN call-setup commands.

13. Computers are connected to this kind of TA with a normal RS-232 cable. The **TA** provides automatic rate adaptation to match whatever data rate your computer supports with ISDN's 64 kbps channel.

14. An example of a more sophisticated **TA** is the ISDN router, which connects to an ISDN line on one side and a Local Area Network on the other.

15. This type of device is able to support many different kinds of computer without special ISDN software, and contains all the intelligence necessary to move traffic over an ISDN link. Because ISDN is purely digital, the effects of noise are largely eliminated, and because the 64 kbps channel is essentially a pure "bit pipe" with no rate negotiation or handshaking involved, there are no modem speed or protocol differences to cause conflicts.

3.3.8 Analog Calls (NON-ISDN Terminals) and ISDN

Types of Non-ISDN Terminals

- ISDN terminals such as DTE, that predate the ISDN standards, are referred to as terminal equipment type 2 (TE2).
- Ex. Terminal with physical interface as RS-232 and host computers with X.25 interface.
- This is the old analog telephone.
- Or old-style fax machine.
- Or modem.
- Or whatever we use to hook up to the analog phone line. It can also be other communications equipment that is handled by a TA (Terminal Adapter).

1. The key characteristic of ISDN is that it is a digital network. However, many of the devices and networks, with which an ISDN user needs to communicate, are not digital, but analog. In order for these two types of device to communicate, the information which they are exchanging - must be converted from one form to the other.

2. In fact, except for data calls between computers across the ISDN network, almost all other types of calls - voice, fax, modems - will all involve some kind of conversion from digital to analog, or vice versa.

3. Much of this conversion takes place without the user's knowledge or intervention and is handled by the networks and devices involved. However, there are instances where an understanding of what is involved will assist in making successful connections and diagnosing problem areas.

4. You need to pay careful attention to the requirements of the ISDN device in use, particularly when sending and receiving faxes. This section provides the background to the various scenarios involved, and the practical implications for the different types of ISDN devices that are available.

3.3.8.1 Voice over ISDN – 1

- ISDN is a **Digital** network. Everything (including sounds such as voice and modem signals) is carried as a stream of bits.

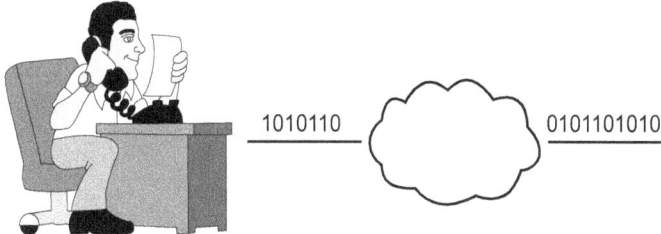

Fig. 3.12: Typical voice over ISDN is represented here

- This means that ISDN telephones need to be able to "digitize" and "un-digitize" sounds.

- This is performed by a device called a **CODEC** (<u>Co</u>der-<u>De</u>coder), which is located inside the telephone.

- The CODEC translates the sounds into bits in one direction, and translates bits into sounds in the opposite direction.

3.3.8.2 Voice over ISDN – 2

- The analog signal originating in the microphone of the telephone handset is sampled and transformed into a stream of bits (64000 of them every second) that is placed on the B channel.

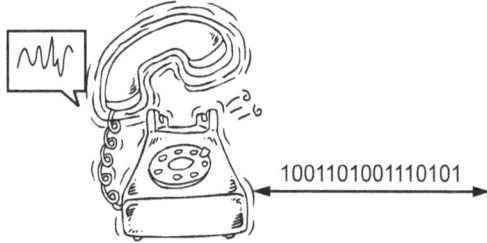

Fig. 3.13: Analog signal sent to the ear-piece of the handset

- Similarly, the incoming bit stream from the B channel is converted back into an analog signal and sent to the ear-piece of the handset.

- B channel is **full duplex**, which means that it can carry data in both directions at once.

3.3.8.3 Voice over ISDN – 3

- The ability to make voice calls from one ISDN telephone to another over a digital B channel is indeed useful. However, the majority of telephones, currently installed worldwide, are analogue devices which are not connected to an ISDN.

- Fortunately, you can make calls between the two networks. For this to work successfully, there has to be a conversion between the bit stream in the B channel and the analog signal required by the PSTN.

Fig. 3.14: Typical voice over ISDN and PSTN network

- CODECs are located at the boundaries of the digital and analog networks.

- Fortunately, you can make calls between the two networks.

- For this to work, the CODECs inside the network and the telephone **must** use the same rules when formatting the bit stream that represents the users' voices.

- Provided both devices are doing the same processing, then the information can be converted by applying the same rules in reverse.

- Given the presence of the CODEC in the network, and adherence to the correct protocols, any device that can be used on the PSTN, such as a modem or a fax machine, can also pass calls into the ISDN.

3.3.8.4 Analog Fax and Modem over ISDN (Scenario-1)

- Another important idea is introduced here; this is the Terminal Adapter.

- A Terminal Adapter (TA) is always necessary to connect non-ISDN devices (such as a serial port of a PC) to the ISDN. However, a TA can also contain a CODEC if it is intended to support analog phones, fax machines and modems.

- In Fig. 3.15, the modem at the top left can plug into the POTS ports on the TA. The TA will then convert sounds generated by the modem on its POTS port into a bit stream (and vice-versa). This bit stream is identical to that created by an ISDN telephone; that's to say it represents sounds.

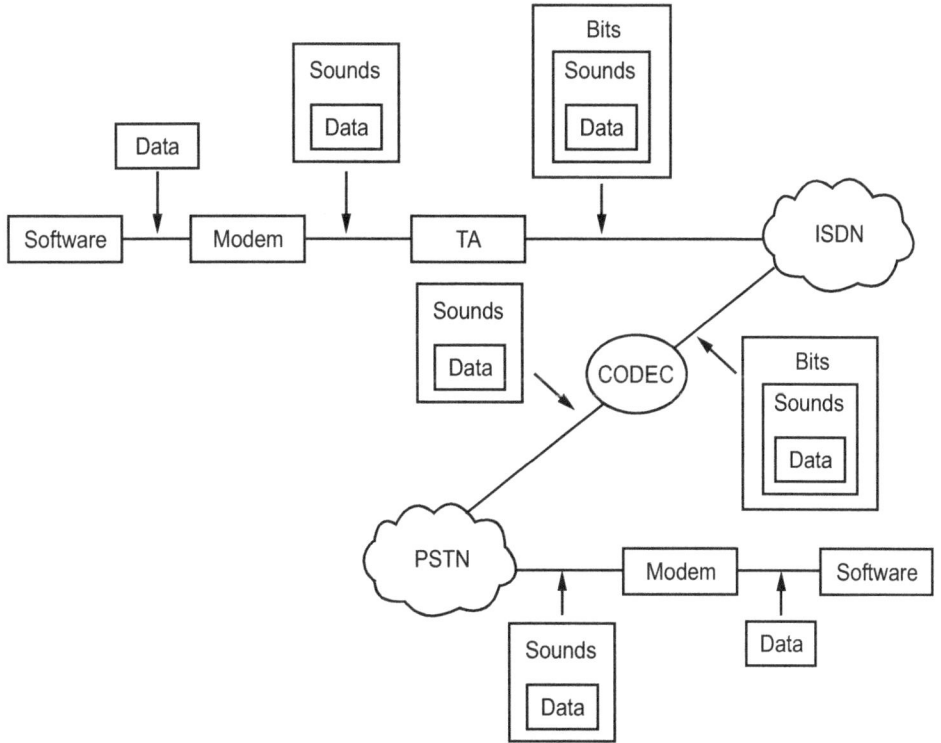

Fig. 3.15: Analog fax and modem over ISDN (scenario-1)

- Starting in the bottom right-hand corner, data leaves the PC as bits that are converted into sounds by the modem. We now have data encapsulated in sounds.

- These sounds cross the PSTN network until they are encapsulated inside a bit stream by the CODEC at the boundary between the ISDN and the PSTN. This bit stream is then passed from the ISDN network to the Terminal Adapter, which contains a CODEC that converts the bit stream back into sounds. These sounds are sent to the modem at the top left, which converts this back into the original data that entered the modem at the bottom left.

- The process runs in the opposite direction to send the data from the PC in the top left-hand corner to the PC in the bottom right-hand corner. This appears to be a lot of work: the data sent across the ISDN has been encapsulated twice.

3.3.8.5 Analogue Fax and Modem over ISDN (Scenario-2)

- The next step in evolving this configuration is to use an internal modem in the PC.

- Logically this is not different from the previous scenario.

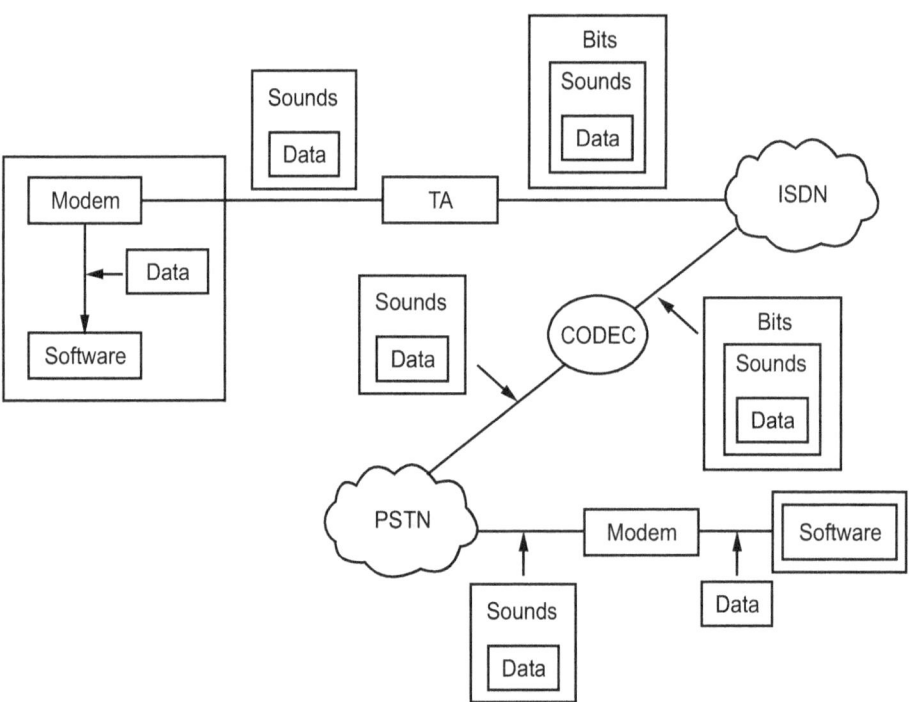

Fig. 3.16: Analog fax and Modem over ISDN (scenario-2)

3.3.8.6 Analog Fax and Modem over ISDN (Scenario-3)

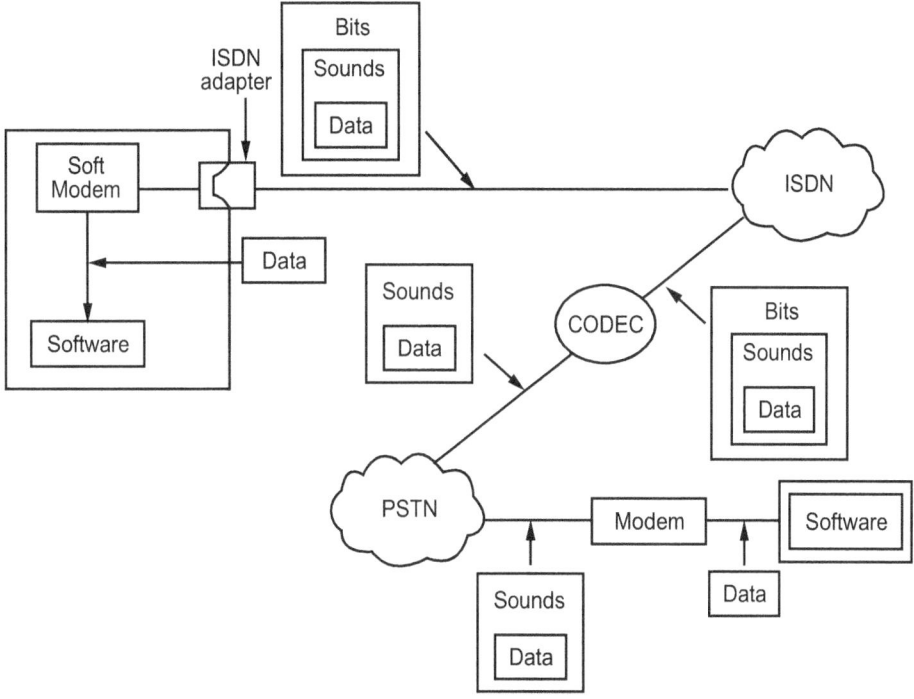

Fig. 3.17: Analog fax and modem over ISDN (scenario-3)

- We could replace the internal modem with an internal ISDN adapter and a driver, which appears to the application software to be a modem.
- In reality, this driver combines the functions of both the modem and the CODEC.
- This driver is known as a **soft modem**.
- A soft modem requires a lot of processing power, since it has to operate in real time.
- The PC is therefore likely to appear a bit sluggish while the connection is active.
- The advantage of this solution is that it can be used with an inexpensive passive ISDN adapter.

3.3.8.7 Analog Fax and Modem over ISDN (Scenario-4)
- The final step in evolving this scenario is to use an ISDN adapter which has a DSP (Digital Signal Processor).
- This takes the very heavy processing load due to the soft modem away from the PC.
- ISDN adapters with a DSP are generally more expensive than passive adapters.

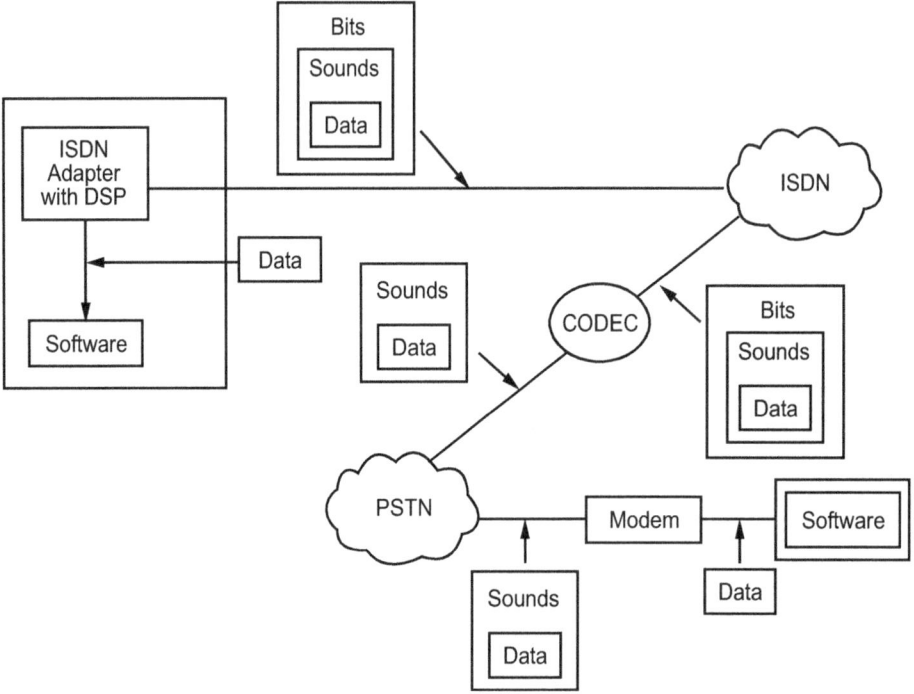

Fig. 3.18: Analog fax and modem over ISDN (Scenario-4)

3.3.8.8 Soft Fax and Soft Modem

- This means that an ISDN adapter with an on-board DSP can also communicate with any device that contains a modem.
- In Fig. 3.19, you can see that we have added a fax machine.

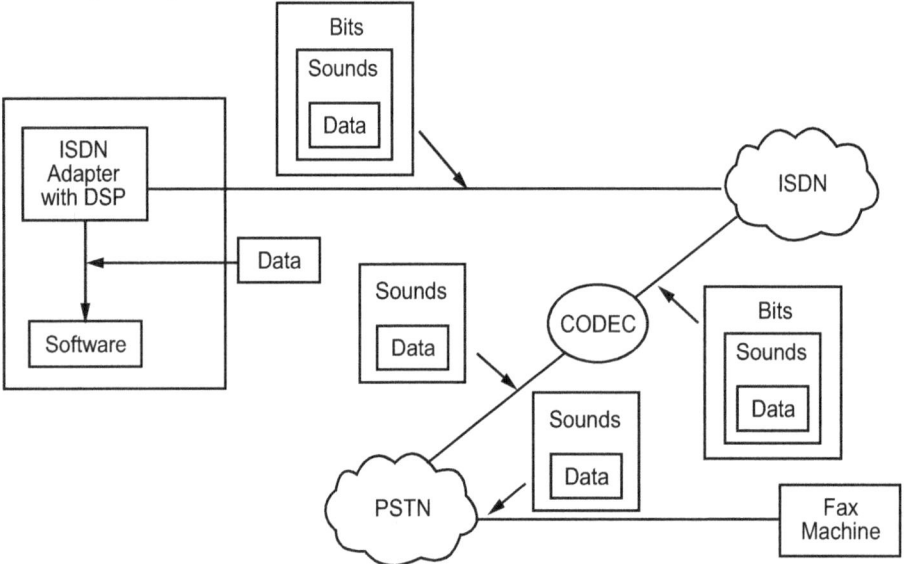

Fig. 3.19: Typical soft fax and soft modem concept implemented

- To perform the job of a modem and a CODEC at the same requires a large amount of processing power.

- DSPs are very powerful processors.

- Nevertheless, you need one DSP for each B channel for which you want to use this technique.

- There is, however, no reason why you couldn't use an ISDN adapter that has a single DSP and a soft modem driver to handle two modem calls at a time.

3.3.8.9 Analog Modems and ISDN

- So who will you call with your brand new ISDN connectivity? The obvious first answer is your Internet Service Provider (ISP).

- Many ISPs are recognizing the performance and reliability improvements of ISDN over modems and are rolling out ISDN services.

- The data applications of ISDN shown so far, all require that both parties in the connection have ISDN or packet data service.

- What if you need to connect with somebody that isn't ISDN capable ? The answer is that you use your analog modem and a TA that supports analog voice connections, or POTS.

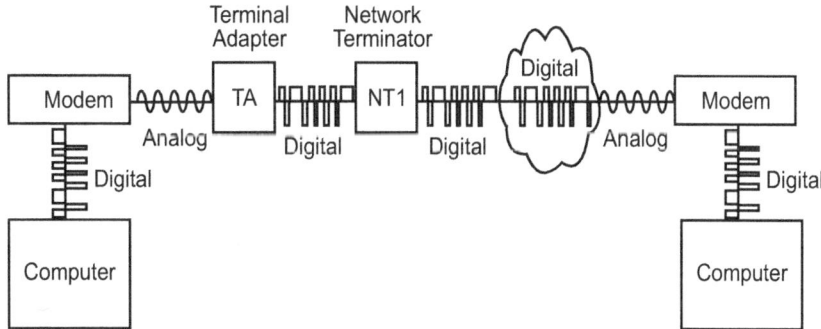

Fig. 3.20: Using analog modems in an ISDN environment

- This kind of TA accepts an ordinary voice or modem audio signal through a standard RJ11 modular jack and digitizes it for transport across the ISDN interface.

- It interprets the touch-tone dialing signals put out by your telephone set or modem and generates the required ISDN call-setup signals.

- If the number you are calling is not an ISDN POP, the telecommunication equipment at the remote end automatically translates the digitized audio back to analog audio, where the destination modem (or human being) hears what it is always heard before ISDN came along.

- In fact, some ISDN TAs include built-in analog modems (sometimes anomalously called "digital modems") just to provide compatibility with existing analog fax and data devices.

- So plan on keeping your modems around at least until the end of the decade; you will still need them occasionally. Fortunately, many TAs provide PSTN's ports without much additional cost, so this is a painless necessity.

Thus we can summarize this ISDN and communication of software, modem and fax machine as follows:

- In ISDN networks everything is carried as a stream of bits.
- Converting digital telephone signals into voice, and vice versa, is done by CODECs.
- Converting data into analog telephone signals, and vice versa, is done by modems.
- A CODEC is the device that allows telephony between an ISDN and the analog network.
- This same CODEC can be used to allow modem and fax calls to cross the same boundary.
- Modems and CODECs always work in pairs - they can be nested together but each must have a partner.
- A Terminal Adapter is an interface between the ISDN and any non-ISDN device, such as a computer or an analog phone.
- If analog devices need to be connected to the ISDN, then the Terminal Adapter will need to perform the function of a CODEC, and have analog (POTS) ports available for modems and fax machines to plug into.
- Internal ISDN adapters can use dedicated chips on the card, or software running on the PC, to implement the digital and analog conversions, thereby removing the requirement for any physical analog devices like fax machines and modems.
- There are three kinds of devices used in data communications with ISDN:
    1. Conventional Modems - These require Terminal Adapter to connect to the ISDN.
    2. ISDN Modems - These combine the functionality of CODEC and modem.
    3. Terminal Adapter - It allows analog devices to connect to the ISDN and contain a CODEC for this purpose.
    4. ISDN Adapters - These merely pass a stream of bits between a protocol driver and the ISDN.

3.3.9 ISDN Equipment and Interface Terminology

U-INTERFACE	**U**-interface is a 2-wire **digital telephone line** that runs from the telephone company's central office (CO) to an NT1 device. The customer is responsible for supplying all the equipments from the U-interface forward.
NT-1 **Network Termination Type 1**	The **NT1** acts as the boundary between the customer premise and the phone company's network. **NT1** is a Basic Rate **ISDN-only device** that converts a service provider's U-interface to a customer's S/T-interface. It can be stand-alone or integrated into a terminal adapter. The **NT1** interface combines the two B channels and the D channel into a single bit stream at the physical level and is also capable of supporting more than one device attached to an ISDN line, sometimes referred to as a multi-drop configuration.
S/T -INTERFACE	S/T-interface is a common way of referring to either an S- or T-interface. The S/T-interface breaks the signal into two paths- **one transmit, one receive**. In an ISDN PBX, the **NT1** connects using the **T**-interface, and the PBX connects using the S-interface. This intermediate track is called **NT2**.
TE1 **Terminal Equipment Type 1**	**TE1** (Terminal Equipment Type 1) is **ISDN-ready** equipment that can directly connect to the ISDN line (often using an **S/ T**-interface). Examples are ISDN phones, ISDN routers, ISDN computers, etc. They are manufactured from the outset to be completely ISDN compatible.
R-INTERFACE	**R**-interface is a **non-ISDN** interface such as an EIA-232 or a V.35 interface. **R**-interface provides a non-ISDN interface between equipment that is not ISDN compatible with the rest of the ISDN network.
TA **Terminal Adapter**	**TA** is a device that allows non-ISDN-ready equipment, such as PCs, to connect to an ISDN line.
TE2 **Terminal Equipment Type 2**	**TE2** is an equipment that **cannot directly connect** to an ISDN line. A common example of this device is a PC, or a non-ISDN-ready router. **TA** must be used to connect to the ISDN line. Examples of TE2 are RS-232 or [X.25] interface based devices, such as personal computers.
SPID **Service Profile ID**	The **SPID** is a number assigned to an ISDN line by the ISDN service provider that identifies certain characteristics of the line. Usually this number is the telephone number **PLUS** 0101 as an identifier.

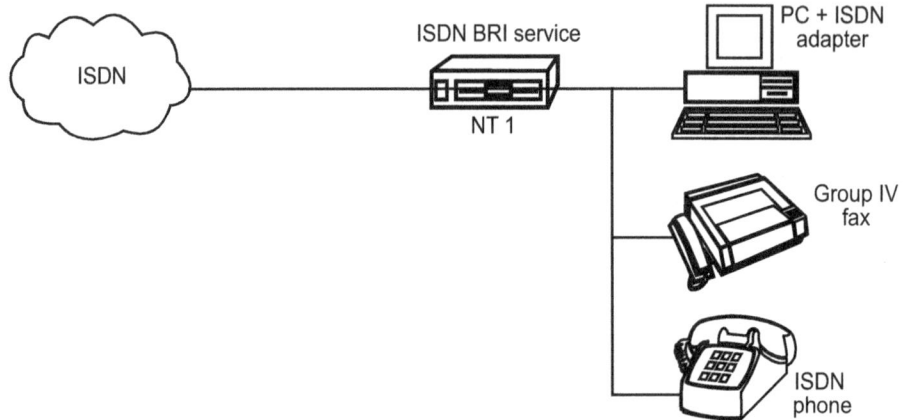

Fig. 3.21: Typical use of NT1 Interface

3.3.9.1 Interfaces

- Generally the **telephone company** provides its BRI customers with a **U-interface**.
- The U-interface is a two-wire (single pair) interface from the phone switch.
- It supports full-duplex data transfer over a single pair of wires, therefore only a single device can be connected to a U-interface.
- This device is called a **Network Termination-1 (NT-1)**.
- The NT-1 is a relatively simple device that converts the 2-wire U-interfaces into the 4-wire **S/T-interface**.
- The S/T-interface supports multiple devices (upto 7 devices can be placed on the S/T bus) because, while it is still a full-duplex interface, there is now a pair of wires for receiving data, and another for transmitting data.
- Today, many devices have NT-1s built into their design.
- Technically, ISDN devices must go through a **Network Termination-2 (NT-2)** device, which converts the T-interface into the S-interface (Note: The S and T-interfaces are electrically equivalent).
- Virtually all ISDN devices include an NT-2 in their design.
- The NT-2 communicates with terminal equipment, and handles the Layer 2 and 3 ISDN protocols.
- Devices most commonly expect either a U-interface connection (these have a built-in NT-1), or an S/T-interface connection.
- Devices, that connect to the S/T (or S) interface, include ISDN capable telephones and FAX machines, video teleconferencing equipment, bridge/ routers, and terminal adapters. All devices, that are designed for ISDN, are designated **Terminal Equipment 1 (TE1)**.

- All other communication devices that are *not* ISDN capable, but have a POTS telephone interface (also called the **R interface**), including ordinary analog telephones, FAX machines, and modems, are designated **Terminal Equipment 2 (TE2)**.
- A **Terminal Adapter (TA)** connects a TE2 to an ISDN S/T bus.
- Going one step in the opposite direction takes us inside the telephone switch.
- Remember that the U-interface connects the switch to the customer premises equipment.
- This local loop connection is called *Line Termination* (LT function).
- The connection to other switches within the phone network is called *Exchange Termination* (ET function).
- The LT function and the ET function communicate via. the **V-interface**.

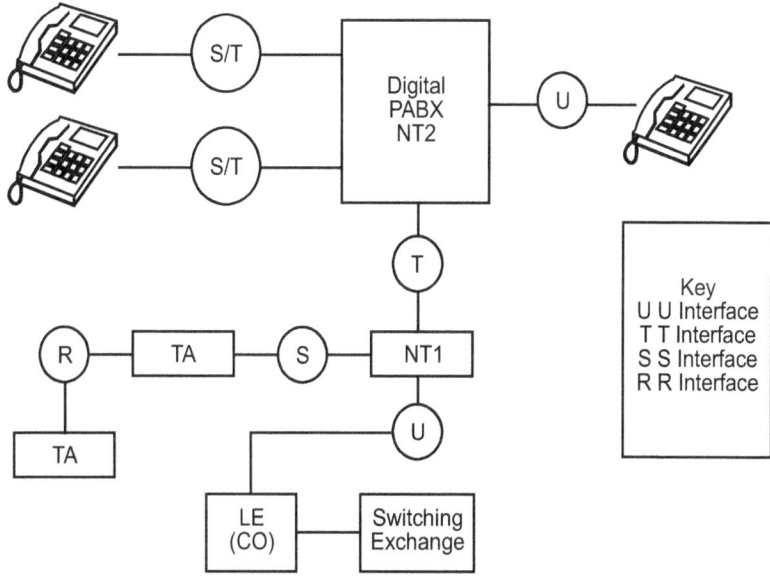

Fig. 3.22: An interface ('reference point') is said to exist between each piece of equipment on the ISDN

3.3.9.2 Examples

NETWORK INTERFACE	RJ-45 for ISDN Basic Rate U-interface (built-in NT1) 128 kbps
DTE INTERFACE	EIA-232 (DB-25) Modem pass through port (3000 only)
DTE DATA RATES	1.2 to 230.4 kbps asynchronous 2400 to 128 kbps synchronous (3010 only)

COMPRESSION	According to standards
PROTOCOLS	Multilink PPP, ITU-T V.120, Clear Channel, Async. BONDING etc.
DIALING SELECTIONS	AT commands, DTR assertion, V.25 bis.
DIAGNOSTICS AND TESTING	Network loopback Remote configuration
ANALOG PORTS	Two standard RJ-11 Each port rings upto three phones within 500 feet
CUSTOM CALLING FEATURES	• Stutter dial tone • Three- and six-way • Conferencing • Call forwarding • Reminder ring • Auto call back • Distinctive ring • Caller ID • Implicit transfer • Visual message waiting indication (Custom calling features must be provided by telephone company.)
ENVIRONMENT	Operating Temperature: 0° to 50°C, (32° to 122°F) Storage Temperature: –20° to 70°C, (–4° to 158°F) Relative Humidity: Upto 95%, non-condensing
PRODUCT INCLUDES	110 V wallmount power supply, CD ROM, one cable to connect ISDN line

3.3.10 ISDN Architectures

1. Basically, network architecture of ISDN is defined to follow an evolutionary path in telecommunication development and different application services.

2. The ISDN architectures play very important role in interfacing and operating the different switching networks and non-switching networks like:

   (a) Circuit switched networks.

   (b) Packet switched networks (Datagram and VC packet).

   (c) Non-switching networks.

   (d) Different signalling networks.

3.　The ISDN architectures are simply categorized for better understanding.

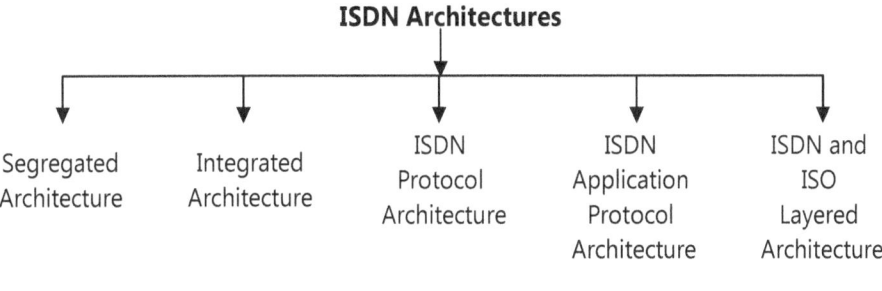

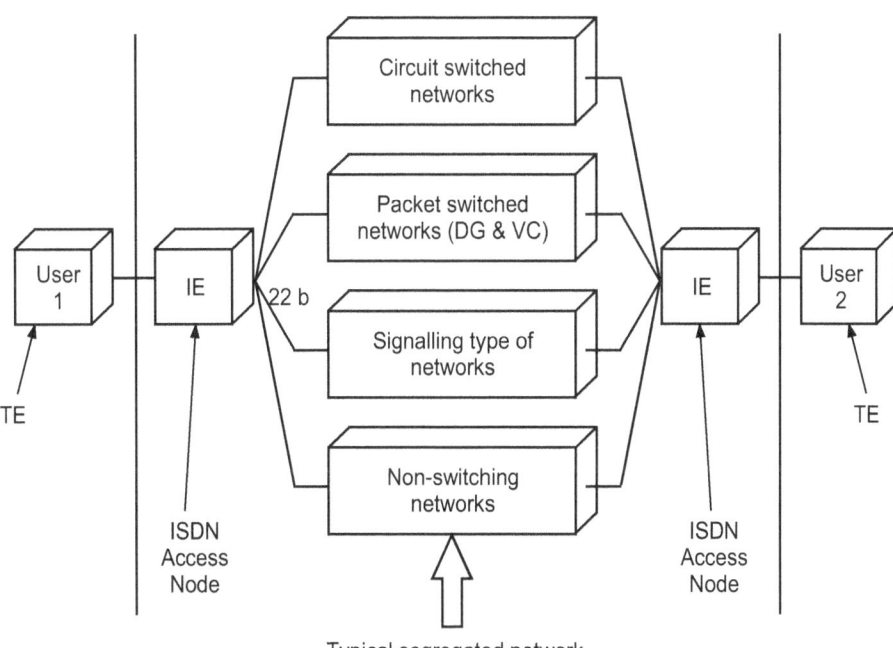

Fig. 3.22 (a): Typical segregated architecture of ISDN

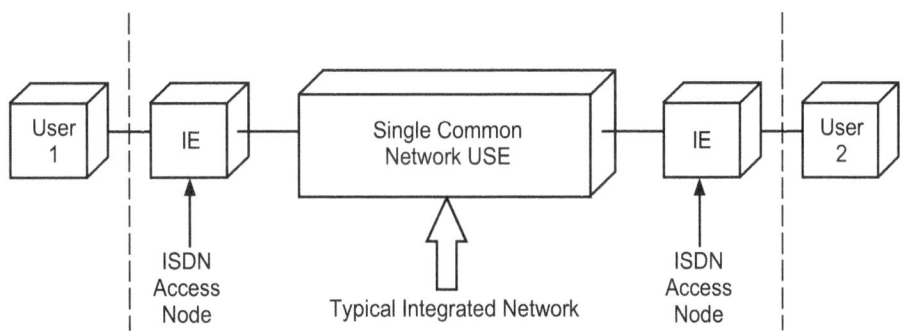

Fig. 3.22 (b): Typical integrated architecture of ISDN

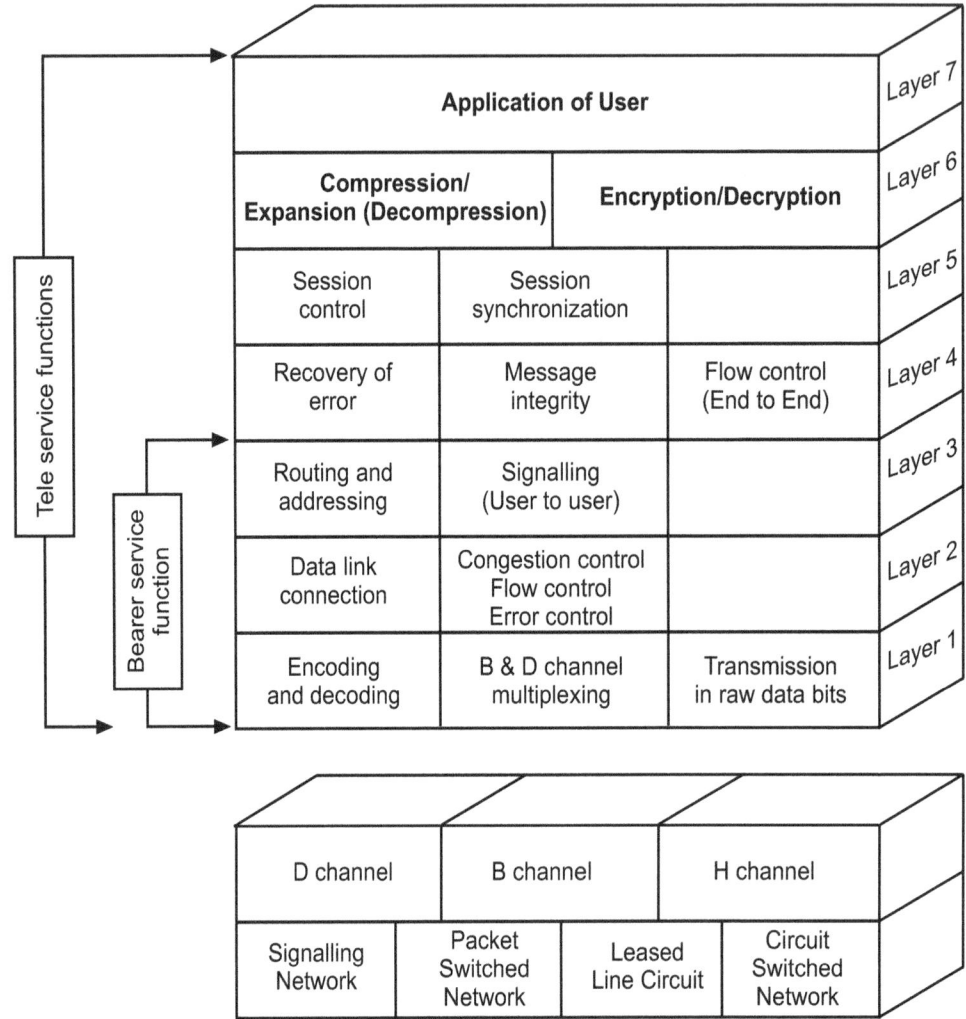

Fig. 3.22 (c): Typical ISDN protocol architecture

4. Thus, Layer 1, Layer 2 and Layer 3 of the ISDN protocol stack is very important.
5. Physical layer (Layer 1) tasks:
    *   Encoding and decoding of digital signals.
    *   Transmission of D, B and H channel data.
    *   Multiplexing to form primary or basic rates of data.
    *   Activation and deactivation of the physical circuits.
6. Datalink Layer (Layer 2) tasks:
    *   Synchronization of trans-reception in data communication.
    *   Establishment and clearing the datalinks.
    *   Flow control at layer 2.
    *   Error control at layer 2.
    *   Congestion control at layer 2.

7. Network layer (Layer 3) tasks:
   • Routing and addressing in network.
   • Signalling (user to user).
   • Multiplexing at network layer level (at level 3).
   • Establishing and clearing network level connection.
   • Multiplexing in internetworking situation.

8. ISDN uses several protocols; which protocol each channel uses is crucial to understanding how ISDN works. ISDN stands for "Integrated Services Digital Networks" and it is a ITU-T (formerly CCITT) term for a relatively new telecommunications service package. ISDN is basically the telephone network turned all-digital end to end, using existing switches and wiring (for the most part) upgraded so that the basic "call" is a 64 kbps end-to-end channel.

9. It is offered by local telephone companies, but most readily in Australia, Western Europe, Japan and portions of the USA.

10. In France, ISDN is known as "RNIS".

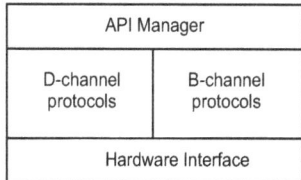

Fig. 3.22 (d): General ISDN protocol architecture with D and B channels

11. Different protocols used are as follows:
    IP: Internet protocol.
    DSSI (Digital Subscriber Signalling System No. 1).
    HDLC: High level datalink control protocol.
    PPP: Point to Point Protocol.

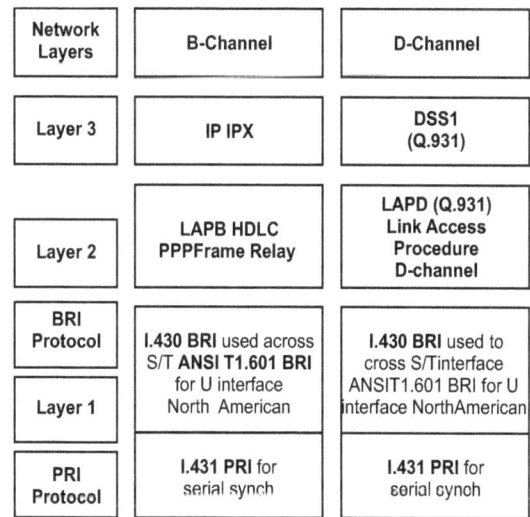

Network Layers	B-Channel	D-Channel
Layer 3	IP IPX	DSS1 (Q.931)
Layer 2	LAPB HDLC PPPFrame Relay	LAPD (Q.931) Link Access Procedure D-channel
BRI Protocol / Layer 1	I.430 BRI used across S/T ANSI T1.601 BRI for U interface North American	I.430 BRI used to cross S/Tinterface ANSIT1.601 BRI for U interface NorthAmerican
PRI Protocol	I.431 PRI for serial synch	I.431 PRI for serial synch

Fig. 3.22 (e): Detail ISDN protocol architecture which uses several protocols now-a-days

12. **ISDN Physical Interfaces – SERIAL INTERFACES used are:**

   - EIA/TIA 232.

   - EIA/TIA – 449.

   - EIA – 530.

   - X.21.

13. An understanding of the format of interfaces and channel type is critical to any analysis of ISDN because they provide the framework through which the protocols and applications flow.

14. ISDN defines a full network architecture as shown in Fig. 3.22 (e). This architecture separates access functions from actual network functions.

15. Thus, different protocols are compatible and fully supported for ISDN communication in today's Internet technology.

16. Numbering and addressing is also very important issue in the ISDN network system.

17. The component of the ISDN address which is used to identify the end point is known as the ISDN number and the component/Entity for identifying the specific instrument/equipment at the end point is called as the ISDN subaddress.

18. The numbering plan for ISDN network follows the following guidelines.

   - Enhanced telephone numbering plan defined by ITU standard is used in ISDN.

   - Numbering plan is independent of nature of the ISDN service (voice, video and data or fax).

   - Numbering plan is independent of routing.

   - ISDN numbers are basically a sequence of decimal digits. (No character or alphabets are allowed).

   - Number is designed in such a way that interworking between ISDNs requires only ISDN numbers and not any other addressing signals or additional digits.

19. Typical ISDN: Message format for user part is shown in Fig. 3.22 (f) which is simple and self explanatory.

20. Typical ISDN address structure is as shown in Fig. 3.22 (g) which is simple and self explanatory.

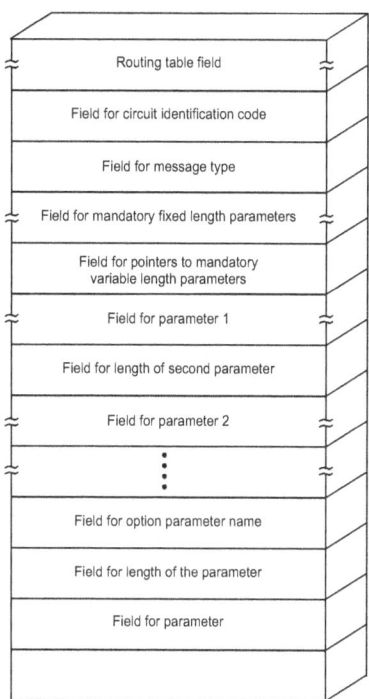

Fig. 3.22 (f): Typical message format for ISDN user part

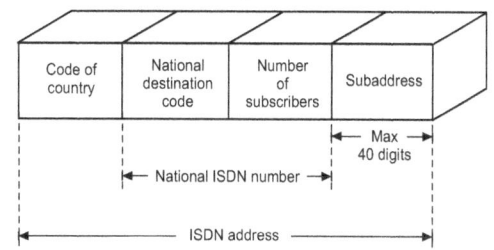

Fig. 3.22 (g): Typical structure of ISDN address

3.3.11 ISDN and OSI Architecture

From the point of view of the OSI architecture, an ISDN line has a stack of three protocols –

- Physical layer.
- Data link layer.
- Network layer (the ISDN protocol, properly).

Network layer (the ISDN protocol, properly) (Layer 3)
Data link layer (Layer 2)
Physical layer (Layer 1)

Fig. 3.23: ISDN line has a stack of three protocols

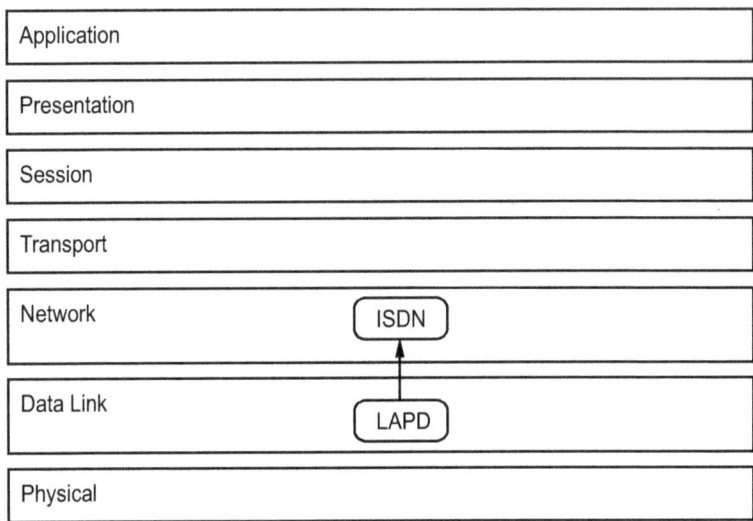

Fig. 3.24: The ISDN is illustrated here in relation to the OSI model

Layer 1 (Physical Layer):

1. ISDN physical layer (Layer 1) frame formats differ depending on whether the frame is outbound (from terminal to network) or inbound (from network to terminal).

2. Both physical layer interfaces are shown in Fig. 3.25.

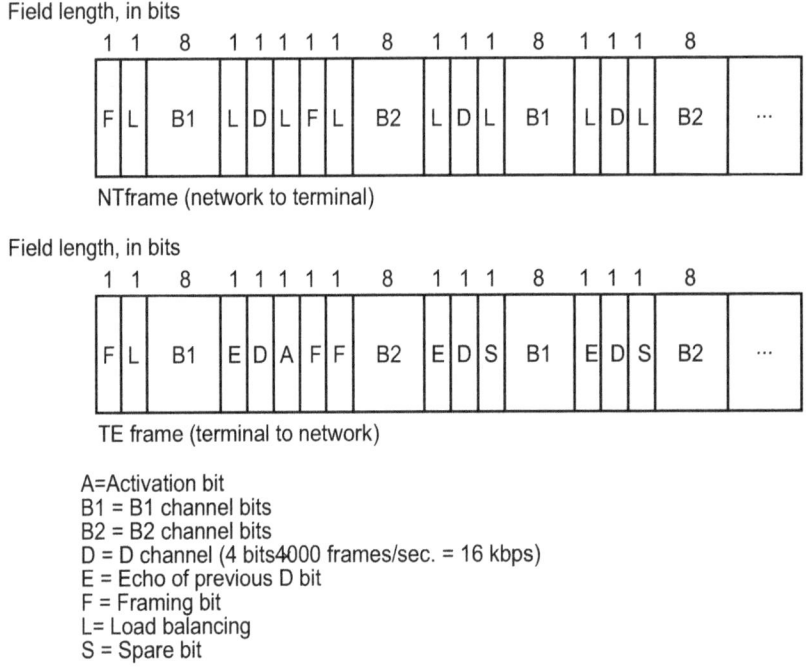

A=Activation bit
B1 = B1 channel bits
B2 = B2 channel bits
D = D channel (4 bits4000 frames/sec. = 16 kbps)
E = Echo of previous D bit
F = Framing bit
L= Load balancing
S = Spare bit

Fig. 3.25: ISDN physical layer frame formats

3. The frames are 48 bits long, of which 36 bits represent data. The bits of an ISDN physical layer frame are used as follows:

   - *F* – Provides synchronization.

   - *L* – Adjusts the average bit value.

   - *E* – Used for contention resolution when several terminals on a passive bus contend for a channel.

   - *A* – Activates devices.

   - *S* – Unassigned.

   - B1, B2, and D – Used for user data (B1 for B1 channel bits and B2 for B2 channel bits).

4. Multiple ISDN user devices can be physically attached to one circuit.

5. In this configuration, collisions can result if two terminals transmit simultaneously.

6. ISDN therefore provides features to determine link contention.

7. When an NT receives a D bit from the TE, it echoes back the bit in the next E bit position.

8. The TE expects the next E bit to be the same as its last transmitted D bit.

9. Terminals cannot transmit into the D channel unless they first detect a specific number of ones (indicating "no signal") corresponding to a pre-established priority.

10. If the TE detects a bit in the echo (E) channel that is different from its D bits, it must stop transmitting immediately.

11. This simple technique ensures that only one terminal can transmit its D message at one time.

12. After successful D message transmission, the terminal has its priority reduced by requiring it to detect more continuous ones before transmitting.

13. Terminals cannot raise their priority until all other devices on the same line have had an opportunity to send a D message.

14. Telephone connections have higher priority than all other services, and signaling information has a higher priority than non-signaling information.

Layer 2 (Data Link Layer):

1. Layer 2 of the ISDN signaling protocol is *Link Access Procedure, D channel*, also known as *LAPD*.

2. As LAPD's acronym indicates, it is used across the **D channel** to ensure that control and signaling information flows and has been received properly.

3. LAPD is similar to *High-Level Data Link Control* (HDLC) [HDLC supports a variety of link types and topologies. It can be used with point-to-point and multipoint links, bounded and unbounded media, half-duplex and full-duplex transmission facilities, and circuit-switched and packet-switched networks].

4. LAPD is similar to *Link Access Procedure, Balanced* (LAPB). [LAPB is best known for its presence in the X.25 (WAN service) protocol stack].

5. As the expansion of the LAPD acronym indicates, it is used across the D channel to ensure that control and signaling information flows and is received properly.

6. The LAPD frame format (see Fig. 3.26) uses *supervisory*, *information*, and *unnumbered* frames.

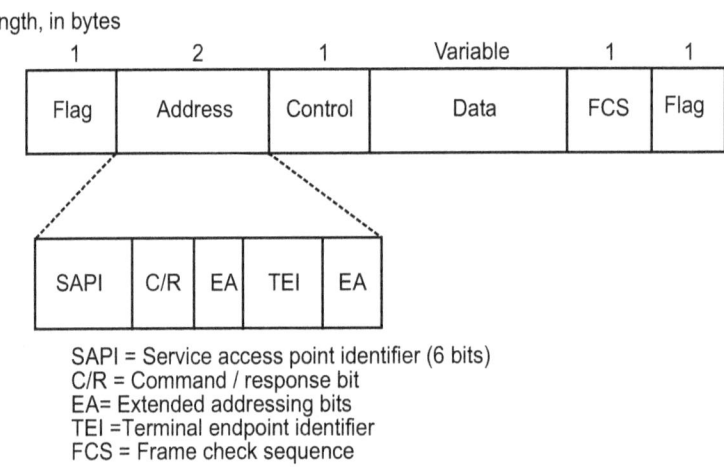

Fig. 3.26: LAPD frame format

7. The LAPD *address* field can be either one or two bytes long.

8. If the extended address bit of the first byte is set, the address is one byte; if it is not set, the address is two bytes.

9. The first address field byte contains the *service access point identifier* (SAPI), which identifies the portal at which LAPD services are provided to Layer 3.

10. The C/R bit indicates whether the frame contains a command or a response.

11. The *terminal end-point identifier* (TEI) field identifies either a single terminal or multiple terminals. A TEI of all ones indicates a broadcast.

12. **FCS:** The Frame Check Sequence (FCS) enables a high level of physical error control by allowing the integrity of the transmitted frame data to be checked. The sequence is first calculated by the transmitter using an algorithm based on the values of all the bits in the frame. The receiver then performs the same calculation on the received frame and compares its value to the CRC.

13. **Window size:** LAPD supports an extended window size (modulo 128) where the number of possible outstanding frames for acknowledgement is raised from 8 to 128. This extension is generally used for satellite transmissions where the acknowledgement delay is significantly greater than the frame transmission times. The type of the link initialization frame determines the modulo of the session and an "E" is added to the basic frame type name (e.g., SABM becomes SABME).

14. **Frame types:**

The following are the Supervisory Frame Types in LAPD:

RR	Information frame acknowledgement and indication to receive more.
REJ	Request for retransmission of all frames after a given sequence number.
RNR	Indicates a state of temporary occupation of station (e.g., window full).

15. **The following are the Unnumbered Frame Types in LAPD:**

DISC	Request disconnection
UA	Acknowledgement frame
DM	Response to DISC indicating disconnected mode.
FRMR	Frame reject
SABM	Initiator for asynchronous balanced mode. No master/slave relationship
SABME	SABM in extended mode
UI	Unnumbered Information
XID	Exchange Information

Layer 3 (Network Layer):

1. Two Layer-3 specifications are used for ISDN signaling.

2. Together, these protocols support user-to-user, circuit-switched, and packet-switched connections.

3. A variety of call establishment, call termination, information, and miscellaneous messages are specified, including SETUP, CONNECT, RELEASE, USER INFORMATION, CANCEL, STATUS, and DISCONNECT.

4. Fig. 3.27 shows the typical stages of an ISDN circuit-switched call.

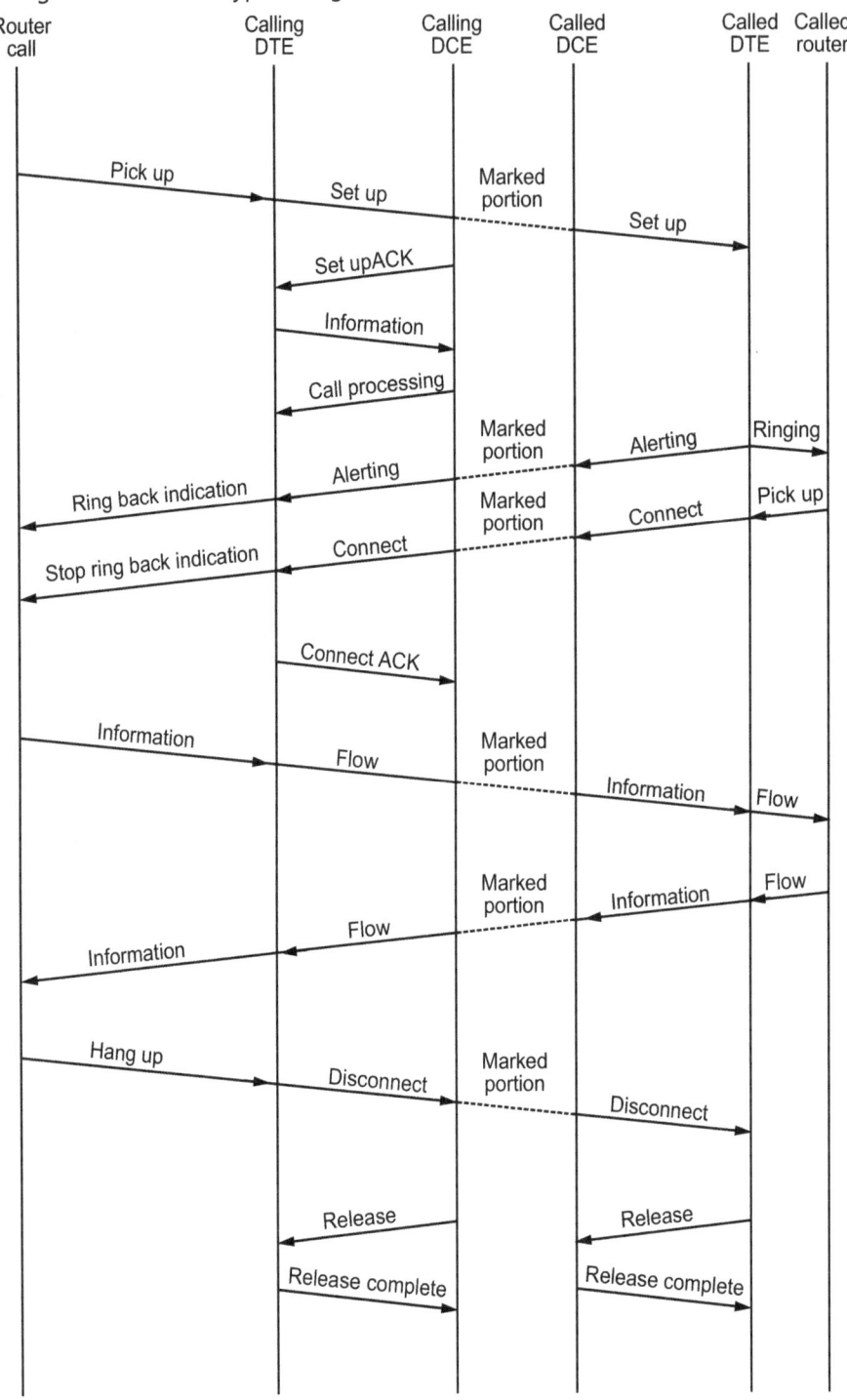

Fig. 3.27: ISDN circuit-switched call stages

3.4 Voice Over Frame Relay

3.4.1 Using Frame Relay to Integrate the Enterprise

Frame Relay Basics:

1. Frame relay is defined as a communication protocol as well as a packet data service.

2. This section will describe frame relay as a packet data service because of its ability to create a Wide Area Network (WAN) that can integrate an enterprise infrastructure.

3. The frame relay service is a high speed packetized data service that consists of physical and logical components.

4. **The physical components include Frame Relay Assemblers Disassemblers (FRADs), access circuits, and frame relay ports.**

5. **The logical components consist of permanent virtual circuits (PVCs).**

6. Frame Relay Assemblers Disassemblers (FRADs) are devices, such as routers, that assemble data into frame relay packets and that transmit the packets through the local access circuits to which they are connected.

7. The local access circuits, whose bandwidths can range from 56 kbps to   1544 Kbps, are digital circuits that connect the FRADs to the frame relay network provider's site.

8. A frame relay port, whose bandwidth equals that of the local access circuit, physically connects the local access circuit to the frame relay network.

9. Frame Relay's logical component differentiates it from the traditional high speed data services that are physical in nature.

10. The logical component of frame relay consists of Permanent Virtual Circuits (PVCs).

11. PVCs are the logical connections that allow the various sites, having physical network access, to communicate among one and other.

12. Each logical connection is defined in the frame relay provider's network and in the FRAD equipment.

13. **Logical connections in the frame relay providers network are software-defined connections that can create many types of network topologies (i.e., hub- and-spoke, full mesh, partial mesh).**

14. Because the connections are defined using software, companies may provide logical connections in a few hours as opposed to the few weeks that are necessary with traditional high speed data services like private lines.

15. In addition to providing the logical connections within the frame relay provider's network, the FRADs must be programmed to send the data to the correct permanent virtual circuit.

16. Every PVC provided in the frame relay network must also be programmed into the FRAD.

17. FRADs are programmed using data link connection identifiers (DLCIs) that associate an identification number to each PVC.

18. Each PVC has a Committed Information Rate (CIR), that is the bandwidth associated to the logical connection.

19. Frame relay networks have the ability to transmit data at a rate higher than that of the CIR. This allows a "bandwidth-on-demand" feature that improves the performance of bandwidth intensive applications.

Frame Relay History:

1. Frame relay is a Data Link Layer protocol that is built on the existing CCITT (Committee Consultative of International Telephone and Telegraphy) X.25 and ISDN standards.

2. Frame relay is often thought of as the next generation packet network succeeding X.25.

3. X.25 was developed about 20 years ago and was designed for use with "noisy" analog lines.

4. To compensate for the errors caused by these "noisy" data links, X.25 checks and corrects the data traversing every data path.

5. This extensive error checking adversely effects the network throughput as compared to frame relay.

6. Sometimes, depending on the packet size, 50% of the X.25 packets, that traverse a data link, are associated with the X.25's error checking rather than with the application's data.

7. Frame relay, on the other hand, realizes its efficiencies by only making error calculations at the source and destination devices rather than making them at each switching node, as does X.25.

8. Error corrections at each switching node are not necessary because today's digital networks have very few errors compared to those on analog networks. (Digital error rates are less than one error in every 1,000,000 bits transmitted.)

9. Since the error verification and correction burden is removed from the network, network response times are greatly improved.

10. These improved network response times improve the response times of applications that traverse the wide area network.

Frame Relay State-of-the-Art:

1. We believe that frame relay's state-of-the-art incorporates the use of multiprotocol routing, Integrated Services Digital Networks (ISDN), dial access, and/or voice networking within the frame relay network.

2. The incorporation of these additional technologies improves the reliability, performance, and flexibility of the frame relay infrastructure.

3. Multiprotocol routing necessitates that the FRAD equipment, which allows multiple protocols to traverse a single PVC.

4. Multiprotocol routing also makes it easier to increase the capacity utilization of the frame relay links (PVCs: Permanent Virtual Circuits) by allowing many different devices, that communicate using different protocols, to use the same PVC.

5. Companies are also using ISDN to enhance the performance and reliability of their wide area network.

6. ISDN is a high speed data network that allows devices to dial one or more   56 kbps data channels.

7. It operates similarly to the standard telephone service, but multiple connections can be made and those connections are at a data rate of 56 kbps or 64 kbps.

8. Wide area network reliability can be increased by having an alternate network (ISDN) on standby in the event that the frame relay network or access circuits fail.

9. Today's FRAD equipment will automatically switch the connections from the frame relay to ISDN in the event of a frame relay failure.

10. Additionally, improved performance can also be realized by increasing the bandwidth on the physical components of the network.

11. FRADs can dial-up additional bandwidth when pre-programmed thresholds are met. For example, FRAD's can enable additional data channels when line utilization exceeds a pre-defined percentage utilization.

12. Today's frame relay networks are also accessible by remote users with "dial-up to frame relay" data connections.

13. "Dial-up to frame relay" capability is usually cost effective because companies neither have to purchase expensive equipment such as terminal servers and authentication servers nor supply administrative support for user IDs, passwords, or security administration.

14. Frame relay is designed as a data only service, but many companies are using specially designed FRADs to deploy voice applications.

15. The specially designed FRADs packetize voice into frame relay packets and transmit them across the network.

16. This allows companies to use their existing data infrastructure to transport voice calls.

17. Voice applications over the frame relay network are not very popular because today's voice networks are very robust from a price, feature and performance standpoint.

18. However, there are some companies that are transmitting voice over frame relay networks in order to reduce telephone expenditures.

Frame Relay Applications:

1. The most popular frame relay application provides companies with Local Area Network (LAN) to LAN communication.

2. This allows companies to integrate their information systems in order to have employees throughout the enterprise to access specific information residing on a LAN somewhere in the enterprise.

3. The devices on the LANs can communicate over the frame relay network regardless of their native protocol.

4. For example, native protocols that can traverse frame relay networks include SNA, DECnet, IPX, TCP/IP, and AppleTalk.

5. Therefore, frame relay has the ability to make the users perceive that the entire company is on one large LAN.

6. Application software such as groupware, e-mail, document sharing, database and many other LAN applications can utilize frame relay technology.

7. Companies are also integrating communication for legacy systems, such as SNA, onto frame relay networks.

8. This allows companies to connect devices such as cluster controllers and front-end processors directly to FRADs in order to use the frame relay network for communications.

9. Frame relay's ability to support both the legacy applications and LAN applications provides an excellent backbone for those companies that are in the process of migrating their information systems from centralized mainframe processing to distributed client/server systems.

10. Companies can turn up legacy applications on the frame relay network and slowly migrate the LAN applications as they are developed.

3.4.2 Frame Relay Technology

1. Today's LANs and computing equipments have the potential to run at much higher speeds and transfer very large quantities of data.

2. With the diversity and complexity of today's networks, management can be a mammoth task if you don't have the proper tools.

3. Each environment is a unique combination of equipment from different vendors.

4. Frame relay, which is a relatively new wide area networking method, is gaining in popularity.

5. It uses a packet-switching technology, similar to X.25, but is more efficient. As a result, it can make your networking quicker, simpler and less costly.

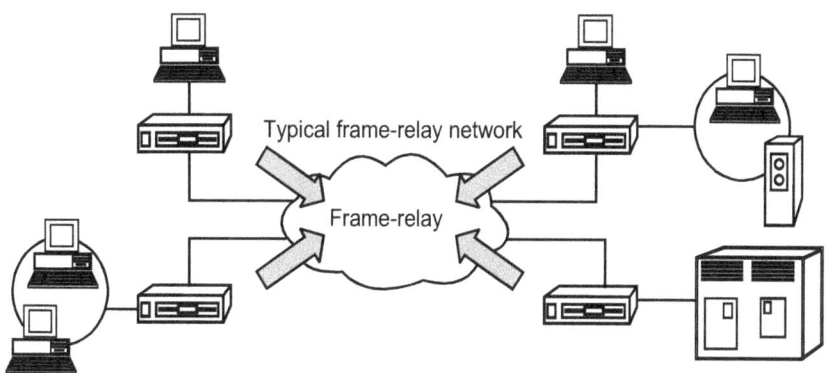

Fig. 3.28: Typical frame relay network connects the different LANs

6. Frame relay was developed to solve communication problems that other protocols could not: the increased need for higher speeds, an increased need for large bandwidth efficiency, particularly for clumping ("bursty" traffic), an increase in intelligent network devices that lower protocol processing, and the need to connect LANs and WANs.

7. Like X.25, frame relay is a packet-switched protocol. But the frame-relay process is streamlined. There are significant differences that make frame relay a faster, more efficient form of networking.

8. A frame-relay network doesn't perform error detection, which results in a considerably smaller amount of overhead and faster processing than X.25.

9. Frame relay is also protocol independent - it accepts data from many different protocols.

10. This data is encapsulated by the frame-relay equipment, not the network.

11. The intelligent network devices connected to a frame-relay network are responsible for the error correction and frame formatting.

12. Processing time is minimized, so the transmission of data is much faster and more efficient.

13. In addition, frame relay is entirely digital, which reduces the chance of error and offers excellent transmission rates. Frame relay typically operates at 56 kbps to 1.544 mbps.

What does Frame Relay do?

1. Frame relay sends information in packets called frames through a shared frame-relay network.

2. Each frame contains all the information necessary to route it to the correct destination.

3. So in effect, each endpoint can communicate with many destinations over one access link to the network.

4. And instead of being allocated a fixed amount of bandwidth, frame-relay services offer a CIR (committed information rate) at which data is transmitted.

5. But if traffic and your service agreement allow, data can burst above your committed rate.

Why Choose Frame Relay?

1. Since frame relay has a low overhead, it's a perfect fit for today's complex networks.

2. You get several clear benefits: First, multiple logical connections can be sent over a single physical connection, reducing your internetworking costs.

3. By reducing the amount of processing required, you get improved performance and response time.

4. And because frame relay uses a simple link layer protocol, your equipment usually requires only software changes or simple hardware modifications, so you don't have to invest a lot of money to upgrade your system.

5. Since frame relay is protocol independent, it can process traffic from different networking protocols like IP, IPX, and SNA.

6. Frame relay is an ideal choice for connecting Wide Area Networks (WANs) that have unpredictable, high-volume, and bursty traffic.

7. Typically, these applications include data transfer, CAD/CAM, and client-server applications.

8. Frame relay also offers advantages for interconnecting WANs. In the past, setting up WANs required the use of private lines or circuit switching over a leased line.

9. Single, dedicated lines are not needed to make each WAN-to-WAN connection with frame relay, reducing costs.

Permanent Virtual Circuits:

1. Essentially, a permanent virtual circuit (PVC) is your dedicated connection through the shared frame-relay network replacing a dedicated end-to-end line.

2. A PVC is needed for each site in the network, just as a private line is. But in a frame relay network, the bandwidth is shared among multiple users.

3. So any single site can communicate with any other single site without the need for multiple dedicated lines.

4. PVCs function via a Local Management Interface (LMI), which provides control procedures.

5. The control procedures function in three ways: link integrity verification initiated by the user device, network status report giving details of all PVCs, and network notification of whether a PVC's status changes from active to inactive or vice versa.

6. Data-Link Connections (DLCs) are PVCs pre-configured by both sides of the connection.

7. The DLC identifier (DLCI) is used as the logical address for frame-layer multiplexing.

Benefits:

- Virtual circuits can exist simultaneously across a given transmission line. In addition, each device can use more of the bandwidth as necessary, and thus operate at higher speeds.

- High reliability.

- Provides a cost-effective way of providing a secure private IP-based network.

- Used as a low cost carrier to replace networks of leased lines.

These factors make frame relay a desirable choice for data transmission. However, they also necessitate testing to determine that the system works properly and that data is not lost. While frame relay does not guarantee data integrity, the protocols transported over it today mainly have their own error correction mechanisms. Thus frames travel very fast and arrive at its destination with very little delay, to the extent that use of frame relay is almost like that of a direct leased line connections, only cheaper.

Advantages of Frame Relay:

Frame relay offers an attractive alternative to both dedicated lines and X.25 networks for connecting LANs to bridges and routers. The success of the frame relay protocol is based on the following two underlying factors:

- Because virtual circuits consume bandwidth only when they transport data, many virtual circuits can exist simultaneously across a given transmission line. In addition, each device can use more of the bandwidth as necessary, and thus operate at higher speeds.

- The improved reliability of communication lines and increased error-handling sophistication at end stations allows the frame relay protocol to discard erroneous frames and thus eliminate time-consuming error-handling processing.

These two factors make frame relay a desirable choice for data transmission. However, they also necessitate testing to determine that the system works properly and that data is not lost.

3.4.3 Frame Relay Structure

1. Standards for the frame relay protocol have been developed by ANSI and CCITT simultaneously.
2. The following discussion of the protocol structure includes the major points from these specifications.
3. The frame relay structure is based on the LAPD (Link Access **Protocol** - Channel D) protocol.
4. In the frame relay structure, the frame header is altered slightly to contain the Data Link Connection Identifier (DLCI) and congestion bits, in place of the normal address and control fields.
5. This new frame relay header is 2 bytes in length and has the following format:

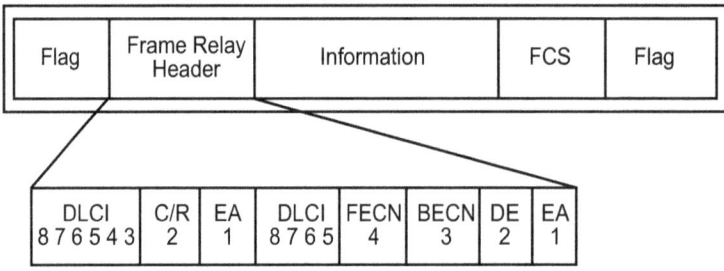

Fig. 3.29: Frame relay header structure

DLCI:

   10-bit DLCI field represents the address of the frame and corresponds to a PVC.

C/R:

   Designates whether the frame is a command or response.

EA:

   Extended Address field signifies upto two additional bytes in the frame relay header, thus greatly expanding the number of possible addresses.

FECN:

   Forward Explicit Congestion Notification (see ECN below).

BECN:

   Backward Explicit Congestion Notification (see ECN below).

DE:

   Discard Eligibility (see DE below).

Information:

   The Information field may include other protocols within it, such as an X.25, IP or SDLC (SNA) packet.

3.4.4 Frame Relay Topologies

Frame relay implementations have been deployed in a number of differing manners. Overall, the ideas behind these implementations are similar. Frame relay supports full mesh, partial mesh, and hub & spoke topologies, as follows:

- **Full Mesh**: The full mesh topology is an "all-to-all" implementation and tends to be the most robust. This topology can be considered to have a form of redundancy built into it because each router has connections to every other router (true redundancy involves multiple paths between each router). Should one connection fail, connectivity to remote networks can still be achieved via another router (as long as it was the link that failed, not the router). This topology also results in the least delay for traffic moving across the network. One disadvantage to the full mesh, however, is that it is the most expensive topology to run.

- **Partial Mesh:** The partial mesh topology is a less expensive cousin of the full mesh. Partial mesh involves redundant (multiple path redundancy, not parallel link redundancy) connections between high volume and/or critical sites co-existing with single connections from lower volume and/or
non-critical sites converging into a central site.

- **Hub and Spoke:** The hub and spoke topology consists of a central site router with connections to all remote sites. This is the most common type of topology implemented in frame relay installations. There are usually very few, if any, redundant connections. Redundant connections are typically provided by ISDN dial backup circuits.

3.4.5 The Future of Frame Relay: Interoperability with Asynchronous Transfer Mode (ATM)

1. The future of frame relay is its inter-operability with the next generation of high speed packetized data service - Asynchronous Transfer Mode (ATM).
2. ATM is a cell-based high speed network designed to transport voice, data, image, and video information.
3. Rather than variable length frames like frame relay, ATM has fixed 53 byte cells.
4. Because the "packets" have a fixed size, their delay time through a network is fixed.
5. This predictable time delay is ideal for isochronous traffic such as voice and video.
6. Many users prefer to connect their systems to ATM networks from frame relay networks rather than from native ATM networks (ATM equipment on location) because of the bandwidth constraints on low speed native ATM connections.
7. Since ATM uses a 53 byte cell with 5 bytes of header information, the native ATM packets contain about 10% overhead due to the protocol.

8. Frame relay, on the other hand, has a packet size ranging from 500 bytes to 4000 bytes and is less susceptible to protocol overhead from consuming bandwidth.

9. Frame relay access to ATM networks will not append ATM's protocol overhead until the data is in the provider's network making the added overhead invisible to the users.

Thus we can summarize the frame relay technique as follows:

- Frame relay is a technology that can create a robust wide area networking fabric that integrates information systems together to form an enterprise network.
- It is an affordable and capable service for supporting today's bandwidth intensive applications as well as those residing on legacy systems.
- Because logical connections are defined in software, it is easy to manage moves, changes, additions, and deletions of logical connections.
- Systems analysts should consider the use of frame relay for corporate applications that incorporate information systems at more than one
  location because of the technologies many technical, financial, logistical advantages.

3.4.6 Additional Possibilities and Benefits Associated with Frame Relay

1. Network managers are constantly seeking new ways to make their company networks more efficient through the use of new and innovative services that are continually being introduced into the market.

2. Often, they are faced with the need to connect remote offices to the corporate backbone to enable access to corporate e-mail, local area networks, mainframe computers, and other corporate services. Frame relay is frequently the technology of choice used to meet these needs.

3. Initially, frame relay gained acceptance as a means to provide end-users with a solution for LAN-to-LAN connections and other data connectivity requirements.

4. Besides providing a flexible and efficient data transport mechanism, frame relay lowered the cost of bandwidth for tying together multi-protocol networks and devices.

5. Over the past few years there has been a migration of legacy traffic such as bisync and SNA from low-speed leased lines onto frame relay.

6. The integration of this so-called legacy traffic with today's LAN-to-LAN connectivity needs provided network managers with a more efficient, flexible, and very cost-effective network.

7. More recently, non-traditional uses are beginning to emerge. Due to advances in areas such as digital signal processing, end-users are beginning to see viable methods, being developed, that incorporate non-data traffic such as voice and video over frame relay.

8. Voice over frame relay (VoFR) technology offers telecommunication and network managers the possibility of consolidating voice and voice-band data (i.e. fax and analog modems) with data services over frame relay.

9. The Frame Relay Forum Technical Committee has developed an Implementation Agreement [FRF.11] in order to allow vendors to interconnect their VoFR-capable equipment.

10. It is anticipated that this work will lay the groundwork for future deployment of VoFR capabilities in multi-vendor and public network environments.

11. Prior to the development of this Implementation Agreement, many equipment vendors developed proprietary methods for implementing voice over frame relay, thus enabling end-users to successfully deploy voice over their frame relay networks.

12. Frame relay will continue to see explosive growth. The acceptance and use of ATM (Asynchronous Transfer Mode, a technology designed with the intent to transport voice, data, and video) will also increase.

13. Both end-users and network service providers will increasingly find that frame relay and ATM do not only coexist, but are complementary; both frame relay and ATM access is offered to, and used by end-users.

14. In addition, service providers have begun to migrate their frame-based networks to ATM-based backbones.

15. The continued use and increased acceptance of frame relay and ATM technologies will bring greater bandwidth and high performance networking to a wider variety of user applications.

16. In addition to giving the reader some insight into how VoFR works, this section will provide an overview of a few of the potential applications of VoFR, some of the considerations faced by end-users, and an overview of the Voice over Frame Relay Implementation Agreement [FRF.11].

17. The intent of this discussion is not to promote or dissuade frame relay users from incorporating voice into their frame relay networks.

18. Instead, it is meant to provide a balanced perspective and information so that readers/users may have more information to decide for themselves as to whether they may benefit from voice over frame relay technology.

3.4.7 Voice Over Frame Relay

3.4.7.1 Theory of Operation

1. Over the years communication networks have become more reliable. Older, low speed, analog connections, which are often susceptible to network-induced errors, are being replaced with higher speed digital links offering relatively error-free performance.

2. In addition, devices communicating between sites have become more intelligent, allowing them to more readily accommodate network delay, and recover from and re-transmit lost data.

3. Unlike most data communications, which can tolerate delay, voice communications must be performed in near real-time.

4. This means that transmission and network delays must be kept small enough to remain imperceptible to the user.

5. Until recently, packetized voice transmission was not possible due to the requirements of voice bandwidth, and the transmission delays associated with packet-based networks.

6. Packetized voice is now possible; low bit rates are attained by analyzing and processing only the essential components of a voice sample, rather than attempting to digitize the entire voice sample (with all the associates pauses and repetitive patterns).

7. Current speech processing technology takes the voice digitizing process several steps further than conventional encoding methods.

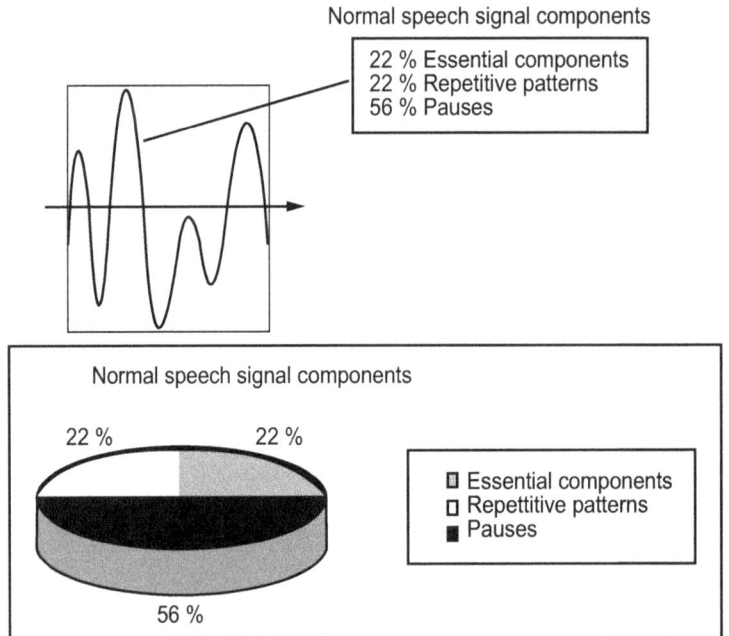

Fig. 3.30: Only 22% of normal speech needs to be sent for high-quality voice communications

8. Human speech is burdened with a tremendous amount of redundant information that is necessary for communications to occur in a natural environment, but which is not needed for a conversation to occur over a communication network.

9. Analysis of a representative voice sample shows that only 22 percent of a typical conversation consists of essential speech components that need to be transmitted for complete voice clarity (Fig. 3.30).

10. The balance is made up of pauses, background noise, and repetitive patterns.

Removal of Repetitive Speech Sounds:

1. Repetitive sounds are inherent in human speech, and are caused by vibrations of the vocal cords.

2. These repetitive sounds (like the 's' in the word *snake* or long 'o' in the word *loan*), are easily compressible.

3. While traveling through the natural environment, perhaps only half of what is spoken will reach the listener's ear.

4. However, in a typical communication network, all of the speech content is transmitted.

5. Transmission of these identical sounds is not necessary; their removal can increase bandwidth efficiency.

Removal of Pauses (Silence Suppression):

1. A person speaking does not provide a continuous stream of information (regardless of how fast he speak).

2. Pauses between words and sentences, and the gaps that occur at the end of one person talking but before the other begins, can also be removed.

3. The pauses may be represented in compressed form and can be re-created at the destination side of the call in order to maintain the natural quality of the spoken communication.

4. The suppression and removal of silent periods can also significantly improve bandwidth utilization.

Voice Frame Formation:

1. The removal of silent periods and redundant information through advanced techniques enables voice to be efficiently "compressed".

2. After the removal of repetitive patterns and silent periods, the remaining speech information may then be digitized and placed into voice packets suitable for transmission over a frame relay network.

3. These packets or frames (both terms are often used interchangeably) also tend to be smaller than the average data frame.

4.   The use of smaller packets helps to reduce transmission delay across a frame relay network.

5.   The concepts introduced above, provide the basis for efficiently using the smallest amount of bandwidth possible for voice transmission over a frame relay network.

3.4.7.2 Using Voice Over Frame Relay

Potential End User Applications:

1.   Telecommunication managers continue to explore alternatives for obtaining the most efficient use of their corporate network resources.

2.   Many network managers have migrated their point-to-point leased communication networks [built in the 1980's with TDM (Time Division Multiplexers) equipment] to public and private frame relay networks.

3.   Since many of these point-to-point leased line networks carried both voice and data, these network managers are interested in meeting not only their data communication needs, but also their voice communication needs.

4.   VoFR (voice over frame relay) offers a potential alternative for carrying voice communications over a frame relay network in order to meet intra-company communication needs.

5.   Current users of frame relay may find that they have "excess" bandwidth available even with the tremendous expansion of applications and increase in data traffic.

6.   And, even when existing bandwidth is efficiently utilized, some network managers might find that the incremental cost for the additional frame relay network bandwidth needed for voice transport is more cost-effective than some of the standard voice services offered by local and long distance carriers.

7.   In other cases, some end-users might find that VoFR is a viable option to be used in place of Off-Premises Extension (OPX) and Private Line Auto Ringdown (PLAR) lines.

8.   Of course, the motivation behind the interest in VoFR will vary.

9.   VoFR has the potential to provide end-users with greater efficiencies in the use of access bandwidth by functionally integrating voice, data, and fax over a single access link.

10. In addition, VoFR has the potential to provide end-users with a cost-effective option for the transport needs of voice traffic between their company locations.

11. As an example, a network manager may choose to integrate a few voice channels and serial data over the frame relay connection between a branch office and corporate headquarters.

12. By transmitting the voice traffic over the frame relay connection, which is already carrying data traffic (Fig. 3.31), the user has the potential to obtain cost-effective intra-company calling and efficient use of network bandwidth.

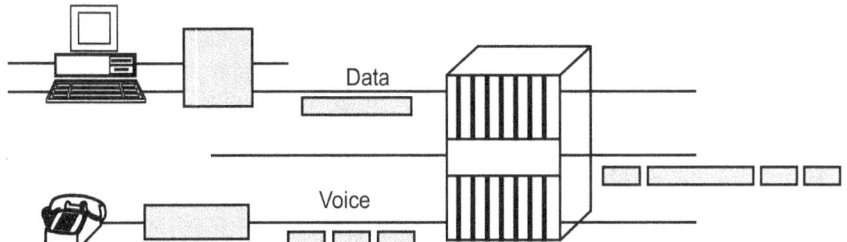

Fig. 3.31: Voice and data being integrated by customer premises equipment

13. The examples provided do not necessarily reflect all the potential possibilities of VoFR.

14. An exploration of the full possibilities and potential for the implementation of VoFR is outside the scope of this chapter.

15. There are many reasons used, and possibilities explored by network managers in their attempt to justify more efficient, flexible, and cost-effective networking capabilities.

16. VoFR represents one of many possible methods that enable users to increase the flexibility and efficiency of their company's network resources.

17. There might, however, be potential trade-offs that the network manager may face when implementing VoFR.

18. Some of the potential trade-offs may include some loss of the quality commonly associated with toll traffic due to VoFR's use of voice compression; the loss of management and administrative benefits associated with carrier voice services (i.e. the loss of consolidated voice billing and invoice itemization, end-user charge back capabilities, and other advanced features such as Caller ID and accounting codes); and the lack of standards defining the acceptable levels of quality for voice transport over a carrier's frame relay network.

19. In addition, carriers offering public frame relay service cannot always guarantee the quality or performance of voice transported over their frame relay networks.

20. In the absence of standards, there are no any specifications, which define the quality of a voice conversation (i.e. delay, tonal and pitch qualities) occurring over the carrier's frame relay service.

21. Since the quality of VoFR is subjective, it is troublesome for the carrier to guarantee complete user satisfaction.

22. The lack of specific voice over frame relay service guarantees and full carrier troubleshooting capabilities is a result of the fact that in today's environment, the implementation of voice over trame relay occurs in equipment on the end-user's premises and outside of the carrier's frame relay network.

23. The potential trade-offs do not necessarily negate the value and promise of VoFR.

24. Significant advances in digital signal processors and compression algorithms often provide voice approaching toll quality.

25. VoFR vendors continue to add advanced capabilities in management and administration capabilities. Future industry work will seek to define standards which define acceptable levels of quality and performance metrics for voice transport through data networks.

26. Some end-users might not be concerned with the potential trade-offs noted; some may find the trade-offs unacceptable in particular situations; others may find that if trade-offs exist, they are outweighed by the potential for
costs savings and efficiencies gained by integrating voice and data over frame relay.

27. In the end, it will be upto the customer to decide.

3.4.7.3 Voice Over Frame Relay Equipment

Common Considerations Faced By Equipment Vendors:

1. **Vendors offering equipment capable of integrating voice and data traffic over frame relay must consider how they will address issues such as compression, echo cancellation, delay and delay variation, frame loss, and traffic prioritization.**

2. Each of these, and other considerations, can affect voice quality.

3. While vendors offering voice over frame relay-capable equipment may have similar objectives regarding quality and performance, each vendor may choose to pursue these objectives through different hardware and software implementations.

4. Common considerations and a few of the many potential methods used to provide voice over frame relay are presented below.

Voice Compression:

1. Compression of voice is a result of the removal of the silent periods and redundant information found in human speech.

2. Voice compression is used to reduce the amount of information needed to recreate the voice at the destination end.

3. Uncompressed digitized voice and fax require a large amount of bandwidth.

4. This often makes it impractical to transmit these signals over low-speed access links. The use of low bit rate voice compression algorithms can make it possible to provide high quality speech while using bandwidth efficiently.

5. Various algorithms are used to sample speech patterns and reduce the information sent - all while retaining the highest possible level of voice quality.

6. A relatively simple ADPCM (Adaptive Delta Pulse Code Modulation) algorithm can reduce the speech data rate to half that of PCM (Pulse Code Modulation), an ITU standard for digital voice coding, which consumes 64 kbps and is optimized for speech quality.

7. PCM is the voice algorithm that is commonly used in telephone networks today.

8. ADPCM may be used in place of PCM, while maintaining about the same voice quality.

9. In addition to ADPCM, there are a number of standard low bit rate voice compression algorithms (e.g., ITU G.729) as well as proprietary algorithms implemented by various vendors, which provide more significant reductions (i.e. upto 10% or less than that of PCM) in the amount of information required to recreate speech at the receiver.

10. Other voice compression algorithms model speech more efficiently (i.e., with fewer bits) by using advanced predictive techniques.

11. These algorithms further reduce the bandwidth required to maintain good voice quality.

12. Implementation of these advanced compression techniques, and meeting their processing demands, is made possible by the use of Digital Signal Processors (DSPs).

13. A DSP is a microprocessor that is designed specifically to process digitized signals such as those found in voice and video applications.

14. In the last ten years, significant advances in the design of DSPs have occurred.

15. This development has allowed manufacturers to bring to market even higher quality digitization algorithms that consume very little bandwidth.

16. The general function of these strategies is to scrutinize the speech signal more carefully in order to eliminate the redundancies in the signal more completely, and to use the available bits to code the non-redundant parts of the signal in an efficient manner.

17. As the available bit rate is reduced from 64 kbps to 32, 16, 8, and 4 kbps or below, the strategies for redundancy removal and bit allocation need to be ever more sophisticated.

18. Low cost general purpose DSP processors and other advanced compression algorithms allow the possibility of accomplishing voice compression within VoFR-capable devices at lower and lower bit rates.

Echo Cancellation:

1. Echo is a phenomenon found in voice networks. Echo occurs when the transmitted voice is reflected back to the point from which it was transmitted.

2. In voice networks, echo cancellation devices are used within a carrier's network when the propagation delay increases to the point where echo results.

3. The longer the distance, the more the delay, and the more likely that echo will result.

4. Voice transmitted over a frame relay network will also face propagation delays.

5. As the end-to-end delay increases, the echo will become noticeable to the end-user if it is not canceled.

Delay and Delay Variation:

1. The bursty nature and variable frame sizes of frame relay may result in variable delays between consecutive packets.

2. The variation in the time difference between each arriving packet is called "jitter".

3. Jitter can impede the ability of the receiving end CPE to smoothly regenerate voice.

4. Since voice is inherently a continuous waveform, a large gap between the regenerated voice packets will result in distorted sound.

5. Equipment vendors can contribute to the mitigation of jitter across the network by employing fragmentation of data packets in order to transmit uniform packet sizes into the network.

6. To avoid dropping speech samples, data can be buffered sufficiently at the speech decoder to account for the worst-case delay jitter through the network.

7. Equipment vendors look to incorporate this capability within their equipment.

Frame Loss:

1. Compressed voice can usually withstand infrequent packet loss better than data can.

2. If a voice packet is lost, most likely the user will not notice.

3. If excessive frame loss occurs, it is equally unacceptable for VoFR and for data traffic.

Traffic Integration - Fax and Modem Support:

1. Vendors implementing VoFR technology appear to be mimicking switched public voice services.

2. Since VoFR supports fax and data modem services as well, end-users, who have high fax traffic volumes between branches and headquarters, will find this ability beneficial.

3. Voice band fax signals are demodulated at the locally connected equipment and transmitted over the network as digital data in a standard packet format.

4. In effect, the local Voice FRAD tricks the fax machine into thinking it is connected to a remote fax machine across an analog network.

5. However, it is difficult to reliably compress fax and data modem signals to achieve the low bandwidth utilization often necessary for the most efficient integration over frame relay.

6. Some vendors have implemented schemes where voice is compressed to a low bit rate, but upon detection of a fax tone, the bandwidth is reallocated to a higher bit rate to allow for faster fax transmission.

Prioritization:

1. Voice, fax and some data types are delay-sensitive.

2. This means that if the end-to-end delay or the delay variation exceeds a specified limit, the service level will get degraded.

3. To minimize the potential for service degradation, vendors can employ a variety of mechanisms and techniques.

4. To minimize voice traffic delay, a prioritization mechanism that provides service to the delay-sensitive traffic can first be employed.

5. Vendors offering equipment capable of integrating voice and data over frame relay may choose to use a variety of proprietary mechanisms to ensure a balance between voice and data transmission needs.

6. Although they may differ, the concept remains essentially the same.

7. For example, each input traffic type may be configured into one of several priority queues.

8. Voice and fax traffic can be placed in the highest-priority queue, for expeditious delivery to the network.

9. Lower-priority data traffic can be buffered until the higher-priority voice and fax packets are sent (Fig. 3.32 below).

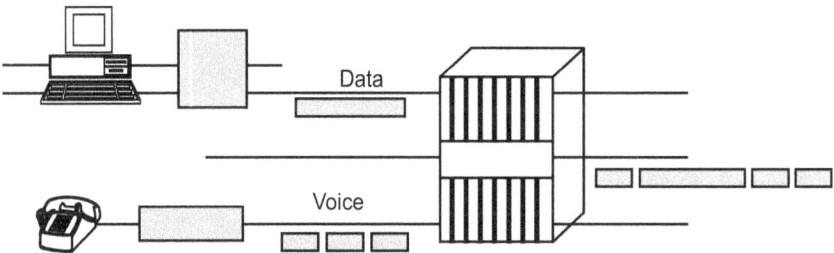

Fig. 3.32: Prioritization places delay-sensitive traffic, such as voice, ahead of lower priority data transmissions

Fragmentation:

1. Fragmentation is used to break up large blocks of data into smaller, less delay-creating frames.
2. This is another means used to ensure the highest level of voice quality possible.
3. Fragmentation attempts to ensure an even flow of voice frames into the network, thus minimizing delay jitter across circuits that carry both, packet-voice and data.

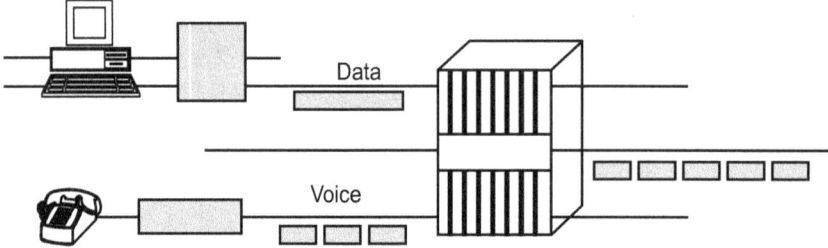

Fig. 3.33: Fragmentation Ensures that High Priority Traffic, such as Voice, does not have to wait to be sent. Long Data Packets can be Interrupted to Send a Voice Packet

4. Fragmentation often involves all of the data in the network, to retain consistent voice quality.
5. This is because even if the voice information is fragmented, delay will still occur if a voice frame is held up in the "middle" of the network, behind a large data frame.
6. This fragmentation of data packets (as shown in Fig. 3.33) ensures that voice and fax packets are not unacceptably delayed behind large data packets.
7. Additionally, fragmentation reduces jitter because voice packets can be sent and received more regularly.
8. Fragmentation, especially when used with prioritization techniques, is used to ensure a consistent flow of voice information.
9. The objective of this and other techniques is to enable VoFR technology to provide service approaching toll quality voice.
10. The Frame Relay Forum recommends the use of the Fragmentation Implementation Agreement [FRF.12] when employing fragmentation for VoFR.

Digital Speech Interpolation:

1. Digital speech interpolation addresses silence suppression.
2. The nature of speech communication entails pauses between words and sentences.
3. Advanced voice compression algorithms, which identify and remove these redundant patterns, effectively reduce the amount of speech information to be transmitted.
4. DSI uses advanced voice processing techniques to detect silence periods and suppress transmission of this information.
5. By taking advantage of this technique, bandwidth consumption may be reduced.

Multiplexing Techniques:

1. Some equipment vendors offering voice FRADs (Frame Relay Access Devices) use different bandwidth optimization multiplexing techniques such as Logical Link Multiplexing and Subchannel Multiplexing.

2. Logical Link Multiplexing allows voice and data frames to share the same PVC (Permanent Virtual Circuit).

3. This can provide savings on carrier PVC charges and increase the utilization of the PVC.

4. Subchannel Multiplexing is a technique used to combine multiple voice conversations within the same frame.

5. By allowing multiple voice payloads to be sent in a single frame, packet overhead is reduced.

6. This may offer increased performance on low speed links.

7. This technique can allow slow speed connections to transport small voice packets efficiently across the frame relay network.

Other Considerations:

1. In addition to providing basic services such as encapsulation of data traffic for transport over the frame relay network, voice capable FRADs may sometimes provide connectivity between PBXs and other voice equipment.

2. As a result, the voice FRAD would have to manage different traffic types and accommodate their different needs.

3. When voice is carried over a frame relay network that employs ATM in the backbone, there is no impact due to the use of the ATM backbone since ATM functions purely as a transport medium.

3.4.7.4 Voice Over Frame Relay Implementation Agreement (FRF.11)

Overview:

1. Frame Relay Forum Implementation Agreements provide an agreed upon basis for vendors and service providers to develop equipment and services that inter-operate.

2. In the case of VoFR, as with many emerging technologies, vendors are often able to develop and deploy capabilities before the various industry and user organizations achieve consensus on uniform standards and implementations.

3. FRF.11 provides an outline for an agreed-upon basis for VoFR so that companies may build equipment and offer services that will be capable of functionally inter-operating with each other.

4. The IA addresses the following:
   - Transport of compressed voice within the payload of a frame relay frame, via the support of a diverse set of voice compression algorithms such as CS-ACELP, LD CELP, MP-MLQ, PCM, etc.
   - Effective utilization of low bit rate frame relay connections.
   - Multiplexing of upto 255 sub-channels on a single frame relay DLCI, such that a single DLCI may contain both voice and data payloads.
   - Support of multiple voice payloads on the same or different sub-channel(s) within a single frame.

3.4.7.5 Reference Model

1. The reference model for VoFR is shown in Fig. 3.34. Using the VoFR feature, it is possible for any type of VFRAD on the left-hand side of Fig. 3.34 to exchange voice and signaling information with any type of VFRAD on the right-hand side of Fig. 3.34.

2. Three types of devices are shown in Fig. 3.34. The top layer shows end-system devices similar to telephones or fax machines; the middle layer shows transparent multiplexing devices similar to channel banks; the bottom layer shows switching system devices similar to PBX's.

3. A VFRAD connects to a frame relay UNI via physical interfaces as defined in [FRF.1.1].

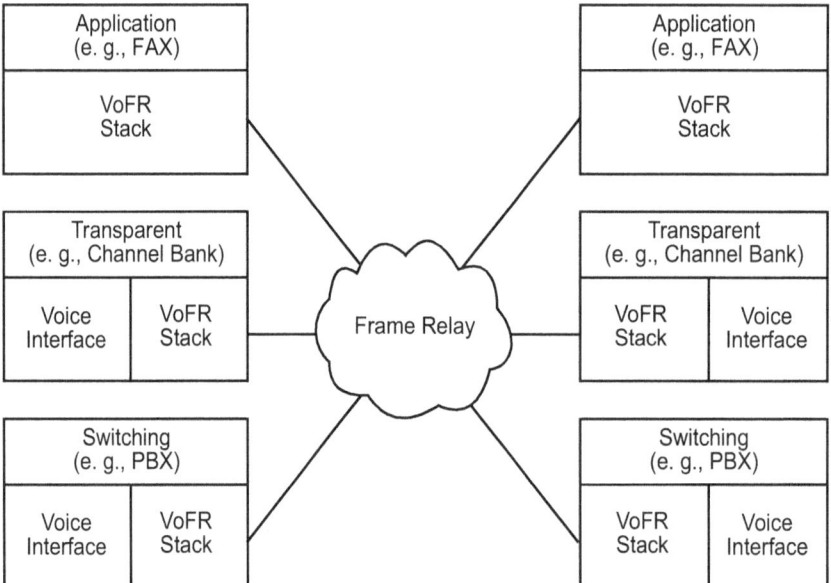

Fig. 3.34: Voice over frame relay network reference model

Thus we can summarize the frame relay technology as follows:

- Frame relay is beginning to evolve from a single, data-only application technology to one with a broad spectrum of uses.
- Integration of voice and data over frame relay represents one of many promising areas of development that could not only benefit end users, but one that could continue to fuel the continued growth of frame relay services and applications.
- Voice over frame relay (VoFR) technology consolidates voice and voice-band data (i.e. fax and analog modems) with data services over the frame relay network.
- It has the potential to provide end-users with greater efficiencies in the use of access bandwidth and to provide end-users with cost-effective transport of voice traffic for intra-company communications.

3.5 ATM Networks

Introduction:

1. Asynchronous transfer mode (ATM) is an advanced implementation of packet switching that provides high-speed data transmission rates to send fixed-size packets over broadband and baseband LANs or WANs.

2. ATM can accommodate:

   - Voice
   - Data
   - Fax
   - Real-time video
   - CD-quality audio
   - Imaging.
   - Multimegabit data transmission.

3. The CCITT defined ATM in 1988 as part of the broadband Integrated Services Digital Network (BISDN), discussed later in this lesson.

4. Because of ATM's power and versatility, it is influencing the development of network communications.

5. It is equally adaptable to LAN and WAN environments, and it can transmit data at very high speeds (155 Mbps to 622 Mbps or more).

ATM Technology:

1. ATM is a broadband cell relay method that transmits data in 53-byte cells rather than in variable-length frames.

2. Fig. 3.35 illustrates an ATM cell. These cells consist of 48 bytes of application information with five additional bytes of ATM header data.

3. For example, ATM would divide a 1000-byte packet into 21 data frames and put each data frame into a cell.

4. The result is a technology that transmits a consistent, uniform packet.

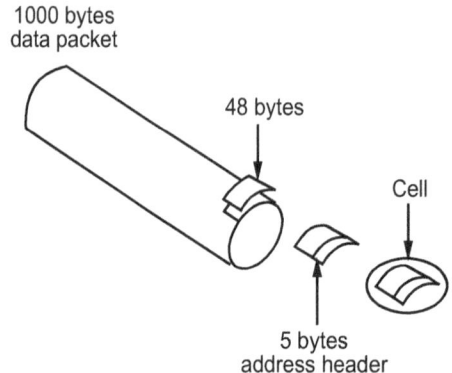

Fig. 3.35: ATM cells have 48 bytes of data and a 5-byte header

5. Network equipment can switch, route, and move uniform-sized frames much more quickly than it can move random-sized frames.

6. The consistent, standard-sized cell uses buffers efficiently and reduces the work required to process incoming data. The uniform cell size also helps in planning application bandwidth.

7. Theoretically, ATM can offer throughput rates of upto 1.2 gigabits per second.

8. Currently, however, ATM measures its speed against fiber-optic speeds that can reach as high as 622 Mbps, most commercial ATM boards will transmit data at about 155 Mbps.

9. As a reference point, at 622 Mbps ATM could transmit the entire contents of the latest edition of the *Encyclopedia Britannica*, including graphics, in less than one second. If the same transfer were tried using a 2400-baud modem, the operation would take more than two days.

10. ATM can be used in LANs and WANs at approximately the same speed in each.

11. ATM relies on carriers such as AT&T and Sprint for implementation over a wide area.

12. This creates a consistent environment that does away with the concept of the slow WAN and the differing technologies used in the LAN and WAN environments.

ATM Components:

1. ATM components are currently available through only a limited number of vendors.

2. All hardware in an ATM network must be ATM-compatible.

3. Implementing ATM in an existing facility will require extensive equipment replacement.

4.   This is one reason why ATM has not been adopted more quickly.

However, as the ATM market matures, various vendors will be able to provide:

- Routers and switches to connect carrier services on a global basis.
- Backbone devices to connect all the LANs within a large organization.
- Switches and adapters that link desktop computers to high-speed ATM connections for running multimedia applications.

5.   **ATM Media:** ATM does not restrict itself to any particular media type. It can be used with existing media designed for other communication systems including:

- Coaxial cable.
- Twisted-pair cable.
- Fiber-optic cable.

6.   However, these traditional network media, in their present forms, do not support all of ATM's capabilities. An organization called the ATM Forum recommends the following physical interfaces for ATM:

- FDDI (100 Mbps)
- Fiber Channel (155 Mbps)
- OC3 SONET (155 Mbps)
- T3 (45 Mbps)

7.   **ATM Switches:** ATM switches are multiport devices that can act as either of the following:

- Hubs to forward data from one computer to another within a network.
- Router-like devices to forward data at high speeds to remote networks.

8.   In some network architectures, such as Ethernet and Token Ring, only one computer at a time can transmit. In Fig. 3.36, three routers are feeding data into the ATM switch and onto the ATM network at the same time.

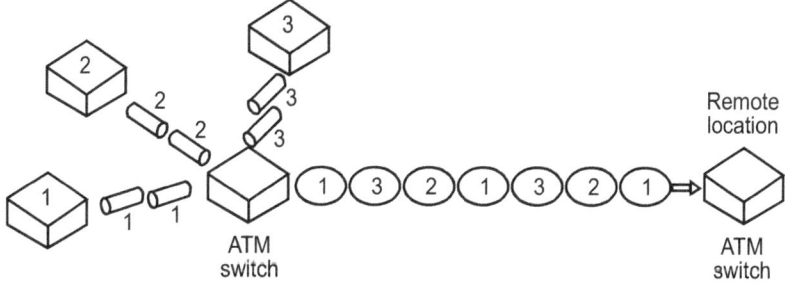

Fig. 3.36: ATM switches act as multiplexers allowing multiple data input

3.5.1 Why ATM?

1. ATM stands for Asynchronous Transfer Mode.
2. ATM is a connection-oriented technique that requires information to be buffered and then placed in a cell.
3. When there is enough data to fill the cell, the cell is then transported across the network to the destination specified within the cell.
4. We can see that ATM is very similar to packet-switched networks, but there are several important differences:
   - ATM provides cell sequence integrity. i.e. cells arrive at the destination in the same order as they left the source. This may not be the case with other packet-switched networks.
   - Cells are much smaller than standard packet-switched networks. This reduces the value of delay variance, making ATM acceptable for timing sensitive information like voice.
   - The quality of transmission links has lead to the omission of overheads, such as error correction, in order to maximize efficiency.
   - There is no space between cells. At times when the network is idle, unassigned cells are transported.
5. These are the techniques that allow ATM to be more flexible than Narrow-band ISDN (N-ISDN), and hence ATM was chosen as the broadband access to ISDN by the CCITT (now ITU - International Telecommunication Union).
6. The broadband nature of ATM allows for a multitude of different types of services to be transported using the same format.
7. This makes ATM ideal for true integration of voice, data and video facilities on one network. By consolidation of services, network management and operation is simplified.
8. However, new terms of network administration must be considered, such as billing rates and quality of service agreements.
9. The flexibility inherent in the cell structure of ATM allows it to match the rate at which it transmits to that generated by the source.
10. Many new high bit-rate services, such as video, are variable bit rate (VBR). Compression techniques create bursty data which is well suited for transmission using ATM cells.

3.5.2 The Protocol Reference Model

1. In a similar way to the OSI 7-layer model, ATM has also developed a protocol reference model, consisting of a control plane, user plane and management plane.
2. The model also incorporates SAPs, SDUs and PDUs that are also mentioned in the OSI layered approach.

3. As the diagram below shows, the User plane (for information transfer) and Control plane (for call control) are structured in layers.

4. Above the Physical Layer rests the ATM Layer and the ATM Adaptation Layer (AAL). Management provides network supervision. **The ATM reference model relates to the lowest two layers of the OSI reference model.**

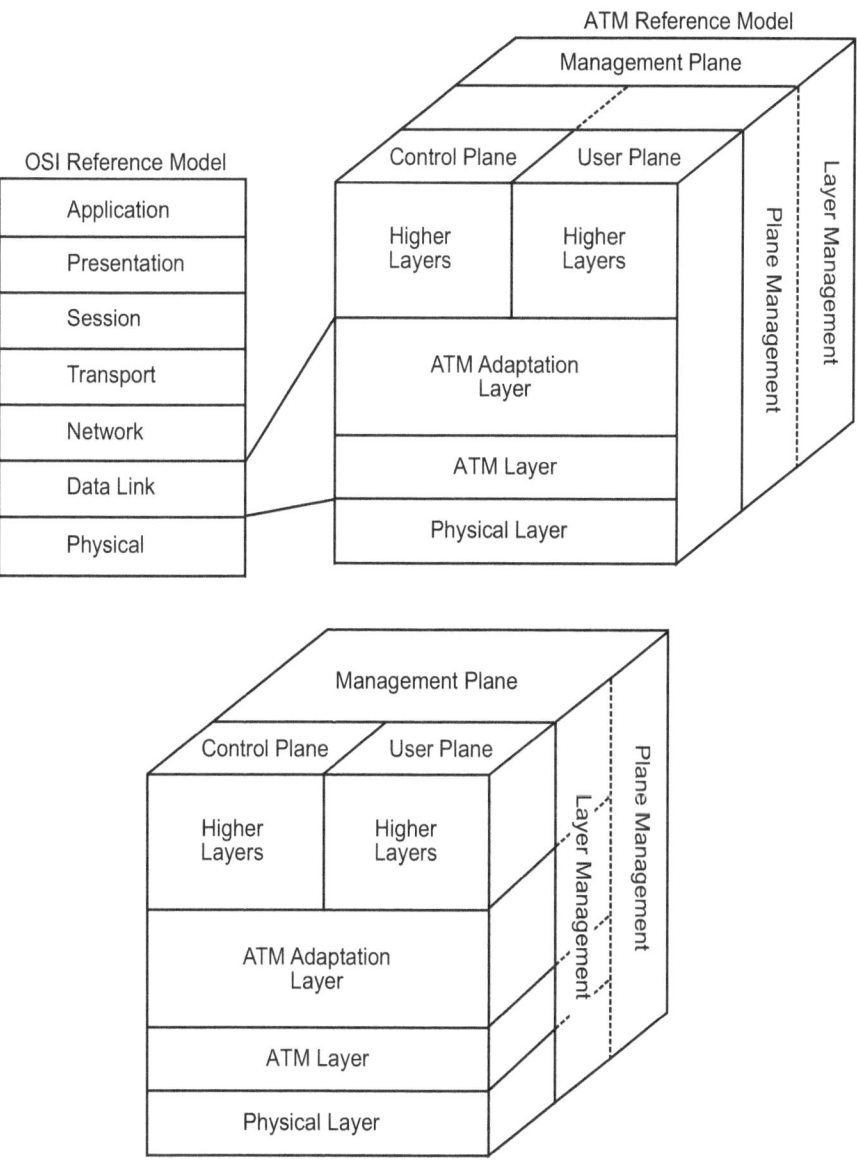

Fig. 3.37: ATM has also developed a protocol reference model, consisting of a control plane, user plane and management plane

The AAL and Physical layers are further divided into sublayers, and the functions of these layers are shown below.

Layer/Sublayer	Function
ATM Adaptation Layer Convergence Sublayer Segmentation and Reassembly Sublayer	Convergence Segmentation and Reassembly
ATM Layer	Generic Flow Control Cell header generation/extraction Cell VPI/VCI translation Cell multiplex and demultiplex
Physical Layer Transmission Convergence Sublayer Physical Medium Sublayer	Cell-rate decoupling HEC header generation/check Cell delineation Bit timing Physical medium

ATM Layer:

Responsibilities:

1. The ATM layer is responsible for transporting information across the network.
2. ATM uses virtual connections for information transport.
3. The connections are deemed virtual because although the users can connect end-to-end, connection is only made when a cell needs to be sent.
4. The connection is not dedicated to the use of one conversation. The connections are divided into two levels:
   - The Virtual Path
   - The Virtual Channel

These are the properties of the VP and VC that allow cell multiplexing. There is a complication in that cell switching requires only the value of the VP identifier, VPI to be known.

Cell Structure:

1. The structure of the cell is important for the overall functionality of the ATM network.

2. A large cell gives a better payload to overhead ratio, but at the expense of longer, more variable delays.

3. Shorter packets overcome this problem, however the amount of information carried per packet is reduced.

4. A compromise between these two conflicting requirements was reached, and a standard cell format chosen.

5. The ATM cell consists of a 5-octet header and a 48-octet information field after the header. This is shown below.

Header 5 bytes	Payload 48 bytes

Fig. 3.38: ATM cell

6. The information contained in the header is dependent on whether the cell is carrying information from the user network to the first ATM public exchange (User-Network Interface - UNI), or between ATM exchanges in the trunk network (Network-Node Interface - NNI).

7. The formats of the two types of header are shown below.

8. Notice the similarity between the two, with only the UNI having a Generic Flow Control, GFC, field.

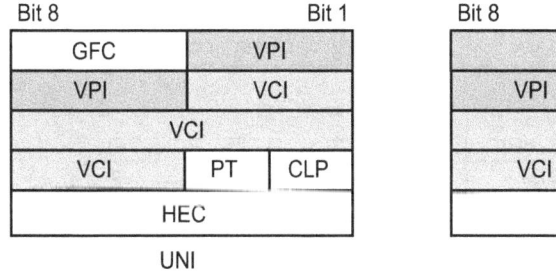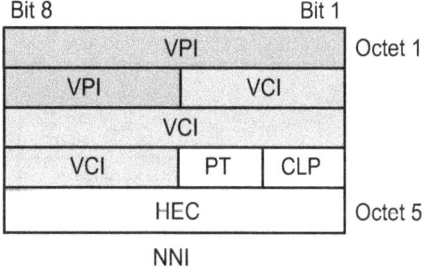

Fig. 3.39: Descriptions of all the fields contained in the ATM cell headers, GFC, VPI, VCI, PT, CLP, HEC, are found in the ATM dictionary

(CLP – Cell Loss Priority, PT – Payload Type, HEC – Header Error Control)

Virtual Channels:

1. The connection between two endpoints is called a Virtual Channel Connection, VCC.

2. It is made up of a series of virtual channel links that extend between VC switches.

3. The VC is identified by a Virtual Channel Identifier, VCI.

4. The value of the VCI will change as it enters a VC switch, due to routing translation tables.

5.   Within a virtual channel link the value of the VCI remains constant.

6.   The VCI (and VPI) are used in the switching environment to ensure that channels and paths are routed correctly.

7.   They provide a means for the switch to distinguish between different types of connection.

8.   There are many types of virtual channel connections, these include:
     •   User-to-user applications: Between customer equipment at each end of the connection.
     •   User-to-network applications: Between customer equipment and network node.
     •   Network-to-network applications: Between two network nodes and includes traffic management and routing.

9.   Virtual channel connections have the following properties:
     •   A VCC user is provided with a quality of service, QoS, specifying parameters such as cell-loss ratio, (CLR), and cell-delay variation, (CDV).
     •   VCCs can be switched or semi-permanent.
     •   Cell sequence integrity is maintained within a VCC.
     •   Traffic parameters can be negotiated, using the Usage Parameter Control, (UPC).

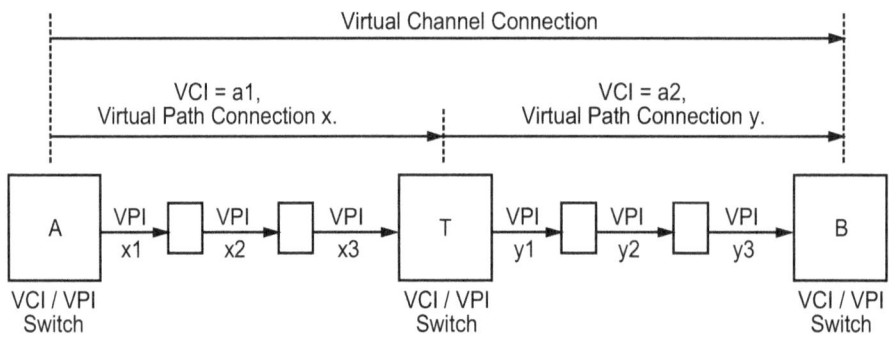

Virtual channel view

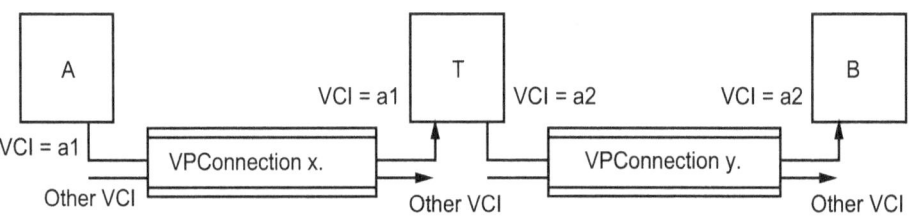

Fig. 3.40: A detailed diagram showing the relationship between virtual channels and paths is shown

Virtual Paths:

1. A virtual path (VP) is a term for a bundle of virtual channel links that all have the same endpoints.

2. As with VCs, virtual path links can be strung together to form a virtual path connection (VPC).

3. A VPC endpoint is where its related VPIs are originated, terminated or translated.

4. Virtual paths are used to simplify the ATM addressing structure.

5. VPs provide logical direct routes between switching nodes via intermediate cross-connect nodes.

6. A virtual path provides the logical equivalent of a link between two switching nodes that are not necessarily directly connected on a physical link.

7. It therefore allows a distinction between logical and physical network structure and provides the flexibility to rearrange the logical structure according to traffic requirements. This is best shown in the diagram above.

8. As with VCs, virtual paths are identified in the cell header with the Virtual Path Identifier (VPI).

9. Within an ATM cross-connect, information about individual virtual channels within a virtual path is not required, as all VCs within one path follow the same route as that path.

ATM Adaptation Layer:

Responsibilities:

1. The ATM Adaptation Layer (AAL) performs the necessary mapping between the ATM layer and the higher layers.

2. This task is usually performed in terminal equipment, or terminal adaptors (TA) at the edge of the ATM network.

3. The ATM network is independent of the services it carries.

4. Thus, the user payload is carried transparently by the ATM network.

5. The ATM network does not process, or know the structure of the payload.

6. This is known as semantic independence.

7. The ATM network is also time independent, as their is no relationship between the timing of the source application and the network clock.

8. All of this independence must be built into the boundary of the ATM network, and falls into the realm of the AAL. The AAL must also cope with:
   - Data flow to application
   - Cell delay variation, CDV
   - Loss of cells
   - Misdelivery of cells

9. It would have been possible to develop seperate AALs for each type of telecommunication service offered, however, the many common factors between services has meant that a small set of AAL protocols is sufficient to cover the envisaged possibilities.

10. A telecommunication service is defined on the following parameters:
    *   Timing relationship between source and destination.
    *   Bit-rate.
    *   Connection mode.

11. Parameters such as communication assurance are treated as quality of service parameters. As a result, four classes of service have been defined.

Class:	A	B	C	D
Timing relationship between source and destination	Required		Not Required	
Bit rateConstant		Variable		
Connection mode	Connection-oriented			Connectionless

Fig. 3.41: There are four classes of service

12. The classes of service are general concepts, but these they are mapped onto different specific AAL types.
    *   Class A: AAL 1.
    *   Class B: AAL 2.
    *   Class C & D: AAL 3/4.
    *   Class C & D: AAL 5.

13. The AAL is organised on two sublayers:
    *   The Convergence Sublayer.
    *   The Segmentation and Reassembly Sublayer.

14. Information pertaining to the CS and SAR is found in the ATM dictionary.

15. The CS, which performs the tasks of processing cell delay variation, synchronisation and handling cell loss, is broken up into two parts:
    *   The Service Specific CS (SSCS)
    *   The Common Part CS (CPCS)

16. Again, information about these two sublayers is found in the dictionary.

17. A diagram below shows the relationship between the layers and sublayers of the AAL.

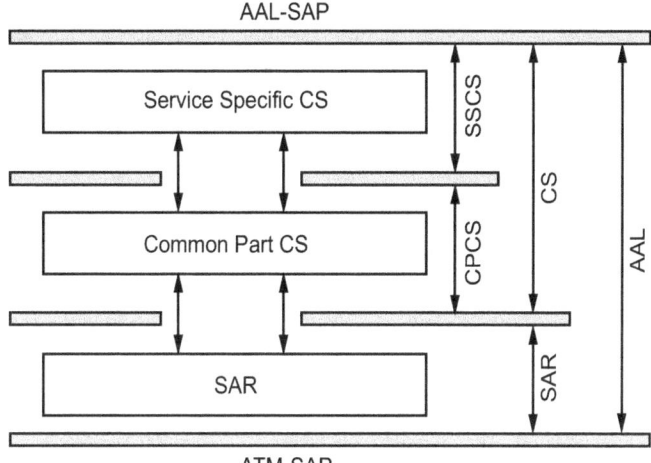

Fig. 3.42: Relationship between the layers and sublayers of the AAL

18. Information that moves between layers of the AAL follows a naming convention.
19. Protocol Data Units (PDUs) contain the information between peer layers, while Service Data Units (SDUs) pass data across Service Access Points (SAPs).
20. This is shown clearly in a diagram in the ATM dictionary.
21. Below is a list of the defined AAL types. Contained with each type is a list of applications suited to that particular AAL.

AAL Type 1:
- Circuit transport to support synchronous (e.g. 64 kBit/s) and asynchronous (e.g. 1.5, 2 MBit/s) circuits.
- Video signal transport for interactive and distributive services.
- Voice band signal transport.
- High quality audio transport.

AAL Type 2:
AAL 2 has not currently been defined, but services for this type may include:
- Transfer of service data units with a variable source bit-rate.
- Transfer of timing information between source and destination.

AAL Types 3/4:
- AAL 3 was designed for connection-oriented data, while AAL 4 for connectionless-oriented data.
- They have now been merged to form AAL 3/4.
- The structure of the layers for an AAL 3/4 is shown in Fig. 3.43.
- Note how the user data for payload does not take up all of the payload area of the cell.

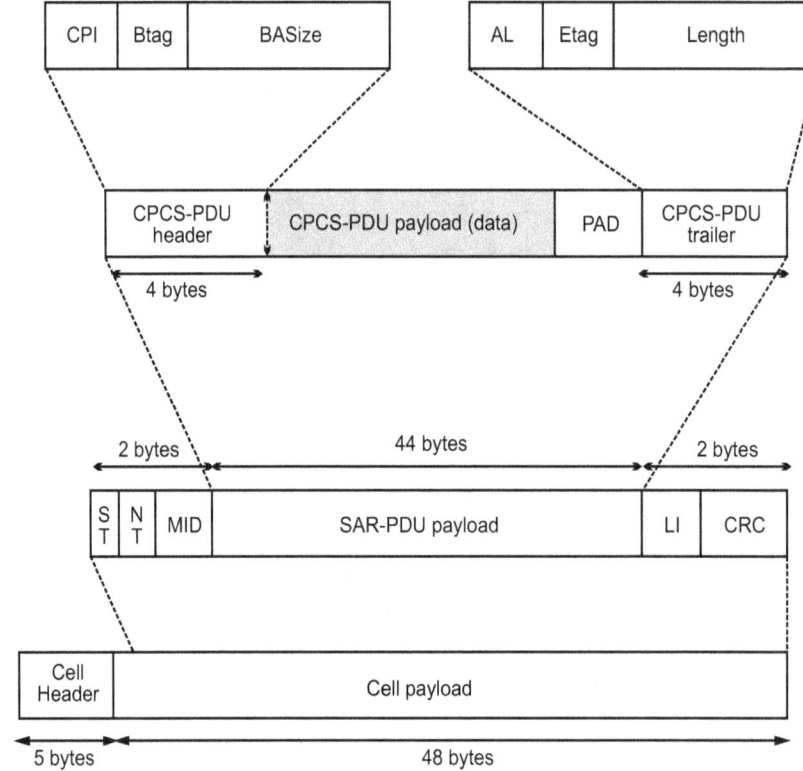

Fig. 3.43: The structure of the layers for an AAL 3/4 is shown in the diagram

- (ST) Segment Type (2 bits): Indicates whether segment is beginning, continuation, end or single segment message.
- (SN) Sequence Number (4 bits): Allows sequence of SAR-PDUs to be numbered modulo 16.
- (MID) Multiplexing Identification (10 bits): Allows for more than one connection over a single ATM-layer connection. The value of the MID must be unique over the current VP only.
- (LI) Length Indicator (6 bits): Indicates the number of bytes of CS-PDU information in the SAR-PDU, as the amount of information may not fill the 44 bytes available.
- (CRC) Cyclic Redundancy Check Code (10 bits): Used to detect errors in the SAR-PDU. This includes the CS_PDU and user data.
- (CPI) Common part indicator (1 octet).
- (Btag) Beginning tag (1 octet).
- (BASize) Buffer Size allocation (2 octets).
- (PAD) Padding (0 to 3 octets).
- (AL) Alignment (1 octet).
- (Etag) End tag (1 octet).
- (length) Length of CPSU-PDU payload (2 octets).

AAL Type 5:

- AAL 5 is designed for the same class of service as AAL 3/4, but contains less overheads.
- It allows the full 48 bytes of payload to be used for transportation of CS-PDU segments, not just SAR-PDU segments.
- There is a CRC field incorporated into the CS-PDU field, as indicated below.

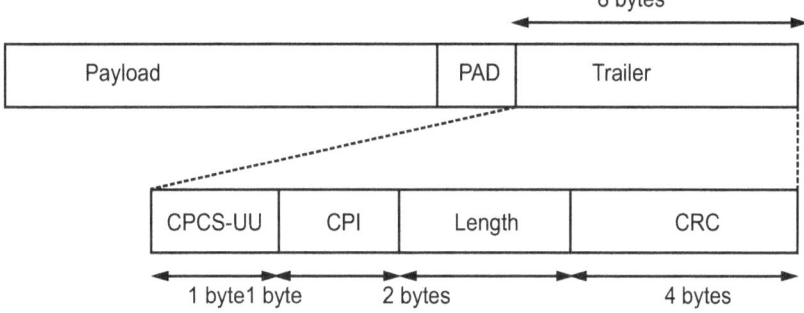

Fig. 3.44: CRC field incorporated into the CS-PDU field

Physical Layer:

Responsibilities:

The physical layer has two sublayers:

- Physical Medium sublayer.
- Transmission Convergence sublayer.

The physical layer is responsible for the transmission of the data across a physical link, in much the same way as the physical layer of the OSI reference model. The diagram below shows the role of the interface between the ATM layer and the physical layer.

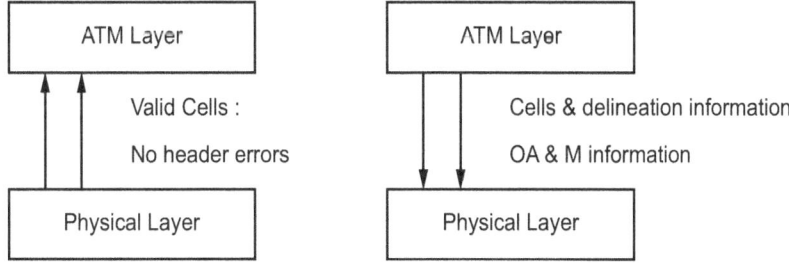

Fig. 3.45: The role of the interface between the ATM layer and the physical layer

Transfer Capacity:

1. The CCITT Recommendation I.432 defines two bit-rates for the physical layer:
    - 155 520 kBit/s.
    - 622 080 kBit/s.

2. The transportation medium may either be electrical or optical, and can use SDH-based or cell-based framing.
3. Different countries are currently introducing SDH (Synchronous Digital Hierarchy) into their network and so this chapter will concentrate on this framing for ATM.
4. The bit rates mentioned above are the gross bit rates of the physical layer and hence contain transportation overheads of the carrier, and also of the layers above the physical layer (ATM Adaptation Layer and ATM Layer).
5. This causes the actual user data bit rate to be less than the gross rate by a significant amount.
6. The values shown in the table below are based on a SDH frame structure. The column "fraction available" shows the ratio of payload to (payload plus header).
7. Thus, a SDH frame (see below) allows 260 bytes of payload and 10 bytes of overhead and pointers.
8. This gives a fraction of 260/270. Similarly for ATM cell formats, payload is   48 bytes and overheads 5 bytes, giving a fraction of 48/(48 + 5) = 48/53.
9. The final value of cell-payload bit rate does not allow for space taken up in the payload by AAL format types and related headers, (e.g. CRCs, MIDs, CPIs, etc).
10. Thus the maximum available bit-rate to the user cannot reach that of the maximum available for cell-payload and is dependent on the AAL type used.

	Fraction available	STM-1 (kBit/s)	STM-4 (kBit/s)
Gross Physical Layer bit-rate	1.0	155 520	622 080
Maximum bit-rate for ATM cells	260/270	149 760	599 040
Maximum bit-rate for ATM payload	48/53	135 631	542 526

Fig. 3.46: Different Bit Rates

3.5.3 Connection-Orientated Service

Signalling Principles:

1. ATM is a connection-orientated technique.
2. A connection within the ATM layer consists of one or more links, each of which is assigned an identifier.
3. A lot of applications, such as Constant Bit Rate (CBR) Services and X.25 data service are best handled by connection-orientated communications.
4. With ATM and other connection-orientated techniques, a connection has to be established before information transfer takes place.
5. ATM uses an out of band signaling system in dedicated Signaling Virtual Channels (SVCs).

6.   There are different types of SVCs for different requirements:

- The Meta-Signalling Virtual Channel (MSVC) is bi-directional and permanent. It is used to establish, check and release point-to-point and selective broadcast SVCs.

- The point-to-point signalling channel is bidirectional and is used to establish, control and release VCCs and VPCs that carry user data.

- Broadcast SVCs are unidirectional and can send signalling messages to all, or select endpoints.

- General SVCs are like Broadcast SVCs, but do not allow selected groups.

Traffic Control:

In order for a broadband network based on ATM to achieve a high level of performance, traffic control capabilities have to be introduced. The CCITT Recommendations are as follows:

- Connection admission control.

- Usage parameter control.

- Priority control.

- Congestion control.

These control mechanisms are outlined below.

Connection Admission Control:

Connection admission control is the set of actions taken by the network at the call setup phase in order to establish whether a VC/VP connection can be established.   A connection can only be established if the network resources are available to provide the required quality of service. The introduction of a new connection should not affect the QoS of other established connections. Source traffic can be identified by parameters such as,

- Peak duration
- Average bit rate
- Burstiness
- Peak bit rate

Usage Parameter Control:

Usage parameter control is the set of actions taken by the network to monitor and control user traffic volume and cell routing validity. Its main purpose is to protect network resources from malicious as well as unintentional misbehaviour, which can affect the QoS parameters of existing connections by detecting violations of negotiated parameters. **UPC** includes monitoring the following functions:

- Validity of VPI/VCI values.
- Monitoring VP/VC traffic volumes to check for violations.
- Monitoring total traffic volumes on links.

Priority Control:

Priority Control is determined using the cell loss priority bit in the cell header. Information can be broken into more and less important parts. Thus different components of the same signal will be treated differently by the network control mechanisms.

Congestion Control:

1. Congestion is defined as a state of network elements in which, due to traffic overload, the network is not able to guarantee a QoS to already established connections and to new connection requests.
2. Congestion control tries to minimise congestion effects and avoid the problem spreading. Congestion control could, for example, reduce the peak bit rate available to a user.

Cell Delay Variation and Queues:

1. As explained above, the small sized cells allow for small delay variation, CDV.
2. This is useful for the transportation of isochronous media, which requires data (especially voice) to be sent at fixed intervals.
3. Small delay variation allows for "virtual" isochronous transmission.
4. Traffic shaping schemes try to shape traffic into isochronous flow, with regular time intervals at the output.
5. The leaky bucket is an example of a traffic shaping scheme.
6. The leaky bucket algorithm uses a buffer of finite size that incoming traffic is placed into.
7. Traffic is allowed to drain out of the bucket and sent on the network at a rate, p. Excess data that cannot fit into the buffer is discarded.
8. The leaky bucket algorithm has the effect of shaping bursty traffic into a flow of equally spaced cells, each being emitted 1/p units of time after the previous cell.
9. The size of the buffer limits the cell delay. Hence to limit CDV, a small buffer is required.

3.5.4 Connectionless Service

1. ATM is connection-orientated communication.
2. However, there are many applications, such as mail services and other data services that are characterized by small amounts of data, sent sporadically.
3. To save time and expense, no connection is established - i.e. a connectionless service. User information is sent in a message containing all necessary addressing and routing information.
4. This is used in local area networks that employ Carrier Sense Multiple Access with Collision Detection (CSMA/CD) network structures (e.g. ethernet).
5. It is possible for ATM to be used in a connectionless configuration.
6. An ATM connectionless data service allows the transfer of information among service subscribers without the need for end-to-end call establishment.
7. A connectionless data service will require the introduction of connectionless servers.
8. The connectionless servers route cells to their destination according to the routing information contained in the cells.
9. The connectionless service sits on top of ATM, i.e. it is not integrated into the functionality of the ATM switch.
10. This requires a direct connection between each user and the connectionless server.
11. These connections can be semi-permanent or switched.
12. The use of direct connection means that only n connections are required for n users.
13. Fig. 3.47 indicates the provision of a connectionless service on ATM.

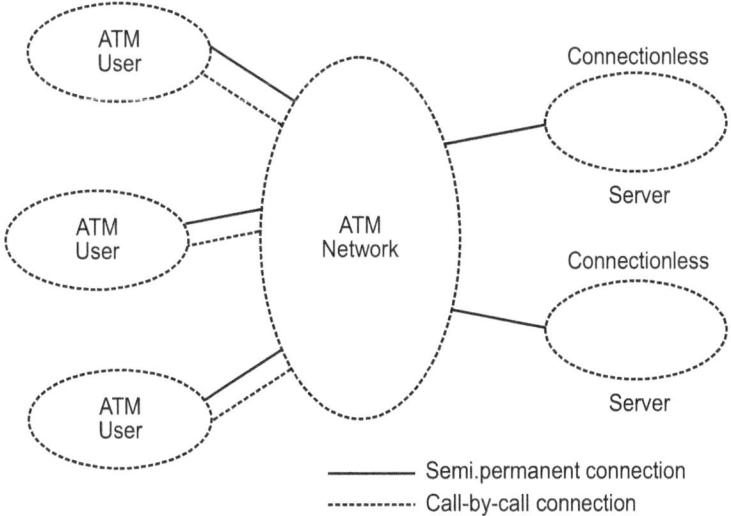

Fig. 3.47

3.5.5 LAN Traffic over ATM

1. The first ATM networks are likely to be installed by companies that have a specific high bandwidth need.

2. These could include single locations, between buildings (across a campus), or across a high speed (E3) link.

3. Other solutions to the joining of LANs exist, such as FDDI. However, these solutions are not suitable for the Wide Area Networks (WANs), and the data must be transformed into something else for transmission.

4. ATM, on the other hand, if used throughout the LAN, then the transition to a MAN or WAN would be "seamless", as the same language and technologies would be used throughout.

5. This is an example of the **scalability** of ATM - the ability to handle different bit rates for different situations, and being able to upgrade to higher rates as technology progresses.

3.5.6 ATM LAN Network Configurations

1. This section of the chapter covers topologies of different ATM network configurations.

2. This includes some migrations towards ATM based solutions, as well as highlighting problems of other non ATM-based solutions.

3. As LANs increasingly require communication with each other, due to multimedia and other bandwidth hungry services, the connections between the LANs become overloaded and create a bottleneck.

4. Although there are alternative solutions to this problem, ATM is the most "future-proof".

5. Note that in the examples given below, ethernet is just one of the services that ATM can interface.

Current Situation:

1. The diagram below shows the current situation in a typical office environment.

2. The Ethernet backbone, that joins together the Ethernet subnetworks, becomes a bottleneck, as only one user can access the backbone at a time, even if they do not require the services of the entire line.

3. A solution to this bottleneck must be found.

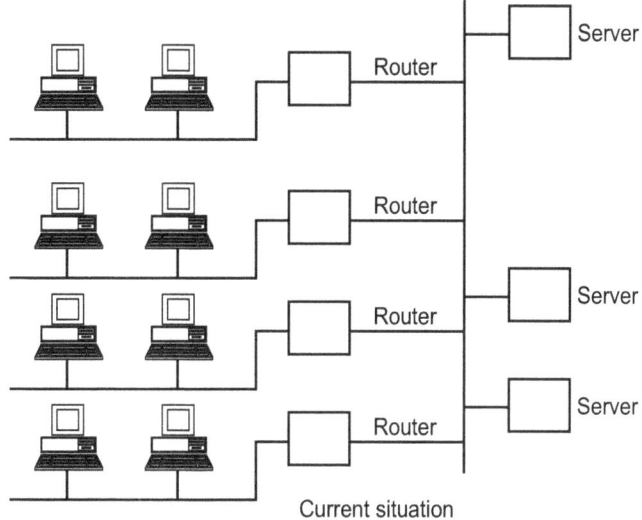

Fig. 3.48: Current situation in a typical office environment

FDDI (Fiber Distributed Data Interface) Solution:

FDDI provides a solution to the bottleneck problem, by increasing the speed of the backbone from 10 MBit/s (in the Ethernet case), to 100 MBit/s (FDDI).

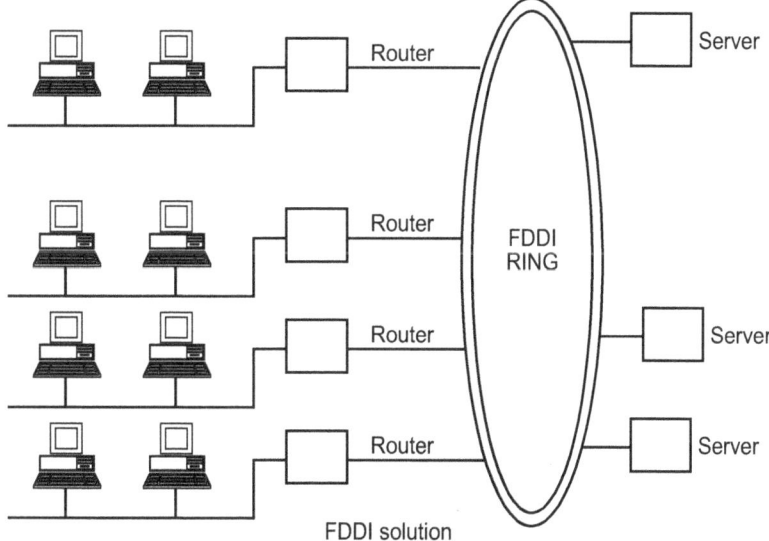

Fig. 3.49: FDDI provides a solution to the bottleneck problem

The problem with this solution, however, is that it is not "future-proof". Future bandwidth hungry applications may soon eat into the 100 MBit/s bandwidth, and the FDDI ring would have to be broken into smaller rings, linked together with routers. Hence the bottleneck returns at the router interface.

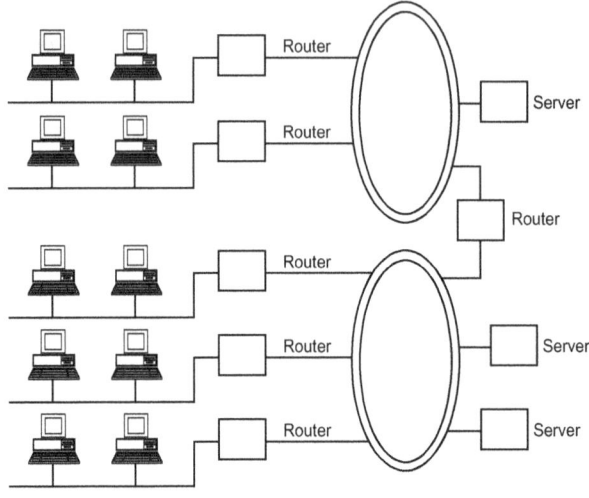

FDDI expansion

Fig. 3.50: FDDI ring would have to be broken into smaller rings, linked together with routers

Interim ATM Solution:

1. ATM can provide a solution to the bottleneck problem by replacing the backbone architecture with an ATM switch.
2. The switch allows higher bandwidths to pass through, as it is not a single access system. i.e. multiple parties can communicate at the same time.
3. This has a cumulative effect on bandwidth, allowing greater throughput.
4. The ATM solution also allows different protocols between the routers and ATM switches (e.g. SDH, E1, E3), so that these connections are upgradable as the demand on that connection increases.

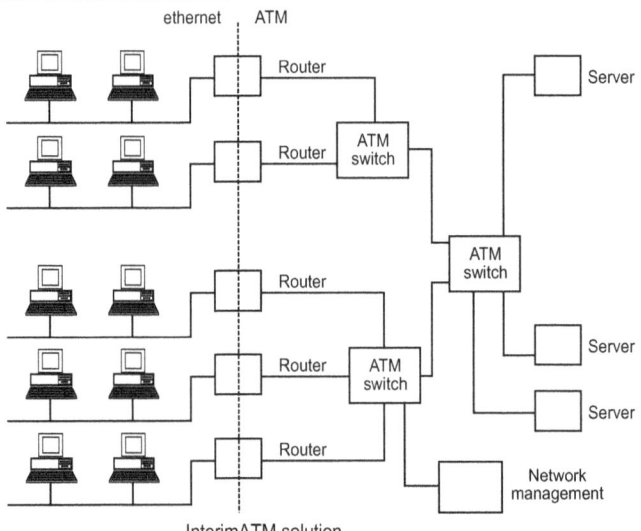

InterimATM solution

Fig. 3.51: ATM can provide a solution to the bottleneck problem by replacing the backbone architecture with an ATM switch

"Virtual LAN" ATM Solution:

1. With the installation of adaptor cards in the ATM switch, (in this example Ethernet), virtual LANs can be created.

2. This means that workstations may be grouped to form a LAN, even though they are separated by physical links.

3. The ATM switch provides the logical connections for the LANs.

4. This allows workstations to be able to move physical location without the need to change LAN.

5. The functionality of this system is provided by network management, that allows the administrator easy access to the entire ATM network through a remote terminal.

Thus ATM is a scalable, flexible and "future-proof" technology that allows for transportation of various forms of information, including data, voice, video or multiples of them. Global standards are being introduced to ensure compatibility. It is primarily for these reasons that ATM was chosen as the method for the implementation of broadband services.

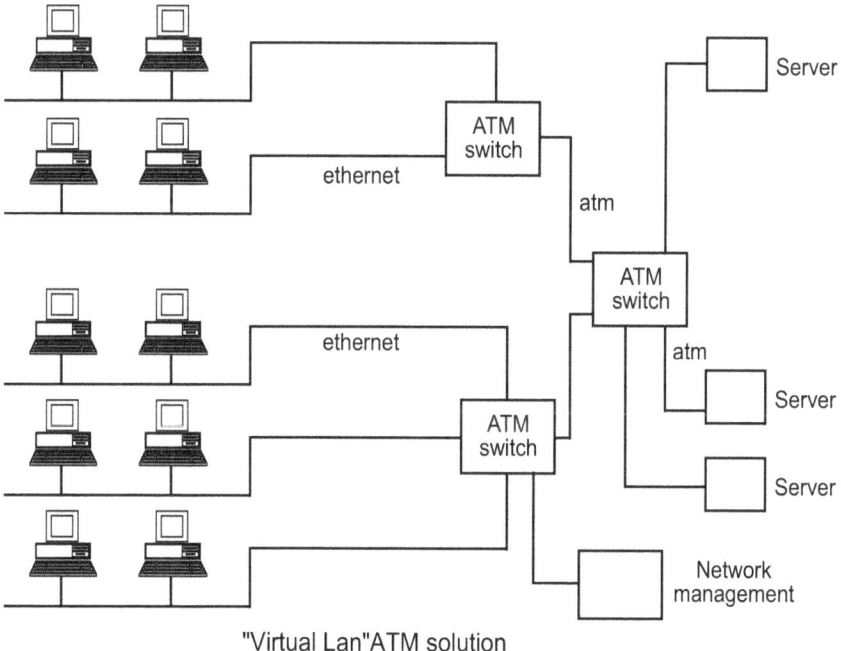

"Virtual Lan"ATM solution

Fig. 3.52: The ATM switch provides the logical connections for the LANs

3.5.7 ATM Devices and ATM Interfaces

1. An ATM network consists of an ATM switch and ATM end systems.

2. The ATM switch handles transmission of cells through the ATM network.

3. Its functions are: accepting the incoming cell from an ATM end station or another ATM switch; reading and updating the cell-header information and switching the cell towards its destination.

4. The ATM end system contains an ATM network interface adapter.

5.   Examples of such end systems are workstations, routers, and LAN switches.

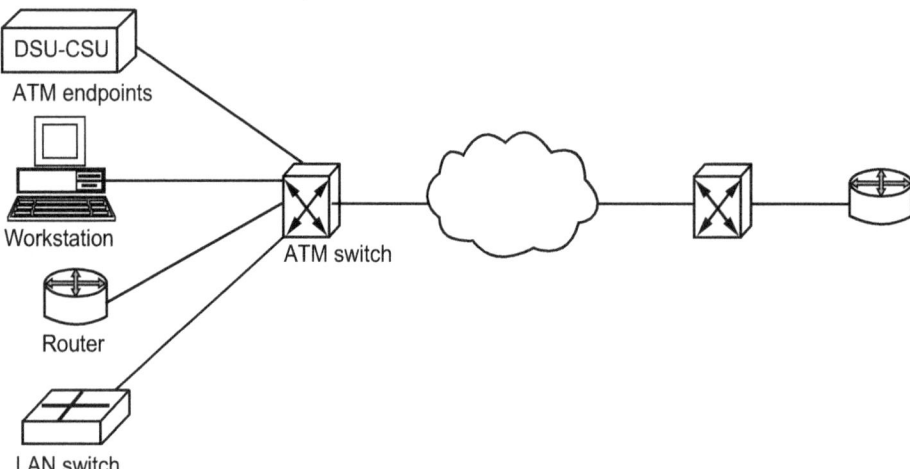

Fig. 3.53: An ATM network

ATM Network Interfaces:

1. An ATM network consists of a set of ATM switches interconnected by point-to-point ATM links or interfaces.

2. ATM switches support two primary types of interfaces: *UNI* and *NNI*.

3. The UNI connects ATM end systems (such as hosts and routers) to an ATM switch. The NNI connects two ATM switches.

4. Depending on whether the switch is owned and located at the customer's premises or publicly owned and operated by the telephone company, UNI and NNI can be further subdivided into public and private UNIs and NNIs.

5. A private UNI connects an ATM endpoint and a private ATM switch.

6. Its public counterpart connects an ATM endpoint or private switch to a public switch.

7. A private NNI connects two ATM switches within the same private organization.

8. A public one connects two ATM switches within the same public organization.

9. An additional specification, the *Broadband Interexchange Carrier Interconnect* (B-ICI), connects two public switches from different service providers.

10. Fig. 3.54 illustrates the ATM interface specifications for private and public networks.

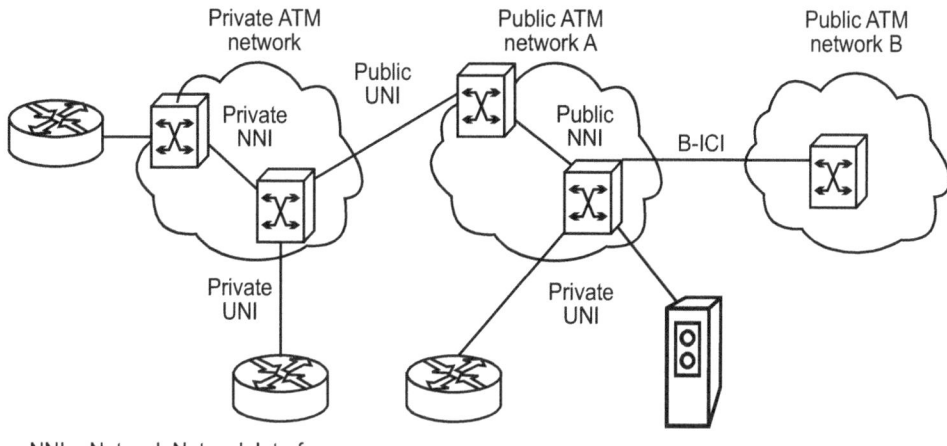

NNI = Network Network Interface
UNI = User Network Interface

Fig. 3.54: ATM interface specifications differ for private and public networks

3.5.8 ATM Cell-Header Format

- An ATM cell-header can be one of the two formats: *UNI* or *NNI*.
- The UNI header is used for communication between ATM endpoints and ATM switches in private ATM networks.
- The NNI header is used for communication between ATM switches. Fig. 3.55 depicts the basic ATM cell format, the ATM UNI cell-header format, and the ATM NNI cell-header format.

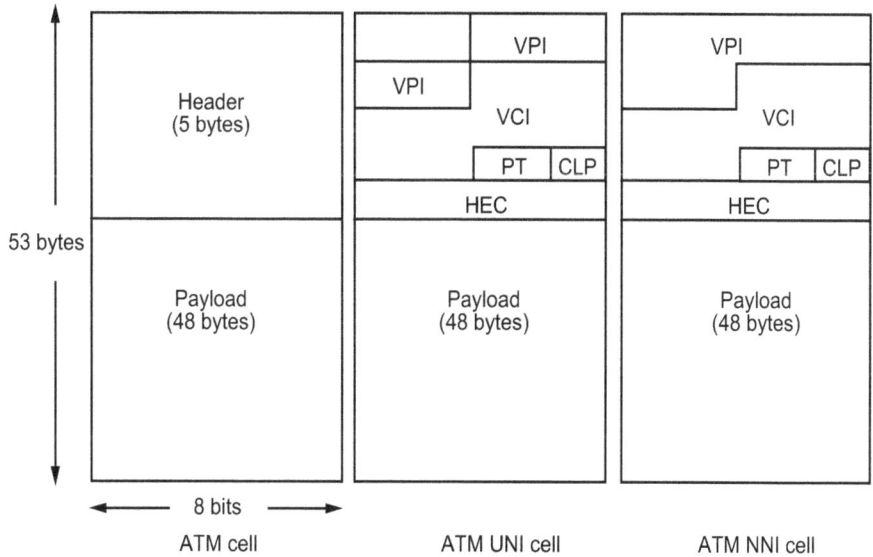

HEC = Header error control   PT = Payload Type   CLP = Cell Loss Priority

Fig. 3.55: An ATM Cell, ATM UNI Cell, and ATM NNI cell-header each containing 48 Bytes of payload

1. Unlike the UNI, the NNI header does not include the Generic Flow Control (GFC) field.
2. Additionally, the NNI header has a Virtual Path Identifier (VPI) field that occupies the first 12 bits, allowing for larger trunks between public ATM switches.

3.5.9 ATM Services

1. Three types of ATM services exist: *Permanent Virtual* Circuits (PVC), *Switched Virtual* Circuits (SVC), and connectionless service (which is similar to SMDS).
2. A PVC allows direct connectivity between sites.
3. In this way, a PVC is similar to a leased line. Among its advantages, a PVC guarantees availability of a connection and does not require call setup procedures between switches. Disadvantages of PVCs include static connectivity and manual setup.
4. An SVC is created and released dynamically and remains in use only as long as data is being transferred. In this sense, it is similar to a telephone call.
5. Dynamic call control requires a signalling protocol between the ATM endpoint and the ATM switch.
6. The advantages of SVCs include connection flexibility and call setup that can be handled automatically by a networking device. Disadvantages include the extra time and overhead required to set up the connection.

Table 3.1: Differences between PVCs and SVCs

PVCs	SVCs
Connected on a permanent basis. Users are charged a flat rate.	Dynamically connected as needed. Users are charged only for time and resources used.
Manually configured, permanent connections. Each PVC must be configured at both end systems and on all ATM switches in the network.	Dynamically signalled. SVCs are configured only on the end systems; they do not require configuration on all ATM switches in the network.
Provisioned when the connection is set up. Bandwidth and services allocated to the PVC are not available to other applications even when not in use.	Can request bandwidth and ATM service quality information needed for a particular connection. Once the connection is released, network resources are made available to other users or applications.
Cannot take alternate routes in the event of a failure in the network.	Can take alternate routes in the event of a failure in the network.

3.5.10 ATM Virtual Connections

1. ATM networks are fundamentally connection-oriented, which means that a *Virtual Channel* (VC) must be set up across the ATM network prior to any data transfer. (A virtual channel is roughly equivalent to a virtual circuit.)
2. Two types of ATM connections exist: *Virtual Paths*, which are identified by Virtual Path Identifiers, and *Virtual Channels*, which are identified by the combination of a VPI and a *Virtual Channel Identifier* (VCI).

3.   A virtual path is a bundle of virtual channels, all of which are switched transparently across the ATM network on the basis of the common VPI. All VCIs and VPIs, however, have only local significance across a particular link and are remapped, as appropriate, at each switch.
4.   A transmission path is a bundle of VPs. Fig. 3.56 illustrates how VCs concatenate to create VPs, which, in turn, concatenate to create a transmission path.

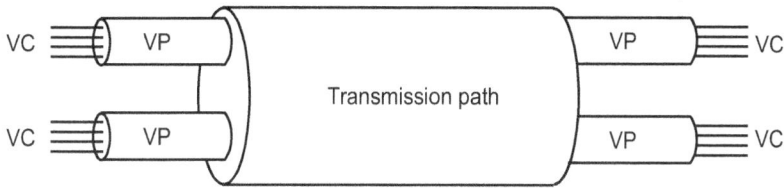

Fig. 3.56: VC concatenate to create VPs

3.5.11 ATM Switching Operations

1.   The basic operation of an ATM switch is straightforward: The cell is received across a link on a known VCI or VPI value.
2.   The switch looks up the connection value in a local translation table to determine the outgoing port (or ports) of the connection and the new VPI/VCI value of the connection on that link.
3.   The switch then retransmits the cell on that outgoing link with the appropriate connection identifiers.
4.   Because all VCIs and VPIs have only local significance across a particular link, these values are remapped, as necessary, at each switch.

3.5.12 ATM Quality of Service (QoS)

1.   ATM supports QoS guarantees composed of *traffic contract, traffic shaping,* and *traffic policing.*
2.   A traffic contract specifies an envelope that describes the intended data flow.
3.   This envelope specifies values for peak bandwidth, average sustained bandwidth, and burst size, among others.
4.   When an ATM end system connects to an ATM network, it enters a contract with the network, based on QoS parameters.
5.   Traffic shaping is the use of queues to constrain data bursts, limit peak data rate, and smooth jitters so that traffic will fit within the promised envelope.
6.   ATM devices are responsible for adhering to the contract by means of *traffic shaping.*
7.   ATM switches can use *traffic policing* to enforce the contract. The switch can measure the actual traffic flow and compare it against the agreed-upon traffic envelope.

8. If the switch finds that traffic is outside of the agreed-upon parameters, it can set the *cell-loss priority* (CLP) bit of the offending cells.

9. Setting the CLP bit makes the cell discard eligible, which means that any switch handling the cell is allowed to drop the cell during periods of congestion.

3.6 B-ISDN and ATM

3.6.1 Introduction

1. B-ISDN is an effort by the telephone companies to develop a single integrated digital network that can be used for voice, video, and data communications.

2. Much of the existing telephone system consists of the old circuit-switching equipment that is based on Alexander Graham Bell's original operator-controlled switching system, although far more automatic.

3. In addition, the phone companies have call management systems and newer data services in place such as frame relay.

4. B-ISDN can provide all these services in an integrated framework that scales upto very high data rates.

5. B-ISDN is a CCITT (now referred to as the ITU) recommendation that defines data, voice, and video transmission operating in the megabit-to-gigabit range.

6. As shown in Fig. 3.57, the underlying transfer mode for implementing B-ISDN is cell switching. Refer to "ATM (Asynchronous Transfer Mode)" and "Cell Relay" for more information.

7. In the carrier networks, ATM cells are delivered across a physical network called SONET (Synchronous Optical Network), which now makes up the trunk topology for most of the phone systems.

8. A similar standard used elsewhere in the world is called SDH (Synchronous Digital Hierarchy). SDH is a CCITT recommendation.

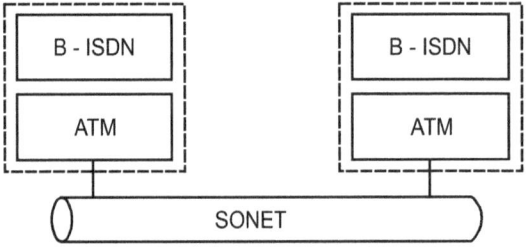

Fig. 3.57: B-ISDN network

9. SONET is the physical transport backbone of B-ISDN.
10. It is a fiber-optic–based networking standard that defines a hierarchy of transmission rates and data framing formats.

11. It is used as a transmission medium to interconnect carrier-switching offices worldwide, and so forms the structure of current and future global communications.

12. B-ISDN, FDDI (Fiber Distributed Data Interface), and SMDS can be transported on SONET networks.

13. SONET is now used as the medium between carrier-switching offices and many customer premises sites.

14. SONET transmission rates start at 51.4 Mbits/sec and increase in 52 Mbits/sec building blocks. Speeds upto 50 Gbits/sec are possible.

15. ATM is the switching technology for B-ISDN and provides B-ISDN users access to the SONET fiber-optic network.

16. Information received at the ATM layer is placed in fixed-length cells, addressed, and transmitted over the SONET network.

17. ATM provides very high-speed switching of these packets between the links attached to the SONET network. ATM takes full advantage of the transmission speeds available on fiber-optic cable.

3.6.2 B-ISDN Architecture

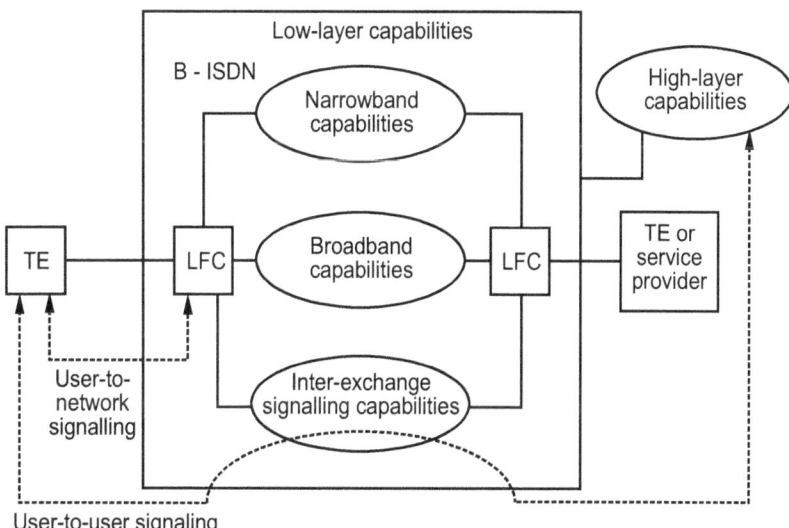

Fig. 3.58: B-ISDN architecture

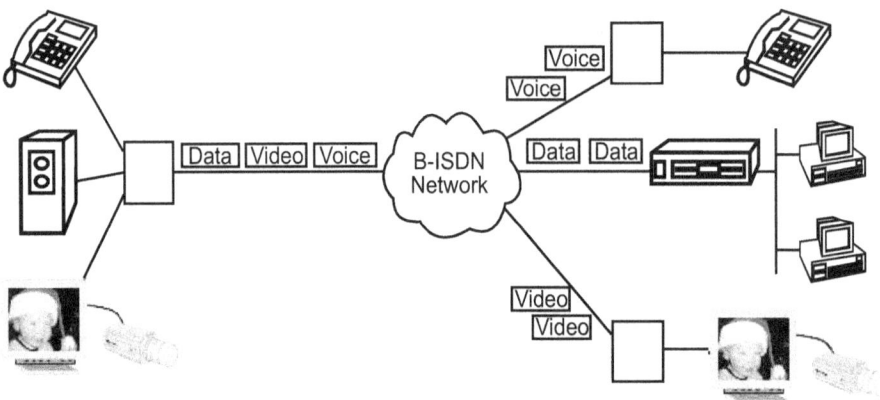

Fig. 3.59: Voice, Video and Data with B-ISDN network

Table 3.2: Typical Broadband Services

Service Categories		Example Services
Interactive Services	Conversational Services	TV Conference
	Messaging Services	Video Mail
	Retrieval Services	Videotex
Distribution Services	Without User Presentation Control	TV Broadcast
	With User Presentation Control	Videography

1. ISDN is a switched service and is designed around intelligent switching components in the carrier network.

2. It allows users to dial any other ISDN point on the network and create a high-speed digital link that can mimic point-to-point T1 lines.

3. However, T1 lines are usually permanently established between two points, while ISDN allows the switching of the line between many different points by the customer.

4. This is due to the intelligent network components. The intelligent network also supports a variety of other services, including call forwarding, caller ID and channel bonding.

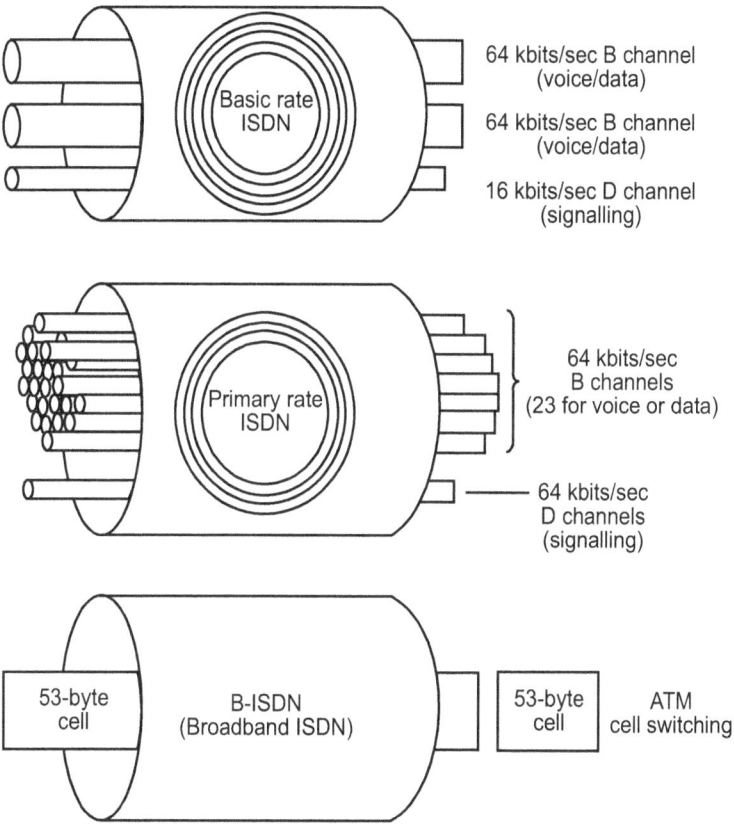

Fig. 3.60: ISDN implementation

5. B-ISDN provides the intelligent telecommunications services above ATM.

6. It manages the establishment of point-to-point and point-to-multipoint connections through the switched network.

7. It supports on-demand, reserved, and permanent services, as well as connection-oriented and connectionless services.

8. The carriers had big plans to use B-ISDN for services like videotelephony, videoconferencing, electronic newspapers, and TV distribution.

9. Now, B-ISDN is rarely discussed. All you hear about is ATM.

10. SONET is the physical transport backbone of B-ISDN. It is a fiber-optic-based networking standard that defines a hierarchy of transmission rates and data-framing formats.

11. It is used as a transmission medium to interconnect carrier-switching offices worldwide, and so forms the structure of the communications network.

12. SONET is now used as the medium between carrier-switching offices and customers.

13. SONET transmission rates start at 51.4 Mbits/sec and increase in 52 Mbits/sec building blocks.

14. ATM is the switching technology for B-ISDN and provides B-ISDN users access to the SONET fiber-optic network.

15. Information received at the ATM layer is placed in fixed-length cells, addressed, and transmitted over the SONET network.

16. ATM provides very high-speed switching of these packets between the links attached to the SONET network.

17. ATM takes full advantage of the transmission speeds available on fiber-optic cable.

18. Note that neither ISDN nor B-ISDN has gained the popularity envisioned by the carriers.

19. IP networking has gained in popularity and the latest trend is to build converged networks where voice travels in packets.

3.7 Voice Over ATM

1. VoATM enables a router to carry voice traffic (for example, telephone calls and faxes) over an ATM network.

2. An ATM network is a cell-switching and multiplexing technology designed to combine the benefits of circuit switching (constant transmission delay and guaranteed capacity) and packet switching (flexibility and efficiency for intermittent traffic).

3. All traffic to or from an ATM network is prefaced with a Virtual Path Identifier (VPI) and Virtual Channel Identifier (VCI).

4. A VPI-VCI pair is considered a single virtual circuit.

5. Each virtual circuit is a private connection to another node on the ATM network.

6. Each virtual circuit is treated as a point-to-point mechanism to another router or host and is capable of supporting bi-directional traffic.

7. Each ATM node establishes a separate connection to every other node in the ATM network with which it must communicate.

8. All such connections are established by means of a Permanent Virtual Circuit (PVC) or a Switched Virtual Circuit (SVC) with an ATM signalling mechanism.

9. This signaling is based on the ATM Forum User-Network Interface (UNI) Specification V3.0.

10. Each virtual circuit is considered as a complete and separate link to a destination node.

11. Data can be encapsulated as needed across the connection, and the ATM network disregards the contents of the data.

12. The only requirement is that data be sent to the ATM processor card of the router in a manner that follows the specific ATM adaptation layer (AAL) format.

13. An ATM connection transfers raw bits of information to a destination router or host.

14. The ATM router takes the Common Part Convergence Sublayer (CPCS) frame, carves it up into 53 byte cells, and sends the cells to the destination router or host for reassembly.

15. In AAL5 format, 48 bytes of each cell are used for the CPCS data and the remaining 5 bytes are used for cell routing.

16. The 5 byte cell header contains the destination VPI-VCI pair, payload type, Cell Loss Priority (CLP), and Header Error Control (HEC) information.

3.7.1 AAL Technology

1. AAL defines the conversion of user information into the ATM cells.

2. AAL protocols perform a convergence function; that is, they take whatever traffic is to be sent across the ATM network, establish the appropriate connections, and then package the traffic received from the higher layers into the 48 byte information payload that is passed down to the ATM layer for transmission.

3. At the receiving level, the AAL layer must receive the information payloads passed up from the ATM layer and put the payloads into the form expected by the higher layer.

4. The AAL layers provide a service to the higher layers that corresponds to the four classes of traffic. AAL1 and AAL2 handle isochronous traffic, such as voice and video, but are not relevant to the router. AAL3/4 and AAL5 support data communications by segmenting and reassembling packets.

5. AAL2 is a bandwidth-efficient, standards-based trunking method for transporting compressed voice, voice-band data, circuit-mode data, and frame-mode data.

6. VoATM with AAL2 trunking provides the following functionality:
   • Increased quality of service (QoS) capabilities
   • Robust architecture
   • Signalling transparency
   • CAS and CCS support

AAL5 is designed to support only message-mode, non-assured operation. AAL5 packets contain 48 bytes of data and a 5 byte header.

3.7.2 Variable Bit Rate Real-Time Options for Traffic Shaping

1. Variable Bit Rate (VBR) is a QoS class defined by the ATM Forum for ATM networks.
2. VBR is subdivided into a Real-Time (RT) class and Non-Real Time (NRT) class.
3. RT VBR is used for connections in which there is a fixed timing relationship between samples, as in the case of traffic shaping.
4. NRT VBR is used for connections in which there is no fixed timing relationship between samples, but which still need a guaranteed QoS.
5. Traffic shaping prevents a carrier from discarding incoming calls from a router.
6. Traffic shaping is performed by configuring the peak, average, and burst options for voice traffic.
7. Burst is required if the PVC is carrying bursty traffic. Peak, average, and burst are required, so the PVC can effectively handle the bandwidth for the number of voice calls.

3.7.3 Voice Over ATM System

1. As real-time voice services have been traditionally supported in the WAN via circuit-based techniques (e.g., via T1 multiplexers or circuit switching), it is natural to map these circuits to ATM CBR PVCs (CBR is constant bit rate) using circuit emulation and ATM adaptation Layer 1 (AAL1).
2. However, there are significant disadvantages in using circuit emulation in that the bandwidth must be dedicated for this type of traffic (whether there is useful information being transmitted or not), providing a disincentive for corporate users to implement circuit emulation as a long-term strategy.
3. For example, a T1 1.544 Mbps circuit requires 1.74 Mbps of ATM bandwidth when transmitted in circuit-emulation mode.
4. This does not downplay its importance as a transitional strategy to address the installed base.
5. As technology has evolved, the inherent burstiness of voice and many real-time applications can be exploited (along with sophisticated compression schemes) to decrease the cost of transmission significantly through the use of VBR–RT connections over ATM.
6. VBR techniques for voice exploit the inherently bursty nature of voice communication, as there are silence periods that can result in increased efficiency.
7. The following silence periods (in decreasing levels of importance) arise:
    *   When no call is up on a particular trunk; that is, the trunk is idle during off-peak hours (trunks are typically engineered for a certain call-blocking probability: at night, all the trunks could be idle).
    *   When the call is up, but only one person is talking at a given time.
    *   When the call is up, and no one is talking.

8. Work is just starting in the ATM Forum on ATM adaptation for VBR voice.

9. The addition of more bandwidth-effective voice coding (e.g., standard voice is coded using 64 kbps PCM) is economically attractive, particularly over long-haul circuits and T1 ATM interfaces.

10. Various compression schemes have been standardized in the industry (e.g., G720 series of standards).

11. Making these coding schemes dynamic, provides the network operator the opportunity to free up bandwidth under network-congestion conditions.

12. For example, with the onset of congestion, increased levels of voice compression could be dynamically invoked, thus freeing up bandwidth and potentially alleviating the congestion while diminishing the quality of the voice during these periods.

13. A further enhancement to the support of voice over ATM is to support voice switching over SVCs.

14. This entails interpreting PBX signalling and routing voice calls to the appropriate destination PBX (see Fig. 3.61).

15. The advantage from a traffic management perspective is that connection admission controls can be applied to new voice calls; under network congestion conditions, these calls could be rerouted over the public network and therefore not cause additional levels of congestion.

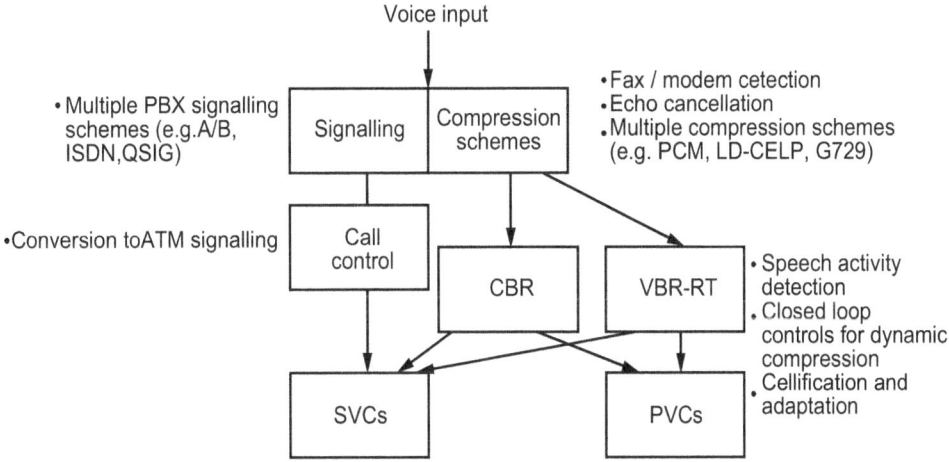

Fig. 3.61: Voice switching over SVCs

The ATM Forum is currently focusing its efforts on voice handled on CBR SVCs. VBR–RT voice is a future standards activity.

3.7.4 Fragmentation

*   It is built into ATM, with its small, fixed-size, 53 byte cells.
*   Very fast ATM switches speed data through the ATM network.

- The high bandwidth associated with ATM reduces congestion problems, providing extremely reliable service.

- Carriers can therefore promise customers Quality of Service (QoS), stipulated in Service Level Agreements (SLAs).

3.7.5 ATM Prioritization

- It is implemented through QoS parameters.

- ATM was designed from the outset to carry voice as well as all types of data.

- ATM Adaptation Layer 1 (AAL1) protocol in ATM's Constant Bit Rate (CBR) service was the de facto standard for VoATM.

- However, this protocol proved inefficient for voice applications.

- CBR, the highest quality class of ATM service, provides Circuit Emulation Service (CES), which transmits a continuous bit stream of information.

- This allocates a constant amount of bandwidth to a connection for the duration of a transmission.

- Although it guarantees high quality voice, CES monopolizes bandwidth that could be used for other applications.

- In addition, in the interest of reducing delay, CES might send the fixed-size ATM cells half empty rather than waiting 6 milliseconds for 47 bytes of voice to fill the cell.

- This wastes over 20 bytes of bandwidth per ATM cell.

- Dynamic Bandwidth Circuit Emulation Service (DBCES) is a variation of CES.

- DBCES does not send a constant bit stream of cells, but transmits only when there is an active voice call (off hook).

- However, like in CES, the cells might remain partially empty. Therefore, using AAL1 for VoATM increases the overhead of voice transmissions and wastes bandwidth.

- AAL2's Variable Bit Rate (VBR-RT) service, as specified in ITU-T recommendation I.363.2, emerged as the standard of choice for VoATM.

- The structure of AAL2 allows for the packing of short packets (1 to 45/64 bytes), also called minicells, into one or more ATM cells. (This resembles Frame Relay's and IP's variable sized fragments.)

- In contrast to AAL1, which has a fixed payload, AAL2 enables a variable payload within cells.

- This functionality provides a dramatic improvement in bandwidth efficiency over structured or unstructured circuit emulation using AAL1.

- In addition, AAL2 supports voice compression and silence suppression and allows multiple voice channels with varying bandwidth on a single ATM connection.

3.7.6 Voice Compression

- It is not necessary in pure-ATM networks, which enjoy ample bandwidth.

- However, in hybrid ATM-frame relay networks (for example, with ATM headquarters and frame relay branches), voice compression is required since frame relay uses voice compression.

- ATM must therefore be equipped to support voice compression that will work with VoFR equipment at the remote site.

3.8 The Need for Interworking

- Since a comprehensive standard has not been adopted for any one technology, it is unrealistic to expect the emergence of inter-operability standards between technologies in the near future.

- Interworking solutions will therefore have to be proprietary.

- It is essential that the inter-operability be transparent to the users, who want to communicate through the network efficiently and without concern for the technological issues involved.

- Due to the lack of inter-operability standards for voice communications over Frame Relay, IP and ATM, vendors must develop proprietary interworking solutions.

- There are many situations in which interworking between technologies is required within a corporate network.

- For example, corporations that are running data and voice over frame relay might require VoIP to extend the network to remote locations that don't have a frame relay infrastructure without deploying additional equipment.

- This may also be required for telecommuters working from home, salespeople working from hotel rooms and resellers that want to access information.

- Consider the configuration below, in which IP is extended to hotels or residential locations.

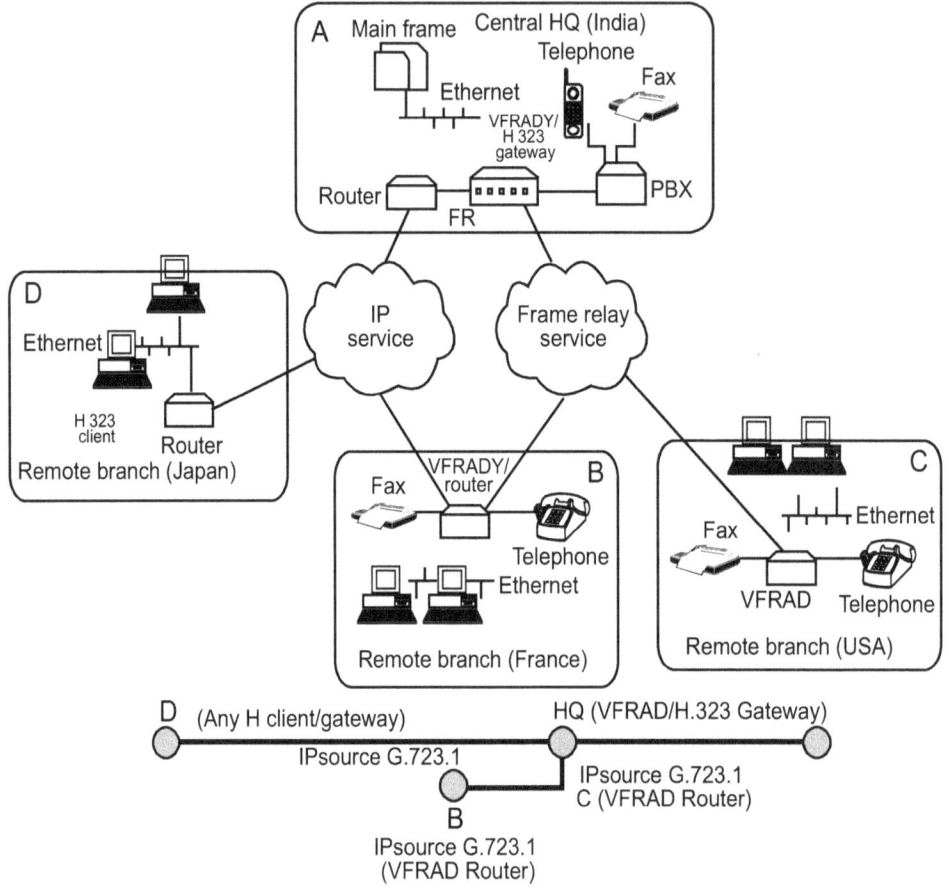

Fig. 3.62: Interworking technology

- Interworking between frame relay and IP is vital in this scenario.

- This is easier said than done, however, as frame relay and IP use different standard voice compression algorithms (ITU G.729 and ITU G.723A, respectively).

- There is also a discrepancy between signalling methods.

- For switched virtual circuits is not widely used as the basis for frame relay voice switching.

- In fact, there is no standard for voice switching in frame relay networks.

- In any case, it does not interwork with VoIP voice switching based on the H.323 protocol stack.

- In large corporate networks with many remote branches using frame relay service and VoFR, there is a need for high speed ATM service in order to support the required amount of traffic at company headquarters.

- In this case there is a need for interworking between frame relay and ATM in general and VoFR and VoATM in particular.

- Another reason for the desirability of multiple voice technology support over the same platform is to enable migration to different technologies without losing the initial investment in existing equipment.

- RAD is developing a pre-standards strategy to facilitate interworking between frame relay and IP.

- The strategy will provide a migration path from frame relay to IP technologies, which can be an important advantage when IP services become available.

- RAD is currently developing an interworking solution between frame relay and IP.

- The VoFR-VoIP product will perform signalling conversion and negotiate with the remote IP product in order to choose a common voice compression algorithm and other parameters.

- Thus without a doubt, the data revolution will only gain momentum in the coming years, with more and more voice traffic moving onto data networks.

- Vendors of voice equipment will continue to develop integrated voice and data devices based on packetized technology.

- Users with ubiquitous voice and data service integrated over one universal infrastructure will benefit from true, seamless, transparent interworking between voice and all types of data. RAD Data Communications will remain in the forefront of industry efforts to provide universal services.

Thus the full implementation of B-ISDN is certainly something worth looking forward to. With the usage of ATM technology as well as the laying of fiber optic cables, the **B-ISDN** would certainly revolutionise the transmission of information. With the extremely high and flexible bit rate, users could be assured of a negligible delay between the sender and receiver.

EXERCISE

1. What are the different problems existing in data and voice integration?
2. What are the different economic advantages of data and voice integration?
3. Write a short note on unified messaging system.
4. Write a short note on "Mixed solutions of voice/data communication".
5. Explain in detail QoS factor in Data-voice communication.
6. Write advantages of integrated voice and data network technology.
7. What are the different applications of integrated voice and data network?

8. How "Integrated voice and data network" is beneficial for a business?
9. Compare circuit switching vs messaging switching technique.
10. Write notes on services provided by ISDN.
11. What are the different types of ISDN terminals?
12. List out different non-ISDN terminals.
13. Write detail note on ISDN devices.
14. Explain ISDN PRI service in detail.
15. Write short note on characteristics of B and D channels.
16. Write a short note on "ISDN equipment and interface terminology".
17. Explain "ISDN protocol stack" in detail.
18. Draw and explain "LAPD" format in detail.
19. Write short note on "Voice over frame relay".
20. What are the different applications of frame relay?
21. What are the different advantages of frame relay?
22. Write about different topologies of frame relay.
23. Draw and explain voice over frame relay network reference model.
24. Draw and explain ATM reference model.
25. Write short note on cell structure of ATM network.
26. Write concept of virtual channels in ATM.
27. What are the responsibilities of ATM adaptation layer?
28. Draw and explain "ATM cell-header format".
29. Write short notes on "ATM QoS".
30. Explain B-ISDN architecture in detail.
31. Write detail note on "Voice over ATM".

Unit IV

GLOBAL SYSTEM FOR MOBILE COMMUNICATION

4.1 Introduction

The Global System for Mobile Communication (GSM) is the most popular standard for mobile phones in the world. In 1982, CEPT set up a committee known as Groupe Special Mobile (GSM), now known as Global System for Mobile Communication. GSM service is used by over 2 billion people across more than 210 countries. It is a second generation (2G) mobile phone system with digital signalling and speech channels. It is an open standard, currently developed by 3GPP. From user point of view, GSM has an advantage of higher digital voice quality and low cost alternative to calls i.e. text messaging. It retains backward compatibility with original GSM phones. e.g. Packet data capabilities were added in the Release '97 version of the standard by means of GPRS. Higher speed data transmission has also been introduced with EDGE in the Release '99 version of the standard.

In this unit, we discuss the various standards for wireless communication system, the various access technologies, cellular communication fundamentals. Further, discussing GSM in detail, starting with GSM architecture and interfaces, radio link features in GSM system, the GSM logical channels and frame structure, speech coding techniques in GSM, the various data and value added services available in GSM. At last, we discuss about privacy and security in GSM.

4.2 Standards for Wireless Communication

The wireless communication is divided into various generations. The International Standards bodies are currently engaged in defining the fourth generation mobile system.

Following is the classification of all the generations of wireless communication.

0G:

- PTT
- MTS
- IMTS
- AMTS

0.5G:

- Autotel/PALM
- ARP

1G:

- NMT
- AMPS
- Hicap
- CDPD
- Mobitex
- DataTac

2G:

- GSM
- iDEN
- D-AMPS
- IS-95/CdmaOne
- PDC
- CSD
- PHS

2.5G:

- GPRS
- HSCSD
- WiDEN

2.75G:

- CDMA, 2000 IXRTT/IS-2000
- EDGE

3G:

- W-CDMA
  - UMTS
  - FOMA
- IXEV-DO/IS-856
- TD-SCDMA
- GAN/UMA

3.5G:

- HSDPA

3.75G:
- HSUPA

4G:
- Frequency bands
- SMR
- Cellular
- PCS

4.2.1 0G – Mobile Radio Telephone

The modern cellular mobile telephony technology was preceded by the mobile radio telephone systems. These are known as zero generation (0G) systems as they are the predecessors of first generation cellular telephones. The technologies used in 0G systems include –
- PTT (Put to Talk),
- MTS (Mobile Telephone System),
- IMTS (Improved Mobile Telephone Service), and
- AMTS (Advanced Mobile Telephone System).

These early mobile telephone systems can be distinguished from earlier radio telephone systems, in that they were available as a commercial service that was part of the public switched telephone network, with their own telephone numbers, rather than part of a closed network such as a police radio or a taxi dispatch system.

4.2.2 0.5G

0.5G is a middle generation between zeroth and first generation. It includes two technologies: Autotel and ARP.

4.2.2.1 Autotel

It is also called as PALM or Public Automated Land Mobile. It is a radiotelephone service which was the 'missing link' between 0G MTS/IMTS and later cellular telephone services. Except voice channel which is analog, for all other supervisory messages (call setup, ringing, channel assignment, etc.), digital signalling is used. It uses existent high power VHF channels. Thus, the system was not cellular.

4.2.2.2 ARP

It was commercially operated in Finland as public mobile phone network. ARP means Autoradiopuhelin i.e. Car Radio Phone. The ARP was a success and reached great popularity, but finally became too congested and was gradually replaced by more modern NMT technology. ARP operated on 150 MHz frequency. Also, ARP did not support handoff. ARP was also expensive. However, in 1990s, handhelds were introduced in ARP, but it never became popular, as there was more modern equipment available in other systems like NMT.

4.2.3 1G

It is the first-generation wireless telephone technology, cellphones. These are analog cellphone standards introduced in 80s and were later replaced by 2G digital cellphones. Radio signals used by 1G networks are analog and 2G is digital. But, both systems use digital signalling to connect the radio towers to the rest of the telephone system. But the call itself is encoded to digital signals in 2G whereas, 1G is only modulated to high frequency. One such standard is NMT (Nordic Mobile Telephone) used in Nordic countries, Eastern Europe and Russia. Others include AMPS (Advanced Mobile Phone System) used in US. TACS (Total Access Communication System) in UK, C-450 in West Germany, Portugal and South Africa, Radiocom 2000 in France and RTMI in Italy.

4.2.4 2G

It is second generation wireless telephone technology. Main difference between 1G and 2G is that the radio signals used by 1G are analog, while 2G networks are digital.

4.2.4.1 2G Standards

2G technologies are of two types: TDMA-based and CDMA-based, depending on the type of multiplexing used.

The main 2G standards are:

- GSM (TDMA-based), originally from Europe, but used worldwide.
- iDEN (TDMA-based), by Nextel in US and Telus Mobility in Canada.
- IS-136/D-AMPS (TDMA-based), used in America.
- IS-95/cdmaOne (CDMA-based), used in America and Asia.
- PDC (TDMA-based), used in Japan.

2G is known as PCS (Personal Communication Services) in US.

4.2.4.2 2G-Capacities, Advantages and Disadvantages

Capacity:

System capacity is increased in two ways by the use of digital signals between handsets and towers.

1. Digital voice data can be multiplexed and compressed much more effectively than analog voice encoding through the use of various CODECS, allowing more calls to be packed into the same amount of radio bandwidth.
2. The digital systems emit less radio power from handsets, thus making the equipment less expensive.

Advantages:
1. The low powered radio signals require less battery power, so phones last much longer between charges and batteries can be smaller.
2. Low power emissions helped address health concerns.
3. All-digital allowed for introduction of digital data services, as SMS and email.
4. A key digital advantage is security and it is harder to eavesdrop on by use of radio scanners. 2G phones are more private than 1G.

Disadvantages:
1. In sparesly populated areas, the weaker digital signals will not be sufficient to reach a cell tower.
2. Analog has a smooth decay curve, while digital has a jagged steppy one. This can be both an advantage and a disadvantage. Under good conditions, digital will sound much better. Under slightly worse condition, analog will have annoying static, while digital has occasional dropouts. With time, digital starts to fail by dropping calls or being unintelligible, while analog just slowly worstens, generally holding a call longer and allowing atleast a few words to get through.
3. With analog system, it was possible to use same phone number by different handsets; but in digital system, it is not possible.
4. Digital calls are free of static and background noise.

4.2.5 2.5G

The 'second and a half generation' is a stepping stone between 2G and 3G cellular wireless technologies. It has implemented a packet switched domain in addition to the circuit switched domain. It does not necessarily provide faster services because bundling of time slots is used for circuit switched data services (HSCSD) as well. 2.5G was invented only for marketing purpose and is not officially defined as 2G and 3G. 2.5G provides some benefits of 3G (e.g. it is packed-switched) and can use some of the existing 2G infrastructure in GSM and CDMA networks. GPRS is 2.5G technology used by GSM operators.

Some protocols, such as EDGE for GSM and CDMA-2000 IXRTT for CDMA, can qualify as 3G, because of data rate above 144 kbps; but are considered by most to be 2.5G or 2.75G, as they are many times slower than 'true' 3G services.

4.2.6 2.75G

2.75G is the term which has been decided on for systems which do not meet the 3G requirements, but are marketed as if they do (e.g. CDMA-2000 without multicarrier) or which do, just meet the requirements but are not strongly marketed as such (e.g. EDGE systems). The term 2.75G has not been officially defined.

4.2.7 3G

It is the third generation technology with ability to transfer both voice and non-voice data. It was introduced on a large commercial scale in Japan. In marketing 3G services, video telephony has often been used as the flag-ship killer application for 3G. But, real life usage of video telephony on 3G network is only a very small fraction of all services. Downloading of music finds very strong demand by customers. 3G networks are not IEEE 802.11 networks. IEEE 802.11 networks are short range, primarily internet access networks, while 3G wireless networks are the evolution of wide area cellular telephone networks which hope to incorporate high speed internet access and video telephony to these networks.

4.2.8 3.5G

3.5G is a transition for 2G and 3G. It has a data rate of 3 Mbps.

High Speed Downlink Packet Access (HSDPA) is a new mobile telephony protocol and is sometimes referred to as a 3.5G technology. In this respect, it extends WCDMA in the same way that EV-DO extends CDMA-2000. HSDPA provides a smooth evolutionary path for Universal Mobile Telecommunication Systems (UMTS) networks allowing for higher data capacity (upto 14.4 Mbps in the downlink). It is an evolution of the W-CDMA standards, designed to increase the available data rate by a factor 5 or more.

HSDPA defines a new W-CDMA channel, the high speed downlink shared channel

(HS-DSCH) that operates in a different way from existing W-CDMA channels, but is only used for downlink communication to the mobile.

4.2.9 3.75G

High Speed Uplink Packet Access (HSUPA) is a data access protocol for mobile phone networks with extremely high upload speeds upto 5.76 Mbps. Similar to HSDPA, HSUPA is considered 3.75G.

4.2.10 4G

This wireless access technology is the fourth generation successor of 3G. The IEEE official name for 4G is "3G and beyond".

1. 4G is the future standard for wireless devices. A Japanese company is testing 4G communication at 100 Mbps while moving and 1 Gbps while stationary. Its first commercial release is planned in 2010.

2. Pervasive network: An amorphous and presently entirely hypothetical concept, where the user can be simultaneously connected to several wireless access technologies and can seamlessly move between them. These access technologies can be Wi-Fi, UMTS, EDGE, etc. Included in this concept is also smart radio/ cognitive radio technology to efficiently manage spectrum use and transmission power as well as the use of mesh routing protocols to create a pervasive network.

Ideally, 4G would provide users with on demand high quality video and audio. Video is one of the big differences between 4G and 3G. 4G may use OFDM (Orthogonal Frequency Division Multiplexing), and also OFDMA (Orthogonal Frequency Division Multiple Access) to better allocate network resources to multiple users. 4G devices may use SDR (Software-defined radio) receivers, which allow for better use of available bandwidth as well as making use of multiple channels simultaneously.

Unlike 3G networks, which are a jumble of circuit and packet switched networks, 4G will be based on packet switching only. This will allow low-latency data transmission.
The competitors in space will be:
>   WiMax - 7.2 million units by 2010.
>   TD-SCDMA - 100 million subscribers (in China) by 2010.
>   Flash OFDM - 13 million subscribers in 2010.
>   UMTS FDD - Valued at $ 2 billion in 2010.

4.3 Access Technologies

4.3.1 Introduction

In this section, the various access technologies for cellular communication are discussed. Thereafter, the spectral efficiencies of all these technologies are discussed.

4.3.2 Wireless System Architecture

The architecture of most digital and analog wireless system is channelized. The most important criteria in wireless communication is the efficient use of the available radio spectrum. Thus, a narrowband channelized systems take an upper hand to the wideband non-channelized systems.

4.3.2.1 Channelized System

A channelized system is one, in which the available spectrum is divided into a number of narrow radio channels, each being allotted a specific carrier frequency. For wireless communication, each of these radio channels are assigned a pair of frequencies, called the forward and reverse channel frequency.

Forward channel frequency is the downlink path frequency i.e. the frequency used for transmission from base station to mobile station. Reverse channel frequency is the uplink path frequency i.e. the transmission frequency from mobile station to base station.

To minimize co-channel interference between transmission and reception, the forward and reverse channels are widely separated.

4.3.2.2 Narrowband Channelized System

In a narrowband channelized system, the output frequency for every individual transmitter is precisely controlled i.e. the transmission from every mobile station is confined within a specific narrow bandwidth, to avoid adjacent channel interference. This demands the use of modulation techniques and also introduces constrains on the design of transmitter and receiver elements esp filters, thus, influencing the cost of mobile station.

The use of efficient technologies can lead to efficient utilization of the available radio spectrum utilization, thus more users within the assigned spectrum and thus increased profits.

4.3.2.3 Narrowband Digital Channelized Systems

The drawbacks of traditional mobile communication are:

1. Limited service area.
2. Poor service performance leading to congestion.
3. Inefficient frequency spectrum utilization.

To overcome these shortcomings of first-generation analog cellular system, digital technologies were used. One of these technologies is Multiple Access.

Multiplexing involves grouping of several channels in a way so as to transmit them simultaneously on the same carrier frequency of a radio link without mixing. At the receiver, demultiplexing is performed to separate the channels.

The multiplexing technologies used in cellular network are:

1. Frequency Division Multiplexing (FDMA).
2. Time Division Multiplexing (TDMA).
3. Code Division Multiplexing (CDMA).

4.3.2.3.1 FDMA - Frequency Division Multiplexing

In this technique, different sub-bands of frequencies are alloted to different users on a continuous time basis. To reduce interference between users allocated adjacent channel bands, guard bands are used to act as buffer zones, as shown in Fig. 4.1.

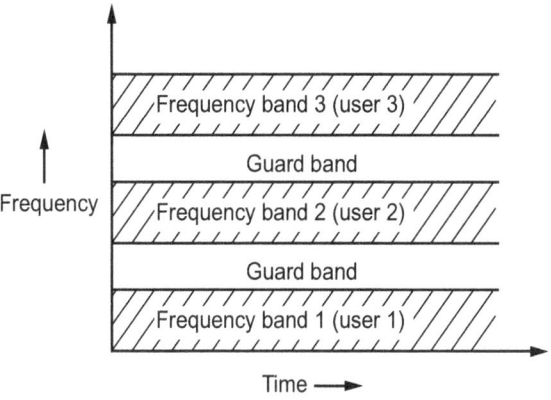

Fig. 4.1

4.3.2.3.2 TDMA - Time Division Multiplexing

In this, each user is allocated the full spectral occupancy, but for a short duration of time, called a time slot. Buffer zones in the form of guard times are inserted between the assigned time slots, to reduce interference between users by allowing for time uncertainty that arises due to system imperfections, esp in synchronization schemes.

Advantages:

1. An advantage of TDMA over FDMA is full power efficiency.
2. TDM is immune to amplitude non-linearities in the channel, as a source of crosstalk.

Disadvantages:

1. The TDM is highly sensitive to dispersion.

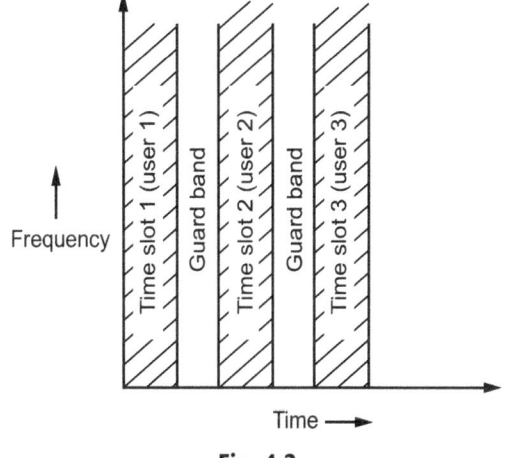

Fig. 4.2

Table 4.1: Comparison of Data Multiplexing Techniques

Parameter	FDM	TDM
Line efficiency	Poor	Good
Channel capacity	Poor	Good
High speed sub-channel	Very poor	Poor
Flexibility	Very poor	Good
Error control	None	None
Multidrop capability	Good	Difficult
Cost	High	Low
Transmission delay	None	Low

4.3.2.3.3 CDMA - Code Division Multiplexing

CDMA is hybrid combination of TDMA and FDMA. Specifically, frequency hopping may be employed to ensure that during each successive time slot, the frequency bands assigned to the users are reordered in an essentially random manner.

An important advantage of CDMA, over both FDMA and TDMA, is that it can provide for secure communication. The frequency hopping mechanism can be implemented through the use of pseudo-noise (PN) sequence, which is a cyclic code with noiselike characteristics.

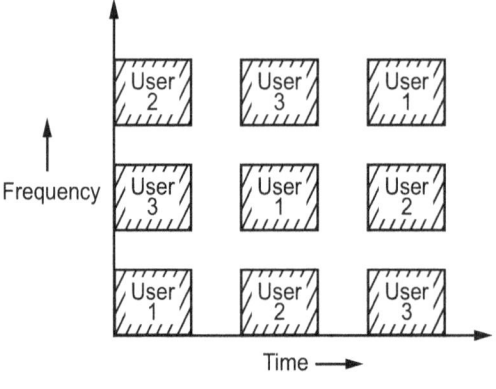

Fig. 4.3

4.3.3 Spectral Efficiency

Spectral efficiency is defined as the efficient use of the available frequency spectrum. Various techniques are employed for an efficient use of a spectrum. A few of them are listed below:

1.   Choice of multiple access scheme.
2.   Reduction of channel bandwidth.

3.   Information compression techniques.
4.   Variable bit rate control.
5.   Improved channel assignment.
6.   Modulation.

Modulation and multiple access spectral efficiencies, combinely help in knowing the overall efficiency of a cellular system.

4.3.3.1 Overall Spectral Efficiency

The overall spectral efficiency can be obtained by combining the modulation and multiple access efficiency.

$$\eta = \eta_m \eta_a$$

where, η is the overall efficiency.

η_m is the modulation efficiency.

η_a is the multiple access spectral efficiency.

4.3.3.1.1 Spectral Efficiency of Modulation

The spectral efficiency of modulation is defined as the total number of available channels in the system divided by the bandwidth and total coverage area.

$$\eta_m = \frac{\frac{B_s}{B_c} \times \frac{N_c}{N}}{B_s \times N_c \times A_c} \qquad \text{... (4.1)}$$

where, η_m is the modulation efficiency (channels/MHz/km^2).

B_s is the system bandwidth (MHz).

B_c is the channel spacing (MHz).

N_c is the total number of cells in the covered area.

N is the frequency sense factor of system.

A_c is the area covered by a cell (km^2).

On solving the above equation, we get,

$$\eta_m = \frac{1}{B_c \times N \times A_c} \qquad \text{... (4.2)}$$

It is seen that modulation efficiency depends only on channel spacing, coverage area of a cell and frequency reuse factor of a system and not on system bandwidth.

The spectral efficiency can also be defined as the total traffic carried by the system divided by bandwidth and total coverage.

$$\eta_m = \frac{\eta_t \times \dfrac{\dfrac{B_s}{B_c}}{N}}{B_s \times A_c} \qquad \text{... (4.3)}$$

$$\eta_m = \frac{\eta_t}{B_c \, N \, A_c} \qquad \text{... (4.4)}$$

where, $\eta_t = \dfrac{B_s}{B_c}$ is the trunking efficiency factor

η_m is modulation efficiency in Erlangs/MHz/km².

η_t is a function of the blocking probability and $\dfrac{B_s}{B_c}$.

4.3.3.1.2 Multiple Access Spectral Efficiency

Multiple Access Spectral Efficiency η_a is defined as,

$$\eta_a = \frac{\text{Total time-frequency domain dedicated for voice transmission}}{\text{Total time-frequency domain available to the system}}$$

It is a dimensionless quantity with an upper limit of unity.

4.3.3.1.2.1 FDMA Spectral Efficiency

In FDMA, spectral efficiency is less due to the guard bands and signalling channels.

$$\eta_a = \frac{B_c N_T}{B_s} \qquad \text{... (4.5)}$$

where, N_T is the total number of voice channels in the covered area.

4.3.3.1.2.2 TDMA Spectral Efficiency

In TDMA, spectral efficiency is reduced due to guard time and synchronization sequence.

For narrowband TDMA,

$$\eta_a = \left(\frac{\tau M_t}{T_f}\right)\left(\frac{B_u N_u}{B_s}\right) \qquad \text{... (4.6)}$$

where, τ is time slot duration

T_f is the frame duration.

M_t is the number of time slots per frame.

B_u is the bandwidth of each user during his time slot.

N_u is the number of users sharing the same time slot in the system, but having access to different frequency sub-bands.

The capacity of a TDMA system is given by,

$$N_u = \frac{\eta_b \mu}{v_f} \times \frac{B_s}{RN} \qquad \text{... (4.7)}$$

where, N_u is the number of channels (users) per cell.

η_b is the bandwidth efficiency factor.

μ is the bit efficiency.

v_f is the voice activity factor.

B_s is the one-way system bandwidth.

R is the information bit rate plus overhead.

N is the frequency reuse factor.

$$\eta = \frac{N_u \times R}{B_s} \text{ bit/sec/Hz} \qquad \text{... (4.8)}$$

η is the spectral efficiency.

Efficiency of a TDMA Frame:

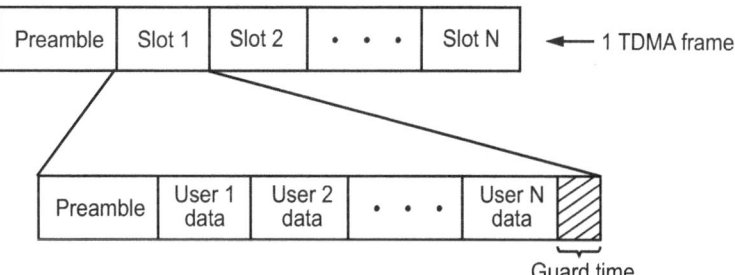

Fig. 4.4: TDMA Frame

$$b_o = N_r b_r + N_t b_p + (N_t + N_r) b_g \qquad \text{... (4.9)}$$

where, b_o is the number of overhead bits/frame.

N_r is the number of bursts per frame

N_t is the traffic bursts/frame.

b_r is the number of overhead bits/reference burst.

b_p is the number of overhead bits/preamble/slot.

b_g is the number of equivalent bits in each guard time interval.

$$b_t = T_f \times R_r \qquad \dots (4.10)$$

where, b_t is the total number of bits/frame.

T_f is the frame duration.

R_r is the bit rate of radio frequency channel.

$$\eta_f = \left(1 - \frac{b_o}{b_t}\right) \times 100\% \qquad \dots (4.11)$$

η_f is the frame efficiency.

$$b_u = RT_f \qquad \dots (4.12)$$

where, b_u is the number of bits/data channel (user)/frame.

R is the bit rate of each channel.

The number of channels per frame is defined as,

$$N_{C/F} = \frac{\text{Total data bits/frame}}{\text{Bits per channel/frame}}$$

$$N_{C/F} = \frac{\eta_f R_r T_f}{RT_f} \qquad \dots (4.13)$$

$$N_{C/F} = \frac{\eta_f R_r}{R} \qquad \dots (4.14)$$

4.3.4 Wideband Systems

Wideband systems use the spread spectrum technology. In this, the entire system bandwidth is available to each user. This often leads to bandwidth wastage. The two types of spread spectrum are Direct Sequence Spread Spectrum (DSSS) and Frequency Hopping Spread Spectrum (FHSS).

4.3.5 Solved Examples

Example 4.1: In a TDMA cellular system, the one-way bandwidth is 40 MHz. The channel spacing is 30 kHz and there are 1333 total voice channels in the system. The frame duration is 40 ms with 6 time slots/frame. The individual user data rate is 16.2 kbps and speech with error protection has a rate of 13 kbps. What is the TDMA system efficiency?

Solution: We know that the TDMA spectral efficiency is given by

$$\eta_a = \left(\frac{\tau M_t}{T_f}\right)\left(\frac{B_u N_u}{B_s}\right)$$

From the example, we get,

T_f = 40 ms, M_t = 6, B_u = 30 kHz, B_s = 40 MHz, N_u = 1333.

Time slot duration τ is calculated as,

$$\tau = \left(\frac{13}{16.2}\right)\left(\frac{40}{6}\right) = 5.35 \text{ ms}$$

$$\eta_a = \frac{5.35 \times 6}{40} \times \frac{30 \times 1333}{40000}$$

$$= 0.802$$

Overhead portion of frame= $1 - 0.802$

$$= 0.198$$

$$= 19.8\%$$

Example 4.2: An IS-54 system has η_b = 0.96, μ = 1.62, v_f = 1.0, information bit rate = 19.5 kbps, frequency reuse factor is 7 and bandwidth of system is 12.5 MHz.
Calculate the capacity and spectral efficiency (η).

Solution: We know that the capacity of a TDMA system is given by

$$N_u = \frac{\eta_b \mu}{v_f} \times \frac{B_s}{RN}$$

$$= \frac{0.96 \times 1.62}{1.0} \times \frac{12.5 \times 10^6}{19.5 \times 10^3 \times 7}$$

$$= 142.41 \simeq 142$$

Spectral efficiency is given by

$$\eta = \frac{N_u \times R}{B_s}$$

$$= \frac{142 \times 19.5}{12.5 \times 1000}$$

$$= 0.22 \text{ bit/sec/Hz}$$

Example 4.3: Calculate the frame efficiency and number of channels per frame of a TDMA system having 3 number of reference bursts per frame, a traffic of 24 frames of 120 ms each with 8 time slots per frame, 148 overhead bits in each of 8 time slots per reference burst. 34 overhead bits in each of 8 time slots per preamble per slot, 8.25 equivalent bits in each of 8 time slots in each guard time interval.

A frame duration of 120 ms and R_r = 270 kbps, R = 25 kbps.

Solution: The number of overhead bits/frame is given by

$$b_o = N_r b_r + N_t b_p + (N_t + N_r) b_g$$

From above data, we get,

N_r = 3

N_t = 24 frames of 120 ms each with 8 time slots/frame

b_r = 148 bits in each of 8 time slots

b_p = 34 bits in each of 8 time slots

b_g = 8.25 bits in each of 8 time slots

T_f = 120 ms

R_r = 270 kbps

R = 25 kbps

$$b_o = 3 \times 8 \times 148 + 24 \times 8 \times 34 + 8 \times 8.25 \times (3 + 24)$$
$$= 11,862 \text{ bits/frame}$$

The total number of bits/frame is given by

$$b_t = T_f \times R_r$$
$$= 120 \times 10^{-3} \times 270 \times 10^3$$
$$= 32,400 \text{ bits/frame}$$

The frame efficiency is given by

$$\eta_f = \left(1 - \frac{b_o}{b_t}\right) \times 100$$

$$= \left(1 - \frac{11862}{32400}\right) \times 100$$

$$= 63.38\%$$

The number of channels per frame is given by

$$N_{c/f} = \frac{\eta_f R_r}{R} = \frac{0.6338 \times 270}{25}$$

$$= 6.84$$

4.4 Cellular Communication Fundamentals

4.4.1 Mobile Cellular Communication

Mobile communication was started in 1975-1980. Initially, in UHF, 800-950 MHz was received for educational program, but later this band was no longer used. So, this band was free to be used by mobile services and hence allotted to mobile services.

Initially, the cellular communication was called 'Traditional Mobile Communication', in which cellular word was missing. The cellular word came into being when the entire area to be served by each group of radios was called 'cells'. Every cell has a transmitting tower of its own. Each cell operates at a different frequency. The 'MTSO', mobile telephone switching office, is situated in one of the cells. Each cell has around 10 km periphery.

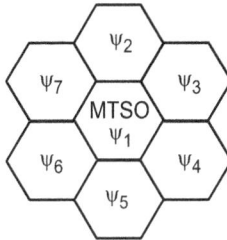

Fig. 4.5: A Simple Cellular System (k = 7)

4.4.2 Hexagonal Cells
The cell coverage depends on the terrain and many other factors. For design convenience, the cell coverage area is assumed to be a regular hexagon. The hexagon use is because of some reasons.
1. It avoids dead spots and full area coverage is achieved.
2. It requires fewer cells.
3. It requires less transmitter sites.
4. It is less expensive.

4.4.3 Elements of Cellular Mobile Radio Design
Some of the important elements of cellular mobile radio design are:
1. Frequency reuse.
2. Co-channel interference reduction factor.
3. Desired carrier to noise ratio.
4. Hand-off.
5. Cell splitting.

4.4.3.1 Frequency Reuse
The cellular system makes an efficient use of available channels by using low-power transmitters to allow frequency reuse at much smaller distances. Thus increasing the number of times each channel may be reused in a given geographical area.

Frequency can be repeated after some distance i.e. safe distance between two channels. This results into efficient frequency spectrum utilization. Distance, after which the frequency is repeated between the cells, is called frequency reuse distance.

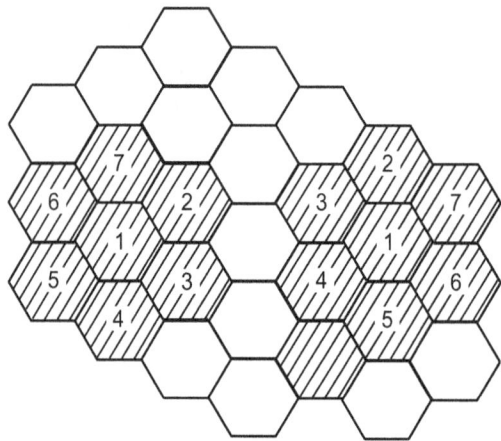

Fig. 4.6: Frequency Reuse

Frequency reuse can either be in time domain or frequency domain. In time domain, it is done by TDMA scheme i.e. allocation of different time slot to the frequency reuse scheme. In frequency domain, it is done by using FDMA scheme i.e. repeat carrier frequency after some time and frequency reuse distance.

4.4.3.1.1 Frequency Reuse Distance
Frequency reuse is the minimum distance between the two identical frequency carriers of the cell, so as to minimize the co-channel interference. The distance depends on the following parameters.

    (i)   Pattern used for cellular communication i.e. K.
    (ii)   Radius of the cell i.e. R.
    (iii) Antenna height.
    (iv) Transmitted power.

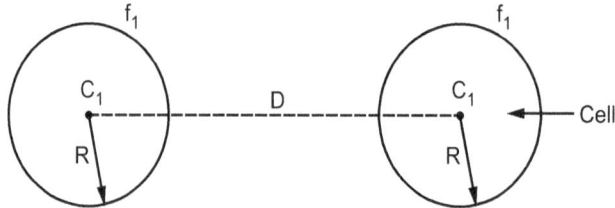

Fig. 4.7: Frequency Reuse Distance

where,   D is the frequency reuse distance

          C is the carrier

$$D = \sqrt{3K} \cdot R \qquad \qquad \text{... (4.15)}$$

4.4.3.2 Co-channel Interference Reduction Factor

The interference of one cell on another identical frequency cell is called co-channel interference. It is experienced both at the cell site and at the mobile stations in the center cell. In a small cell system, interference will be the dominating factor and the thermal noise can be neglected. The interference will be maximum if the cells are in adjacent tiers.

The co-channel interference reduction factor (q) is given by,

$$q = \frac{D}{R} \qquad \qquad ...(4.16)$$

where,   D is the distance between the two identical cells

R is the radius of the cell

$$\text{Interference, } I \propto \frac{D}{R} \qquad \qquad ...(4.17)$$

C is the power/signal strength

I_k is the interference of the kth cell

i is the number of tiers.

$$\frac{C}{I} = \frac{C}{\sum\limits_{k=1}^{k_i} I_k} \qquad \qquad ...(4.18)$$

Using equation (4.17),

$$\frac{C}{I} = \frac{C}{\sum\limits_{k=1}^{k_i} \left(\frac{D_k}{R_k}\right)^r} \qquad \qquad ...(4.19)$$

where, r is the proportionality constant, which is the propagation path-loss slope and it depends upon the terrain environment.

$$\frac{C}{I} = \frac{C}{\sum\limits_{k=1}^{k_i} \left(\frac{R_k}{D_k}\right)^{-r}} \qquad \qquad ...(4.20)$$

Using equation (4.16),

$$\frac{C}{I} = \frac{C}{\sum\limits_{k=1}^{k_i} \frac{1}{q_k^{-r}}} \qquad \qquad ...(4.21)$$

$$\frac{C}{I} = \frac{C}{\sum\limits_{k=1}^{k_i} q_k^{r}} \qquad \qquad ...(4.22)$$

where, $2 \leq r \leq 5$ and usually, r = 4.

In designing mobile cellular structure, the interference due to first tier, second tier and so on is calculated and it is obvious that interference due to first tier is dominated, whereas interference due to second and other tier is negligible, hence, can be neglected in mathematical modelling.

Co-channel interference can even be reduced by using directional antennas.

4.4.3.3 Carrier to Noise Ratio

From equation (4.22), we see that the carrier to noise ratio is decided by q_k, i.e. the co-channel interference factor of the kth cell.

For analog systems using FM, normal cellular practice is to specify the C/I ratio to be 18 dB or higher, based on subjective tests. A C/I ratio of 18 dB is the measured value for the accepted voice quality from present day cellular mobile receiver.

4.4.3.4 Hand-off Mechanism

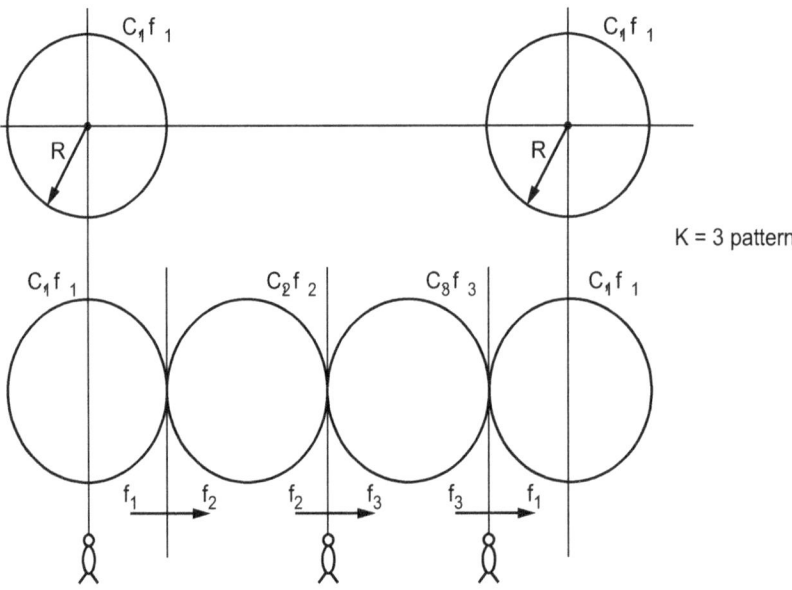

Fig. 4.8: Hand-off Mechanism

Hand-off is a mechanism which is necessary in mobile cellular communication. It is a process of changing the frequency automatically by the system without user intervention, while crossing from 1 cell site to another.

The conditions for hand-off are:

(i) When the signal strength received at the cell site is less than −100 dBM.

(ii) When C/I goes below 18 dB due to high interference.

(iii) When the mobile unit reaches loop holes due to geographical layout of that side.

4.4.3.4.1 Two Level Hand-off Mechanism

To avoid unnecessary hand-offs due to loop holes, 2-level hand-off mechanism is used. Hand-off should take place at proper time and place.

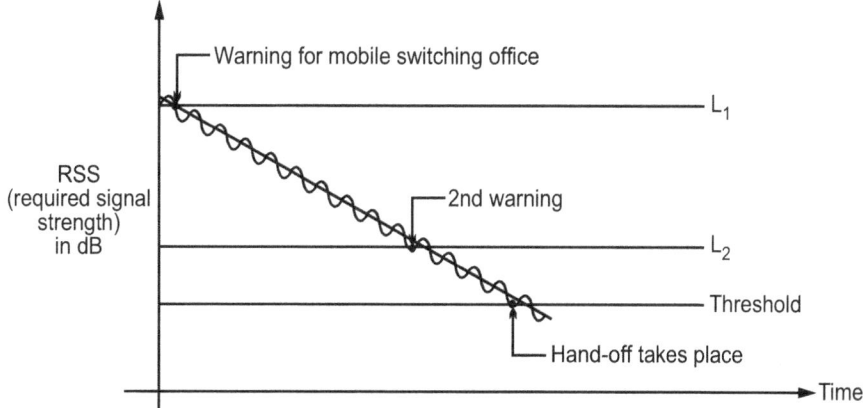

Fig. 4.9: RSS Vs. Time Graph

The above graph shows three levels L_1, L_2 and threshold of required signal strength. When the signal strength reaches L_1, a warning is given to the mobile switching office for hand-off. When the RSS falls further to L_2, another warning is given if another cell site is not free. Further, on reaching the threshold, hand-off takes place.

4.4.3.5 Cell Splitting

Cell is splitted into smaller when the traffic increases. The cell area or the individual component coverage area of the system is divided into more cell areas. This increases the amount of channel reuse, thus increasing subscriber serving capacity.

However, there is an increase in the hand-off rate per subscriber.

Cell splitting is of two types:

(i) Permanent and

(ii) Dynamic

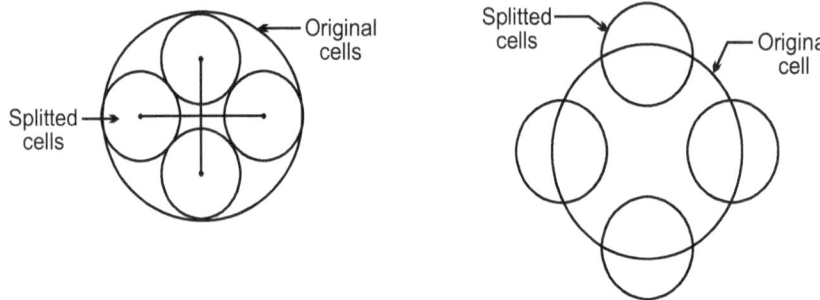

Fig. 4.10: Cell Splitting

In the above cell splitting example, the original cell is divided into 4 cells for load sharing. In the first figure, the new cells occupy the same area as that of the original cell, but in the second figure, the new cells can even occupy another cell area which is not so crowdy. One tower is divided in four towers. Thus, power required by individual tower is less.

4.4.3.5.1 Permanent Cell Splitting
It is done by planning ahead of time. Advantage of this method is that another frequency can also be used.

4.4.3.5.2 Dynamic Cell Splitting
It is done using software algorithm. It is done after analyzing all cell sites and traffic condition in a city. Whenever need is there, a cell is splitted and when no traffic is there, it can be recombined.

4.4.4 Blocking Probability

Blocking probability (P_b) is the probability of blocking calls out of N number of calls generated in a busy hour condition. Offered load is the load carried by a particular service in a busy hour condition. It is measured in Erlangs. It is given by,

$$A = \frac{\text{Average calling time} \propto \text{Total customers}}{60} \qquad ... (4.23)$$

The number of customers per channel M_0 is given by,

$$M_0 = \frac{\text{Number of customers}}{\text{Number of channels}} \qquad ... (4.24)$$

The number of calls supported by a system in a busy hour condition is given by,

$$Q_i = \frac{A \times 60}{1.76} \qquad ... (4.25)$$

The trunking efficiency or the degradation factor is given by,

$$\eta_e = \frac{Q_{i\,(1c)} - 2Q_{i\,(2c)}}{Q_{i\,(1c)}} \qquad ... (4.26)$$

where, $Q_{i\ (1c)}$ is the number of calls supported by a 1 carrier system.

$Q_{i\ (2c)}$ is the number of calls supported by a 2 carrier system.

As the number of carriers in a market grows, the trunking efficiency (η_e) degrades further for a fixed blocking probability.

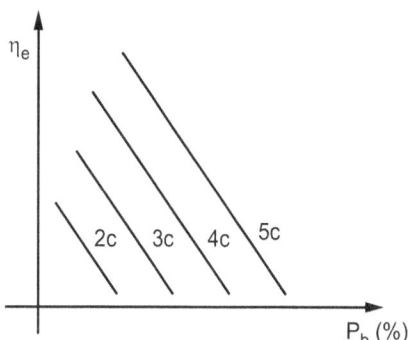

Fig. 4.11: η_e Vs. P_b graph

η_c is the ratio of number of calls per hour per cell to the total number of subscribers/ customers.

The number of subscribers per cell is a function of Q_i and η_c.

$$M_i \quad = \quad f(Q_i, \eta_c) \qquad\qquad \text{... (4.27)}$$

4.4.5 Solved Examples

Example 4.4: In an area 666 channels are available and are shared between 7 cells. The blocking probability is 2%. Calculate the offered load (using the Erlangs' table).

Solution: Using the data given, the number of channels per cell (N) is calculated as,

$$N \quad = \quad \frac{666}{7} \simeq 95 \text{ channels/cell}$$

Given: $P_b = 2\% = 0.02$

Using Erlangs' table, the offered load $A_1 = 83.14$ erlangs

Example 4.5: Calculate the offered load for a 2 carrier system if there are 333 channels shared by 7 cells and $P_b = 2\%$. Thus, using example 4.4, calculate the trunking efficiency.

Solution:

Part 1: Number of channels per cell (N) = $\frac{333}{7}$ = 47.5 channels/cell.

$$P_b = 2\% = 0.02$$

Thus, the Erlangs' table, the offered load $A_2 = 38$ erlangs.

Part 2: Trunking efficiency is given by

$$\eta_e = \frac{Q_{i\,(1c)} - 2Q_{i\,(2c)}}{Q_{i\,(1c)}}$$

Q_i from equation (4.25) is,

$$Q_{i1} = \frac{A_1 \times 60}{1.76}, \quad Q_{i\,2} = \frac{A_2 \times 60}{1.76}$$

Q_{i1} is the number of calls supported by 1 carrier system.

Q_{i2} is the number of calls supported by 2 carrier system.

$$Q_{i1} = \frac{83.14 \times 60}{1.76} = 2832.95 \text{ calls/hr}$$

$$Q_{i2} = \frac{38 \times 60}{1.76} = 1295.45 \text{ calls/hr}$$

$$\therefore \quad \eta_e = \frac{2832.95 - 2 \times 1295.45}{2832.95}$$

$$\therefore \quad \eta_e = 8.5\%$$

Example 4.6: The maximum calls per hour Q_i in 1 cell is 3000 and the average calling time is 1.76 min. The blocking probability is 2%. Calculate the offered load in the system and number of channels.

Solution: We have,

$$Q_i = \frac{A \times 60}{1.76}$$

$$\therefore \quad A = \frac{Q_i \times 1.76}{60}$$

$$= \frac{3000 \times 1.76}{60}$$

$$= 88 \text{ erlangs}$$

$$P_b = 2\%$$

Using Erlangs' table, $N = 102$ channels

Example 4.7: There are 50 channels in a cell, to handle all the calls and the average time is 100 sec per call. How many calls can be handled in this cell with $P_b = 0.002$.

Solution: Given: $N = 50$, $P_b = 0.002$

From Erlangs' table,

Offered load, $A = 40.3$

From equation (4.25),

$$Q_i = \frac{A \times 60}{T}$$

$$= \frac{40.3 \times 60}{100/60}$$

$$= 1450.8$$

∴ 1451 calls can be handled by exchange in busy hour condition.

Example 4.8: Calculate the number of subscribers, if 1000 calls are initiated per hour per cell.

Solution: We know that,

$$\eta_c = \frac{\text{Number of calls/hr/cell}}{\text{Total number of subscribers/customers}}$$

∴ Number of subscribers $= \dfrac{10,000}{\eta_c}$

η_c normally lies between 0.7 to 0.8

Assuming $\eta_c = 0.8$,

$$\text{Number of subscribers} = \frac{10,000}{0.8}$$

$$= 1250$$

Example 4.9: During the busy hour, the number of calls per hour (Q_i) for 10 cells are:

Cell 1 → 2000
Cell 2 → 1500
Cell 3 → 3000
Cell 4 → 500
Cell 5 → 1000
Cell 6 → 1200
Cell 7 → 1800
Cell 8 → 2500
Cell 9 → 2800
Cell 10 → 900

If $\eta_c = 0.6$ and $\eta_c = 0.8$, calculate the number of subscribers in the cell.

Solution:

Total number of calls/hr/cell = 2000 + 1500 + 3000 + 500 + 1000 + 1200 + 1800 + 2500
+ 2800 + 900

= 17200

We know that number of subscribers (M) is,

$$M = \frac{\text{Total number of calls/hr/cell}}{\eta_c}$$

Case 1: η_c = 0.6

$$M = \frac{17200}{0.6}$$
$$= 28{,}600$$

Case 2: η_c = 0.8

$$M = \frac{17200}{0.8}$$
$$= 21500$$

4.5 GSM Architecture and Interfaces

4.5.1 GSM Architecture

GSM was originally defined by ETSI as a European digital cellular telephony standard. GSM interfaces defined by ETSI lay the ground work for a multivendor network approach to digital mobile communication. The GSM, Public Land Mobile Network architecture is as shown below in Fig. 4.12.

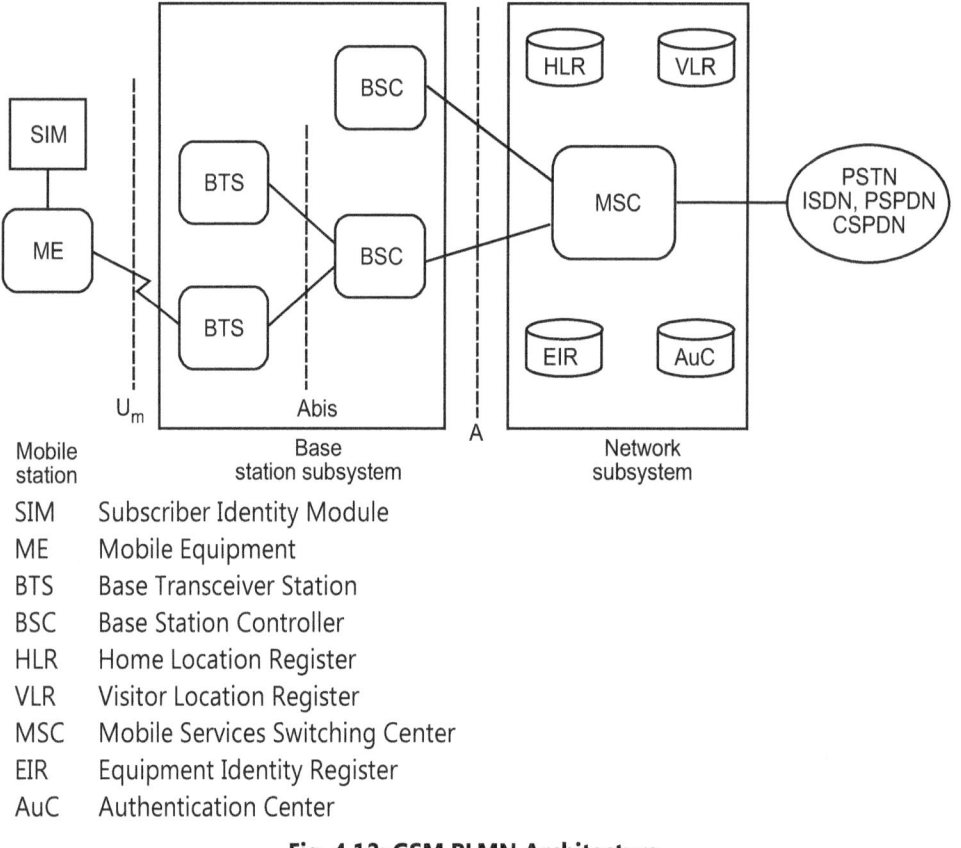

SIM	Subscriber Identity Module	
ME	Mobile Equipment	
BTS	Base Transceiver Station	
BSC	Base Station Controller	
HLR	Home Location Register	
VLR	Visitor Location Register	
MSC	Mobile Services Switching Center	
EIR	Equipment Identity Register	
AuC	Authentication Center	

Fig. 4.12: GSM PLMN Architecture

A Public Land Mobile Network (PLMN) includes the following system entities:

- Mobile - Services Switching Center (MSC).
- Home Location Register (HLR).
- Visitor Location Register (VLR).
- Equipment Identity Register (EIR).
- Authentication Center (AuC).
- Base Station System (BSS).
- Base Transceiver Station (BTS).
- Base Station Controller (BSC).
- Mobile Station (MS).
- Operation and Maintenance Center (OMC).
- Other Network Elements.

4.5.2 GSM Subsystem Entities

Fig. 4.12 shows the functional entities of the GSM and their logical interconnection. All the functional entities are described below.

4.5.2.1 Mobile-Services Switching Center (MSC)

The switching functions for all mobile stations located in the geographic area covered by its assigned BSSs is performed by MSC. It also interfaces with the PSTN (Public Switched Telephone Network) as well as with the other MSCs and other system entities, such as HLR, in the PLMN.

The functions of MSC are –

- Management of MSC-BSS signalling protocol.
- Management of required logical radio-link channel during calls.
- Call handling that copes with mobile nature of subscriber (e.g. paging).
- Handling location registration and ensuring interworking between mobile station and VLR.
- Control of inter-BSS and inter-MSC handovers.
- Acting as a gateway MSC to interrogate the HLR.
- Exchange of signalling information with other system entities.
- Standard functions of a local exchange switch in the fixed network.

4.5.2.2 Home Location Register

The identities of mobile subscribers, their service parameters and their location information are stored in the home location register (HLR). The HLR contains –

- Identity of mobile subscriber.
- ISDN directory number of mobile station.
- Subscription information on teleservices and bearer services.
- Service restrictions (if any).
- Supplementary services.
- Location information for call routing.

4.5.2.3 Visitor Location Register

The VLR contains –

- Identity of mobile subscriber.
- Any temporary mobile subscriber identity.
- ISDN directory number of mobile.
- A directory number to route calls to a roaming station.
- Location area where the mobile station is registered.
- Copy of the subscriber data from the HLR.

4.5.2.4 Equipment Identity Register (EIR)

When a mobile station accesses the system, during equipment validation procedure, the EIR is accessed. It contains the identity of mobile station equipment which may be valid, suspect or known as fraudulent. EIR contains –

- White or valid list – List of valid MS equipment identifies.
- Crrey or monitored list – List of suspected mobiles under observation.
- Black or prohibited list – List of mobiles for which service is barred.

4.5.2.5 Authentication Center (AuC)

- AuC contains subscriber authentication data called authentication keys (k_i).
- AuC generates security related parameters needed to authorize service using k_i.
- AuC generates unique data pattern called a cipherkey (k_c) needed for encrypting user speech and data.

4.5.2.6 Operations and Maintenance Center (OMC)

The centralised maintenance and diagnostic heart of the BSS is OMC. It allows the network provider to operate, administer and monitor the functioning of the BSS.

4.5.2.7 Base Station System (BSS)

The characteristics of BSS are –

- It is responsible for communicating with mobile stations in cell areas.
- One BSC controls one or more BTSs and can perform inter BTS and intra BTS hand-offs.
- The BTS serves one or more cells in the cellular network and contains one or more transceivers (TRXs).
- The TRX serves full duplex communication to the MS.
- In the GSM network implementation of Lucent technologies the BSC includes the Transcoder/Rate Adapter Unit (TRAU). The TRAU adapts the transmission bit rate of the A-interface (64 kbps) to Abis (16 kbps).

BSSs are of different types as given below:

- BSS can be an integrated (Intg) or a distributed (Dist) BSS. An Intg is a BSS, which has BSC and BTS functionality located in the same physical unit. In distributed BSS, BTS and BSS are physically separated.
- BSS can have internally (Int) or externally (Ext) located speech transcoding. Speech transcoding to 64 kbps takes place either in BSC for BSS types 1, 4 and 5 or external to BSS for BSS types 2, 6 and 7. For BSS type 3, transcoding takes place in BTS.
- The Abis interface uses multiplexing (Mult) or Rate Adapter (RA) on its links. The first option means that four 16 kbps links are multiplexed into one 64 kbps channel. The latter option means that no multiplexing of the 16 kbps channels takes place.

4.5.2.8 Mobile Station (MS)

The terminal equipment used by wireless subscriber supported by GSM wireless system is represented by MS.

The two entities of MS are –

- Subscriber Identity Module (SIM).
- Mobile Equipment.

Validity checks made on the MS equipment are performed independently of the authentication checks made on the MS subscriber information.

Functions of MS are:

- Radio transmission termination.
- Radio channel management.
- Speech encoding/decoding.
- Radio link error protection.
- Flow control of data.
- Rate adaptation of user data to the radio link.
- Mobility management.
- Performance measurements of radio link.

4.5.2.9 Some Network Elements

MSC can interface to some other network elements like Billing and Service center. Billing center polls the disk record, where the call accountings are stored by MSC, to collect the billing data. Service Center is responsible for SMS (Short Message Service).

4.5.2.10 Power Classes

The MSS can have different maximum RF power level transmission based on which GSM-900 has 5 power classes and GSM-1800 has 3 power classes.

Table 4.2: MS Power Classes

Class		I	II	III	IV	V
Max RF Power (in watts)	GSM-900	–	8	5	2	0.8
	GSM-1800	1	0.25	4	–	–

4.5.2.11 Operation and Maintenance Center (OMC)

The security based on validation of identities of various telecommunications entities is handled by OMC. AuC and EIR are the centers where these functions are performed.

The maintenance and remote operations of PLMC is done by OMC. It monitors and controls these functions.

4.5.3 GSM Interfaces

GSM interfaces are used for connection of various nodes in GSM network. There are different GSM interfaces, defined as below.

4.5.3.1 U_m Interface

It is also known as Air Interface or Radio Interface. It is the most important part in any mobile radio system and interfaces MS and BTS (Base Transceiver Stations).

It supports maximum spectral efficiency and universal use of any compatible mobile station in a GSM network.

The radio interface uses the Link Access Protocol on D_M Channel ($LAPD_M$).

4.5.3.2 Abis Interface

Abis interfaces are vendor specific. It interfaces BSC and BTS. The interface comprises traffic and control channels. Functions implemented at Abis interface are:
1. Traffic channel transmission, terrestrial and radio channel management.
2. Voice-data traffic exchange.
3. Signalling exchange between BSC and BTS.
4. Transporting synchronization information from BSC to BTS.

This interface supports two types of communication links:
1. Traffic channels at 64 kbps.
2. Signalling channels at 16 kbps.

The two messages handled by traffic management procedure part of the signalling interface are transparent and non-transparent. Messages between MS and BSC-MSC are transparent messages and they do not require analysis by BTS. But, BTS analysis is required by non-transparent messages.

4.5.3.3 A-Interface

It is the interface between BSC and MSC. The physical layer of A-interface is a 2 Mbps standard CCITT digital connection.

4.5.3.4 Proprietary M-Interface

It is the interface between physical BSC and the TRAU. TRAU is included in BSC in the GSM network implementation of lucent technologies. The TRAU adapts transmission bit rate of A-interface (64 kbps) to A_{bis}-interface (16 kbps).

4.5.3.5 Interface between other GSM Entities

MAP is used to transfer information between GSM PLMN entities. Mobile application and several Application Service Elements (ASEs) are contained in MAP.

4.6 Radio Link Features in GSM System

4.6.1 Radio Link Aspects

GSM networks operate in four different radio frequencies. The most popular bands are 900 MHz or 1800 MHz. 850 MHz and 1900 MHz bands are used in some parts of USA and Canada as 900 MHz and 1800 MHz were already allocated.

The uplink frequency band for 900 MHz is 890-915 MHz and the downlink frequency band is 935-960 MHz. This 25 MHz bandwidth is further divided into 124 carrier frequency channels, each 200 kHz apart.

Time division multiplexing is used to allow speech channels per radio frequency channel. Each TDMA frame contains 8 radio time slots; with a frame duration of 4.615 ms and transmission channel data rate is 270.833 kbps. The transmission power in the handset is limited to a maximum of 2 watts in GSM 850/900 and 1 watt in GSM 1800/1900.

Linear Predictive Coding (LPC) is used in GSM to reduce bit rate. The vocal tract is mimiced by the parameters of LPC filter. A residual signal is left behind by the signal which passes through this filter. Speech is encoded at 13 kbps.

A GSM network has cells of four different sizes - macro, micro, pico and umbrella cells. The coverage area of each cell varies according to the implementation environment. Cell radius depends on antenna height, gain and propagation conditions from a couple of hundred meters to several tens of kilometers. The longest distance, the GSM specification supports in practical use, is 35 km (22 miles).

Gaussian Minimum Shift Keying (GMSK) modulation is used in GSM. In GMSK, the signal to be modulated onto the carrier is first smoothed with a Gaussian LPF before being fed to a frequency modulator, which reduces adjacent channel interference.

4.6.2 Interference-Reducing Mechanism

Following are the mechanisms used by GSM to reduce interference:

1.   Dynamic Power Control (DPC).

2.   Discontinuous Transmission (DTX).

3.   Slow Frequency Hopping (SFH).

4.6.2.1 Discontinuous Transmission (DTX)

Discontinuous transmission is a GSM feature in which speech is transmitted only when there is speech available to transmit. The average interference is reduced by 3 dB if the transmitter is active only 50% of the time. This would also help in power consumption reduction by mobile phones. However, a voice activity detector (VAD) is used to initiate switching process. If its operation is imperfect, there might be clipping in speech. Noise contrast between client and active periods is another disadvantage of DTX. The DTX can be used to improve the quality of uplink only without additional gains in capacity. The capacity advantage is achieved by decreasing reuse distance because DTX has a greater impact when the system is interference limited.

A Silence Indicator (SID) every 480 ms is sent by a mobile to provide comfort noise level information to BS so that the person on the far end can hear some low level noise and cannot conclude that the link is down.

4.6.2.2 Dynamic Power Control

To achieve effective communication with the BTS, MS is instructed by GSM network to use only minimum power level necessary.

The received power level, the quality of received signal, and ID codes for upto 6 neighbouring BSS are measured by HS. Similarly, the BS measures the received power level and signal quality, the distance and transmit power of each MS.

The signal level values in GSM in dBm is in the range of –110 dBm to –48 dBm. These levels are mapped in 63 levels with a gap of 10 dBm each. The quality level value in GSM is determined by the bit error rate, BER is mapped to 8 levels ranging from 0.2% to 12.8%. For the BS to send the information to MS, the BS should determine the minimum required transmit power. The power output is nominally controlled in 2 dB steps, for the BTS, to provide better co-channel interference performance.

The battery life of a mobile set can be increased and interference can be reduced with the use of minimum transmitting power to access the network.

4.6.2.3 Slow Frequency Hopping (SFH)

To reduce the required C/I ratio and improve performance in multipath fading environment, slow frequency hopping is used in GSM.

By invoking SFH, chance of losing the radio link is reduced when the mobile passes through areas of fade and poor reception. It is even important in case of hand-offs.

SFH improves the signal quality in GSM because the hop rate is less than the message bit rate in SFH.

The hopping rate in GSM is equal to 1/frame duration or $1/4.1615 \times 10^{-3}$ i.e. 216.7 hops per second. A mobile transmits at one frequency during a time slot and hops to a different frequency before the next time slot.

Rayleigh Fading, which causes a fade upto 40 to 50 dB on the received signal and radio link may be lost, is overcome by frequency hopping.

Interference diversity is provided by frequency hopping. Frequency hopping improves system capacity by reducing C/I requirement from 12 dB to 9 dB.

4.6.3 Future Techniques for Interference Reduction in GSM

With the increased demand for spectrum to serve mobile users, further techniques are being planned to reduce the interference in GSM. Some of them are as given below:
- Channel Management.
- Advanced Antenna Technology.

4.6.3.1 Channel Management

There are mainly three types of channel borrowing schemes:
- Dynamic Channel Allocation (DCA).
- Hybrid Channel Assignment (HCA).
- Channel Borrowing Without Locking (CBWL).

A central pool of channels is used in Dynamic Channel Allocation (DCA). For use in a call, a channel is borrowed from this pool by a BS; which is then returned to the pool after the call is completed. Self organizing channel assignment algorithm is used in DCA.

In Hybrid Channel Assignment, some channels are permanently assigned to each BS and rest are borrowed from a central pool. To avoid co-channel interference, a channel locking scheme is used.

In Channel Borrowing Without Locking, each BS is allocated channel. Channel borrowing is used, if all channels of BS are occupied and a new call arrives. Some advantages of CBWL over DCA and HCA are –

1. It exhibits better performance even in heavy traffic load.
2. Control and management tasks are simplified in CBWL as channel borrowing at a BS does not require global information about channel usage in the system.
3. User can borrow channels from any of the adjacent BSS.
4. No additional infrastructure cost is there.

4.6.3.2 Advanced Antenna Technology

A smart of intelligent antenna reduces interference. It is a group of core RF technologies that control directional antenna arrays by means of digital signal processing algorithms. It manages the incoming signals to maximize performance after evaluating signal conditions of each transmitted/received signal. It optimizes the signal characteristics by assigning specific weight to each of the incoming signal. It does all real time decision, thus helping in interference reduction.

4.7 GSM Logical Channels and Frame Structure

4.7.1 Multiple Access and Channel Structure

All users share the limited resource of the radio spectrum. TDMA/FDMA is used to divide the bandwidth among maximum number of users. In FDMA, the 25 MHz bandwidth is divided into 124 carrier frequencies spaced 200 kHz apart. Each base station is assigned one or more carrier frequencies. These carrier frequencies are further divided in time using TDMA.

'Burst period' is the fundamental unit of time in TDMA. It is equal to $15/26 = 0.577$ ms approximately. A TDMA frame is made up of 8 burst, thus, it lasts for around $8 \times 0.577 = 4.615$ ms, which is the basic unit of a logical channel. One physical channel is one burst period per TDMA frame. Number and position of burst periods define the channel. All these definitions are cyclic with a cycle period of approximately 3 hours. Broadly, channels can be divided into two types:

- Dedicated channels – allocated to MS.
- Common channels – Used by MSs in idle mode.

4.7.2 GSM Logical Channels

User information and control signals are constantly transmitted between the MS and the BS. Logical channels are used for these transmissions. Different logical channels are used for different physical channels. The two basic logical channels in GSM are –

- Traffic Channel (TCH).
- Control Channel (CCH).

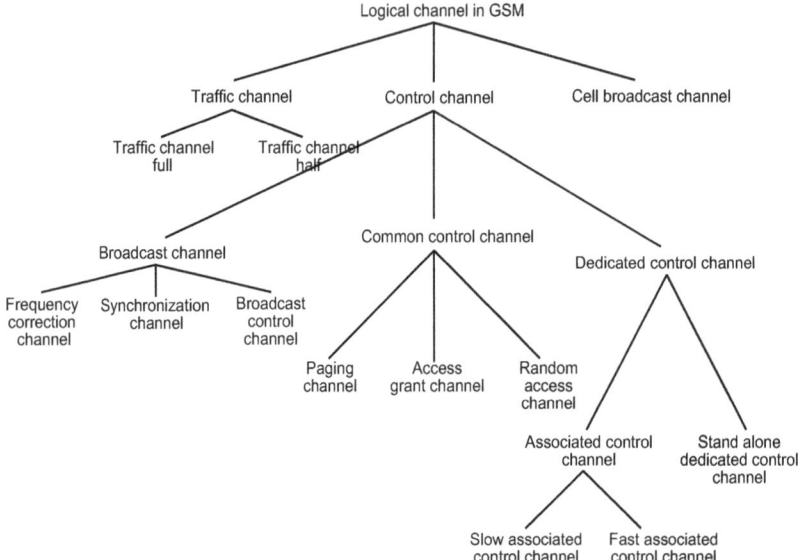

Fig. 4.13: GSM Logical Channels

4.7.2.1 Traffic Channels

Speech and data are carried by the traffic channel (TCH). A TCH is defined as a group of 26 TDMA frames of 120 ms duration, similar to the definition of the length of a burst period. In the 26 frames, 24 are used as TCH, 1 for SACCH (Slow Associated Control Channel) and 1 is unused. TCHs for uplink and downlink are separated in time by 3 burst periods, so that the MS do not have to transmit and receive simultaneously; resulting in a simplified electronics. Above was the description of full rate TCHs. Half rate TCHs are also defined, but not implemented yet. Full rate speech coding is at 13 kbps; whereas for half rate, it is 7 kbps. This doubles the capacity of a system.

Standalone Dedicated Control Channels (SDCCH) are eighth rate TCHs, they are also specified and used for signalling.

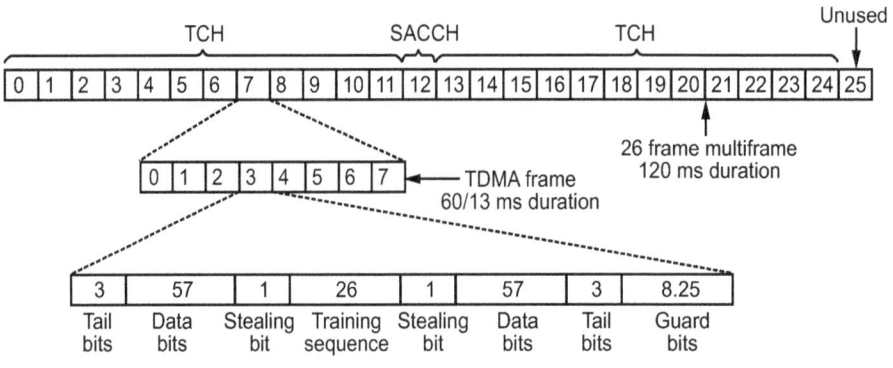

Fig. 4.14: Burst Organization, TDMA Frames and Multiframes for Speech and Data

4.7.2.2 Control Channels

Channels used by mobiles in idle as well as dedicated modes are called control channels (CCH). In idle mode, mobiles use CCH to exchange the signalling information required to change to dedicated mode. The surrounding BSs hand-offs and other information are monitored by mobiles in dedicated mode. The common channels are defined within a S1-frame multiframe, so that dedicated mobiles using the 26-frame multiframe TCH structure can still monitor control channels.

The common channels include:
1. **Broadcast Control Channel (BCCH):** It is used to continuously broadcast, on the downlink, information about BS identity, frequency allocations and frequency hopping sequences.
2. **Frequency Correction Channel (FCCH) and Synchronization Channel (SCH):** It is used to synchronize the mobile to the time slot structure of a cell by defining the boundaries of burst periods and time slot numbering. In a TDMA frame, on time slot 0, every cell in a GSM network broadcasts exactly 1 FCCH and 1 SCH.
3. **Random Access Channel (RACH):** It is the slotted ALOHA channel used by the mobile to request access to the network.
4. **Paging Channel (PCH):** It is used to alert the MS of an incoming call.
5. **Access Grant Channel (AGCH):** It is used to allocate an SDCCH to a mobile for signalling after a request on the RACH in order to obtain a dedicated channel.

4.7.3 GSM Frame Structure

The forward and reverse bands are divided into 200 kHz channels called Absolute Radio Frequency Channel Numbers (ARFCN), in which each of the 8 users for a full rate channel utilizes the same ARFCN and occupies a unique time slot per frame. Out of the 156.25 bits, 8.25 bits are used for guard band, 6 start and stop bits are used to prevent adjacent time slot overlap. 148 bits are transmitted at 270.833 kbps. 8 time slots of 4.615 ms duration and 1250 bits constitute a single full rate GSM frame, with a frame rate of 216.667 frames/s. The 13th and 26th frames are used for control purpose.
Refer to Fig. 4.14.

4.7.4 GSM Bursts

There are five different types of bursts used in GSM. The GSM bursts are of the following types:
*   Normal burst.
*   Synchronization burst.
*   Frequency correction burst.
*   Access burst.
*   Dummy burst.

4.7.4.1 Normal Burst

3	57	1	26	1	57	3	8.25
Tail bits	Data bits	Stealing bit	Training bits	Stealing bit	Data bits	Tail bits	Guard time

Fig. 4.15: Normal Burst

A normal burst is used to carry data and most signalling. It contains 156.25 bits, made up of two 57 bit information bits, 26 bit training sequence for equalization, 1 stealing bit for each information block (FACCH), 3 tail bits at each end and an 8.25 bit guard sequence. The tail bits are used to provide start and stop bit patterns. The 156.25 bits are transmitted in 0.577 ms, giving a gross bit rate of 270.833 kbps. The guard bit is used to prevent overlap between adjacent time slots during transmission. It is an empty space.

4.7.4.2 Synchronization Burst

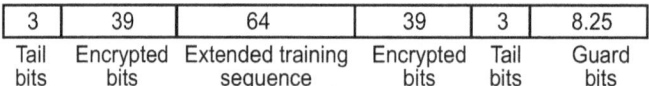

3	39	64	39	3	8.25
Tail bits	Encrypted bits	Extended training sequence	Encrypted bits	Tail bits	Guard bits

Fig. 4.16: Synchronization Burst

Synchronization burst is used for time synchronization of mobile, thus, having a long synchronization sequence of 64 bits. The information of the TDMA frame alongwith the BTS identification code (BSIC) is carried by the 78 encrypted bits.

To protect user information, the TDMA frame is broadcast over an SCH after ciphering the information.

4.7.4.3 Frequency Correction Channel Burst

3	142	3	8.25
Tail bits	Fixed all zeroes	Tail bits	Guard bits

Fig. 4.17: Frequency Correction Burst

The frequency burst is used on FCCH and is used for frequency synchronization. It contains a fixed all zero sequence of 142 length causing the modulator to deliver an unmodulated carrier with an offset of 1625/24 kHz above the nominal frequency.

4.7.4.4 Access Burst

3	48	36	3	60
Tail bits	Synchronization sequence	Encrypted message	Tail bits	Additional guard time

Fig. 4.18: Access Burst

The access burst is shorter than the normal burst and is used only on the RACH. The additional guard period is to protect for burst transmission from an MS that does not know the timing advance when it first access the system. It is used for random access. The transmission distance from BS to MS is 35 km.

4.7.4.5 Dummy Burst

3	58	26	58	3	8.25
Tail bits	Mixed bits	Training bits	Mixed bits	Tail bits	Guard time

Fig. 4.19: Dummy Burst

Dummy burst is sent from BTS. It carries no information. The fixed bits are defined as modulating bit states.

4.8 Speech Coding in GSM

4.8.1 Speech Coding

GSM is a digital system. So, speech which is inherently analog, has to be digitized. The current telephone system uses PCM (Pulse Code Modulation). With a output bit rate of 64 kbps, which is too high to be feasible over a radio link, it also contains redundancy in the 64 kbps signal.

The speech coding used by GSM is Linear Predictive Coding (LPC) which has a long term predictor loop with a regular excited pulse. This was after study of several speech coding algorithms on the basis of subjective speech quality and complexity related to cost, processing delay and power consumption.

In Linear Predictive Coder, information from previous samples is used to predict the current sample. The signal is represented by the coefficients of the linear combination of the previous samples plus an encoded form of the residual i.e. the difference between the predicted and actual sample. The total bit rate is 13 kbps. Speech is divided into 20 ms sample, each of which is encoded as 260 bits. This is full-rate speech coding. In North America, GSM 1900 operators have implemented an enhanced full rate speech coding algorithm (EFR), which provides an improved speech quality using 13 kbps bit rate.

4.8.2 Vocoders

Vocoders are used for human speech production. They are parametric digitizers. Sound pressure waves radiated from lips produce human speech. Vocal cords are excited by the air compressed in the lungs, in two modes. The vocal cords vibrate and produce quasiperiodic voice sounds, when generating voice sounds. Voice cards are not used to produce voice in case of unvoiced sounds.

In vocoders, a set of source parameters is generated to characterize the input signal close for a given period of time. Though, in vocoders, the synthetic speech quality is relatively low, but it has an advantage of low bit rate. Vocoders can be frequency domain or time domain. But frequency domain vocoders are more advantageous than time domain vocoders.

4.8.3 Speech Codecs

In a GSM cell phone, the audio data from microphone is sampled at 8 kHz with a resolution of 13 bits, thus giving a source data rate of 104 kbps. GSM has an option of 4 codecs to perform compression.
- Enhanced full rate codec.
- Adaptive multirate codec.
- Half rate speech codec.
- Full rate speech codec.

A modified Linear Predictive Coder (LPC) acts as a full rate speech codec, it models the human vocal tract as a series of cylinders of different widths. Speech sounds are generated by forcing air through these cylinders. The LPC coder models this with a set of simultaneous equations. Two techniques are used to enhance the quality of LPC in GSM as a standard LPC cannot provide the quality of speech required for a telephone system. The two techniques are –
- Regular Pulse Excitation (RPE).
- Long Term Prediction (LTP).

Thus, the full rate codec is described as a RPELTP linear predictive coder; which is given an input speech data of 160 samples, 20 ms duration and 13 bit resolution.

Table 4.3: Relative encode and decode complexity compared to full rate vocoders

Codec	Bit Rate (kbps)	Compression Ratio	Codec Type
Full rate	13	8	RTE-LTP LPC
EFR	12.2	8.5	ACELP
Half Rate	5.6	18.4	VSELP
AMR	12.2 to 4.75	8.5 to 21.9	ACELP

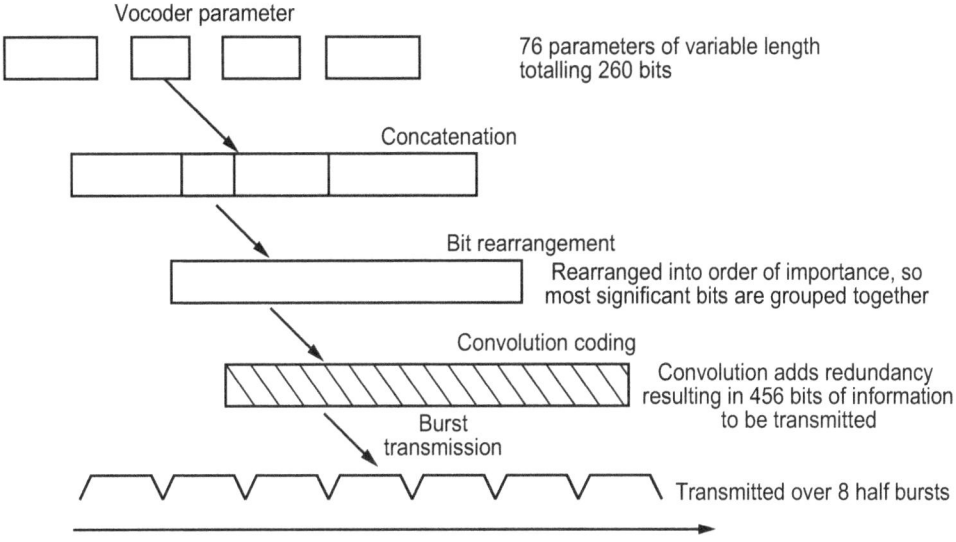

Fig. 4.20: Example of a Full Rate Speech Transmission

4.8.4 GSM Vocoders

4.8.4.1 Full Rate Vocoder

Linear Predictive Coding with Regular Pulse Excitation (LPC-RPE) is the GSM vocoder. Speech is processed by encoder in 20 ms block, 260 bits thus giving an output rate of 13 kbps.

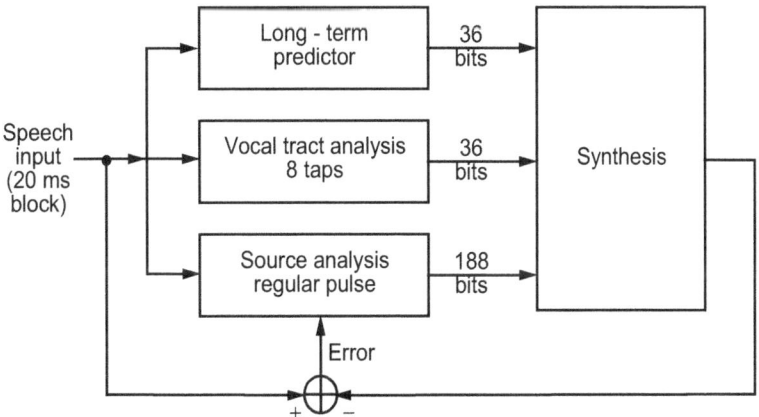

Fig. 4.21: GSM Full Rate LPC - RPE Vocoder

Major parts of an encoder are –

- Linear prediction analysis.
- Long term prediction.
- Excitation analysis.

The linear prediction analysis consists of a 8-tap filter having 8 log-area ratios, each having 3, 4, 5 or 6 bits, thus, giving a resultant of 36 bits.

The pitch and gain is estimated by the long-term predictor. 7 bits of lag coefficient and 2 bits of gain coefficients are provided by each estimate. The regular pulse excitation analysis gives an output of 188 bits.

4.8.4.2 Half Rate Vocoder

The Vector Self Excited Linear Predictor (VSELP) acts as the half rate GSM vocoder with a bit rate of 5.6 kbps. VSELP is similar to CELP family, except that it uses more than 1 separate excitation codebook, which are separately scaled by their respective excitation gain factor. It has 4 modes of operation, it can operate in any of the four modes depending on the grade of voice detected in the speech. 28 bits per 20 ms frame are encoded. Long-Term Predictor (LTP) gain decides the mode of operation.

4.9 Data Services in GSM

4.9.1 Data Interworking

Voice band modems (1200-56000 baud) are used for low speed data transmission over telephone network. The uses of data networks are:

- Accessibility to electronic mail, remote computers.
- Transfer of files, facsimile.
- Internet accessibility.
- Transaction services like credit and validation.

The mobile systems have not been designed for transmission of non-voice signals, so they must possess the capability to do protocol conversion to support services using voice band modem. This provision of the protocol conversion in the MS is called interworking. Interworking is possible only if the air interface supports a data rate higher than the basic data rate of the voice-band modem.

In digital cellular phones, there is a digital port. But, since RS-232 connector is too large for the mobile phones, some special form of connector is used. Each manufacturer uses its own type of connector. Infrared serial port is used in many of the mobile phones.

Three types of MSs are defined by GSM standard.

- **Type 0 station:** They either do not support data services, or have all data functionality fully supported within the phone.
- **Type 1 MS:** They have separate ISDN terminal and support S-interface. A data terminal is connected to ISDN terminal as most ISDN terminals do not include data terminal equipment.
- **Type 2 MS:** In type 2 MS, an X-series terminal (X.21, X.25) or a V series terminal (V.32) is supported directly by R interface. MS usually has to perform a rate adaptation as the data rates for terminal and data path to the BTS are different.

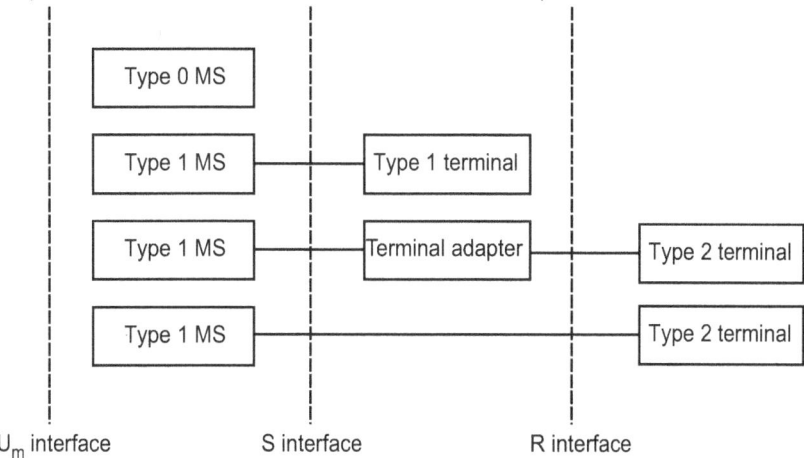

Fig. 4.22: Terminal Adaptation for GSM MSS

4.9.2 Data Services in GSM

There are two types of data services in GSM.

- **Circuited switched data:** This data can be to an ISDN connection, to an analog modem or to a fax machine.
- **Packet switched data:** It connects to a packet network. It is via. the signalling.

4.9.2.1 Interconnection for Switched Data

The transmission of vocoded voice in the physical layer of GSM is at 13 kbps. So for data to be transmitted, 13 kbps is the maximum data rate supported. A modem is required to interconnect voice band modem in the analog wireline network.

Circuit switched data is supported at 300 to 9600 baud rate, for higher data rate, i.e. to operate at around 56 kbps, GSM phones have to use multiple time slots and aggregate the slots; but this reduces the capacity of the cell.

To connect to a terminal, PC and other items to MS, terminal adapters are required. L2R protocol and RLP are used on the radio link.

4.9.2.2 Group 3 Fax

Wireline to wireline service over analog voice band or ISDN facilities is known as Group 3 Fax. An adapter function is installed in the GSM network and at the GSM MS, as GSM does not transmit analog voice or ISDN at 64 kbps. Two modems will be required, if connection is to another MS. Depending on the other end of connection (ISDN or analog), modem may be a digital ISDN modem or analog fax modem. The protocol stack for operation of the system is similar to the X.25 stack.

4.9.2.3 Packet Data on the Signalling Channel (PDS)

Data transfer in GSM network of very small data packets on radio interface signalling channels for applications that use small amounts of data with a throughput of 600-9200 bps and with a call duration of a few seconds is enabled by a bearer service known as PDS. PDS is used for data transfer between a mobile user and packet data network (e.g. X.25 or IP) or between a mobile user and a host directly accessing an MSC or a PDS-Service 2 support node. But, PDS is not defined in GSM specification. PDS is of two forms –
  • PDS - Service 1.
  • PDS - Service 2.

4.9.2.4 User to User Signalling

An ISDN service used by a user to send small data to another user in association with a call is called user to user signalling. SS7 network is used for data transmission via. signalling message. The data can be sent in any of the below situations.
  • Call setup.
  • Call termination signalling.
  • During alerting.
  • During the call.

128 octets is the maximum length of message associated with each signalling message.

In case of connection to an ISDN phone, MSC passes the user to user information via. SS7 messages to and from the wireline ISDN network. The two MSCs communicate directly or via. wireline network in case of GSM to GSM user to user messages.

4.9.3 SMS

SMS, is similar to the paging service, but in GSM system, SMS consists of –
  • Message entry features.
  • Administration features.
  • Message transmission capabilities.

The GSM system and the SMS Messaging Center (SMSMC) together make up the SMS system. During SMS, there is an exchange of short alphanumeric messages between an MS and the GSM system and between the GSM system and an external device capable of transmitting and optionally receiving short messages. The SMSMC can either be physically integrated into the GSM system or can be separate.

An SMS teleservice provides:
- Option of specifying priority level.
- Future delivery time.
- Message expiration interval.
- One or more of a series of short, predefined messages.

In some teleservices, sender can even request for acknowledgement that the MS has received the message. The administration features of SMS are –
- Message storage.
- Profile editing.
- Verification of receipt.
- Status inquiry capabilities.

Broadcast messaging service is available to MSS on GSM paging channel as well as to MSS in a call on a GSM traffic channel. GSM system supports two types of SMS.
- Point-to-Point Service.
- SMS Cell Broadcast (SMS CB).

4.9.3.1 Point-to-Point Service

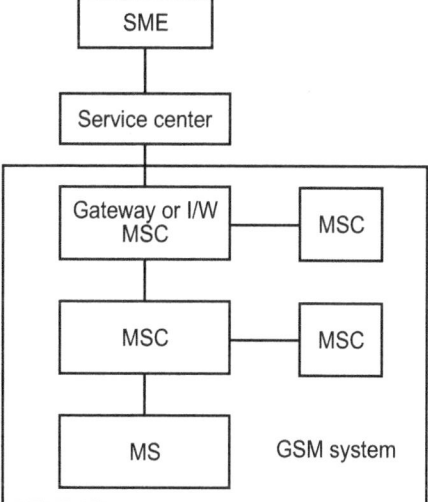

Fig. 4.23: Architecture of SMS

In point-to-point service, to enter the message in the GSM system, sender sending a short message has to interact with a SME (Short Message Entity). The user can interact with SME via.

- email.

- phone call to an operator who takes the message and enters it into the system.

- call to a voice response system that accepts DTMF tones.

The SME sends the message to MSC which forwards it to the MS. In roaming state, a gateway MSC receives the message and forwards it to the destination MSC. But, SME is not defined in GSM standard and is considered outside GSM architecture.

4.9.3.2 SMS Cell Broadcast

In this, same message is broadcast to multiple MSs.

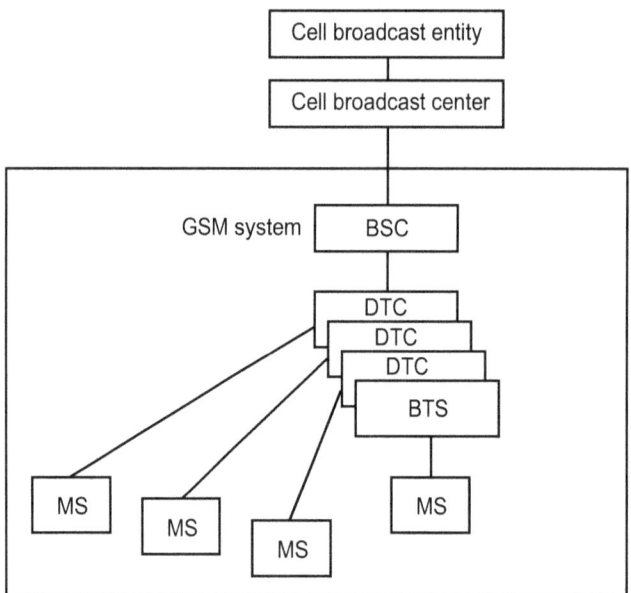

Fig. 4.24: Architecture of SMSCB

Providing the same information to many MSs in the system, is the main purpose of this service. Cell Broadcast Entity, is the information provider that originates the information. Cell Broadcast Entity forwards the information to the cell broadcast center, which broadcasts it to one or more BSCs. BSCs forward it to BTSs for transmission over air. GSM does not define the interface between cell broadcast center and BSC, it is a matter of agreement between the operators of each network element.

4.9.4 GSM GPRS

The packet capabilities of GSM are extended to higher data rates and longer messages by GSM GPRS. In addition to sending messages to point-to-point and point-to- multipoint, two new nodes are added to the network to support GPRS.

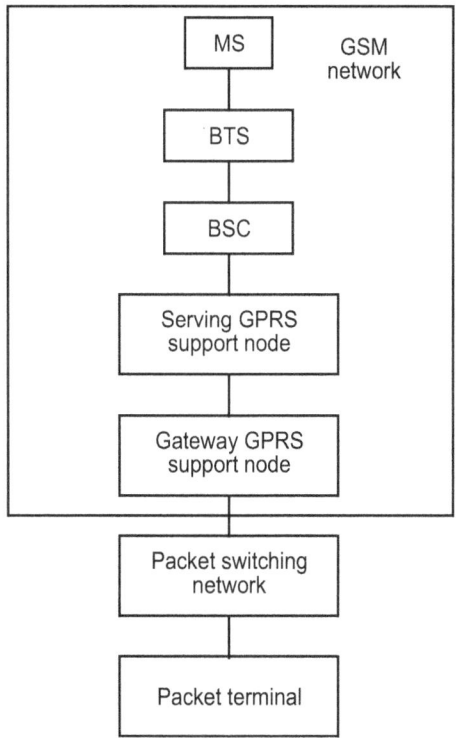

Fig. 4.25: GPRS Network Architecture

In the service area, serving GPRS support node communicates with MS; then the gateway GPRS support node communicates to packet switching network outside the GSM network. Three new channels are added on the radio channel.

- **Packet Broadcast CCH:** System information is transmitted to all packet MSs in the area of a cell by this channel.

- **Packet Common CCH:** It has four sub-channels.

  - **Packet PCH:** It is used to page MSs.

  - **Packet Random Access Channel:** It is used for MSs to access the network for initiation of transmissions or responds to pages.

  - **Packet Access Grant Channel:** Resource assignments to an MS is send through this subchannel.

  - **Packet Notification Channel:** It is used to send multicast information to MSs.

- **Packet TCH:** To transmit data packets between MS ad BS, this uplink and downlink channel is employed. It is also used to send control information to/from MSs using Packet Associated CCH.

GPRS is a packet radio system, thus, its characteristics are same as that of ALOHA system.

GPRS is a low data rate service.

4.10 Value Added Services in GSM

A group of communication capabilities that the service provider offers to the subscriber in GSM is known as telecommunication services. The telecommunication services are divided into three types:

- **Bearer Services:** These services provide the subscriber, the capacity to transmit signals between access points.

- **Teleservices:** It is a type of value added service which provides the subscriber with necessary capabilities like terminal equipment functions to communicate with other subscribers.

- **Supplementary Services:** These are provided as supplementary to the telecommunication services.

4.10.1 Teleservices

Some of the teleservices offered by GSM are –

- **Speech Transmission:** It may be during simple telephony or during an emergency call.

- **Short Message Services (SMS):** SMS can be transmitted as mobile terminating point-to-point or mobile originating or it might be a cell broadcast to many MS.

- Storage and handling of messages.

- Access to videotex.

- Transmission of teletext.

- Transmission of facsimile.

On comparing the teleservices supported by GSM and ISDN, we find that messaging and paging teleservices are offered only by GSM and not by ISDN. Whereas, the services which are offered by both GSM and ISDN are circuit speech i.e. telepony, emergency call, point-to-point SMS, cell broadcast message, alternate speech/fascimile group 3, automatic facsimile group 3 service, voice band modem (3.1 kHz audio). Some other services are there which are offered by ISDN, but not by GSM.

4.10.2 Supplementary Services

These services are offered along with basic telecommunication services as supplement.

Some of the supplementary services offered by GSM are –

1. **Number identification services:** It consists of the following tasks.

   - **Presentation of identified calling number:** The ISDN number of the incoming call is displayed on the GSM phone when this service is active.

   - **Restricted identification of calling number:** The calling party can activate this service, so that its number will not be displayed on the GSM phone.

   - **Presentation of the connected number identification:** The ISDN number of the telephone, where call is made, is displayed when this service is activated.

   - **Restricted identification of connected number:** The called party can restrict the display of its ISDN number where the call is completed.

   - **Identification of malicious call:** A user can identify an incoming call as malicious if this service is activated.

2. **Call offering services:**

   - **Unconditional call forwarding:** It routes all calls to a GSM phone to another number.

   - **Call forwarding mobile busy:** When the GSM phone is busy and this service is activated, all calls are routed to another number.

   - **Call forwarding no reply:** When GSM phone does not answer any calls, all calls are routed to another number.

   - **Call forwarding mobile not reachable:** When GSM phone is off or out of range, all calls are forwarded to another number.

   - **Transfer of all:** In this, ongoing call can be transferred to another number.

   - **Mobile access hunting:** Calls can be made to multiple phones in sequence if this service is activated.

3. **Call completion services:**

   - **Call waiting:** When a GSM phone is busy, another incoming call will generate an indication.

   - **Call holding:** A GSM phone can receive a second call by temporary holding the ongoing call.

   - **Completion of call to busy subscriber:** A GSM subscriber requests the network to monitor a busy phone and connect to it when it becomes idle.

4. **Multiparty services:**

- **Three party service:** It allows simultaneous communication between three phones.
- **Conference calling:** It allows simultaneous communication between three to five phones.

5. **Community of interest services:**

- **Closed user group:** In this, a group of GSM users can communicate among each other.

6. **Charging services:**

- **Advice of charge:** It displays the charge associated with an established call.
- **Free phone service:** In this a free phone number will pay for all incoming calls.
- **Reverse charging:** It allows payment for an incoming call on a selective basis.

7. **Additional information transfer service:**

- **User to user signalling:** A GSM phone can send user data to another GSM or ISDN phone.

8. **Call restriction services:**

- Barring all originating calls.
- Barring all outgoing international calls.
- Barring calls except home country calls.
- Barring incoming calls when in roaming.
- Barring all incoming calls.

4.11 Privacy and Security in GSM

GSM system provides user privacy, it has security controls that eliminates cloning fraud. As there is no encryption in the identity of a subscriber, cellular fraud is extensive in analog cellular system.

There are four mechanisms which ensure privacy and security in GSM:

1. The system is designed to authenticate the subscriber using shared secret cryptography.
2. SIM card stores the subscriber's security information.
3. The secrecy of the cryptographic algorithms and keys for authenticating the subscriber and providing voice privacy are maintained by GSM operators. SIM card and authentication center store these algorithms.
4. The cryptographic keys are not shared with other GSM administration.

4.11.1 GSM Security

USIM is introduced by UMTS. It uses a longer authentication key to give greater security, pulse authenticating the network and user. Confidentiality and authentication is provided by security model, but it provides limited authorization to non-repudiation.

Over the air privacy is ensured by A5/1 and A5/2 stream ciphers. The key to any GSM ciphering, which is never sent over air interface, is K_i, the crypto variable stored on the SIM card. A5/1 and A5/2 algorithms have series weakness. A5/2 can be broken in real time in a cipher text only attack. The operators may replace the cipher with a stronger one as the GSM system supports multiple algorithms.

4.11.2 Wireless Security

Wireless security is one of the basic concerns in GSM. Both privacy of communication and authentication of user is of vital importance during wireless communication.

4.11.2.1 Privacy of Communication

The important points considered in the privacy of communication are –

- **Call setup information:** During call setup, the called number, calling number, and service request should be sent in a secure way.
- **Speech:** Speech is encrypted to avoid interception by hackers on air waves.
- **Data:** Data should also be encrypted.
- **User location** should also be secured, this is done by encrypting user ID.

4.11.3 SIM Card

User's subscription information and phone book are stored in a detachable smart card called subscriber identity module i.e. SIM card. It allows the user to retain his information after switching handsets. Operators can also be changed by simply changing the SIM. SIM locking is a facility, by which some operators allow only single SIM for a handset, but it is illegal in some countries.

Location information, encryption key and encryption key sequence numbers are stored and update on the SIM after each call.

4.11.4 Security Algorithms used in GSM

GSM uses some security algorithms, some of them are –

1.   A3 algorithm.
2.   A8 algorithm.
3.   A5 algorithm.

4.11.4.1 A3 Algorithm

It is the authentication algorithm. It computes the signed response (SRES) using K_i on SIM card and random number (RAND) from BS. A3 algorithm is unique for each GSM administration and thus is secret.

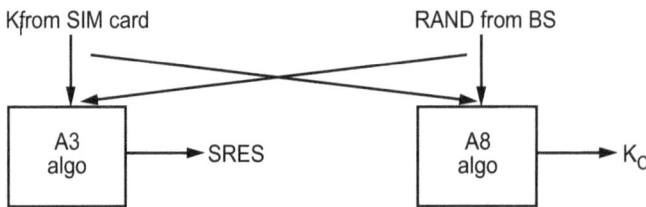

Fig. 4.26: GSM Authentication using A3 and A8 Algorithm

4.11.4.2 A8 Algorithm

It is the privacy key generation algorithm used for voice and data privacy. It uses RAND from BS and K_i from SIM to generate K_C, a private key.

4.11.4.3 A5 Algorithm

It is the encryption algorithm, to encrypt transmitted data on DCCH and TCH. Privacy key K_C and 22 bit long and 4.6 ms long TDMA frame is input to the algorithm. Block 1 and Block 2 are the two outputs of A5 algorithm which are used for encryption by BS and handset respectively.

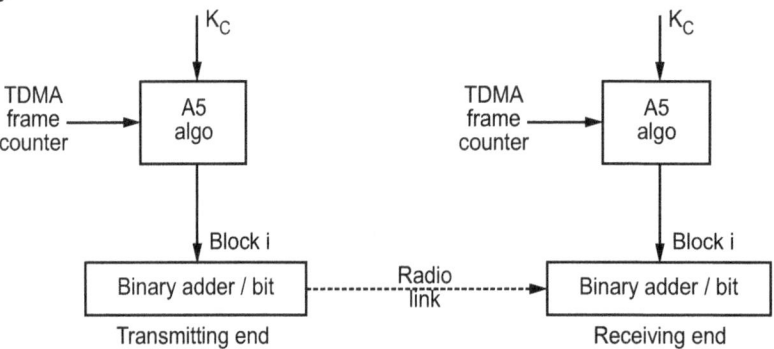

Fig. 4.27: A5 Algorithm used in Encryption and Decryption of DCCH and TCH

4.12 Summary

In this chapter, we presented the basics of GSM communication. Starting with the different types of standards for wireless communication system, in which we presented the various generations of communication. Then, we discussed about the various access technologies for GSM communication like TDMA, FDMA, CDMA. Then, we discussed the fundamentals of cellular communication. Later, we went deep into GSM and discussed the GSM architecture and interfaces, the various radiolink features in GSM system. Later, we went on to discuss the logical channels and frame structure used in GSM. Speech coding techniques used in GSM are also discussed. GSM offers various data services and value added services which are also discussed in this unit. Last but not the least, we discussed about the privacy and security issues related to GSM. Thus, at the end, we got some fundamental and basic idea about the GSM system.

EXERCISE

1. Explain cellular communication fundamentals.

2. Explain the following terms:

    (a) GSM architecture

    (b) GSM subsystem entities

3. Explain the radio link aspects and interference-reducing mechanism.

4. Explain the GSM logical channels and frame structure.

5. How speech coding is done in GSM? Also explain the GSM vocoders.

6. Explain the following terms:

    (a) Data services in GSM

    (b) Value added services in GSM

7. Explain the privacy and security in GSM.

8. In the GSM 900 digital channelized cellular system, the one way bandwidth is 15 MHz. The channel spacing is 250 kHz. 8 users share each channel and three channels per cell are used for control. Calculate the spectral efficiency if the area of a cell is 8 km², total coverage area is 4000 km², average number of calls per user during the busy hour is 1.2,

average holding time of a call is 100 s, call blocking probability is 2% and frequency reuse factor is 4.

What is the efficiency of the system with 10, 30, 50 and 90 MHz?

9. In a IS-54 system, η_b = 0.96, μ = 1.62, voice activity factor v_f = 1.0, information bit rate = 21.5 kbps, frequency reuse factor is 7 and system bandwidth is 19 MHz. Calculate the capacity and spectral efficiency of this system.

Unit V

CODE DIVISION MULTIPLE ACCESS

5.1 Introduction of CDMA

Code Division Multiple Access is the fastest - growing digital wireless technology. CDMA is an advanced digital technology that can offer more capacity than analog technologies and TDMA.

Advantages of CDMA:

- Speech quality is far superior than to any other digital cellular technology.
- CDMA provides the most cost-effective solution for cellular operators.
- Low prices and good performance in voice quality, system reliability, and battery life.
- CDMA is superior in signal security.
- Low power consumption which makes enable CDMA handset to 4 hours of talk time or 48 hours of standby time.
- CDMA systems have fewer dropped calls than with GSM.
- Internet access is also possible in CDMA technology.

Drawbacks of CDMA:

(1) Analog technology is ahead in availability as compared with IS-95 CDMA.

(2) One drawback for CDMA customers is that there are some limitations on roaming capabilities.

5.2 Major Attributes of CDMA Systems

1. **Projected CDMA system capacity** is much higher than that of existing analog/ digital systems.

The system capacity is increased because of improved coding gain/modulation scheme, voice activity, three-part sectorization, and reuse of the same spectrum in every cell and all sectors.

2. **QoS (Quality of Service):** CDMA takes advantage of multipath fading to enhance communications and voice quality. In this system, each mobile station selects the three strongest multipath signals and coherently combine them to produce an enhanced signal. But in narrow-band systems fading creates a degradation in signal quality. By using soft hand-off, CDMA also eliminates the ping-pong effect.

Ping-Pong Effect: Ping-Pong effect occurs when the mobile is near a border between cells and the call is rapidly switched between two cells. Due to this effect, there is chance of a dropped call, increase a load on switching equipment, also effect in hand-off noise.

But in CDMA's soft handoff, a connection is made to the target cell while maintaining the connection with the serving cell, both operating on the same carrier frequency. This ensures a smooth transition between cells and also undetectable to the subscriber. But other system (TDMA) use a break-before-make connection which requires change in frequency and then there is a chance of dropped call also increases hand-off noise.

3. CDMA is a more economical because it requires fewer cell sites and no costly frequency reuse pattern. This system requires less average transmitting power which means battery life will be longer.

5.3 IS-95 System Architecture

For the personal communication system, many reference models were proposed. The TR-45 reference model, with some minor changes in element names was adopted by TR-46 standard group. A model similar to the TR-45/46 model was proposed by TIPI. To overcome some mobility problems in the above architecture, two other architectures - wireless intelligent network and reference model - are introduced.

5.3.1 TR-45/TR-46 Reference Model

The TR-45/TR-46 reference model is an enhancement of the TR-45 reference model for personal communication system. It supports only terminal mobility. The main elements of the reference model are described below.

5.3.1.1 Mobile Station

It enables user access to services from the network and terminates the radio path on the user side.

5.3.1.2 Base Station

It consists of a Base Transceiver System and Base Station Controller. It connects to mobile switching center and terminates the radio path.

- **Base Transceiver System:** It is either located with the base station controller or independently. It terminates the radio path on the network side. BTS consists of one or more transceivers placed at a single location.

- **Base Station Controller:** It controls and manages the BTSS. It exchanges messages with BTS and MSC.

5.3.1.3 Mobile Switching Center

It acts as an interface between wireless network and wireline network and also between two wireless networks. Functions of MSC include:

- Call handling.
- Management of required logical radio-link channel during calls.
- Management of MSC-BSS signalling protocol.
- Handling location registration.
- Control of inter-BSS and inter-MSC handovers.
- Acting as a gateway MSC to interrogate the HLR.
- Exchange of signalling information with other system entities.

5.3.1.4 Home Location Register

The HLR contains the identities of mobile subscribers, their service parameters and their location information. It may be independent of MSC or an integral part of it. Many MSCs are served by a single HLR.

5.3.1.5 Data Message Handler

It collects the billing data.

5.3.1.6 Visitor Location Register

The VLR contains the subscriber parameters and location information for all mobile subscribers currently located in the geographical area controlled by the VLR. VLR contains:

- Identity of mobile subscriber.
- Any temporary mobile subscriber identity.
- ISDN directory number of mobile.
- A directory number to route calls to a roaming station.
- Location area where the MS is registered.
- Copy or part of the subscriber data from the HLR.

5.3.1.7 Authentication Center

It contains the subscriber authentication data i.e. the Authentication Keys. AUC generates security related parameter needed to authorize service. It generates a unique data pattern called a Cipher Key needed for encrypting user speech and data.

5.3.1.8 Equipment Identity Register

The EIR is accessed during the equipment validation procedure when a MS accesses the system. It contains the identity of mobile station equipment.

5.3.1.9 Operation and Management Center

The OMC is the centralized maintenance and diagnostic heart of BSS. It allows the network provider to operate, administer and monitor the functioning of the BSS.

5.3.1.10 Interworking Functions

It is used for communication of MSC with other networks.

5.3.1.11 External Networks

Other communication networks include – PSTN, ISDN, PLMN and PSPDN.

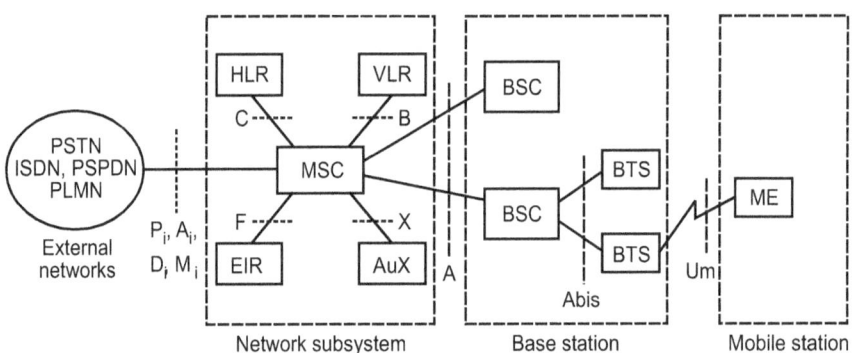

Fig. 5.1: TR-45/46 Reference Model

5.3.1.12 Interfaces

There are various interfaces defined between various elements of the system. Some of them are listed below:

- **A interface:** It is the interface between MSC and BSC, it defines SS7, ISDN BRI/PRI and frame relay transport protocols.

- **AUS interface:** It connects BTS to BSC.
- **UM interface:** Interface between base station and mobile station.
- **B interface:** Connects MSC to VLR.
- **C interface:** Connects MSC to HLR.
- **F interface:** Connects MSC to EIR.
- **X interface:** Connects MSC to auxiliary equipment.
- **A$_i$ interface:** MSC to PSTN. It is defined as an analog interface using multifrequency or dual tone multifrequency signalling.
- **P$_i$ interface:** MSC to PSPDN, it is defined by packet network connected to MSC.
- **M$_i$ interface:** MSC to PLMN.
- **D$_i$ interface:** MSC to ISDN. It is a digital interface.

5.3.2 Functional Model Based on Reference Model

The functional entities in the functional model help in developing several physical scenarios.

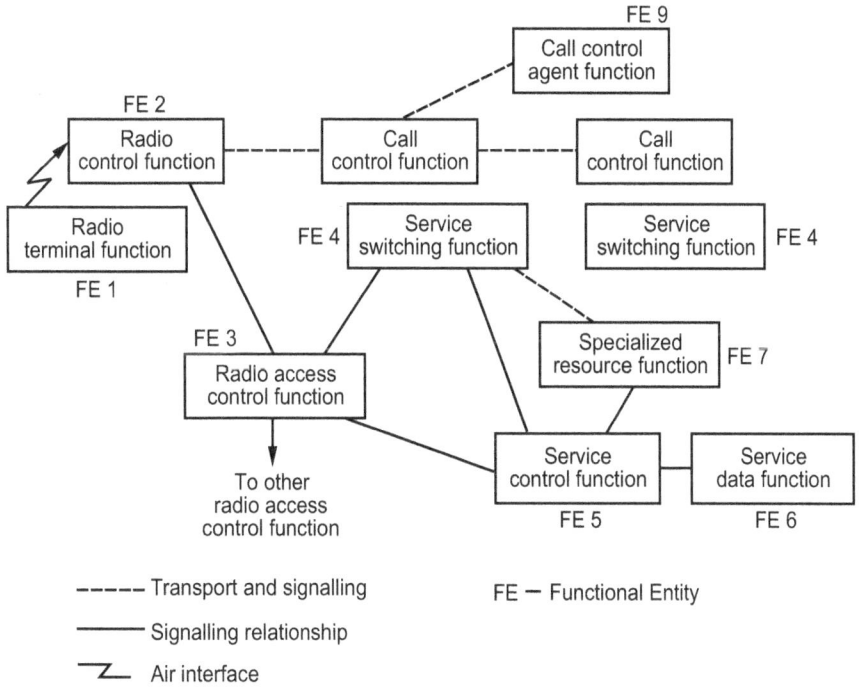

Fig. 5.2: Functional Model

The call control and mobility management messages are carried by the physical interface between radio system (RS) and switching system platform (SSP). All the functional entities are grouped into RS and SSP as shown in figure.

The various functional entities are as defined below:

- **Radio Terminal Function Entity:** It is the subscriber unit. The only physical interface is to the radio system through air interface.

- **Radio Access Control Function and Radio Control Function Entity:** They are included in the radio system. The air interface specific functions are isolated from other interfaces when these two functional entities are combined. There is only one physical interface to switching system platform to carry both call control and mobility management signalling.

- **Call Control Function and Service Switching Function Entity:** They are included in switching system platform. They provide interface to international calls, network repair and maintenance centers and operator services.

- **Specialized Resource Function and Data Interworking Function:** They are contained in the internet protocol. SSP and mobility management platform are its two physical interfaces.

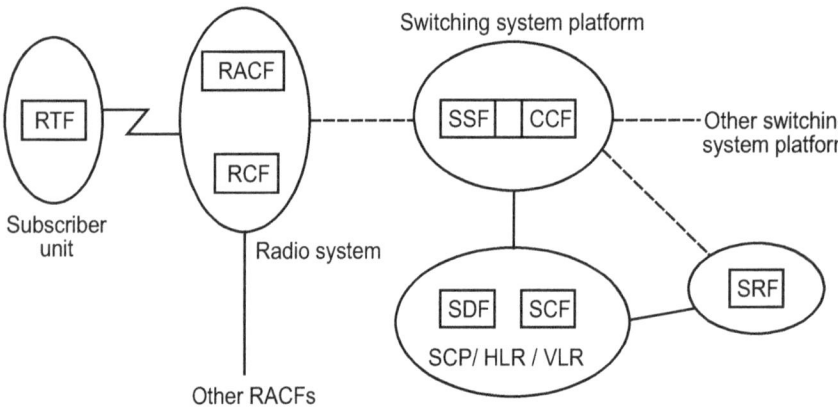

Fig. 5.3: Grouping According to Functional Entities

5.3.3 Wireless Intelligent Network

Intelligent Network is a set of protocols defined initially for wireline network by BellCore. Later, it was also adopted for wireless network.

5.3.3.1 Communication Control Panel for Intelligent Network

The functional elements are discussed one by one on the mobile side and network side.

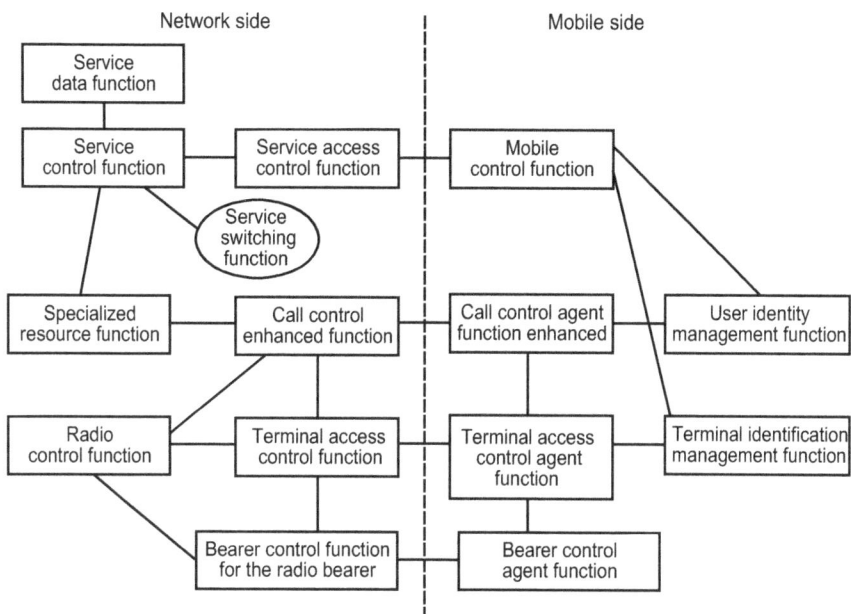

Fig. 5.4: Communication Control Plane

5.3.3.1.1 The Functional Elements on the Network Side of the Communications Control Plane

- **Bearer Control Function:** It provides the bearer functions required for hand-offs.
- **Bearer Control Function for the Radio Bearer:** It provides the necessary functions for selection of bearer functions and radio resources. It performs hand-off processing and detects and responds to pages from the networks.
- **Call Control Function Enhanced:** Call and connection control are provided by it.
- **Service Access Control Function:** Mobility management function is provided by it.
- **Service Control Functions:** Service and mobility control logic and call processing are provided by it.
- **Service Data Function:** Data storage and data access in support of mobility management and security data for the network is provided by these functions.
- **Specialised Resource Function:** It provides the specialized functions needed to support execution of IN services.
- **Service Switching Function:** It provides interaction between CCF' and SCF.
- **Terminal Access Control Function:** It provides control of the connection between the MS and the network.

5.3.3.1.2 Functional Entities on the Mobile Side

- **Bearer Control Agent function:** It maintains, establishes, modifies and releases bearer connection between MS and network.
- **Call Control Agent Function Enhanced:** It provides call processing functions of the MS.

- **Mobile Control Function:** It provides mobility management functions of the MS.
- **Terminal Access Control Agent Function:** It supports the functions necessary to select bearer function and radio resources.
- **Terminal Identification Management Function:** It stores the terminal related security information.
- **User Identification Management Function:** It provides user related security information similar to TIMF.

5.3.3.2 The Intelligent Network Functional Reference Model for PCS

Many of the functional entities of the IN model and ITU model are same except some elements.

- **Radio Terminal Function:** All the functionality of the mobile side of the reference model is contained.
- **Radio Access Control Function:** It provides mobility management function and is similar to SACF.
- **Radio Control Function:** It provides same function as by TACF, BCFr and BCF in ITU model.
- **Call Control Agent Function:** It provides access to the wireless network by wireline users.
- **Service Management Function:** It provides the network management functions for each functional element.

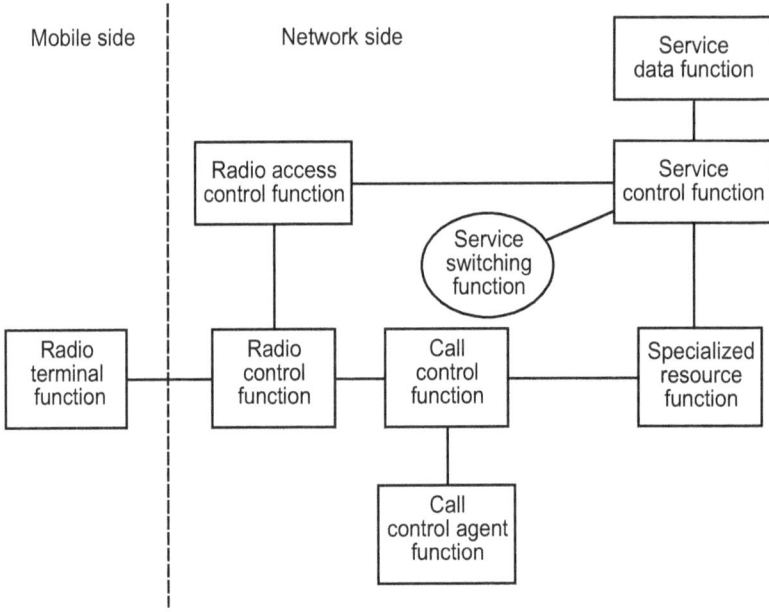

Fig. 5.5: WIN Model for PCS

5.4 Is-95 CDMA Air Interface

5.4.1 TIA is-95 Cdma System

The TIA IS-95 CDMA and the AMPS operate on the same frequency. For Band Class 0, the reverse link frequency is from 869 to 894 MHz and forward link is from 824 to 849 MHz. The modulation used is QPSK. The chip rate is 1.2288 Mcps, nominal data rate is 9.6 kbps, filtered bandwidth is 1.23 MHz, convolution with viterbi coding is used. Interleaving with 20 ms span is used with error control coding.

5.4.1.1 Forward Link

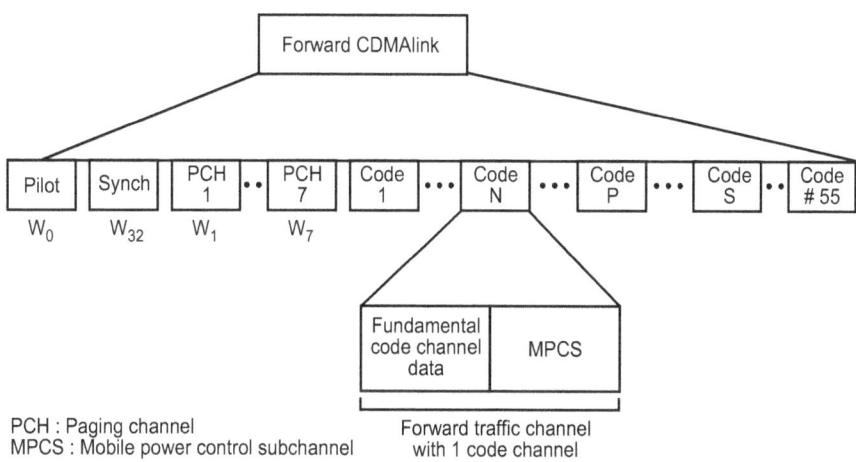

PCH : Paging channel
MPCS : Mobile power control subchannel

Fig. 5.6: Structure of Forward Link Channel

The forward link channel consists of –
- One pilot channel.
- 1 synchronization channel.
- 7 paging channels.
- Number of forward traffic channels.

One forward fundamental code channel and may be 1 to 7 forward supplemental code channels are there in forward traffic channel.

Walsh function is used to modulate information on each channel, then a quadrature pair of PN sequences (chip rate = 1.2288 Mcps) is used to modulate the information. Code channel number 0 is assigned the pilot channel. Code channel number 32 is given to sync channel, if present. Code channel numbers 1 to 7 are assigned to paging channels.

The sync channel data rate is 1200 bps, it is convolutionally encoded to 2400 bps repeated to 4800 bps. 4 walsh symbols are used by interleaved symbols.

To generate forward traffic channel data, speech is encoded using a variable rate vocoder.

The MS is provided with system information and instructions, plus acknowledgement messages following access requests on the mobile stations' access channels using the paging channels.

All 64 channels are combined to single I and Q channels. Reference for all MSs is provided by the pilot CDMA signal transmitted by a BS.

The strongest signal component is found by MS by processing the pilot channel. When the MS identifies the strongest pilot offset by processing the multipath components from the pilot channel correlator, it examines the signal on its sync channel which is locked to the pseudorandom binary sequence signal on the pilot channel.

The MS accesses the paging channel and listens for system information. When acquisition and synchronization is complete, the MS enters the idle state. Call is initiated after listening to the assigned channel. The MS recovers the speech data when paging channel informs that voice traffic is available.

5.4.1.2 Reverse Link

The reverse and forward channels are separated by 45 MHz at cellular frequency and 80 MHz at PCS frequency. The chip code (32,768) is same for reverse and forward link. The reverse link channels are either access or reverse traffic channels. A reverse traffic channel is further subdivided into a single fundamental code channel and 0 to 7 supplement code channels. There are 32 access channels and 62 traffic channels. The access channel (4800 bps) is used by MS to communicate non-traffic information.

The radio system can correctly decode the information from an individual MS, each assigned a PN code. The data is convolutionally encoded, block interleaved and modulated by modulation symbols transmitted for each 6 code symbols. The data rates may be 9600, 4800, 2400 or 1200 bps. The rate of spreading PN sequence is fixed at 1.2288 Mcps, so that each walsh chip is spread by 4 PN chips.

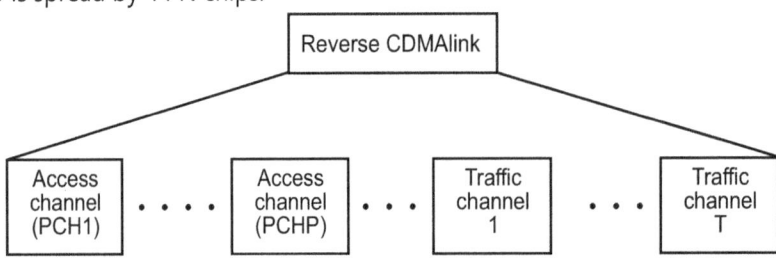

Fig. 5.7: Reverse link Channel Structure

The period for pilot PN sequence is 26.666 ms and chip rate is 1.2288 Mcps. 75 pilot PN repetitions every 2 seconds. Offset quadrature phase shift keying spread modulation is used.

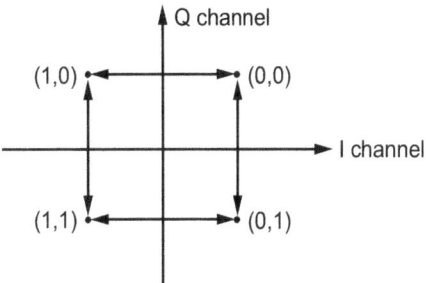

Fig. 5.8: Signal Constellation of OQPSK

5.5 Physical and Logical Channels of IS-95 CDMA

5.5.1 Introduction

IS-95 channels can be segmented into physical channels and logical channels. Thus, classification can be given as follows.

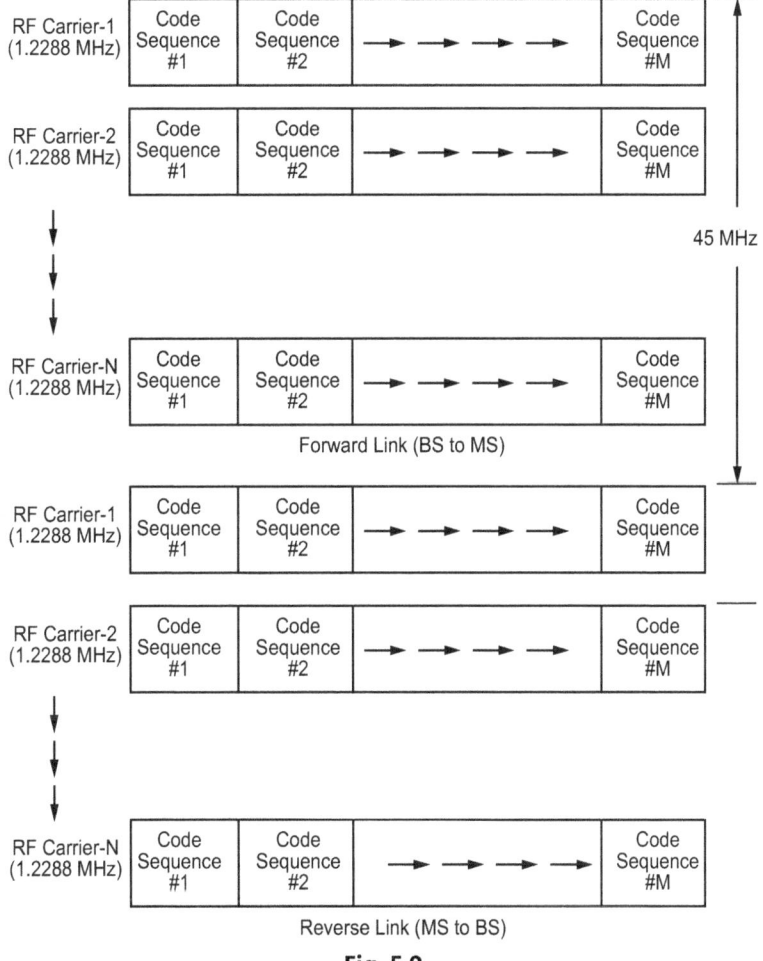

Fig. 5.9

5.5.2 Physical Channels of IS-95 System

1. Physical channels are defined in terms of an RF frequency and a code sequence.
2. There are 64 walsh codes available for the forward link (BS-MS) providing 64 logical channels.•
3. On the reverse link channels are identified by long PN code sequences.
4. In IS-95 CDMA carrier band, center frequencies are denoted by AMPS (Advanced Mobile Phone Service) channel numbers.
5. One CDMA carrier requires 41, 30 kHz AMPS channels to provide a CDMA carrier B.W. of 1.23 MHz.
6. 1.23 MHz bandwidth of a CDMA carrier makes the minimum center frequency separation between two carriers at 1.23 MHz.
7. Fig. 5.32 indicates the forward and reverse link respectively. Forward link is BS to MS and reverse link is MS to BS.
8. MS indicates Mobile Station and BS indicates Base Station.

5.5.3 Forward/Reverse Link and Physical Channel

5.5.3.1 Forward Link

Definition:

The forward link in an IS-95 system is the link from the base station to a mobile subscriber.

The physical channel is the approximately 1.25 MHz of bandwidth occupied by the CDMA signals.

Note: *The forward link physical channel is the approximately 1.25 MHz of band-width centered at the frequency of the forward link. For example, the B-band primary center frequency is 881.52 MHz.*

Application:

1. Four different types of signals or channels may be transmitted on the forward link in IS-95 systems.
2. These signal types are the pilot, and the **Synchronization**, paging, and traffic channels.
3. There is one pilot, upto and typically just one **Synchronization** channel, upto seven paging channels, and typically between 55 and 61 traffic channels depending on the number of paging channels.
4. The total power transmitted on the forward link is divided among the four channel types with the pilot usually allocated more power than any other signal.
5. The total number of forward-link channels, transmitted at one time, cannot exceed 64, the number of **Walsh words** available.
6. The **Walsh words** allow separation of the individual channels or signals at their designated receivers in spite of the fact that all the signals occupy the same physical channel. **Walsh words** are orthogonal or mutually non-interfering, which allow

them to be separated and distinguished from one another in the absence of multipath on the forward link.

7. Each forward link channel from a given base station is spread by the same Pseudo-random Noise (PN) sequence.

8. This spreading, along with the use of the **Walsh words**, produces wideband PN signals which allow universal reuse of the available frequencies with acceptable levels of interference.

9. Universal reuse increases capacity and facilitates soft and softer hand-offs.

10. The wideband spread signals also allow some multipath paths to be resolved and combined constructively by the RAKE-receiver fingers.

11. This provides IS-95 signals with multipath protection and actually uses multipath power to increase the signal strength.

Example:

1. The total power in a forward link is typically 8 Watts or 39 dBm.

2. This produces a power spectral density over the 1.25 MHz (61 dBHz) physical bandwidth of about −22 dBm/Hz.

3. With a path attenuation of 130 dB, the signal arrives at a mobile at about −152 dBm/Hz, well above thermal noise.

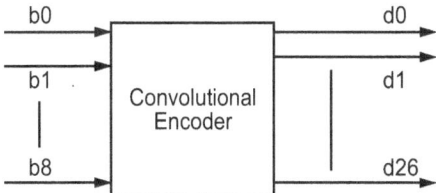

Fig. 5.10: Forward Link (Base Station to Mobile Station) and Reverse Link (Mobile Station to Base Station) in CDMA Frequency Division Duplex (FDD) System

5.5.3.2 Reverse Link

Definition:

The reverse link in an IS-95 system is any link from a mobile subscriber to a base station.

1. **Note:** In IS-95 cellular systems operating in the 800 MHz band, the physical channel of the reverse link is the approximately 1.25 MHz of bandwidth centered at a frequency 45 MHz below the physical channel of the forward link.

2. In PCS (Personal Communication Systems) operating in the 1900 MHz band, the physical channel of the reverse link is 80 MHz below the physical channel of the forward link.

Application:

1. Two different types of signals or channels may be transmitted on the reverse link in IS-95 systems.

2. These signal types are the Access Channels and the Traffic Channels.

3. There can be as many as 32 access channels per paging channel associated with any one pilot.

4. The number of reverse-link traffic channels is generally determined by the system self-interference.

5. The total number of reverse-link channels supporting calls in progress equals the total number of forward-link traffic channels also supporting the same number of calls.

6. Therefore, the number of traffic channels cannot exceed 63, the maximum number of Walsh words available to traffic, even though there are many more than this number of long code offsets which uniquely identify the individual access channels and mobile users.

Example:

1. The access and traffic messages on IS-95 reverse links use rate 1/3 convolutional coding, interleaving, and a binary symbol rate of 28.8 ksym/sec.

2. The symbols are partitioned into blocks of 6 and used to select one of 64 Walsh words, which are the orthogonal waveforms in the 64-ary orthogonal modulation scheme used on the reverse link.

3. Redundant symbols potentially created by symbol repetition are removed by the data burst randomizer.

4. The 64-chip Walsh words are spread by the output of the long code generator and the Offset QPSK PN spreader before being transmitted.

5. The output of the data burst randomizer causes the reverse-link signal from each mobile to have a variable duty cycle on a frame-to-frame basis.

6. For full-rate Vocoder frames, the duty cycle is unity. For half, quarter, and eighth-rate frames, the duty cycle equals the frame rate.

Bit Adder:

The bit adder simply adds a string of 8 zeros to each frame. This is to reset the Viterbi decoder used at the decoding unit. The new frame lengths and the corresponding bit rates are shown in Table 5.2.

Table 5.1: Data Rates after Zero Padding

Data Rate	Frame Length
9600 bps	192
4800 bps	96
2400 bps	48
1200 bps	24

Convolution Encoder:

The encoder used is a convolution encoder of constraint length K = 9 and rate 1/3. The encoding is important to make the data less susceptible to channel noise, as the redundancy added by coder reduces the probability of error due to non-ideal channel. The convolution encoder is described using a generator matrix that introduces memory in the data stream and hence at the decoding end, a sequence detection has to be performed using a Viterbi decoder. In the project, the encoder used was with a generator matrix of G1 = [0 0 1], G2 =[0 1 0]; G3 = [1 0 0];

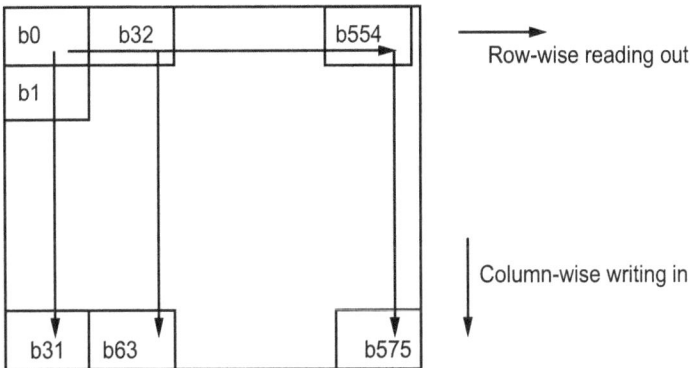

Fig. 5.11: Convolutional Encoder

This becomes a trivial case of just a repetition code for simplicity of implementation. Since there is no memory introduced in this case, the decoding requires a simple un-repeater instead of a Viterbi decoder. The bit rates after encoding are given in Table 5.2.

Table 5.2: Data Rates after Coding

Data Rate	Frame Length
28800 bps	576
14400 bps	288
7200 bps	144
3600 bps	72

Block Interleaver:

The purpose of the interleaver is to reduce burst errors. The channel coding and error correction capabilities of the convolution encoder is limited to random errors, and does not help much in case of burst errors. The interleaver scrambles the data so that even though the channel introduced burst errors on a sequence of bits, the errors on the actual information bits is random and hence independent. The interleaver used is a block or matrix of size 32 × 18, the incoming data is written into the matrix column-wise and read out row-wise. Thus any two adjacent code bits are now separated by 18 bits. This operation however, introduces delay in the processing, and so the total processing time is 20 ms.

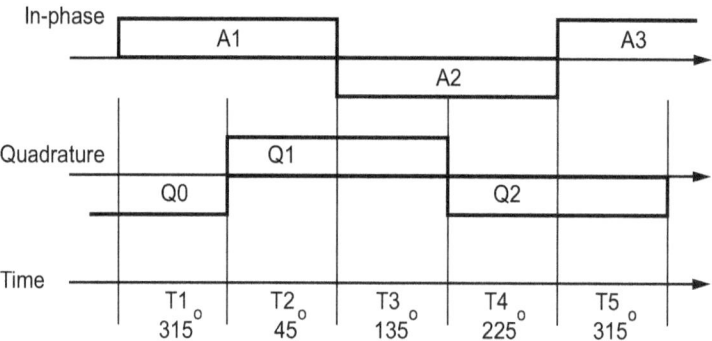

Fig. 5.12: Block Interleaver

Reading from the interleaver: b0,b32,b64...b554,b1...562, b31..b575.

5.5.4 Walsh Words

Definition:

A group of 2N vectors or words, which contains 2N binary elements which with themselves and their logical inverses, form a mutually orthogonal set.

Note: Every Walsh word of a given length is orthogonal to all other Walsh words of that length and all inverses of the other Walsh words of that length.

Application:

1. IS-95 uses Walsh words having 64 chips to identify the logical channels on the forward link.

2. The logical channels are separable from the aggregate of forward-link CDMA signals based on the orthogonality of the Walsh words and their inverses.

3. The orthogonality of the Walsh words is also used on the reverse link in the 64-ary orthogonal modulation scheme.

4. The critical property of the Walsh words used on both the forward and reverse links is their orthogonality. The Walsh words do not, in general, have uniformly distributed power spectra and do not generally have low cross-correlation at arbitrary time shifts.

5. Therefore, the PN codes are used to provide this uniform power distribution over the physical channel and to provide low correlation between shifted versions of the transmitted signals.

Example:

1. Walsh words may be produced using the simple iterative scheme illustrated below.

2. The rule is to produce the next matrix of Walsh words by repeating the entire present matrix to the right and to the bottom and to repeat with all signs or states reversed to the diagonal.

$$\begin{matrix} W & W \\ W & \overline{W} \end{matrix}$$

0000	0000 0000
0101	0101 0101
0011	0011 0011
0110	0110 0110
	0000 1111
	0101 1010
	0011 1100
	0110 1001

5.5.5 Modulation Scheme

5.5.5.1 Offset or Staggered QPSK

Application:

1. The mobile-subscriber unit uses Offset QPSK (OQPSK), which is sometimes also called Staggered QPSK (SQPSK).

2. The advantages in amplifier design, when SQPSK is used, include tighter control of out-of-band emissions and better efficiency in converting prime DC power to transmitted RF power.

3. These advantages are particularly important when the mobile is a handset powered by batteries.

4. In IS-95, SQPSK is used as the PN spreading modulation on the reverse links. Hence, the delay introduced is one-half of a chip duration.

5. At the PN chipping rate of 1.2288 Mchip/sec, a chip duration equals 813.80 nsec requiring a delay of 406.90 nsec.

6. In IS-95, this delay is introduced into the Q or "quadrature" element as opposed to the I or "in-phase" element.

7. The fact that offsetting chip timing in SQPSK makes it impossible to have 180° transitions is illustrated in the example below.

5.5.5.2 Offset or Staggered QPSK

Example:

1. The "in-phase" chips are denoted by A1, A2, etc. and the "quadrature" chips are denoted by Q0, Q1, etc.

2. The offset chip streams are shown in the Fig. 5.35 on the following page.

3. The in-phase chip stream is depicted at the top of the figure and the delayed quadrature stream is shown just below it. At the bottom of the figure, time is shown in units equal to one-half of a chip duration.

4. Note that the quadrature chip stream is delayed one-half of a chip relative to the in-phase stream.

5. During T1 and T2, the in-phase chip remains at A1. The quadrature stream changes chip values beginning at T2, but A1 cannot change at this time.

6. Hence, only the value of one of the chips in the two streams can ever change at the same time.

7. When the in-phase chip remains unchanged, the phase must lie in either the first or fourth quadrants (in-phase positive) or in the second or third quadrants (in-phase negative).

8. A change in the quadrature chip value can at most change the phase by one quadrant or 90°.

9. When the quadrature chip remains unchanged, the phase must lie in either the first or second quadrants (quadrature positive) or in the third or fourth quadrants (in-phase negative).

10. A change in the in-phase chip value can at most change the phase by one quadrant or 90°.

11. The phase values during each time unit are as shown in the figure. In this example, the phase advances by 90° in each successive time unit.

12. This phase pattern corresponds to the in-phase and quadrature chip patterns equaling each other for a short time.

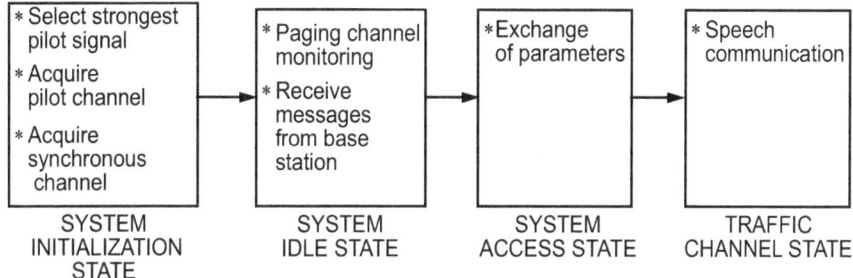

Fig. 5.13: Offset chip streams are shown typically in OQPSK

5.5.6 Symbol Repetition

Definition:

The process of repeating the symbols of an input data stream to produce a new output symbol stream whose symbol rate is an integer times greater than the rate of the input stream.

Application:

1. All the channels in IS-95 use symbol repetition except the pilot channel.
2. In the case of the synchronization channel, the primary purpose in repeating the symbols to produce a 4.8 ksym/sec stream from a 2.4 ksym/sec stream appears to be to improve signal reliability by transmitting the symbols of the message twice with interleaving.
3. Increasing the symbol rate on the access channels from 14.4 ksym/sec to 28.8 ksym/sec improves reliability and also produces a 28.8 ksym/sec stream, which is common to all reverse-link channels.
4. In all other cases, the primary motivation appears to be to produce a convenient common symbol rate.
5. The forward link, for example, repeats each symbol of the half-rate paging channel to increase the symbol rate from 9.6 ksym/sec to 19.2 ksym/sec, which is the same rate as in the full-rate paging channels.
6. Forming the common 19.2 ksym/sec rate allows the use of one interleaver and one decimator to scramble the paging messages.
7. In the case of half-rate paging, repeating the paging symbols also improves the reliability of the channel, which has no power control.
8. The forward and reverse traffic channels are both greatly simplified using repetition. The four possible rates produced by the variable rate Vocoder are transformed to a common rate.

9. This allows common circuitry following the repetition function.

10. In the case of the traffic channels, after repetition is used to form a convenient common symbol rate, some other function is used to achieve the capacity increase associated with the voice activity factor.

11. On the forward traffic links, the repeated symbols are transmitted, but at a reduced power level which keeps the energy per bit fixed.

12. On the reverse traffic links, the average power is reduced by eliminating in the data burst randomizer the redundant bits produced by repetition.

13. **The resulting transmitted signal has a duty cycle equal to 1, 1/2, 1/4, and 1/8 when the Vocoder bit frame rate is full-rate, 1/2, 1/4, or 1/8 respectively.**

5.5.7 Logical Channels

Definition:

A logical channel is an individual CDMA signal, which can be separated or isolated from an aggregate of CDMA signals which occupy the same physical bandwidth or channel.

Note: The term logical channel is used because, while the signals all use the same physical channel or bandwidth at the same physical time, there is something about their mathematical or "logical" structure, which allows them to be separated or isolated from one another. The logical structure in CDMA is in the orthogonality between Walsh words and the near orthogonality, which exists between short segments of long PN codes.

Application:

1. The logical channels, or means by which individual signals are separated, on the forward link are the **Walsh words** .

2. After the PN chips common to the received forward-link signals have been removed, the resulting stream is the sum of time-aligned (or nearly so) **Walsh words** which may have different amplitudes and different polarities depending on the data symbols.

3. Each of these individual **Walsh words** can be isolated or separated from this stream by using a correlator or a filter matched to the Walsh word assigned to that mobile.

4. Ideally, there is no interference from any other Walsh word at the output of the correlators at the time the polarity of the data symbol is measured. Multipath and possible nonlinearities in the transmitter and receiver in practice produce some interference.

5. On the reverse link from a mobile to its base station, orthogonality or near orthogonality is achieved by the random nature of short segments of long PN code sequences.

6. The Walsh-word symbols used on the reverse link are transmitted at a rate of 4800 per second.

7. At the PN chipping rate of 1.2288 Mchips/sec, each Walsh word is spread by 256 random PN chips.

8. The **Walsh words** from different mobiles are spread by different segments of 256 chips.

9. At the base receiver, a signal is multiplied by a synchronized PN code which agrees in all 256 chips with the chips used to spread the Walsh word to which this channel of the receiver is tuned.

10. Signals, to which the receiver is not tuned, also have their 256 PN chips multiplied by the receiver's 256 chips.

11. Now, however, the two segments of 256 chips agree and disagree in about the same number of individual chip multiplications.

12. Hence, the product of the two different 256-chip segments averaged over the Walsh-word is near zero; i.e., the segments are nearly orthogonal.

5.5.7.1 Pilot Channel

Definition:

The base-to-mobile forward-link channel which is modulated only by the pilot PN spreading codes common to all signals transmitted from a given base station.

Application:

1. The pilot channel provides several critically important functions to the forward links in IS-95 systems.

2. As its definition states, the pilot channel is only modulated by the PN spreading codes.

3. This facilitates the process of generating a time synchronized replica at the receiver of the PN spreading sequences used at the transmitter to modulate the synchronization, paging, and traffic channels transmitted from that base station.

4. The power of the pilot is an indication to the mobile of its ability to successfully use the signals from the base station transmitting that pilot.

5. The individual pilots are recognizable based on a specific offset of the short pilot PN sequences which have a period of exactly 215 chips.

6. The pilot channel also provides the coherent reference signal needed to demodulate the coherent Binary Phase Shift Keying (BPSK) modulation used on the forward link.

7. The pilot channel, when processed by the pilot searcher, also identifies the multipath-delay structure on which the mobile receiver bases its decisions of how best to use its RAKE-receiver fingers.

8. To provide all these important functions reliably, the power level, at which the pilot channel is transmitted, is typically higher than the power used on any other channel.

9. A pilot-power level of 2 Watts is not unusual. With a total forward-link power output of say 8 Watts, the pilot power is usually of the order of 25% of the total forward-link power.

5.5.7.2 Synchronization

Definition:

The process of bringing two signals or the wideband components of two signals into time alignment is called synchronization. The process is applied most frequently in digital communication systems.

Application:

1. Whenever a symbol stream is combined with a same or higher rate Walsh-chip word or PN-chip sequence at the transmitter for scrambling, spreading, or addressing; the combining process must eventually be reversed or undone at the receiver to recover the symbol stream.

2. In each case, the signal s (t) is in effect multiplied by a wideband signal PN (t) and the transmitted signal is of the form PN (t) s (t).

3. After propagation delay, the received signal is of the form PN (t – τ) s (t – τ).
    At the receiver, a local replica of the PN or Walsh generator produces a signal PN (t – x), where x is an adjustable timing offset.

4. The receiver forms the product PN (t – x) PN (t – τ) s (t – τ).

5. The synchronization circuit adjusts x so that it is close enough to τ that PN (t – x) PN (t – τ) is approximately PN (t – τ)2, which is always one.

6. This recovers s (t – τ), the desired signal. This process applies to PN spreading and despreading, **Privacy Scrambling** and descrambling, and encoding and decoding of **Walsh words** on the forward link in IS-95.

Example:

1. Several schemes have been developed to synchronize two digital streams.

2. In one method used in Direct Sequence (DS) spread spectrum systems, initially the **PN generator** at the receiver, while the same generator as used at the transmitter, is clocked at a slightly different rate causing the chip rate of the receiver sequence to be slightly different than the chip rate of the signal received.

3. Hence, the PN signals PN (t – x) and PN (t – τ) tend to slide by one another as time passes because their rates differ.

4. A circuit continually monitors the product PN $(t - x)$ PN $(t - \tau)$ s $(t - \tau)$. The power in this signal will be spread over a wide bandwidth whenever x and $-\tau$ differ by more than about half a chip time.

5. When x and $-\tau$ differ by less than half a chip, the power in PN $(t - x)$ PN $(t - \tau)$ s $(t - \tau)$ lies mostly within the bandwidth of s (t).

6. The synchronization circuit detects this condition and sets the chipping rate at the receiver equal to the chipping rate at the transmitter.

7. Other tracking circuitry brings the two signals into closer alignment and keeps them aligned.

8. When the received signal is very weak, the product PN $(t - x)$ PN $(t - \tau)$ s $(t - \tau)$ may be processed for an extended period of time.

9. In such cases it is best if s $(t - \tau)$ does not change over the processing interval. This is done in the IS-95-pilot case.

5.5.7.3 Synchronization Channel

Definition:

It is the forward-link base-to-mobile channel on which the IS-95 synchronization messages are transmitted.

Application:

1. The synchronization channel carries the synchronization message at a rate of 1200 bits/sec.

2. The bits are protected by rate 1/2 convolutional encoding, yielding 2400 sym/sec, and then repeated for protection to form a stream at 4800 sym/sec.

3. The 4800 sym/sec stream is interleaved 128 symbols at a time spanning exactly 26.666... msec, which equals the period of the pilot code.

4. Walsh word 32, consisting of 32 binary zeros followed by 32 binary ones is used to identify the synchronization channel.

5. The 32 zeros and 32 ones of Walsh word 32 may be viewed as a square wave which is zero for about 26.04 μsec and then one for 26.04 μsec having a bandwidth of about 38.4 kHz.

6. This signal is then PN spread to the approximate 1.25 MHz of the physical channel by the pilot PN codes.

7. Power control is not used on the synchronization channel.

5.5.7.4 Synchronization Message

Definition:
It is the message transmitted on the forward-link base-to-mobile synchronization channel.

Application:
1. The synchronization message contains the first information bits actually demodulated by the mobiles.
2. Prior to demodulating the synchronization message, the mobile has only acquired a pilot PN code at a suitable power level.
3. The synchronization message contains critical information needed by the mobile receiver to progress have knowing the pilot to having the information needed to demodulate the other forward-link channels.
4. This information includes the pilot offset of the pilot the mobile has acquired.
5. This information allows the mobile to know where to search for the pilots in the neighbour list.
6. System time, the time of day in the IS-95 system, is based on Global Positioning Satellite (GPS) time.
7. The system time is used to synchronize system functions. For instance, the PN generators on the reverse link use zero offset relative to the even numbered seconds in GPS time.
8. However, the mobiles only know system time at the base stations plus an uncertainty due to the propagation delay from its base station to the mobile's location.
9. The state of the long code generator at system time is also sent to the mobile in the synchronization message.
10. This allows the mobile to initialize and run its long code generator very nearly in time synchronism with the long code generators in the base stations.
11. The synchronization message also notifies the mobile of the paging channel data rate, which may be either 4800 or 9600 bits/sec.
12. The transmission of the synchronization message begins at the same time that a period of the PN pilot begins and ends within three PN pilot code periods.
13. Three PN pilot code periods equal exactly 80 msec and this 80 msec interval is called a synchronization super frame.
14. The system time sent in the synch message is a time with respect to the time at the end of the super frame (end of the third pilot period) in which the synchronization message ends.
15. To account for propagation and signal processing delays, the system time sent to the mobile is the GPS time of day exactly 320 msec after the end of the super frame in which the synchronization message would end on the zero offset pilot.

16. That is, assuming that the pilot is the zero offset pilot, the system time is 4 synch super frames or 12 PN pilot-code periods into the future with respect to the end of the super frame in which the synchronization message ends.

17. The mobile can recognize the end of the message and the end of the PN pilot-code which first occurs after the end of the message.

18. It then counts 12 pilot-code periods and adjusts for the actual PN code offset knowing the PN code offset which is contained in the synchronization message.

5.5.7.5 Paging Channel

Definition:

It is a base-to-mobile forward-link communication channel used to send control, call set-up, and paging messages when the mobile is not in the traffic mode.

Application:

1. There are upto 7 paging channels available to each base station.

2. While the mobile is not in the traffic mode, the base sends orders and messages to the mobile on the paging channel. It receives responses and requests via the mobile's access channel.

3. The data rate on the paging channels is either 9600 or 4800 bits/sec.

4. The paging traffic is protected by rate 1/2 convolutional encoding, interleaving, and scrambling using a paging channel mask.

5. The nth paging channel, n equal 1 upto 7, is always assigned the nth Walsh word.

6. There is no power control on the paging channel. The pilot PN code offset used to spread the paging channels is the same as used to spread all the other signals transmitted by a given base station.

5.5.7.6 Paging Messages

Definition:

The signals sent on the paging channels to either convey system overhead or signalling messages or to notify a mobile that it is being paged.

Application:

1. The paging channels carry two different types of messages.

2. One type is the signalling or overhead, control, and supervision messages and the second type is the signal sent to mobiles to notify them that they are being paged.

3. The paging channels are the primary means of sending signalling messages to the mobile subscribers.

4. These signalling messages are discussed under a separate topic entitled Signalling Messages.

5. The paging messages to a mobile are scrambled for privacy using a paging long code mask.

6. The mobile receiver is able to generate a replica of the scrambling signal by appropriately setting the mask of its long code generator.
7. The mobile is able to set the appropriate 42-bit mask by knowing the paging channel number and the offset of the pilot code used by its current base station.
8. All messages to mobiles on a certain paging channel are scrambled in the same way.
9. A mobile being paged is addressed or identified by at least the first 24 binary bits of its 34-bit Mobile Station Identification Number (MIN), which is the binary representation of its 10-decimal-digit telephone number.
10. The length of the body of the paging message is specified in the message. The maximum length of the paging messages is 1184 bits.
11. The paging channel can operate in either the continuous or slotted modes.
12. The purpose of the slotted mode is to allow the mobile to power-down some of its receiver circuitry to conserve battery power.

5.5.7.7 Access Channel

Definition:

A mobile-to-base communication channel used primarily for control and sending short messages such as call origination, page response, and registration.

Application:

1. In IS-95, upto 32 access channels are associated with the pilot offset of a particular base station.
2. The mobile uses an access channel to transmit to a base station when it is not in the traffic mode.
3. Overhead or control data and short messages are sent to the base station at a rate of 4800 bits/second.
4. Mobile transmit power control and randomized timing are used to control or limit contention, which is the simultaneous reception of access messages at the base station.
5. An access channel is identified by its unique long code mask, which in part depends on the pilot offset of the base station to which the mobile is transmitting.

Example:

1. After the mobile initially acquires the pilot of a base station and reads the data on the **synchronization** channel, it transmits to the base station on an access channel.
2. This is the first indication that the base station has that the mobile is present and active.
3. All communications with the base station occur using the access channel until the mobile is placed in the traffic mode.
4. Individual access messages are contained in short "bursts" of data called probes.
5. Groups of randomly, but closely, spaced probes are called sequences.
6. An access attempt consists of a few probe sequences.

7. Closed-loop power control, incrementally increasing power, and randomized timing between access probes is used during an access sequence.

8. The access channel uses rate 1/3 convolutional coding, times 2 symbol repetition, interleaving, 64-ary orthogonal modulation, long-code scrambling with an offset based on an access-channel mask for privacy, and quadrature PN spreading using offset or staggered QPSK.

9. The initial portion of each access probe, called the probe preamble, uses a bit pattern which facilitates acquisition by the receiver at the base station.

5.5.8 A Comparison between IS-95 and other 2nd Generation Cellular Phone Systems

IS-54/136 GSM	IS-95
TDMA/FDMA	CDMA
Hard Hand-off	Soft Hand-off
Open-loop and Slow Power Control	Close-loop and Faster Power Control
Fixed Rate Vocoder	Variable Rate Vocoder

5.6 IS-95 CDMA Call Processing

5.6.1 Introduction

Mobile station goes through different IS-95 call processing states for acquiring traffic channel.

Each call processing state in turn consists of many substates.

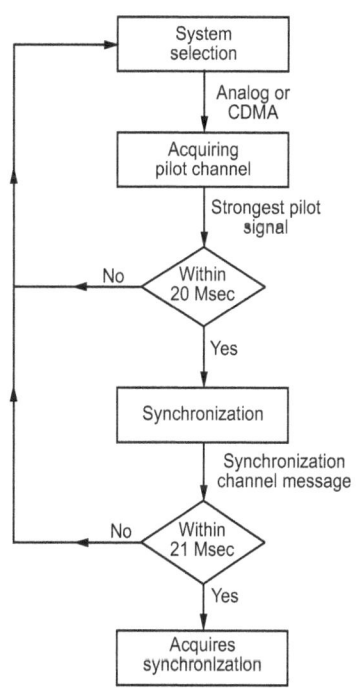

Fig. 5.14: Process of Acquiring Traffic Channel

5.6.2 System Initialization State

In this state, mobile selects the system to use, then selects the strongest pilot and synchronizes with the CDMA carrier.

(i) Selecting system: The dual mode cellular unit selects the system (analog or CDMA). The choice depends on the service provider. Accordingly, it sets the parameters after selecting the system.

(ii) Selecting pilot channel: In this state, mobile searches for the strongest signal and acquires the corresponding pilot channel.

Mobile enters into synchronization state if pilot channel is acquired within 20 msec, otherwise it returns to previous state   i.e. system selection state.

(iii) Synchronization: In this state, mobile searches for synchronization channel message. After receiving this message within 21 msec, the mobile stores system configuration and timing information, otherwise returns back to system selection state.

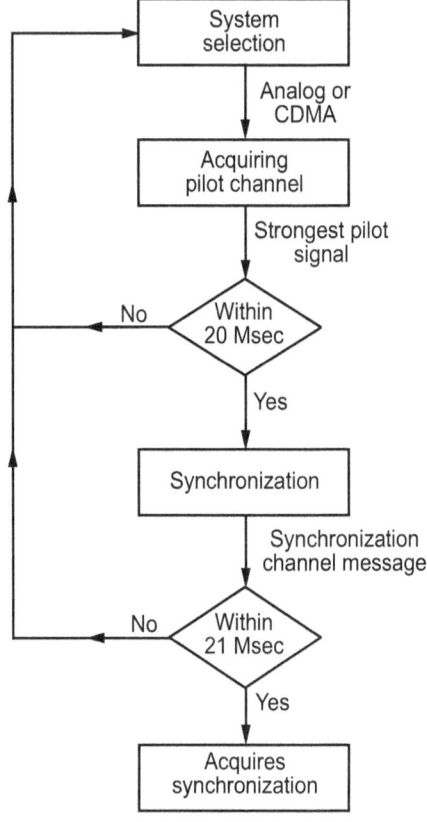

Fig. 5.14

5.6.3 Idle State

After acquiring synchronization, mobile enters into idle state. Walsh code for primary paging channel and paging channel rate is set.

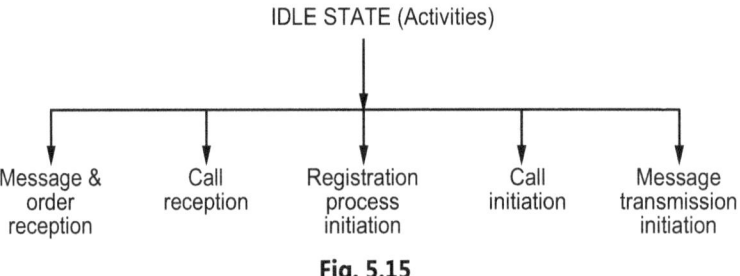

Fig. 5.15

In case of non-slotted mode, paging and control data for mobile can be received in any paging channel slot.

In slotted mode, channel is divided into slots of 80 ms, the slots are called as paging channels slots.

In slotted mode operation, the mobile station monitors the paging channel only during certain assigned slots. Battery power can be saved by stopping the mobile processing when slot is not being monitored.

There is a more pages field in slotted page message, which determines the performance or further action.

When this field is 0, the slots contain no more messages, so mobile stops scanning that channel. If filed is not 0, mobile searches for more messages in the channel slots.

5.6.3.1 Acknowledgement Procedure

The message sent to the mobile on paging channel from base station has the following attributes –

(i)   Address field.

(ii)   Acknowledgement required sequence number.

(iii)   Message sequence number.

(iv)   Other fields including data field.

OTHER FIELD	ADDR_TYPE	ACK_REQ	MSG_SEQ

If the ACK_REQ field of the message from base station is 1, then following is transmitted by mobile.

OTHER FIELD	ADDR_TYPE	ACK_REQ	ACK_SEQ	VALID_ACK
	I	1	I	1

I: addr_type/msg sequence number of msg requiring ack

When slotted page message has its ACK_REQ field = 0, the following set of acknowledgement is sent by mobile to base station.

OTHER FIELD	ADDR_TYPE	ACK_REQ	ACK_SEQ	VALID_ACK
	I	0	I	0

5.6.3.2 Idle Hand-off

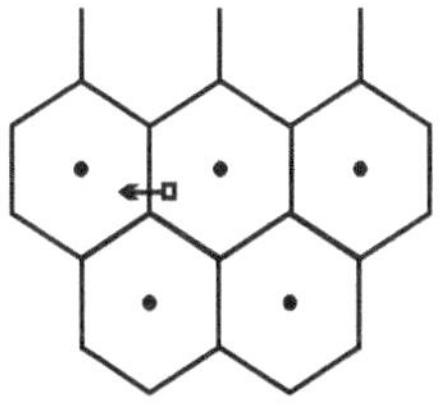

Fig. 5.16: Cell

Basically, the physical area is divided into number of hexagonal shapes i.e. for coverage.

When a person moves from one cell to another, he moves away from current cell's network to network of another cell.

When the mobile in such case receives the pilot signal which is stronger than current one, it hands over to that pilot channel. This process is called as hand-off. During this process of hand-off, the call is not disconnected and user even don't know that he has moved from one cell to another.

Pilot channels are identified by short PN offsets. There are three pilot sets in idle mode –

  (i)   Active pilot set

  (ii)   Neighbour pilot set

  (iii) Remaining pilot set

For each pilot set, one search window is specified, which searches for direct as well as multipath components of pilot signal. When stronger pilot signal is determined, hand-off takes place. Mobile operates in non-slotted more unless it receives one message from new channel and then resumes slotted operation.

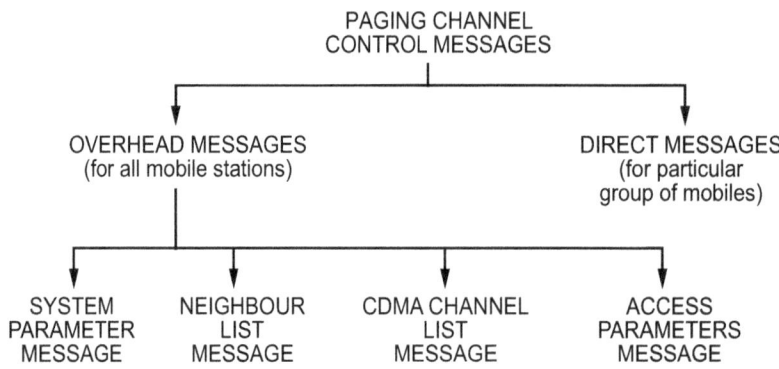

Fig. 5.17

5.6.4 System Access State

The system access state includes the following substates.

  (i)   Overload information update: Monitoring of paging channel unit is done in the substate till current set of configuration messages is received.

(ii) Mobile station origination attempt: Origination message to base station is sent from mobile station. This generally happens if user initiates a call.

(iii) Page response: Page response message is send to base station, when mobile receives general page message or slotted page message.

(iv) Registration access: Registration message is send by mobile station to base station.

(v) Mobile station order/message response: If a mobile receives message or order which requires acknowledgement or response, mobile sends a response to message received from base station.

(vi) Mobile station message transmission: Data burst messages generated by user are send to the base station.

(vii) PACA channel: PACA stands for Priority Access Channel Assignment. If the base station responds with an authentication request, the mobile responds in this substate.

5.6.5 Mobile Control on Traffic Channel

(i) Call Origination: Following states describe the call origination process.

First in traffic channel initialization substate, mobile verifies that it can receive the forward traffic channel and begins transmission. The primary traffic packets are exchanged with base station. The mobile station disconnects call after finishing with it.

(ii) Call Termination: Very first step is traffic channel initialization. Then mobile waits for an alert with an information message like data (phone num) or voice.

Then the mobile waits for the user to answer the call, the conversation takes place after this and after the conversation is over, mobile disconnects the call.

5.6.6 CDMA Registration

Registration is the process by which base station is notified by the mobile about:

(i)   its location

(ii) its status

(iii) identification

(iv) slot cycle and other characteristics.

IS-95 supports nine different forms of registration.

(i) Power up registration: Mobile registers when it is powered, or switches from one system to another.

(ii) **Power down registration:** When the mobile is power down, it registers to the system informing that it is no longer active.

(iii) **Time based registration:** In this case at regular time intervals, the mobile is registered to the system.

(iv) **Distance based registration:** A mobile station registers when the distance between current base station and base station in which it last registered exceeds the threshold value.

(v) **Zone-based registration:** When a mobile enters from one zone to another, it registers to the new zone.

(vi) **Parameter change registration:** When any of the following parameters are modified, the mobile registers to the system.

(a) Preferred slot cycle index.

(b) The station class mark.

(c) The call termination enabled indicator.

(vii) **Ordered registration:** Mobile registers when base station asks it to do so.

(viii) **Implicit registration:** When mobile successfully sends an origination message or page response message, the base station can infer the mobile station's location. This is implicit registration.

(ix) **Traffic channel registration:** Whenever the base station has registration information for a mobile that has been assigned to a traffic channel, the base station can notify the mobile that it is registered.

5.6.7 Authentication

Secret key known as A-key is used to authenticate mobile station. Only authentication centre of mobiles home system and mobile station are aware of A-key.

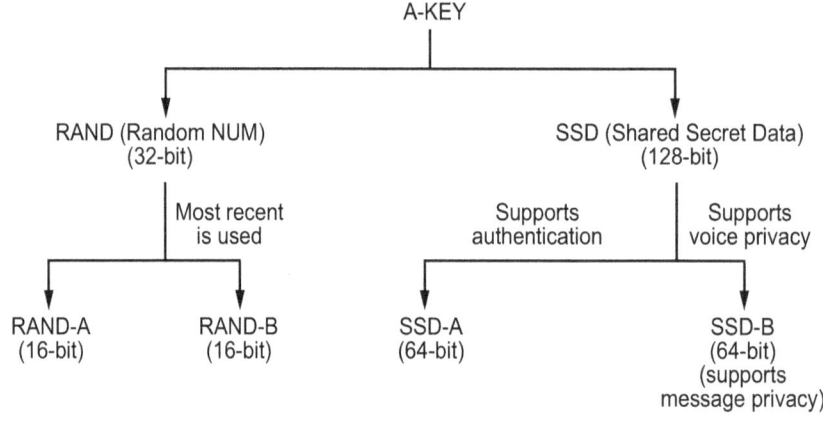

Fig. 5.18

5.7 CDMA 2000 System

5.7.1 Overview Of CDMA Technology

1. The world is demanding more from wireless communication technologies than ever before as more people around the world are subscribing to wireless.

2. Add in exciting Third-Generation (3G) wireless data services and applications - such as wireless email, web, digital picture taking/sending, assisted-GPS position location applications, video and audio streaming and TV broadcasting - and wireless networks are doing much more than just a few years ago.

3. This is where CDMA technology fits in.

4. CDMA consistently provides better capacity for voice and data communications than other commercial mobile technologies, allowing more subscribers to connect at any given time, and it is the common platform on which 3G technologies are built.

5. CDMA is a "spread spectrum" technology, allowing many users to occupy the same time and frequency allocations in a given band/space.

6. As its name implies, CDMA (Code Division Multiple Access) assigns unique codes to each communication to differentiate it from others in the same spectrum.

7. In a world of finite spectrum resources, CDMA enables many more people to share the airwaves at the same time than do alternative technologies.

8. The CDMA air interface is used in both 2G and 3G networks. 2G CDMA standards are branded cdmaOne and include IS-95A and IS-95B.

9. CDMA is the foundation for 3G services: the two dominant IMT-2000 standards, CDMA2000 and WCDMA, are based on CDMA.

10. **cdmaOne: The Family of IS-95 CDMA Technologies**: cdmaOne describes a complete wireless system based on the TIA/EIA IS-95 CDMA standard, including IS-95A and IS-95B revisions. It represents the end-to-end wireless system and all the necessary specifications that govern its operation. cdmaOne provides a family of related services including cellular, PCS and fixed wireless (wireless local loop).

11. **CDMA2000: Leading the 3G revolution:** CDMA2000 represents a family of ITU-approved, IMT-2000 (3G) standards and includes CDMA2000 1X and CDMA2000 1xEV technologies. They deliver increased network capacity to meet growing demand for wireless services and high-speed data services. CDMA2000 1X was the world's first 3G technology commercially deployed (October 2000).

12. **CDMA Deployments:** CDMA is the fastest growing wireless technology and it will continue to grow at a faster pace than any other technology. It is the platform on which 2G and 3G advanced services are built.

5.7.2 CDMA 2000 is 3G Technology

1. Third Generation (3G) is the term used to describe the latest generation of mobile services, which provide better quality voice and high-speed data, access to the Internet and multimedia services.

2. The International Telecommunication Union (ITU), working with industry bodies from around the world, has defined the technical requirements and standards as well as the use of spectrum for 3G systems under the IMT-2000 (International Mobile Telecommunications-2000) program.

3. The ITU requires that IMT-2000 (3G) networks, among other capabilities, deliver improved system capacity and spectrum efficiency over 2G systems and that they support data services at minimum transmission rates of 144 kbps in mobile (outdoor) and 2 Mbps in fixed (indoor) environments.

4. Based on these requirements, in 1999, the ITU approved five radio interfaces for IMT-2000 standards.

5. Three of the five approved standards (CDMA2000, TD-SCDMA, WCDMA) are based on CDMA.

6. CDMA2000 is also known by its ITU name, IMT-2000 CDMA Multi-Carrier (MC).

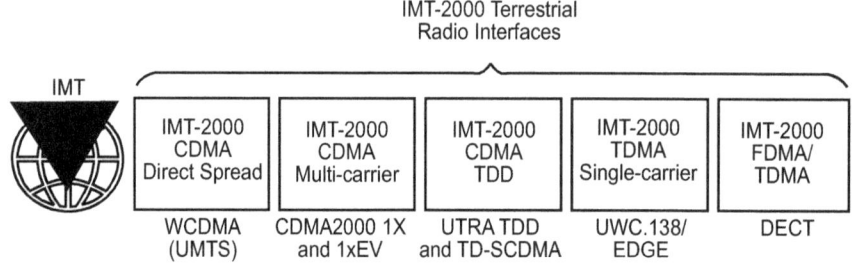

Fig. 5.19: Indicates the IMT-2000 Terrestrial Radio Interfaces

7. By the end of 2005, there were close to 170 commercial CDMA2000 (1X and 1xEV-DO) and WCDMA systems serving more than 275 million users across all continents. CDMA2000 is the most widely deployed 3G technology today.

8. CDMA is expected to become the dominant wireless platform worldwide in the future, as 3G CDMA (CDMA2000 and WCDMA) take market leadership from second-generation (2G) GSM.

5.7.3 The CDMA2000 Family of Technologies

CDMA2000 represents a family of standards and includes CDMA2000 1X and CDMA2000 1xEV-DO technologies.

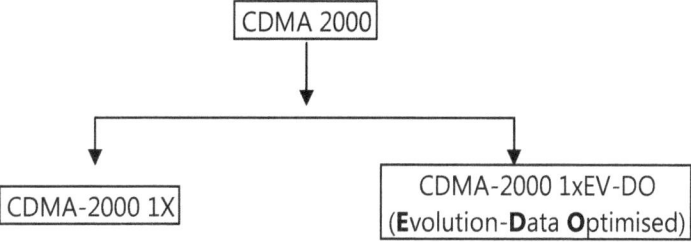

1. **CDMA2000 1X** can nearly triple the voice capacity of cdmaOne networks and delivers peak packet data speeds of 153 kbps (Release 0) or 307 kbps (Release 1) in mobile environments in a single 1.25 MHz channel.

2. CDMA2000 1xEV-DO (**Ev**olution-**D**ata **O**ptimized) is a data centric technology that allows operators to offer advanced data services like:

    • CDMA2000 1xEV-DO Release 0 delivers upto 2.4 Mbps data speed; in commercial networks it delivers 300-600 kbps in a single 1.25 MHz channel, the highest data rates of any wireless technology deployed today. It supports the most advanced data applications, such as MP3 transfers and video conferencing, TV broadcasts, video and audio downloads. It has been commercial since 2002.

    • CDMA2000 1xEV-DO Revision A (Rev A) delivers peak data speeds of 3.1 Mbps on the downlink and 1.8 Mbps on the uplink and incorporates quality of service (QoS) controls to manage latency on the network. With Rev A, operators will be able to introduce advanced multimedia services, including voice, data and broadcast over all-IP networks. Rev A will be commercially available in 2H 2006.

    • CDMA2000 Revision B (Rev B) standard will be published in the first half of 2006. Rev B introduces a 64-QAM modulation scheme, and will deliver peak rates of 73.5 Mbps in the forward link and 27 Mbps in the reverse link through the aggregation of 15 1.25 MHz carriers within 20 MHz of bandwidth. A single 1.25 MHz carrier and an aggregated 5 MHz carrier in the forward link will deliver a peak rate of upto 4.9 Mbps and 14.7 Mbps, respectively. In addition to supporting mobile broadband data and OFDM-based multicasting, the lower latency characteristics of Rev B will improve the performance of delay-sensitive applications such as Voice over Internet Protocol (VoIP), push-to-talk over cellular, video telephony, concurrent voice and multimedia, and massive multiplayer online gaming. Rev B will be commercial in 2008.

3. CDMA2000 1X and CDMA2000 1xEV-DO are backward compatible with cdmaOne.

5.7.4 Advantages of CDMA 2000

1. CDMA2000 benefited from the extensive experience acquired through several years of operation of cdmaOne systems. As a result, CDMA2000 is a very efficient and robust technology. It delivers the highest voice capacity and data throughput using the least amount of spectrum, and it can be used to provide services in urban as well as remote areas cost effectively.

2. The unique features, benefits, and performance of CDMA2000 make it an excellent technology for high-voice capacity and high-speed packet data. Since CDMA2000 1X supports both voice and data services on the same carrier, it allows operators to provide both services cost efficiently. CDMA2000 1xEV-DO is optimized for data and is capable to support large volumes of data traffic at broadband speeds. 1xEV-DO is well suited to provide high-speed data services to its mobile subscribers and/or broadband access to the Internet.

3. Due to its optimized radio technology, CDMA2000 enables operators to invest in fewer cell sites and deploy them faster, ultimately allowing the service providers to increase their revenues with faster Return On Investment (ROI).

4. The CDMA2000 evolutionary path was designed to minimize investment and the impact to an operator's network without service interruption for the end-user. This has been achieved through backward and forward compatibility, hardware reuse, in-band migration and hybrid network configuration. This unique feature of CDMA2000 technologies has provided operators a significant time-to-market advantage over other 3G technologies.

5.7.4.1 Key Advantages of CDMA2000 Technologies

1. Increased voice capacity
2. Higher data throughput
3. Multicast services
4. Frequency band flexibility
5. Migration path
6. Serves multiple markets
7. Supports multiple service platforms
8. Full backward compatibility
9. For more information on CDMA2000 technology click on the topic of interest below.
10. Increased battery life
11. Synchronization
12. Power control
13. Soft hand-off
14. Transmit diversity
15. Voice and data channels

16. Traffic channel
17. Supplemental channels
18. Turbo coding
19. Connectivity to ANSI-41, GSM- MAP and IP networks
20. Full backward compatibility
21. Improved service multiplexing and QoS management
22. Flexible channel structure in support of multiple services with various QoS and variable transmission rates
23. Multicast services

5.7.5 Increased Voice Capacity

1. The spectral efficiency of CDMA2000 1X permits high traffic deployments in a small amount (1.25 MHz channel) of spectrum. CDMA2000 1X can provide voice capacity of nearly three times that of cdmaOne systems with Selectable Mode Vocoders (SMV) and antenna diversity techniques.
2. CDMA2000 delivers 4-8 times higher voice capacity than TDMA-based technologies.
3. CDMA2000 1X supports 35 traffic channels per sector per RF (26 erlangs/sector/RF) using the EVRC vocoder.
4. Voice capacity improvement in the forward link is attributed to faster power control, lower code rates (1/4 rate), and transmit diversity (for single path Rayleigh fading).
5. In the reverse link, capacity improvement is primarily due to coherent reverse link.

5.7.6 Higher Data Throughput

1. Today's commercial CDMA2000 1X networks support a peak data rate of 153 kbps (Rel. 0) or 307 kbps (Rel. 1).
2. CDMA2000 1xEV-DO enables peak rates of upto 2.4 Mbps (Rev. 0) or 3.1 Mbps on the downlink, and 1.8 Mbps on the uplink (Rev A). 1xEV-DO networks deliver the highest data speeds commercially available today.

5.7.7 Average Data Throughput

CDMA2000 1X	60-100 kbps
CDMA2000 1xEV-DO	400-800 kbps

5.7.8 Multicast Services

1. With the introduction of EV-DO Release 0 and followed by EV-DO Revisions A and B, operators have the ability to offer multicast services, "one to many" delivery, which allows transmitting the same information to an unlimited number of users without the need to rebroadcast the information multiple times.

2. Multicast functionality offers significant advantages to operators and users.

3. For operators, it allows a vast range of high-revenue generating services with minimum network resources at low cost. For the end-user, multicast services provide access to multimedia content, such as TV broadcasts, MP3 audio files, movies, etc., and a higher quality of services.

4. For 1xEV-DO Rel 0, the multicast functionality is referred to as Gold Multicast and for 1xEV-DO Rev A, it is called Platinum Multicast.

5.7.9 Frequency Band Flexibility

CDMA2000 can be deployed in most cellular and PCS spectrum. CDMA2000 networks have already been deployed in the 450, 800, 1700, 1900 and 2100 MHz bands.

5.7.10 Migration Path

CDMA2000 provides a direct migration path to 3G for first generation (1G) and second generation (2G) systems. CDMA2000 systems have been deployed by Greenfield, cdmaOne, TDMA and analog operators.

5.7.11 Serves Multiple Markets

1. CDMA2000 technologies support both fixed (Wireless Local Loop – WLL) and mobile services and can be used by operators to provide affordable voice services and broadband data access in urban, as well as remote areas, cost-effectively.

2. While CDMA2000 technologies are mostly deployed by operators to offer mobile services, in many developing regions, i.e., Africa and South East Asia, CDMA2000 WLL technology is used to provide voice and data services to communities.

5.7.12 Supports Multiple Service Platforms

CDMA2000 can be used with various operating systems (Palm and PocketPC), application platforms (JAVA and BREW), WAP, and emerging wireless technologies (WiFi and Push-to-Talk).

5.7.13 Full Backward Compatibility

1. CDMA2000 is backward compatible with cdmaOne, and 1xEV-DO is backward compatible with both CDMA2000 1X and cdmaOne through multi-mode devices.

2. Backward compatibility assures service transparency for the end user and smooth integration of 2G and 3G networks for the operator.

5.7.14 Increased Battery Life

CDMA2000 significantly enhances battery performance. Benefits include:

- Quick paging channel operation,
- Improved reverse link performance,
- New common channel structure and operation,
- Reverse link gated transmission,
- New MAC states for efficient and ubiquitous idle time operation.

5.7.15 Synchronization

1. CDMA2000 is synchronized with the Universal Coordinated Time (UCT).
2. The forward link transmission timing of all CDMA2000 base stations worldwide is synchronized within a few microseconds.
3. Base station synchronization can be achieved through several techniques including self-synchronization, radio beep, or through satellite-based systems such as GPS, Galileo, or GLONASS.
4. Reverse link timing is based on the received timing derived from the first multipath component used by the terminal.
5. **There are several benefits to having all base stations in a network synchronized:**
   - The common time reference improves acquisition of channels and hand-off procedures since there is no time ambiguity when looking for and adding a new cell in the active set.
   - It also enables the system to operate some of the common channels in soft hand-off, which improves the efficiency of the common channel operation.
   - Common network time reference allows implementation of very efficient "position location" techniques.

5.7.16 Power Control

1. The basic frame length is 20 ms divided into 16 equal power control groups.
2. In addition, CDMA2000 defines a 5 ms frame structure, essentially to support signalling bursts, as well as 40 and 80 ms frames, which offer additional interleaving depth and diversity gains for data services.
3. Unlike IS-95, where Fast Closed Loop Power Control was applied only to the reverse link, CDMA2000 channels can be power controlled at upto 800 Hz in both the reverse and forward links.
4. The reverse link power control command bits are punctured into the F-FCH or the F-DCCH (explained in later sections) depending on the service configuration.

5. The forward link power control command bits are punctured in the last quarter of the R-PICH power control slot.

6. In the reverse link, during gated transmission, the power control rate is reduced to 400 or 200 Hz on both links.

7. The reverse link power control sub-channel may also be divided into two independent power control streams, either both at 400 bps, or one at 200 bps and the other at 600 bps. This allows for independent power control of forward link channels.

8. In addition to the closed loop power control, the power on the reverse link of CDMA2000 is also controlled through an Open Loop Power Control mechanism.

9. This mechanism inverses the slow fading effect due to path loss and shadowing. It also acts as a safety fuse when the fast power control fails.

10. When the forward link is lost, the closed loop reverse link power control is "freewheeling" and the terminal disruptively interferes with neighbouring.

11. In such a case, the open loop reduces the terminal output power and limits the impact to the system.

12. Finally, the Outer Loop Power drives the closed loop power control to the desired set point based on error statistics that it collects from the forward link or reverse link.

13. Due to the expanded data rate range and various QoS requirements, different users will have different outer loop thresholds; thus, different users will receive different power levels at the base station.

14. In the reverse link, CDMA2000 defines some nominal gain offsets based on various channel frame format and coding schemes.

15. The remaining differences will be corrected by the outer loop itself.

5.7.17 Soft Hand-off

1. Even with dedicated channel operation, the terminal keeps searching for new cells as it moves across the network. In addition to the active set, neighbour set, and remaining set, the terminal also maintains a candidate set.

2. The step-by-step procedure with multiple thresholds and timers used in CDMA2000 ensures that the resource is only used when beneficial to the link and pilots are not constantly added and removed from the various lists, therefore limiting the associated signalling.

3. In addition to intrasystem, intrafrequency monitoring, the network may direct the terminal to look for base stations on a different frequency or a different system.

4. CDMA2000 provides a framework to the terminal in support of the inter-frequency handover measurements consisting of identity and system parameters to be measured.

5. The terminal performs required measurements as allowed by its hardware capability.

6. In case of a terminal with dual receiver structure, the measurement can be done in parallel.

7. When a terminal has a single receiver, the channel reception will be interrupted when performing the measurement. In this instance, during the measurement, a certain portion of a frame will be lost.

8. To improve the chance of successful decoding, the terminal is allowed to bias the power control loop and boost the transmit power before performing the measurement.

9. This method increases the energy per information bit and reduces the risk of losing the link in the interval.

10. Based on measurement reports provided by the terminal, the network then decides whether or not to hand-off a given terminal to a different frequency system.

11. It does not release the resource until it receives confirmation that hand-off was successful or the timer expires.

12. This enables the terminal to come back in case it could not acquire the new frequency or the new system.

5.7.18 Transmit Diversity

1. Transmit diversity consists of de-multiplexing and modulating data into two orthogonal signals, each of them transmitted from a different antenna at the same frequency.

2. The two orthogonal signals are generated using either Orthogonal Transmit Diversity (OTD) or Space-Time Spreading (STS).

3. The receiver reconstructs the original signal using the diversity signals, thus taking advantage of the additional space and/or frequency diversity.

4. Another transmission option is directive transmission. The base station directs a beam towards a single user or a group of users in a specific location, thus providing space separation in addition to code separation.

5. Depending on the radio environment, transmit diversity techniques may improve the link performance by upto 5 dB.

5.7.19 Voice and Data Channels

The CDMA2000 forward traffic channel structure may include several physical channels:

- The Fundamental Channel (F-FCH) is equivalent to functionality Traffic Channel (TCH) for IS-95. It can support data, voice or signalling multiplexed with one another at any rate from 750 bps to 14.4 kbps.

- The Supplemental Channel (F-SCH) supports high rate data services. The network may schedule transmission on the F-SCH on a frame-by- frame basis, if desired.

- The Dedicated Control Channel (F-DCCH) is used for signalling or bursty data sessions. This channel allows for sending the signalling information without any impact on the parallel data stream.

The reverse traffic channel structure is similar to the forward traffic channel.

- It may include R-PICH,
- A Fundamental Channel (R-FCH),
- And/or a Dedicated Control Channel (R-DCCH),
- And one or several Supplemental Channels (R-SCH).
- Their functionality and encoding structure is the same as for the forward link with data rates ranging from 1 kbps to 1 Mbps. (It is important to note that while the standard supports a maximum data rate of 1 Mbps, existing products are supporting a peak data rate of 307 kbps).

5.7.20 Traffic Channel

1. The traffic channel structure and frame format is very flexible.
2. In order to limit the signaling load that would be associated with a full frame format parameter negotiation, CDMA2000 specifies a set of channel configurations.
3. It defines a spreading rate and an associated set of frames for each configuration.
4. The forward traffic channel always includes either a fundamental channel or a dedicated control channel.
5. The main benefit of this multichannel forward traffic structure is the flexibility to independently set up and tear down new services without any complicated multiplexing reconfiguration or code channel juggling.
6. The structure also allows different hand-off configurations for different channels.
7. For example, the F-DCCH, which carries critical signalling information, may be in soft hand-off, while the associated F-SCH operation could be based on a best cell strategy.

5.7.21 Supplemental Channels

1. One key CDMA2000 1X feature is the ability to support both voice and data services on the same carrier.

2. CDMA2000 operates at upto 16 or 32 times the FCH rate - also referred to as 16x or 32x in Release 0 and A, respectively. In contrast to voice calls, the traffic generated by packet data calls is bursty, with small durations of high traffic separated by larger durations of no traffic.

3. It is very inefficient to dedicate a permanent traffic channel to a packet data call.

4. This burstiness impacts the amount of available power to the voice calls, possibly degrading their quality if the system is not engineered correctly.

5. Hence, a key CDMA2000 design issue is assuring that a CDMA channel carrying voice and data calls simultaneously do so with negligible impact to the QoS of both.

6. Supplemental Channels (SCHs) can be assigned and deassigned at any time by the base station.

7. The SCH has the additional benefit of improved modulation, coding, and power control schemes.

8. This allows a single SCH to provide a data rate of upto 16 FCH in CDMA2000 Release 0 (or 153.6 kbps for Rate Set 1 rates), and up to 32 FCH in CDMA2000 Release A (or 307.2 kbps for Rate Set 1 rates).

9. Note that each sector of a base station may transmit multiple SCHs simultaneously, if it has sufficient transmit power and Walsh codes.

10. The CDMA2000 standard limits the number of SCHs a mobile station can support simultaneously to two.

11. This is in addition to the FCH or DCCH, which are set up for the entire duration of the call since they are used to carry signalling and control frames as well as data.

12. Two approaches are possible: individually assigned SCHs, with either finite or infinite assignments, or shared SCHs with infinite assignments.

13. For bursty and delay-tolerant traffic, assigning a few scheduled fat pipes is preferable to dedicating many thin or slow pipes.

14. The fat-pipe approach exploits variations in the channel conditions of different users to maximize sector throughput.

15. The more sensitive the traffic becomes to delay, such as voice, the more appropriate the dedicated traffic channel approach becomes.

5.7.22 Turbo Coding

1. CDMA2000 provides the option of using either turbo coding or convolutional coding on the forward and reverse SCHs.

2. Both coding schemes are optional for the base station and the mobile station, and the capability of each is communicated through signalling messages prior to the set up of the call.

3. In addition to peak rate increase and improved rate granularity, the major improvement to the traffic channel coding in CDMA2000 is the support of turbo coding at rate 1/2, 1/3, or 1/4.

4. The turbo code is based on 1/8 state parallel structure and can only be used for supplemental channels and frames with more than 360 bits.

5. Turbo coding provides a very efficient scheme for data transmission and leads to better link performance and system capacity improvements.

6. In general, turbo coding provides a performance gain in terms of power savings over convolutional coding.

7. This gain is a function of the data rate, with higher data rates, generally providing more turbo coding gain.

5.7.23 Advantages of CDMA 2000 1xEV-DO

5.7.23.1 Value Propostion for End Users

Good User Experience for All Device Platforms and Application Types: End users experience peak data rates upto 2.4 Mbps with 1xEV-DO devices. End users are able to have a wireline-equivalent experience using their laptops with a full suite of applications. PDAs can use richer content, and smartphones are accommodated at the appropriate data rate.

Dual-mode Devices: End users can select devices that offer both 1X voice and 1xEV-DO high-speed data services. These dual-mode devices can hand off to 1X packet data services if users move out of 1xEV-DO coverage and also monitor voice calls when in 1xEV-DO data sessions.

Attractive Monthly Service Prices: End users can take advantage of new service pricing plans, due to 1xEV-DO's lower cost per bit. Based on the CDMA2000 network architecture, the system has the ability to track usage by volume (bytes, packets), as well as the traditional tracking of usage by time.

Always-on Service: 1xEV-DO provides an "always-on" user experience. Once a device is powered on, the end user only logs in once, and the subsequent sessions can be started without having to log in again. When a user comes out of dormancy, the connection time is less than 0.5 second. This is an important advantage of the service offering, since it allows the user's natural state to be dormancy, where the device does not utilize any radio resources and has minimal power consumption.

Ubiquitous Coverage and Service Availability in All Environments: 1xEV-DO is the only megabit Internet service available today that operates in all environments. End users enjoy the high data rates in mobile, portable, and fixed environments. Therefore, end users can use 1xEV-DO's high-speed data services in the same manner as they use mobile voice services today. 1xEV-DO takes the desktop experience and extends it to all wireless environments.

5.7.23.2 Competitive Advantage for Operators

The 1xEV-DO system provides significant and fundamental competitive advantages for operators:

Spectral Efficiency: 1xEV-DO uses spectrum very efficiently and provides the highest capacity (aggregate peak capacity of 7.4 Mbps in a 3-cell sector) with a 1.25 MHz frequency carrier. This enables the best and most economical use of an operator's spectrum resources.

High Service Quality: By separating voice and packet data services on different frequency carriers, voice quality is maintained at its highest level and packet data services have higher peak data rates (2.4 Mbps).

Increased Revenue Opportunity: The higher capacity of the 1xEV-DO system accommodates a large number of users, increasing the revenue potential for operators. The megabit data rates attract high-value customers desiring to purchase data services along with their voice service. 1xEV-DO targets all market segments, ranging from mobile professionals to consumers.

Higher Profit Margins: Because 1xEV-DO has higher capacity while essentially using the same amount of network resources, it delivers the lowest cost per bit for packet data.

Leverage from Existing Capital Investments: 1xEV-DO can be highly integrated into CDMA2000 and cdmaOne systems, leveraging operators' existing capital investments. 1xEV-DO can be highly integrated into existing base stations, and can use the same PDSN, BSC, cell sites, towers, antennas, and network plans.

5.7.23.3 Time-to-Market Advantage for Manufacturers

Proven, Low-risk Technology: 1xEV-DO has been extensively tested in the field and provides a proven and low-risk solution for device and infrastructure manufacturers.

High-volume CDMA2000 Cost Curves: 1xEV-DO uses the same RF components as used in CDMA2000 and cdmaOne systems and devices. These RF components have high-volume cost curves, and enable manufacturers to benefit from cost savings associated with mainstream components.

5.7.23.4 Services and Products

Applications and Services: From basic communications to streaming video entertainment and m-commerce transactions, 1xEV-DO enables a wireless lifestyle that allows users the freedom and flexibility to have their wireless world at their fingertips. Operators can offer existing applications at lower costs, introduce data intensive applications, and look forward to a new breed of wireless applications which follow wireline Internet trends with the addition of mobility and position location customizations. The wide variety of applications include.

Communications:

- E-mails with large attachments
- Multimedia messaging
- Chat

Information:

- Web browsing with multimedia and graphical content
- Large file transfer
- Intranet access
- Video news clips
- Graphical stock quotes and trends
- Database queries
- Scheduling

Entertainment:

- Streaming audio and video
- Download of audio and video clips
- Graphics and picture downloads
- Games
- Photographs
- Movie previews

Position Location:

- Navigation / maps
- Real-time traffic alerts

- Graphical weather alerts
- Friend finder

Transactions:

- M-commerce
- Stock trades
- E-cash
- Reservations

Devices:

1xEV-DO enhances the end user's experience with more robust applications across the full range of devices. From handsets to wireless video players, to telematic devices, 1xEV-DO enables a broad array of devices for personal or professional use.

Integrated Devices:

- Handset / Smartphone
- PDA
- PDA with voice
- PC including laptops, notebooks, tablets, etc.
- Media appliances including wireless cameras, wireless MP3 players, wireless video players, etc.

Wireless Network Adapters:

- Handset / Smartphone with Bluetooth/USB
- PC Card
- Compact Flash Module
- Fixed Access Terminal with USB/Ethernet

Network:

The 1xEV-DO airlink is extremely flexible and offers multiple architectural options for various deployment scenarios depending on specific market and business cases. 1xEV-DO systems are well positioned to heavily leverage existing CDMA and IP networks.

- Integrated Architecture
- Complementary Architecture
- Distributed Architecture

5.7.24 CDMA 2000 Architecture

Fig. 5.65 depicts the general architecture of cdma2000. Development of the cdma2000 Family of standards has, to the greatest extent possible, adhered to the architecture by specifying different layers in different standards.

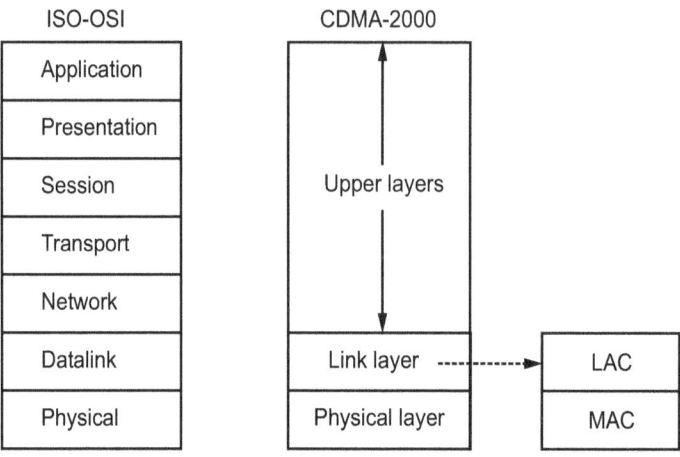

Fig. 5.20: Typical ISO-OSI Reference Model and CDMA2000 Model

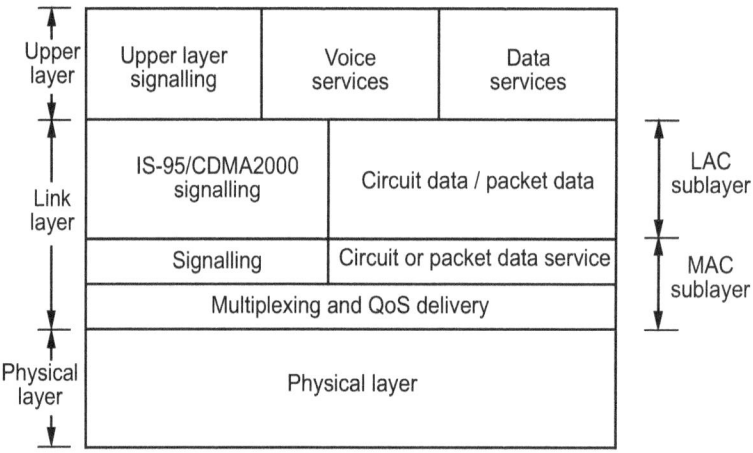

Fig. 5.21: CDMA2000 Architecture

5.7.24.1 CDMA2000 Upper Layer

1. This layer has the provision of upper layer signalling, voice services and data services applications.

2. Upper layer signalling contains IS-95 layer circuit signalling and CDMA2000 upper layer signalling.

3. Voice services include voice telephony services, PSTN access, IP telephony and mobile to mobile communication.

4. Data services include circuit data services and packet data services.

5. Circuit data services like ISDN and B-ISDN emulation services play important application for industries and different organizations.

6. Packet data services like TCP/IP network, connection-oriented and connectionless services are having huge applications in communication field.

5.7.24.2 CDMA2000 Link Layer

1. The second layer in CDMA 2000 architecture is link layer.

2. Link layer is divided into two sublayers:

    (a) Link Access Control (LAC) Sublayer.

    (b) Media Access Control (MAC) Sublayer.

3. LAC Sublayer manages the reliable transmission and reception between two different systems.

4. LAC Layer is responsible for the flow control, error detection and error correction between different communicating users.

5. LAC Layer supports IS-95 signalling and CDMA2000 signalling techniques and hence their protocols.

6. CDMA2000 also supports the MAC sublayer. MAC sublayer provides the following three important functions:

    (a) MAC control signalling.

    (b) Circuit or packet data delivery.

    (c) Multiplexing and QoS delivery.

5.7.24.3 CDMA2000 Physical Layer

1. The physical layer provides coding and modulation services for the set of logical channels used by the multiplexing and QoS layer.

2. The different physical channels are classified as –

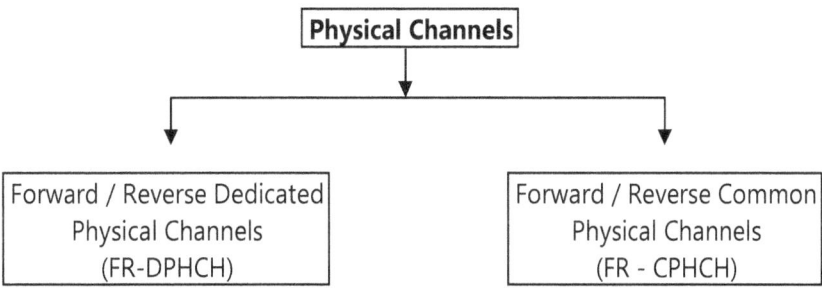

3. Forward dedicated channels carry information between the base station and a specific mobile unit. Common channel carries information from base station to a set of mobiles. Here, we have to consider point-to-point communication.

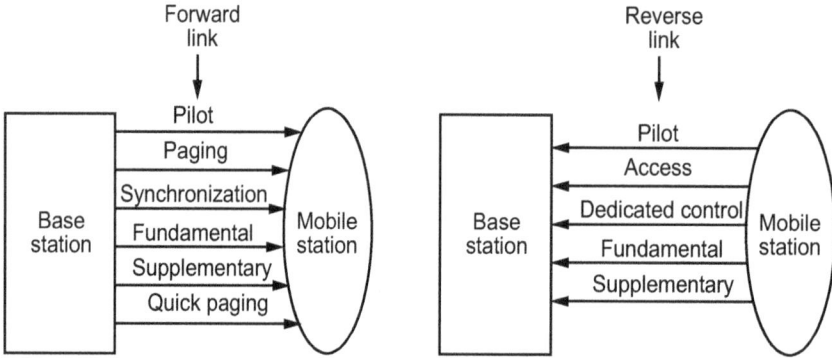

Fig. 5.22: CDMA2000 Physical Channels

4. CDMA2000 may be configured in a variety of ways, depending on the system's requirements and constraints.

5. CDMA2000 accepts both single carrier and multiple carrier implementations; it also proposes a Time Division Duplex (TDD) mode, which will be discussed in the next section.

6. Also the different channels corresponding to the physical layer of CDMA2000 system is discussed here.

7. For both FDD (Frequency Division Duplex) and TDD (Time Division Duplex) implementation, the physical layer channels are the same.

8. Channels are prefixed with an *R* for Reverse link channels (from the Mobile to the Base Station) and with *F* for forward link channels (from the Base Station to the Mobile unit).

9. **Physical channels are classified in two distinct groups: Dedicated and Common channels and are discussed in section 5.11.25.**

10. Dedicated Physical Channels (DPCH) offer a point to point connection while Common Physical Channels (CPCH) offer a point to multi-point access. Here is a list of the channels of CDMA2000:

5.7.25 Dedicated Physical Channel (DPHCH)

5.7.25.1 Forward Dedicated Physical Channel

1. Fundamental Channel (F-FCH):

Designed to transport dedicated data.

2. **Supplemental Channel Type (F-SCHT):**
   These are channels allocated dynamically to meet a required data rate.
3. **Dedicated Control Channel (F-DCCH):**
   Transports mobile-specific control informations.
4. **Dedicated Auxiliary Pilot Channel (F-DAPICH)** *(optional)*:
   This channel is used with antenna beam-forming and beam-steering techniques to increase the coverage or data rate towards a particular user.

5.7.25.2 Reverse Dedicated Physical Channel

1. **Fundamental Channel (R-FCH):**
   Similar to F-FCH; designed to transport dedicated data.
2. **Supplemental Channel Type (R-SCHT):**
   These are channels allocated dynamically to meet a required data rate.
3. **Dedicated Control Channel (R-DCCH):**
   Transports mobile-specific control informations.
4. **Pilot Channel (R-PICH):**
   Provides the capabilities for coherent detection.

5.7.26 Common Physical Channel (CPHCH)

5.7.26.1 Forward Channels

1. **Pilot Channel (F-PICH):**
   This channel provides capabilities for soft *hand-off* and coherent detection.
   Hand-off is a procedure where a mobile with an on-going call changes channel and/or base station under the supervision of the network.
2. **Common Auxiliary Pilot Channel (F-CAPICH):**
   Also provides capabilities for soft *hand-off* and coherent detection.
3. **Common Channel Type (F-CCHT):**
   - **Paging Channel (F-PCH):** Enables paging functions. Also provides a means for short burst data communications.
   - **Common Control Channel (F-CCCH):** Also provides a mean for paging functions, but it supports different data rates. It also provides capability for short burst data communications.
   - **Sync Channel (F-SYNC):** Provides the mobile station with system information and synchronization.

5.7.26.2 Reverse Channels

1. **Access Channel (R-ACH):** Multiple access channel where mobile stations communicate messages to the base station.
2. **Common Control Channel (R-CCCH):** Similar to the R-ACH, but it is meant to transport control information.

5.7.27 Pilot Channels

1. CDMA2000 includes *Pilot* symbols for both the uplink and the downlink.
2. Pilot symbols are known symbols sent by the transmitter so that the receiver is able to detect the phase of the signal thus enabling the capability for coherent detection.
3. It also allows the receiver to estimate the properties of the channel through which the signals travel.
4. On the downlink, the F-PICH carries the Pilot symbols.
5. The F-PICH is shared among the users for an efficient use of the available bandwidth.

5.7.28 Chip Rates

1. CDMA2000 supports a range of chip rates; all can be expressed by:
   N × 1.2288 Mcps, N = 1, 3, 6, 9, 12. When N > 1, there are two ways by which CDMA2000 can spread the signal.
2. The first one, **Multi-Carrier**, basically de-multiplexes the message signal into N information signals and spreads each of those on a different carrier, at a chip rate of 1.2288 Mcps.
3. The second one, **Direct-Spread**, simply spreads the message signal directly with a chip rate of N × 1.2288 Mcps.
4. In the Multi-Carrier mode, each carrier has an IS-95 signal format. The two methods are illustrated next:

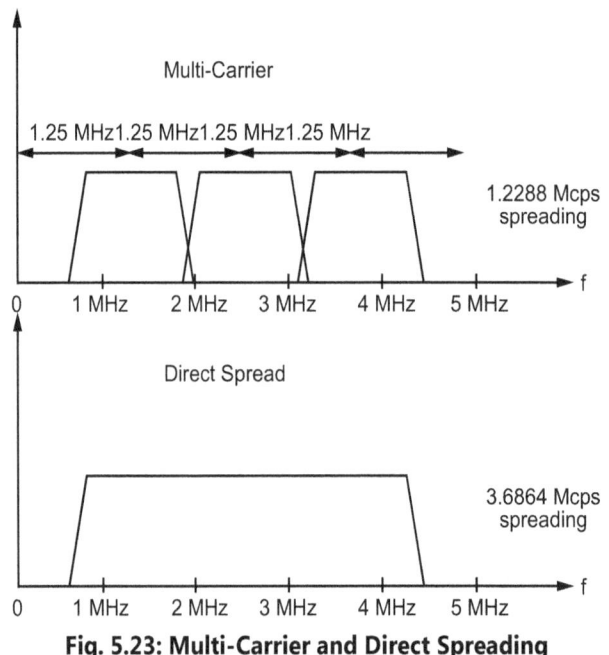

Fig. 5.23: Multi-Carrier and Direct Spreading

5.7.29 Modulation and Spreading

5.7.29.1 Single Carrier

Downlink:

1. The following diagram illustrates the modulation and spreading process for downlink single carrier CDMA2000.
2. The input consists of a single channel which is already coded, punctured and interleaved according to the CDMA2000 specifications.
3. Each channel has different possible configurations but the modulation and spreading process is the same for all channels.

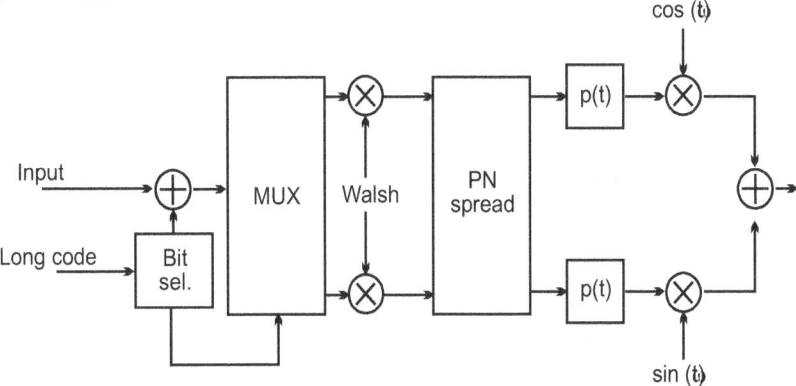

Fig. 5.24: The Modulation and Spreading Process for Downlink Single Carrier CDMA2000

4. First, a long PN code scrambles the channel. The rate of the scrambling code depends on the code rate of the input. Only the PCH, DCCH, FCH and SCH are scrambled.
5. Then the MUX maps the codes to polar form, transfers the serial data to parallel and also provides the possibility of puncturing the data stream, to insert a bit for power control (indicated by the *Bit Sel.* box).
6. A Walsh code running at the chip rate (1.2288 Mcps) then multiply the data.
7. The same code is used for both the In-Phase and Quadrature component.
8. Each channel gets a different Walsh code assigned and might be of different length (OVSF codes), to adjust the Spreading Factor to the data rate required.

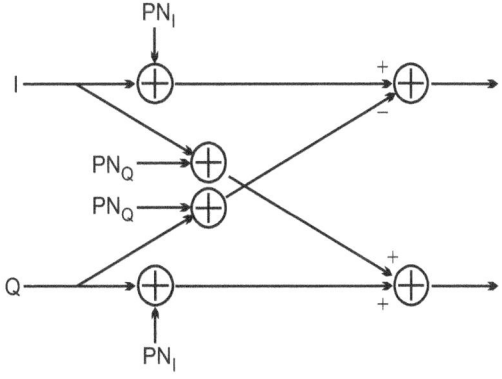

Fig. 5.25: Complex Spreading Procedure

9. The data is then complex PN multiplied, also at the chip rate.
10. This is accomplished using the set-up illustrated in the *Complex Spreading* diagram. PN_I and PN_Q are two different PN sequences.

11. Finally, the information is modulated, using p(t) as a waveform, which is the same as the one used in IS-95.

12. The same structure is used for *Direct Spread*, but the chip rate is modified to N × 1.2288 Mcps.

Uplink:

1. The following figure illustrates the uplink modulation and spreading process.

2. The channel illustrated here is the Reverse Dedicated Channel.

3. It consists of a Reverse Pilot Channel, which is always present, a Reverse Fundamental Channel (R-FCH), one or more Reverse Supplemental Channel (R-SCH) and a Reverse Dedicated Control Channel (R-DCCH). The R-FCH, R-SCH and R-DCCH may not always be used.

4. Each channel is spread with a Walsh-Hadamard codeword as indicated in the diagram. Channels which require higher data rates, get a smaller codeword.

5. The R-DCCH is spread with the sequence (00001111), the R-FCH with the sequence (0011), the R-SCH is spread with (01) if there is only one supplemental channel present or (0101) if two are used.

6. The second supplemental channel would then be spread with the sequence (0110).

7. It is also possible to have more supplemental channels by using longer Walsh-Hadamard codewords.

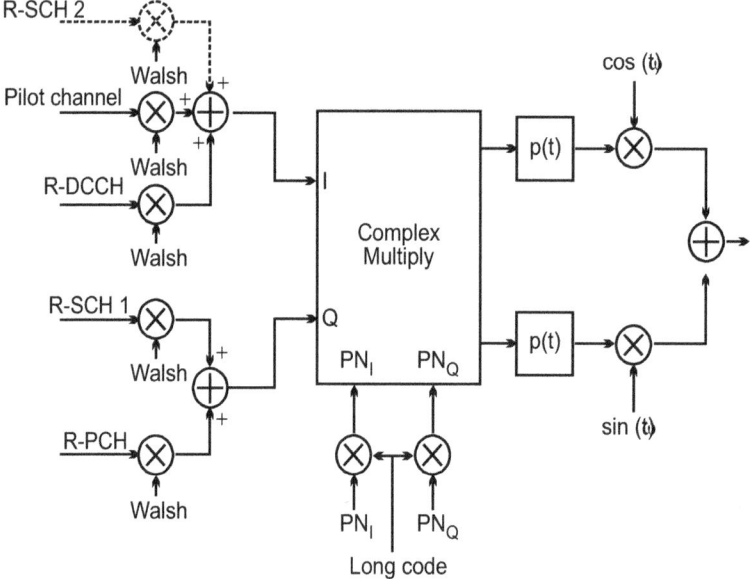

Fig. 5.26: Uplink Modulation and Spreading

8.   The spread Pilot Channel and the R-DCCH are mapped to the In-Phase component.

9.   The spread R-FCH and R-SCH are mapped to the Quadrature component.

10. Both components are then complex multiplied by the two PN sequences provided, PN_I and PN_Q, which are themselves multiplied by a long code.

11. The complex multiplication process was illustrated in the previous diagram.

12. The two PN sequences have the same properties as their IS-95 equivalents and have a period of 2^{15} chips.

13. The mobile station aligns the PN sequences in time with the synchronization channel so that their state is known by the base station.

14. The long code has a period of $2^{42} - 1$ chips.

15. The reverse link supports Direct Spread CDMA for chip rates that are multiples of the basic 1.2288 Mcps.

16. Chip rates of 3X, 6X, 9X and 12X, which correspond to 3.6864 Mcps, 7.3728 Mcps, 11.0592 Mcps and 14.7456 Mcps respectively, are supported.

5.7.29.2 Multi-Carrier

Downlink:

1.   Fig. 5.72 illustrates the structure of downlink multi-carrier CDMA2000.

2.   It is very similar to the single carrier implementation.

3.   After scrambling (if applicable), the user data is demultiplexed to feed the N IQ-Modulators (N = 3, 6, 9 or 12) so that each frequency carries part of the data stream.

4.   The N carriers are Walsh modulated to the chip rate of 1.2288 Mcps.

5.   The Walsh codes may be different for each.

6.   As for the single carrier case, provision is made to puncture the data stream to add a bit for power control. It is also indicated by the *Bit Sel.* box.

7.   The carriers are located on a different frequency with a spacing of 1.25 MHz between each.

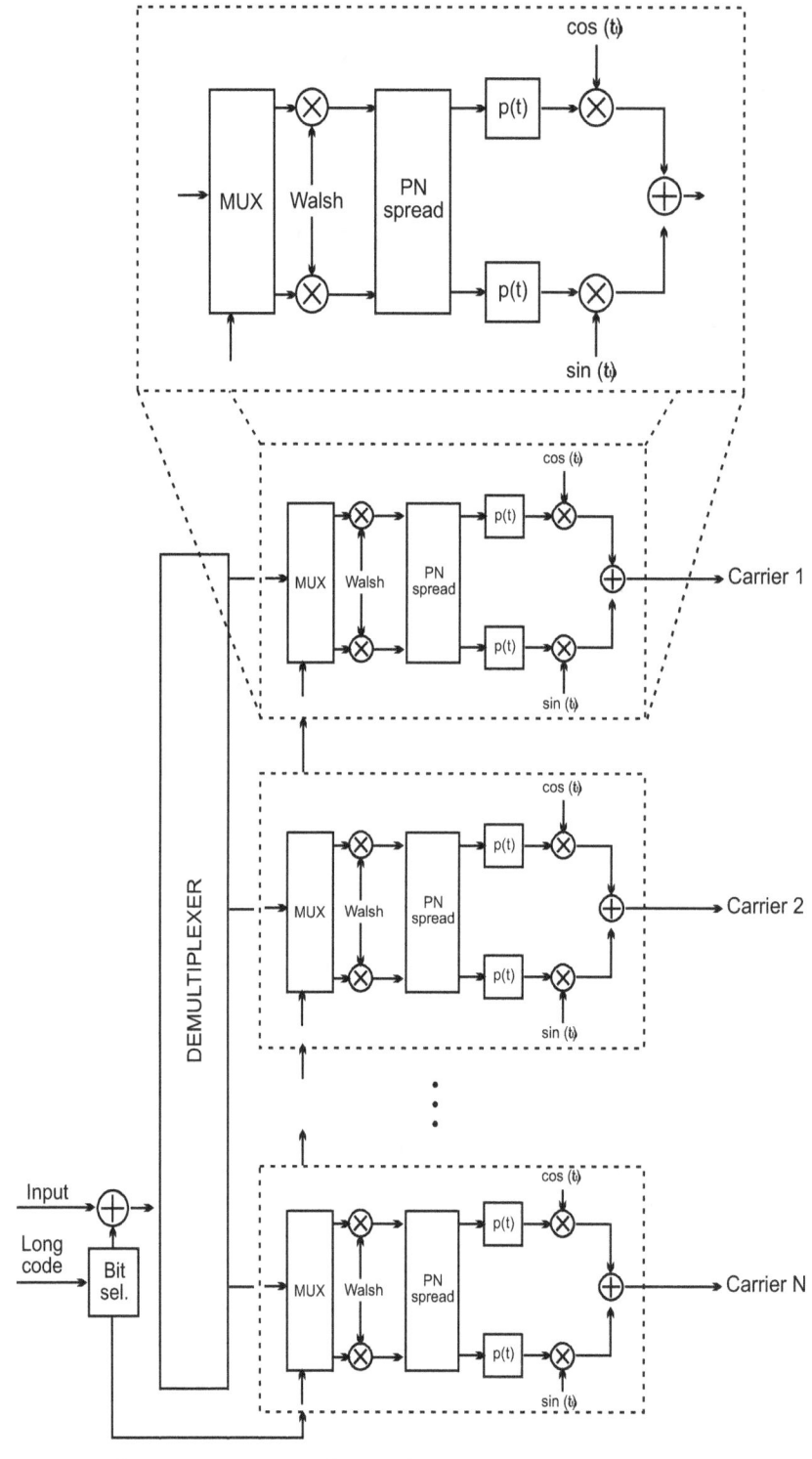

Fig. 5.27: Structure of Downlink Multi-Carrier CDMA2000

Uplink:

There is no Multi-Carrier implementation for the uplink connection.

5.7.30 Bandwidth Usage

Depending on the factor N mentioned previously and on the type of spreading used, the bandwidth, that CDMA2000 requires, varies. The 3 dB bandwidth for each band (transmit and receive) is defined here for the three types of spreading:

Single Carrier:

$BW_{3dB} = 1.2288$ MHz

Multi-Carrier:

$BW_{3\,dB} = (N-1) \times 1.25$ MHz $+ 1.2288$ MHz, where N = 3, 6, 9, 12

Direct Spread:

$BW_{3\,dB} = N \times 1.2288$ MHz, where N = 3, 6, 9, 12.

CDMA2000 allocates guard regions of 625 kHz, on each sides of the allocated bandwidth, to prevent interference with neighbouring bands. So the figure for the total bandwidth must include these two guard regions.

5.7.31 Pulse Waveform

The pulse waveform for the transmission is the same as the one defined for IS-95.

5.7.32 Frame Structure

CDMA2000 supports two frame lengths, depending on the channel used: 5 ms and 20 ms. For voice data, frames of 20 ms are used to enhance the demodulation performance through longer interleaving span.

5.7.33 Other Characteristics

CDMA2000 plans to use multiple antennas to enhance the performance of the transmission link. Note that the multi-carrier implementation is particularly well suited for diversity systems since the signal to be transmitted is already demultiplexed in multiple carriers. Provision is also made to use multiple antennas in the direct-spread implementation.

Thus Here is a quick summary of the important transmission characteristics of CDMA2000 (FDD):

1. Modulation chip rate: $N \times 1.2288$ Mcps

2. Pulse Shaping: same as IS-95

3. Modulation:

(a) Uplink:
- BPSK Data modulation
- QPSK Spreading modulation

(b) Downlink:
- QPSK Data modulation
- QPSK spreading modulation

4. Detection: Coherent for both uplink and downlink.

5. Channel Spacing: $(N + 1) \times 1.25$ MHz.

5.7.34 Transmit Diversity

1. As the demand for wireless services has grown, there has been an increased usage of wireless data services, such as wireless e-mail, Web browsing and instant messaging with many services now incorporating high data rate multimedia capabilities for simultaneous voice, image, and real-time video transfer.

2. Such services will inevitably lead to a shift from the present asymmetrical uplink and downlink traffic load to a more evenly balanced load.

3. As traffic demand continues to outstrip the supply of network capacity, the cellular operators must continuously seek alternative means for enhancing system capacity, throughput, coverage, and range to maintain an acceptable quality of service and to remain competitive in the marketplace.

4. A wide range of solutions has historically been employed to meet these performance challenges.

5. These solutions typically fall into four broad categories — regulatory, network design, standards, and radio technology.

6. Regulatory solutions involve the introduction of new or shared RF spectrum, allocated to specific operators or designated for specific types of services.

7. Unfortunately, these solutions are limited by the available spectrum resources and often require many years to implement.

8. Network design involves modifications to a carrier's wireless network infrastructure and RF planning, and is perhaps the most common approach employed for enhancing system performance.

9. Operators continuously seek to optimize their RF utilization by regularly deploying new base station sites, adding additional sectors to existing sites, and by adjusting their RF frequency plans to reduce interference, increase capacity and improve coverage.

10. While these solutions are very effective, they can be quite costly and time-consuming to implement, and are plagued by increasingly strict zoning regulations that can make new site acquisition difficult or impossible.

11. A standards body solution, in which new protocols and revisions to existing protocols are developed to facilitate the introduction of new performance enhancing technologies or network architectures, is often too time-consuming and requires years of work in the standard bodies to release new revisions and introduce significant performance enhancements.

12. Radio technology is perhaps the most promising means currently available for improving system performance in a timely and cost effective manner.

13. Transmit diversity offers an advantage in the forward link of the cdma2000 system by balancing the spectrum efficiency in the uplink and downlink.

14. Three schemes for performing transmit diversity are mentioned in this paragraph.

15. Orthogonal transmit diversity, time switched transmit diversity, and selection transmit diversity for communication environments.

16. In particular, transmit diversity technique will introduce and evaluate a new technique for dramatically improving performance of a code division multiple access (CDMA) cellular network.

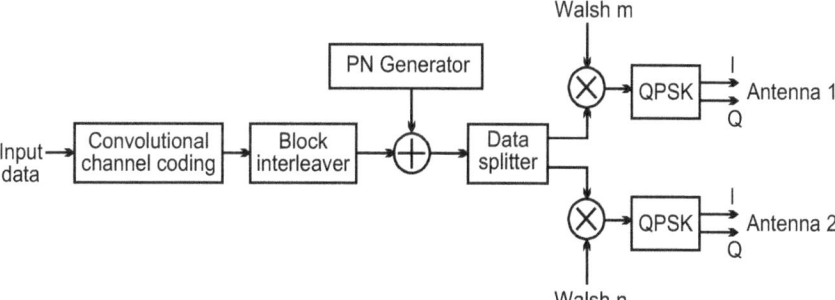

Fig. 5.28 (a): Transmitter for Orthogonal Transmit Diversity

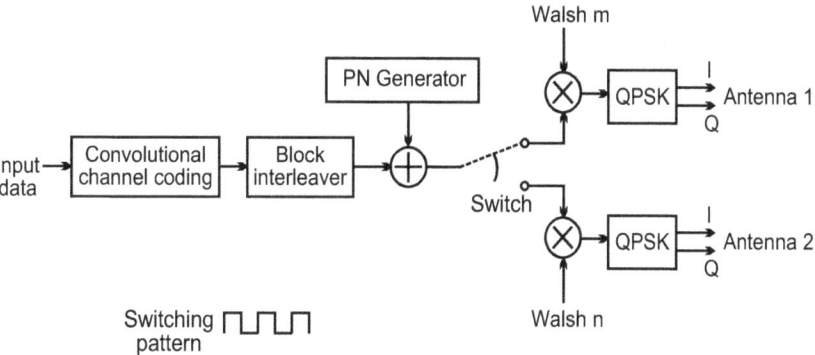

Fig. 5.28 (b): Transmitter for Time Switched Transmit Diversity

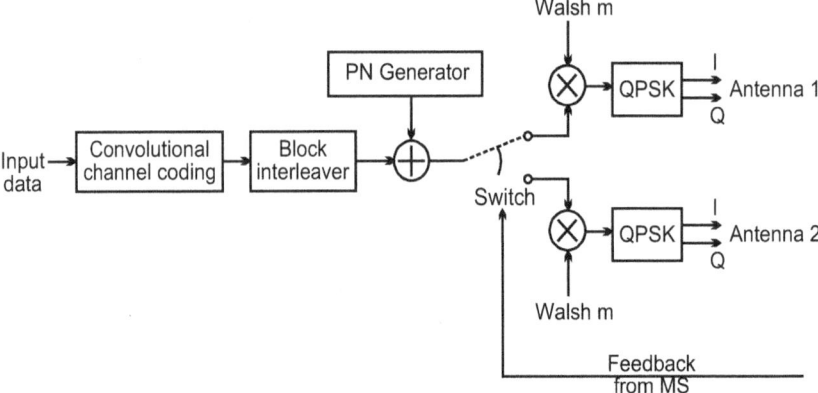

Fig. 5.28 (c): Transmitter for Selection Transmit Diversity (STD)

Orthogonal Transmit Diversity:

1. Orthogonal Transmit Diversity (OTD) is implemented in the transmitter as shown in Fig. 5.73 (a).

2. The coded and interleaved bits are split into two different streams for simultaneous transmission over different transmit antennas.

3. Different Walsh spreading codes are used for both streams to maintain the orthogonality.

4. In order to maintain the effective number of Walsh codes per user as in single antenna transmission, the spreading length is doubled.

Time Switched Transmit Diversity:

1. Time Switched Transmit Diversity (TSTD) is implemented in the transmitter as shown in Fig. 5.28 (b).

2. Unlike OTD where both the antennas are used all the time, in TSTD each user uses only one of the antennas at any instant of time.

3. The same Walsh code is used for transmission on both the antennas and the length of these codes is the same as in single antenna transmission.

4. The different users could be forced to shift between antennas using identical or different pseudo random switching patterns.

5. Switching them pseudorandomly means that on the average half the users will use one antenna and hence the capacity and crest factor of the power amplifiers are reduced.

6. As in the case of OTD, two different pilots are needed for coherent detection.

Selection Transmit Diversity:

1. Selection Transmit Diversity (STD) is implemented as shown in Fig. 5.28 (c).

2. The instantaneous transmit antenna used in TSTD may not yield the highest SNR at the MS receiver.

3. Ideally, we want the transmitter to choose that antenna that yields the highest received SNR.

4. However, this is not possible because the transmitter does not know the state of the channel between the BS (Base Station) and MS (Mobile Station).

5. Hence a feedback channel is used from the MS to the BS, indicating which of the two antennas has a higher SNR.

6. To prevent a large reduction in the reverse link capacity, a one-bit Antenna Selection (AS) message is sent from the mobile to the base station.

7. An important consideration is how the performance is affected by the AS rate, the delay in implementing the AS command and error in the AS feedback.

8. Ideally, the rate of feedback should be matched to the channel variations, the delay is zero and the feedback channel error rate is also zero.

9. However, using a variable rate feedback scheme is complicated and a fixed rate scheme must be used for ease of implementation.

10. It is proven practically with different applications that the performance of STD is better than OTD and TSTD.

5.7.35 WCDMA vs. CDMA2000

1. According to the technology, investment reusability, gradual investments, simpler service migration, more attractive services (primarily roaming) and a better long-term terminal market, combine to make this decision rather simple.

2. GSM operators who face difficulties to find spectrum for a WCDMA deployment, for example, in different countries, should rather use EDGE (Enhanced Data for Global Evolution) as bridging technology until spectrum for WCDMA becomes available, than choosing a CDMA2000 evolution.

3. For CdmaOne operators, the generally preferable path is to evolve its network to CDMA2000 1X (which has similar service-enabling capabilities to GPRS) and then on to DO and/or DV.

4. Spectrum availability, investment reusability, gradual investments, simpler service migration and lack of CDMA/WCDMA terminals, combine to make this a straightforward decision.

5. For a TDMA operator we view both WCDMA- and CDMA-based evolution paths as feasible.

6. High economies-of-scale, more attractive services (primarily roaming) and a more attractive long term terminals market all speak for WCDMA.

7. Against these factors stand the prospects of simpler spectrum management, gradual investments enabled by AMPS (Advanced Mobile Phone System)/ CDMA terminals and higher investment reusability, which speak in favour of CDMA2000.

8. Whichever option is adopted, the TDMA operators will have to make sure that they have the solid backing of its suppliers to provide them with confidence in making this difficult decision.

9. An overall conclusion is that GSM/GPRS will continue to dominate the global market for years to come and WCDMA will be the dominant 3G technology in the long term, considering the dominance of existing 3G networks and already made decisions on GSM-to-WCDMA evolution.

Table 5.9

Parameter	W-CDMA	cdma2000
Carrier spacing	5 MHz	3.75 MHz
Chip rate	4.096 MHz	3.6864 MHz
Data modulation	BPSK	FW – QPSK; RV - BPSK
Spreading	Complex (OQPSK)	Complex (OQPSK)
Power control frequency	1500 Hz	800 Hz
Variable data rate implement	Variable SF; multicode	Repet, puncturing, multicode
Frame duration	10 ms	20 ms (also 5, 30, 40)
Coding	Turbo and convolutional	Turbo and convolutional
Base stations synchronized	Asynchronous	Synchronous
Base station acquisition/ detect	3 setp; slot, frame, code	Time shifted PN correlation
Forward link pilot	TDM dedicated pilot	CDM common pilot
Antenna beam forming	TDM dedicated pilot	Auxiliary pilot

5.8 Summary

1. It is proven that, based on an in-depth analysis of industry data, the worldwide migration to 3G is accelerating, as evidenced by the proliferation of CDMA2000.

2. CDMA2000 is creating competition by driving down the cost of delivering voice, multimedia messaging and broadband data services across the globe.

3. In fact, many operators who choose GSM in the past are making wholesale network changeovers to CDMA2000 to remain competitive and increase their earnings.

4. In the last few years, many operators, all of whom had a choice of several 2G and 3G technologies, selected CDMA2000.

5. Around many of these operators were GSM operators.

6. 3G CDMA2000 enables operators to lower the cost of delivering voice and data, while supplementing their voice and SMS revenue with lucrative, value-added services.

7. Within few years of its introduction, 3G has reached millions of subscribers worldwide.

8. More than 30 million subscribers are added every quarter, and the 3G adoption rate has far exceeded that of any other wireless technology.

9. In leading markets, such as Japan, Korea and the United States, the number of 3G subscribers has already surpassed that of 2G subscribers.

10. Other regional and emerging markets are expected to follow their lead.

11. Western Europe will be the next region to witness the inevitable cross-over of having more 3G than 2G subscribers.

12. CDMA2000 is now available in 72 countries, and in every major world market on all six continents.

13. CDMA2000 is flexible enough to satisfy the wireless communication needs of densely populated urban markets as well as sparsely populated rural markets.

14. In fact, CDMA2000 is bridging the digital divide in many countries offering affordable voice and broadband data access to millions of users in remote areas who have limited purchasing power.

15. For subscribers, the rapid growth of CDMA2000 serves both personal and enterprise demands by offering a broad range of applications, such as VoIP, multimedia messaging, high-speed video, mobile commerce, position location, and broadband Internet access.

16. With close to millions of subscribers, CDMA2000 offers next generation services with economies of scope and scale that are comparable to GSM.

17. CDMA2000 adds nearly millions of new subscribers every month, and close to 80% of the entire 3G subscriber base uses CDMA2000 devices and services.

18. CDMA2000 offers subscribers a very large selection of devices, from notebook PC embedded EV-DO modules that download email files with large attachments, to entry-level handsets that cost less than US$50 and enable consumers to download ringtones, wallpapers and daily prayers.

19. CDMA2000 supports more devices from more suppliers than any other technology.

20. For the remainder of the decade, the everyone expects CDMA2000 to continue offering the most innovative and most affordable selection of 3G devices.

21. In all, CDMA2000 offers the highest performance technology and most economical set of network characteristics - all the while preserving operators' investments through easy backward- and forward-compatible upgrades.

22. CDMA2000 is based on open standards that are specified and promulgated by the ITU (IMT-2000), 3GPP2 and TIA/EIA.

23. The CDMA2000 evolution path is also capable of maximizing the performance of various applications by integrating and concurrently assigning multiple airlinks, such as CDMA, TDM, OFDM and OFDMA, and using Multiple Input Multiple Output (MIMO) and Spatial Division Multiple Access (SDMA) techniques.

24. Within the next few years, CDMA2000 1xEV-DO is expected to deliver peak data rates between 100 to 500 Mbps, depending upon the level of mobility, using 20 MHz of bandwidth.

EXERCISE

1. What do you mean by Ping-Pong effect? How CDMA eliminates the Ping-Pong effect?

2. Explain major attributes of CDMA systems.

3. Explain TIA IS-95 CDMA system.

4. Explain logical channels.

5. How typical messages are carried over the logical channels of the forward and reverse link?

6. Explain the substates of the system initialization state.

7. Explain the registration and authentication procedures of CDMA.

8. Draw the flow diagrams for CDMA call origination, call termination and call release.

9. Explain CDMA2000 layering structure.

10. Explain the improvements of CDMA2000 over CDMAone.

11. Explain the data services in CDMA2000, also the mapping of logical channel.

12. Write down the major technical differences between CDMA2000 and W-CDMA.

Unit VI

IP TELEPHONY

6.1 Introduction to Voice Networks

6.1.1 Analog Voice Network

1. Public switched telephone networks are communication systems that are available to the public to allow users to interconnect communication devices.

2. Public telephone networks within countries and regions are standard integrated systems of transmission and switching facilities, signalling processors and associated operations support systems that allow communication devices to communicate with each other when they operate.

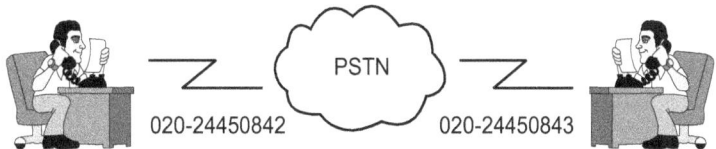

Fig. 6.1: Typical Analog Voice Network

3. A telephone call may consist of an ordinary voice transmission using a telephone, a data transmission when the calling party and called party are using modems, or a facsimile transmission when the two parties are using fax machines.

4. Where a telephone call has more than one called party, it is referred to as a conference call.

5. Calls are usually placed through a network (such as the Public Switched Telephone Network) provided by a commercial telephone company.

6. If the caller's wired phone is directly connected to the calling party, when the caller takes their telephone off-hook, the calling party's phone will ring.

7. This is called a hot line. Otherwise, the calling party is usually given a tone to indicate they should begin dialing the desired number.

8. In some cases, the calling party cannot dial calls directly, and is connected to an operator who places the call for them.

9. Preceding, during, and after a telephone call is placed, certain tones signify the progress and status of the telephone call.

10. **A dial tone** signifying that the call is ready to be placed either:

- a ringing tone signifying that the calling party has yet to answer the telephone.

- a busy signal (or engaged tone) signifying that the calling party's telephone is being used in a telephone call to another person.

11. Status tones such as STD notification tones (to inform the caller that the telephone call is being trunk dialled at a greater cost to the calling party), minute minder beeps (to inform the caller of the relative duration of the telephone call on calls that are charged on a time basis), and others a tone (sometimes the busy signal) to signify that the called party has hung up.

6.1.2 Digital Voice Network

1. Above discussion is related to the typical analog voice network. Let us discuss the digital voice networks.

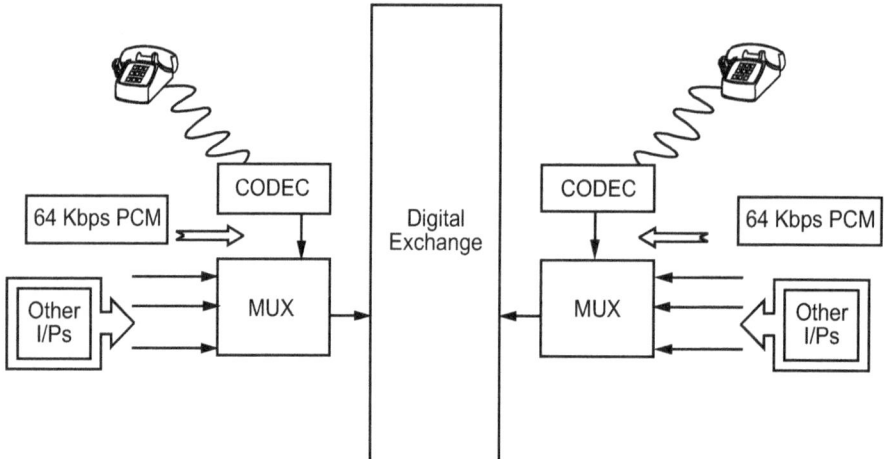

Fig. 6.2: Typical Digital Voice Network

2. Generally above network is commonly referred to as a T1 line or circuit.

3. That circuit was developed to relieve cable congestion in metropolitan areas by providing a transport mechanism for 24 digitized voice conversation to be simultaneously carried over one cable.

4. To do so, each voice conversation is digitized using a technique called pulse code modulation (PCM).

5. Under PCM, an analog voice conversation is digitized at 64 kbps.

6. To provide information that enables one conversation to be distinguished from another and switched into and out of a group of conversations, framing bits must be added to the T1 data flow.

7. Those framing bits operate at 8000 bps and carry control information, error-detection information, and a limited data-link capability.

8. This capability, for example, enables two private branch exchanges (PBXs) to communicate with one another while transporting 24 voice conversations on a T1 circuit interconnecting the PBXs.

9. The 24 channels, each operating at 64 kbps, result in an operating rate of 1.536 Mbps.

10. When the 8 kbps framing information is added to the T1 line, its operating rate becomes 1.544 Mbps.

11. Communication carriers also offer low-speed digital services operating at data rates from 2.4 kbps upto 56 kbps, using time-division multiplexers to group multiple low-speed digital circuits onto a 64 kbps circuit.

12. The 64 kbps circuit, in turn, is connected to a channel on a carrier's T1 line, which represents the basic backbone infrastructure used for transporting voice, data, and video across entire country.

6.1.3 VoIP Voice Network

1. Internet telephony refers to communication services like voice, facsimile, and/or voice-messaging applications that are transported via the Internet, rather than the public switched telephone network (PSTN).

2. The basic steps involved in originating an Internet telephone call are conversion of the analog voice signal to digital format and compression/ translation of the signal into Internet Protocol (IP) packets for transmission over the Internet. The process is reversed at the receiving end.

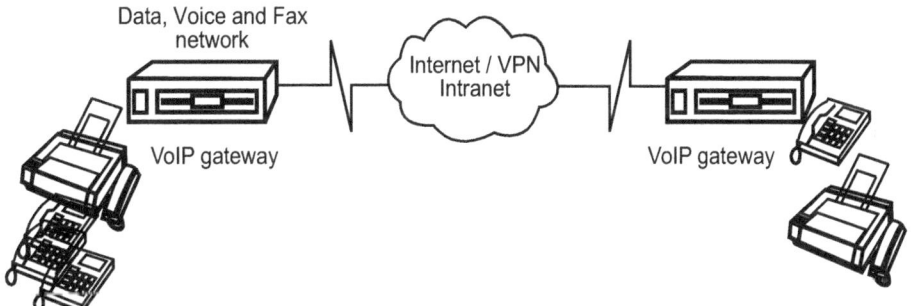

Fig. 6.3: Typical VoIP N/W (Voice Network) with VoIP Gateway

3. Initially, convert the dialed number to an IP address.

4. Secondly, establish connection to remote gateway.

5. Thirdly, send voice over the data network.

6. Finally, receive voice over the data network at receiver end.

7. This feature allows VoIP to operate over frame relay and ATM networks autonomously.

8. More importantly, VoIP operates over typical LANs to go all the way to the desktop.

9. In this sense, VoIP is more of an application than a service, and VoIP protocols have evolved with this in mind.

10. VoIP protocols fall into two general categories: centralized and distributed.

11. In general terms, centralized models follow a client/server architecture, while distributed models are based on peer-to-peer interactions.

12. Both architectures have advantages and disadvantages.

13. Distributed models tend to scale well and are more resilient (robust) because they lack a central point that could fail.

14. Conversely, centralized call control models offer easier management and can support traditional supplementary services (such as conferencing) more easily, but they can have scaling limits based on the capacity of the central server.

15. Hybrid and networking models being developed also offer the best of both approaches.

16. The strong pressures driving the integration of voice and data networks have resulted in various solutions to the problem, each with its own strengths and weaknesses. Three general approaches exist:

    - **Voice over IP**
    - **Voice over ATM**
    - **Voice over Frame Relay**

6.2 VoIP Technology

6.2.1 Introduction

(A) Need:

1. In the past, voice and data networks have been kept separate.

2. A key reason for this is that legacy network technologies could not meet the diverse performance requirements of voice and data.

3. Advances in networking technology, including fast Ethernet, wire-speed switching and Policy-Based Quality of Service management, have made it possible to build converged voice and data networks.

4. Converged networks enable a new generation of integrated voice/data applications.

5. For example, users of web-based e-commerce applications can view product information while talking with customer service agents in a call center.

6. With converged networks this can be done through a single network connection.

7. The focus of most converged network strategies is voice over IP (VoIP).

8. VoIP refers to the transmission of telephone conversations over a packet-switched IP network.

9. **This IP network could be as small as a single subnet, private LAN, or as large as the public Internet.**

(B) The Technical difference between VoIP and Traditional PSTN:

1. Current telephone networks are used for the same purpose (voice transmission), but require complex circuit switching to route calls to their destination.

2. As VoIP uses existing IP technology, it uses packet switching to send information - directing only the "packets" of voice data to their destination.

3. As you can imagine, this requires much less infrastructure and logistics than legacy telecommunication technologies - saving a considerable amount of money for the user.

4. If an company requires several phone connections, they must get cables routed through the building, spend money on equipment, wait days for phone numbers to be assigned etc...

5. With VoIP, you can use existing infrastructure (a PC) with free software and communicate for free with other VoIP users. You might not even need trailing wires if you are using a wireless network.

6. This technology has numerous advantages over the current system, mainly in cost reduction, but also in future capacity and capabilities. It would not be difficult to combine VoIP with other existing technologies such as streaming video.

7. Major telecoms companies often use VoIP "in the middle" of the virtual connection of your phone call, especially in long-distance or transatlantic calls.

8. Many users are unaware that their call is converted from PSTN (Public Switched Telephone Network) to VoIP and then back to PSTN to the receiver of the call.

(C) Ways to Connect to VoIP Services:

1. There are several methods for communicating over VoIP, ranging in ease of use and cost:

   - **Personal Computer** - A standard PC can act as a VoIP receiver to make free calls, as long as it is connected to the recipient computer over a network (the internet or a LAN).

   - **Analog Telephone Adapter** - This adapter interfaces your standard house phone to connect to your PC/Router to make calls.

   - **IP Phone -** It is a dedicated hardware phone that connects to a network socket on your router. This can make and receive calls all in a separate unit.

2. The cheapest and easiest method of trying VoIP is by using your PC as the VoIP gateway, and is great for VoIP to VoIP calls - as they are usually free.

3. All you need is a microphone and speakers, although a headset is usually preferable.

4. There is plenty of free VoIP software around, and many of these allow you to call normal phone for a small charge (almost always cheaper than land line rates).

5. **Analog Telephone Adapters** (VoIP gateways) allow you to connect your old telephone to your PC/Router for direct calling.

6. Some ATAs require software to be installed to act as a gateway for the phone to function. This method was very popular until dedicated IP phones arrived.

7. IP Phones look exactly like a normal telephone, expect they plug directly into your router to communicate directly with another VoIP gateway, server or phone.

8. No computer or software is required and it can be used completely independently as long as an internet connection exists. This is the best option for a serious user.

9. Dial-up users will find VoIP impractical to use, as it requires more bandwidth than can be provided. Any broadband user should be able to fully utilize VoIP without any problems.

(D) Features of VoIP:

VoIP benefits users/customers, service providers, and equipment makers:

1. **Users benefit by new applications based on converged voice and data networks. For example, VoIP**

   - Eliminates long distance charges over LANs and WANs.

   - No need to maintain separate voice and data networks in the enterprise.

   - Enables web call centers.

- Supports multi-media conferencing and collaboration.
- Provides unified messaging (using a phone or PDA to access both email and voice mail; appropriate conversions are performed using text-to-speech and speech recognition systems).

2. **Service providers benefit with more efficient use of their networks. For example,**
   - Voice packets can be sent along with data over a single network.
   - Compression techniques can be applied to send more voice packets over the same bandwidth, thus enabling more VoIP connections (normal voice channels require 64 kbps; this bandwidth can be reduced to 6.4 kbps by using compression techniques such as G.723; further compression has a noticeable negative effect on voice quality).
   - A single network can be used for transmitting both, voice and data.

3. **Equipment makers will benefit from the new types of equipment and software. For example,**
   - VoIP gateways for converting analog voice to IP packets and vice versa. This allows the use of PSTN for the last mile connection to the phone users.
   - IP phones (phones which convert voice to IP packets and vice versa; no an IP connection is needed for such phones - a voice connection is not required).

(E) Applications of VoIP:

VoIP will be used, for example, in
- Backhaul carrier networks,
- Converged data and voice networks,
- Converged data and voice appliances such as IP PBXs, and
- Always-on cellular phones.
- VoIP can be used to avoid very high tariffs on normal international voice connections over the public telephone networks (many countries have very high telephone tariffs) - VoIP packets go over the data networks and are not subject to voice telephony tariffs; using VoIP over private networks can save upto 80% in costs,

(F) Benefits for the Enterprise:

Originally regarded as a novelty, VoIP technology is attracting more and more users worldwide because of the benefits it offers to the enterprise, service provider, and ultimately, the consumer.

Cost Savings: Users can bypass long-distance carriers and their per-minute usage rates and run their voice traffic over the Internet for a flat monthly Internet-access fee.

IP networks can be significantly less expensive to operate and maintain. The simplified network infrastructure of an Internet Telephony solution cuts costs by connecting IP phones over the LAN wiring system and eliminates the need for dual cabling.

Internet Telephony can also eliminate toll charges on site-to-site calls via global four-digit dialing. And, by using the extra bandwidth on your WAN for IP Telephony, you leverage the untapped capabilities of your existing data infrastructure to maximize the return on your current network investment.

Portability and flexibility: Employees are no longer confined by geographic location. IP telephones work anywhere on the network, even over a remote connection. Service can be extended to remote sites and home offices over cost-effective IP links.

Simplicity and consistency: A common approach to service deployment can allow cost-savings with the use of common management tools, resource directories, and a consistent approach to network security.

The ability to network existing PBXs using IP can bring new values to the enterprise. For example, the ability to consolidate voice mail onto a single system, or to fewer systems, makes it easier for voice mail users to network.

Ubiquity: Internet Telephony is supported over a wide variety of transport technologies. A user can gain access to just about any business system, whether it is through an analog line, a DSL line, a LAN, Frame Relay, ATM (Asynchronous Transfer Mode), SONET or wireless.

Operational Agility: You can add new services and users to the network with fewer burdens on the existing system. This can pave the path for more revenue-earning possibilities.

(G) Benefits for the Service Provider:

SPs (Service Providers) can look forward to enterprises outsourcing their data and voice requirements through them. An existing service provider can benefit in many ways.

Low network capital cost: The SP has already established a MAN or a WAN for data transport. Adding voice services does not require heavy capital expenditure. Packet infrastructure is cheaper than switching infrastructure and offers better granularity and flexibility than circuit switches. Moreover, a distributed switching infrastructure can provide modularity.

Transport cost: Since SPs can add voice services over the same network, the cost of data transport will increase in the beginning. But with economies of scale due to business volumes, the cost will reduce substantially. An SP can also interconnect with other major PSTN carriers to extend its reach and use minutes at a competitive rate.

Bandwidth cost: SPs can use many ways to control bandwidth cost. It can use compression techniques to increase capacity, billing can be based on usage, and the flexibility of IP can be used to get efficient bandwidth prioritization.

Operational cost: Operational costs will not increase very much because skill sets required to manage the VoIP infrastructure are common. You don't need specialized VoIP personnel in your organization. Some vendors even promise that you can maintain unmanned sites in your network.

New services: An SP can offer a range of new services to the consumer like long distance calls, calling cards, Voice VPN, UM (Unified Messaging), and mobile services.

6.2.2 VoIP on the LAN

1. With VoIP on the LAN, telephone conversations are converted to a stream of IP packets and sent over an Ethernet network.
2. This network is usually restricted to a building or campus.
3. As VoIP technology matures, new conversion methods may emerge.
4. Regardless of the method that is used to convert VoIP traffic for LANs, VoIP traffic will always traverse the LAN as a stream of IP packets.

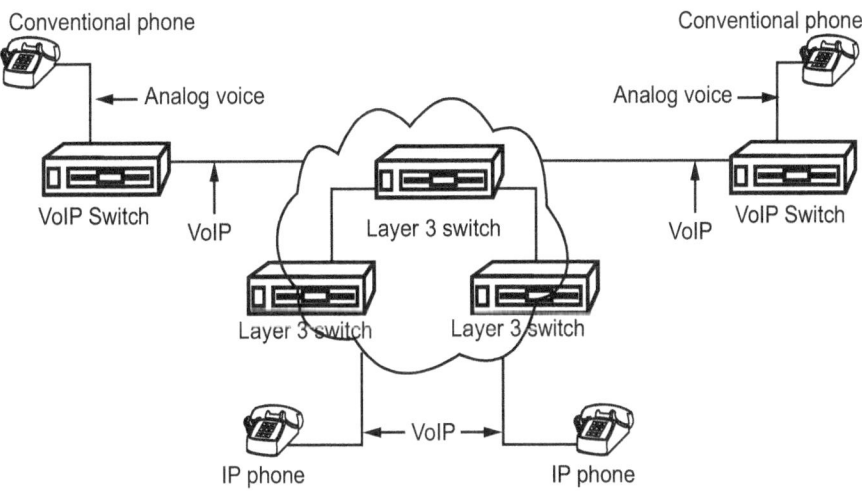

Fig. 6.4: VoIP on the LAN

6.2.3 Quality of Service and Infrastructure

6.2.3.1 VoIP QoS Requirements and QoS Solutions

VoIP QoS Requirements:

1. H.323, the global standard for packet-based multimedia communication like VoIP, provides telephone functionality that is comparable to the public switched telephone network.

2.   But the other key requirement for successful VoIP communication is QoS.

3.   Voice communication requires networks with very low latency, low jitter and minimal packet loss.

Two factors drive these QoS requirements:

   • Very high user expectations.

   • The technical requirements of real-time voice communication.

4.   Telephone users have very high expectations because they are accustomed to the QoS provided by the PSTN and private PBX-based networks.

5.   These connection-oriented, circuit-switched networks provide each user with dedicated bandwidth for the duration of each call.

6.   The result is extremely low latency, jitter, and minimal disruption due to "noise" on the connections.

7.   Low latency allows users to carry on natural conversation.

8.   Users differ in their delay tolerance, but a good rule of thumb is to limit one-way delay to about 150 milliseconds (ms).

9.   This delay budget includes the processing delays introduced by the end systems plus the latency of the network.

10. When codecs (coders/decoders) in VoIP terminals compress voice signals, they introduce three types of delay:

   • **Processing delay: the time required for the codec to encode a single voice frame.**

   • **Look ahead delay: the time required for a codec to examine part of the next frame while encoding the current frame.**

   • **Frame delay: the time required for the sending system to transmit one frame.**

11. The following are some commonly used ITU-T standard codecs and the amount of one-way delay that they introduce:

   • G.711 uncompressed 64 kbps speech adds negligible delay.

   • G.729 encodes speech at 8 kbps and adds a one-way delay of about 25 ms.

   • G.723.1 encodes speech at 6.4 kbps or 5.3 kbps and adds a one-way delay of about 67.5 ms.

12. In general, greater levels of compression introduce more delay and require lower network latency to maintain good voice quality.

VoIP QoS Solutions:

There are three techniques that can be used (separately or in combination) to improve network QoS:

1. **Controlling networking environment:** You have to provide a controlled networking environment in which the capacity can be pre-planned and adequate performance can be assumed. This would generally be the case with a private IP network or an Intranet that is owned and operated by a single organization.

2. **Using management tools:** You can use management tools to configure the network nodes, monitor performance, and manage capacity and flow on a dynamic basis. Traffic can be prioritized by location, by protocol, or by application type. This allows real-time traffic to be given precedence over non-critical traffic. Queuing mechanisms can also be manipulated to minimize delays for real-time data flows.

3. **Adding control protocols and mechanisms**: You can add control protocols and mechanisms that help to avoid or alleviate the problems inherent in IP networks. Protocols like RTP (Real Time Protocol) and RSVP (Reservation Protocol) can also be used to provide greater assurances of controlled QoS within the network. Other mechanisms like admission controls and traffic shaping may also be used to avoid overloading a network.

6.2.3.2 Building the Right Infrastructure to Support Voice over IP

1. One of the key challenges in implementing VoIP is to design and build an IP-based network that meets QoS requirements and is comparable in performance to conventional circuit-switched telephone networks.

2. The high latency forwarding and best-effort delivery provided by traditional software based routers is generally not acceptable for streaming traffic like VoIP because it does not provide maximum latency guarantees or minimum bandwidth guarantees.

3. From the perspective of an IP-based Ethernet network, a VoIP packet containing part of a telephone conversation is not different than a data packet containing part of an e-mail.

4. Both packets are received on an ingress port of an Ethernet switch and need to be forwarded out the egress port of an Ethernet switch. From the perspective of the end points, different types of traffic have very dissimilar requirements.

5. **VoIP traffic is a real-time process.**

6. To complete a successful VoIP session, the network must be able to support the streaming of VoIP packets between the two end-points for the duration of the telephone conversation. VoIP traffic requires a network to guarantee bandwidth and capacity for VoIP traffic.

7. To support VoIP traffic consistently and reliably, a network must be able to provide three things:

- **Packet-forwarding latency that does not exceed the maximum tolerable level for a VoIP conversation.**
- **Packet-forwarding jitter, which is the variation in latency over time, that does not exceed the maximum tolerable level to sustain a VoIP session.**
- **Guaranteed network bandwidth and capacity for VoIP sessions during periods of network congestion.**

8. In other words, a network needs to provide performance – low latency and low jitter – and protection – QoS.
9. Most VoIP sessions require one-way latency of not more than about 150 milliseconds.
10. This delay budget is reduced by any delays introduced by codecs in the end systems.
11. When round-trip delays exceed approximately 300 ms., natural human conversation becomes difficult.
12. Depending on the type of voice-compression method used, each one-way VoIP transmission requires between 32 kbps to 64 kbps of bandwidth.
13. Some compression methods, such as G.729, take the bandwidth required below 8 kbps.
14. Bandwidth required for VoIP sessions is relatively low. The challenge is to make that bandwidth available regardless of network utilization.

6.2.4 Voice over IP on the WAN

1. VoIP traffic can be sent over a variety of IP-based wide area networks (WANs).
2. An IP-based WAN can be one of the following:
    - A private enterprise WAN made up of leased lines, a frame relay service or an ATM service,
    - A public IP carrier,
    - The public Internet.
3. One of the main reasons for implementing VoIP over the WAN, is cost savings.
4. Cost savings can be immediate when long distance phone calls are diverted from the Public Switched Telephone Network (PSTN) and sent over an existing IP-based WAN.
5. Running VoIP traffic on the WAN can be done in several ways:
    - If the voice traffic is coming from a PBX, a VoIP gateway will then be required to convert voice traffic from the PBX into IP packets for transmission over the IP-based WAN. Similarly, a VoIP gateway will be required at the other end to convert VoIP traffic back into the format used by the PBX. **The IP-based WAN can be a private data network, a public IP carrier or the public Internet.**
    - If the voice traffic has already been converted to VoIP traffic on the LAN, then the VoIP traffic will be transmitted over the IP-based WAN like any other IP data traffic.

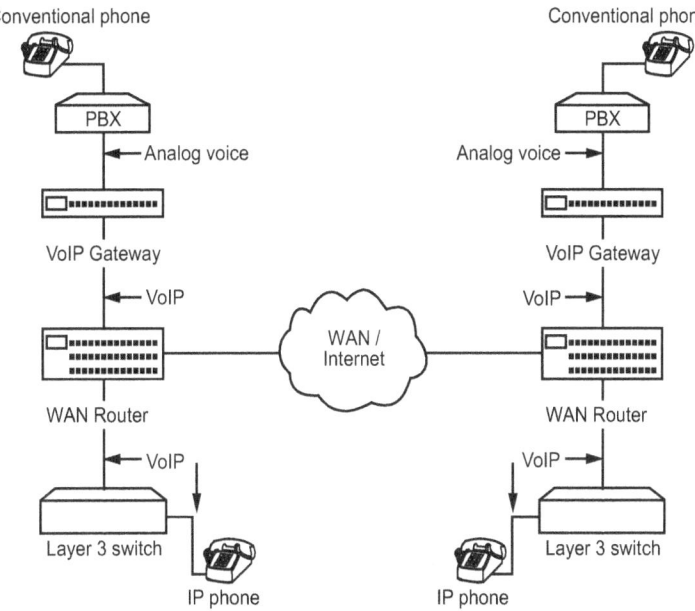

Fig. 6.5: VoIP on the WAN

6.2.5 An Overview of Voice-over-IP Standards and Protocol

1. International Telecommunications Union (ITU-T) Recommendation H.323 is a global standard for packet based multimedia communications, including VoIP. H.323 can be implemented on WANs or LANs.
2. H.323 is often referred to as an "umbrella " standard because it references by a number of other standards that support multimedia communications.
3. **H.323 is a set of network components and protocols that support real-time audio, video, and data communications.**
4. The following diagram shows the components that make up an H.323 VoIP network.

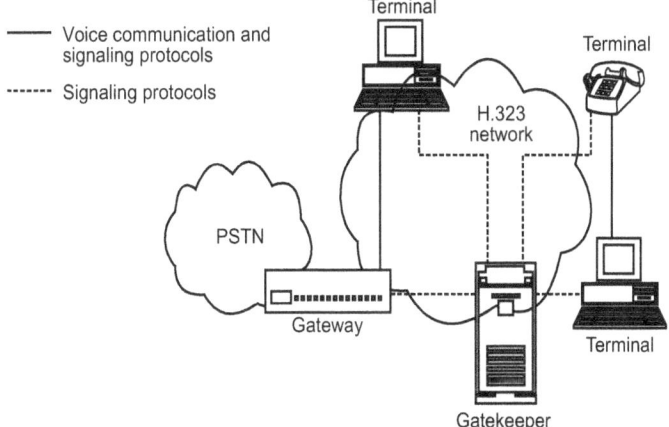

Fig. 6.6: Components of an H.323 VoIP Network

5. These components support real-time voice communications between end users and provide PBX-like network control functions.

6. Terminals are the end-user devices that support two-way, real-time voice communications across H.323 networks.

7. The most common terminal types are:

- **IP phones** – This option uses a telephone with a built-in codec and embedded H.323 software, network interface card (NIC) and IP protocol stack. The IP phone is plugged directly into an Ethernet LAN just as a PC or other Ethernet station would be.

- **PC phones** – This option uses PC software and hardware to enable a PC to become a VoIP phone on the network. This option is very similar to the IP phone option with one major difference, the PC phone typically has one NIC that will be used for both VoIP packets and data packets. In the case of an IP phone, the NIC is dedicated to only processing VoIP packets.

- **Gateways** enable communications between H.323 VoIP users and users of non-H.323 networks, most often the public switched telephone network (PSTN) or private PBX-based networks. Gateways allow users of conventional phones to communicate with VoIP users.

- **Multipoint Control Units (MCU)** are optional H.323 components that support multipoint conferencing, commonly called conference calls.

- **Gatekeepers** provide control functions similar to those provided by PBXs and carrier switches in conventional voice networks. These devices control call setup and they can provide additional functions such as call forwarding, conference calling, and call waiting.

6.2.5.1 H.323 Protocols

1. H.323 defines the data stream formats and protocols that endpoints use to communicate with one another.

2. It also defines the management and control protocols used between terminals, gatekeepers, gateways and MCUs.

3. The following diagram shows the protocol stack implemented by H.323 endpoints (terminals and gateways) in VoIP networks.

Table 6.1: Protocol stack implemented by H.323 endpoints in a voice-over-IP network

Audio Application	Video Application	Terminal Control and Management				
Audio Codecs G.711 G.729 G.723.1	Audio Codecs G.711 G.729 G.723.1	Real-Time Control Protocol	H.225.0 Registration, Admission, and Status	H.225.0 Call Signalling	H.245 Control Signalling	T-120 Data
Real-Time Protocol (RTP)						
User Datagram Protocol (UDP)				Transmission Control Protocol (TCP)		
Internet Protocol (IP)						

4. Codecs digitally encode and decode audio or video signals for transmission across an H.323 network.

5. In VoIP networks only audio codecs are used.

6. Codecs differ in the encoding techniques that they use and the bit rate of their digital output streams.

7. Codec compatibility is essential to VoIP inter-operability. Endpoints cannot speak to one another, unless they use compatible codecs.

8. H.323 end points must support at least one audio codec – the G.711 standard.

9. This ensures basic inter-operability between all H.323 terminals. The G.711 standard encodes audio at 64 kbps and supports the pulse code modulation (PCM) that is widely used to encode voice on the PSTN.

10. Other audio codecs may optionally be implemented. Some of these codecs and their transmission rates are:

    •   G.723.1 = 6.4 kbps or 5.3 kbps

    •   G.728 = 16 kbps

    •   G.729 = 8 kbps

11. Note that these standards use less bandwidth than G.711 because they compress audio signals.

12. These compression algorithms take advantage of the repetitive patterns found in human speech.

13. Network designers should be aware that these low-bandwidth codecs output digital voice in very short frames – typically 10 to 30 bytes in length.

14. In addition to compression, most VoIP terminals also implement silence suppression to eliminate network traffic during pauses in conversations.

6.2.5.2 Real-Time Protocols

1. Digitized audio and video streams are transported between endpoints by the real-time protocol (RTP).

2. RTP is a connection-oriented, end-to-end protocol that is designed to transport delay-sensitive information.

3. RTP identifies the encapsulated payload type and includes sequence numbers and time stamps that can be used to synchronize real-time information flows.

4. RTP uses the connectionless, unreliable UDP transport protocols rather than TCP because retransmission delays disrupt real-time audio and video streams.

5. The real-time control protocol (RTCP) works with RTP to provide sending software with feedback on the quality of service being experienced by the receiver.

6. RTP reports QoS parameters including packet loss and the amount of jitter being experienced.

7. The sender can adjust transmission rates based on this feedback.

6.2.5.3 Signalling Protocols

1. Endpoints use the H.225 Registration, Admission, and Status (RAS) protocols to register with a gatekeeper.

2. The H.225 RAS protocol runs over UDP.

3. The H.225 Call Signalling standard is the protocol that endpoints use to set up and release connections.

4. H.225 messages are transported on TCP connections.

5. After a call is set up, end points use H.245 Control Signalling to exchange information about their capabilities.

6. For example, endpoints negotiate the use of audio codecs to ensure that both ends of the conversation are "speaking " the same language.

7. H.245 messages are transported on TCP connections.

6.2.6 The Promise of Voice over IP

1. For over a decade, now the prospect of using the internet to carry voice calls has been 'next years technology'.

2. Although there has not yet been any revolution in the way we route our phone calls, a number of enabling technologies, services and providers are now in place which can finally deliver a reliable, high-quality solution at very low cost.

3. Most businesses and individuals, who are serious internet users, now have un-timed and effectively un-limited connection to the internet.

4. Users can spend all day downloading data from the other side of the world at no added cost.

5. And yet, when those same users make a phone call, they are charged by the minute, whether the call is local, national or international.

6. In practice, the data may well travel over exactly the same route, on the same wires, owned by the same people.

7. Only the billing mechanism and price is different. Wouldn't it be better for the end user if the telephone call went with the internet traffic with the attendant price saving?

8. **Another attractive application** for many businesses would be to connect home workers and sub-offices.

9.   The only on-going cost at each site would be the charge for an always-on internet connection.

10. The remote sites could use the internet connection to log-in to the main office network and also run their telephones as extensions to the main office phone system.

11. **A third use of Voice-over-IP technology** is to replace the expensive telephone system that most companies require.

12. The idea is to use existing computer hardware such as servers and Ethernet cabling to handle telephone traffic.

13. Telephone system functions such as call-transfer and hold could be handled by software and telephone devices could just be plugged into a network point instead of dedicated wiring.

14. The three applications outlined above can be summarised as:
     •   Long-distance call routing.
     •   Point-to-point connections.
     •   In-house PBX systems.

We consider each of these applications in greater detail and look further at the hardware in our article "The Promise of Voice over IP".

6.2.6.1 The Hardware in VoIP

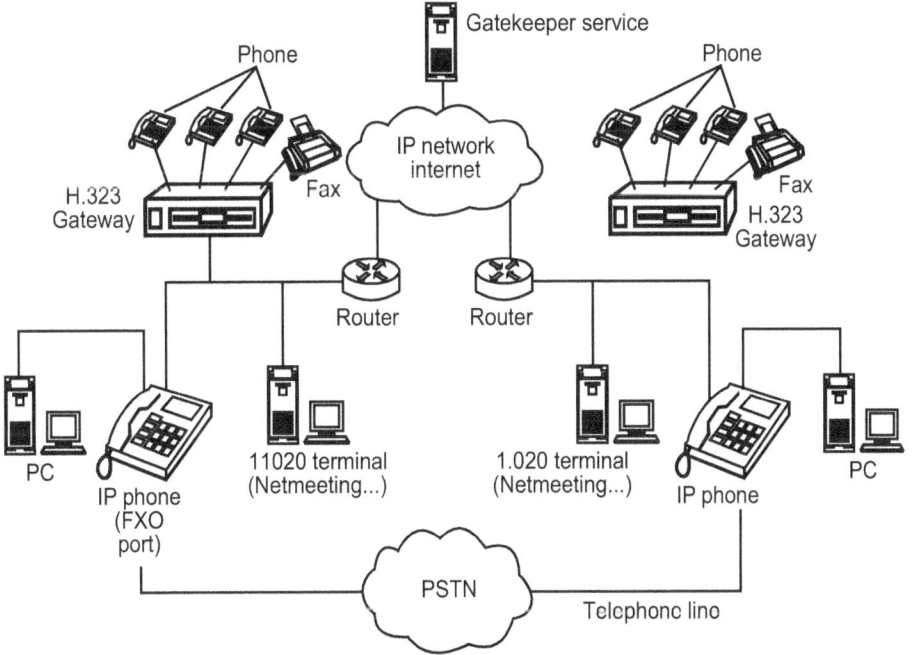

Fig. 6.7: Typical Hardware Requirement in VoIP

6.2.6.2 VoIP Phones

- VoIP Phones connect directly to your LAN via an RJ45 ethernet connection and provide quick and easy access to internet based telephony.

Fig. 6.8: Typical VoIP Phones

6.2.6.3 Gateways

- A VoIP Gateway is a device, which connects a telephone device or line to a computer network.

- On the computer connection side, devices may just have an ethernet connection or they may incorporate a cable-modem or ADSL modem.

- All the products available from Solwise have 10/100 Mbps ethernet ports for their network side connection.

- At the telephone side, all the Solwise products provide standard analog (also called PSTN or POTS) connections.

- These connections come in two flavours:

FXS	Used with devices like phones, fax machines or PBX trunk ports.
FX0	Connected to a trunk line from BT or a PBX extension.

6.2.6.4 The Channel

- In principle, you can use a VoIP gateway to communicate with anyone else on the internet who is similarly equipped, or has software to drive their PC/Soundcard.

- For best performance, it is preferred that both ends have some for of broadband connectivity.
- A more common use is to connect two or more sites for free calls between the sites.
- There may already be a data-link between the sites or the prospect of free-calls may be the spur to set this up.
- Each telephone conversation requires a channel of less than 10 k, so any data-link from 64 k up would be reasonable as long as it is fairly stable, has a small delay and is not already congested.
- Suitable choices for the channel are –
  1. Direct wired/RF/IR/Microwave ethernet connection
  2. Leased Line
  3. ISDN/ADSL/Cable Modem/dialup
- Of these the most 'asked about' is the last. Here is a list of requirements for such a dial-up account system.
  1. Must have fixed (though not necessarily public) IP.
  2. ISPs must not block VoIP protocols (some ISP's may have a vested interest in not allowing you to do telephone calls via the internet).

6.2.7 CODECS

1. Codecs are software drivers that are used to encode the speech in a compact enough form that they can be sent in real time across the Internet using the bandwidth available.
2. Codecs are not something that VoIP users normally need to worry about, as the VoIP clients at each end of the connection negotiate between them which one to use.
3. VoIP software or hardware may give you the option to specify the codecs you prefer to use.
4. This allows you to make a choice between voice quality and network bandwidth usage, which might be necessary, if you want to allow multiple simultaneous calls to be held using an ordinary broadband connection.
5. Your selection is unlikely to make any noticeable difference when talking to PSTN users, because the lowest bandwidth part of the connection will always limit the quality achievable, but VoIP-to-VoIP calls using a broadband Internet connection are capable of delivering much better quality than the plain old telephone system.
6. A broadband connection is desirable to use VoIP, though it is certainly possible to use it over a dial-up modem connection if a low-bandwidth, low-fidelity codec is chosen.

7. Table 6.2 lists some commonly used codecs.

Table 6.2

Codec	Algorithm	Bit rate (kbit/s)	Bandwidth (kbit/s)
G.711	Pulse Code Modulation (PCM)	64	87.2
G.722	Adaptive Pulse Code Modulation (ADPCM)	48	66.8
G.726	Adaptive Differential Pulse Code Modulation (ADPCM)	32	55.2
G.728	Low-Delay Code Excited Linear Predication (LD-CELP)	16	31.5
iLBC	Internet Low Bitrate Coded (ILBC)	15	27.7
GSM	Regular Pulse Excited (RPE)	13	30.1
G.729a	Conjugate Structure Algebraic-Code Excited Linear Prediction (CS-CELP)	8	31.2
G.723.1a	MP-MLQ	6.4	21.9
G.723.1	ACELP (Algebraic-Code Excited Linear Prediction)	5.3	20.8

8. The bit rate is an approximate indication of voice quality or fidelity, however, it is only approximate.

9. Codecs, that use pulse code modulation, all give high fidelity, and you will detect little or no difference between any of them.

10. The G.728 codec will give much better quality than the only nominally lower rate GSM codec, because the algorithm it uses is much more sophisticated.

11. However, the GSM codec uses less computing power, and so will run on simpler devices.

12. The bandwidth gives an indication of how much of the capacity of your broadband Internet connection will be consumed by each VoIP call.

13. The bandwidth usage is not directly proportional to the bit rate, and will depend on factors such as the protocol used.

14. Each chunk of voice data is contained within a UDP packet with headers and other information.

15. This adds a network overhead of some 15 - 25 kbit/s, more than doubling the bandwidth used in some cases.

16. However, most VoIP implementations use silence detection, so that no data at all is transmitted when nothing is being said.

17. Insufficient bandwidth can result in interruptions to the audio if VoIP uses the same Internet connection as other users who may be downloading files or listening to music.

18. For this reason, it is desirable to enable the Quality of Service "QoS" option in the TCP/IP Properties of any computer running a software VoIP client, and to use a router with QoS support for your Internet connection.

19. This will ensure that your VoIP traffic will be guaranteed a slice of the available bandwidth so that call quality does not suffer due to other heavy Internet usage.

6.2.8 A Converged Networking Environment

1. VoIPs core benefit is its ability to make next generation converged network a reality.

2. In a converged network environment, telephony and data signals are transmitted as packets over the data network.

3. A typical office has a separate network for data transmission and voice (telephone).

4. The data transmission network uses a switch to connect workstations and segment them.

5. The switches are connected to a router, which in turn connects to the corporate WAN or a SPs WAN network.

6. The voice network in the office has a PBX, on which telephone lines from the local exchange terminate.

7.   All the telephones in the office are connected to the PBX.

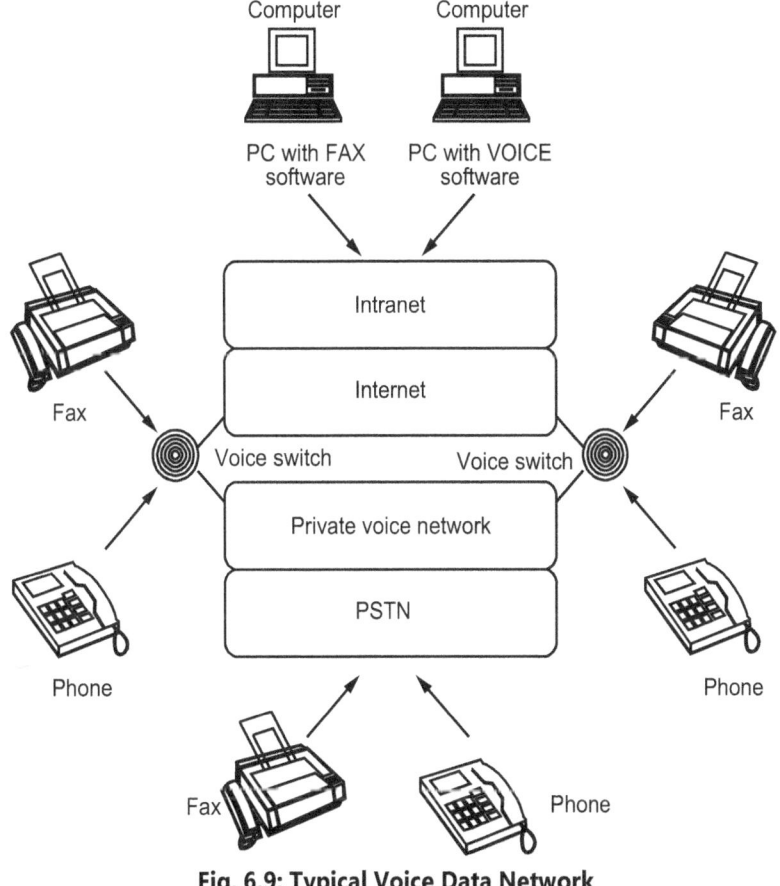

Fig. 6.9: Typical Voice Data Network

8. A converged network can enable you to transmit voice over existing data network.

9. Resources, that have traditionally been restricted to data, can now be used for telephony.

10. This maximizes the efficiency of your network.

11. The traditional voice circuits can be used as backup or even eliminated.

12. It simplifies your network architecture.

13. A single infrastructure is capable of carrying both, data and telephony traffic.

14. You don't need to pull separate cables for services.

15. This approach reduces repair time and streamlines network installations and reconfigurations.

16. Network deployments and reconfigurations are simplified, and service can be extended to remote sites and home offices over cost-effective IP links.

17. A future VoIP network will include IP-based PBXs (I-PBXs), which will emulate the functions of a traditional PBX.

18. These will allow both standard telephones and multimedia PCs to connect to either the PSTN or the Internet, providing a seamless migration path to VoIP.

19. An I-PBX can also combine the features of today's switches and routers and could become the gateway for variety of value-added services like directories, message stores, firewalls and other network-based servers.

20. Such a VoIP system would also combine real-time and non real-time communications.

6.2.9 VoIP Advantages

VoIP offers your small / home business several advantages over "traditional" telephone services. Assuming you choose a solution that allows you to use phone numbers in exactly the same way as you did before, you can count on:

1. **Lower cost:** Setup fees are typically very low and savings can be felt after only one month of service. Many VoIP providers offer "flat-fee" "all-you-can-eat" plans that don't carry any per-minute charges except for international calls, which are significantly cheaper than with traditional phone companies.

2. **Obtaining more control over your phone services:** Your VoIP service can often be configured and managed via extranet web sites; you can examine the log of phone calls, archive messages in the digital format; change account set-up directly; receive billing information, and so on.

3. **Gaining more flexibility in physical location:** Because VoIP does not "tie" you to a particular location, you can relocate anywhere where you can get reliable Internet access without any disruptions to your phone service. You can keep your number and work from your office, home, hotel, etc. in the same way.

4. **Improving business processes and increasing sales:** There are tools to make you more flexible and more accessible to your customers. You can utilize call routing to take calls on your cell phone when your main number is not available. You can also order "alternative" phone numbers with almost any area code for your VoIP line and thus allow your customers to call you on a "local" number.

6.2.10 VoIP Drawbacks

It would not be fair not to mention several drawbacks that are currently associated with VoIP deployment:

1. Call quality depends on your Internet connection. If your Internet connection is not reliable, you may experience drop-outs and sound distortion. (With that said, most cable and DSL lines are adequate for VoIP).
2. Unclear regulatory environment. Government still has not decided on whether or not VoIP is going to be regulated as tightly as phone services are.

6.3 Issues in Voice Communication Over Networks

1. As the IP network was primarily designed to carry data, it does not provide real-time guarantees, but only provides best effort service, which is inadequate for voice communication.
2. Upper layer protocols were designed to provide such guarantees. Further, as there are several vendors in the market implementing these protocols, conformance to standards and inter-operability issues have become important.
3. The major issues governing transfer of a voice stream over the Internet or using Internet protocols are listed below.

6.3.1 Bandwidth Requirement

1. In the analog world, the voice transmission frequency spectrum requirement is 0 to 3.4 kHz in the base band, and is nominally called a 4 kHz voice channel for convenience.
2. For digital telecommunication, the signal is sampled at twice the rate. The minimum-sampling rate required is thus 8 kHz. If each sample contains 8 bits, the digital bandwidth required works out to be 64 kbps.
3. Quality voice requires sampling at 8 kHz. The bandwidth then depends on the level of quantization. With linear quantization at 8 bits/sample or at 16 bits/sample, the bandwidth is either 64 kbps or 128 kbps.
4. Further, the quantization (e.g. PCM) is modified by using an **A law** or **µ-law** companding curve.

5. In order to communicate Quality-grade voice (or similarly, other real-time applications such as moving video), two different approaches can be attempted:
    • To transmit information of the highest quality over unrestricted bandwidth or
    • To reduce the bandwidth required for transmitting information (voice) of a given quality.

6. Stated differently, decisions are required regarding what information should be transmitted and how it should be transmitted.

7. Compression and decompression (CODEC) of digital signals is a means of reducing the required bandwidth or transmission bit rate.

8. Certain source data are highly redundant, particularly digitized images such as video and facsimile.

9. If, for example, a digital signal contains a string of zeroes, it will be economical to transmit a code indicating that a string of zeros follows along with the length of the string.

10. Many different algorithms for compression and decompression of digital codes have been constructed.

11. Pulse code modulation (PCM) and adaptive differential PCM (ADPCM) are examples of "waveform" CODEC techniques.

12. Waveform CODECs are compression techniques that exploit the redundant characteristics of the waveform itself.

13. In addition to waveform CODECs, there are source CODECs that compress speech by sending only simplified parametric information about voice transmission; these CODECs require less bandwidth.

14. Source CODECs include linear predictive coding (LPC), code-excited linear prediction (CELP) and multipulse-multilevel quantization (MP-MLQ).

15. Coding techniques for telephony and voice packet are standardized by the ITU-T in its G-series recommendations.

16. Some algorithms for voice compression and decompression are given in the Table 6.3 below.

Table 6.3: Coding algorithms

Input Range	Transmission Rate	Standard
Linear Predictive Coding Algorithm	64 kbps	LPC-10 G.711
Code Excited Linear Prediction CELP)	8 kbps	6.729 G.729 A
32 kbps Adaptive Differential Pulse Code Modulation (ADPCM)	32 kbps	G.721

6.3.2 Mean Opinion Score (MOS)

1. Each CODEC provides a certain quality of speech. The quality of transmitted speech is a subjective response of the listener.

2. A common benchmark used to determine the quality of sound produced by specific CODECs is the mean opinion score (MOS).

3. With MOS, a wide range of listeners judge the quality of a voice sample (corresponding to a particular CODEC) on a scale of 1 (bad) to 5 (excellent).

4. The scores are averaged to provide the MOS for that sample. The Table 6.4 shows the relationship between CODECs and MOS scores.

Table 6.4: Compression methods and MOS scores

Compression Method	Bit Rate (kbps)	Framing Size (ms)	MOS Score
G.711 PCM	64	1.25	4.1
G.729 CS-ACELP	8	10	3.92
G.729 × 2 Encodings	8	10	3.27
G.729 × 3 Encodings	8	10	2.68
G.729a CS-ACELP	8	10	3.7

5. Although it might seem logical from a resource usage standpoint to convert all calls to low bit-rate CODECs to save on infrastructure costs, there are drawbacks to compressing voice.

6. One of the main drawbacks is signal distortion due to multiple encodings (called tandem encodings).

7. For example, when a G.729 voice signal is tandem-encoded three times, the MOS score drops from 3.92 (very good) to 2.68 (unacceptable). Quality-grade voice refers to MOS scores of 4 or above.

6.3.3 Delay

1. A very important design consideration in implementing voice communications networks is minimizing one-way, end-to-end delay.

2. Voice traffic is real-time traffic and if there is too long a delay in voice packet delivery, speech will be unrecognizable.

3. An acceptable delay is less than 200 milliseconds. Delay is inherent in voice networking and is caused by a number of different factors.

There are basically two kinds of delay inherent in today's telephony networks:

- **Propagation delay** caused by the characteristics of the speed of light travelling via. a fiber-optic-based or copper-based medium of the underlying network.

- **Handling delay (also called serialization delay)** caused by the devices that handle voice information and have a significant impact on voice quality in a packet network. This delay includes the time it takes to generate a voice packet. DSPs may take 5 ms to 20 ms to generate a frame and usually one or more frames are placed in a voice packet. Another component of this delay is the time taken to move the packet to the output queue. Some devices expedite this process by determining packet destination and getting the packet to the output queue quickly. The actual delay at the output queue, in terms of time spent in the queue before being serviced, is yet another component of this handling delay and is normally
around 10 ms. A CODEC-induced delay is considered as a handling delay.
The Table 6.5 shows the delay introduced by different CODECs.

Table 6.5: Codec-Induced Delays

CODEC	Bit Rate (kbps)	Compression Delay (ms)
G.711 PCM	64	5
G.729 CS-ACELP	8	15
G.729a CS-ACELP	8	15

6.3.4 Serialization Delay

1. Serialization delay is the amount of time - a router takes to place a packet on a wire for transmission.

2. Fragmentation helps to eliminate serialization delay, but fragmentation, doesn't help without a queuing mechanism in place.

3. For example, if a 1000 byte packet enters a router's queue and is fragmented into ten 100 byte packets, without a queuing mechanism in place, a router will still send all 1000 bytes before it starts to send another packet.

4. Conversely, if there is a queuing mechanism in place, but no fragmentation, voice traffic can still fail.

5. If a router receives a 1000 byte packet in its queue and begins sending this packet in an instant before it receives a voice packet, the voice packet will have to wait until all 1000 bytes are sent across the wire, before entering the queue, because once a router starts sending a packet, it will continue to do so until the full packet is processed.

6. Therefore, it is essential that there is a method for a router to break large data packets into smaller ones, and a queuing strategy in place to help voice packets jump to the front of a queue ahead of data packets for transmission.

6.3.5 End-to-End Delay

End-to-end delay depends on the end-to-end signal paths/data paths, the CODEC, and the payload size of the packets.

6.3.6 Jitter

1. Jitter is variation in the delay of arrivals of voice packets at the receiver.
2. This causes a discontinuity of the voice stream.
3. It is usually compensated for by using a play-out buffer for playing out the voice smoothly.
4. Play-out control can be exercised both in adaptive or nonadaptive play-out delay mode.

6.3.7 Echo Cancellation

1. Echo is hearing your own voice in the telephone receiver while you are talking.
2. When timed properly, echo is reassuring to the speaker.
3. If the echo exceeds approximately 25 ms, it can be distracting and cause breaks in the conversation.
4. In a traditional telephony network, echo is normally caused by a mismatch in impedance from the four-wire network switch conversion to the two-wire local loop and is controlled by echo cancellers.
5. In voice over packet-based networks or VoIP, echo cancellers are built into the low bit-rate CODECs and are operated on each DSP.
6. Echo cancellers are limited by design by the total amount of time they will wait for the reflected speech to be received, which is known as an echo trail. The echo trail is normally 32 ms.

6.3.8 Reliability

1. Traditional data communication strives to provide reliable end-to-end communication between two peers.
2. They use checksum and sequence numbering for error control and some form of negative acknowledgement with a packet retransmission handshake for error recovery.
3. The negative acknowledgement with subsequent re-transmission handshake adds more than a round trip delay to transmission.
4. For time-critical data, the retransmitted message/packet might therefore be entirely useless.
5. Thus, VoIP networks should leave the proper error control and error recovery scheme to higher communication layers.

6. They can thus provide the level of reliability required, taking into account the impact of the delay characteristics.

7. Therefore, UDP is the transport level protocol of choice for voice and like communications. Reliability is built into higher layers.

8. Audio data is delay-sensitive and requires the transmitted voice packets to reach the destination with minimum delay and minimum delay jitter.

9. Although TCP/IP provides reliable connection, it is at the cost of packet delay or higher network latency.

10. On the other hand, UDP is faster compared to TCP.

11. **However, as packet sequencing and some degree of reliability are required over UDP/IP, RTP over UDP/IP is usually used for voice and video communication.**

6.3.9 Inter-operability

1. In a public network environment, in order for products from different vendors to inter-operate with each other, they need to conform to standards.

2. These standards are being devised by the ITU-T and the IETF. H.323 from ITU-T is by far the more popular standard.

3. However, SIP/MGCP standards from IETF are rapidly gaining more acceptance as relatively light weight and easily scalable protocols.

6.3.10 Security

1. On the Internet, since anybody can capture packets meant for someone else, security of voice communication becomes an important issue.

2. Some measure of security can be provided by using encryption and tunneling.

3. Usually, the common tunneling protocol used is Layer 2 Tunneling Protocol, and the common encryption mechanism used is Secure Sockets Layer (SSL).

6.3.11 Integration with PSTN and ISDN

1. IP Telephony needs to co-exist with traditional PSTN for still some more time.

2. It means that both PSTN and IP telephony networks should appear as a single network to users.

3. This is achieved through the use of gateways between the Internet on the one hand and PSTN or ISDN on the other.

6.3.12 Scalability

1. As succeeding VoIP products strive to provide Telco-grade voice quality over IP as is true for PSTN, but at a progressively lower cost, there is a potential for high growth rates in VoIP systems.

2. In such a scenario, it is essential that these systems be flexible enough to grow into large user markets.

6.4 Typical Voice Call Handling in a VoIP Application

1. It is useful to understand what happens at an application level when a call is placed using VoIP.
2. Fig. 6.10 describes the general flow of a two-party voice call using VoIP.

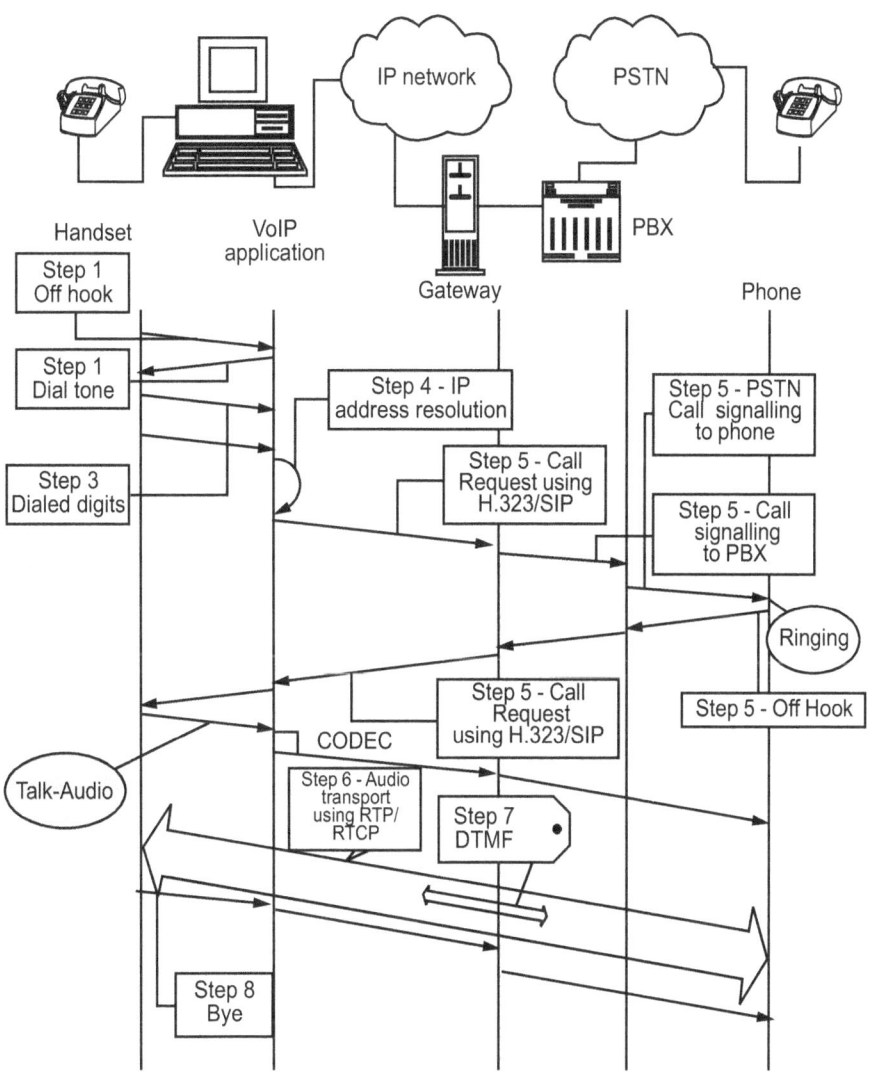

Fig. 6.10: Typical VoIP Call Handling

Table 6.6: Typical VoIP call handling

Step	Action
Step 1	The user picks up the handset; this signals an off-hook condition to the signalling application part of VoIP.
Step 2	The session application part of VoIP issues a dial tone and waits for the user to dial a telephone number.
Step 3	The user dials the telephone numbers; those numbers are accumulated and stored by the session application.
Step 4	After enough digits are accumulated to match a configured destination pattern, the telephone number is mapped to an IP host via. the dial-plan mapper. The IP host has a direct connection to either the destination telephone number or a PBX that is responsible for completing the call to the configured destination pattern.
Step 5	The session application then runs the session protocol (H.323 or SIP/MGCP) to establish a transmission and a reception channel for each direction over the IP network. If the call is being handled by a Private Branch Exchange (PBX), the PBX forwards the call to the destination telephone. If Resource Reservation Protocol (RSVP) has been configured, the RSVP reservations are put into effect to achieve the desired QoS over the IP network.
Step 6	The coder-decoder compression schemes (CODECs) are enabled for both ends of the connection and the conversation proceeds using Real-Time Transport Protocol/User Datagram Protocol/Internet Protocol (RTP/UDP/IP) as the protocol stack.
Step 7	Any call-progress indications (or other signals that can be carried inband) are cut through the voice path as soon as end-to-end audio channel is established. Signaling that can be detected by the voice ports (for example, inband dual-tone multifrequency (DTMF) digits after the call setup is complete) is also trapped by the session application at either end of the connection. It is carried over the IP network, encapsulated in the Real-time Transport Control Protocol (RTCP) using the RTCP application-defined (APP) extension mechanism.
Step 8	When either end of the call hangs up, the RSVP reservations are torn down (if RSVP is used) and the session ends. Each end becomes idle, waiting for the next off-hook condition to trigger call setup.

6.5 H.323 Standard

    1.   The H.323 standard has been developed by the ITU-T for equipment manufacturers and vendors who provide Voice over IP service.

2. It provides technical recommendations for voice communication over LANs assuming that no Quality of Service (QoS) is being provided by LANs.

3. It was originally developed for multimedia conferencing on LANs, but was later extended to Voice over IP.

4. The first and second versions of H.323 were released in 1996 and 1998 respectively. Currently, version 4 of H.323 is under consideration.

6.5.1 Components of H.323

The H.323 standard proposes an architecture that is composed of four logical components, viz. Terminal, Gateways, Gatekeepers and Multipoint Control Units (MCUs). The architecture schematic is depicted in the following diagram. The various components are described subsequently.

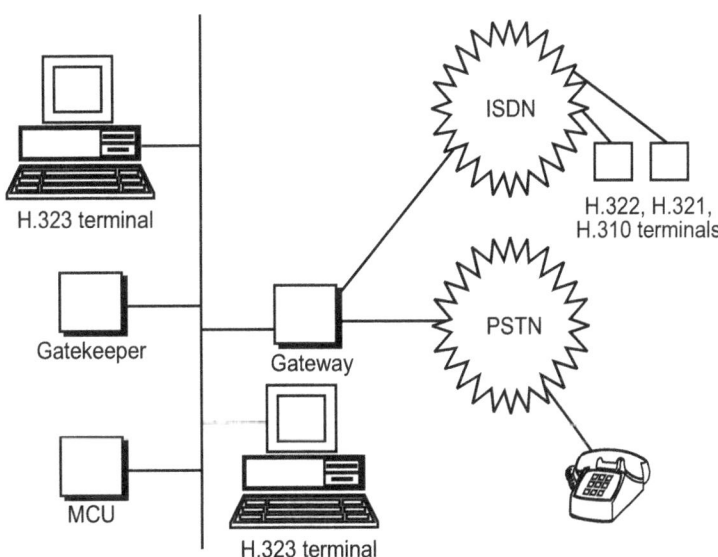

Fig. 6.11: VoIP H.323 Architecture

Terminals:

1. These are LAN client endpoints that provide real-time, two-way communications.

2. All H.323 terminals are required to support H.245, H.225, Q.931, Registration Admission Status (RAS) and Real-time Transport Protocols (RTP).

3. H.245 is used for controlling channel usage, while H.225 or Q.931 are used for call signalling, call setup and teardown.

4. RTP is used as a media transport protocol that carries the voice traffic.

5. RAS is used by the endpoint for interacting with the gatekeeper. H.323 terminals may also use T.120 data conferencing protocols, video codecs and support for MCU.

6. An H.323 terminal can communicate with either another H.323 terminal, a H.323 gateway or a MCU.

Gateways:

1. An H.323 gateway is an endpoint on the network that provides for real-time, two-way communications between H.323 terminals on the IP network with other ITU terminals on a switch-based network like PSTN or to another H.323 gateway.

2. The gateways handle different transmission formats.

3. Gateways are optional devices in the H.323 architecture because terminals in a single LAN can communicate directly with each other without using a gateway.

4. Only if the communication needs to span to other networks such as the PSTN, a gateway will be required.

5. In such cases, H.245 and Q.931 protocols are used by the participating endpoints and the intermediate gateway.

Gatekeepers:

1. This is an important component of the H.323 architecture and functions as its "manager".

2. It is the central point for all calls within its zone and provides services to the registered endpoints.

3. A zone is the aggregation of the gatekeeper and the registered endpoints.

4. A gatekeeper performs functions such as address translation, admissions control, call signalling, call authorization, call management and bandwidth management.

Multipoint Control Units (MCU):

1. The MCU acts as an endpoint on the network for providing capability for three or more terminals and gateways to participate in a multipoint conference.

2. The MCU consists of a mandatory Multipoint Controller (MC) and an optional Multipoint Processor (MP).

3. The MC's functions are to determine the common capabilities of conferencing terminals, using the H.245 protocol. It, however, does not perform multiplexing of audio, video and data streams.

4.   The multiplexing of these media streams is handled by the MP under control of the MC.

6.5.2 H.323 Protocol Stack

1.   A schematic description of the H.323 protocol stack is given in the following diagram.

2.   The unreliable but low latency UDP is used to transport audio, video and registration packets.

3.   Whereas the reliable but slow TCP is used for data and control packets in call signalling, the T.120 protocol is used for data conferencing.

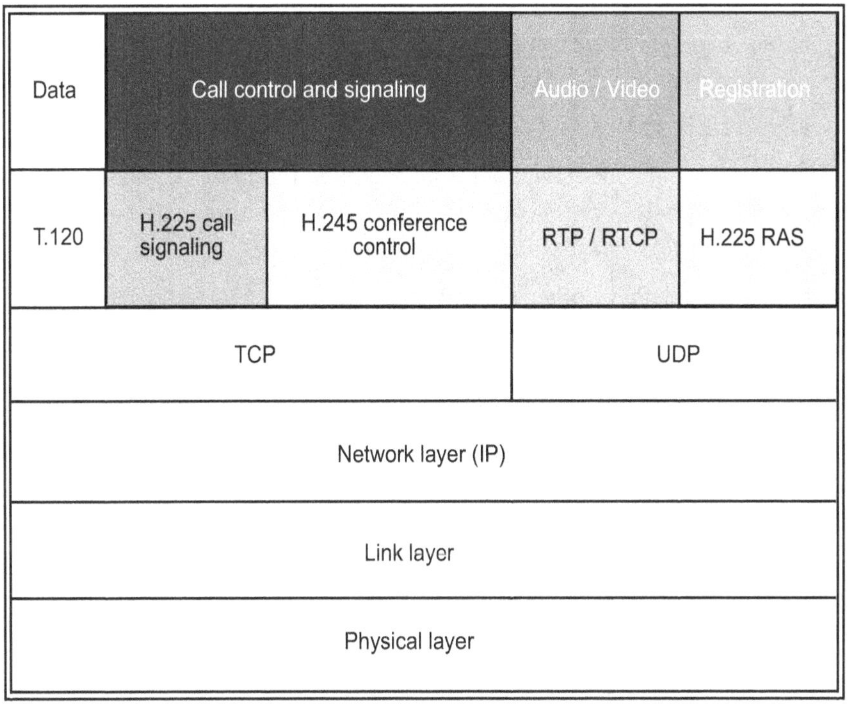

Data	Call control and signaling		Audio / Video	Registration
T.120	H.225 call signaling	H.245 conference control	RTP / RTCP	H.225 RAS
TCP			UDP	
Network layer (IP)				
Link layer				
Physical layer				

Fig. 6.12: H.323 Protocol Stack

6.5.3 Control and Signalling in H.323 System

1.   H.323 provides three control protocols – H.225/Q.931 call signalling, H.225/RAS call signalling and H.245 media control.

2.   The H.225/Q.931 is used for call signalling control.

3.   The H.225/RAS channel is used for establishing a call from the source to the receiving host.

4.   After the call is established, H.245 is finally used to negotiate the media streams.

H.225/RAS:

1. This RAS (Registration, Admission and Signalling) channel is used between the endpoints and the gatekeeper.

2. RAS uses unreliable UDP and hence also implements timeouts and retry count mechanisms for incorporating reliability.

3. RAS procedures used by endpoints encompass gateway discovery, endpoint registration, endpoint location, admission, bandwidth negotiation and status change.

H.225/Call Signalling:

1. This channel is used to carry H.225 control messages. In networks that do not contain a gatekeeper, call signalling messages are exchanged directly between endpoints using the Call Signalling Transport Address.

2. In this case, it is assumed that the calling endpoint knows the called endpoints.

3. However, in networks containing gatekeepers, the initial admission message can take place between the calling endpoint and the gatekeeper, using the gatekeeper's RAS channel Transport Address.

4. This call signalling is done over TCP.

H.245 Media and Conference Control:

1. After establishment of a call, the H.323 systems use the H.245 media control protocol to negotiate and establish all the media channels to be carried by RTP/RTCP.

2. This protocol is used to perform functions such as determination of master and slave in a multi-party conference, capability exchange, media channel control and conference control.

H.323 Call Setup:

Given below is a set of steps required for setting up a H.323 call.

- Discover a gatekeeper that would manage the endpoint.
- Register the endpoint with the gatekeeper.
- Endpoint enters the call setup phase.
- Capability exchange between the endpoints.
- Call is established.
- After calling, the call can be terminated by either party.

H.323 Implementations:

1. One of the most popular H.323 implementation available in the market is from Radvision.

2. Its H.323 stack is widely used by service providers.

3. Some of the other H.323 implementations available in the market are from Elemedia, Cisco, Micom, Nortel, Vocaltec, Neura Solutions and Ericsson.

6.6 MEGACO AND H.248

6.6.1 Megaco/H.248: Media Gateway Control Protocol

1. Megaco/H.248, the Media Gateway Control Protocol, is for control of elements in a physically decomposed multimedia gateway, which enables separation of call control from media conversion.

2. The Media Gateway Control Protocol (Megaco) is a result of joint efforts of the IETF and the ITU-T Study Group 16.

3. Therefore, the IETF defined Megaco is the same as ITU-T Recommendation H.248. Megaco is the IETF name and H.248 is the ITU-T name.

4. Megaco/H.248 addresses the relationship between the Media Gateway (MG), which converts circuit-switched voice to packet-based traffic, and the Media Gateway Controller (MGC, sometimes called a call agent or softswitch, which dictates the service logic of that traffic).

5. Megaco/H.248 instructs an MG to connect streams coming from outside a packet or cell data network onto a packet or cell stream such as the Real-Time Transport Protocol (RTP).

6. Megaco/H.248 is essentially quite similar to MGCP from an architectural standpoint and the controller-to-gateway relationship, but Megaco/H.248 supports a broader range of networks, such as ATM.

7. There are two basic components in Megaco/H.248: terminations and contexts. Terminations represent streams entering or leaving the MG (for example, analog telephone lines, RTP streams, or MP3 streams).

8. Terminations have properties, such as the maximum size of a jitter buffer, which can be inspected and modified by the MGC.

9. Terminations may be placed into contexts, which are defined as when two or more termination streams are mixed and connected together.

10. The normal, "active" context might have a physical termination (say, one DS0 in a DS3) and one ephemeral one (the RTP stream connecting the gateway to the network).

11. Contexts are created and released by the MG under command of the MGC.
A context is created by adding the first termination, and it is released by removing (subtracting) the last termination.

12. A termination may have more than one stream, and therefore a context may be a multistream context. Audio, video, and data streams may exist in a context among several terminations.

6.6.2 Protocol Structure - Megaco/H.248 (Media Gateway Control Protocol)

- All Megaco/H.248 messages are in the format of ASN.1 text messages. Megaco/H.248 uses a series of commands to manipulate terminations, contexts, events and signals. **The following is a list of the commands:**

1. **Add** - The Add command adds a termination to a context. The Add command on the first termination in a context is used to create a context.

2. **Modify** - The Modify command modifies the properties, events and signals of a termination.

3. **Subtract** - The Subtract command disconnects a termination from its context and returns statistics on the termination's participation in the context. The Subtract command on the last termination in a context deletes the context.

4. **Move** - The Move command atomically moves a termination to another context.

5. **AuditValue** - The AuditValue command returns the current state of properties, events, signals and statistics of terminations.

6. **AuditCapabilities** - The AuditCapabilities command returns all the possible values for termination properties, events and signals allowed by the Media Gateway.

7. **Notify** - The Notify command allows the Media Gateway to inform the Media Gateway Controller of the occurrence of events in the Media Gateway.

8. **ServiceChange** - The ServiceChange command allows the Media Gateway to notify the Media Gateway Controller that a termination or group of terminations is about to be taken out of service or has just been returned to service. ServiceChange is also used by the MG to announce its availability to an MGC (registration), and to notify the MGC of impending or completed restart of the MG. The MGC may announce a handover to the MG by sending it ServiceChange command. The MGC may also use ServiceChange to instruct the MG to take a termination or group of terminations in or out of service.

- All of these commands are sent from the MGC to the MG, although ServiceChange can also be sent by the MG.

- The Notify command, with which the MG informs the MGC that one of the events the MGC was interested in has occurred, is sent by the MG to the MGC.

- There are two basic constructs in Megaco: terminations and contexts (see Fig. 6.13).

- Terminations represent streams entering or leaving the MG (for example, analog telephone lines, RTP streams, or MP3 streams).

- Terminations have properties, such as the maximum size of a jitter buffer, which can be inspected and modified by the MGC.

- A termination is given a name, or TerminationID, by the MG. Some terminations, which typically represent ports on the gateway, such as analog loops or DS0s, are instantiated by the MG when it boots and remain active all the time.

- Other terminations are created when they are needed, get used, and then are released. Such terminations are called "ephemerals" and are used to represent flows on the packet network, such as an RTP stream.

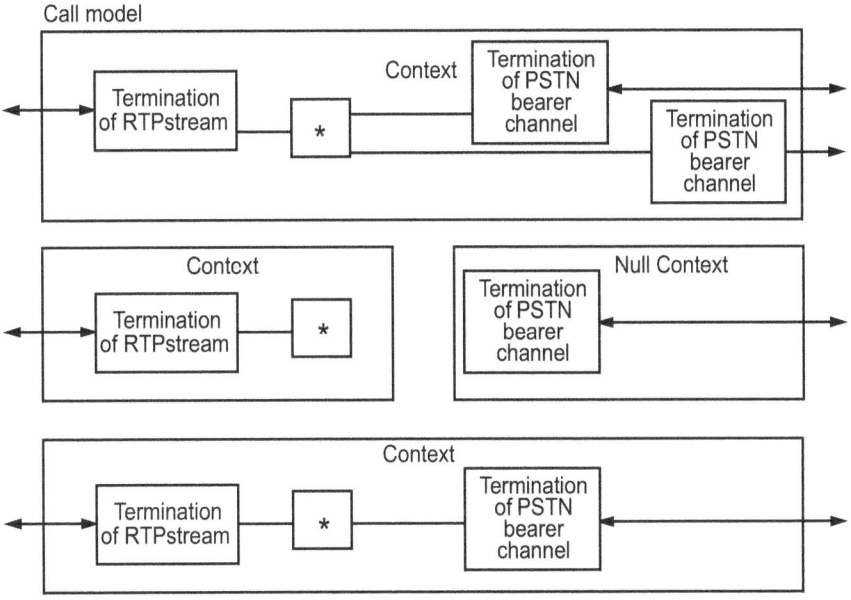

The * represents the mixing property of the context
(all terminations "hear" all other terminations)

Fig. 6.13: This Figure is an Example of Terminations as they relate to contexts in a MEGACO-Based Implementation

6.6.3 Data Connection's MGCP/Megaco Product Family

The DC-MGCP and DC-Megaco/H.248 software products are high function, flexible, portable protocol implementations, which allow vendor to quickly and easily build MGCP and/or Megaco/H.248 based products for –

- residential gateways
- trunking gateways
- other media gateway devices
- Call Agents or SoftSwitches
- enhanced service platforms (such as IVR Interactive Voice/Video Response announcement servers).

DC-MGCP and DC-Megaco both consist of a core protocol stack implementation plus a toolkit that allows customization of the protocol support to match the level provided by the Typical Vendor application. This largely avoids the Vendor application having to provide code for valid protocol messages that it does not support, as these can be rejected during parsing.

6.6.4 SIP and MGCP/Megaco

1. MGCP/Megaco and SIP are not peers; they can and will coexist in converged networks.
2. There are, however, a number of issues surrounding implementations that will influence future directions and capabilities.
3. As discussed in the Architecture section, MGCP/Megaco does not constitute a complete system: a session initiation protocol is required between gateway controllers.
4. SIP is eminently suitable and is a requisite where there is more than one softswitch.
5. A more contentious area of discussion, is the use of MGCP/Megaco to control end-points.
6. A media gateway could be an IP phone but, due to the service limitations this imposes, this is likely to be unpopular.
7. MGCP/Megaco would only be able to support basic IN-type services in a dumb black phone.
8. For advanced services (i.e. anything more sophisticated than IN services), SIP is required to reside both in the endpoints and above the signalling network, acting as the service intelligence. The issue that then arises is where should services reside?
9. Softswitch vendors would prefer the service intelligence to reside in the IP Central Office, tied into the softswitch architecture.

10. This perspective holds firm in the short-term where emphasis on convergence means that the interconnect point between a circuit-switched environment and an IP network will be a major focus.

11. In this scenario, SIP application servers reside with the softswitches in the IP Central Office with MGCP/Megaco controlling multiple media gateways across the network, delivering services to all endpoints.

12. As the legacy circuit-switched network diminishes in importance, and focus shifts squarely onto the IP infrastructure, then this model will become increasingly imbalanced and irrelevant. The softswitch function will need to evolve away from the interconnect point.

13. In a pure IP environment, service creation would be distributed across the network.

14. This is the model that has produced the startling innovations that we have seen on the Internet: anyone with a few dollars and a good idea has the opportunity to give it a try.

15. The Application Service Provider model can be extended to offer voice-type services.

16. ASPs, ISPs, or even the end-users themselves can create their own SIP services; after all, SIP's similarity to other Internet protocols makes it a familiar programming language to web developers.

17. A SIP-centric implementation would use MGCP/Megaco only for internally controlling an IP telephony gateway. SIP application servers would distribute services throughout the network via SIP proxy servers.

SIP	MGCP/Megaco
Peer-to-peer signalling protocol.	Can be used as a control protocol for delivering services across the network.
A session initiation protocol required between separate softswitches*.	Used for internally controlling an IP telephony gateway.
Client-server architecture.	Master-slave architecture.
"Pure" IP solution.	An interim solution for co-existing. networks - "PSTN over IP".
Horizontal architecture that re-uses Internet elements.	Mirrors the signalling and control architecture of IN.
Intelligent clients.	Assumes dumb end-points.
Abstracts the signalling layer from the network.	Pre-supposes the existence of hardware.
"New world" approach - simple open and horizontal.	"Old world" Decentralized, controlled and vertical.

   *   SIP and MGCP/Megaco are complementary in certain ways and mutually exclusive in others.

6.6.5 SIP, H.323 and MGCP/Megaco

1. A number of signalling protocols have been developed in different camps to address the need for real-time session signalling over packet-based networks.

2. Each of these protocols has different origins and different supporters with differing priorities.

3. H.323 was developed in the Enterprise LAN community as a video-conferencing technique and has much in common with ISDN signalling protocols such as Q.931.

4. MGCP/Megaco comes from the telecommunication engineering world and is closely associated with intra-domain control of softswitches and media gateways etc.

5. The IETF developed SIP, reusing many familiar Internet elements: SMTP, HTTP, URLs, MIME, DNS.

6. Despite all being signalling protocols, they are not equals and peers - they can and will coexist; however, there is some debate as to what extent.

6.7 Session Initiation Protocol

1. Session Initiation Protocol or SIP is the IETF standard for voice or multimedia session establishment over the Internet.

2. It was proposed as a standard (RFC 2543) in Feb. 1999.

3. Its original author was Henning Schulzrinne.

4. SIP is an application level protocol used for call setup management and teardown.

5. SIP is used in association with its other IETF sister protocols like the SAP, SDP and MGCP (MEGACO) to provide a broader range of VoIP services.

6. The SIP architecture is similar to HTTP (client-server protocol) architecture.

7. It comprises requests that are sent from the SIP user client to the SIP server.

8. The server processes the request and responds to the client. A request message, together with the associated response messages, makes a SIP transaction.

9. SIP makes minimal assumptions about the underlying transport protocol and itself provides reliability and does not depend on the underlying protocol's characteristics.

10. SIP depends on Session Description Protocol (SDP) for negotiation of session parameters such as codec identification and media.

11. It supports user mobility through proxy servers and redirecting requests to the user's currently registered location.

Some major SIP features are as follows:

Feature	Description
Call setup	Session establishment with agreed call parameters between the two endpoints.
Renegotiate call parameters	Renegotiate session parameters while the call is in progress.
User location	Determination of the end system to be used for communication, given the user's email style address.
User availability	Determination of the willingness of the called party to engage in a conversation.
User capabilities	Determination and negotiation of the media and call parameters to be used in the session.
Call handling	Transfer and termination of the call.

6.7.1 SIP Components

The SIP architecture specifies two components as given below.

1. User Agents
2. SIP Servers

1. User Agents:

A SIP User Agent is an end system (end point) acting on behalf of the user. It consists of two parts:

- **User Agent Client (UAC):** This is the user client portion, which is used to initiate a SIP request to the SIP servers or the UAS.
- **User Agent Server (UAS):** This is the user server portion that listens and responds to SIP requests. Note: User = UAC + UAS

2. SIP Servers:

The SIP architecture describes the following types of network servers to help in the SIP call setup and services.

- **Registration Server:** This server receives registration requests from SIP users and updates their current location with itself.
- **Proxy Server:** This server receives SIP requests and forwards them to the next-hop server, which has more information of the called party.
- **Redirect Server:** This server on receipt of the SIP request, determines the next-hop server and returns the address of the next-hop server to the client instead of forwarding the request to the next-hop server itself (as in the case of SIP proxy).

6.7.2 SIP Messages

SIP defines the following major messages between the client and server.

INVITE	Request to invite a user (called party) to a call.
ACK	Acknowledgement to start reliable exchange of invitation messages.
BYE	To terminate (or transfer) the call between the two endpoints.
OPTIONS	Request to get information about the capabilities of a call.
REGISTER	To register information of current location with a SIP registration server.
CANCEL	Request to terminate search of a user or "ringing".
INFO	Mid-call information (e.g. ISUP, DTMF).
PRACK	Provisional Acknowledgement
COMET	Pre-condition met.
SUBSCRIBE	Request to subscribe to an event.
NOTIFY	Notify subscribers.

6.7.3 Typical Sip Call Setup

The following diagram describes a typical voice call session setup over the Internet using SIP.

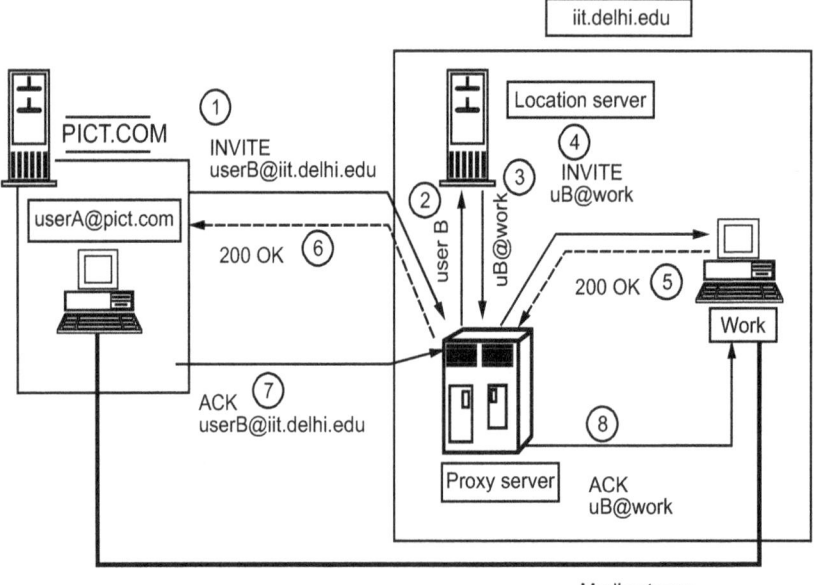

Fig. 6.14: SIP – Basic Operation

In this diagram, a SIP client "userA@pict.com" creates an INVITE message for "userB@iit.delhi.edu" to invite the latter to a voice call. Given below is a step-by-step description.

1. UserA (userA@pict.com) sends an INVITE message meant for UserB (userB@iit.delhi.edu) to the SIP proxy server of iit.delhi.edu domain. Alternately, this message would have been sent to the SIP proxy server of pict.com domain, which in turn would have forwarded this to the SIP proxy server of the iit.delhi.edu domain. The proxy server tries to obtain the IP address of the SIP server that will handle the requests for the requested domain.

2. The proxy server of iit.delhi.edu domain consults the location server to determine the current address of UserB.

3. The location server returns the current address of UserB, which is uB@work.

4. The proxy server then sends INVITE to uB@work. The proxy server inserts its address in the via field of the Invite message.

5. UAS of UserB responds to the proxy server with 200 OK message.

6. The proxy server in turn sends a 200 OK response back to userA@pict.com.

7. UserA@pict.com then sends an ACK message destined for UserB via the proxy server.

8. The proxy server forwards the ACK message to uB@work.

9. After both the parties agree to participate in the call, an RTP/RTCP channel (media stream) is opened between the two endpoints for transporting voice.

10. After transmission is complete, the session is torn down, using the BYE and ACK messages between the two participating endpoints.

6.7.4 SIP Implementations

1. Although SIP is relatively new, it has already been implemented by several companies.

2. The implementations encompass SIP proxy and redirect servers; User agents on MS Windows, Linux, etc.; Ethernet Phones; Softswitches; firewalls, SIP-H.323 translators and unified messaging systems.

3. Some of the current ongoing implementations are being done by companies such as dynamicsoft, Hughes Software Systems, Cisco, Ericsson, Hewlett Packard, Lucent, Nokia, Nortel, Siemens, Telogy, Iwatsu Electric and Vovida.

4. Universities such as Carnegie-Mellon University and Columbia University are actively developing the standard through their implementations.

5. The SIP stack can also be found as Open Source software. Companies such as Vovida or dynamicsoft have SIP stacks in the Open Source arena.

6.8 Comparison between H.323 and SIP

1. SIP is a relatively new protocol as compared to H.323 and hence, has been able to avoid all the problems associated with H.323.
2. Because H.323 had been initially designed, keeping ATM and ISDN in mind, it was not suited to control voice traffic over IP networks.
3. The earlier version of H.323 is inherently complex with large overheads and is thus inefficient for IP networks, where bandwidth is a premium commodity.
4. On the other hand, as SIP has been designed keeping the Internet in mind, it has been able to better address and circumvent the complexity and extensibility issues. SIP is "HTTP-ish", i.e. it reuses most of the HTTP header fields, encoding rules, error codes and authentication mechanisms.
5. SIP uses only 37 header fields as compared to hundreds of elements in the H.323 header.
6. This "HTTP-ish" characteristic of SIP enables it to be lightweight and also gives it the potential of becoming a more popular protocol, such as HTTP, over the Internet.
7. H.323 uses a binary representation for its messages.
8. This is based on ASN.1 syntax. The SIP, however, is a text-based protocol such as HTTP.
9. SIP is more scalable, whereas H.323 has limited scalability, as it was initially designed for use within a single LAN.
10. The newer versions of H.323 have, however, managed to address this issue.
11. Loop detection techniques in complex multi-domain searches in H.323 are limited and not very scalable.
12. This is done in a limited manner in H.323 by maintaining message states. However, in SIP, this is done efficiently by checking the path history stored in the message header and thus it can be done in a stateless manner.

Table 6.7

Feature	H.323	SIP
Architecture	Stack Implementation	Element Implementation
Complexity	Complex	Simple
Standards body	ITU	IETF
Protocol	Mostly TCP	Mostly UDP
Protocol Encoding	Binary (ASN.1, Q.931)	Text (HTTP-ish)
Server processing	State-full	State-less, Transaction-oriented
Addressing	Flat alias, E.164, email	SIP, E.164, URLs
Call Setup delay	V1: 6-7 × RTT to V3: 1.5-2.5 × RTT	1.5 × RTT
Mid-call failure	Fail	Live
Loop Detection	V1: No, V3: Path Value	Yes – "via" field, time, hops
Manageability	Yes	No
Call control	Yes	Yes

6.9 Related VoIP Protocols

The following diagram depicts the relationship of SIP, H.323 and other related protocols.

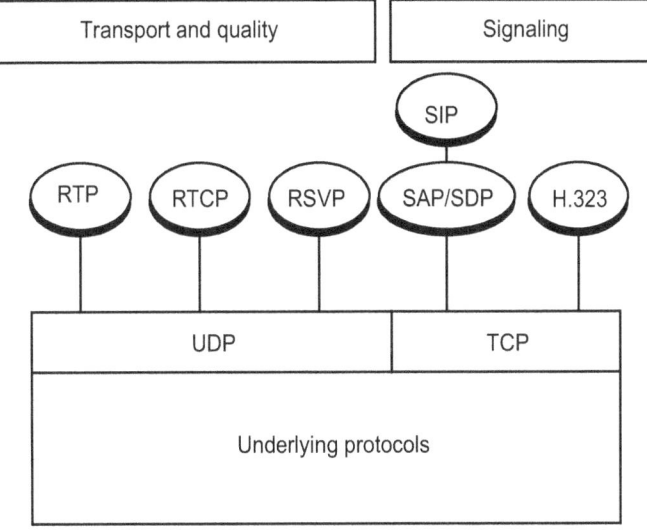

Fig. 6.15: SIP, H.323 and Other Protocols

6.9.1 Session Description Protocol (SDP)

1. SDP is an IETF specified protocol (RFC2327) that helps in describing multimedia sessions.
2.   It is used for session announcements, session invitation, etc.
3. For example, the SDP payload gets included in the SIP INVITE packet to convey information about the sender to the recipient and vice versa, before participating in the session.
4. This allows media information to be similarly shared between the parties. An SDP payload includes the following information:
    *   Session name and purpose
    *   Address and port number
    *   Start and stop times
    *   Media information
    *   Bandwidth requirement
    *   Contact information
5. The above information is conveyed in text format.
6. In general, SDP must convey sufficient information to enable a party to join a session and also to announce the resources to be used in a multiparty conference.
7. The media information that SDP sends is: type of media (audio or video), transport protocol (RTP, UDP, etc.) and media format (MPEG video, H.263 video, etc.).

6.9.2 Session Announcement Protocol (SAP)

1. The SAP protocol is used for advertising multicast conferences and multicast sessions.

2. A SAP announcer periodically multicasts announcement packets to a well known multicast address and port (port number: 9875).

3. The SAP listener listens to the well known SAP address and port and learns of the multicast scopes using the Multicast Scope Zone Announcement Protocol.

4. A SAP announcer is unaware of the presence or absence of SAP listeners.

5. A SAP announcement is multicast with the same scope as the session it is announcing, thus ensuring that the recipients of the announcement can also be potential recipients of the session being advertised.

6. If a session uses addresses in multiple administrative scope ranges, it is necessary for the announcer to send identical copies of the announcement to each administrative scope range.

7. It is alright for multiple announcers to announce a single session, thus ensuring robustness of the protocol.

8. The intervening time period between announcements is decided such that the total bandwidth used by all the announcements in a single SAP group is less than a pre-configured limit.

9. Each announcer is required to listen to all the announcements in its group in order to determine the total number of sessions being announced in the group.

10. One of the protocol's objectives is to announce the existence of long-lived wide area multicast sessions and involves a large startup delay before a complete set of announcements is heard by a listener.

11. SAP proxy caches can also be deployed to reduce the inherent delays in SAP.

12. SAP proxy is expected to listen to all SAP groups in its scope and maintain an up-to-date list of all announced sessions along with the last receipt time of each announcement. SAP also contains mechanisms to ensure the integrity of session announcements, announcement encryption and also to authenticate the origin of an announcement.

6.9.3 Media Gateway Control Protocol (MGCP)

1. MGCP defines the communication between "Call Agents" (call control elements) and gateways.

2. It is an IETF specification. Call Agents are also called Media Gateway Controllers.

3.   It is a control protocol that monitors the events on IP phones and gateways and instructs them to send media to specified addresses.

4.   MGCP has evolved from two earlier protocols – the Simple Gateway Control Protocol and the Internet Protocol Device Control.

5.   As per recommendations, the call control intelligence is located outside the gateway in the call agents.

6.   These call agents are assumed to have synchronized with each other and they issue coherent commands to the gateways under their control.

7.   The issued commands are executed by the gateways in a master/slave manner. MGCP defines the concepts of "Endpoints" and "Connections" to describe and establish voice paths between two participants.

8.   Similarly, it has defined "Events" and "Signals" to describe set-up or teardown of sessions.

9.   MGCP is intended to be a simple protocol for enabling development of reliable and cheap local access systems.

10. Accordingly, the programming complexity is concentrated into the call agent.

Creating Connections:

Call agents create connections at each endpoint that will participate in a call. If the endpoints are located on different gateways managed by the same call agent, then the creation of a connection is done using the following steps.

- The call agent asks the first gateway to create a connection on the first endpoint. The response sent by the gateway includes the session description that contains relevant information required by other parties to be able to send packets to the newly created connection.

- The call agent then sends the session description of the first connection to the second gateway and requests it to create a connection on the second endpoint. The second endpoint and subsequently the second gateway responds and includes its own session description.

- The call agent then uses a modify-connection command to provide this second session description to the first endpoint.

Communication can now occur between the two endpoints.

On the other hand, if the two gateways are controlled by different call agents, then MGCP requires that the two call agents synchronize by exchanging information between themselves, using the agent signalling protocol. This will enable the call agents to issue synchronous commands to the different gateways.

Commands:

1. The media gateway control interface is implemented as a set of transactions.

2. These transactions are composed of a pair consisting of a command and an associated mandatory response.

3. There are eight types of MGCP commands.

4. **These commands are used to create, modify and delete connections, audit endpoints and connections, to send notification requests or to notify and finally reset or restart connections.**

6.10 Multimedia Networking: Goals and Challenges

1. On today's Internet, multimedia networking is playing an important role.

2. Computer networks used to carry computer data only.

3. Today, they are also used for internet telephony, multimedia conferencing, transmission of lectures and meetings, distributed simulations, network games and other real-time applications.

4. Future application areas with real-time requirements might include telemedicine, distributed workgroups, distance learning and telecommuting.

5. Multimedia networking is to build the multimedia on network and distributed systems, so different users on different machines can share image, sound, video, voice and many other features and to communicate with each under these tools.

6.10.1 Challenges of Real-time

1. Multimedia networking face many technical challenges like real-time data over non-real-time network, high data rate over limited network bandwidth, unpredictable availability of network bandwidth.

2. First, multimedia applications usually require much higher bandwidth than traditional textual applications.

3. High-bandwidth network protocols such as Gigabit Ethernet, FDDI, and ATM are expected to make the networking of digital video and audio practical.

4. The basis of Internet, TCP/IP and UDP/IP, provides the range of services needed to support both small and large scale networks.

5. Second, almost all multimedia applications require the real-time traffic which is very different from non-real-time data traffic.

6. If the network is congested, the only effect on non-real-time traffic is that the transfer takes longer to complete.

7. In contrast, real-time data becomes obsolete if it doesn't arrive in time.

8. As a consequence, real-time applications deliver poor quality during periods of congestion.

9. On the other hand, bandwidth is not the only problem.

10. For most multimedia applications, the receiver has a limited buffer, if the data arrives too fast, the buffer can be overflowed and some data will be lost, also resulting in poor quality.

11. Therefore, protocols for real-time applications must be worked out before the real multimedia time comes.

6.10.2 Multimedia over Internet

1. Running multimedia applications over packet-switched networks like the Internet is very attractive.

2. First, the infrastructure often is already in place.

3. Adopting existing datagram networks and Internet connections will save expensive software development.

4. Second, this approach seems more economical and easier to manage than separate datagram and real-time networks.

5. In contrast to dedicated lines or connections, LAN and WAN technologies provide a relatively inexpensive, plentiful, but shared bandwidth over bigger and bigger networks.

6. Because of its shared nature, at first glance, datagram networks do not seem suitable for real-time traffic.

7. Packets are routed independently across shared networks, so transit times vary significantly.

8. Variations in transit delays are called jitter.

9. A class of real-time applications called playback applications aims to solve the jitter problem.

10. Playback applications aim to solve the jitter problem by buffering at the receiver.

11. Adaptive applications adapt to changing delays and work well on moderately loaded datagram networks.

12. They can deal with jitter caused by short-lived bursts, and they can tolerate occasional lost packets during brief periods of congestion.

13. However, parts of the Internet are often heavily loaded.

14. The price tag attached to shared bandwidth is congestion, leading to jitter and packet loss.

15. At certain times of the day, some audio multicasts are unintelligible because of more than 30% packet loss.

16. While real-time traffic contributes heavily to congestion because of large bandwidth requirements, it also suffers more from congestion than non-real-time traffic.

17. The only effect of congestion on non-real-time traffic is that a transfer takes longer to complete.

18. In contrast, real-time data becomes obsolete if it doesn't arrive in time.

19. As a consequence, real-time applications deliver poor quality during periods of congestion.

20. To cope with congestion, several approaches have been proposed in which the application adapts to the available bandwidth by switching to a different encoding.

21. Adaptive encoding mechanisms help to keep up useful service during congestion, but they are not a general solution.

22. Real-time applications are useless when the available bandwidth drops below a certain minimum bandwidth or when transit times vary so much that interactivity is impossible.

6.10.3 Solutions

1. The underlying problem is that different classes of applications require different services.

2. For example, a file transfer application requires that some quantity of data is transferred in an acceptable amount of time, while internet telephony requires that most packets get to the receiver in less than 0.3 seconds.

3. If enough bandwidth is available, best-effort service fulfills all of these requirements.

4. When resources are scarce, however, real-time traffic should be treated differently.

5. The Integrated Services working group in the IETF (Internet Engineering Task Force) developed an enhanced Internet service model that includes best-effort service and real-time service.

6. **The Resource Reservation protocol (RSVP), together with Real-time Transport Protocol (RTP), Real-Time Control Protocol (RTCP), Real-Time Streaming Protocol (RTSP), provides a working foundation for this architecture that is a comprehensive approach to provide applications with the type of service they need in the quality they choose.**

6.11 How does RSVP Work?

1. When an application in a host (end system) requests a specific QoS for its data stream, RSVP is used to deliver the request to each router along the path(s) of the data stream and to maintain router and host state to provide the requested service.

2. Although RSVP was developed for setting up resource reservations, it is readily adaptable to transport other kinds of network control information along data flow paths.

3. A host uses RSVP to request a specific *Quality of Service* (QoS) from the network, on behalf of an application data stream.

4. RSVP carries the request through the network, visiting each node the network uses to carry the stream.

5. At each node, RSVP attempts to make a resource reservation for the stream, see Fig. 6.16.

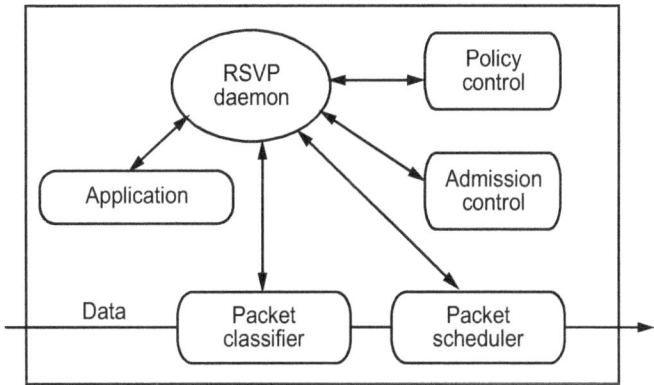

Fig. 6.16: Reservation at a Node on the Data Flow Path

6. In order to make a reservation at a node, the RSVP daemon calls two local decision procedures, admission control and policy control.

7. Admission control determines whether the node has sufficient available resources to supply the requested QoS.

8. Policy control determines whether the user has administrative permission to make the reservation.

9. If either check fails, the RSVP program returns an error notification to the application process that originated the request.

10. If both checks succeed, the RSVP daemon sets parameters in a **packet classifier** and **packet scheduler** to obtain the desired QoS.

11. The packet classifier determines the QoS class for each packet and the scheduler orders packet transmission to achieve the promised QoS for each stream.

12. The reservation requests are receiver-oriented, and merge when they progress up the multicast tree.

13. The reservation for a single receiver does not need to travel to the source of a multicast tree; rather it travels only until it reaches a reserved branch of the tree. See Fig. 6.17.

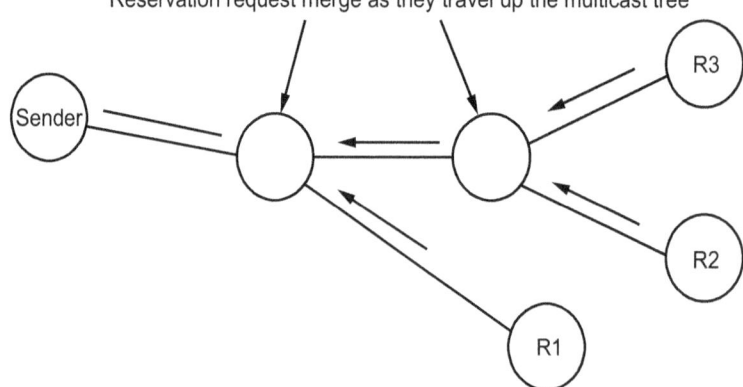

Reservation request merge as they travel up the multicast tree

Fig. 6.17: Reservation Requests Merge

14. This leads to a primary feature of RSVP viz. scalability. RSVP can scale to very large multicast groups. While the RSVP protocol is designed specifically for multicast applications, it may also make unicast reservations.

15. RSVP reserves resources for *simplex* data streams, i.e., it reserves resources in only one direction on a link, so that a sender is logically distinct from a receiver. However, the same application may act as both sender and receiver.

16. RSVP protocol mechanisms provide a general facility for creating and maintaining distributed reservation state across a mesh of multicast delivery paths.

17. RSVP transfers reservation parameters as opaque data (except for certain well-defined operations on the data), which it simply passes to admission control and to the Packet Scheduler and Classifier for interpretation.

18. RSVP is also designed to utilize the robustness of current Internet routing algorithms.

19. RSVP does not perform its own routing; instead it uses underlying routing protocols to determine where it should carry reservation requests.

20. As routing changes paths to adapt to topology changes, RSVP adapts its reservation to the new paths wherever reservations are in place.

21. This modularity does not rule out RSVP from using other routing services.

22. Current research within the RSVP project is focusing on designing RSVP to use routing services that provide alternate paths and fixed paths.

23. RSVP runs over IP, both IPv4 and IPv6. Among RSVP's other features, it provides opaque transport of traffic control and policy control messages, and provides transparent operation through non-supporting regions.

6.11.1 RSVP Features

(A) RSVP supports multicast or unicast simplex data delivery. RSVP is fundamentally designed for multicasting as well as unicasting, and it treats data flow as one-directional. It distinguishes the roles of data sender (e.g., hosts H1, H2 in Fig. 6.18) from data receiver (hosts H3, H4, H5 in Fig. 6.18), although in many cases the same application will play both the roles.

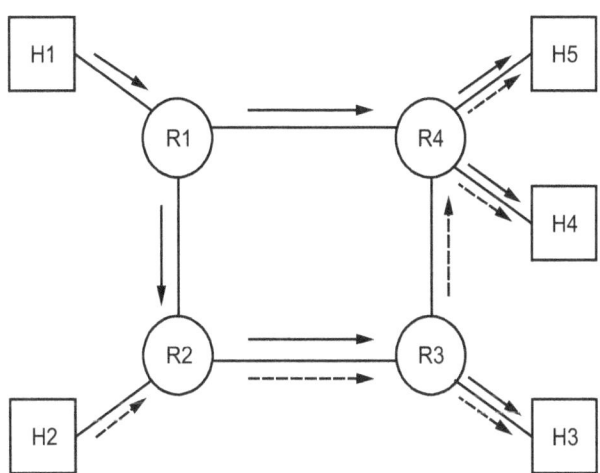

Fig. 6.18: A Simple Network with the Multicast Routing Trees. The Dotted and Solid Lines Depict the Routing Trees of H2 and H1 Respectively

(B) RSVP handles heterogeneous receivers: Different hosts on the same multicast delivery tree may have different capabilities and therefore need different QoS.

(C) RSVP is receiver-oriented: To efficiently handle heterogeneous receivers and dynamic group membership, RSVP makes receivers responsible for requesting resource reservations. Each receiver can request a QoS that is tailored to its particular requirement, by sending RSVP reservation messages upstream towards the senders.

Fig. 6.19 shows RSVP reservation messages flowing upstream. Just as the data branches out in routers R1, R3, and R4 in Fig. 6.19, so the reservation messages going upstream are "merged". Thus, a single reservation message need only flow upstream until it is merged with another reservation.

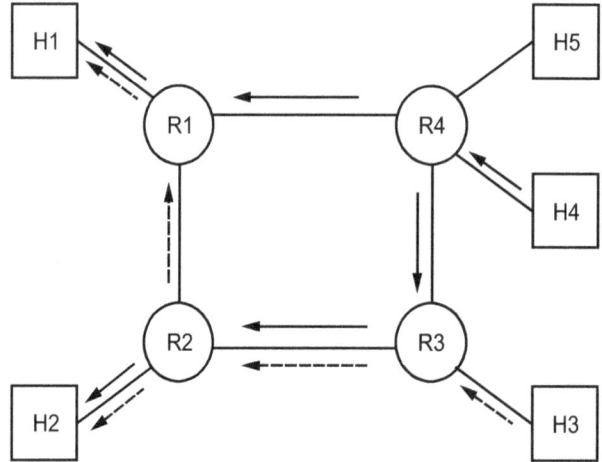

Fig. 6.19: RSVP Reservations are sent Upstream Towards the Sender. The Dotted and Solid Lines Depict the Sink Trees of H3 and H4 Respectively

(D) RSVP adapts to changing group membership as well as changing routes: For dynamic adaptability and robustness, RSVP maintains "soft state" in the routers. The only permanent state is in the end systems, which periodically send their RSVP control messages to refresh the router state. In the absence of refresh, RSVP state in routers will time out and be deleted.

(E) RSVP is not a routing protocol: The RSVP daemon consults the local routing protocol(s) to obtain routes. RSVP is designed to operate with existing and future unicast and multicast routing protocols. Thus, a host sends IGMP messages to join a multicast group, but it uses RSVP messages to reserve resources along the delivery path(s) from that group.

6.12 RTP (Real-time Transport Protocol)

1. As discussed in the first section, because of their unpredictable delay and availability, TCP/UDP are not suitable for applications with real-time character.

2. The real-time transport protocol (RTP) is a thin protocol providing support for applications with real-time properties, including timing reconstruction, loss detection, security and content identification.

3. RTP can be used without RTCP if desired.

4. RTP can transport independently so that it could be used over CLNP (Connectionless Network Protocol), IPX (Internetwork Packet Exchange) or other protocols.

5. RTP is currently also in experimental use directly over AAL5/ATM.

6.12.1 How does RTP Work?

1. There are two transport layer protocols in the Internet protocol suite, TCP and UDP.
2. TCP provides a reliable flow between two hosts.
3. It is connection-oriented and thus cannot be used for multicast.
4. UDP provides a connectionless unreliable datagram service.
5. To use UDP as a transport protocol for real-time traffic, some functionality has to be added.
6. Functionality, that is needed for many real-time applications, is combined into RTP, the **real-time transport protocol.**
7. Applications typically run RTP on top of UDP as part of the transport layer protocol, as shown in Fig. 6.20.

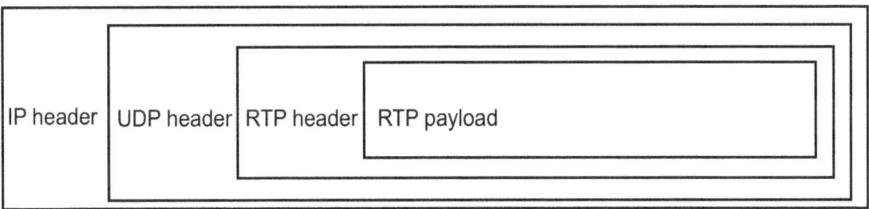

Fig. 6.20: RTP Data in an IP Packet

8. In practice, RTP is usually implemented within the application. RTP is designed to be independent from the underlying transport protocol and can be used over unicast as well as multicast.

9. To set up an RTP session, the application defines a particular pair of destination transport addresses (one network address plus a pair of ports for RTP and RTCP).

10. In a multimedia session, each medium is carried in a separate RTP session, with its own RTCP packets reporting the reception quality for that session.

11. For example, audio and video would travel on separate RTP sessions, enabling a recipient to select whether or not to receive a particular medium.

12. An audio-conferencing scenario can illustrate the use of RTP.

13. Suppose each participant sends audio data in segments of 20 ms duration.

14. Each segment of audio data is preceded by an RTP header, and then the resulting RTP message is placed in a UDP packet.

15. The RTP header indicates the type of audio encoding that is used, e.g., PCM. Users can opt to change the encoding during a conference in reaction to network congestion or, for example, to accommodate low-bandwidth requirements of a new conference participant.

16. Timing information and a sequence number in the RTP header are used by the receivers to reconstruct the timing produced by the source, so that in this example, audio segments are contiguously played out at the receiver every 20 ms.

RTP consists of two closely-linked parts:

- The real-time transport protocol (RTP), to carry data that has real-time properties.

- The RTP control protocol (RTCP), to monitor the quality of service and to convey information about the participants in an on-going session. The latter aspect of RTCP may be sufficient for "loosely controlled" sessions, i.e., where there is no explicit membership control and set-up, but it is not necessarily intended to support all of an application's control communication requirements.

6.12.2 Protocol Structure - RTP (Real-Time Transport Protocol)

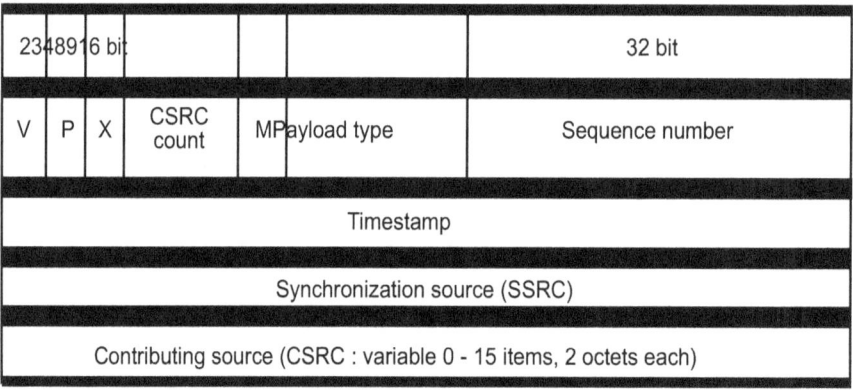

Fig. 6.21: Protocol Structure - RTP (Real-Time Transport Protocol)

This includes –

- **V** - Version. Identifies the RTP version.
- **P** - Padding. When set, the packet contains one or more additional padding octets at the end, which are not part of the payload.
- **X** - Extension bit. When set, the fixed header is followed by exactly one header extension, with a defined format.
- **CSRC count** -Contains the number of CSRC identifiers that follow the fixed header.

- **M - Marker.** The interpretation of the marker is defined by a profile. It is intended to allow significant events such as frame boundaries to be marked in the packet stream.
- **Payload type** - Identifies the format of the RTP payload and determines its interpretation by the application. A profile specifies a default static mapping of payload type codes to payload formats. Additional payload type codes may be defined dynamically through non-RTP means.
- **Sequence number** - Increments by one for each RTP data packet sent, and may be used by the receiver to detect packet loss and to restore packet sequence.
- **Timestamp** - Reflects the sampling instant of the first octet in the RTP data packet. The sampling instant must be derived from a clock that increments monotonically and linearly in time to allow synchronization and jitter calculations.
- **SSRC** - Synchronization source. This identifier is chosen randomly, with the intent that no two synchronization sources within the same RTP session will have the same SSRC identifier.
- **CSRC -** Contributing source identifiers list. Identifies the contributing sources for the payload contained in this packet.

6.12.3 RTP Features

- RTP provides end-to-end delivery services for data with real-time characteristics, such as interactive audio and video.
- Applications typically run RTP on top of UDP to make use of its multiplexing and checksum services. But efforts have been made to make RTP transport-independent so that it could be used on other protocols.
- RTP itself does not provide any mechanism to ensure timely delivery or provide other quality of service guarantees, but relies on lower-layer services to do so. RTP assumes that the underlying network is reliable and delivers packets in sequence.
- RTP is a protocol framework that is deliberately not complete. A complete specification of RTP for a particular application requires a profile specification or/and a payload format specification.
- RTP doesn't assume anything about the underlying network, except that it provides framing. Its original design target was the Internet, but it is intended to be protocol-independent. For example, test runs of RTP transmissions over ATM AAL5 and IPv6 are in progress.
- Field PT (payload type) of the RTP header identifies within seven bits the media type and encoding/compression format of the payload. At any given time, an RTP sender is supposed to send only a single type of payload, although during transmission, change of payload types may occur (e.g. in reaction to bad receiving rate feedback from the receiver via RTCP packets).

- RTP provides functionality suited for carrying real-time content, e.g. a timestamp and control mechanisms for synchronizing different streams with timing properties. Because RTP/RTPC is responsible for controlling the flow of one media stream, it will not automatically synchronize various streams. This has to happen at application level.

- The basis for flow and congestion control is provided by RTCP sender and receiver reports. We distinguish transient congestion and persistent congestion. By analyzing the inter-arrival jitter field of the sender report, we can measure the jitter over a certain interval and indicate congestion before it becomes persistent, hence resulting in packet loss.

6.13   RTCP: Real-Time Transport Control Protocol (or RTP Control Protocol)

The Real Time Transport Control Protocol (RTP control protocol or RTCP) is based on the periodic transmission of control packets to all participants in the session, using the same distribution mechanism as the data packets. The underlying protocol must provide multiplexing of the data and control packets, for example, using separate port numbers with UDP.

6.13.1 RTCP Performs Four Functions

1. RTCP provides feedback on the quality of the data distribution. This is an integral part of the RTP's role as a transport protocol and is related to the flow and congestion control functions of other transport protocols.

2. RTCP carries a persistent transport-level identifier for an RTP source called the canonical name or CNAME. Since the SSRC identifier may change if a conflict is discovered or a program is restarted, receivers require the CNAME to keep track of each participant. Receivers may also require the CNAME to associate multiple data streams from a given participant in a set of related RTP sessions, for example, to synchronize audio and video.

3. The first two functions require that all participants send RTCP packets, therefore the rate must be controlled in order for RTP to scale upto a large number of participants. By having each participant send its control packets to all the others, each can independently observe the number of participants. This number is used to calculate the rate at which the packets are sent.

4. An OPTIONAL function is to convey minimal session control information, for example, participant identification to be displayed in the user interface. This is most likely to be useful in "loosely controlled" sessions where participants enter and leave without membership control or parameter negotiation.

Functions 1 to 3, SHOULD be used in all environments, but particularly in the IP multicast environment. RTP application designers SHOULD avoid mechanisms that can only work in unicast mode and will not scale to larger numbers. Transmission of RTCP may be controlled separately for senders and receivers for cases such as unidirectional links where feedback from receivers is not possible.

6.13.2 Protocol Structure - RTCP (RTP Control Protocol)

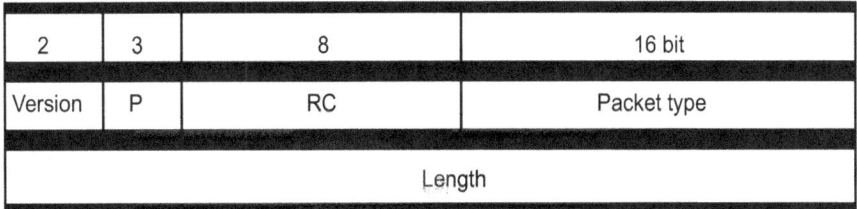

2	3	8	16 bit
Version	P	RC	Packet type
Length			

Fig. 6.22: Typical Protocol Structure - RTCP (RTP Control Protocol)

This includes –

- **Version -** Identifies the RTP version, which is the same in RTCP packets as in RTP data packets. The version defined by this specification is two (2).

- **P - Padding:** When set, this RTCP packet contains some additional padding octets at the end which are not part of the control information. The last octet of the padding is a count of how many padding octets should be ignored. Padding may be needed by some encryption algorithms with fixed block sizes. In a compound RTCP packet, padding should only be required on the last individual packet because the compound packet is encrypted as a whole.

- **RC -** Reception report count, the number of reception report blocks contained in this packet. A value of zero is valid. Packet type contains the constant 200 to identify this as an RTCP SR packet.

- **Length -** The length of this RTCP packet in 32-bit words minus one, including the header and any padding. (The offset of one makes zero a valid length and avoids a possible infinite loop in scanning a compound RTCP packet, while counting 32-bit words avoids a validity check for a multiple of 4.)

6.14 UDP: User Datagram Protocol

1. UDP is a connectionless transport layer (layer 4) protocol in OSI model, which provides a simple and unreliable message service for transaction-oriented services.

2. UDP is basically an interface between IP and upper-layer processes.

3.   UDP protocol ports distinguish multiple applications running on a single device from one another.

4.   Since many network applications may be running on the same machine, computers need something to make sure the correct software application on the destination computer gets the data packets from the source machine, and some way to make sure replies get routed to the correct application on the source computer.

5.   This is accomplished through the use of the UDP "port numbers".

6.   **For example, if a station wished to use a Domain Name System (DNS) on the station 128.1.123.1, it would address the packet to station 128.1.123.1 and insert destination port number 53 in the UDP header.**

7.   **The source port number identifies the application on the local station that requested domain name server, and all response packets generated by the destination station should be addressed to that port number on the source station.**

8.   Unlike the TCP, UDP adds no reliability, flow-control, or error-recovery functions to IP. Because of UDP's simplicity, UDP headers contain fewer bytes and consume less network overhead than TCP.

9.   **UDP is useful in situations where the reliability mechanisms of TCP are not necessary, such as in cases where a higher-layer protocol might provide error and flow control, or real time data transportation is required.**

UDP is the transport protocol for several well-known application-layer protocols, including Network File System (NFS) , Simple Network Management Protocol (SNMP) , Domain Name System (DNS) and Trivial File Transfer Protocol (TFTP).

6.14.1 Protocol Structure - UDP User Datagram Protocol Header

16	32 bit
Source port	Destination port
Length	Checksum
Data	

Fig. 6.23: Protocol Structure - UDP User Datagram Protocol Header

This includes –

•   **Source port** - Source port is an optional field. When used, it indicates the port of the sending process and may be assumed to be the port to which a reply should be addressed in the absence of any other information. If not used, a value of zero is inserted.

- **Destination port** - Destination port has a meaning within the context of a particular Internet destination address.
- **Length** - It is the length in octets of this user datagram, including this header and the data. The minimum value of the length is eight.
- **Checksum** - The sum of a pseudo header of information from the IP header, the UDP header and the data, padded with zero octets at the end, if necessary, to make a multiple of two octets.
- **Data** - Contains upper-level data information.

6.15 Introduction to Speech Coding Technologies

Pulse Code Modulation (PCM) is a method of converting an analog signal into digital form. The information contained in instantaneous samples of analog signal is represented by digital words in a serial bit stream.

Apart from PCM, there are many other methods of converting analog signal into digital form. To list a few –

(i)   Delta Modulation (DM).

(ii)   Differential Pulse Code Modulation (DPCM).

(iii)   Adaptive Delta Modulation (ADM).

In communication systems, it is always better to use digital communication than analog communication because of the advantages of digital communication such as –

1.   Digital communication has better noise performance i.e. it can withstand channel noise and distortion, provided they are within limits.

2.   The hardware is inexpensive. There is also flexibility in implementation of circuit.

3.   It is possible to multiplex signals from several sources.

4.   Regenerative repeaters can be employed in long distances communication.

5.   Low error rate, high fidelity and security are the advantages offered by digital signals as they can be coded accordingly.

6.   Digital signal storage is relatively easy and inexpensive.

Of course, the bandwidth requirement for digital transmission is more than that of analog. But above advantages make digital communication a preferred choice over analog.

6.15.1 PCM Generation and Reconstruction

The PCM signal is generated by carrying out three basic operations.

(i)   Sampling,   (ii) Quantizing,   (iii) Encoding.

The reconstruction involves –

(i)   Decoding,   (ii) Filtering (LPF).

The block diagram of PCM system is shown in Fig. 6.24. Let us discuss this in detail.

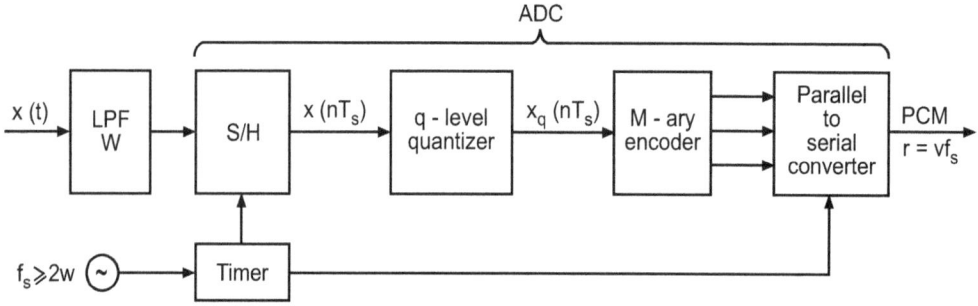

(a) PCM Transmitter

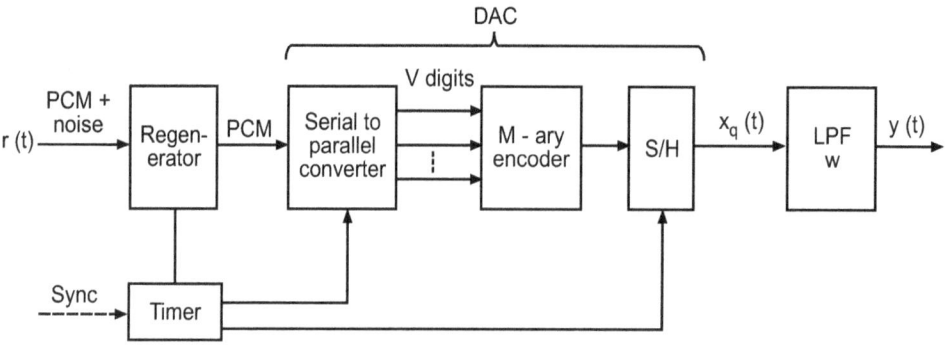

(b) PCM Receiver

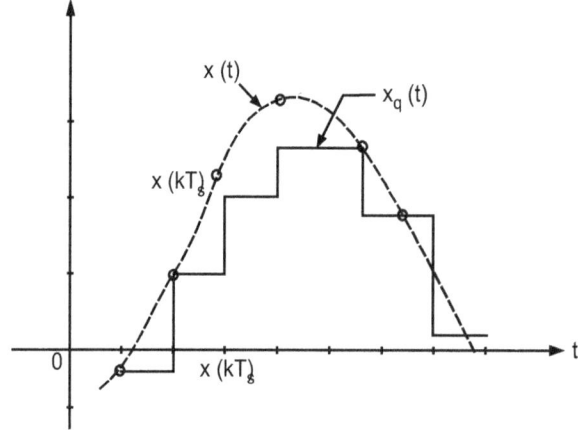

(c) Reconstructed Waveform

Fig. 6.24

6.15.1.1 Low Pass Filter

In order to convert an analog signal into digital form, we need to first sample the signal. In order to avoid the effect of aliasing resulting form under sampling, we need to limit the signal in bandwidth. Hence, we pass the signal which is time limited and hence having infinite bandwidth through a low pass filter. This filter is also called **antialias filter.**

6.15.1.2 Sampling

The low pass filtered analog signal is sampled with sampling rate slightly above Nyquist rate. This will create a guard band ($f_s > 2W$) to facilitate use of practical low pass filter for reconstruction. The sampling operation generates a flat-top PAM signal as shown in Fig. 6.25.

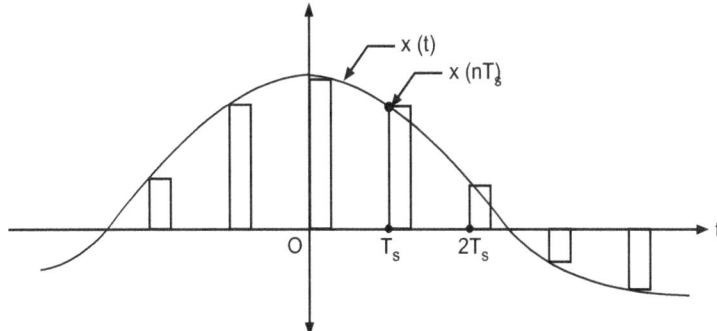

Fig. 6.25: Sampling Process

6.15.1.3 Quantizing

Sampling processes train of samples with amplitude depending on the instant of sampling i.e. $g(nT_s)$. If the signal $x(t)$ ranges from $+A$ to $-A$, there will be infinite levels $g(nT_s)$ can assume between this range. In order to convert the samples into bit stream, we need to limit the number of levels of sampled signal. For this the amplitude range $(-A, A)$, is divided to finite number of levels and the sampled amplitude is approximated to nearest possible level. This process is called quantizing. It is shown in Fig. 6.26.

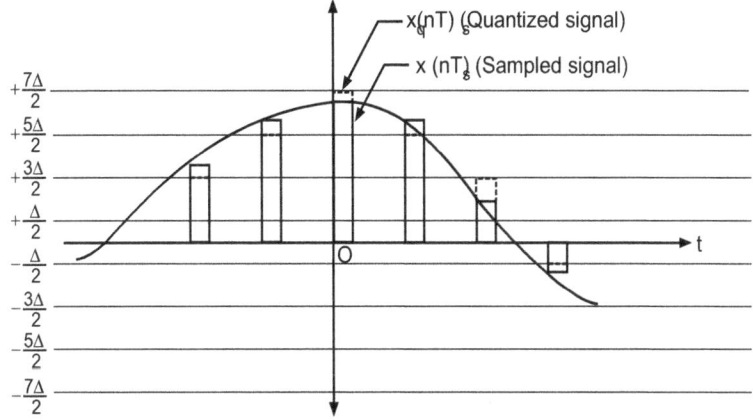

Fig. 6.26: Quantization Process

The difference between the two adjacent representation levels is called step size (Δ). Quantizer can be of uniform or non-uniform type. In uniform quantizer, the representation levels are uniformly spaced. In non-uniform quantizer, the approximated levels are spaced non-uniformly.

The quantizer characteristics can be midtread or midrise type. The input-output characteristics of these types of quantizers are shown in Fig. 6.27 (a) and (b).

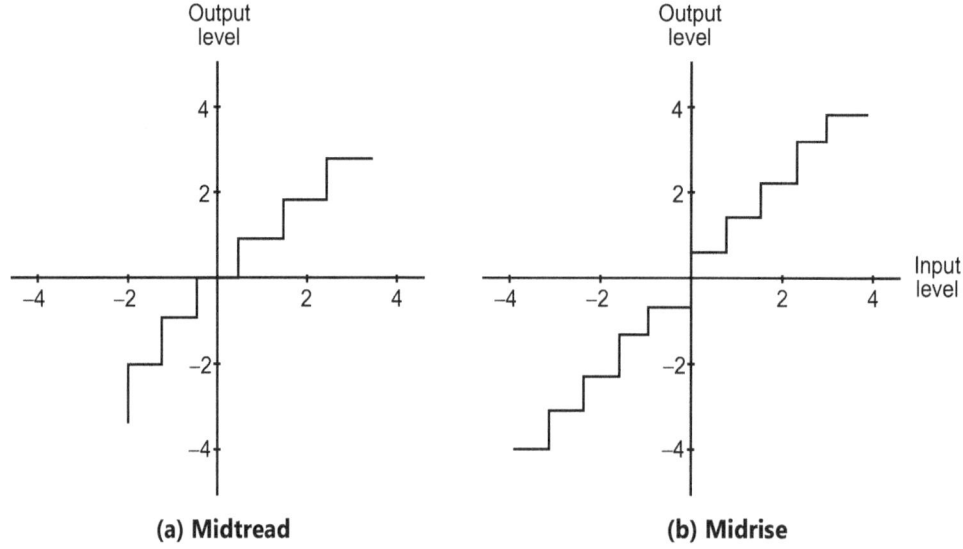

(a) Midtread   **(b) Midrise**

Fig. 6.27: Quantization Types

6.15.1.4 Encoding

The quantized signal x_q (nT_s) can be converted into digital format. This process is called encoding. The signal can be encoded using any one of the following techniques.

   (i)   **Binary code:** It represents each quantized amplitude into 0's and 1's.

   (ii) **Ternary code:** It represents each quantized level into three levels.

   (iii) **M-ary code:** It represents each quantized amplitude into M levels. (More than 3).

However, maximum advantages over the effect of noise in transmission medium is obtained by using a binary code. It is because binary symbols withstand relatively high level of noise and are easy to regenerate.

There are several ways to establish one-to-one correspondence between representation level and code word. e.g. We can use an encoder which makes 'n' sequential comparisons to generate n-bit code word. The level is compared with a voltage obtained by a combination of reference voltages proportional to 2^7, 2^6, 2^5, ..., 2^0. Hence, if we are using 3-bit PCM, then we can have $2^3 = 8$ quantization levels into which we have to divide the signal amplitudes – A_{max} to + A_{max}. The quantized output can be encoded in 3-bit format as follows.

Table 6.8

Quantized Level	Encoder Output
$-A_{max}$	000
$-A_{max}/4$	001
$-2A_{max}/4$	010
$-A_{max}/4$	011
$+A_{max}/4$	100
$+2A_{max}/4$	101
$+3A_{max}/4$	110
$+A_{max}$	111

The number of bits required for encoding a sample depends on number of quantization levels. If there are L quantization levels, then number of bits required for encoding a sample will be $\log_2$ L. In other words, if we use v bits for encoding, there will be 2^v quantization levels.

6.15.1.5 Regeneration

The most important feature of PCM system lies in ability to control distortion and noise. This is achieved by reconstructing the PCM signal by means of chain of regenerative repeaters located at sufficiently close spacing. It consists of circuit which reshapes the distorted signal into clean pulses.

6.15.1.6 Decoding

The first operation in the receiver is to regenerate the received pulses (1's and 0's). These pulses are regrouped into code words and decoded into quantized signal.

The decoding process involves generating a pulse whose amplitude is linear sum of 1's and 0's in the codeword (similar to binary to decimal conversion). This process is also called Digital to Analog Conversion (DAC).

6.15.1.7 Reconstruction Filters

The decoded output (DAC output) is staircase waveform. A low pass filter, whose cut-off frequency is equal to message bandwidth W Hz, is used to smoothen out the DAC output as shown in Fig. 6.24 (c).

6.15.1.8 Bandwidth Requirement of PCM

How much bandwidth is required for transmission of PCM signal? If the signal bandwidth is W Hz, then it requires to be sampled at a rate 2W samples per second.

If each sample is encoded into v bits, then the bit rate i.e. number of bits per second will be,

$$\text{Bit rate (r)} = \text{Number of samples per second} \propto \text{Number of bits per sample}$$

$$\therefore \qquad r = f_s \times v$$

$$\therefore \qquad \boxed{r = vf_s} \qquad \qquad \text{... (6.1)}$$

Therefore, bandwidth needed for PCM will be,

$$B_T = \frac{1}{2} \times r = \frac{1}{2} vf_s \qquad \qquad \text{... (6.2)}$$

The minimum bandwidth requirement for transmission of PCM signal will be when $f_s = 2W$

$$\therefore \qquad (B_T)_{min} = \frac{1}{2} v \times 2^W v \times W \qquad \qquad \text{... (6.3)}$$

Example 6.1: An analog signal with maximum frequency 3 kHz is transmitted using binary PCM. The number of quantization levels used are 16. Find minimum bandwidth requirement.

Solution: Given: $\qquad$ W $= 3$ kHz

$\qquad$ Number of quantization levels $= L = 16$

$\qquad \therefore \quad$ Sampling rate, $f_s = 2 \times W$

$$= 2 \times 3 = 6 \text{ kHz}$$

Since, $L = 2^v$

Number of bits per sample (v) $= \log_2 L$

$$= \log_2 16$$

$$= 4$$

$\therefore$ Bit rate of this system,

$$r = v \times f_s$$

$$= 4 \times 6 \text{ kHz}$$

$$= 24 \text{ kHz}$$

Minimum bandwidth required,

$$(B_T)_{min} = \frac{1}{2} \times v \times f_s$$

$$= \frac{1}{2} \times 24$$

$$= 12 \text{ kHz}$$

6.15.2 Quantization Noise

The process of quantization introduces quantization error in the PCM signal. This is because sampled output is approximated to nearest level. If signal x (t) is sampled at a rate $\frac{1}{T_s}$ then x (nT_s) will be the sample at $t = nT_s$. Let us say that it is approximated to x_q (nT_s) after quantization. The error difference $q = x(nT_s) - x_q(nT_s)$ is called quantization noise.

Quantizer output for a typical input signal is shown in Fig. 6.28 (a). The plot of quantization error alongwith the quantized signal is shown in Fig. 6.28 (b).

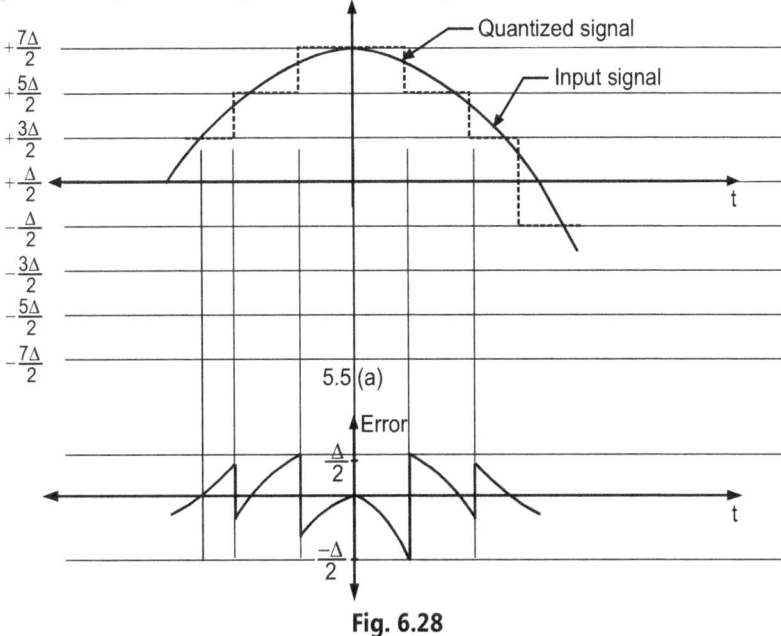

Fig. 6.28

It can be seen from the quantization error graph that the quantization error takes on any value between $+ \Delta/2$ and $- \Delta/2$. Thus, it is uniformly distributed random variable with zero mean. Let us denote this variable as Q. The probability density function for Q is plotted in Fig. 6.29.

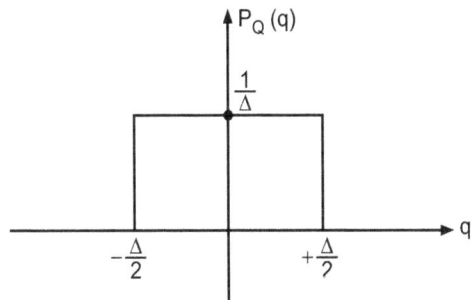

Fig. 6.29: PDF of Quantization Error

Hence,
$$p_Q(q) = \begin{cases} \dfrac{1}{\Delta} & ; \quad -\dfrac{\Delta}{2} \le q \le +\dfrac{\Delta}{2} \\ 0 & ; \quad \text{Otherwise} \end{cases} \qquad \dots (6.4)$$

The variance can be calculated as,

$$\sigma_Q^2 = \int_{-\Delta/2}^{\Delta/2} q^2\, p_Q(q)\, dq$$

$$= \int_{-\Delta/2}^{\Delta/2} q^2 \times \dfrac{1}{\Delta}\, dq$$

$$= \dfrac{1}{\Delta} \left[\dfrac{q^3}{3} \right]_{-\Delta/2}^{\Delta/2}$$

$$= \dfrac{\Delta^2}{12} \qquad \dots (6.5)$$

This variance is mean square value of quantization noise. Since mean value is zero, $[E(X^2)] = \sigma_X^2 - m_X^2$]. Hence, this is quantization noise power.

∴   Quantization noise power,

$$P_{Nq} = \dfrac{\Delta^2}{12}$$

Let us consider an input whose amplitude ranges from $-A_{max}$ to $+A_{max}$. Assuming uniform quantizer of midrise type, step size is given by,

$$\Delta = \dfrac{2\,A_{max}}{L} \qquad \dots (6.6)$$

where, L is the number of representation levels.

Let v be number of bits per sample.

∴ $L = 2^v$ $\dots (6.7)$

or $v = \log_2 L$ $\dots (6.8)$

∴ $\Delta = \dfrac{2\,A_{max}}{2^v}$ $\dots (6.9)$

Hence, quantization noise will be,

∴ $$P_{Nq} = \dfrac{\Delta^2}{12} = \dfrac{4\,A_{max}^2}{2^{2v} \times 12} = \dfrac{A_{max}^2}{3L^2}$$

$$= \dfrac{A_{max}^2}{3 \times 2^{2v}} \qquad \dots (6.10)$$

Therefore, the output signal-to-noise ratio of uniform quantizer will be,

$$\left(\frac{S}{N}\right)_0 = \frac{P_s}{P_{Nq}}$$

$$= \left(\frac{3\,P_s}{\frac{2}{A_{max}}}\right) \times 2^{2v} \qquad \qquad \dots (6.11)$$

This equation shows that signal-to-noise ratio is proportional to bits per sample v. This is obvious from the fact that more number of bits per sample will increase number of levels which in turn will decrease step size. But then this will require more bandwidth as, $B_T = \frac{1}{2}\,vf_s$.

If input signal is a sinusoidal signal, then signal power is,

$$P_s = \frac{A_{max}^2}{2}$$

$$\therefore \qquad \left(\frac{S}{N}\right)_0 = \frac{3 \times A_{max}^2/2}{A_{max}^2} \times 2^{2v}$$

$$= \frac{3}{2}\,2^{2v} \qquad \qquad \dots (6.12)$$

$$\therefore \qquad \left(\frac{S}{N}\right)_0 \text{ in dB} = 10\,\log_{10}\left(\frac{3}{2}\,2^{2v}\right)$$

$$= 10\,\log_{10}\frac{3}{2} + 10\,\log_{20} 2^{2v}$$

$$= 1.8 + 20\,v \times \log 2$$

$$= 1.8 + 6\,v \text{ dB} \qquad \qquad \dots (6.13)$$

Following Table 6.9 shows various values of L and v with corresponding (SNR)$_0$.

Table 6.9

L (Levels)	v (bits / sample)	SNR (dB)
256	8	49.8
128	7	43.8
64	6	37.8
32	5	31.8

Analog signals such as voice and music are specified in terms of crest factor. Crest factor is defined as ratio of peak to r.m.s. value.

$$\text{i.e.} \qquad \text{Crest factor} = \frac{\left|x\,(t)\right|_{max}}{\sigma_x} \qquad \qquad \dots (6.14)$$

If x (t) is normalised, i.e. $\left|x\,(t)\right|_{max} \leq 1$, then mean square value $\sigma_x^2 \ll 1$ implies large crest factor.

Now, consider the equation for signal to noise ratio.

$$\left(\frac{S}{N}\right)_0 = \frac{3\,P_S}{A_{max}^2} \,\infty\, 2^{2V}$$

If x (t) is normalised i.e. $\left|A_{max}\right| \leq 1$,

$$\therefore \qquad \left(\frac{S}{N}\right)_0 = 3 \infty P_S \infty 2^{2V} = 3\,P_S\,L^2$$

P_S is the signal power at the destination. If we normalise P_S i.e. $P_S \leq 1$, then,

$$\left(\frac{S}{N}\right)_0 \text{ in dB} = 10 \log (3 \infty 2^{2V}\,P_S)$$

$$= 4.8 + 6\,v\, dB \quad \text{(Putting } P_S = 1) \qquad\qquad ... (6.15)$$

e.g. voice telephone PCM system have v = 8. Hence, the signal-to-noise ratio for this system is,

$$\therefore \qquad \left(\frac{S}{N}\right)_0 \leq 52 \text{ dB}$$

Signals with large crest factor will have this ratio much less than 4.8 + 6 v. Since in case of these signals,

$$10 \log (3 \times 2^{2V} \times P_S) < 4.8 + 6\,v$$

as

$$\sigma_X^2 = P_S << 1$$

6.15.3 Multiplexing and Synchronization

One of the advantages PCM has is, number of signals can be simultaneously transmitted over a single channel. This is possible with time division multiplexing of the signals. There is a time available between two samples of same source where we can accommodate samples from other sources. Of course, the signalling rate (bit rate) will increase and bandwidth requirement also. Consider a case of N identical sources having maximum frequency N Hz. If these sources are sampled at rate f_S and then multiplexed then the signalling rate will be,

$$r = N \times v \times f_S \text{ bps}$$

where, v is the number of bits used per sample.

Hence, bandwidth requirement will be,

$$B_T = \frac{1}{2} \times r = \frac{1}{2} N \times v \times f_S \text{ Hz} \qquad\qquad ... (6.16)$$

The minimum bandwidth required will be for

$$f_S = 2W$$

$$\therefore \qquad (B_T)_{min} = \frac{1}{2} \times N \times v \times 2 \times W$$

$$= N \times v \times W \, Hz \qquad \qquad ...(6.17)$$

But multiplexing warrants timing operations at transmitter and receiver to be synchronized properly. Hence, we require a local clock at the receiver to keep the same time as that of clock at the transmitter.

Example 6.2: The bandwidth of TV video plus audio signal is 4.5 MHz. If this signal is converted to PCM bit stream with 1024 quantization levels, determine number of bits/sec. generated by the PCM system. Assume that the signal is sampled at a rate 20% above Nyquist rate.

Solution: Given:

$$W = 4.5 \, MHz$$

$$L = 1024$$

Now, v

$$= \log_2 L$$

$$\therefore \qquad v = \log_2 1024 = 10 \, bits$$

$$Nyquist \, rate = 2 \times W$$

$$= 2 \times 4.5$$

$$= 9 \, MHz$$

$$Sampling \, rate = 9 + 0.2 \times 9$$

$$= 10.8 \, MHz$$

$$\therefore \qquad Bit \, rate = \frac{1}{2} \times v \times f_s$$

$$= 10 \times 10.8 \times 10^6 \, bits/sec.$$

$$= 108 \times 10^6 \, bits/sec. = 108 \, Mbps$$

Example 6.3: The output signal-to-noise ratio of 10-bit PCM was found to be 30 dB. The desired SNR is 42 dB. It was decided to increase SNR to desired level by increasing number of quantization levels. Find fractional increase in transmission bandwidth required for this increase in SNR.

Solution: Given:

$$\left(\frac{S}{N}\right)_{01} = 30 \, dB$$

$$v_1 = 10$$

$$\therefore \qquad \left(\frac{S}{N}\right)_{01} = 1000$$

$$\left(\frac{S}{N}\right)_{02} = 42 \, dB = 15{,}849$$

$$\left(\frac{S}{N}\right)_{01} = \frac{3 P_s}{A_{max}^2} \times 2^{2V_1}$$

$$\left(\frac{S}{N}\right)_{02} = \frac{3 P_s}{A_{max}^2} \times 2^{2V_2}$$

$$\therefore \quad \frac{10,000}{15,849} = \frac{2^{2V_1}}{2^{2V_2}}$$

$$0.63095 = \frac{2^{2V_1}}{2^{2V_2}}$$

$$0.63095 \times 2^{2V_2} = 2^{2V_1}$$

$$\log_2 0.63095 + 2 v_2 = 2 v_1$$

$$- 0.6644 + 2 v_2 = 2120$$

$$v_2 = 10.33322$$

$$\therefore \quad v_2 \simeq 11$$

$$\text{Bandwidth required for first case} = \frac{10 f_s}{2}$$

$$\text{Bandwidth required for second case} = \frac{11 f_s}{2}$$

$$\therefore \quad \text{Fractional increase in BW} = \frac{11 - 10}{10}$$

$$= 0.1$$

$$\therefore \quad \text{Fractional increase in BW} = 10\%$$

Example 6.4: A telephone signal with cut-off frequency of 4 kHz is digitized into 8-bit PCM sampled at Nyquist rate. Calculate baseband transmission bandwidth and quantization S/N ratio.

Solution: Given:

$$W = 4 \text{ kHz}$$

$$v = 8$$

$$\therefore \quad f_s = 8 \text{ kHz}$$

$$\text{Bit rate, } r = v f_s$$

$$= 8 \times 8$$

$$= 64 \text{ kbps}$$

$$\therefore \quad \text{Bandwidth, } B_T = \frac{1}{2} \, r$$

$$= \frac{1}{2} \times 64 \text{ kHz}$$

$$= 32 \text{ kHz}$$

For voice signal, $\left(\frac{S}{N}\right)_0 = 4.8 + 6\,v$

$$= 4.8 + 6 \times 8$$

$$= 52.8 \text{ dB}$$

Example 6.5: A signal m (t) bandlimited to 3 kHz is sampled at a rate $33\frac{1}{3}$ % higher than Nyquist rate. The maximum acceptable error in the sample amplitude (the minimum quantization error) is 0.5% of peak amplitude m_p. The quantized samples are binary coded. Find minimum bandwidth of a channel required to transmit the encoded binary signal. If such 24 channels are time division multiplexed, determine minimum transmission bandwidth.

Solution: Given: W = 3 kHz

$\therefore$ Nyquist rate = 6 kHz

$\therefore$ Sampling rate = 6 kHz + $33\frac{1}{3}$ % of 6 kHz

$$= \ 6 + 2$$

$$= 8 \text{ kHz}$$

Maximum quantization error = $\pm \dfrac{\Delta}{2}$

$\therefore$ $\dfrac{\Delta}{2}$ = 5% of Λ_{max}

$\therefore$ $\dfrac{\Delta}{2}$ = 0.005 A_{max}

Δ = 0.01 A_{max}

Now, L $= \dfrac{2\,A_{max}}{\Delta}$

$\therefore$ L = $\dfrac{2\,A_{max}}{0.01 \times A_{max}}$

$$= 200$$

$\therefore$ v = $\log_2 L$

$\therefore$ v = $\log_2 200$

$$\approx 7.6$$

$\therefore$ v = 8

Transmission bandwidth requirement (minimum),

$$(B_T)_{min} = v \times W$$
$$= 8 \times 3$$
$$= 24 \text{ kHz}$$

If 24 channels are multiplexed, then, bandwidth requirement,

$$B_T = N \times v \times W$$
$$= 24 \times 18 \times 3$$
$$= 576 \text{ kHz}$$

Example 6.6: An audio signal has its spectral components limited to frequency band of 0.3 to 3.3 kHz. A PCM signal is generated with sampling rate of 8000 samples/sec. The required output signal to quantizing noise ratio is 30 dB.

    (i)   Calculate the minimum number of uniform quantization levels required.

    (ii)   How many minimum number of bits per sample are needed?

    (iii)   Calculate minimum system bandwidth required.

Solution: Given: $W = 3.3 \text{ kHz}$ (Maximum frequency)

$$f_s = 8 \text{ kHz}$$

We have, $\qquad\qquad \left(\dfrac{S}{N}\right)_{dB} = 4.8 + 6v$

$\therefore \qquad\qquad\qquad 30 = 4.8 + 6v$

$\therefore \qquad\qquad\qquad v = 4.2 \text{ bits}$

$\therefore \qquad\qquad\qquad v = 5 \text{ bits}$

$\qquad\qquad$ Number of levels $= 2^v$

$$= 2^5$$
$$= 32$$

Minimum transmission bandwidth required,

$$(B_T)_{min} = v \times W$$
$$= 5 \times 3.3$$
$$= 16.5 \text{ kHz}$$

6.15.4 Non-Uniform Quantization and Companding

In case of uniform quantizer, the representation levels are uniformly spaced i.e. step-size remains constant for the entire range. In case of music and speech signals, the range of voltage variations is very high because of loud talks and weak talks. In other words, the crest factor of these signals is very large. If uniform quantization is used in such signals, the weak passages will have more quantization errors compared to loud passages.

Non-uniform quantization can be used in such signals, so that weak passages are given protection at the expense of loud passages. The step-size is increased as the separation of the input-output amplitude characteristic is increased. The quantization error $x (nT_s) - x_q (nT_s)$ is therefore, variable. The PDF of which is shown in Fig. 6.30.

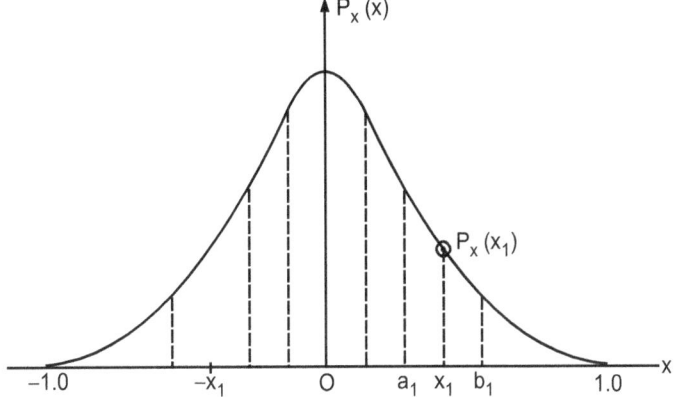

Fig. 6.30: Message PDF with Non-Uniform Quantization Bands

The quantization levels are closely spaced near $x = 0$ and widely spaced for large values of $|x(t)|$ as shown in Fig. 6.31.

The quantization noise power in this case can be calculated as below. If we consider a sample value $x(nT_s)$ in the band $a_i < x < b_i$ which is to be quantized to x_i, the quantization error will have mean squares value given by,

$$\overline{q_e^2} = \int_{a_i}^{b_i} (x_i - x)^2 \, p_x(x) \, dx \qquad \dots (6.18)$$

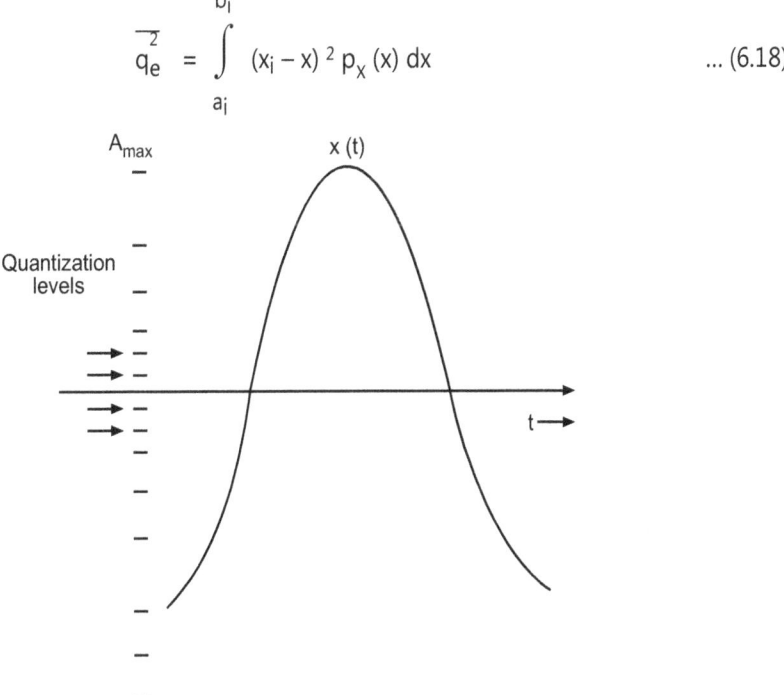

Fig. 6.31: Non-uniform Quantization

If there are total L levels, then the quantization noise will be sum of all mean square values given by,

$$\sigma_q^2 \;=\; 2 \sum_{i=1}^{L/2} \overline{q_e^2} \qquad\qquad \text{... (6.19)}$$

$b_i - a_i = \Delta_i$ is small enough for the approximation,

$$p_X(x) \;\simeq\; p_X(x_i) \qquad \text{Over each integration band}$$

$$\therefore \qquad \overline{q_e^2} \;=\; p_X(x_i) \int_{x_i - \Delta_i/2}^{x_i + \Delta_i/2} (x_i - x)^2 \, dx \qquad\qquad \text{... (6.20)}$$

$$= p_X(x_i) \times \frac{\Delta_i^3}{12} \qquad\qquad \text{... (6.21)}$$

$$\text{and} \qquad\qquad \sigma_q^2 \;=\; \frac{1}{6} \sum_{i=1}^{L/2} p_X(x_i)\, \Delta_i^3 \qquad\qquad \text{... (6.22)}$$

If all the intervals are equal i.e. for uniform quantizer,

$$\Delta_i \;=\; \frac{2}{L} \qquad\qquad\qquad p_X(x_i) \;=\; \frac{1}{2}$$

$$\therefore \qquad\qquad \sigma_q^2 \;=\; \frac{1}{6} \times \frac{1}{2} \times \left(\frac{2}{L}\right)^3 \times \left(\frac{L}{2}\right) \qquad\qquad \text{... (6.23)}$$

$$= \frac{1}{3L^2} \;=\; \frac{1}{3} \times \frac{1}{\left(\dfrac{2}{\Delta_i}\right)^2} \;=\; \frac{\Delta_i^2}{12}$$

which is quantization noise for uniform quantizer.

6.15.4.1 Compander

It is possible to minimize quantization noise by proper selection of a_i, b_i and x_i. But, then this will require knowledge of signals PDF. This will also require custom tailored hardware. Hence, in practice, a compressed signal is applied to uniform quantizer. The compression characteristics are shown in Fig. 6.32.

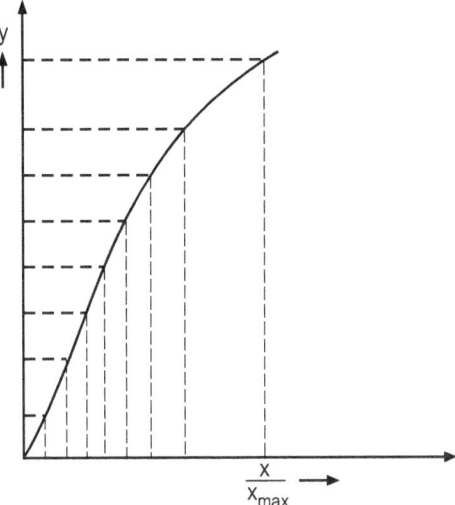

Fig. 6.32: Compression Characteristics

The horizontal axis is normalised input signal $|x(t)|/x_{max}$. The vertical axis is output signal.

The compressed sample must be restored to their original values at receiver by using an expander with complimentary characteristics of compressor. The compressor and expander together are called compander.

One important point here is that, when we compress a signal, its bandwidth will increase. But we are not compressing the original analog signal, but the sampled version of analog signal. And as long as number of samples per second do not change, there will be no change in bandwidth. The post detection signal-to-noise ratio for companded PCM will be P_s/σ_q^2, where, σ_q^2 is given by equation (6.22) rewritten here,

$$\sigma_q^2 = \frac{1}{\sigma} \sum_{i=1}^{L/2} p_X(x_i) \, \Delta_i^3$$

Let us now find σ_q^2 for the compressor curve. The curve is drawn in Fig. 6.33.

It is a normalised curve and shows positive part only since it is odd symmetric. [i.e. $y(x) = -y(|x|)$].

The slope of this curve is $y'(x) = \dfrac{dy(x)}{dx}$.   ... (6.24)

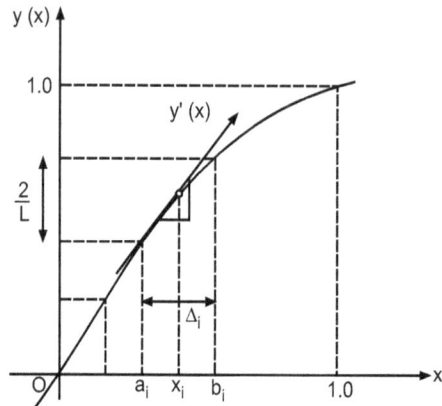

Fig. 6.33: Compressor Curve

The value of slope at $x = x_i$ can be given by,

$$y'(x_i) = \frac{(2/L)}{\Delta_i} \qquad \text{... (6.25)}$$

$\therefore$

$$\Delta_i^2 = \frac{(2/L)^2}{[y'(x_i)]^2}$$

$$= \frac{4}{L^2 [y'(x_i)]^2} \qquad \text{... (6.26)}$$

Hence, equation (6.22) becomes,

$$\sigma_q^2 = \frac{1}{6} \sum_{i=1}^{L/2} p_x(x) \times \frac{4}{L^2 [y'(x_i)]^2} \times \Delta_i$$

$$= \frac{2}{3 L^2} \sum_{i=1}^{L/2} \frac{p_x(x_i)}{[y'(x_i)]^2}$$

$$\simeq \frac{2}{3 L^2} \int_0^1 \frac{p_x(x)}{[y'(x)]^2} \, dx \qquad \text{... (6.27)}$$

Converting summation to integration $h_i \to dx$

$\therefore$

$$\left(\frac{S}{N}\right)_0 = \frac{P_s}{\sigma_q^2} = \frac{3 L^2 \times P_s}{I_y} \qquad \text{... (6.28)}$$

where,

$$I_y = 2 \int_0^1 \frac{p_x(x)}{[y'(x)]^2} \, dx \qquad \text{... (6.29)}$$

It can be seen from above expression that if $I_y < 1$, then $\left(\frac{S}{N}\right)_0 > 3 \, L^2 \, P_s$ meaning companding improves PCM performance by reducing quantization noise.

A-Law and μ-Law:

In practice, there are two compression laws which are in use viz. μ-law and A-law, μ-law is used in North America and Japan and A-law is used in Europe and rest of the world and international routes. The μ-law is defined as,

$$y(x) = \frac{\log_e\left(1 + \mu\frac{|x|}{x_{max}}\right)}{\log_e(1 + \mu)} \; Sgn\left(\frac{x}{x_{max}}\right) \qquad \frac{|x|}{x_{max}} \le 1 \; ... (6.30)$$

μ is called compression parameter which determines degree of compression. x_{max} is maximum input level that can be quantized without overload. The plot of y (x) against x/x_{max} is shown in Fig. 6.34.

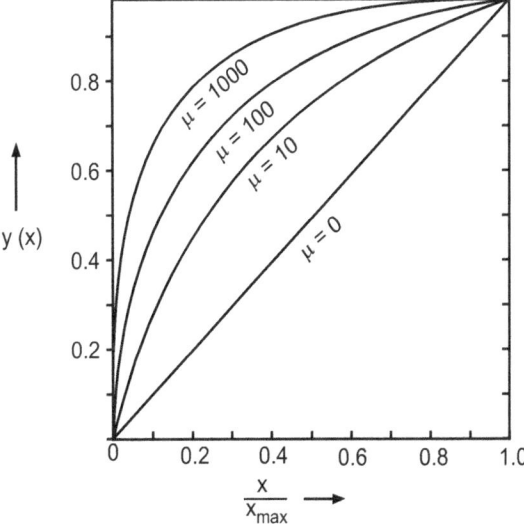

Fig. 6.34: μ-law Characteristics

μ = 0 represents uniform quantization. For better performance, values of μ above 100 are performed. An optimum value of μ = 255 is used in practice.

We can find y' (x) to find $\left(\frac{S}{N}\right)_0$ of μ-law compander.

$$y'(x) = \frac{\mu}{\log_e(1 + \mu)} \times \frac{1}{1 + \mu|x|} \qquad\qquad ... (6.31)$$

where, $|x|$ is normalised input i.e. $|x| \le 1$.

Substituting equation (6.31) in equation (6.29),

$$I_y = 2\int_0^1 P_x(x) \times \frac{[\log(1 + \mu) \cdot (1 + \mu|x|)]^2}{\mu^2} \; dx$$

$$= \frac{[\log(1+\mu)]^2}{\mu^2} \times 2 \int_0^1 p_x(x)(1 + 2\mu|x| + \mu^2 x^2)\,dx$$

$$= 2[\log(1+\mu)]^2 \times \left[2 \int_0^1 p_x(x)\,dx + 4\mu \int_0^1 |x| p_x(d)\,dx \right.$$

$$\left. + 2\mu^2 \int_0^1 x^2 p_x(x)\,dx \right]$$

$$\therefore \qquad I_y = \frac{[\log_e(1+\mu)]^2}{\mu^2} \times (1 + 2\mu \times m_x + \mu^2 \sigma_x^2) \qquad \ldots (6.32)$$

Substituting equation (6.32) in equation (6.27),

$$\therefore \qquad \sigma_q^2 = \frac{3}{L^2}\left[\frac{\log_e(1+\mu)}{\mu} \right]^2 (1 + 2\mu m_x + \sigma_x^2)$$

$$\therefore \qquad \left(\frac{S}{N}\right)_0 = \frac{\sigma_x^2}{\sigma_q^2}$$

$$= \frac{3L^2}{[\log_e(1+\mu)]^2} \times \frac{\mu^2 \times \sigma_x^2}{(1 + 2\mu m_x + \sigma_x^2)}$$

$$\therefore \qquad \left(\frac{S}{N}\right)_0 = \frac{3L^2}{[\log_e(1+\mu)]^2} \infty \frac{1}{\left(1 + \dfrac{2m_x}{\mu\sigma_x^2} + \dfrac{1}{\mu^2 \sigma_x^2}\right)} \qquad \ldots (6.33)$$

Since $|x|$ is normalised m_x and σ_x^2 are both less than one. Hence, the second term can be neglected.

$$\therefore \qquad \left(\frac{S}{N}\right)_0 = \frac{3L^2}{[\log_e(1+\mu)]^2} \qquad \ldots (6.34)$$

$$\left(\frac{S}{N}\right)_0 dB = 6.02 v + \alpha \qquad \ldots (6.35)$$

where, $\qquad \alpha = 4.77 - 20\log_{10}[\log_e(1+\mu)]$

We need m_x and P_s to find exact $\left(\dfrac{S}{N}\right)_0$ of μ-law.

Experimentally it is observed that PDF of voice signal is given by,

$$p_X(x) = \frac{\lambda}{2} e^{-\lambda|x|}$$

$\therefore$ $$P_s = \sigma_x^2 = \frac{2}{\lambda^2} \qquad \text{and } m_X = E[X] = \frac{1}{\lambda} = \sqrt{\frac{P_s}{2}}$$

For $\mu = 255$, if we substitute above values in equation (6.32), we get,

$$I_y = 4.73 \times 10^{-4}(1 + 361\sqrt{P_s} + 65{,}025\,P_s)$$

If we plot $\left(\dfrac{S}{N}\right)_0$ against P_s, it can be seen that it remains constant over wide range of P_s as

shown in Fig. 6.35. The figure also shows $\left(\dfrac{S}{N}\right)_0$ graph without companding for comparison.

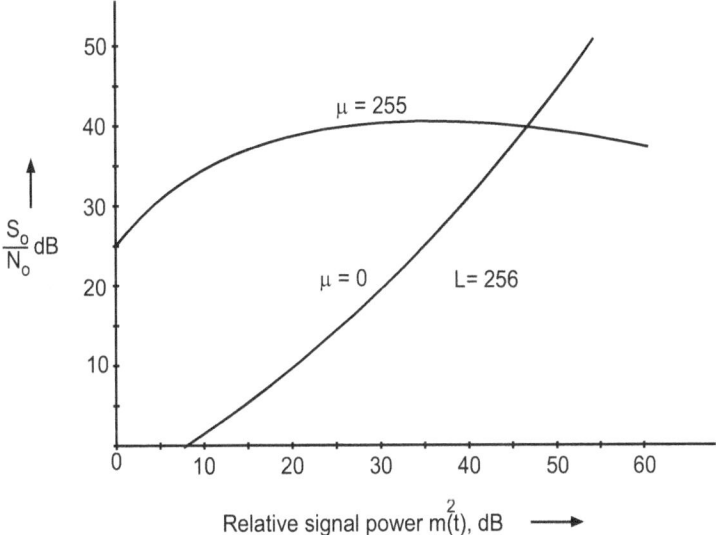

Fig. 6.35: Signal to Quantization-noise Ratio in PCM with and without Compression

Thus, μ-law companding provides fixed value of $\left(\dfrac{S}{N}\right)_0$ despite wide variations in P_s.

The **A-Law** compander is defined as,

$$y(x) = \frac{A\,|x|/x_{max}}{1 + \log_e A} \qquad\qquad 0 \le \frac{|x|}{x_{max}} \le \frac{1}{A} \quad \dots (6.36)$$

$$= \frac{1 + \log_e(A\,|x|/x_{max})}{1 + \log_e(A)} \qquad \frac{1}{A} \le \frac{|x|}{x_{max}} \le 1$$

A is called compression parameter and its practical values are near 100.

For uniform quantization, A = 1.

The plot of y (x) against normalised input $\dfrac{|x|}{x_{max}}$ is shown in Fig. 6.36.

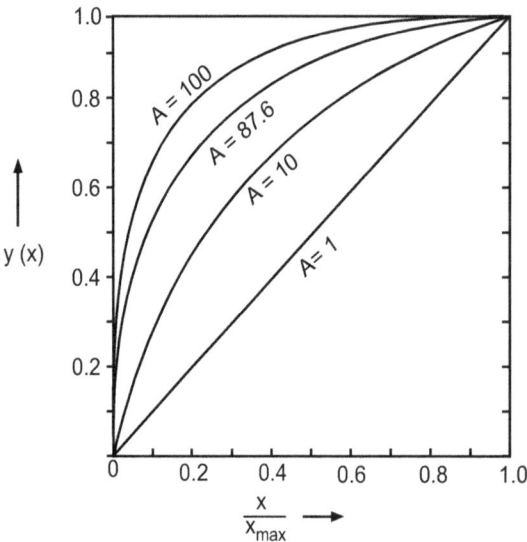

Fig. 6.36: A-law Characteristics

The signal to noise ratio for A-law compander is given by,

$$\left(\frac{S}{N}\right)_0 = \frac{3L^2}{[\log_e (1 + A)]^2} \qquad \text{... (6.37)}$$

$$\left(\frac{S}{N}\right)_0 \text{ in dB} = 6.02 + \alpha \qquad \text{... (6.38)}$$

where, $\alpha = 4.77 - 20 \log_{10} (1 + \log_e A)$

The logarithmic compressors like A-law and μ-law are implemented in practice using semiconductor diodes, as their V-I characteristic resembles compressor.

Another approach is to use linear approximation to the logarithmic characteristic.

Example 6.7: A signal of bandwidth 4 kHz is transmitted using a binary companded PCM with μ = 100. Calculate transmission bandwidth and output signal-to-noise ratio for –

    (i)   64 quantization levels.

    (ii) 256 quantization levels.

Comment on the results of transmission bandwidth of output SNR.

Solution: Given: W = 4 kHz

                      μ = 100

(i)   L = 64, v = 6

SNR ratio for PCM with µ-law is given by,

$$\left(\frac{S}{N}\right)_0 = \frac{3 \times L^2}{[\log_e (1 + \mu)]^2}$$

$$= \frac{3 \times 64 \times 64}{(\log 101)^2}$$

$$= 576.92$$

∴ $$\left(\frac{S}{N}\right)_0 \text{ in dB} = 10 \log 576.92$$

$$= 27.49 \text{ dB}$$

Bandwidth requirement (B_T) $= 6 \times 4 = 24$ kHz

(ii)   L = 256, v = 8

$$\left(\frac{S}{N}\right)_0 = \frac{3 \times L^2}{\log_e (1 + \mu)^2}$$

$$= \frac{3 \times 256 \times 256}{[\log_e (101)]^2}$$

$$= 9230.71$$

$$\left(\frac{S}{N}\right)_0 \text{ in dB} = 39.65 \text{ dB}$$

Bandwidth requirement, $B_T = n \times W = 8 \times 4 = 32$ kHz

6.15.5 pcm with Noise

The analog signal received at the receiver end of PCM system is corrupted by noise. Two types of noises are present in it.

(i)   Quantization noise caused by quantizer at the transmitter, the detailed analysis of which is covered earlier.

(ii)   Bit errors in recovered PCM signal. The bit errors are caused by channel noise and improper channel filtering.

In addition to this, there can be aliasing noise caused by filtering at transmitter end done purposely when the signal is not strictly bandlimited. Another distortion like aperture effect, might occur due to flat-top sampling.

6.15.5.1 Decoding Noise

Due to channel noise, an erroneous bit can occur in the codeword, which will result in decoding of wrong quantization level. This error is termed as **decoding noise.**

Let us analyse this noise for PCM with uniform quantization.

Let P_e be bit error probability $<< 1$.

v be number of bits in a codeword.

The probability of one error in a word will be vP_e, when $P_e << 1$. Probability of two or more errors can be negligibly small.

Consider a received codeword $b_0, b_1, b_2, ..., b_{v-1}$.

An error in the mth bit shifts the decoded level by an amount $= \dfrac{2}{L} \times 2^m$. Hence, the mean square error over the v bit positions will be,

$$\overline{e_m^2} = \frac{1}{v} \sum_{m=0}^{v-1} \left(\frac{2}{L} \times 2^m\right)^2 \qquad \text{... (6.39)}$$

$$= \frac{4}{vL^2} \cdot \sum_{m=0}^{v-1} 4^m$$

$$= \frac{4}{vL^2} \times (4^v - 1)/3$$

$$= \frac{4}{3v} \times \frac{L^2 - 1}{L^2} \qquad (\because 4^v = 2^{2v} = L^2)$$

$$\simeq \frac{4}{3v} \qquad \text{... (6.40)}$$

The decoding noise power will be,

$$\sigma_d^2 = vP_e \times \overline{e_m^2}$$

$$\simeq \frac{4}{3} vP_e \times \frac{4e}{3v} \qquad \text{... (6.41)}$$

$$\simeq \frac{4}{3P} P_e$$

The quantization noise power,

$$\sigma_q^2 = \frac{1}{3L^2} \qquad \text{... (6.42)}$$

Total destination noise power,

$$N_0 = \sigma_q^2 + \sigma_d^2 = \frac{1}{3L^2} + \frac{4}{3} P_e$$

$$= \frac{1 + 4L^2 P_e}{3L^2}$$

$$\therefore \qquad \left(\frac{S}{N}\right)_0 = \frac{3L^2}{1 + 4L^2 P_e} \ P_s \qquad \qquad ... (6.43)$$

If $P_e << \dfrac{1}{4L^2}$,

$$\left(\frac{S}{N}\right)_0 = 3L^2 P_s \qquad \qquad ... (6.44)$$

and if $P_e >> \dfrac{1}{4L^2}$,

$$\left(\frac{S}{N}\right)_0 = \frac{3}{4P_e} \ P_s \qquad \qquad ... (6.45)$$

Hence for small P_e, quantization noise is more significant; whereas for large P_e, decoding noise dominates.

The error probability P_e is determined from received signal-to-noise ratio $\left(\dfrac{S}{N}\right)_R$

i.e. $P_e = Q\left[\sqrt{\left(\dfrac{S}{N}\right)_R}\ \right]$

As $\left(\dfrac{S}{N}\right)_R$ falls below a particular threshold value, there is sharp decline in detected output

signal-to-noise ratio $\left(\dfrac{S}{N}\right)_D$. This is called threshold effect. It is caused by increasing errors.

Below the error threshold $P_e >> \dfrac{1}{4L^2}$, the errors occur frequently causing totally wrong reconstruction of waveforms.

6.15.5.2 Error Threshold

The PCM error threshold level is the point where decoding noise $\left(\dfrac{S}{N}\right)_D$ falls by 1 dB. But it is not possible to analyse error threshold from this definition. Hence, we will assume that decoding errors are negligible if $P_e << 10^{-5}$. Then we can obtain condition on $\left(\dfrac{S}{N}\right)_R$ for polar M-ary signalling.

$$P_e \ - \ 2\left(1 - \frac{1}{M}\right) Q\left[\sqrt{\frac{3}{M^2 - 1} \times \left(\frac{S}{N}\right)_R}\right] < 10^{-5}$$

Solving for minimum value of $\left(\dfrac{S}{N}\right)_R$,

$$\left(\frac{S}{N}\right)_{R_{th}} = 6\,(M^2 - 1)$$

This equation says, if $\left(\dfrac{S}{N}\right)_R < 6\,(M^2 - 1)$, then PCM output cannot be reconstructed satisfactorily due to decoding noise.

We also have analog transmission parameter.

$$v = \frac{S_R}{N_0\,W}$$

$$= \left(\frac{B_T}{W}\right) \times \left(\frac{S}{N}\right)_R$$

For PCM, $B_T >> \dfrac{r}{2} \geq v\,W$

$\therefore$ $$v_{th} = \left(\frac{B_T}{W}\right)\left(\frac{S}{N}\right)_{R_{th}}$$

$$\cong 6 \times \frac{B_T}{W} \times (M^2 - 1)$$

$\therefore$ $$v_{th} = 6\,v\,(M^2 - 1)$$

Hence, given v and M, we can find v needed for PCM above threshold. This will help in comparing PCM with other methods.

6.15.6 Comparison of PCM and Analog Modulation

1. Analog modulation methods like FM, PPM exhibit reduction of wideband noise above their threshold level.

PCM also has the property of wideband noise reduction above the threshold.

Let the sampling frequency be close to Nyquist rate 2W.

$\therefore$ $B_T \simeq v\,W$

$L = M^v$ where, $M = 2$ in case of binary PCM

$\therefore$ $L = M^b$ where, $b = \dfrac{B_T}{W}$ (bandwidth ratio)

Since, $$\left(\frac{S}{N}\right)_0 = 3\,L^2\,P_s$$

$$\left(\frac{S}{N}\right)_0 = 3\,M^{2b}\,P_s$$

This expression shows that there is an exponential reduction of noise above threshold. The plot of various modulation types is shown in Fig. 6.37.

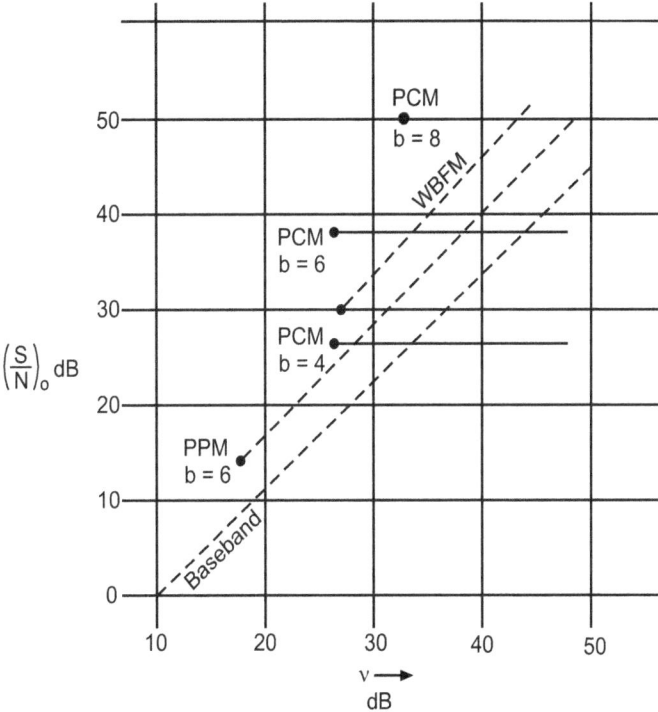

Fig. 6.37: Performance of PCM and Analog Modulation

It is seen that beyond threshold (indicated by dot), PCM does not offer any improvement in signal-to-noise ratio. Hence, PCM should be operated just above threshold for power efficiency. With same value of b, PCM has better $\left(\dfrac{S}{N}\right)_0$ ratio near threshold.

2. PCM allows one of regenerative repeaters for reshaping the pulses for long distance transmission. Analog modulations do not offer this advantage.

3. Digital multiplexing is possible with PCM, which offers advantage of transmission of signals from variety of sources (data, voice, images, etc.) on same channel.

Analog modulation schemes do not offer this advantage.

4. PCM is not suited for all applications. e.g. in radio transmission, $\left(\dfrac{S}{N}\right)_0$ ratio of 60 dB is required. For this, the bandwidth ratio required for PCM would be above 8; whereas, FM can offer this at b = 8. Moreover, FM has more simpler hardware at transmitter and receiver. In general, PCM is not suitable for most single channel applications because of bandwidth requirement and hardware complexity.

Example 6.8: A binary channel with r_b = 3600 bits/sec. is available for PCM voice transmission. Find appropriate values of bits/sample, number of quantization levels and sampling frequency if W = 3.2 kHz.

Solution:

$$f_s \geq 2W$$

$\therefore$ $$f_s \geq 2 \times 3.2 \geq 6.4 \text{ kHz}$$

(i)   Now, $$v \cdot f_s = r_b$$

$\therefore$ $$vf_s = 36000$$

$\therefore$ $$v \leq \frac{36000}{6400}$$

$\therefore$ $$v \leq 5.6$$

$\therefore$ $$v = 5$$

(ii) $$L = 2^v$$

$$= 2^5$$

$$= 32$$

(iii) $\therefore$ $$f_s = \frac{r_b}{v}$$

$$= \frac{36000}{32}$$

$$= 7.2 \text{ kHz}$$

Example 6.9: A PCM system of video signal with f_s = 10 MHz requires signal-to-noise ratio of 50 dB for signal power = 1. Calculate signalling rate. Repeat above for signal power = 0.1.

Solution: Given:

$$f_s = 10 \text{ MHz}$$

$$\left(\frac{S}{N}\right)_0 = 50 \text{ dB}$$

(i) $P_s = 1$

$\therefore$ $$\left(\frac{S}{N}\right)_0 = 3 L^2 P_s$$

$$= 3 L^2$$

$$= 3 \times 2^{2v}$$

$$\left(\frac{S}{N}\right)_0 \text{dB} = 10 \log_e [3 \times 2^{2v}]$$

$$= 4.8 + 6v$$

$\therefore$ $50 = 4.8 + 6\,v$

$$v = 7.583$$

$\therefore$ $v = 8$

$\therefore$ Signalling rate, $r = v \cdot f_s$

$$= 8 \times 10 \times 10^6$$

$$= 80 \text{ Mbps}$$

(ii) $P_s = 0.1$

$\therefore$ $\left(\dfrac{S}{N}\right)_0 = 3\,L^2 \times P_s$

$$= 3 \times 2^{2v} \times 0.1$$

$\therefore$ $\left(\dfrac{S}{N}\right)_0$ in dB $= 10 \log (3 \times 2^{2v} \times 0.1)$

$$= 4.8 + 6\,v - 10$$

$$50 = 4.8 + 6\,v - 10$$

$\therefore$ $v = 9.2$

$\therefore$ $v = 10$

       Signalling rate, $r = v \cdot f_s$

$$= 10 \times 10 \text{ MHz}$$

$$= 100 \text{ Mbps}$$

Example 6.10: What is minimum size of memory required to store 10 minutes of sampled and quantized voice assuming signal-to-noise ratio is 35 dB and $f_s = 8$ kHz.

Solution: Given: $\left(\dfrac{S}{N}\right)_0 = 35$ dB

$$f_s = 8 \text{ kHz}$$

    Storage time $= 10$ min.

$$\left(\dfrac{S}{N}\right)_0 = 4.8 + 6\,v$$

$$35 = 4.8 + 6\,v$$

$\therefore$ $v = 5$

$\therefore$ $v = 5$

$$\text{Signalling rate} \ = \ v \cdot f_s$$
$$= \ 5 \times 8 \times 10^3$$
$$= \ 40 \times 10^3 \text{ bps}$$

$\therefore$ Memory required for 10 min. storage
$$= \ 40 \times 10^3 \times 10 \times 60$$
$$= \ 24 \times 10^6 \text{ bits}$$
$$= \ 24 \text{ Mbits}$$

6.16 Delta-sigma Modulation

In delta modulation which we have seen earlier, we take derivative of incoming signal. Then at the receiver end, we integrate (accumulate) the signal. If this signal is added with noise, then the demodulated signal is going to accumulate the errors due to noise. Hence, we integrate the signal before delta modulation. This scheme is called Delta-Sigma Modulation, to be precise Sigma-Delta Modulation. It has following advantages:

1. We can eliminate the accumulator at the receiver and receiver circuit will be very simple.

2. The low frequency contents are pre-emphasized.

3. Adjacent samples of input given to delta modulator are more correlated with each other. It reduces variance of error signal improving system performance.

Fig. 6.38 (a) shows the transmitter and receiver for delta-sigma modulator. The 1-bit DM signal is produced by multiplying pulse generator and the hard-limiter output because of integration used at the transmitter. We need a differentiator at the receiver end to compensate for the pre-emphasis. But then integrator-differentiator combination will cancel out each other and we need only low pass filter at the receiver. Similarly, we can combine the two integrators into one at the transmitter end. The modified block diagram is shown in Fig. 6.38 (b).

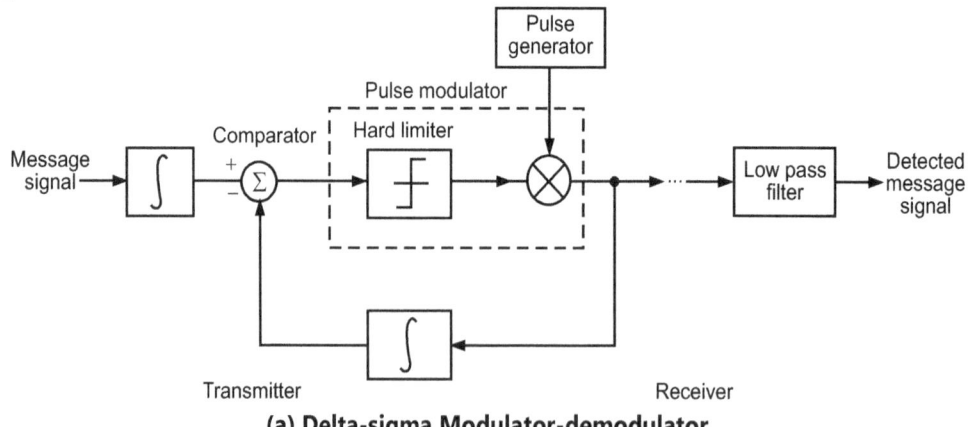

(a) Delta-sigma Modulator-demodulator

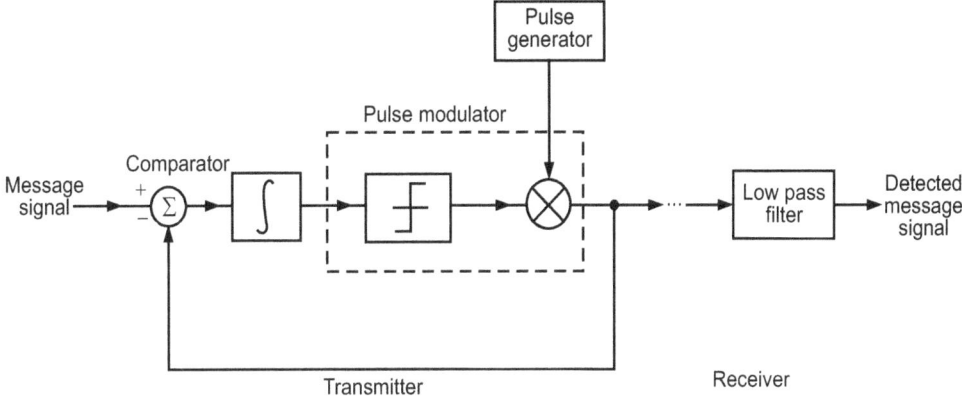

(b) Delta-sigma Modulator-demodulator

Fig. 6.38

6.17 Adaptive Delta Modulation

Slope-overload and granular noise are major problems associated with delta modulation. To tackle this, the step-size Δ is made adaptive to the variations in input signal m (t). When the signal is varying fast, step-size is increased and for slow varying signal, step-size is decreased. It can be observed from DM waveforms that, when there is slope overload, the error signal e (t) has same polarity; whereas for slow varying signal, the polarity alternates. This information can be used to adapt the step-size. The method implementing this technique of adaptive step-size is called Adaptive Delta Modulation (ADM).

Fig. 6.39 (a) shows the ADM transmitter. The transmitter is similar to DM transmitter except that step-size controller is added in ADM. The quantizer output will decide whether step-size should be increased or decreased. If output of quantizer is positive, step-size controller will increase step-size and vice versa. The ADM waveforms are shown in Fig. 6.39 (b).

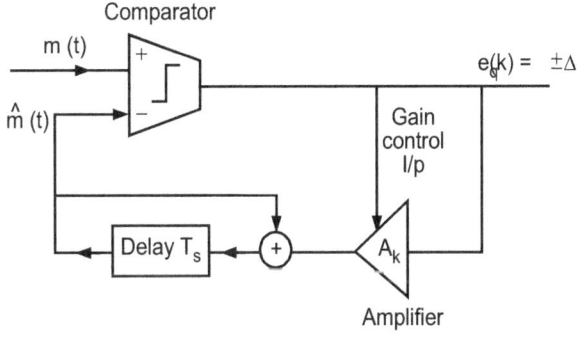

(a) ADM Transmitter

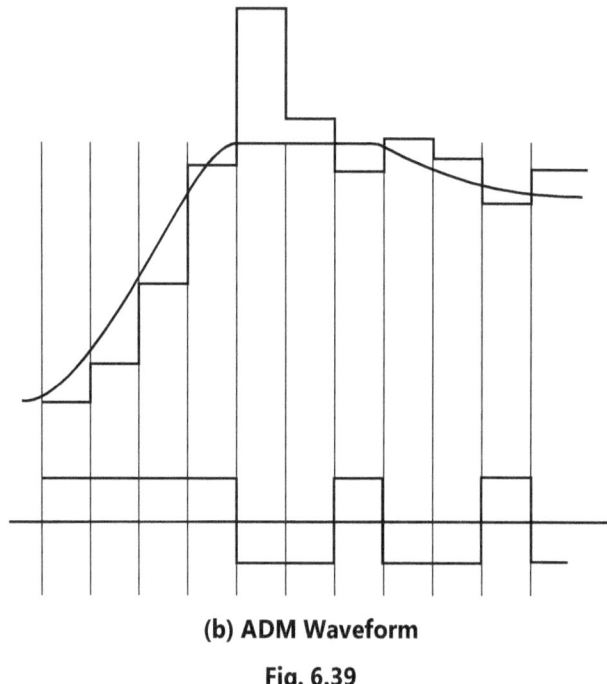

(b) ADM Waveform

Fig. 6.39

It can be seen from the waveform that if step-size is Δ at a particular instant and the signal is increasing, at the next sample instant it will become 2Δ, then 3Δ, etc. till the signal is rising. When the signal is falling or remaining constant, step-size will decrease by Δ. (Here, Δ is minimum step-size).

The accumulator will keep on accumulating previous values of quantized error signal [e_q (k)] to generate $\hat{m}_q$ (k). The signal is compared with current quantized sample m_q (k) to generate the output to be transmitted.

In the receiver, there is step-size generator. It generates step-size depending on past and present input to it as below.

Table 6.10

Past Input	Present Input	Step-size
1	1	Increase
1	0	Decrease
0	1	Decrease
0	0	Decrease

The steps are accumulated to generate a staircase waveform which is smoothened by a low pass filter to reconstruct the original signal m (t).

Advantages of ADM:

(i)   Dynamic range of ADM is better than DM because of variable step-size.

(ii)   Because of reduction in slope overload, signal-to-noise ratio is improved.

(iii) Bandwidth requirement for ADM is reduced because slope overload is reduced.

(iv)   Simple hardware implementation than PCM.

(v)   Less costly than PCM.

(vi)   1-bit output per sample.

6.17.1 Continuously Variable Slope Delta Modulator (CVSD)

In case of simple delta modulation, there is variation of signal-to-noise ratio with signal power. At low signal power, the S/N ratio is considerably smaller than the high signal power S/N ratio (provided there is no slope overload). We can modify the DM system as shown in Fig. 6.40.

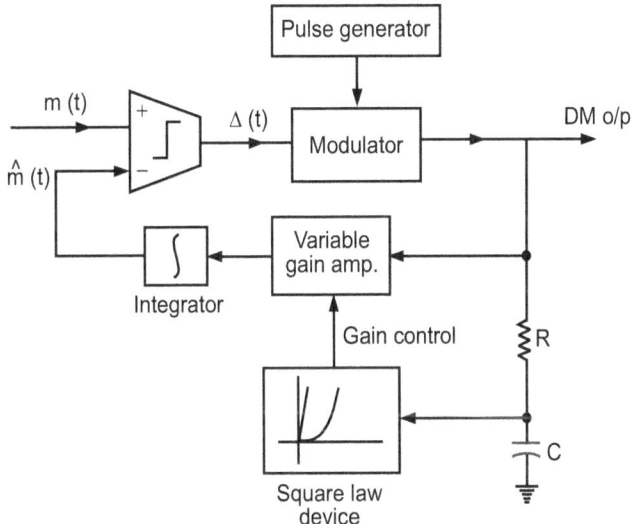

Fig. 6.40: Continuously Variable Slope Delta Modulation (CVSD)

A variable gain amplifier is used before integrator. The amplifier is driven by gain-control voltage. The gain of amplifier is low when gain control voltage is zero. Gain of amplifier increases with increase in gain control voltage. The R–C circuit serves as integrator. The voltage across capacitor is given to square law device which actually produces gain control voltage. Square law device always produces positive voltage. For small input signal m (t), the step-size will be kept small. The step-size is increased for large voltage. Hence, noise power is small for small input and it increases for large input. Hence, S/N ratio remains constant over large region of input power levels. There will be considerable reduction in slope overload since step-size is largest in slope overload region.

Advantage of CVSD:

The bit rate of CVSD is almost half of companded PCM. For voice signal, PCM requires 64 kbps, whereas CVSD requires 32 kbps.

Disadvantage of CVSD:

It is not suitable for time sharing application (multiplexing).

6.18 Differential PCM

When voice signal is sampled at a rate higher than Nyquist rate, adjacent samples do not change much. When we transmit such signal using PCM, we will be transmitting more redundant information. This redundancy can be reduced by transmitting the difference between two adjacent samples i.e. m (k) and m (k – 1). We transmit the differences m (k) – m (k – 1) by using PCM. These differences will be quite smaller than the sample values. Hence, less number of quantization levels are required. This will reduce the bit rate and in turn, bandwidth requirement. For example, if we use 8-bit PCM to encode signal with range – A_{max} to + A_{max}, 256 levels will be required. If you use DPCM, the difference signal m (k) – m (k – 1) = ± 2Δ can be encoded in just four levels and two bits per sample will be required. But then this produces large quantization errors. The quantization errors can be reduced by using sampling rate higher than Nyquist rate. If we do this, the bit rate increases. The situation in DPCM can be improved by using predictor. The predictor will give the best possible estimate of current value of input sample $\hat{m}$ (k) . This value can be predicted from past values of signal. The difference,

$$e \; (k) \;\; = \; m \; (k) - \hat{m} \; (k)$$

is quantized and encoded. The transmitter circuit is shown in Fig. 6.41 (a).

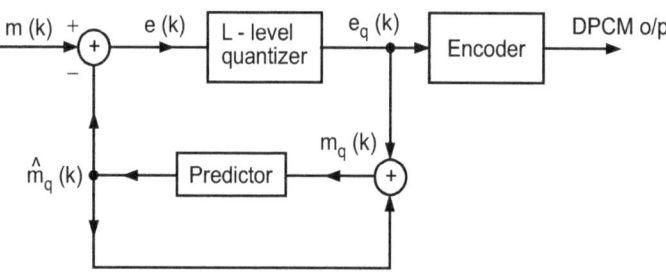

Fig. 6.41 (a): DPCM Transmitter

The predictor should have a facility to store past values and an algorithm to predict the next required increment. A tapped-delay-line filter can be used as shown in Fig. 6.41 (b).

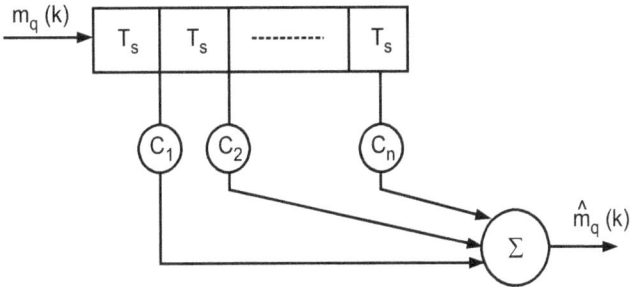

Fig. 6.41 (b): Predictor Circuit

The quantizer output will be,

$$e_q(k) = e(k) + q(k)$$

where, $q_e(k)$ is quantization error.

The filter output will be

$$m_q(k) = \hat{m}_q(k) + e_q(k)$$

∴ $$m_q(k) = \hat{m}_q(k) + e(k) + q(k)$$

But, $$\hat{m}(k) + e(k) = m(k)$$

∴ $$m_q(k) = m(k) + q(k)$$

The $m_q(k)$ is quantized version of m (k). Thus, if our predicted value $\hat{m}_q(k)$ is better, e (k) will be small. Then, quantizer with a given number of levels can be adjusted to produce quantization errors with less variance compared to standard PCM system.

The receiver for DPCM is shown in Fig. 6.42.

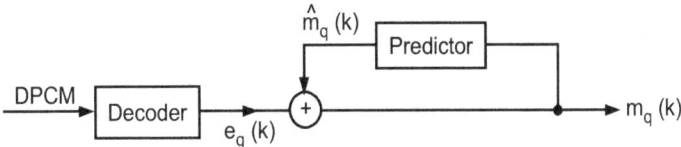

Fig. 6.42: DPCM Receiver

The decoder converts the binary signal into quantized error signal $e_q(k)$. The next part will keep on accumulating the quantized error signal $e_q(k)$ by adding $e_q(k)$'s with the output of prediction filter. The same type of prediction filter is used as that of transmitter. The receiver output $m_q(k)$ will be differing from original signal m (k) only by quantization error q (k). This is termed as the prediction error.

Signal-to-Noise Ratio for DPCM:

The signal-to-noise ratio of output of DPCM is given by,

$$(SNR)_0 = \frac{\sigma_m^2}{\sigma_q^2}$$

where, σ_m^2 is variance of original input signal m (k) and σ_q^2 is variance of quantization error. We can write above equation as,

$$(SNR)_0 = \frac{\sigma_m^2}{\sigma_e^2} \times \frac{\sigma_e^2}{\sigma_q^2}$$

where, σ_e^2 is variance of prediction error.

$$\therefore \quad (SNR)_0 = G_p \times \frac{\sigma_e^2}{\sigma_q^2}$$

where, G_p is called prediction gain or processing gain defined by,

$$G_p = \frac{\sigma_m^2}{\sigma_e^2}$$

If we use L levels for quantizing error signal e (k), then as already derived from PCM, signal-to-noise ratio is

$$\frac{\sigma_e^2}{\sigma_q^2} = 3 L^2 \times P_s$$

Thus, signal-to-noise ratio for DPCM is given by,

$$(SNR)_0 = G_p \times 3 L^2 P_s$$

The SNR for DPCM is enhanced by prediction gain G_p.

The DPCM system and DM system are similar, except that in DM, we have 1-bit quantizer and there is single delay element instead of prediction filter. Thus, DM is 1-bit version of DPCM.

DPCM will suffer from slope overload for fast varying signal just like DM. DPCM has quantization noise similar to PCM.

Example 6.11: If DPCM predictor has predictor gain of the order of 6 dB, show that DPCM word needs one less bit than that of binary PCM, all other factors remaining same.

Solution: Given: $\quad G_p = 6$ dB

$$\therefore \quad G_p = 3.98 \simeq 4$$

SNR for PCM:

$$(SNR)_{PCM} = 3 L_1^2 \times P_s$$

where L_1 is the number of quantization levels of PCM.

SNR for DPCM:

$$(SNR)_{DPCM} = G_p \times 3 L_2^2 P_s$$

where L_2 is the number of quantization levels of DPCM.

$$\therefore \qquad 3 L_1^2 \times P_s = G_p \times 3 L_2^2 P_s$$

$$\frac{L_1^2}{L_2^2} = 4$$

$$\frac{L_1}{L_2} = 2$$

$$\therefore \qquad L_1 = 2 L_2$$

$$\therefore \qquad 2^{2v_1} = 2 \infty 2^{v_2}$$

$$v_1 \log_2 2 \, v_1 = \log_2 (2 \infty 2^{v_2})$$

$$\therefore \qquad v_1 = \log_2 2 + v_2 \log_2 2$$

$$v_1 = 1 + v_2$$

$\therefore$ Hence, number of bits of PCM is one more than number of bits of DPCM.

6.19 LPC Speech Synthesis

Speech consists of a sequence of 'voiced' and 'unvoiced' sounds that are passed through a filter. Voiced sounds are generated by the vibrations of the vocal words. Unvoiced sounds are generated when speaker pronounces words with hissing sound.

Linear Predictive Coding (LPC) is a method of representing speech signal into digital format. We need not transmit the actual speech waveform generated by a speaker. Instead, we transmit the information related to synthesizing the waveform in encoded format. By doing this, we will be operating at a very low bit rate of the order 3 to 8 kbps. Of course, the resulting reproduced voice is of artificial quality. Systems, that generate speech in this manner, are called **vocoders**.

Fig. 6.43 (a) shows speech synthesizer. It has two input generators, one for voiced sounds and another for unvoiced sounds, a variable gain amplifier and a filter in a feedback loop. The unvoiced sounds are generated by noise source and voiced sounds by an impulse generator. Frequency of impulse generator is the fundamental frequency of vibration of vocal cords. The filter represents the effect of mouth throat and nasal passages.

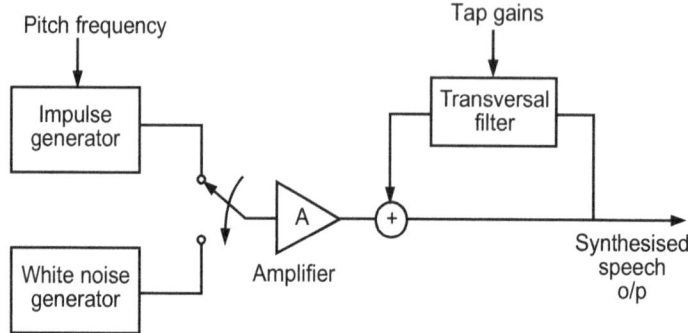

Fig. 6.43 (a): Speech Synthesizer

Now let us consider the LPC transmitter shown in Fig. 6.43 (b).

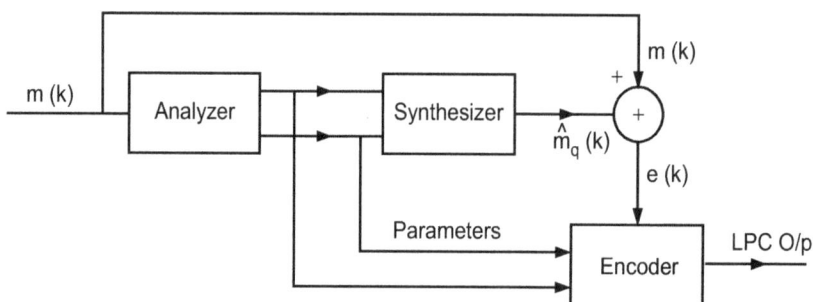

Fig. 6.43 (b): LPC Transmitter

Speech signal from a speaker is analysed and the necessary parameters are generated. The synthesizer uses these parameters to generate approximate version of the signal. The synthesizer output and input signal are compared to generate error signal. This error signal along with the parameters is encoded and transmitted as LPC signal.

Fig. 6.43 (c) depicts receiver for LPC system. The parameter values of quantized error are used to reconstruct the speech signal.

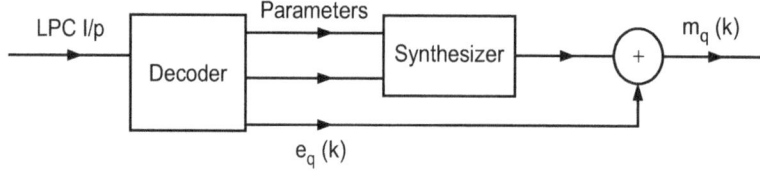

Fig. 6.43 (c): LPC Receiver

An LPC codeword has 80-bits. They are distributed as below.

    1 bit for recognising voiced/unvoiced sound.

    6 bits for pitch frequency.

    5 bits for amplifier gain.

    6 bits each for 10 tap gains of the filter.

    and 8 bits for error.

The filter has 10 tap gains. The parameters are updated every 10 to 25 ms. This is equivalent to sampling at 40 to 100 Hz. Hence, the LPC has bit rate equal to 80 × 40 (3200) to 80 × 100 (8000) bps.

6.20 Comparison of Various Speech Coding Technologies

Table 6.11

Parameter for comparison	PCM	ADPCM	DM	ADM
1. Bits per sample	Variable	Variable	One	One
2. Step-size	Fixed in simple PCM variable in companded PCM	Fixed	Fixed	Variable
3. Maximum Quantization error	$\pm \dfrac{\Delta}{2}$	$\pm \dfrac{\Delta}{2}$	$\pm \Delta$	$\pm \Delta$
4. Quantization Noise	$\dfrac{\Delta^2}{12}$	$\dfrac{\Delta^2}{12}$	$\dfrac{\Delta^2}{3}$	$\dfrac{\Delta^2}{3}$
5. Complexity of circuit	Complex	Complex	Less complex	More complex than DM
6. Bit rate for voice encoding (kbps)	56-64	32-48	64-128	48-64
7. Cost	Costly	Costly	Cheapest	Cheap
8. Synchronization requirement	Yes	Yes	No	No
9. Signalling rate	High	Lower than PCM	Lower if no slope overload, highest if slope overload	Lower than DM
10. Bandwidth requirement	Higher	Lower than PCM	Lower if no slope overload, highest if slope overload	Lower than DM
11. SNR	$3\,L^2\,P_s$	$G_p\ 3\ L^2\ P_s$	$\dfrac{3}{\Delta^2} \times \dfrac{f_s}{W} \times P_s$	Better than DM.

6.21 Speech Codecs

1. Codecs are software drivers that are used to encode the speech in a compact enough form that they can be sent in real time across the Internet using the bandwidth available.

2. Codecs are not something that VoIP users normally need to worry about, as the VoIP clients at each end of the connection negotiate between them which one to use.

3. VoIP software or hardware may give you the option to specify the codecs you prefer to use.

4. This allows you to make a choice between voice quality and network bandwidth usage, which might be necessary if you want to allow multiple simultaneous calls to be held using an ordinary broadband connection.

5. Your selection is unlikely to make any noticeable difference when talking to PSTN users, because the lowest bandwidth part of the connection will always limit the quality achievable, but VoIP-to-VoIP calls using a broadband Internet connection are capable of delivering much better quality than the plain old telephone system.

6. A broadband connection is desirable to use VoIP, though it is certainly possible to use it over a dial-up modem connection if a low-bandwidth, low-fidelity codec is chosen.

7. The Table 6.12 below lists some commonly used codecs.

Table 6.12

Codec	Algorithm	Bit rate (kbit/s)	Bandwidth (kbit/s)
G.711	Pulse Code Modulation (PCM)	64	87.2
G.722	Adaptive Pulse Code Modulation (ADPCM)	48	66.8
G.726	Adaptive Differential Pulse Code Modulation (ADPCM)	32	55.2
G.728	Low-Delay Code Excited Linear Prediction (LD-CELP)	16	31.5
iLBC	Internet Low Bitrate Coded (ILBC)	15	27.7
GSM	Regular Pulse Excited (RPE)	13	30.1
G.729a	Conjugate Structure Algebraic-Code Excited Linear Prediction (CS-CELP)	8	31.2
G.723.1a	MP-MLQ	6.4	21.9
G.723.1	ACELP(Algebraic Code-Excited Linear Prediction)	5.3	20.8

8.   The bit rate is an approximate indication of voice quality or fidelity, however it is only approximate.

9.   Codecs, that use pulse code modulation, all give high fidelity, and you will detect little or no difference between any of them.

10.   The G.728 codec will give much better quality than the only nominally lower rate GSM codec, because the algorithm it uses is much more sophisticated.

11.   However, the GSM codec uses less computing power, and so will run on simpler devices.

12.   The bandwidth gives an indication of how much of the capacity of your broadband Internet connection will be consumed by each VoIP call.

13.   The bandwidth usage is not directly proportional to the bit rate, and will depend on factors such as the protocol used.

14.   Each chunk of voice data is contained within a UDP packet with headers and other information.

15.   This adds a network overhead of some 15 - 25 kbit/s, more than doubling the bandwidth used in some cases.

16.   However, most VoIP implementations use silence detection, so that no data at all is transmitted when nothing is being said.

17.   Insufficient bandwidth can result in interruptions to the audio if VoIP uses the same Internet connection as other users who may be downloading files or listening to music.

18.   For this reason, it is desirable to enable the Quality of Service "QoS" option in the TCP/IP properties of any computer running a software VoIP client, and to use a router with QoS support for your Internet connection.

This will ensure that your VoIP traffic will be guaranteed a slice of the available bandwidth so that call quality does not suffer due to other heavy Internet usage.

6.21.1 Speech Codecs in Detail

ITU-T G.711 - Voice Codec:

Description:

G.711 is a ITU-T recommendation for compression of voice frequency signals used in telephony networks. The module is bit exact compliant to ITU-T G.711 test vectors. This algorithm converts 128 kbps linear (PCM) to and from either 64 kbps A-law or μ-law PCM.

Features:

- Full duplex mode of operation.
- All the ITU-T test vectors bit exact verified.
- Optimized for high performance on proprietary DSP core.

Configuration:

- Used in conversion from or to μ or A-law to linear PCM.
- Used with ITU-T recommendations G.726.

Typical Applications:

- Multimedia products.
- Videophones.
- Cordless phones.
- Digital satellite system.
- DCME, ISDN, PSTN etc.

ITU-T G.722 - Speech Codec:

Description:

ITU-T recommendation G.722 is Sub-Band Adaptive Differential Pulse Code Modulation (SB-ADPCM) based audio coding system. It has a bandwidth of 50 to 7000 Hz., which is used for a variety of higher quality speech applications. The G.722 full duplex algorithm converts 256 kbps linear (PCM) to and from, 64, 56 or 48 kbps. The latter two modes allow an auxiliary data channel of 8 and 16 kbps respectively to be provided within the 64 kbps by making use of bits from the lower sub-band. The G.722 module is bit compliant with the ITU G.722 test vectors.

Features:

- Full duplex mode of operation.
- All ITU-T test vectors are bit exact verified.
- Allows auxiliary data channels.
- Implemented on a proprietary DSP core with SIMD (single instruction, multiple data) super scalar architecture.
- Can handle multiple instances/channels.

Configuration:

- Operates on 16 kHz Sampling rate with14 bits per sample as input.

- Operates on a pair of samples or on a frame of 40/80/160 samples.

- Auxiliary data channels of 8 kbps or 16 kbps can be added to the output of the encoder. This is external to the codec.

- The decoder can operate on 64 kbps, 56 kbps or 48 kbps as required.

- Multiple instances environment compatible.

- Line echo cancellation.

Typical Applications:

- Multimedia products.

- Videophones.

- Cordless phones.

- Digital satellite system.

- DCME (Digital Circuit Multiplication Equipment), ISDN, PSTN.

- Digital leased lines.

- Voice store and forward systems, etc.

ITU-T G.726 - Speech Codec:

Description:

This speech codec is Adaptive Differential Pulse Code Modulation (ADPCM) based codec recommended by ITU-T. The G.726 algorithm converts a 64 kbps A-law or µ-law or 128 kbps linear PCM channel to and from a 40, 32, 24, or 16 kbps channel.

This codec is multiple instance capable.

Features:

- Full and half duplex mode of operation.

- All the ITU-T test vectors are bit exact verified.

- Capable of operating on single sample or on frames.

- Can operate on multiple instances/channel.

- Conversion of PCM to and from A-law and µ-law is done using ITU-T recommendation G.711.

Configuration:

- Direct interface to 8 kHz PCM data stream.
- Line echo cancellation can be done.
- Coder selection can occur at run time.
- Multiple instance compatible.
- Implementation available on proprietary SIMD architecture.
- Seamless integration with RTP/RTCP, DTMF, **VAD (Voice Activity Detection)** and jitter management,
- RTOS implementation optional.

Typical Applications:

- Multimedia products
- Videophones
- Cordless phones
- Digital satellite system
- DCME, ISDN, PSTN
- Digital leased lines
- Voice store and forward systems

ITU-T G.729A - Speech Codec:

Description:

This ITU-T recommendation is reduced complexity implementation of G.729. This implementation provides coding of speech and audio signals used in multimedia applications at 8 kbps using **Conjugate-Structure Algebraic-Code –Excited Linear Prediction (CS-ACELP).** This module is bit exact compliant with all the ITU-T test vectors. Typical input rates include µ or A-law 64 kbps PCM or 128 kbps linear PCM providing a compression ratio of upto 16 : 1.

Features:

- Full duplex and half duplex mode of operation.
- Multiple instance/channel compatible.
- All ITU-T test vectors are bit exact verified.
- Common compressed speech frame stream to support systems with multiple codecs.
- Voice Activity Detection and Comfort Noise Generation.
- Optimized implementation.

Configuration:

- Direct interface to 8 KHz. PCM data stream. (µ or A-law).
- Line echo cancellation.
- Operates on 10 msec frame.
- Can be used for compression of audio used in multimedia applications at a very low bit rate.
- Can be a part of H.324/H.323, MGCP (Media Gateway Control Protocol), SIP.
- VAD and **CNG (Comfort Noise Generator)** compatible.
- Coder selection can occur at run time.
- Data modem systems compatible.
- Multiple instance/channels compatible.
- Seamless integration with RTP/RTCP, DTMF, VAD and jitter management.

Typical Applications:

- Voice over IP (VoIP).
- Digital satellite systems.
- Voice/Fax/Data relay systems.
- Multimedia products.
- DCME, PSTN, ISDN.
- Digital leased lines.
- Voice store and forward.
- Video phones and cordless telephones.
- Land digital mobile radio.

ITU-T G.729B - Speech Codec:

Description:

G.729B is ITU-T recommendation G.729 modified to achieve a reduction in the transmitted bit rate by exploiting silent periods in human speech. This implementation provides coding of speech and audio signals used in multimedia applications at 8 kbps using Conjugate-Structure Algebraic-Code –Excited Linear Prediction (CS-ACELP). This module is bit exact compliant with all the ITU-T test vectors. It has a one-way algorithmic delay of 15 msec. Typical input rates include µ or A-law 64 kbps PCM or 128 kbps linear PCM providing a compression ratio of upto 16 : 1.

Features:

- Full duplex and half duplex mode of operation.

- Multiple instance/channel compatible.

- All ITU-T test vectors are bit exact compatible.

- Common compressed speech frame stream to support systems with multiple codecs.

Configuration:

- Direct interface to 8 kHz PCM data stream. (μ or A-law).

- Line echo cancellation.

- Can be used for compression of audio used in multimedia applications at a very low bit rate.

- Can be a part of H.324/H.323, MGCP, SIP.

- VAD and CNG compatible.

- Where multiple speech coders are available, then coder selection can occur at run time.

- Data modem systems compatible.

- Multiple instance/channels compatible.

- Seamless integration with RTP/RTCP, DTMF, VAD and jitter management.

- RTOS (Real time operating system) implementation.

Typical Applications:

- Voice over IP (VoIP).

- Digital satellite systems.

- Voice/Fax/Data relay systems.

- Multimedia products.

- DCME, PSTN, ISDN.

- Digital leased lines.

- Voice store and forward.

- Video phones and cordless telephones.

- Land digital mobile radio.

ITU-T G.729AB - Speech Codec:

Description:

G.729AB is ITU-T recommendation G.729A modified to achieve a reduction in the transmitted bit rate by exploiting silent periods in human speech and reducing the complexity of the algorithm. This implementation provides coding of speech and audio signals used in multimedia applications at 8 kbps using Conjugate-Structure Algebraic-Code –Excited Linear Prediction (CS-ACELP). This module is bit exact compliant with all the ITU-T test vectors. It has a one-way algorithmic delay of 15 msec. Typical input rates include µ or A-law 64 kbps PCM or 128 kbps linear PCM providing a compression ratio of upto 16 : 1.

Features:

- Full duplex and half duplex mode of operation.
- Multiple instance/channel compatible.
- All ITU-T test vectors are bit exact compatible.
- Common compressed speech frame stream to support systems with multiple codecs.

Configuration:

- Direct interface to 8 kHz PCM data stream. (µ or A-law).
- Line echo cancellation.
- Can be used for compression of audio used in multimedia applications at a very low bit rate.
- Can be a part of H.324/H.323, MGCP, SIP.
- VAD and CNG compatible.
- Coder selection can occur at run time.
- Data modem systems compatible.
- Multiple instance/channels compatible.
- Seamless integration with RTP/RTCP, DTMF, VAD and jitter management.
- RTOS implementation.

Typical Applications:

- Voice message recorded announcements.
- Digital satellite systems.
- Voice/Fax/Data relay systems.
- Multimedia products.
- DCME, PSTN, ISDN.

- Digital leased lines.
- Voice store and forward.
- Video phones and cordless telephones.
- Land digital mobile radio.

ITU-T G.729E - Speech Codec:

Description:

G.729E is ITU-T recommendation G.729 modified to achieve a bit rate of 11.8 kbps. This is ratified in September 1998 by the ITU as highest bitrate member of G.729 family of codecs.

G.729 annex E is designed to surpass the level of robustness and quality offered by the public switched telephone network (PSTN). And for this reason, is the favorite candidate for solutions that are used in competing the legacy telephone system, like the various initiatives from cable providers to offer local telephony services.

Its excellent capability to transport general audio, like music and background elements, makes it a logical choice for remote surveillance, conferencing and announcements within call waiting applications.

Features:

- Full duplex and half duplex mode of operation.
- Multiple instance/channel compatible.
- All ITU-T test vectors are bit exact compatible.

Configuration:

- Direct interface to 8 kHz PCM data stream. (μ or A-law).
- Line echo cancellation.
- Can be used for compression of audio used in multimedia applications.
- Can be a part of H.324/H.323.
- Coder selection can occur at run time.
- Data modem systems compatible.
- Multiple instance/channels compatible.

Typical Applications:

- Voice over IP (VoIP).
- Voice/Fax/Data relay systems.
- Multimedia products.

- Conferencing.

- Remote surveillance.

- Voice store and forward.

- Video phones and cordless telephones.

- DSL (Digital Subscriber line).

6.22 Wireless Codecs

6.22.1 AMR-NB (Adaptive Multirate Narrowband Voice Compression Standard)

The AMR narrowband codec is the 3GPP mandatory standard codec for narrowband speech and multimedia messaging services over 3G wireless systems based on evolved the GSM core network **[WCDMA(Wideband CDMA), EDGE, GPRS (General Packet Radio Service)]**. (**EDGE**, or the Enhanced Data Rate for Global Evolution, is the new technique in the Global Internet Connectivity scene. EDGE provides upto three times the data capacity of GPRS. EDGE is a new modulation scheme that is more bandwidth efficient. EDGE is the new name for **GSM 384**. The technology was named GSM 384 because of the fact that it provided Data Transmission at a rate of 384 kbps. It consists of the 8 pattern time slot, and the speed could be achieved when all the 8 time slots were used).

AMR initially developed for the GSM system, the single most deployed 2G mobile telecommunication system worldwide, AMR was also standardized by the European Telecommunications Standards Institute (ETSI) in 1999.

The AMR (Adaptive Multi-Rate) codec standard is a speech coding algorithm operating on narrowband (200-3400 Hz) signals at variable bit rates in the range of 4.75 to 12.2 kbps.

Technical Highlights:

- Only narrowband speech codec offering eight different bit rates that can be adapted according to network congestion, thus enabling significant enhancement of QoS.

- Voice Activity Detector (VAD) functionality included.

- Comfort Noise Generation (CNG) included.

- Discontinuous Transmission (DTX) functionality included.

- Proof speech coding technology tested in various operating conditions in the selection and characterization phases of the ETSI and 3GPP standardization.

- Bridge between packet network and wireless applications, eliminating the need for transcoding and the resulting degradation in quality.

Benefits:

AMR narrowband is several steps ahead of its direct speech compression competitors:

- 3GPP has adopted AMR, which contains codecs that are widely used in 2G mobile systems.

- This standard is the only narrowband technology offering such a complete range of built-in features. In most other cases, VAD, CNG, or the different bit rates are optional. AMR narrowband provides end-to-end solutions to various applications. The package comprises not only the codec, but also VAD, CNG, DTX, payload and storage formats, and hooks to media file formats.

- For VoPN (Voice over packet network), the eight available bit rates open the door to a striking QoS improvement. AMR flexibility enables the development of applications that control the bit rate according to the network characteristics.

- Coded AMR media can be encapsulated in the 3GP or MPEG-4 file formats and used along the entire delivery chain in multimedia applications.

- AMR is a proven technology that can be applied anywhere low bit rate speech coding is important, for example, in toys.

Without doubt, this technology is paving the way to network convergence — and it will be integrated into millions of applications, as its predecessors were. By implementing AMR narrowband today, companies are gaining a competitive edge, as they are building on a technology that is guaranteed to be around for some time.

Applications:

- Multimedia services for 3G mobile communication systems.
- Voice over IP.
- Audio and videoconferencing.
- Portable audio devices.
- Unified Messaging.
- Internet applications.
- Digital radio broadcasting.

6.22.2 AMR-WB (A Clear Sound and Rich Voice Revolution)

Most speech coding systems in use today are based on telephone-bandwidth narrowband speech, nominally limited to about 200-3400 Hz and sampled at a rate of 8 kHz. This limitation built into the public switched telephone network (PSTN) dates back to the first transcontinental telephone service at the beginning of the 20th century and imposes a constraint on communication quality.

Today, the increasing penetration of end-to-end digital networks such as the second- and third-generation wireless systems (2G and 3G) and voice over packet networks permits the use of wider speech bandwidth.

This wider speech bandwidth offers communication quality significantly surpassing that of the PSTN in intelligibility and naturalness, giving an experience that is equivalent to face-to-face interaction.

Technical Background:

The AMR-WB speech codec utilizes the ACELP (Algebraic Code Excitation Linear Prediction) technology, which is also employed in the AMR narrowband and EFR speech codecs as well as in ITU-T G.729 and G.723.1 at 5.3 kbit/s, among others. The AMR-WB speech codec consists of nine speech codec modes with bit rates of 23.85, 23.05, 19.85, 18.25, 15.85, 14.25, 12.65, 8.85 and 6.6 kbps. AMR-WB also includes a background noise mode that is designed to be used in discontinuous transmission (DTX) operation in GSM and as a low bit rate source-dependent mode for coding background noise in other systems. In GSM, the bit rate of this mode is 1.75 kbps.

Comparison of Wideband Speech Coding Standards:

Table 6.13

Recommendations	G.722	G.722.1	AMR-WB/G.722.2
Bit rate (kbps)	48, 56, 64 (embedded)	24, 32	23.85, 23.05, 19.85 18.25, 15.85, 14.25, 12.65, 8.85, 6.6
Type	Sub-band ADPCM	Transform Coding	Algebraic Code Excited Linear Prediction (ACELP)
Delay (ms): – Frame Size – Lookahead	 0.125 1.5	 20 20	 20 5
Quality	Commentary (at 64 kbps)	Poor speech performance in some operating conditions. Scope of standard limited to hands-tree and low packet loss rates. Good music performance	Good speech performance at rates 12.65 kbit/s and higher: 15.85 >= G.722@56 23.05 >= G.722@64

Recommendations	G.722	G.722.1	AMR-WB/G.722.2
Complexity	10 MIPS	< 15 MIPS	38 WMOPS
RAM (Kwords)	1	2	5.3
Fixed point	Bit-exact	Bit-exact C	Bit-exact C
Floating point	None	Exists in Annex B	In ANSI-C code
VAD/DTX/CNG	None	None	Included
Principal applications	ISDN, video conferencing	Same as G.722 plus VoPN	Same as G.722.1 plus 3G wireless

WMOPS (Weighted Million Operations Per Second) an ITU-T measure of computational complexity, similar to MIPS. WMOPS are roughly equivalent to MIPS for fixed-point processors.

Technical Highlights:

The AMR-WB codec includes:

- **A set of fixed-rate coding modes, which can be adapted according to network congestion, thus ensuring significant enhancement of QoS.**

- With a bandwidth ranging from 50 to 7000 Hz, AMR-WB not only improves the intelligibility and naturalness of speech, but also adds a feeling of transparent communication and eases speaker recognition.

- Voice Activity Detector (VAD) functionality.

- Discontinuous Transmission (DTX) functionality in GSM and Source-Controlled Rate (SCR) functionality in 3G.

- In-band signalling for codec mode transmission.

- Bridge between wired and wireless applications.

- Interoperability across different wired and wireless applications.

Benefits:

Wideband speech coding results in major subjective improvements in speech quality. Compared to narrowband telephone speech, low-frequency enhancement in AMR-WB from 50 to 200 Hz contributes to increased naturalness, presence, and comfort. The high-frequency extension from 3400 to 7000 Hz provides better fricative differentiation (for example, between words like **fin and thin**), and therefore higher intelligibility.

- The adoption of AMR-WB by ETSI/3GPP and ITU-T (where it is referred to as G.722.2) is of significant importance because, for the first time, the same codec has been adopted for wireless as well as wired services. This eliminates the need for transcoding and eases the implementation of wideband voice applications and services across a wide range of communication systems and platforms.

- Not only does AMR-WB provide superior voice quality over the existing narrowband standards, but it is also very robust against transmission errors due to multi-rate operation and adaptation.

- The AMR-WB package comprises not only the codec but also VAD, CNG, DTX (Discontinuous Transmission), payload and storage formats, and hooks to media file formats. AMR-WB provides end-to-end solutions to a variety of applications and is the only wideband technology offering such a complete range of built-in features.

Applications:

The naturalness of wideband speech coding is a significant feature in high-fidelity telephony and in extended telecommunications processes such as audio teleconferencing and program broadcasting. Application areas for wideband speech include:

1. Multimedia services for 3G mobile communication systems.
2. Wideband telephony over packet networks.
3. Audio and video teleconferencing.
4. Digital radio broadcasting.
5. Internet applications such as:
   - Broadcasting and streaming.
   - Chat and virtual reality immersion environments.
   - Multimedia real-time collaboration tools.
   - Archiving and distribution of narrative content.
   - Network-based language-learning applications.

VoIP:

Compared to narrowband telephony, AMR-WB wideband speech coding delivers very noticeable improvements in speech quality and comprehensibility which are sure to please customers.

Digital Terminals:

Digital handsets and digital terminals allow for improved sound quality because they are not tied to the traditional 4 kHz limitation. Equipment at both ends must share similar "hi-fi" capacity if they want to establish a call using a wideband payload. PCs, PDAs, cell phones and IP phones are perfectly suited for the wideband experience.

Enterprise:

An office is a perfect environment, in which to implement a wideband experience, whether the environment is centralized in one building or distributed across remote offices linked by packet networks. A noteworthy feature of AMR-WB/G.722.2 is that it behaves like a narrowband codec when it connects to legacy systems to make calls to non-wideband devices.

Conferencing:

Conferencing is one of the primary drivers for wideband speech communication. Conferencing emulates the face-to-face experience, and to achieve this goal, superior speech quality is required. Developers of conferencing equipment are among the early adoptors of wideband codecs.

Increasing On-net Traffic:

VoIP system integrators have noticed that "interfacing" their VoIP cloud with the legacy PSTN requires a large amount of equipment (media gateways, SS7 gateways, echo cancellers). Wideband experience will boost the use of IP terminals on both ends, helping to reduce the number of:

- Legacy terminals used by your customer base.
- "Outgoing" off-net calls to legacy terminals (thus increasing on-net IP-to-IP calls).

6.22.3 VMR-WB (Variable Rate Multi-Mode Wideband) - Source-controlled Variable Bit Rate Wideband Compression

The Variable Rate Multi-Mode Wideband (VMR-WB) codec is the mandatory speech codec for cdma2000 wideband telephony and multimedia streaming services. Designed by Nokia and VoiceAge, VMR-WB is based on the AMR-WB/G.722.2 codec. VMR-WB operates in the range from 0.8-13.3 kbps, including one mode of operation (mode 3) that is inter-operable with AMR-WB/G.722.2 (at 12.65 kbps and below).

Quality:

This table compares the quality of VMR-WB with source control at several average bit rates for a speech signal that is 60% active speech and 40% background noise/ silence.

Table 6.14

VMR-WB mode	VMR-WB at average bit rate	Quality	G.722 at fixed bit rate
1	5.5 kbps	=	56 kbps
2	4.5 kbps	>	48 kbps
3*	6.7 kbps	=	56 kbps

* Inter-operable with AMR-WB/G.722.2.

Technical Background:

VMR-WB is a source-controlled variable bit rate (VBR) codec. The VBR speech coding concept is crucial for optimal operation of CDMA systems (such as cdmaOne and cdma2000). In source-controlled VBR coding, the codec operates at several bit rates, and a rate selection mechanism is used to determine the bit rate suitable for encoding each speech frame based on the characteristics of the speech signal (e.g., voiced, unvoiced, transient, background noise). The goal is to attain the best speech quality at a given average data rate (ADR). The codec can operate in different modes by tuning its rate selection algorithm to obtain different ADRs. Codec performance is improved by increasing the ADR. The system imposes the mode depending on the network capacity and the desired quality of service. This gives the codec a mechanism of trade-off between speech quality and system capacity.

Rate Sets:

CDMA systems use rate sets comprised of 4-bit rates referred to as full-rate (FR), half-rate (HR), quarter-rate (QR), and eighth-rate (ER). CdmaOne and cdma2000 systems support two rate sets, referred to as Rate-Set I and Rate-Set II. The following table shows the source-coding bit rates and corresponding channel bit rates inclusive of error protection bits for variable-rate codecs with a rate selection mechanism operating in Rate-Set I and Rate-Set II.

Table 6.15: Operating rates of a variable-rate codec with rate selection mechanism operating in Rate-Set I and Rate-Set II

	FR	HR	QR	ER
Rate-Set I:				
Source-coding bit rate (kbps)	8.55	4.0	2.0	0.8
Channel bit rate including error detection bits (kbps)	9.6	4.8	2.4	1.2
Rate-Set II:				
Source-coding bit rate (kbps)	13.3	6.2	2.7	1.0
Channel bit rate including error detection bits (kbps)	14.4	7.2	3.6	1.8

Operating Modes:

VMR-WB has four operating modes in Rate-Set II and one in Rate-Set I.

Modes 0 to 3 operate in Rate-Set II. Modes 0, 1, and 2 are specific to CDMA systems with mode 0, providing the highest quality and mode 2 is the lowest ABR (**available bit rate**). Mode 3 is inter-operable with AMR WB/G.722.2 at 12.65 kbps and below. Its ADR (**Average Data Rate)** is slightly higher than the ABR of mode 0.

Mode 4 is compliant with cdma2000 Rate-Set I with an ADR slightly lower than mode 2 and with quality equivalent to or better than mode 2.

VMR-WB Operating Modes:

Table 6.16

VMR-WB mode	Description	Approximate speech average data rate (kbps)	Bit rate for 40% speech activity (kbps)
0	"Premium"	12.8	5.7
1	"Standard"	10.5	4.8
2	"Economy"	8.1	3.8
3	Inter-operable with AMR-WB/G.722.2	13.3	6.1
4	Rate-Set I mode	~ 8.1	~ 3.8

The system selects one of the operational modes depending on the traffic conditions. The transition from one mode to another is seamless and memoryless (i.e., there is no transition period to achieve the ADR of the new mode), and there is no need to transmit the mode information to the decoder. The system can also force maximum and minimum rates.

Narrowband Operation:

The narrowband codecs developed in CDMA for Rate-Set I operation consist of QCELP8 (IS-95), EVRC (IS-127), and SMV. In Rate-Set II operation, QCELP13 (IS-733) is used.

QCELP is Qualcomm code excited linear prediction. While the design of VMR-WB focused on wideband input and output signals, VMR-WB accepts narrowband input signals sampled at 8 kHz, and it can synthesize narrowband speech. The codec lookahead varies depending on the sampling frequency of the input and the output, being 13.75 ms for wideband input and output and 15.0625 ms for narrowband input and output.

Technical Highlights:

- Equipped with an integrated efficient noise reduction (NR) algorithm with adjustable maximum allowed reduction.
- Uses a sophisticated frame error concealment technique making it very robust for background noise and channel impairments.
- Delivers high quality at very low bit rates.
- Includes DTX (Discontinuous Transmission) for VoIP.
- RTP payload format is defined.

Applications:

- For wired, Wi-Fi, and cdma2000 wireless networks.

VMR-WB Standard for cdma2000 Telephony:

Approved as a standard by 3GPP2, the VMR-WB codec was also adopted by the 3GPP2 as the mandatory speech codec for cdma2000 wideband telephony services.

6.22.4 AMR Wideband Plus (AMR-WB+) Wideband Speech Plus High-Quality Audio

Emerging end-to-end digital communication systems enable the use of wideband audio coding in a large and varied collection of applications for mobile environments. Applications include streaming services for music, news, and sports as well as multimedia messaging services for person-to-person and business-to-person communications.

Now a breakthrough technology AMR Wideband Plus (AMR-WB+) — addresses mixed speech and audio content at low bit rates.

As an extension of the AMR wideband standard, the AMR-WB+ audio codec combines advanced audio coding technology with unrivaled speech coding technology, allowing service providers to deliver consistent high-quality audio while making efficient use of their transmission capacity.

In addition to delivering the same rich, natural sounding speech as its predecessor, AMR-WB+ delivers high-quality music, speech-over-music, and speech-between-music, making it perfectly suited to low-bit-rate mixed-content audio applications such as 3GPP Packet-Switched Streaming (PSS), Multimedia Messaging Services (MMS), Multimedia Broadcast/Multimedia Service (MBMS) and IP Multimedia Subsystem (IMS) Messaging Service and Presence Service.

Technical Background:

Selected as an audio codec standard by ETSI/3GPP, AMR-WB+ utilizes a hybrid of two technologies: **ACELP and TCX, respectively Algebraic Code Excited Linear Prediction and Transform Coded Excitation**. ACELP technology is in 15 international telecommunications standards, including AMR narrowband and AMR-WB as well as in ITU-T G.729 and G.723.1 at 5.3 kbps.

The AMR-WB+ codec has a wide bit-rate range, from 6-48 kbps. Mono rates are scalable from 6-36 kbps, and stereo rates are scalable from 7-48 kbps.

In the 3GPP standardization tests for audio codecs, AMR-WB+ performed better than the other codec for all content types at low bit rates (upto 20 kbps). At 20 kbps in stereo mode, AMR-WB+ is equivalent when music, speech and mixed contents are averaged, and performs better for both speech and mixed content. In mono mode,
AMR-WB+'s quality at 15.25 kbps is equivalent to the other codec's at 20 kbps, and its quality at 9.75 kbps is equivalent to the other codec's at 16 kbps. AMR-WB+ therefore provides bandwidth efficiencies of 25% to 40% to deliver equivalent quality.

Technical Highlights:

The AMR-WB+ codec is characterized by these important features:
- Hybrid ACELP/TCX codec provides consistent performance across both speech and audio content types, including music, speech-between-music, and speech-over-music.
- High-efficiency parametric stereo (HE-PS) provides high-fidelity stereo image reproduction at lowest bit rates.
- Coding modes can be adapted according to network congestion and desired quality of service (QoS). High scalability from
  – 6 to 36 kbps for mono.
  – 7 to 48 kbps for stereo.
- Low decoder complexity for PSS/MMS decoder, resulting in low power consumption:
  – Less than 8 WMOPS for mono.
  – Less than 15 WMOPS for stereo.
  – MMS (Multimedia Messaging Service) encoder complexity comparable to AMR-WB codec.
- Small incremental increase in footprint compared to AMR-WB codec.

AMR-WB+ at a Glance:

Table 6.17

Bits rate (kbps)	Mono: 6-36 kbps Stereo: 7-48 kbps		
Type	ACELP®/TCX		
Encoded bandwidth	Ranges from 50 Hz - 7.2 kHz upto 50 Hz - 19.2 kHz		
Delay (ms): Frame size Lookahead	 80 40		
Quality	• For speech, performance better than or equal to AMR-WB. • For music performance **better than or equal to** AAC Plus in most tests, and at low bit rate (less than 18 kbps) audio performance better than AAC Plus.		
Complexity (WMOPS)	**Decoder** Mono 8 Stereo 15	**MMS encoder** Stereo 36	**PSS encoder** Stereo 62
RAM + ROM (Kwords)	Mono 22.6 Stereo 27.3	Stereo 36.1	Stereo 40
PROM (Kwords)	Mono 4.0 Stereo 4.9	Stereo 6.8	Stereo 6.8
Fixed-point	Bit-exact C available for encoder and decoder		
Floating-point	C-code available for encoder and decoder		
Principal applications	PSS, MMS, MBMS, IMS Messaging Service and Presence Service		

IP Multimedia Subsystem **(IMS)**, Multimedia Broadcast and Multicast Service **(MBMS)**, Packet Switched Streaming **(PSS)**, Multimedia Messaging Service **(MMS)**.

Benefits:

To secure broad-based acceptance of 3GPP multimedia services, service providers must meet subscribers' expectations of high-quality audio at a fair price. AMR-WB+ provides the best quality in mobile environments for mixed content: speech and audio (music and other audio). The 3GPP PSS/MMS selection exercise for low rate audio codecs demonstrated that

AMR-WB+ provides equal or better performance, for any content, than any codec available in the 3GPP Release 5 specifications. An additional benefit to subscribers, and therefore to service providers, is the low decoder complexity, which is directly related to implementability on low-cost mass market devices and the battery life of the mobile handset.

To deliver services at a fair price, service providers must operate at the lowest possible cost, making efficient use of bandwidth. Low bit rate transmission is particularly important for MMS services, in which message sizes are limited. At the commercially relevant low bit rates of 14 and 18 kbps for mono and stereo, respectively, AMR-WB+ clearly satisfies this requirement.

To ensure the quality and cost-efficiency of AMR-WB+ implementations, the AMR-WB+ codec is offered with open specifications for decoder and encoder. As well, source code both in floating-point and fixed-point arithmetic is available. And in order to facilitate fast time-to-market, favourable licensing terms have already been established. Details can be found here.

When providers of streaming and multimedia messaging services consider the need to balance the consistent quality of the signal against deployment costs, it's clear that AMR-WB+ is certain to create more revenue for the mobile industry than any other codec of its type.

Applications:
Server-Based Streaming (PSS):
• Music and other audio content in mono and stereo • Movies • Video clips • News programming • Sports events • Audio books • Commercial advertisements • Access to multimedia information systems • Interactive gaming • "Infotainment".

Multimedia Messaging Services (MMS):
• Person-to-person messaging • Application-to-person messaging • Instant messaging.

Multimedia Broadcast/Multicast Service (MBMS):
• Live TV • Radio programming • Multi-player interactive gaming • Commercial advertisements.

IP Multimedia Subsystem (IMS) Messaging Service and Presence Service:
• Immediate messaging • Session-based messaging.
Download Services:
• Hi-fi ringtones • Music • Video clips • Movie trailers • Audio books

6.22.5 GSM EFR

In comparison to the GSM Full Rate codec (GSM-FR), GSM-EFR has improved speech quality and better robustness to network impairments. This codec provides one of the rates of AMR.

The GSM-EFR implementation is fully compliant with the ETSI GSM 06.60 Enhanced Full Rate (EFR) speech transcoding specification.

Technology:

Table 6.18

Encoded bandwidth	~ 200 - 3400 Hz
Standardized	ETSI
Coding type	ACELP (Algebraic Code Excited Linear Prediction)
Bit rate	12.2 kbps
Delay (ms): Frame size Lookahead	20 0
Quality	Toll
Complexity: MIPS RAM (words)	15 - 20 4 K

Applications:

- Digital telephony – Wi-Fi, VoIP, wireless (GSM, GPRS, EDGE)
- Audio and videoconferencing
- Media players
- Media servers
- Media gateways
- Content creation tools
- PDA/handset-hosted applications

6.22.6 GSM FR

GSM FR was the first digital speech coding standard used in GSM digital mobile phone systems. Its bit rate is 13 kbps. The VoiceAge GSM-FR implementation is fully compliant with the ETSI GSM 06.10 Full Rate (FR) speech transcoding specification.

Technology:

Table 6.19

Encoded bandwidth	~ 200 - 3400 Hz
Standardized	ETSI
Coding type	RPE-LTP (Regular Pulse Excitation with Long-Term Prediction)
Bit rate	13 kbps
Delay (ms): Frame size Lookahead	20 0
Quality	< Toll
Complexity: MIPS RAM (words)	4.5 1 K

Applications:

- Digital telephony – Wi-Fi, VoIP, wireless (GSM, GPRS, EDGE).
- Audio and videoconferencing.

6.22.7 GSM HR

The GSM-HR codec was developed for the purpose of increasing network capacity, but it achieves this through a trade-off where quality is less than toll. The GSM-HR implementation is fully compliant with the ETSI GSM 06.20 Half Rate (HR) speech transcoding specification.

Technology:

Table 6.20

Encoded bandwidth	~ 200 - 3400 Hz
Standardized	ETSI
Coding type	VSELP (Vector Sum Excited Linear Prediction)
Bit rate	6.5 kbps
Delay (ms): Frame size Lookahead	20 5
Quality	< Toll
Complexity: MIPS RAM (words)	30 4 K

Applications:

- Digital telephony – Wi-Fi, VoIP, wireless (GSM, GPRS, EDGE).
- Audio and videoconferencing.

6.23 Wireless Codecs (GSM Codecs) in Detail

1. The transmission of speech from one point to another over GSM mobile phone network is something that most of us take for granted.

2. The complexity is usually perceived to be associated with the network infrastructure and management required in order to create the end-to-end connection, and not with the transmission of the payload itself. The real complexity, however, lies in the codec scheme used to encode voice traffic for transmission.

3. The GSM standard supports four different but similar compression technologies to analyse and compress speech.

4. **These include full-rate, enhanced full-rate (EFR), adaptive multi-rate (AMR), and half-rate.**

5. Despite all being lossy (i.e. some data is lost during the compression), these codecs have been optimized to accurately regenerate speech at the output of a wireless link.

6. In order to provide toll-quality voice over a GSM network, designers must understand how and when to implement these codecs.

7. To help out, this article provides a look inside how each of these codecs works. We will also examine how the codecs need to evolve in order to meet the demands of 2.5 and 3G wireless networks.

6.23.1 Speech Transmission Overview

1. When you speak into the microphone on a GSM phone, the speech is converted to a digital signal with a resolution of 13 bits, sampled at a rate of 8 kHz—this 104,000 b/s forms the input signal to all the GSM speech codecs.

2. The codec analyses the voice, and builds up a bit-stream composed of a number of parameters that describe aspects of the voice.

3. The output rate of the codec is dependent on its type (see Table 6.21), with a range of between 4.75 kbit/s and 13 kbit/s.

Table 6.21: Different Coding Rates

Codec	Bit Rate (k/sec)	Compression	Codec type (see text)
Full Rate	13	8	RTE-LTP
Enhanced Full Rate (EFR)	12.2	8.5	ACELP
Half Rate	5.6	18.4	VSELP
AMR 12.2	12.2	8	ACELP
AMR 10.2	10.2	10.2	ACELP
AMR 7.95	7.95	13.1	ACELP
AMR 7.4	7.4	14.1	ACELP
AMR 6.7	6.7	15.5	ACELP
AMR 5.9	5.9	17.6	ACELP
AMR 5.15	5.15	20.2	ACELP
AMR 4.75	4.75	21.9	ACELP

4. After coding, the bits are re-arranged, convoluted, interleaved, and built into bursts for transmission over the air interface.

5. Under extreme error conditions, a frame erasure occurs and the data is lost, otherwise the original data is re-assembled, potentially with some errors to the less significant bits.

6. The bits are arranged back into their parametric representation, and fed into the decoder, which uses the data to synthesize the original speech information.

6.23.2 The Full-Rate Codec

1. The full-rate codec is a **regular pulse excitation, long-term prediction (RPE-LTP)** linear predictive coder that operates on a 20 ms frame composed of one hundred sixty 13-bit samples.

2. The vocoder model consists of a tone generator (which models the vocal chords), and a filter that modifies the tone (which models the mouth and nasal cavity shape) [Fig. 6.44].

3. The short-term analysis and filtering determines the filter coefficients and an error measurement, the long-term analysis quantifies the harmonics of the speech.

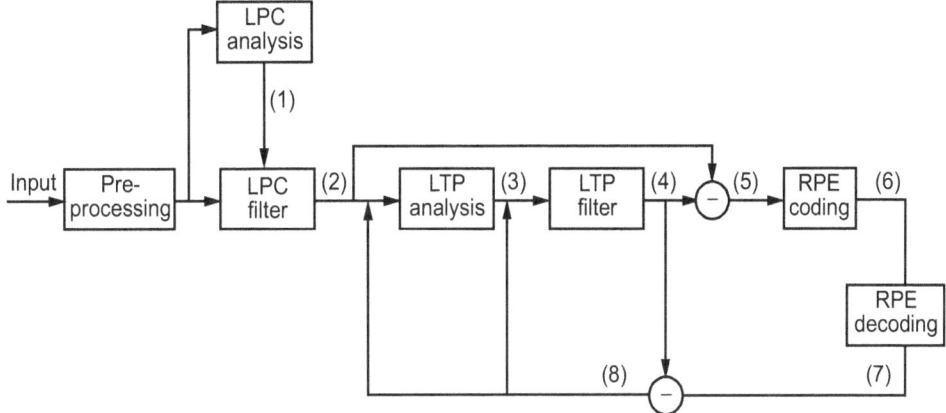

(1)   Reflection coefficients, converted to Log Area Ratios for transmission.
(2)   Short-term residual signal.
(3)   LTP lag and gain parameters.
(4)   Short-term residual estimate (prediction).
(5)   Long-term residual signal.
(6)   RPE Parameters.
(7)   Reconstructed long-term residual signal.
(8)   Reconstructed short-term residual signal.

Fig. 6.44: Diagram of a Full-rate Vocoder Model

4.   As the mathematical model for speech generation in a full-rate codec shows a gradual decay in power for an increase in frequency, the samples are fed through a pre-emphasis filter that enhances the higher frequencies, resulting in better transmission efficiency. An equivalent de-emphasis filter at the remote end restores the sound.

5.   The short-term analysis (linear prediction) performs autocorrelation and Schur recursion on the input signal to determine the filter ("reflection") coefficients.

6.   The reflection coefficients, which are transmitted over the air as eight parameters totalling 36 bits of information, are converted into **log area ratios (LARs)** as they offer more favourable companding characteristics.

7.   The reflection coefficients are then used to apply short term filtering to the input signal, resulting in 160 samples of residual signal.

8.   The residual signal from the short-term filtering is segmented into four sub-frames of 40 samples each.

9.   The **long-term prediction (LTP)** filter models the fine harmonics of the speech using a combination of current and previous sub-frames.

10. The gain and lag (delay) parameters for the LTP filter are determined by cross-correlating the current sub-frame with previous residual sub-frames.

11. The peak of the cross-correlation determines the signal lag, and the gain is calculated by normalising the cross-correlation coefficients.

12. The parameters are applied to the long-term filter, and a prediction of the current short-term residual is made.

13. The error between the estimate and the real short-term residual signal—the long-term residual signal—is applied to the RPE analysis, which performs the data compression.

14. The **Regular Pulse Excitation (RPE)** stage involves reducing the 40 long-term residual samples down to four sets of 13-bit sub-sequences through a combination of interleaving and sub-sampling.

15. The optimum sub-sequence is determined as having the least error, and is coded using **APCM (adaptive PCM)** into 45 bits.

16. The resulting signal is fed back through an RPE decoder and mixed with the short-term residual estimate in order to source the long-term analysis filter for the next frame, thereby completing the feedback loop (Table 6.22).

Table 6.22: Output Parameters from the Full Rate Codec

Parameter	Number of Parameters	Total bits per frame
LARs	8 per frame	36 bits
LTP lag	1 per subframe (7 bits)	28 bits
LTP gain	1 per subframe (2 bits)	8 bits
RPE grid position	1 per subframe (2 bits)	8 bits
Block amplitude	1 per subframe (6 bits)	24 bits
RPE Pulses	13 per subframe (3 bits each)	156 bits
Total		**260 bits per frame**

6.23.3 The Enhanced Full-Rate Codec

1. As processing power improved and power consumption decreased in **digital signal processors (DSPs)**, more complex codecs could be used to give a better quality of speech.

2. The EFR codec is capable of conveying more subtle detail in the speech, even though the output bit rate is lower than full rate.

3. The EFR codec is an **algebraic code excitation linear prediction (ACELP)** codec, which uses a set of similar principles to the RPE-LTP codec, but also has some significant differences.

4. The EFR codec uses a 10th-order linear-predictive (short-term) filter and a long-term filter implemented using a combination of adaptive and fixed codebooks (sets of excitation vectors).

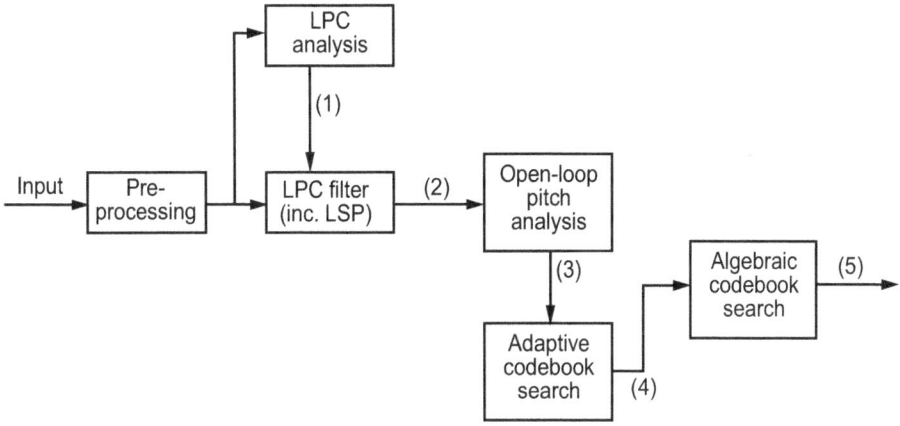

(1)   Direct form short-term coefficients.
(2)   Line Spectral Pair representation of short-term coefficients.
(3)   Lag estimate to seed adaptive codebook search.
(4)   Adaptive code index and gain.
(5)   Fixed code index and gain.

Fig. 6.45: Diagram of the EFM Vocoder Model

5.   The pre-processing stage for EFR consists of an 80 Hz high-pass filter, and some downscaling to reduce implementation complexity.

6.   Short-term analysis, on the other hand, occurs twice per frame and consists of autocorrelation with two different asymmetric windows of 30 ms in length concentrated around different sub-frames.

7.   The results are converted to short-term filter coefficients, then to line spectral pairs (for better transmission efficiency) and quantized to 38 bits.

8.   In the EFR codec, the adaptive codebook contains excitation vectors that model the long-term speech structure. Open loop pitch analysis is performed on half a frame, and this gives two estimates of the pitch lag (delay) for each frame.

9.   The open-loop result is used to seed a closed-loop search for speed and reduced computation requirements.

10.   The pitch lag is applied to a synthesizer, and the results compared against the non-synthesized input (analysis-by-synthesis), and the minimum perceptually weighted error is found. The results are coded into 34 bits.

11.   The residual signal remaining after quantization of the adaptive codebook search is modelled by the algebraic (fixed) codebook, again using an analysis-by-synthesis approach.

12.   The resulting lag is coded as 35 bits per sub-frame, and the gain as 5 bits per sub-frame.

13.   The final stage for the encoder is to update the appropriate memory ready for the next frame.

6.23.4 Going Adaptive

1. The principle of the AMR codec is to use very similar computations for a set of codecs, to create outputs of different rates.

2. In GSM, the quality of the received air-interface signal is monitored and the coding rate of speech can be modified. In this way, more protection is applied to poorer signal areas by reducing the coding rate and increasing the redundancy, and in areas of good signal quality, the quality of the speech is improved.

3. In terms of implementation, an ACELP coder is used. In fact, the 12.2 kbit/s AMR codec is computationally the same as the EFR codec.

4. For rates lower than 12.2 kbit/s, the short-term analysis is performed only once per frame.

5. For 5.15 kbit/s and lower, the open-loop pitch lag is estimated only once per frame.

6. The result is that at lower output bit rates, there are a smaller number of parameters to transmit, and fewer bits are used to represent them.

6.23.5 The Half-Rate Codec

1. The air transmission specification for GSM allows the splitting of a voice channel into two sub-channels that can maintain separate calls.

2. A voice coder that uses half the channel capacity would allow the network operators to double the capacity on a cell for very little investment.

3. The half-rate codec is a **vector sum excitation linear prediction (VSELP)** codec that operates on an analysis-by-synthesis approach similar to the EFR and AMR codecs.

4. The resulting output is 5.7 kb/s, which includes 100 b/s of mode indicator bits specifying whether the frames are thought to contain voice or no voice.

5. The mode indicator allows the codec to operate slightly in different manner to obtain the best quality.

6. Half-rate speech coding was first introduced, but the public perception of speech quality was so poor, that it is not generally used today.

7. However, due to the variable bit-rate output, AMR lends itself nicely to transmission over a half-rate channel.

8. By limiting the output to the lowest 6 coding rates (4.75 - 7.95 kbps), the user can still experience the quality benefits of adaptive speech coding, and the network operator benefits from increased capacity.

9.   It is thought that with the introduction of AMR, use of the half-rate air-channel will start to become much more widespread.

6.23.6 Computational Complexity

Table 6.23 shows the time taken to encode and decode a random stream of speech-like data, and the speed of the operations relative to the GSM full-rate codec.

Table 6.23: General Encoding and Decoding Complexity

Codec	Encoding (mS)	Decoding (mS)	Relative Encode	Relative Decode
Full Rate	0.41	0.16	1.0	1.0
Enhanced Full Rate (EFR)	9.02	0.86	22.0	5.4
Half Rate	8.31	1.30	20.3	8.1
AMR 12.2	8.99	1.11	21.9	6.9
AMR 10.2	8.31	1.12	20.3	7.0
AMR 7.95	8.70	1.07	21.2	6.7
AMR 7.4	8.10	1.07	19.8	6.7
AMR 6.7	8.53	1.08	20.8	6.8
AMR 5.9	7.19	1.44	17.5	9.0
AMR 5.15	6.40	1.38	15.6	8.6
AMR 4.75	7.71	1.08	18.8	6.8

1.   The full-rate encoder operates on a non-iterative analysis and filtering, which results in fast encoding and decoding.

2.   By comparison, the analysis-by-synthesis approach employed in the CELP codecs involves repetitive computation of synthesized speech parameters.

3.   The computational complexity of the EFR/AMR/half-rate codecs is therefore far greater than the full-rate codec, and is reflected in the time taken to compress and decompress a frame.

4.   The output of the speech codecs is grouped into parameters (e.g. LARs) as they are generated (Fig. 6.46).

5.   For transmission over the air interface, the bits are rearranged, so the more important bits are grouped together.

6. Extra protection can then be applied to the most significant bits of the parameters that will have biggest effect on the speech quality if they are erroneous.

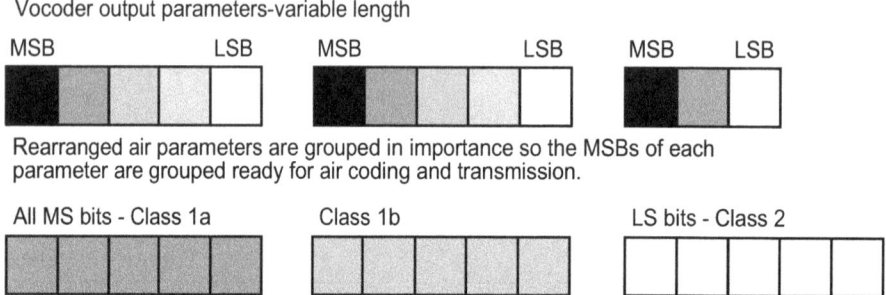

Fig. 6.46: Diagram of Vocoder Parameter Groupings

7. The process of building the air transmission bursts involves adding redundancy to the data by convolution.

8. During this process, the most important bits (Class 1a) are protected most, while the least important bits (Class 2) have no protection applied.

9. This frame building process ensures that many errors occurring on the air interface will be either correctable (using the redundancy), or will have only a small impact on the speech quality.

6.24 Transcoder Technologies

6.24.1 Transcoding Introduction

1. **Transcoding** is the direct digital-to-digital conversion from one (usually lossy) codec to another.

2. It involves decoding/decompressing the original data to a raw intermediate format (i.e. PCM for audio or YUV for video), in a way that mimics standard playback of the lossy content, and then re-encoding this into the target format.

3. PCM is pulse code modulation, whereas in YUV, Y stands for the luminance component (the brightness) and U and V are the chrominance (colour) components.

4. Transcoding can also refer to recompressing files to a lower bitrate without changing formats.

5. Compression artifacts are cumulative, therefore transcoding between lossy codecs causes a progressive loss of quality with each successive generation.

6.   For this reason, it is generally discouraged unless unavoidable.

7.   Transcoding can be found in many areas of content adaptation, however, it is commonly used in the area of mobile phones content adaptation.

8.   In the world of mobile content, transcoding is a must due to the diversity of mobile devices.

9.   This diversity requires an intermediate state of content adaptation in order to make sure that the source content will adequately present on the target device one sent to it.

10.   For example, when using a camera phone to take a digital picture, you are actually creating a high resolution JPEG image, usually at least $640 \infty 480$ with 24 bits of colour.

11.   However, when sending the image to another phone, this high resolution image might be transcoded to a lower resolution image with less amount of colour in order to better fit the target device's screen size and colour limitation (i.e. $120 \infty 160$ and 16 bits of colour).

12.   This size and colour reduction does not only improve the user experience on the target device, but is sometimes the only way for content to be sent between different mobile devices.

13.   One of the most popular technologies, in which transcoding is used is MMS (Multimedia Messaging System), which is the technology used to send or receive messages with media (Image, Sound, Text and Video) between mobile phones.

6.24.2 Internet Transcoding for Universal Access

1.   More and more pervasive devices, such as personal digital assistants (PDAs), hand-held computers, smart phones, TV browsers, wearable computers, and other mobile devices are gaining access to the Internet and other multimedia-rich information sources.

2.   However, the capabilities of these devices, to receive, process, store and display Internet content, vary widely.

3.   Given the variety of client devices, it is difficult for Internet content publishers to tailor the content to individual devices.

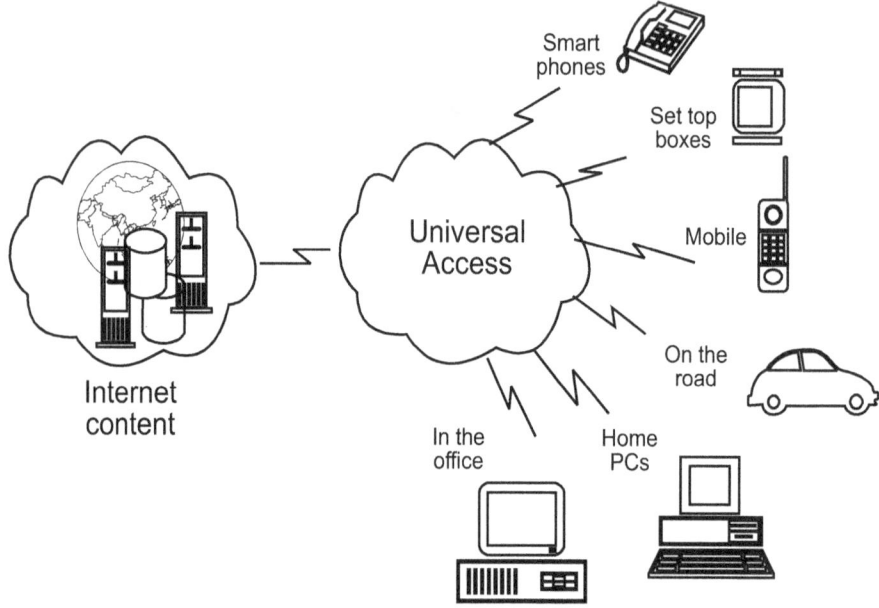

Fig. 6.47: Transcoding for Universal Access

4.   Enabling universal access of multimedia content has become increasingly important.

5.   Universal access describes the mechanism for adapting multimedia content to the constraints of the client devices.

6.   As an example, a smart phone can access a text document through the use of text-to-speech synthesis.

7.   To enable universal access in the coming age of pervasive computing, vendors are developing a system that tailors the content of web pages for pervasive computing devices.

8.   This tailoring process is called **transcoding**.

9.   The transcoding system adapts video, images, audio and text to the individual pervasive devices using a new framework that allows the content to be summarized, translated and converted, on the fly.

6.24.3 DTMF

DTMF (Dual Tone Multiple Frequency) signalling system is used for touch-tone dialing. Each of the 16 digits are signified by pairs of tones, one from a "low" group - 697 Hz, 770 Hz, 852 Hz, 941 Hz - and the other from a "high" group - 1209 Hz, 1336 Hz, 1477 Hz, 1633 Hz. DTMF receivers detect the presence of these tones while eliminating background noise and allowing for distortions introduced by the network.

Technical Specifications:

- Supports generation and detection of 16 DTMF digits.
- Conformance to ITU Q.23 and Q.24 standards.
- Configurable frame length.
- Configurable parameters (power level, power twist and the on-off duration of the lower and higher frequencies).
- Multichannel, Re-entrant implementation.
- Optimized implementation.

Applications:

- Telecommunications (public or private telephone exchanges; telephony and line test equipment).
- Voice Mails , Voice Response Systems.
- Remote control of computer and telephone equipment.

6.24.4 Line Echo Canceller

Echo Canceller implements line echo cancellation algorithm conforming to ITU specifications. It can be configured to cancel echo tails of lengths 16 ms to 128 ms. The Echo canceller implements the following components:

- Adaptive filter for estimating the echo.
- Double talk detector for disabling the filter adaptation during the periods of double-talk.
- Non linear processor for suppressing the residual echo.
- 2100 Hz tone detector to disable the echo cancellation.

Technical Specifications:

- Multi-channel, Re-entrant implementation.
- C-callable API for initialization and echo cancellation.
- Echo tail length configurable from 16 to 128 ms.
- Rapid Convergence.
- Low residual echo.
- Robust double talk detection, without divergence or clipping.
- Robust performance against narrowband signals and background noise.
- Fast convergence on echo path changes (during call forwarding).

Applications:
- Conventional telephone networks.
- Voice over IP or Voice over ATM.
- Voice communication with Satellite / Wireless networks.

6.24.5 Acoustic Echo Canceller (AEC)

Acoustic Echo Cancellers are used to cancel out the echo produced by the acoustic path between the speaker and microphone in hands-free telephone and video/audio conferencing solutions (mobile phones, speaker phones, IP phones). Acoustic echo is caused due to the reflections from the walls and objects present in the environment (for example, echo from inside of a car for hands free telephone or room walls for conferencing solutions). Acoustic Echo Canceller (AEC) is a proprietary algorithm to remove the acoustic echo from speech.

Technical Specifications:
- Efficient adaptive algorithm removes the echo and enhances the speech quality.
- Robust double talk detection (can detect double talk even in presence of 20 dB gain in the echo path).
- Fast convergence (> 20 db / sec).
- Programmable filter length (delay).
- Comfort Noise Generator (CNG) is included.
- Non-Linear Processor (NLP) for reducing non-linear residual echo.
- Re-entrant, multi-channel implementation.
- C-callable APIs.

Applications:
- IP phones / Speaker phones / Video phones / Feature phones.
- Multimedia / Telecommunication products.
- Audio conferencing / Video conferencing.
- Handsfree systems.

6.24.6 Typical Echo Canceller

1. The aim of echo cancellation is to remove any of the loudspeaker output from the microphone output, whether caused by direct or indirect propagation.

2. Dealing with the direct propagation path is not so much of a problem, as the same signal being used to drive the loudspeaker can be appropriately subtracted from the microphone output.

3. However it is the indirect path that pose a much greater problem, as there exist thousands of potential acoustic paths.

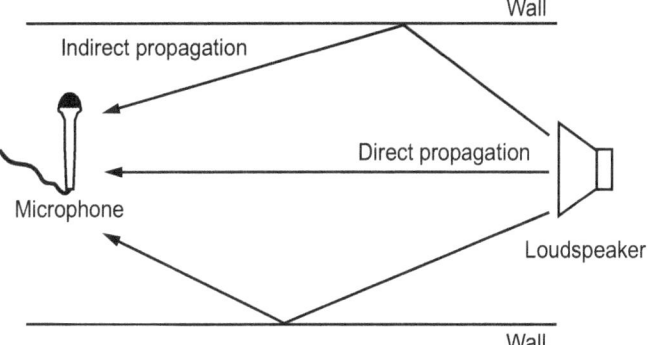

Fig. 6.48: Direct and Indirect Acoustic Paragraph Paths

4. To overcome the problem, use is made of an echo canceller, which performs two main functions.

5. Firstly, the echo canceller estimates the echo paths within the environment, by comparing the signal being used to drive the loudspeaker, and that of the microphone output.

6. Using cross correlation, the weightings of an algorithm are decided upon, whereby applying the loudspeaker signal as input, gives a close approximation to the actual microphone output signal.

7. The second function of an echo canceller is then to subtract the estimated echo signal from the actual microphone output signal, with the hope that the estimation closely matches the actual echo signal.

8. As can be appreciated, the echo canceller must perform rapidly for such real time use, and it is the subject of the type of algorithm chosen, and the mathematical accuracy that determines the computational burden.

9. Additionally, as the echo canceller requires constant adaptation to the acoustic environment, the computational burden is further increased by the need for adaptive filtering.

10. Considering an environment as a system with an input of speech, and an output consisting of an acoustic echo, we can think of an environment as having an impulse response.

11. Simply by drawing the curtains, moving a chair, or closing a door, the impulse response is significantly altered.

12. The most commonly used adaptive filter used within echo cancellers has a tapped delay line structure, which basically means this just involves an algorithm with many tap weights, each of which model the acoustic environment.

13. The two most common algorithms for updating the tap weights of the filter are the Least Mean Square algorithm, and the **Recursive Least Square (RLS) algorithm**.

14. Fast types of the latter have been developed with a significantly reduced computational burden, and thus their use is rather more favoured - more exotic and efficient algorithms exist.

15. Further levels of algorithmic classification lead to three subclasses of RLS algorithm, however we shall only investigate the use of the Fast Transversal Filter.

16. Different Experiments have shown that for effective echo cancellation, use is required of either 24-bit fixed point, or 32-bit floating point calculations, and that use of 16-bit fixed point arithmetic provides unsatisfactory results.

17. The degree of echo reduction is basically dependent upon the number of taps, the arithmetic precision, and the impulse response of the room.

18. As designers only have control over the first two issues, researchers are continually working upon devising more computationally efficient algorithms.

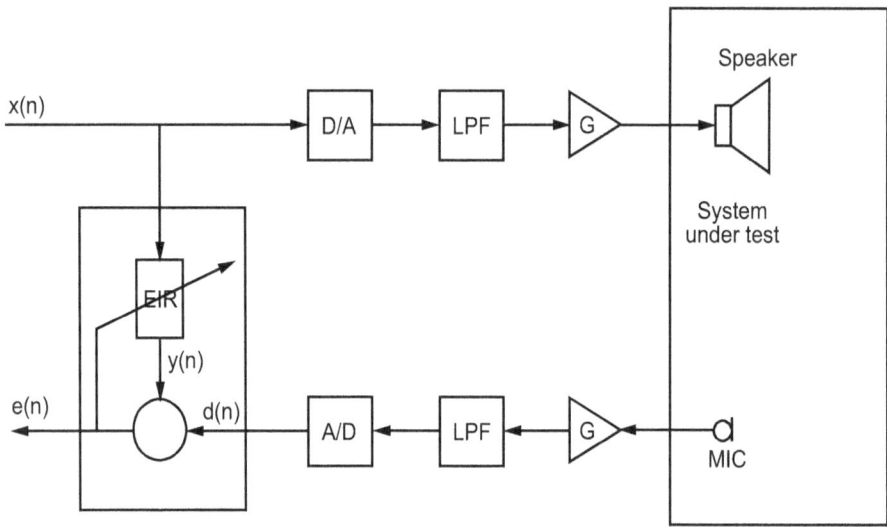

Fig. 6.49: A Model of a Basic Echo Cancelling System

19. The system consists of a loudspeaker, a microphone, analog-to-digital, and digital-to-analog converters, amplifiers, low-pass filters, and an echo canceller consisting of an adaptive filter.

20. where,

x(n) denotes the nth sample from the far end speaker,
d(n) is the actual echo signal detected by the microphone after low pass filtering,
y(n) is the estimated echo signal from the echo canceller,
and e(n) is the residual echo after subtraction heard at the far end.

21. The performance of echo cancellers is commonly measured by a quantity called the Echo Return Loss Enhancement, which is defined as,
ERLE(n) = 10 log { E[d(n)*d(n)] / E[e(n)*e(n)] }
where,
E[d(n)*d(n)] is the expected value of the received echo signal power,
and E[e(n)*e(n)] is the residual echo signal power.
(Effective echo cancellation requires an ERLE of at least 30 dB or better.)

22. A consideration to bear in mind is when both speaking parties talk at the same time, commonly called double-talk.

23. In terms of the local microphone, it detects the local speaker's voice, and also the voice of the far end speaker via the loudspeaker.

24. Now as the tap weights of the local adaptive filter are based upon the local microphone and local loudspeaker signals, the weights diverge from the previous single-talk values, because the voice of the local speaker is taken as noise.

25. However, as speech signals are highly complex and variable, the adaptive filter is unable to cope with the far end speech, the local speech, and the local acoustic echo, and the result is poor echo cancellation.

26. Note this doesn't mean we are back to the half-duplex operation of voice controlled switching, as a speaker can easily interrupt another speaker using this method.

27. Note that the above argument applies equally as well when reversed to consider the far end microphone.

6.24.7 VAD / CNG / DTX

1. **VAD (Voice Activity Detection) / DTX (Discontinuous Transmission) / CNG (Comfort Noise Generator)** are used to reduce the transmission rate during inactive speech periods while maintaining an acceptable level of output quality.

2. VAD classifies the input signal into active speech, inactive speech or background noise.

3. Based on the VAD decisions, DTX inserts Silence Insertion Descriptor (SID) frames during the silence intervals.

4. During silence, SID's are periodically sent to the CNG module, which generates ambient noise during periods of inactive speech on the receive side.

5. The purpose of a Voice Activity Detection (VAD) algorithm is to distinguish between speech and noise (inactive) regions in a speech signal.

6. It is an important problem because it has applications in speech recognition, speech coding and echo cancellation.
7. In the speech recognition, VAD improves recognition-accuracy significantly.
8. While in the speech coding, it aids in improving the system resource utilization in conjunction with comfort noise generator (CNG) during periods of speech absence by selectively encoding and transmitting data.
9. It is a complicated problem because of the variety and time-varying nature of the noise in the speech signal.
10. Due to this complexity, the VAD algorithms are susceptible to Clipping and False detection errors.
11. A number of solution methods have been proposed in the literature for VAD:
    - Heuristics based VAD algorithms.
    - The G.729-Annex B VAD algorithm.
    - Statistical Model based VAD algorithms.
    - Higher Order Statistics based VAD algorithms.
    - Misc VAD algorithms.

Technical Specifications:
- Robust algorithm, works under a variety of background noise conditions.
- Uses an adaptive smoothing algorithm to avoid clipping of speech at active to inactive speech transition regions.
- Efficient Noise Generation.
- Support for **discontinuous transmission (DTX)** of inactive frames (based on changes in inactive speech signal).
- Speech detection at low signal-to-noise ratios.
- Adapts to changing background noise.
- Re-entrant, multi-channel implementation.
- Configurable frame size.
- C-callable APIs.

Applications:
- Voice Over Packet Systems.
- Digital Telephone Answering Machines.
- Speech Enhancers.

6.24.8 Typical Voice Activity Detection
1. Any inaccuracies in the calculation of N(F) will cause distortion in the reproduced clean speech signal, either because of over or under subtraction.
2. Thus one must be able to clearly distinguish between clean speech, noise, and (clean speech + noise), and it is here where the Voice Activated Detector (VAD) serves its purpose.

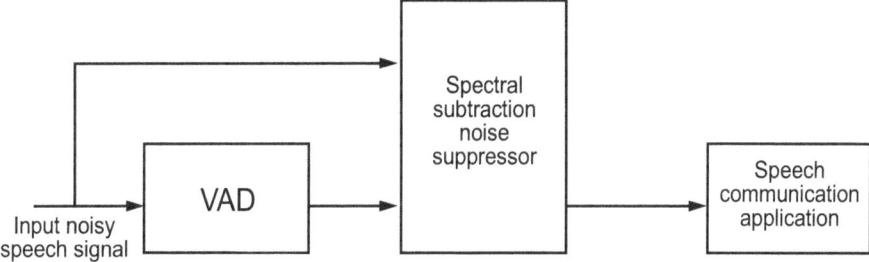

Fig. 6.50: A Voice Activity Detector

3.   Provided any background noise is stationary over relatively long periods of time, the spectral characteristics of the noise will be very similar from frame to frame of the microphone output signal.

4.   In principle then, it should be possible to detect the presence of speech by looking for deviations from the spectral characteristics of the background noise.

5.   Early VAD's could only operate with restricted background noise with signals of SNR around 30 dB, however current VAD's can effectively deal with SNR's as low as 0 dB.

6.   Research is still needed for VAD operation in environments with highly complex noise, however for use in noisy environments, the plots below show that the background noise can be taken as simple white Gaussian.

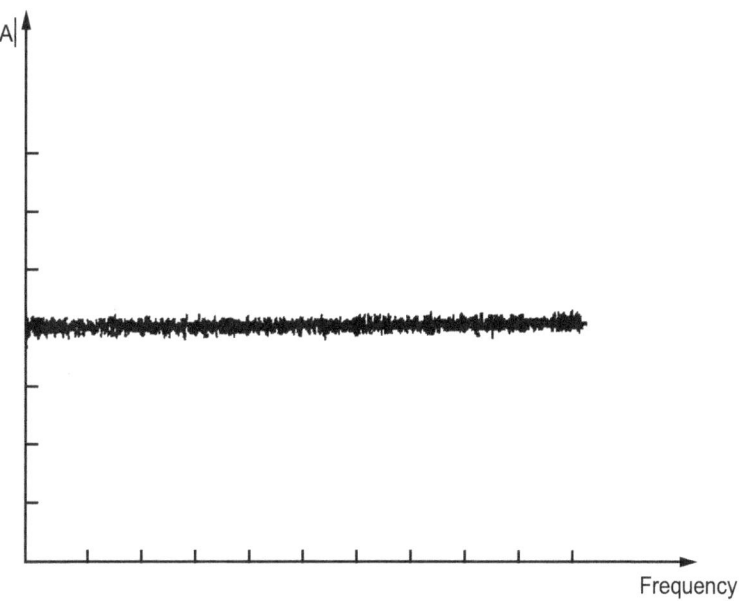

Fig. 6.51: A Spectral Noise Plot of a System Under Test

6.24.9 Packet Loss Concealment (PLC)

1. Packet Loss Concealment is used to recover from lost frames/packets in packet based telephony systems.
2. It is used to avoid unnecessary artifacts, glitches caused due to packet loss, so that the speech quality remains within the human tolerable limit.
3. Typical Packet Loss Concealment algorithm is normally based on ITU-T standard which can generate synthetic data (noise, silence or speech) depending upon the past speech history.
4. Packet Loss Concealment is a technique used to mask the effects of lost or discarded packets.
5. PLC is generally effective only for small numbers of consecutive lost packets, for example, a total of 20-30 milliseconds of speech, and for low packet loss rates.
6. Packet loss can be bursty in nature - with periods of several seconds during which packet loss may be 20-30 percent.
7. The average packet loss rate for a call may be low, however, these periods of high loss rate can cause noticeable degradation in call quality.
8. PLC algorithms typically involve either replaying the last packet received ("replay") or some more sophisticated algorithm that uses previous speech samples to generate speech.
9. Simple replay algorithms tend to lead to "robotic" sounding speech when multiple consecutive packets are lost.
10. More sophisticated algorithms can provide reasonable quality at 20% packet loss rates, however can consume DSP bandwidth and hence reduce the
    number of channels that can be supported in, for example, a high density gateway.
11. If PLC is not enabled, then users may report difficulty in understanding speech due to short gaps. If PLC is used but is not effective, then the problem is likely to be bursts of packet loss or periods of high discard rate.

Technical Specifications:
*   Improved quality even with a packet-loss of upto 15%.
*   Re-entrant, multi-channel implementation.
*   C-Callable APIs.

Applications:
*   IP Telephony.
*   Speech Enhancers.

6.24.10 Call Progress Tones (CPT)

Call Progress Tones are audible tones set from switching systems to calling parties to show the status of calls. The **Call Progress Tones (CPT) generator** resides at the Local Exchange and is used to generate the tones to be sent to the Terminal Equipment. CPT detectors are used in Terminal Equipments for machine recognition of tones.

Typical Call Progress Tones supports the following tones:
- Dial tone, Recall dial tone.
- Ringing tone, Ringing tone (PABX).
- Busy tone and Congestion tone.
- Special information tone.
- Warning tone.
- Waiting tone.
- Record tone.
- Executive override tone.
- Intercept tone.
- Confirmation tone.

Technical Specifications:
- Supports generation and detection of call progress tones.
- Supports for all tones.
- Configurable parameters (single or dual frequency, frequency ranges, modulation).
- Re-entrant, multi-channel implementation.
- C-callable APIs.

Applications:
- Telecommunication.
- Billing Systems.
- Voice over Packet Systems.
- Automatic Dialers.

6.24.11 Caller Identification (CLI or Caller-ID)

Caller Identification (also known as Caller-ID) is a method of transmitting the information of the caller to the called subscriber via a burst of FSK or DTMF data during the On-hook/Off-hook state of Telephony Equipment. The On-hook transmission of CLI is through FSK or DTMF burst known as type 1, whereas Off-hook transmission is with FSK burst known as type 2.

Technical Specifications:
1. **Transmission:**
   - FSK and DTMF Caller ID transmission formats for Off-hook operation as per standards.
2. **Reception:**
   - Detection of the dual tone alerting signal as specified.
   - Detection of the dual tone alerting signal as specified for Off-hook data reception.
   - Demodulating the FSK data as specified for Off-hook operation.
3. Supports Single Data Message Format (SDMF) and Multiple Data Message Format (MDMF).

4. Re-entrant multi-channel implementation.
5. C-Callable APIs.

Applications:

- Telecommunication.
- Voice over Packet systems.
- Automatic Dialers.

6.25 Products and Applications

Industry Products:

Products belonging to important categories of the Voice over IP market and their typical features are described in the following table.

Table 6.24

Category	Products	Categorywise Typical Features
Gateways	3COM Gateway Cisco systems DE-30 + Gateway Lucent Technologies MICOM V/IP Gateway Neura Solutions Access Plus F200 IP Nortel Networks CVX SS7 Gateway Pathstar Access Server Radvision H.323 Stack VocalTec Series 2000 Gateway	• LAN - based gateways, which can be installed on a LAN without reprovisioning of network resources. • Multiple O/S support. • Analog/Digital (T1/E1) link support. • Interfaces to existing communications equipment like PABXs and telephones and no need for networking re-provisioning. • QoS Support. • Billing and Account Record Processing. • Security e.g. PGP. • SS7 signalling. • Codec support. • Inter-operability, Bellcore's NEBS compliance. • H.323 support. • SIP/MGCP support. • Network manageable e.g. SNMP • Web-based remote management. • Scalable. • High availability.

Category	Products	Categorywise Typical Features
Gatekeepers	Elemedia H.323 Gatekeeper GK2000S Ericsson H.323 Gatekeeper Nortel Network's IP connect Radvision H.323 Gatekeeper VocalTel Gatekeeper	• Admissions control and RAS • H.323 support. • Dial Plan Management. • Centralized accounting and billing. • Network security. • Web-based service management. • Web-based network management. • SNMP support. • Scalabilty.
Softswitches	Lecent Softswitch	• Multi-signal inter-operability between SS7, Q.931, H.323, SIP. • PSTN/ISDN to IP gateway • Scalable. • Multiple-User style configurable. • Programmable. • Java based portable application.
IP Telephones	Cisco IP Phones Selsius IP Phones	• IP enabled. • Configurable IP address. • LAN enabled. • Programmable features. • Audio quality voice. • Speaker phone. • LCD displays. • Caller identification. • Line status. • Directory. • Compatible with other H.323 devices. • Supports Ms NetMeeting-like conferencing solutions.
PC-based Soft Phones	Microsoft NetMeeting Netscape CoolTalk VocalTec IP phone White Pine CU-SeeMe Pro	• PC to phone capability - requires ITSP authorization. • Video capability. • Audio/video conferencing using conferencing servers. • Data collaboration – e.g. white boarding to share documents. • Chat. • Auto call handling and answering. • Directory service.

Voice over IP Services:

Some typical Voice over IP services available in the market are listed below.

Table 6.25

Category	Services	Description and Typical Features
PC to Phone Services	VocalTec Surf & Call Dialpad.com	This service uses gateways to convert signals and voice to IP. • "Click to Talk"/"Click to Fax" types of service. • Call center application support for e-commerce. • Nearly free long distance call tariffs. • Free downloadable software from the Internet.
PC to PC Services	Microsoft NetMeeting VocalTec IP phone TalTalk.com.	• Can be provided without gateways. • Audio and video multi-conferencing capabilities. • Data collaboration facilities. • Application share services.
Phone to Phone Services	America Online at ~x cents/min long distance over IP AT&T at ~x cents/min long distance over IP IDT Corporation at ~x cents/min	• Local access remains the same as PSTN. • Trunk routes as IP networks. • Reduced rates. • Same PSTN customers are retained.
Prepaid calling card based services	AcculinQ at ~x cents/min USATEL VIA ONE prepaid calling card	• Prepaid calling card based. • Call from anywhere.
Unified Messaging Services	Glenayre Unified Messaging Service Cisco AVVID	• All types of messages – email, voice mail, video mail, paging, SMS, are integrated into one browser-based user interface.

Category	Services	Description and Typical Features
Network Services	Level 3's IP Crossroad Service Qwest Virtual Network Service	• These provide quality of service over IP networks. • Dedicated network trunks and resources, akin to company's intranet. • Large geographical reach. • Multimedia capability. • Low cost. • Intended for corporate use.
Services for service providers	ITXC Delta Three IP Telephony for carriers Ericsson IP Telephony for carriers Cisco/VocalTec hybrid end-to-end services for carriers and service providers Cisco AVVID	• Intended for Telephone carriers and Internet service providers, prepaid calling card companies, call back companies and ITSPs. • Billing. • Scaleable service. • Manageable service.

6.26 Summary

1. The market place is rapidly moving towards convergence of services onto a single user-end device.

2. In doing so, it is moving away from circuit-switched to packet networks.

3. Service providers have already realized the cost benefits of integrating media over the same packet network devices.

4. They are aggressively defining and implementing standards enabling delivery of multimedia over packet-based networks.

5. These cost benefits are being gradually passed over to the user slowly, because of telecom regulatory issues and enormous investments in old technology by telecom monopolies across the world.

6. The Internet has revolutionized the nature of business and societal behaviour with an exponentially increasing Internet penetration.

7. The ubiquitous multimedia terminal, whose current outputs are the multimedia desktops, wireless handsets, and Internet- enabled TVs, are increasingly being seen as the indispensable tool to conduct business and social engagements.

8. User expectations of converged multimedia applications have multiplied manifold.

9. To meet these requirements, service providers need to quickly transition from circuit switched technologies to packet networks and implement protocols and standards, as discussed in this unit.

10. This transition is still in the nascent stage, as the major issues of Quality of Service, scalability and security of packet networks need to be substantially enhanced to the level of circuit-switched networks.

11. Major telecommunications companies, who have enormous investments in traditional networks, have been slow, but are increasingly committed to making this transition.

12. However, data network service providers and router manufacturers, who were already committed to this transition, have to scale up and extend the capabilities of their equipment.

13. Cisco and other similar companies, who belong to the data world, have been exceedingly successful in driving this convergence and in increasing user expectations.

14. Traditional Telecommunications, however, have been pushed to recognize the eventuality of converged networks because of decreasing returns from traditional networks and applications.

15. A host of other new wave companies have also joined this convergence market place with innovative new applications or by providing efficient mechanisms for implementing convergence.

16. Some of the newer breed of service-providers are increasingly looking into IP networks to deliver quality video and voice to their subscribers.

17. A case in point are the Cable Network operators who are leveraging their wide subscriber base and packaging voice conferencing, video on demand and Internet connectivity along with their traditional video broadcast services.

18. They are providing broadband optical fiber access to the curb or to the users home and using IP as the network layer.

19. Most of the protocols that have been discussed in this paper, currently have host based implementations.

20. This is mainly because the protocols are evolving.

21. However, with increasing popularity and acceptance, very soon an increasing percentage of their implementations would be in the embedded domain.

22. End user devices including active network nodes will use these protocols as implemented on chips.

23. At this point, it has become increasingly necessary for the IT industry to understand, master and further the mechanics of convergence and integrate with it.

24. In the near future, we are going to witness the emergence of native Internet HTTP-ish protocols, which will be more efficient, scalable, secured and which will guarantee quality similar to traditional networks.

25. Application architectures will increasingly accommodate these new protocols and deliver a wider range of innovative services, for which organizations would need to plan accordingly.

EXERCISE

1. Compare analog voice network and digital voice network.

2. What are the needs of VoIP technology?

3. Write the technical difference between VoIP and traditional PSTN.

4. What are the different ways to connect to VoIP services?

5. What are the different features of VoIP?

6. What are the different applications of VoIP?

7. Write short note on "VoIP QoS requirements and QoS solutions".

8. Explain the concept "VoIP over LAN".

9. Explain the concept "VoIP over WAN".

10. Explain H.323 protocols in detail.

11. Explain real time protocols and their operation in detail.

12. What are the different signalling protocols used in VoIP?

13. Write detail note on "CODECS".

14. What are the different advantages of a VoIP technology?

15. What are the different drawbacks of VoIP?

16. Explain typical voice call handling in VoIP application.

17. Explain components of H.323 in detail.

18. Draw and explain H.323 protocol stack.

19. Write short note on "MEGACO and H.248".

20. Write short note on Session Inition Protocol.

21. Compare H.323 and SIP.

22. Write short notes on:

   (a) RSVP

   (b) RTP

   (c) RTCP

   (d) PCM and ADPCM for voice

   (f) Speech codecs

23. Explain wireless codecs in detail.

24. Compare the different "wideband speech coding standards".

25. Write short note on "full rate codec".

26. Write short note on "Echo canceller".

27. Explain voice activity detection in detail.

28. Explain the concept of "Packet Loss Concealment (PLC)".

www.ingramcontent.com/pod-product-compliance
Lightning Source LLC
Chambersburg PA
CBHW080040130726
47907CB00019B/2357